Finders Keepers,
Losers Weep

A Novel of Innocence Betrayed and the Search for Restitution

Carl Douglass

Neurosurgeon Turned Author Writers with Gripping Realism

Since 1978

PO Box 221974 Anchorage, Alaska 99522-1974
books@publicationconsultants.com—www.publicationconsultants.com

ISBN 978-1-59433-383-5
eISBN 978-1-59433-384-2
Library of Congress Catalog Card Number: 2013942190

Manufactured in the United States of America.

DEDICATION

D edicated to the advocates of concealed-carry gun permits and to those who labor for the eradication of gun related crime and violence in the United States and in the world.

The Salt Lake Tribune, Sunday, May 18, 1997
by Jim Woolf
Police Raid Turns Businessman's American Dream Into Nightmare

Tears well up in Rafael Gomez' eyes as he unrolls plans for a Mexican-style shopping center he hoped to build on the corner of 400 South and Redwood Road in Salt Lake City.

"I'm thinking of selling it all," says the 42 year old businessman. "This has changed everything."

The change came April 25 about 3:30 p.m. when a group of 75 heavily armed police officers burst through the metal door at Gomez' tortilla factory and Mexican food store-Panaderia La Diana, 56 S. 900 West.

They were dressed in black with bullet-proof vests and scarves over their faces. Brandishing rifles and pistols, they ordered everyone—some 90 employees and customers—down on the floor and handcuffed them.

Gomez, who was standing near the door when the police arrived, says he was struck in the face as they poured in. He isn't sure what hit him but witnesses think it was a rifle butt. As he fell to the ground, he struck his head on the concrete floor. When the business owner tried to stand and ask what was happening, he claims to have been kicked in the back and ordered to stay down.

He says a police officer pointed a rifle at the head of his 6 year old son. And Graciela Zamora, a secretary at the business, says an officer dragged her to the floor by her hair.

Police believed more than tortillas were being made in this factory. A confidential informant told them drugs and possibly weapons were being handled there, too.

So, Salt Lake City police officers took no chances as they assembled one of Utah's larges multi-agency law enforcement efforts for the raid. The team included the Salt Lake County Sheriff's Office, Davis County Sheriff's Office, Utah Attorney General, FBI, Internal Revenue Service, Drug Enforcement Administration, and Immigration and Naturalization Service...

Two shots were fired through the door handle on a utility closet near Gomez' office by officers who mistakenly believed it was locked. "I guess they were frightened," says the businessman...

The raid was a failure.

No street drugs or weapons were found in the business. A small quantity of heroin and cocaine but no weapons were confiscated from a few drug dealers working a corner near the parking lot.

7

Salt Lake City police Capt. Marty Vuyk says none of the officers reported hitting Gomez or anyone else during the raid. "But with the number of guys going through the door, someone may have inadvertently hit him."

[A subsequent article in the same newspaper reported: A 3rd district judge has thrown out felony drug charges against the owner of a Mexican food store that was the target of a controversial police raid...Gomez' attorney, Michael Martinez, called it a "stereotype raid", in which Gomez, his employees, and customers were lumped with area drug dealers.]"

Note: A decal appears on the doors of all of the marked Salt Lake City police cars that arrived at the scene of the raid. It reads: To Protect and Serve.

The Salt Lake Tribune, Saturday, October 6, 2012
Police raid wrong home, point gun at 76-year-old

"Mistake: Chief apologizes, places at least one officer on leave during investigation. By Nate Carlisle

"Narcotics detectives in Salt Lake City used a battering ram on Wednesday to knock down a door and execute a search warrant on the wrong house, frightening the home's 76-year-old resident.

"This was a mistake," Police Chief Chris Burbank said Friday. "It should not have happened."

"The woman living at the home near 200 E. Hubbard Ave. (935 South) was not injured, though a police officer pointed a gun at her as officers entered the home. ['She was petrified. She didn't know what to think. This was traumatizing to her,' said the woman's son Raymond Zaelit.]. Burbank said he has placed one officer on administrative leave while the police department investigates how the mistake was made."

"...The task force received what is called a "no-knock" warrant, meaning a judge gave police permission to force their way inside the house without announcing themselves...Before obtaining warrants to search a home for drugs, police typically obtain evidence of drugs or drug crimes there, then conduct surveillance on the home and provide the judge with an address and physical description of the home."

"...We did not do our due diligence on this one," Burbank said.

PROLOGUE

On Friday, February 18, 2022, at ten-thirty in the morning, the forty-sixth President of the United States announced her resignation from office. She was entering the third year of her second term, and her declaration preceded her formal arrest by federal officers by a scant five minutes and obviated the need for the added disgrace of impeachment. The seminal event that brought about her downfall had seemed so inconsequential and forgettable when it occurred; and even at this moment of high crisis, the president was not altogether converted to the seriousness of her mistake. Oh, she recognized the readily apparent legal ramifications that enveloped her; but in her heart-of-hearts, her own part in the drama that enfolded her still seemed to be trivial. She was the first to admit that in the last half of 2021—and for the first two months of the new year, though she tried to concentrate on something else, anything else—the Randolph Kennedy Affair consumed her every waking thought and even intruded on the solace of her sleep. Even as she stepped forward to be arrested, the incident still seemed to be too minor to warrant all of this tumult.

CHAPTER ONE

Randolph Armstrong Kennedy had nothing of the appearance of a giant killer or toppler of powerful leaders. Immediately prior to the series of incidents that now ensnarled the second woman president of the United States, Mr. Kennedy possessed all of the personal and socioeconomic qualities of the voiceless middle middle class. Had his name appeared on a list, the rather disdainful president would dismissively have characterized him squarely with the hordes of "little people" whom she despised—in private— served—in public—and manipulated; and from whom she drew her political breath without bothering to have any of their names or faces come into focus.

He had no claim to fame or notoriety, bore no titles, held no political office, and had no aspirations for any of that. He belonged to no political party, splinter group, or special interest organizations. He voted only sporadically and never with enthusiasm. He tended to vote *against*. Before the "affair" that bore his name and rocked the nation into a constitutional crisis had its inception, Randolph Kennedy was an entrenched member of the silent majority— content to gripe about his taxes, but to pay them anyway, to watch television, take walks, and to have picnics. His ambition was to provide a modest and stable living for his wife of four years whom he considered his best friend, comfortable lover, and family business partner, and for their three year old daughter whom he adored, spoiled, and considered to be the most beautiful and charming human ever to grace the planet.

Randolph was an accountant, a CPA, one of the gray functionaries of one of the faceless big eight national accounting firms. He was one of those people whose clients presumed that he materialized out of the office wall paper for their convenience. He was a man of spare personal interests extracurricular to his work and his family. He maintained memberships in organizations only as he needed to for his occupation. He subscribed to no religious organization and espoused no causes. He was a bland individual with acquaintances instead of real friends; and he was not controversial, opinionated, nor colorful enough to have enemies.

Randolph Kennedy was regular looking—six feet tall, one hundred eighty pounds on a spare, somewhat stringy frame. His hair was a muddy blond with just the hint of a curl if he let it grow long enough. He had slightly off-color yellowed teeth, a nose that was not perfectly straight; and his eyes were set a shade too close together to let him be considered handsome. His face was more rugged than most women preferred and more intelligent and insightful than most people found comfortable. He had long fingers and strong hands that he usually kept in his pockets out of self-consciousness. He tended not to make eye contact with people, seldom laughed out loud, and never pushed himself or his opinions. His occupation as an accountant was perfect for him; he could have been the poster boy for the profession. Randolph passed as easily unnoticed as a good spy—even in a small gathering and was lost in a crowd.

Randolph was a patient, even plodding, sort of a man—a man who paid attention to details. He was of placid disposition, slow to anger, and never swore or lost his temper. He had never raised his voice to his wife or child. He did not easily react to slights or inconveniences that might have provoked a more temperamental man; and he prided himself on being a peaceful person, even a peacemaker. That was the trait his wife admired most having come from a boisterous, argumentative family. He was willing to listen to his clients, his family, and his acquaintances without feeling any particular need to argue or even to state his own opinion. When something did finally rise to exceed his threshold of concern, he was surprisingly strong and assertive, another trait his wife liked—her man made her feel safe.

Ivan Slavich met his modest personal needs and his moderate recreational chemical requirements by performing odd jobs when he could not make ends meet by his principle occupation as a thief. Ivan was an easygoing man who—under the best of conditions—was less than convinced about the desirability of steady work; and when he had accumulated enough free money to score a few good hits of heroin—his chemical of choice—he was erratic and unreliable for days on end. One of the jobs he contracted during one of his more extended periods of instability was the construction of a garden fence for Randolph Kennedy and his wife, Irene.

Ivan was feeling shaky the day he answered the Kennedy's want ad in the *Carpenter's Listing of Caldwell County.*

"Hello," the woman's quiet voice said when he called.

"Uh, hello," Ivan stammered slightly into the phone.

He took a breath to steady the tremulousness in his voice.

"I read your notice in the *Carpenter's Listings.* I'm the next up on the union list; so, I'm a-callin' about the job you wanted done."

"Oh, good," answered the woman. "I'm Irene Kennedy. My husband and I need a fence around our back yard. We have a little girl who likes to stray off. And we wanted to enclose a little area for a garden. Do you do that kind of work, Mr...?"

"Slavich's my name, Ivan Slavich."

He was doing better now that there was a regular flow to the conversation.

"I'm something of an expert in fences. What kinda thing you have in mind, Missus?"

It was immaterial to him to tout his expertise even though this would be the first fence he had ever built. He needed the job, and the only thing that mattered was his needs. How much could there be to making a stupid fence?

"It's Mrs. Kennedy, Mr. Slavich. We don't want anything too fancy...or too expensive. I'd like one of those aluminum or plastic kinds that holds up in all kinds of weather, one that can handle our tough winters. A picket fence, I guess."

"I think we can make one outta wood better. Look better, anyhow. And it'll be cheaper and look better. Not as cheap lookin', you know? How big's your place?"

"Well, Mr. Slavich, I still want to have a plastic one. Our place is a standard city lot, not real big."

"Whatever. I'll come by tomorra mornin' and make a estimate. You be there then?"

"What time did you have in mind, Mr. Slavich?"

"How 'bout 'round 'leven?"

Ivan did not ordinarily do mornings.

"All right. It can't be any later because I have a church group meeting at noon that is a must for me."

"I'm famous for comin' when I says, and I do the work I says, Missus. You kin count on me."

It did not matter to Ivan that neither statement reflected any consistent truth. He needed the job—as crappy as it was—and whatever it took to get it was okay.

"That will be a refreshing change. I will have my husband take off work to meet with you. See you tomorrow."

"Yeah," he said.

He hung up. That had not been so bad. His hand was shaky. He needed a fag. He fumbled in his grimy denim pockets for the last of his Lucky Strikes. He needed the real thing. He was having a nicky fit now. He had had to portion out his cigarettes and had less than a pack for the whole day. It was going to be a bummer of a day. He knew that what he really needed was the sweet release of some smack, but for that he needed money. The motto from his scummy dealer—given with a grin that would cause a dentist to wince—was "in God we trust, all others pay cash." Nothing else good was showing itself on the horizon; so, he was resigned to the need to do some kind of square work.

Ivan was at the Kennedy's place fifteen minutes early—enough to give them the impression of punctuality—but not enough for him to appear eager. He had had no choice but to get up early that morning because he found himself on the hard ground outside his trailer—must not have made it all the way indoors after his toot that night. The suit and his wife—Ivan guessed she was his wife since they probably did not allow live-ins out here in snooty suburbia, he sneered to himself—came out of the house as he was walking off the perimeter of the yard.

"Mr. Slavich, I presume?" the suit greeted.

"Yeah, 'at's right. I'us just doin' some calculatin'."

"We won't interfere until you're finished. Let us know," Randolph Kennedy said patiently.

"Jist 'nother minute. I'll do the figurin'."

Ivan made an elaborate facial demonstration of his mental efforts. The Kennedys watched patiently as the small man consulted his notes and made a few additions and subtractions with a well chewed, blunt carpenter's pencil. His nails were grimy and bitten to the quick. The man's eyes were rheumy, and he blinked frequently—the stigma of an alcoholic or a drug addict. He had a swarthy vulpine face, and his eyes moved quickly and furtively, like a fox's. His was not a face to inspire immediate confidence.

It was worth going high, Slavich figured. The suit and his Stepford Wife looked like pretty easy marks.

"It'll come ta $4200 even, includin' labor. I have ta work for scale, ya know," Ivan said, keeping his voice serious and businesslike.

He suppressed a chuckle at his own cheekiness.

Randolph Kennedy looked at the carpenter with unfeeling Visigothan blue eyes—his business look—making the smaller Slavic man feel uneasy.

"Seems high to me, Mr. Slavich. Mind if I take a look at your notes on the costs of the materials?" Randolph said after a brief eye-to eye with Slavich which caused the workman to drop his gaze.

"Oh, they're just scratchin's. You wouldn't be able to read my writin' I'm worsen a doctor," Slavich replied with an unpleasant grey toothed smile.

Randolph shook his head.

"I have done a lot of preliminary investigation myself. Even retail and adding something for inflation, we can get the vinyl fencing for around $1300. Labor at scale shouldn't take the total beyond a combined sum of $2800 at the outside. That seems more like it."

Working to keep his contempt for the prospective employers from his face, Ivan mocked to himself, "'*a combined sum'. How prissy.*"

He had misjudged the man. He wished he had only the pretty little wife to work with.

"*Oh, well,*" he mused, "*can't have everything.*"

Out loud he said, "Depends on whether you want the posts dug in and cemented. That cost's a pretty penny. Lotsa hard work, too. I'm a tellin' you. I'd have to get a good $3600 to a...$3800 if you want it that way."

It was as polite as he could muster.

Randolph shook his head and looked directly at Ivan. Ivan did not like that.

"Tell you what I could do. I'll buy the supplies and materials, and you give me the exact measurements and requirements and do the labor. Union scale $70 an hour. Am I right?" Kennedy said flatly, the picture of courtesy and fair-mindedness.

Slavich gritted his teeth to suppress an angry retort. He didn't like this unreasonable robot standing there staring at him.

Kennedy continued to stand so that Slavich had to face the sun. Slavich didn't like that either. The man's eyes were unrestrained; but his face—as craggy as the Irish coast from which his ancestors had sprung—was fixed and unrevealing. It was obvious to Slavich that the man wasn't going to budge. He really wasn't going to like this guy.

"That cuts me outta even my little profit, Mr. Kennedy. I'm not a wealthy man…like yourself."

Randolph almost smiled at that.

"I have a family and bills to pay. I'm just a workin' stiff. Whatta you say to a total of thirty-three hunnert…for everythin'? Now, that's about as rock bottom as you can get, believe you me."

"I have figured the total of $3000 as being generous. I figure a profit margin of eleven percent for you, over and above top scale wages. That is my top figure."

To Randolph Kennedy, this discussion was uncomfortably close to the haggling for every good and service he had needed in Morocco when he lived in that Muslim desert as a study abroad student in college. He had not liked haggling or confrontation then, and he did not like dealing with Slavich and his peasant mentality now. He was bored with the grimy little man's greedy demands and was about to dismiss him and to find someone else.

"Gimme a second for some more figurin'," Slavich said.

His eyes were angry now, but he worked to keep his emotion to himself. This was going to be harder than he had expected.

"Take your time," Randolph replied evenly.

"I guess I kin do it for that. It'll be a tough one. You drive a hard bargain; but I need the work, I have ta admit," Slavich said after a few more grimaces of concentration and self-pitying grunts.

He looked at Randolph as if the tall, lean, athletic man had inadvertently spit on him.

Randolph nodded his agreement and said, "Now, I have a few conditions. If you can agree to them, we can draw up a simple contract and get underway."

Ivan glared in the direction of the clean-cut suburbanite without actually meeting the man's eyes. They were too much for a hung-over man to take.

"I want the job done in two weeks or less. If you do it in that time, I'll give you a bonus of five percent, and I will knock off five percent from the three thousand for every week it takes you beyond a twenty-five day maximum," Randolph continued, ignoring the displeasure of the carpenter.

"Hey, man, I never heard of no sucha thing. What's this five percent business?" Ivan interjected, betraying some excitement.

"It's called incentive, Mr. Slavich. Incentive."

Slavich had a blank look on his face. He hated it when big shots used big words to put him down.

"I expect you to have the job done on time," Kennedy went on. "I will not have our yard torn up all summer while you do other jobs, or…activities. I've learned my lesson from past experience with tradesmen. I have no intention of being burned again."

"*Who did this guy think he was?*" Ivan said to himself angrily.

He tried again.

"You have my solemn word on it. I'd get this job done in less'n two weeks. My *word*."

Ivan's demeanor was approaching obsequiousness. He was sure his earnest and forthright honesty was showing through. His most fetching smile came across to Randolph as more fox like than its cherubic intent.

"Good, Then you'll have no trouble with signing a written contract to that effect, right?"

"Ivan gritted his decayed teeth.

"I guess not," he grudgingly replied.

He felt that he had snookered somehow, and he did not like it at all.

"We're making progress," Randolph said with infuriating evenness.

He sneaked a glance at his watch. It was almost eleven forty-five. He had a client appointment; and Irene had her church responsibility, both at noon. It was time to end this.

"Now for my second condition. I will pay for the materials up front, but only for those that actually appear on my property. I will pay you one quarter of your labor costs in advance and the rest when you finish the job to my satisfaction."

Ivan looked as if he had another doubt or question.

"Another incentive," Randolph concluded without smiling.

The lawn sprinklers came on to the left of them. Ivan jumped and looked startled.

"I need half the labor before I start; that's union," he groused.

He had been hoping for full payment in advance way back when he still considered this hard-faced fascist an easy mark.

Randolph knew the union rules because he had checked in advance; they did not specify any up-front payment.

"I'll make a small compromise," he said. "You show me a week's good steady progress, and I'll give you another quarter of the final labor tab at that time. That's better than the union rules require. We both know that."

Nothing about Ivan's face indicated that he recognized that the homeowner had caught him in a lie. He had had practice. The man had done his home-work. Ivan had to grant him that much.

"Okay, all right," Slavich said. "Let's shake on it."

He extended his hand, embarrassed at the fine tremor and sweaty palm. It had been a week and a half since his last fix. He had a monkey on his back and was feeling loose-boweled and fatigued. He had a headache coming on.

Randolph ignored Ivan's proffered hand, a fact that was not lost on the workman and which he added to his growing list of slights from the snotty big shot.

Randolph said, instead, "We can do better than a handshake, Mr. Slavich. We can draw up a contract. Why don't you finish up your calculations about the work, and I'll go to my computer and type us up a document."

Ivan grunted. He hated computers. They never made mistakes, apparently; they never forgot anything like a guy's rap sheet; and they were totally unforgiving. They were a rich man's tool to put down the working poor—a cop and D.A. tool. He was going to take it in the shorts again, he figured.

Irene followed her husband into the house.

"I would probably have paid that creepy man $4200 like he originally asked. I'm glad you were here, Randy. We probably would never have seen him again. You know, I don't feel right about him. I don't trust him. And I certainly have no intention of being alone around here while he's on the job. Don't you think we should look around some more? There has to be someone better than this guy," she said.

Irene was a small woman, even dainty, and was assiduously clean in her person, dress, yard, and house. The evident ground-in grime on Slavich's clothes and skin and under his nails made her very uncomfortable.

"I'm afraid they're all alike. Besides, you recall that he's the only one we have heard from. This is too small a job to attract anybody with a regular job or business. He'll be okay. We just have to be all over him like a cheap K-Mart blue light suit, and I think he'll come up with a decent fence for us in some reasonable period of time," Randolph answered her with more conviction than he felt.

"Cheap suit," Irene laughed. "You and your Texas expressions. You haven't been closer to Texas or the South than Colorado or Ohio. What an affectation," she said to him teasingly.

She shook her head mock scoldingly, the movement causing her luxuriant honey-blond hair to ripple like corn silk in a Nebraska breeze, emphasizing her amusement. Irene was a genuine beauty, as delicate as a porcelain doll.

He laughed at himself.

"It was the best I could do on short notice."

Irene never let him get away with the smallest thing.

In five minutes they had a contract, and both Randolph and Ivan signed it. Randolph gave the man a check for $750 and pretended that he did not see Ivan's hand when it came out for a final gentlemen's hand shake. Ivan hid his anger poorly, turned and left.

At the end of one week, Ivan had placed one-half of the uprights of the fence in three foot deep post holes and had cemented them in place. Randolph made his inspection and had Ivan remove and replace three of them because they were out of alignment. After a stormy protest, Ivan tore the posts out with a vengeance and put in new ones.

"That good enough now, *sir?*" he growled, surly and out of sorts.

"Much better. Here's a check for $900 for materials to complete the work. Remember, there's a bonus in it if you do the job ahead of time."

Randolph seemed thoroughly condescending to Ivan as he handed over the check. Ivan whined inwardly, mocking Randolph. *"Remember, there's a bonus in it…"* Ivan had to forego his only pleasure and work for a full week without having a fix because there would be no more money if he did not get the work done; and the suit guy watched the bottom line of expenditures like a hawk. For a measly two hundred fifty bucks. Big deal!

Ivan's resolutions were not kept. He was able to shop lift some jewelry and to get it fenced for $300. He felt no pain for the next fourteen days. It was well over two weeks before Ivan reappeared at the Kennedy's house and began putting on the transverse slats of the fence. This time only Irene Kennedy was at home. She immediately walked out to where Ivan was working, feeling a pervading sense of apprehension.

"Mr. Slavich, my husband told me to inform you that the five percent deductions in your pay were in effect. He wants the rest of this work done promptly."

"I'm workin'; I'm workin'. No call to get on your high horse. I been sick."

He looked sick—pasty grey skin and anorexic sick. Irene thought the man had probably not had a decent meal, make than any meals, in the two weeks he had been absent from the job. His eyes and nose were runny, and he unconsciously and repeatedly swiped the mucous under his nose with his sleeve as if he had a nervous tic. The pupils of his eyes were constricted making it seem like he only had irises, a rather eerie look.

Slavich worked until three in the afternoon that day. The craving was too much. He headed back to the city and his cache and the peace that went with it. The peace lasted four weeks, and he had another month stay in the hospital being treated for septicemia and renal failure.

Randolph and Irene found another fence builder—a non-union man—and the job was completed in a week with a bonus for the workman. The job and Slavich were forgotten. Five weeks after he abandoned the work site, Ivan Slavich knocked on the door of the white aluminum sided Kennedy house.

Irene opened the door and was instantly happy that she had remembered to lock the storm insulator door. She was unpleasantly jarred and even a little frightened to see the dissolute workman standing before her.

"Yes, Mr. Slavich. What is it?" she asked, somewhat more abruptly than she might have intended.

"Come for my money, Missus," he said without pleasantry or preamble.

"What money?"

"Don't play no dummy with me, lady. You owe me the better part a thousand bucks, an' ya know it. I come to collect what I got comin'. Pay me, and I'm gone."

"You were paid for the work you did."

Her voice quavered which annoyed her.

"You abandoned the job. My husband contacted the union. They sent a man out who looked over the job, told us he didn't have time, but recommended a friend—a nonunion guy. They—the union that is—told us to refer you to them if there was any difficulty with you. So, Mr. Slavich, I'm referring you to the union."

The telephone rang, startling both of them. She was carrying a cordless phone and had forgotten it as the conversation with the nasty little man progressed.

"Hello," she answered without taking her eyes away from Slavich.

"Oh, Randy, I'm so glad you called right now. That guy who took off in the middle of our fence building project just came to the door demanding money. He is still here, won't go away. What should I do?"

She paused to listen, then said, "Not really. I don't think he said anything exactly threatening. He just seems upset. Menacing is more like it."

She listened again for a moment, then concluded the conversation with, "Bye. Be quick."

She lowered the phone.

"My husband is on his way here now. He'll be here any minute. You can leave now or wait out by the street. I would rather that you did not stay on this side of the fence."

"I ain't leavin'. I come for my money, and I ain't leavin' 'thout it. You hearin' me, lady?"

He tried the door handle and pushed on the glass. Now he was frankly menacing. Irene stood facing him through the glass without acknowledging him. She started to close the door to the house.

"You deaf, woman? I said, I come for my money. Now fork it over, or there's gonna be real trouble. You don't know who you're messin' with. Nobody jacks Ivan Slavich around. I want you should know that, little lady. You oughta know that good."

His face was flushed with anger, and his yellowed crooked teeth were bared like a snarling pit bull. He rattled the outer door impotently.

He had gone from menacing to threatening, and the diminutive woman was frightened. Irene closed the front door and bolt locked it. Slavich stood there for a minute looking as if he were trying to think and having a difficult time of it. He kicked the door a couple of times, then backed down the three cement steps of the front porch. He hurriedly walked around the house trying every window and door, but Irene was quicker than him. He stood on the porch again glaring. Finally, he stormed down the neat little front walk to his dilapidated Ford pickup.

Randolph pulled into the driveway of his house about ten minutes later. Slavich was still sitting in the front seat of his pickup. The two men alighted from their vehicles at the same time and walked towards each other. Irene could see them talking, but could not hear anything even after opening the front door and the porch storm door. The gist of the conversation could be inferred, however. Her tall, athletically built, and healthy husband was standing calmly, speaking infrequently, shaking his head in an unmistakable and implacable 'no'. The expression on his face was bland, but then it always was. It took a lot to rattle or rile up Randolph Kennedy. His facial expression was the same infuriating one he wore when the two of them had a fight, always a one-sided fight.

The small, disheveled workman was gesticulating, stomping his foot occasionally, and from time to time pointing in the direction of the fence. Finally, he made an obscene middle finger gesture to her husband and climbed back into his truck, slamming the driver's side door. Randolph stood aside—still unperturbed—until the angry tradesman drove away, scattering gravel from a jack rabbit start and careering up the narrow gravel driveway, running over border plants. It looked as if he were going to run down the mail box; but at the last second, he got control and sped onto the main road.

"Tell me, what did he say? What did you say? Don't leave out the details," Irene demanded as soon as Randolph entered the house.

"Nothing much," Randolph started to say.

"Just like a man. You have a five minute shouting match with a degenerate who was threatening to me; and you say, 'nothing much' was said."

Irene showed her ire easily, unlike her poker faced husband.

"I was trying to tell you. It was *nothing much*. And I didn't shout. I don't shout." He furrowed his eyebrows at his wife.

"He kept telling me that we owed him money for the entire fence because it was his job in the first place. I told him what I thought of that idea. Then he demanded a couple of hundred dollars in compensation for the work he had done. I reminded him that we had already overpaid him. I even said that we expected him to give us our $250 back that he took and never did the rest of the work for. He gave me the finger—told me where I could go—and stomped off. That's it. We've seen the last of that lowlife. Now, let's forget him and splurge. Let's go out and get a Big Mac and a Coke. I'm feeling expansive right now."

Irene laughed and shook her head at her husband. He was about as exciting and expansive as his most recent suggestion, but she realized how comfortable and safe she felt when he was around. It was not exactly something he said or did, and he was only average muscular or tough looking. It was just something self-assured and strong in his manner that made her feel her sense of security. And she knew that—behind his bland exterior and unflappable demeanor—he had steel in his spine. He was not a man to mess with. And it was his job to protect her; it was a comfort.

"Wow," she said, "this mood doesn't strike you very often. I'd better take advantage."

They brought their grease burgers, fries, and Cokes home and sat on their friendly old couch in front of the television to eat. Randolph turned to the news.

"Today, the president announced a broad reaching new program in the continuing war on drugs that was started by President Bush in 2004. We have her message in full then a brief response from the Republicans."

The white haired anchorman turned his head towards the studio monitor. The TV image changed to that of the president.

"My fellow Americans, ladies and gentlemen of the viewing audience. A great national debate has been underway in the past year on the subject of what should be done to halt the scourge of illicit drugs in this country. No single element of our society is nearly so destructive or costly. The Congress has debated the issue of sparing the American people the cost and simply making all of those addictive drugs legal. After all—it was argued—what could be worse than the escalating war being waged by successful and powerful drug lords from a dozen producing countries? The question came down to the acceptance of either of two bills before the Congress and the Senate: one for legalization of these poisons, and one for dramatically toughening the attack on the monsters who produce and sell the drugs. In the latter bill was a unique provision, one that this administration has fought to have enacted for three years running. That proviso—an unpopular one with the radical fringe groups of the far left and with drug users—states simply that the Congress shall provide monies; and the executive branch shall provide a program to interdict the trafficking in illicit drugs at the level of both the manufacturers and sellers and of the purchasers and users.

"We have too long railed against the producer nations, and they have considered us hypocrites for not seeing the problem as they do: America constitutes the world's largest market for illicit drugs. We citizens of the United States—they have argued—should clean up our own house. We should stop the users and purchasers by criminalizing the use of these drugs effectively by attaching real consequences to violation of our drug laws—serious laws with strong teeth in the prosecution of these crimes. I am pleased to tell you—my fellow Americans—that the Congress has done its part today. They have passed a law and moved it by express channels to my desk for my signature—a law that makes it a crime to have illicit drugs in *any* quantity in one's possession. Illicit drug possession will be a federal crime and conviction will carry with it a mandatory jail sentence. This represents truly zero tolerance for the first time in our nation's war on drugs. We have always gone after the producers and traffickers, now we are taking off the gloves and are going after the users.

"We, the people, are going to win the war on drugs. It has been suggested that I am somehow soft on crime because I am a woman, or because I am a Democrat and a liberal, even a secret liberal. My record in office these nearly four years has been unswervingly in favor of law and order. Let no one—friend or foe—mistake my resolve. The war on drugs is going to be won during my administration, and we are not going to put our tails between our legs and tell the drug lords that they have won. They will not even get a compromise. No, my fellow Americans, we are going to win outright. We are going to pursue the drug manufacturers, pushers, users and their confederates, the illegal arms merchants and traffickers into their hiding places, businesses, and even their homes. At last we are going to unfetter our law enforcement personnel; we are going to 'cry havoc and let loose the dogs of war' as Shakespeare so aptly phrased it. We—the people—are taking back our streets and our communities—civil libertarians and their arguments notwithstanding. We have had enough.

"Therefore—effective today—I am forming a working special police force charged with the responsibility of stamping out the twin scourges of illicit drugs and the guns that serve as their criminal enforcement. I will demand an end to any factional rivalries in the law enforcement agencies and will seek to curtail the abuses coming from civil rights laws that the criminals hide behind. In my capacity as president and using the authority vested in my office, I declare this drug and arms criminal syndicate a direct threat to the national security of the United States.

On that basis, certain of the civil rights enjoyed by the common citizens of our country will be temporarily suspended in the pursuit and prosecution of the criminals. Law abiding citizens have nothing to fear and will be able to carry on their ordinary activities free of harassment. However, the working force that will carry the war against the criminal elements into the places where they live, hide, and do their filthy business, will be most vigorous in carrying out the new laws. The law enforcement arm of the war will be called the Final Battle in the War on Drugs and Illegal Firearms Task Force—the Final Battle Group—or FBG, for short. This force will bring about the end of the drug cartels and international arms syndicates operating in our country. You have my solemn word on that. Thank you and good night."

"Let's watch *The Sorcerers*, Randy. All you ever want to watch is the news. I'm tired of the news. It's my turn to choose," Irene insisted.

"Here, the clicker's yours. I'm pretty disgusted by the promises of the president and all the rest about getting tough on crime. I'll wait and see what they actually do."

"I think President Vantassa is getting her re-election campaign ready. They start earlier every go-around," Irene added.

"What's *The Sorcerers*? Randolph asked.

He found it difficult to keep up with the dizzying schedule of twice yearly changes in the programming of the sitcoms and primetime dramas.

Irene rolled her eyes theatrically. Randy had to be from another planet. Everyone knew *The Sorcerers*.

"You remember, the one with that old actor—Rick Shroeder—the sci-fi action thriller set in Third World countries."

She smiled indulgently at her social cipher of a husband.

"The combination travelogue, religious message, and hero worship starring an aging former hunk?"

"That wouldn't be my characterization, but you've got the right one. I like it, okay? Stop belittling things I like. And, I'll thank you not to groan or roll your eyes when we watch it."

Her husband could be positively exasperating.

"Sure, it's okay. I heard a guy at work describing it. He said that the main characters in their special squad…"

"The Magic of Truth squad," Irene added.

"Yeah, the Magic of Truth squad. Anyway, this guy in my office said that the members of the squad say a prayer before every mission, a variation of the old Alcoholics' Anonymous prayer. 'God grant me the serenity to accept the things I cannot change, the courage to change the things I can, the wisdom to know the difference, and the overwhelming firepower to enforce my changes.'"

"You're terrible," Irene laughed affectionately, savoring her little victory.

She settled against him to enjoy the early part of evening before Annette returned from her visit to Grandma Kennedy's.

CHAPTER TWO

Sergeants Hodges and Proventura finished their cheese nachos and shakes, mutually belched in appreciation of the finer things in life, shared a brief laugh at their manners, and started up their black and white. The two men— partners for twelve years—were as comfortable as an old married couple. Both of them were up for detective this go-around, and it was their fondest hope that they would make it at the same time and would eventually be able to work together on the dick squad.

The two men took pride in their clean records. They had survived the sweep of 2009 that cleaned fourteen bad apples from the department. After extensive grilling and investigation of every member of the force, the two men had been given a clean bill of health by IA. Although—at the time, it had seemed Gestapoish-both sergeants had to admit now—six years later—the department was a much better place to work.

"Take her down Ackard, Mike. Let's check out the needle alleys. Since President Vantassa's speech, the green light's been on to bring in the little creeps and make life hard for them. I'm in the mood," Giovanni Proventura requested.

Mike Hodges turned off Main, left on Principia, and right onto Ackard. He slowed down, and the two police officers began a professional scanning of the rat and needle and pusher infested alleyways leading off the degenerating old street.

"Nothin' on my side, Mike," said Giovanni as they began to pass out of the worst blocks in the area.

"Mine, neither," said Mike, yawning and thinking of the three hours and two coffees that lay between him and the end of shift.

"Hey, wait a minute. Somethin's goin' down. Look…there by the Seven-Eleven," Mike said abruptly.

Three men—maybe more—were lurking in the shadows of the alley. Light glinted off white packages. A sleeve rolled up. The men were paying no attention to the street.

"Roll her down about twenty yards, Mike. Let's tippy-toe back and give the boys a bit of a surprise."

The cruiser glided to a stop. The officers quietly eased themselves out of their respective doors and left them ajar to avoid noise.

"Easy out here, partner whispered Giovanni, "These're mean streets."

Neither man had to suggest that the other watch his back. They took protection by the partner for granted after their long partnership.

"I'll go across the street and come back from that side; you take the near side, Giovanni, okay with you?"

"Yeah. Don't take no chances. Keep your weapon out and the safety off. Don't give the scumbags an even break, pard. We're goin' to be dicks, and these punks are not goin' to interfere."

Giovanni's voice was insistent.

"I'm with you all the way," Mike replied softly.

The two officers silently worked their way in the street shadows until each of them was in position. Giovanni held up three fingers. Mike signaled his understanding. Giovanni slowly folded down his fingers: three, two, one.

"Freeze, scumbags!"

"Nobody move a finger!"

The four men in the alley jumped several inches off the ground in total surprise. They must have thought they were invisible, and the realization that they had been seen was overwhelming. That they were under the guns of two determined cops had a paralytic effect. Only one of them tried to bolt. He received a nightstick coup across the back of his head for his trouble. The other three men were as docile as cornered rabbits awaiting the inevitable.

Ivan Slavich cursed his foul luck, the same rotten timing that had dogged him all of his life. He had the tourniquet around his arm and the needle in his antecubital vein when the cops burst in and ruined the party. He dropped his fix in the filth of the alley floor. He cursed.

"Assume the position against the wall. You know the drill. Spread 'em," Mike ordered, tapping one man on his back and another on the medial parts of both knees with his nightstick to emphasize his authority and by way of instruction.

28

There was some sniveling and grumbling, but easy acquiescence was achieved from all four men. The petty criminals all realized that there was no place to run; they were in a box alley. They were no match against two burly cops, and none of them was inclined to increase the charges against himself. They assumed the position and patiently endured the patting down and handcuffing.

Giovanni read them their rights, then the two officers herded the three men back to the squad car and stuffed them into the back—all still uncomfortably handcuffed with their hands behind them. The addicts were booked into the central jail and given a macaroni and cheese dinner, the slop de jour.

The following morning, Ivan Slavich's public defender came to see him in the interview room. Ivan was feeling ragged. The fix of horse he had missed the night before had been the first he had been able to afford for two weeks. He had counted on getting a little bread from the work job he had done for that Kennedy couple out in the 'burbs; and, getting nothing there for all his honest efforts, Ivan had finally had to knock over a little gas station on Rembrandt and Fifth two days ago. Things were tight, and last night had been his first chance to score a fix. The cops had come at the worst possible time; and now Ivan—one more day without his intravenous nirvana—was in a bad way. He had a hard time thinking.

"I'm Ruben Sanchez-Perez," the elderly, down-at-the-heels attorney said and reached out to shake Ivan's hand.

Ivan wiped a dribble of snot from his nose with the back of his blaze orange prison jumper sleeve. He wiped his hand assiduously and shook the attorney's hand.

"I've been assigned to your case, Ivan. You don't mind if I call you Ivan, do you?" asked the diminutive Latino attorney, a nervous, tired looking man with hair pomaded across his head from left to right to cover a conspicuous bald spot.

"Why should I mind, it's my name, ain't' it? Ivan responded grumpily. "Let's have it straight, counselor. What'em I up against here?"

"I took time to go over your rap sheet before I came in here, Ivan. This is the way it is. It doesn't look that good. I mean, to be blunt, you are a three time loser. What with President Vantassa's new program to get tough on little sellers and users, you're looking at a life sentence in calendar college as a career criminal. I kid you not," Ruben said soberly.

His accent was a soft Puerto Rican patois, fairly common in the city even before PR became a state four years previously. Ivan paid it no mind. He had more important fish to fry.

"You sayin' I'm gonna go up to grey bar city for the rest of my natural days, man? That what you're sayin'? For a two-bit little drug sale? What kinda mouthpiece are you? Can't you do no better'n that?"

Ivan let out a long, exasperated sigh.

"This is what I am telling you, my friend. If you don't come up with a fantastically good story between now and the time of your arraignment, you are goin' up river, Mr. Slavich. And you are going to stay up. You get my drift? There's nothing I can do for you. Maybe you shoulda thought of that before you got into your third felony."

"When's the arraignment?"

"Day after tomorrow."

"I gotta think of somethin' 'tween now and then, that right?"

Sanchez-Perez thought that at the rate this dim bulb was burning out his brain, prison was probably the best thing that could happen to him; but he did not say so. Instead, he took in a patient breath and started to explain the situation again.

"That's about it. You need extenuating circumstances; and they'd better be mighty heart wrenching, is all I've got to say. No more of that weenie stuff about murdering your parents and begging for mercy because you're an orphan. Or else you have to hand over some real juicy bit of state's evidence that makes them want to give you the key to the city. Otherwise, I'll make all my pitiful little pleadings, and do all my lawyer things; but they're going to hang you anyways. Think hard," Ruben said, pointing his bony finger for emphasis.

Ruben figured that it would be 'thinking hard' for the poor sniveler, Ivan, to tie a pair of lace-up shoes.

Ivan looked at Ruben through watery, itchy eyes. The man looked dead serious. Ivan felt like someone had just walked on his grave.

Ivan Slavich was not intelligent even when his brains were not fried with smack. If he were smart, he would not be in the fix he was in. During those infrequent times when he was sober and not in D.T.s, or narcotics withdrawal, Ivan did possess a certain feral street cunning. At the best of times, he functioned like a cornered weasel. In his favor was the fact that he was off drugs, not by choice; but it had been weeks since his last fix. The down side of his present condition was that he was off drugs and in the throes of withdrawal—generalized muscle aches, anxiety and uncontrollable nervousness, hypersensitivity to light, noise, and touch, runny nose, and loose bowels. By past experience, Ivan knew that he would be going into a hypercerebration phase shortly; and he would be able to come up with a cogent thought process temporarily until he crashed. His pattern had always been to be able to think better, faster, longer, and harder when he was between fixes, that is, when he could not produce the wherewithal to buy his next bit of nirvana in the form of beautiful China White. He hated the hyperalert feeling, but today this man who was the unfortunate product of a disadvantaged childhood realized that he had to come up with something unique and compelling if he was going to be spared a fate worse than death—life in prison without access to dope with a bunch of big guys that wanted to be his friends—his special friends.

The uncomfortable but useful hyperalert phase hit him in the night. He went into his third night without sleeping, but he thought with the intensity of a forest fire. Finally—in the depths of his weasel mind—a thought germinated; and a plan took root and grew. Three hours before his scheduled arraignment, Ivan Slavich had worked it all out.

"Good morning, Mr. Slavich," sparkled Ruben Sanchez-Perez, exuding an inappropriately light spirit into the somber gray interview room. "Ready for our arraignment, are we?"

"*Who's we?*" Ivan thought sourly.

He was strung-out.

"Whatchu got for me?" he demanded of his court-appointed attorney.

"Motion to dismiss based on your having been an innocent passerby caught in a dragnet with a police rush to judgment. I also have a motion for release on bail on your own recognizance owing to your strong ties to the community and your deep commitment to your job and family. You do have a job, right?"

"I'm between positions, as they say."

"Family?"

"Uh, uh. Parents kicked my out when I was sixteen. Wife kicked me out after two years of supporting me. Nobody else."

Sanchez-Perez shook his head.

"And so what if I don't?"

"To be perfectly frank, it won't matter a hoot in hell. The judge is going to have your sheet and your last sentencing review in front of him, and he's not going to believe one good thing I have to offer about you. Can't imagine why," Ruben said suppressing a dubious look

"Thanks for the vote of confidence."

"Just the facts, man, just the facts, as good old Sergeant Friday used to say back in one of the early cop shows."

Ivan drew a blank. He was not into history himself.

"So…straight. What's my chances of walkin' today? I got important things to attend to," whined Ivan, still keeping the note of defiance of authority in his voice.

"Between slim and none, about like a fart in a windstorm. About that much, by my reckoning," Sanchez-Perez responded bluntly.

"Then I ain't got no choice. I ain't no snitch by nature, but a man's gotta do what a man's gotta do. A guy has to take care of hisself first, don't he? I got a little tidbit that the pigs would love to have. A big tidbit, actually."

"It will need to be, Ivan. You are going to have to produce something they really want or you are going upstate for a long, long stay. Now, what is this electrifying news you have for the minions of the law, hmmh?" Sanchez-Perez asked, looking over his half glasses with a dubious gaze.

"It ain't for you to know, my man. It's ears only stuff for the proper authorities," Ivan said coyly.

Ruben rolled his eyes.

"No, I'm tellin' you man, I got to give this to the ATFers. I know somethin' about some hot stuff. They always wanna look good in the press and all. Here's their big chance. Get 'em on the horn, man. They're gonna love me, I swear. Time's a wastin'!" Ivan's voice had crescendoed an octave.

Ivan's enthusiasm was mounting so much that even Ruben-Sanchez—for all his world-weary cynicism—thought there might be the slightest hint of truth in what the little weasel was saying.

"You'd better really have something, Ivan. You screw this up, and the arraignment will take all of thirty seconds. They'll run you out of there by the seat of your pants, give you a serious marv, and right to jail without you picking up your two hundred dollars or passing go. You understand? And I am not able to vouch for anything you say because you have chosen not to confide in your court appointed lawyer. This is the last thing I am going to say on the subject. I am repeating myself, and I don't like to do that."

The attorney hoped that Ivan had not caught the sigh of relief in his voice.

"Just get on the horn, man. Get those ATFers in here. I'll light up their lights."

The arraignment was continued. Three agents from the Treasury Department's Federal Bureau of Alcohol, Tobacco, and Firearms arrived in the interview room of the central jail at three that afternoon, all of them

feeling a mixture of corrosive doubt just for being in the place and of tin-
gling anticipation that this could be the opportunity for a career making
public bust. During any average working day, every agent—whether he or
she admitted it or not—fantasized about the big bust, the media adulation,
the departmental commendation, and the meritorious promotion. Ruben
Sanchez-Perez had always been a straight shooter about this sort of thing
despite being the lowest form of human—a mouthpiece for scumbag crooks.
They had only a couple of hours to lose if nothing came of the meeting; it was
a slack time in the office.

Ivan Slavich was brought into the interview room shackled. His wrist
shackles were locked to the screw bolt on the utilitarian metal table. His
attorney sat beside him.

"I don't think it's necessary to keep his hands cuffed for this meeting. Okay
if you loosen up a bit?" Agent Drake asked the guard.

"Your funeral," the guard replied and unlocked Ivan's wrists. "I'll be right
outside the door if you need me," the guard, a slight black woman added.

The three ATF agents shared a look of fleeting amusement. Each of them
outweighed the guard by fifty pounds, and the skinny prisoner by a good
seventy-five pounds. The idea that the puny jailbird sitting in front of them
posed any kind of threat was a laugh.

Drake removed the smile from his eyes and thanked the guard. When the
attendant had left the bare utilitarian room, Drake introduced himself and
the other two agents to Sanchez-Perez and Slavich.

"I'm Drake, Henry Drake, Special Agent of the ATF. This is Darren Platte."

He pointed to the neckless man on his right who looked like he would
choke on his tie before the day was done.

"And this is Agent Tomworthy, Phil Tomworthy," he said and nodded
towards the younger of the two silent agents.

The young man had the features and dull face of a professional body
builder. He looked uncomfortable in the suit that must have belonged to his
little brother. Ruben Sanchez-Perez thought the man would be more at home
in WWF trunks; for that matter, they all looked like they were still in the beer
hall putsch phase of their careers.

The attorney accepted Drake's hand and gave it a desultory shake.

He introduced himself and said, "And this is Mr. Ivan Slavich, my client.
He has something for your ears only, he says." He turned to Slavich, "you
want me to leave, Ivan? I don't advise it, by the way."

"Yeah, man. You leave. This's between me and the ATFers."

Ivan reached over and shook Drake's hand and nodded at the other two agents who did not seem inclined to make bodily contact.

Ruben eased himself out of his chair and went to the door. He knocked, and the guard let him out.

Ivan watched until his attorney had left the room.

Then, with a conspiratorial look, he asked, "First thing I wanna know is what's in this for me?"

"Depends on what you've got for us, Mr. Slavich," Henry Drake responded noncommittally.

"Supposin' it's real juicy. Like maybe you guys learn somethin' as makes you look like big shot police officers. In the six o'clock news and all like that. Supposin' that?"

"I'm waiting, Mr. Slavich. I haven't heard anything that gives me the hots yet. I'm making no promises."

But Drake's pulse had gone up a notch.

"Like, say maybe I could tell you where the most important arms clearing house is right here in this city. Like, maybe it's the biggest bust you ever done. What would you have to say to that, huh?"

"If you can give me useful particulars, I'd be interested," said Drake, becoming more interested.

"So, like I ast in the beginning, 'what's in it for me'?"

Despite the reflexive doubtful nature that came from his long history of dealing with scumbags, Drake felt himself getting hooked.

"What're you after, Slavich?"

"I got me a little heat over a nothin' drug deal. Just possession. Not sellin', and nothin' big. But there's a little complication like. My lawyer, old Sanchez Perez—the spic there—he says I'm lookin' at bein' a three-strike loser. They gonna put me away as some sorta career criminal or somethin'. Don't seem right ta me. Now, maybe you could get this dippy little charge dropped, and I maybe could make like the ducks and get the flock outta here. You did what I'm sayin'?"

"I would consider putting in a good word in the right set of ears, Mr. Slavich. I still haven't heard anything concrete. Why should I believe anything you say? Why shouldn't I just think you're trying to get outta this hole and would say anything to accomplish that end?"

"'Consider' ain't good enough. I want a hard promise, official like."

Slavich was playing his best role—the hard-nosed jailhouse negotiator.

"Now, here's the clincher. I got a record as an official RCI. You call Agent Hatcher—Abe Hatcher at the DEA. He has my Registered Confidential Informant record. I done good by them. The stuff I give them guys is pure gold. You ast him. That's how I got that Reliable Confidential Informant title. You gotta be good; they don't just pass those credentials out to anybody, ya know. Then we'll get down to serious business. I ain't about to give my stuff away. My momma didn't raise no fools. We gotta work out a mutual trust, like Hatcher always says. You call him. He'll…uh, what do you call it…vouch for me."

"No time like the present. Darren, get hold of Hatcher. Verify this guy if you can. If you need to, I'll talk to him. I've known him for a while. Tell Hatcher he's supposed to cooperate now that Vantassa's made herself the generalissimo in the FBG, the latest final war on drugs."

"Yeah, boss. Be right back."

Flatte left the room.

The other three men sat in strained silence. Drake lit up a cigarette in violation of jail rules and calmed his habitual urges with a nearly blissful look descending over his mean features as he took a deep, inhaling drag. Slavich looked so needy that Drake finally relented and gave him a puff on his own cancer stick. Tomworthy was a Mormon and did not smoke. He moved to the rear of the room to protect himself as best he could from the second-hand poisonous vapors.

Flatte returned and quietly huddled with the other two ATF agents. He retook his seat at the table.

"Well, Mr. Slavich, seems that Abe Hatcher thinks you are an A-1 snitch. Let's hear what you've got to say," said Drake.

"We don't use the word 'snitch' no more. It ain't professional. I'm a RCI. First, I have your promise that I walk or no info, no deal. Period."

Drake sighed the sigh of a man who has just been bettered in a marked negotiation.

"If your info is good, you walk. Maybe even today. I'm feeling generous. Now get on with it."

"I want this in writing, soon's I get done."

"You'll get it if the info's good."

"Okay, I know you are a man of your word, a federal officer and all. It's good enough for me. This is the straight skinny. I have some contacts, see. Like the kind of contacts I get in my line of work as an RCI, maybe. They took me to a certain house where there was some crack and some Big H. They

35

thought I was some kinda pusher, maybe even a middleman. I let them think that all along, although I don't do nothin' like that. I was like doin' undercover stuff. You gotta believe me there."

Ivan's countenance fairly shone with the purity of his heart, and the battle hardened ATF agents were touched by his sincerity. At least their faces showed him that.

"Get on with the facts," interrupted Drake brusquely.

He crushed out his cigarette butt.

"I'm gettin' there. Keep your shorts on. Anyhow, like I was sayin' when I was so rudely interrupted…"

Three pairs of eyes rolled back in their sockets as if on a cue from the film's director. Ivan acted as if he had not seen them.

"These perps took me to their place. I mean, where they got their pieces and moved some contraband."

"Meaning dope."

"Yeah."

"That's it? You give us the address, and you think we do the big forgiveness for you? I'm here to tell you, Slavich, that's not going to be enough. How do I know that the whole operation hasn't flown the coop?"

"Easy, man. That's the best part. I was just there. Last week, I think it was. They got dope there all right. And for you guys, the sweetness in the pot. They got a basement full of guns, too. Big, fancy, new stuff. Machine guns, bazookas, grenades, and all like that. I ain't no expert on weapons, bein' a peaceful sorta guy, but I'm tellin' ya, they could start World War III pretty handy. I swear it on a stacka bibles."

"Here, Slavich, write down the address. Maybe we'll check it out. We can't afford slipups in this business. If the address is a phony or if the raid doesn't pan out, there'll be hell to pay. You hear what I'm saying, Slavich?"

"So, you're sayin' I gotta rot in here, all my business arrangements goin' into the toilet while you guys take your sweet time over at the office drinkin' coffee and eatin' a Krispy Kreme before you get around to checkin' this all out. That ain't right. I ain't no dummy."

"Maybe there's something we could do to move this business along faster. How about if you go back to the place and check it out for us. See if the stuff…see if it's still there. What about that idea? Gets you outta here faster."

"Maybe gets me killed, too. Ever think of that?"

Ivan was pleased with his performance, especially with the spur of the moment embellishments. It was this native ingenuity that made him a good RCI, he praised himself. He gave himself a couple of 'attaboys'.

"You're a pretty clever and resourceful guy. You know, you help us in this matter, and you got friends in the ATF as well as over at the DEA. A guy can't have too many friends, especially in your line of work, if you get my meaning. Right, Slavich? And friends don't forget their friends."

"If you say so," Ivan said, thinking hard now.

He had not counted on this. He was doing great up to this point. His psyche told him he could do it. Why not? They were right; he was clever.

"All right. Tell you what I can do. I check it out and give you a call. You guys got ona them throw away cell phones? I could call you on it right after I check it out undercover. You can be ready to break down the doors soon's I call. How's that?"

"Sound's all right. How do we know you won't fake it then book?"

"Hey, that's uncalled for. I'm a RCI, remember. You checked me out with Hatcher, remember. I gotta rep to uphold."

Tomworthy leaned over and whispered to Drake, "the guy thinks he's the SAC. I don't know, but I think he believes he's an important cog in the law and order machine."

Drake whispered back, "I know it sounds completely hokey, but I believe the guy. I must be getting soft in the head."

Tomworthy smiled.

"Me, too," he grudgingly agreed.

"You'll have to swear to your findings on an affidavit before a judge; so's, we can get a warrant. You willing to commit to that?"

"Then I get to go?"

Ivan tried not to whine or sound like he was begging. He needed his medicine bad, but he wanted to keep up the appearance of having the upper hand.

"That's our end of the bargain. You just keep in touch after that; that's all we ask."

"You bet, man," Ivan said. "*In a pig's eye*," he murmured inwardly. "You keep me on your RCI list or whatever you call it at your place, and I'm your man. Shake on it," he said.

Ivan solemnly shook the hand of each ATF agent to seal the deal—a contract among gentlemen. It was good enough for him until he had a written contract in hand.

And it was good enough for the Bureau of Alcohol, Tobacco, and Firearms. The two ATV agents took a side trip to the men's room and washed their hands thoroughly before setting off for the surveillance trip. Ivan Slavich—good as his word—took the agents out to the suburbs. While they filmed with a long-range digital camcorder, Ivan knocked on the door, and after several minutes of wheedling conversation, worked his way into the house. He was inside for about ten minutes. He left all smiles; the woman who answered the door appeared very pleased as well.

The U.S. agents and Ivan Slavich drove directly from the suburbs to the chambers of U.S. District Court Judge, Hyrum Petersen. He heard out the agents, then had Slavich himself give his presentation of the facts regarding the criminal activity taking place in the specified location. Ivan was getting better with practice. He related how he had wormed his way downstairs to the basement of the house on the pretext of checking out the goods for big money interests he represented. There he had seen a huge stash of rocket propelled grenade launchers, mortars, fully automatic machine guns, assault rifles, bales of money, and detergent boxes that were filled with baggies of China White. He had seen boxes piled on boxes of "commercial candy" that were in reality containers of individually wrapped rock cocaine.

Ivan was a thoroughly convincing confidential informant. He had braved the lair of the lion; the judge said so; and he deserved respectful treatment, however grudging. Judge Petersen oversaw the working of the agreement between the federal government and Ivan Slavich, RCI and witnessed the signatures. The ATF agents kept one copy, Ivan a second original. The deal was consummated, and another round of handshakes—this time including the judge—sealed the solemn arrangement.

Ivan had not been entirely candid about the visit to the Randolph and Irene Kennedy residence in the suburbs. What he left out was that he presented himself at the door—hat in hand—and with a completely abject penitent manner. He begged the lady's pardon, blaming his behavior on demon rum and his helplessness around evil drugs and pushers. He had even shed a tear. Irene Kennedy, by nature a soft and forgiving woman had bought the whole yarn. He never left the entryway of the house; and, certainly, he never stepped near the basement. As he left to meet the ATF agents he had thought to himself that there oughta be an Oscar for real life dramatic performances like his.

Judge Petersen made a copy of the agreement and Ivan's sworn affidavit and filed it in his records. He filled in the blanks on the warrant form and made a Xerox copy for his records.

He handed Agent Drake the warrant and said, "All right, gentlemen, go strike a blow for the right. President Vantassa will be proud of your work today." He turned to Ivan. "And, Mr. Slavich, thank you. You have done your part as a good citizen; I trust this event will mark a turning point in your life."

Ivan nodded his head self-deprecatingly. Drake, Tomworthy, and Flatte knew they had chosen the right judge for their warrant.

Back on the street, Ivan stepped up to Agent Drake and said, "Look, man, I'm kinda short right now. Think you could arrange a little advance on some of the CI pay? I mean, I did 'brave the lion's den' like the judge said."

"Don't press your luck, Slavich," was Drake's terse comment on Ivan's suggestion. "And don't even think about leaving town, neither."

"No way, José," Slavich said wagging his head enthusiastically. "I want in on more of the easy CI money; and like, I'm a good citizen willin' to do my bit."

Behind his back, Darren Flatte mimed placing his finger down his throat.

Drake, Flatte, and Tomworthy examined the documents to be certain everything was in order. It was simple. They had an open-ended warrant to search the premises for any and all illegal weapons and illicit chemicals and paraphernalia of drug manufacture. They had a blank check to identify all evidence relating to a conspiracy to commit acts of racketeering and to further the interstate transport of illegal firearms and drugs. Drake opined that this had to be an open and shut RICO case; they would be able to take away everything the perps owned, even their visible and invisible means of support—spoiled fruit from a rotten tree.

The name and address checked out with the phone book, telephone and utility company records. Randolph Armstrong Kennedy and his wife, Irene, in their sweet little white picket-fenced suburban home and with his job as a CPA, had the perfect cover. Discreet interviews with neighbors and co-workers revealed that no one knew a thing about the illegal activities. Drake warned the task force that these people were clever and probably dangerous. They would have to go in full force, and they would have to cover each others' backs.

"It's a jungle out there," he said, and smiled.

CHAPTER THREE

The names of Randolph Armstrong Kennedy and his wife, Irene, first passed the desk of President Muriel Vantassa on the second of April during the course of a meeting of the FBG. Within two days after her televised speech, the initials had stuck. Nobody had the patience for the cumbersome formal title of Final Battle in the War on Drugs and Illegal Weapons Task Force. Even Final Battle Group seemed uncomfortably pompous; so, by unspoken agreement, the government, the media, and the citizens all gravitated to the simple, FBG.

DEA, ATF, FBI, Army and Navy Investigative Services, and the Coast Guard representatives all submitted names and brief descriptions of the plans of raiding parties to the Attorney General, Margaret Thaler, who—in turn—passed them over President Vantassa's desk for her pro forma signature. There was little attendant discussion, and all raids were approved. Warrants were in order; Thaler was a stickler for technical legal details—a quality that endeared her to the president—because it kept her office squeaky clean and above criticism. That attention to detail ensured that the Office of the President would remain as pure as Caesar's wife. Eighty-seven raids had already been completed without a single foul-up, and the criminals arrested in the raids had entered the cumbersome judicial process amidst an orgy of media coverage. The latest batch of criminals amounted to an additional sixty-four named individuals and unlimited spaces for John Does.

"Good work, ladies and gentlemen," President Vantassa praised. "It feels good to be on the side of the angels and well under way after all the months of planning, doesn't it?"

"Does everybody have the same trouble we have in getting a little work done?" Irene asked Randoloph. "Sometimes I wish you were as handy as David Gabler."

Her reference was to their next door neighbor who had missed his calling by becoming an obstetrician. David was the quintessential handyman, able to build, remodel, wire and rewire, plumb, paint, or fix anything made of wood, metal, or plastic. He had three garages full of big boy's toys that were the envy of every inept man in the neighborhood. He was also a nice, generous guy ready to help anybody anytime. When Irene brought up Randolph's failings, he hated David. Not really—but every time the man's name came up—he had to smile and recall an old joke. Happiness is knowing that your brother-in-law who doesn't gamble, swear, smoke, miss church, or cheat on his income tax...has gonorrhea. David's name came up frequently enough in the course of this current repair job in their kitchen that even Randolph's vaunted patience was wearing thin. He ruefully thought that it wouldn't be so bad if David got just a little dose.

Randolph sighed and resolved not to take the bait this time.

"I will call Heckler's Construction for the umpty-umph time tomorrow. There is no call to leave that hole right in front of our kitchen door. And yes—I know that David could fix it—and that we have not been able to get in or out of that door for ten days. It's a death trap; but we paid Heckler's; and I am determined that they—not David—are going to finish their work. Last time, old Heckler told me they had to send for a special brass fitting for the gas line and that it would only take a day to finish lining the hole; so, it can provide storage space once they have that exotic fitting in place. They must have sent to Novosibirsk. Let's not argue about it. There's nothing we can do tonight. How about dinner in front of the tube? Did Annie get back from Grandma's? "

"Oh, something different," Irene said sweetly, "and Annie's been here for half an hour."

Randolph gave her a look.

"Isn't it almost Annie's bedtime?" he asked.

She laughed.

"It's only seven, five to. We'll be lucky to put her down by eight...or even nine. She had a two hour nap this afternoon."

He shrugged in minor defeat. He sat down at the card table set up in the corner of the kitchen and started to clean his handgun, a Glock .40. Randolph was an avid target shooter and spent two evenings a week at the indoor range run by the county sheriff's department and the NRA. He was licensed to own the gun—a rarity now since President Vantassa's successful implementation of legislation that required the confiscation of all guns except for hunting rifles and handguns registered with law enforcement agency shooting ranges. The new law required him to account for every bullet fired, and ammunition could only be purchased at the range. He was careful only to take home one loaded clip for fear of accidentally losing a round or two and having to account for them with endless paperwork.

"Don't make a mess, dear, okay?" I have my readers' club here tomorrow. I haven't got time to clean up again before they get here. Do you have a newspaper under you, Randy?"

"Yes, dear."

It was a ritual with them. She asked him the same questions every time he cleaned his gun—twice a week. He loved his gun and the tiny measure of freedom of choice for his own activities that it afforded. She hated the weapon with an inborn abhorrence. For her, guns were the quintessence of violence and brutality. Irene could not be comfortable whenever the thing was in view, and she could find an endless litany of faults until it was once again put away in the gun safe. It bothered her that her mild-mannered Clark Kent of a husband should like guns, should actually possess one and keep it in her house. She considered it a character flaw of Randy's that he was proficient in its use.

The gun was one area where the couple could not communicate.

When she broached the subject of his ability with firearms, he deflected the conversation or closed it with a terse, "I know it's not what a proper gentleman does, but I like to shoot. I do it legally in one of the few venues left in our country for legal gun use. I don't hurt anyone, and I don't commit crimes with my gun. I really don't want to discuss it."

And that was that.

Irene groused that her husband was a stubborn man for all of his exaggerated calmness. He could be allowed one foible, she supposed. He was a prince in most other ways, she thought fondly even when she was miffed at him.

He sat at the card table lovingly oiling his hand gun, and she finished the preparations on her platter of couscous; so, they could enjoy something special in front of the TV.

"Be ready in fifteen minutes, Randy. Maybe you could tear yourself away from your life's passion long enough to wash Annie's hands by then?" she asked petulantly.

He smiled indulgently at her. She was something of a nag at times, but she was the best thing that had ever happened to him. He decided that he would keep her anyway.

AG Thaler faxed the final go-ahead to all teams at 1920. Drake's team had been ready to roll for thirty minutes before the fax came through to the machine in their van.

"Mount up," he said. "The Dragon Lady has spoken. We have written authorization. Be careful out there."

The seven agents clambered into two nondescript black Dodge sedans, impeded by their own bulk and by their impressive personal artillery.

At 1950 they were all in place for the assault. The vehicles were parked one block above and the other a block below the Kennedy drug and arms distribution house. Radio command was set up in the backyard. The Kennedys had no dog, which made entry that much easier. Cops hate dogs as much as do burglars. Agent Jack Bailey—the rookie—manned the radio and sat sullenly in the shadows of the elm trees, grossing about having to miss the action. At the front entrance, Agent Flatte held the door ram poised at the ready with agents Drake and Michael Larsen on either side of the door ready to rush in. Agents Tomworthy and Doug Carter from DEA stood on either side of the rear kitchen door with Agent Stefan Yoblanski holding the heavy door ram for that entryway.

CHAPTER FOUR

"**D**ear, it's five to, the food's ready," Irene called from the family room. "Does that mean it's on the coffee table, or does that mean that it is almost cooked, and you want me to be seated in place; so, it won't get cold?"

It was another of their spoken rituals. Randolph Kennedy had asked wife the same question for the entire four years of their marriage in response to her announcement that a meal was 'ready'. She always said that the meal was on the table, and he always sat down—without complaint—while she actually brought the meal to the table. By now it was one of those comfortable man and wife jokes that could just as well have been assigned a number. Irene could have called out number "twenty-five"; and Randolph would have come to the table; and the two of them would have a small affectionate laugh. Irene was laughing now as Randy recited his part in the marital play.

He captured Annie after a short raucous chase and took the protesting sprite into the bathroom to wash her hands. She was like every other kid, hated to have her hands washed and pitched a fit if her rights were violated by a forced face washing. Her curly corn silk hair flew about as her head bobbed and shook during her struggles to free herself. He tickled her into submission— evoking a peal of musical laughter from the little imp—and did no more than a halfway job of cleaning his daughter's grimy little fingers. Randolph was not nearly as strong a believer in the germ theory as his fastidious wife.

"We're on our way," he yelled at Irene as he put Annie down.

He walked back to the kitchen table to put his gun away in the gun safe. Randolph was punctilious about gun safety as he was about most of the activities of his life. He had the added incentive of protecting his adored little girl from any accidental contact with the dangerous weapon.

Dinner was noisy, messy, and full of hilarity as Annie recounted the imagined activities of her day. She was a theatrical, unselfconscious child; and her stories were models of fractured syntax, non sequiturs, and wondrous imagination that never failed to charm and amuse her parents.

When they finished, the family division of labor was enforced. Randy began gathering up the dishes and utensils, and Irene swept Annie up in her arms and marched into the little girl's bedroom. Randy put the dishes in the sink, rinsed them off; and placed them in the dish washer.

Annie ran to her parents' bathroom and Scotch taped to Randolph's mirror a small round note to her dad the size of a penny. In her childish scribble, it read "luv". She returned to her bedroom and snuggled with her mom. Randolph heard the melodious voice of Annie's mother singing the bedtime song the little curly headed girl always wanted.

Sleep my child, and peace attend thee,

All through the night.
Guardian angels, God will send thee,
All through the night.
Soft the drowsy hours are creeping,
Hill and dale in slumber sleeping,
I, my loving vigil keeping,
All through the night.

Angels watching gather round thee,
All through the night.
In thy slumber, they surround thee,
All through the night.
They will let no fear alarm thee,
No foreboding shall disarm thee,
They will let no peril harm thee,
All through the night.

"They're separating. The male perp is in the kitchen; looks like the woman and the kid headed for the kid's bed room. We'll have to watch out for the kid. I have 2012. We'll go on my count at 2015. The perp'll be in motion and off guard. We'll get to him before he can get comfortable.

The three radio stations verified the message from the team leader.

Agent Bailey whispered from his post in the backyard, "All clear out here. No activity, no guards, no apparent security devices."

"No more chatter, I have 2013 and 45 seconds. Everybody synchronize, and get ready. This is the last communication before my count," Drake whispered and looked at his watch, mentally counting the digital numbers as they appeared.

Randolph picked up his handgun, worked the clip in and out of its receptacle, and slid the cocking action back and forth to ensure its smooth well oiled function. He picked up the gun's holster in his left hand preparatory to putting the holstered gun away in the safe.

"It's almost the news," he called softly to Irene who was still rocking Annie to sleep.

"Counting," said Agent Drake. Every man in the team felt a final surge of adrenaline. This was the show. This the time their teamwork training paid off. They prided themselves at being the best of the best. At least—Drake was fond of pointing out—none of them had shot a member of the team yet.

Drake's harsh whisper was the only sound any of them heard…"three, two, one."

With the last number uttered, Agents Yoblanski and Flatte crashed their respective door rams into the cheap synthetic doors of the perp's house and crime site, easily knocking them off their hinges. By prearrangement, Agents Tomworthy in the rear and Larsen in the front burst through the openings thus created, followed directly by Drake and Carter.

The sound of the doors being splintered off their hinges blasted like a cannonade through the house. Randolph looked at the kitchen entryway and was startled to his core to see Agent Tomworthy take his first heavy step into Randolph's home. The sound from the front hallway was slightly muted by its greater distance from him. Randolph could not react to an attack coming from two directions. Agent Tomworthy tromped his heavy foot through the flimsy particle board of the downed kitchen door. His momentum propelled him forward, through the door, and down into Mr. Heckler's open pit in the kitchen floor. His right tibia and fibula neatly snapped off midshaft. The young officer involuntarily screamed as the bone shards ripped through his muscles and bared themselves outside the skin. Agent Carter crashed over the top of his fellow agent and hurtled forward onto the back of the hapless Tomworthy further destroying the already mangled leg. It was a surreal unfunny Keystone Kops action.

Reflexively reacting to the unannounced intruders, Randolph adopted a leg forward shooting stance, pointed the muzzle of his Glock .40 directly at agent Carter and fired a single round.

The hot projectile hit Carter—a family man with four children—dead center in the forehead as he pitched forward in his fall into the kitchen. He fell over Agent Tomworthy causing another eruption of pain and screaming from the man with the broken leg. Randolph fired a second shot; this round entered the face of the already stricken Agent Tomworthy. Phil Tomworthy died with an expression of pain and astonishment still etched on his face.

Drake bolted into the front entryway pushing Larsen aside and bolted in the direction of the gunshots.

"Who fired?" he yelled.

He knew instinctively that this raid was not going to go down easily.

Darren Flatte followed close at Drake's heels. He rushed past the family room catching Irene Kennedy with his peripheral vision as she jumped up from her rocking chair holding the pink pajama clad baby. He did not have long enough to see the look of utter bemusement on the face of the beautiful blond woman. The movement from the bedroom was a blur to Flatte. It triggered a primeval response. He whirled and loosed a three-round burst from his MAC-10 machine pistol. All three hollow-point plastic man-killer bullets ripped through the curly-haired baby's chest without dissipating any of their energy. They continued through to make three holes in Irene Kennedy's chest no more than two centimeters apart. She and her little girl, Annette Caroline Kennedy—named for the daughter of President John F. Kennedy, Randolph's idol, and now the middle-aged dowager of the famous political family—were both dead before they hit the floor. Annie's tiny chest was nearly cut in half, and Irene had two explosive strikes to her heart and a third that pulverized her ascending aorta.

The local news continued to play on the bed sheet sized TV screen Randolph and Irene had all but mortgaged their home to buy.

Randolph heard the second set of gun shots and the footfalls rapidly approaching him from behind. He took two large steps to place himself in the far corner of the kitchen away from the carnage at the door. Less than two seconds had elapsed since the doors came crashing down.

Agent Bailey heard the shots—and on his own initiative—radioed for backup. It sounded like the start of a war in there, and he was crazy with worry for his teammates. He weighed the possibility that Drake would excoriate him afterwards for acting without orders, but he decided that calling was the lesser of evils.

With the opposition down in the bed room, the remaining agents—Drake in the lead—followed in close file by Flatte and Larsen from the front and Yoblanski from the rear, advanced on the kitchen. Randolph knelt in his corner out of direct sight of the intruders. His mind raced. His worst nightmare was happening. He had heard of house jackings on the news; but that was like a lot of news, something that happened to someone else. It was only an act of God that he had happened to have his Glock in his hand at the exact moment or his whole family would be dead. He was unaware that his wife and daughter had been gunned down. He fought to clear his mind.

Drake stuck his machine pistol—an Uz—into the kitchen and sprayed the room with bullets before making an athletic roll across the floor. Randolph shot the agent in the left buttocks as he was at the top of his roll. Randolph's aim was still low as Flatte came rushing in looking right, closely followed by Yablonski looking left. Randolph fired again and caught Flatte in his pubis, immediately below the lower margin of his bullet proof vest. Flatte shrieked in mortal agony. His last thought before the mercy of unconsciousness and death overtook him was that his pecker had just been shot off.

Somewhere in the primeval fighting portion of Randolph's brain, it registered that his assailants were wearing protective chest coverings and helmets. There was no time for coherent thought. He made the adjustment and fired at Yablonski, hitting him in his left eye just as he turned in the direction of his killer in the corner. The entry wound was .40 centimeter in diameter; the ragged exit wound from Yablonski's head was 8.5 centimeters across. The agent did not have a chance. For a fraction of an absurd second, Randy had a flash that Irene would not appreciate the mess in her immaculate kitchen. Larsen stumbled into the room, tripped up by Flatte's fall. He was shot in the head and died instantly.

Yablonski had been a brave man, but not a quick thinker. He had seen his fellow agents and teammates go down and had reacted with the reflexes of a hero. He entered the house from the kitchen door and had had to step on the bodies of his fallen comrades to stand on the floor. He had fired his MAC-10 at chest level as he had been trained, but he had not anticipated that his opposition would be firing from a point well below waist high. He became a bona fide hero—a dead one—for his mistake.

Drake was a tough man. He curled on his side, gritting his teeth against the pain of his buttock wound and fighting to remain conscious. He fired one burst of three rounds in Randolph's direction. One of the slugs ripped through Kennedy's tense lateral abdominal muscles inflicting a pain like a hot poker stab, but without causing any serious damage.

Randolph fired his last three rounds into the center of Drake's chest as he lay on the floor facing up at him with his gun blazing fire. The flack jacket prevented penetration of Randolph's bullets, but the harsh concussive impacts and the new series of alarming pains were enough to render the already shocked senior agent unconscious.

Sirens converged on the heretofore placid neighborhood from every direction. Policemen and women—ill informed as to which was the crime scene home, the one involved in the raid—crashed into two wrong houses momentarily before entering the Kennedy residence. They came in through every window and opening where doors had once hung. They found a totally bewildered, pale, shocky appearing, bloody Randolph Kennedy kneeling over the bodies of his wife and daughter amidst the carnage and destruction that had once been his home, his safe retreat from the world. He had dropped his empty gun somewhere in the hallway, and now he was totally unarmed and defenseless.

Agent Bailey pushed his way through the house distractedly identifying the bodies of his fallen ATF and DEA teammates.

When he came face to face with Randolph Kennedy, he declared, "That's the perp."

Then he walked back outside white-faced and vomited into the geranium pot.

CHAPTER FIVE

City police handcuffed the totally docile Randolph Kennedy's hands behind his back. The police officers—especially the new set of ATF agents—were still pumped with excitement that was fueled by the mounting rage over the deaths of their fellows. Randolph stood numbly between the two police officers who had taken him into custody and were waiting for a squad car to come to them for transport to the station. Agent Jack Bailey snarled something unintelligible as he walked by the trio, causing Randolph to turn and look the agitated agent directly in his narrowed inflamed eyes. There was a brief staring-down contest, and neither man blinked. Bailey made as if to turn away; then, almost as an afterthought, he turned and smashed the defenseless prisoner full in the face with a ham-sized fist, dropping him to the ground.

A second overheated ATF agent, who had walked up to stand beside Bailey, was caught up in the moment of hysteria, and he aimed two ferocious kicks into the fallen man's ribs before one of his fellow agents dragged him away muttering, "it won't help, and the perp might get a civil rights case out of it. Remember Rodney King."

Randolph's right eye and cheek now featured a new perceptible swelling as he was raised to his feet and shoved into the squad car. The officer took care to see to it that Randolph's head collided with the car door frame. The police sped away with lights and sirens to avoid any further escalation of the already dangerous confrontation.

He was taken to central admitting, fingerprinted and photographed. He was then thrown into a holding cell, rehandcuffed. The jail doctor, as was required, came to do the admission history and physical.

"Nasty wound on your belly, Kennedy," the doctor announced once he had completed his cursory examination. "That'll need a laparotomy."

"What's a laparotomy?" Randolph asked suspiciously.

"Open your belly, an operation to see if you have a bowel or blood vessel injury on the inside. Can't tell without it."

"I want to see my own doctor. No offense, but I want a second opinion, doc.'"

"I'm all there is, Kennedy, like it or lump it. You are the guest of the city right now, and you don't have any options. Medically, you just do as I say."

"Are you the surgeon?" Randolph asked dubiously.

The man seemed shaky. His fingers were tobacco stained; and over a strong smell of Bay Rum cologne, Randolph was sure he detected the faint scent of alcohol.

"No. We'll have to call one in."

"I'll wait."

"I guess you will. You aren't about to be going anyplace for a long while. I understand you declared war on the United States government. They don't take kindly to that kind of thing. Cop killers don't fare too well in the system. A bit of advice—you're in no position to be pushy or choosy."

It was another hour before the surgeon arrived. His examination was more thorough and painful. He probed the bullet entrance wound on the side of Randolph's abdomen with a gloved finger and a cotton-tipped swab. He pushed a finger of his other hand deep into the larger exit wound. He could almost bring the two finger tips together. The pain was excruciating. The grisly-faced old surgeon seemed to take a measure of perverse satisfaction at his prisoner-patient's discomfort.

"Well," he said finally. "I can't tell for sure if that bullet perforated your peritoneum. Only way is to do an abdominal exploration, a laparotomy. I kinda don't think it did. Your belly seems pretty benign: good bowel sounds, no rebound. It's your call, Kennedy. I recommend surgery, but you can refuse and sign an AMA release."

"What's an AMA release?"

"Oh, yeah, we docs use too much jargon. That's against medical advice."

"*And CYA,*" thought Randolph.

He was familiar with that set of initials. Randolph feared the system after the events of the evening. He feared being helpless under the anesthetic and feared an operation at the hands of a surgeon whose first loyalty and interest was not his patient. Randolph feared surrendering what little control he had more than he feared some future infection.

"I'll wait. No surgery," he announced with finality.

He was left alone for a time. His ribs hurt; he was developing new places of hurt as every slow minute went by. The ATF thugs had inflicted several memorable injuries, but Randolph decided that they were relatively minor—just painful. Besides he had a much deeper hurt—one that was not ever going to heal. The reality of his wife's and child's deaths was beginning to sink in now that he was alone, and the adrenaline rush of defending himself against an imminent enemy had subsided. Randolph had a stark knowledge of what he had lost; Annie—his daughter—had been the fun and sense of wonderment in his life. Irene—the trusted wife and friend of a naturally reticent and solitary man—had been his stabilizing factor—the abscissa to his ordinate—the balance to all of his planning. She was his young lover and his heart's friend; they were at once Krishna and Radha, Ulysses and Penelope. He would never forget Irene and Annie's killers.

Two teams of interrogators attempted to question Randolph at intervals through the night. One team was from the ATF and the FBI, and the second was from the local prosecuting attorney's office.

"I will not talk to you until I see a lawyer and have him present," was Randolph's unchanging refrain no matter how many times he was asked and no matter how progressively more exhausted he became.

The overt and unrelenting hostility of the questioners convinced him that the teams did not have the slightest interest in the truth; rather, they wanted him to recite a confession of their making; and they were not going to go away until they had what they wanted. Randolph was adamant: no attorney, no conversation; he would remain silent until the lawyer appeared. The teams read him his Miranda rights, threatened, cajoled, begged, persuaded, whispered, and shouted. Finally, Randolph was unshakable in his belief that the hostility of the interrogators was such that he needed protection from them, and the interrogators had to admit that the cop killer was going to persist in demanding his rights. They backed off for the rest of what remained of the night.

Randolph was extremely tired, and the reality of his wife's and daughter's deaths was beginning to penetrate through the fog of his cognitive processes. His tragedy became his sole focus now that the adrenaline and emotion that surrounded the raid had entirely dissipated, and the mental battle with his law enforcement tormentors was over. Randolph was numb and weak—enveloped by ennui. He was too fatigued to feel the full passion of either anguish for his loss or fury for the injustice he had suffered and apparently was going to continue to endure.

He could not sleep, even after the last interrogation team left him alone in his cell at four o'clock in the morning. His mind just could not quit. His thought processes were erratic, benumbed, and he was unable to hold onto a coherent thought process. His ideas ricocheted from anger to sadness to bewilderment to mundane concerns that it was trash day; and he would not be there to put out the cans; and Irene would scold him. The lawn needed mowed.

Shortly after six in the morning, two corrections officers came to his cell and announced that he had still another visitor.

"Skip it," Randolph snapped presuming that it was another set of interrogators. "I have the same message as last time and the time before that—wait until I see my lawyer."

His voice was devoid of emotion, and his speech was methodical and flat.

"Don't give us a hard time, buddy. We were sent to get you. You come. What you do with your visitor is up to you. Now, get up and follow us."

Randolph put up no more argument, and he meekly offered his wrists for cuffing. The guards also fitted ankle shackles as they had each time he had been taken from his cell.

He was again seated on the hard steel chair; and his wrist cuffs—applied overly tightly—were locked to the screw ring on top of the bare, none too clean steel table. The two guards stepped back. A woman—about forty—dressed in a severe gray suit and light beige cotton blouse, was escorted by a third guard to the other end of the long table. She wore no makeup or jewelry. Her face was calm; and—for her age—almost unlined. Her face was outwardly Botticellian—neither severe nor unpleasant—but all business. Her shining straight black hair was streaked with gray hairs about which she had no evident self-consciousness. Her skin was the color of rich cream, all the more white in contrast to the intense blackness of her thick hair. She had a vaguely unidentifiable exotic look, the ethnicity of which could evoke a plethora of unanswered speculations.

"Hello, my name is Mary Tomlinson," she said. "I am from the ACLU. I have taken the liberty—the presumption—that you might need our help. The public defender's office doesn't know I'm here yet. You might even have a private criminal defense attorney in mind. I think the ACLU is best equipped to deal with the U.S. government. Frankly, they don't always…I'll amend that; they don't *ever* act in good faith when one of their own is a victim or one of them is accused. The public defender's office is too busy and too weak to deal with Big Brother—and unless I miss my bet—you don't have the money to afford a top-flight defense attorney on your own."

She looked levelly at the shackled man at the other end of the table, studying him before he responded.

"I think I'm the one being accused, Ms. Tomlinson. I don't see how I am in any position to be on the offensive, although any decent and objective judge would see me as the victim here."

"You're half right, Mr. Kennedy. You are indeed the accused. From what I could glean even from the overtly biased cops, you shouldn't be. You are wrong if you expect something called justice. At least your lay definition of the term, or decency or objectivity from a federal judge. Justice is what happens in a courtroom, and that has little to do with the truth or what really happened. Federal judges protect their own interests which coincide with those of the government of the United States, quite conveniently. Starting today, you are going to be tried and convicted in the news media. Vilified, is a more apt term. By the end of the week, every school kid in the country is going to know you as a slathering pedophilic dope-smuggling terrorist and wanton slayer of innocent police officers who are one and all born-again Christians, family men, and dog lovers. They are—to a man—all martyrs and heroes."

She delivered the entire speech without altering her nearly beatific facial expression, but a little color rose in her cheeks.

Randolph shook his head. His exhaustion prevented him from thinking clearly enough to deal with what this hard talking woman who was saying. His whole body drooped.

"I'm sorry. Sometimes I forget the human side to this kind of thing. Your wife and daughter…I'm sorry," Ms Tomlinson offered.

Her expression was genuinely sympathetic now.

"Thanks," he said quietly.

He slumped forward and was silent. His usually tanned and active face now seemed pasty and void of interest.

"Talk to the PD, but don't commit to anything until you talk to me again. You need me. I can help. Sleep on it."

Ms. Tomlinson motioned to the guards to take him away.

Randolph had never had much sympathy for the ACLU or its causes. They always seemed to be on the wrong side defending the degenerates, the commies, and the crazies. It was a deeply sobering thought that he was considered to be a prime candidate to be an ACLU symbol of their ongoing fight against the power of big governments violating the supposed rights of the little people. His problem was to decide whether or not he fit into the category of people who needed that kind of help. He was innocent of anything.

He knew it, and everyone else should know it. It was a nightmare from which he did not seem to be able to wake up.

Two factors that happened in close succession made for an easy decision. Randolph slept for four hours. At one o'clock in the afternoon, he was taken to see the public defender who provided the first deciding factor.

"Mr. Kennedy. I am Rudolph Swaze. I have been appointed to defend you since I understand that you don't have the means to secure your own private attorney. I have reviewed the facts of the case, and I'll be blunt."

Swaze glanced down at his watch, obviously intent on getting through the schedule of his busy day.

"I see no viable alternative except to cop a plea."

Sensing that Randolph did not know the exact definition of the police-attorney jargon, Swaze added, "Plead guilty and make a deal with the prosecution."

Randolph looked more surprised than angry at the suggestion, but manifested a significant measure of both emotions in his weary, lined face. He did not speak.

The attorney's next communication was a corollary.

Swaze leaned a little closer and said, "You can plea-bargain for a light sentence by turning state's evidence against your accomplices. Finally, if none of the plea-bargain attempts is successful; you can plead guilty and throw yourself on the mercy of the court. This is your first offense, I presume. I think we could get the charge of aggravated murder tossed, and you would be able to get only life without the possibility of parole."

"Lucky me," muttered Randolph ruefully. "I am innocent. I am a victim. I will plead innocent. I need an attorney who is ready to defend me from the arraignment to the Supreme Court if that's what it takes. I need an attorney who will do a thorough investigation, who will pursue my case in the courts, in the media, on the streets, and in the back rooms. I need to be defended by an attorney who believes in me, one who is not too busy to care about me."

"Look, Kennedy, you killed four cops. The case against you is air tight. The Public Defender's Office of Hopewell, Virginia does not have the resources to fight lost causes. We are not going to be a party to a circus. We are not going to pursue this routine matter anywhere beyond the court of jurisdiction. I will give you a good defense; I have already outlined the options; it's up to you now."

He paused, smiling at the thought from this simpleton client that his case was some sort of grand precedent setter. The man was a dummy. That opinion was evident on the attorney's bored face.

"And there is nothing grandiose about your case, Mr. Kennedy. The Supremes won't give you the time of day. Get real."

"Thank you for coming to see me, Mr. Swaze. I will not be needing your services."

"Your funeral, my friend, but nobody is going to force you."

Swaze got up, strode briskly to the interview room door and knocked three times on the steel. He departed without a backward glance or comment.

The second decisive factor that convinced Randolph to accept the offer from the ACLU was the newspaper. To his surprise, his request to see a copy of the day's paper was granted. Banner headlines read: "LOCAL ARMS MERCHANT IN SHOOT-OUT WITH ATF". The article occupied the portion of the front page above the fold and in the right two columns. It presented Randolph as a known criminal with a lengthy rap-sheet and suggested ties to the latest Colombian cartel. He was described as having a long record of drug and arms offenses, according to unnamed ATF and FBI sources. The article described the incident as an ambush of police officials set up with the aid of an accomplice. There was no mention of his wife and daughter.

After he ate his carbohydrate lunch, Randolph asked the guard to let him use the phone. He called Mary Tomlinson and signed on as a client of the American Civil Liberties Union.

CHAPTER SIX

President Vantassa's FBG task force met in emergency session the day following the Randolph Kennedy house shoot-out. It was the only item on the agenda. Attorney General Thaler quickly mentioned the other thirty-two raids carried out—all successfully—over the last two days, and moved quickly on to the Kennedy case.

"It looks like the perp was lying in wait for our guys," Ms. Thaler told the assembled law enforcement officials and the president. "I don't have any idea how he knew they were coming, but he obviously did. Agent Drake—who led the raid and barely survived it—reported that he suspects the ATF's informant, a usually reliable CI. At this point in time, there is no good evidence linking the CI to Kennedy except for his reported visits to Kennedy's house, one of which was witnessed by the agents. We'll be monitoring phone logs as soon as the FBI can review them."

Muriel Vantassa had not risen to occupy the highest office in the world by being gullible or slow-witted. She was famous for her insightful ability to cut to the core or a situation and to examine the fundamental kernel hidden away.

"Margaret…" the president paused for a moment in thought, then went on, "by tomorrow morning I want a full report on the informant who signed the affidavit that led to the warrant that in turn led to the raid. I want to see a detailed raw data description of all surveillance of the suspect house and its occupants. I want to see the full record of the evidence that convinced that judge to sign a warrant. And—for good measure—it is in order for the FBG and me to review all evidence—and I underline all—that links the residents of that particular house to any criminal activity. Get me a rundown on the law enforcement personnel who participated in the planning and execution of the raid. For some reason I am getting mental images of the wackos at Waco, and I don't mean the religious fanatics inside the compound.

"I am also thinking of the debacle at Ruby Ridge, of the silliness in Jordan, Montana, of two notorious mistaken raids on residences in the last decade of the previous century—where, unlike this raid—no one was hurt. Clinton's administration took gas for the raid on the Mueller family in St. Charles, Missouri. I am loath to have the same cloud descend over the presidency during my watch, if you catch my drift. Now, what are you doing about damage control for the time being?"

Thaler knew that she had been skewered and had just received a scolding by the president. The attorney general blanched briefly.

"Madame President, we've started the full court press in the media to make our case—a proper law and order action—against a hardened criminal secretly operating in the midst of a nice family community. When we're done, even his own mother won't have this Kennedy fellow over to dinner. We've sequestered all of the law enforcement officers involved, even peripherally. We are going ahead with the criminal case with the utmost care and dispatch. We're trying to get the perp to cop a plea and to save everyone the pain and expense of a drawn out trial. We've had a busy day."

The president was quiet for a few minutes, her face thoughtful and frowning. No one in the room was brave or foolish enough to interrupt one of President Vantassa's famous brooding silences.

Finally, the president broke her silence, "This is what I want all of you to do. Right now—and until further notice from me—I want you to put a lid on it. Establish a news blackout. This is to be kept *sub judice* within our task force, and I will have the scalp of anyone in any federal agency who leaks a word. There is too much at stake here. My whole drug war to end all drug wars program can be fatally jeopardized by us painting this guy as the Great Satan and beating him half to death in the news or in the courtroom only to find out that he is—in fact—nothing more than the innocent victim some renditions of this affair show him to be. This government cannot be seen to be violating the eleventh commandment in the prosecution of this program of ours, certainly not in the early stages. It is too early on in its development. We stand to risk too much. Now get me the objective information I have to have. Any questions?"

The chief ATF agent looked askance at the director of the FBI.

"What's the eleventh commandment, Ted?" he whispered.

He knew it was another of Vantassa's oblique references whose meaning was known only to her inner circle, of which Ted Coleman was one.

"Thou shalt not commit nincompoopery," Ted leaned over and said into the ATF chief's ear with a rueful tone.

The head of the DEA was the only one to venture a response to the president's request for questions.

"And, Madam President, what are we going to do if it turns out that we have really stepped in it this time?"

The 'we' to whom he had reference was patently obvious—the ATF. The long simmering inter-service rivalry between the two services was barely kept from boiling over publicly by the iron hand of the president.

"Well, Carl, I guess we'll have to deal with that eventuality when we come to it. Let's get to work on the tasks at hand, what do you say, gentlemen…and lady?"

Immediately after her reply, the president rose, abruptly signaling adjournment.

There were no further announcements from the government in any news media and no leaks from anyone, an unheard of situation that, besides driving reporters crazy, perplexed Mary Tomlinson. She knew better than to trust her good luck.

"We can concentrate on getting you ready for the grand jury instead of working on our own press campaign. That's a real plus, Randy," she said. "Precious resources can be focused on the main task—our case in chief. Now let me tell you about the grand jury system and what you can expect."

Mary spent an hour describing the federal grand jury system: how it got started in England in 1215 when the barons forced King John at Runnymede Meadow to sign the Magna Carta guaranteeing that a person could be bound over for trial only upon information or indictment by twelve out of twenty-three of his peers. The concept of presumption of innocence until being proved guilty originated there, she told him. Ms. Tomlinson dwelled particularly on how it came to be that a witness before the grand jury could not have his or her attorney present. She explained—in a contemptuous tone—that an appearance before a grand jury was not an adversarial process; rather, it was a one-sided presentation of information by the prosecution and that double jeopardy could occur; failure to indict by one grand jury could lead to an appearance before a second jury.

"Prosecutors are sheepherders in their communications with the jury. They all abuse the process flagrantly in favor of their side of the case. They don't have to present exculpatory evidence; there is no mechanism for opposing counsel to object or to elicit testimony or to present evidence in the accused's behalf; and no examination of adverse witnesses. The jury in there today is only going to hear the government's side of the case. In fact, there is no law or rule that even requires that the person under suspicion of having committed a felony must be present. It doesn't matter if the evidence against the defendant is insufficient or incompetent. In a case where the Bank of Nova Scotia sued the United States and in the famous Calandra case, this fact was established by precedent that has never been reversed. The record in favor of federal prosecutors before federal grand juries is nearly 97 percent for accused tax violators and only a little less for criminal matters."

She took a deep breath.

"I don't even get to respond with information that helps my case, even if it's relevant?"

She shook her head.

"You have to understand that it is not the grand jury's job to find the truth. They are empowered only to decide whether or not to proceed to the adversarial system of a judge and jury as you know it—the petit jury—where the truth can be tested, including both sides of a case."

Randolph thought he did not have the chance of the proverbial snowball in hell. He felt as if he had fallen down Alice's rabbit hole into a world he could not understand. His only contribution to the conversation was a small expression of self-pity.

"I was the victim of the government. Now, I get to be the victim of the government again in a starchamber court. Then—if I understand the system correctly—I get to be the victim one more time when they try me in federal court. It's like standing in line for a movie and having a guy come up and punch you in the face for no reason. Then, he gets you hauled before the magistrate for bashing his knuckles on your nose. Truth, justice, and the American way. It's more like slavery, lynching, and kangaroo courts—the American way," he almost spat.

"Finished?" Mary asked, no sympathy on her face and none in her voice.

"Um hmmh," Randy muttered.

Under her tough exterior, she grieved for him. He had lost his wife and daughter; his house was a shambles, nearly completely destroyed; and he had not been able to return to work. There had been broad hints that he would be fired. He was bearing up rather well, all things considered.

"Sorry," Randy said, subdued. "I hate whiners as much as you must."

"You've got a right, Randy, but it won't help. Remember, this is only one step in a long process—presuming that you don't have a miracle; and they no-bill you. Let's get down to work and prepare you for the gauntlet. I am going to ask you a bunch of very tough questions. Try to anticipate the ones you might get in front of the grand jury. Don't take offense, but I have to know. You and I can not afford any surprises. Whatever you do, don't lie to me in the tiniest degree."

"Go ahead."

"Did you or do you use illegal drugs—even marijuana that you don't inhale like that president said a while back—what's his name?"

Randolph shrugged. He could not recall that president's name, and he did not think it mattered. The old excuse had become imbedded in the culture and would probably be the only lasting legacy left to history by a distant past president.

"Never. Don't now, didn't then. Nobody in my family ever has. My wife was a health nut."

"Okay. Did you in the past or do you now participate in any way—financially, physically, or by influence—in the trafficking of illegal drugs?"

"No, again."

"Do you own a gun?"

"Yes, a Glock .40. It's properly registered. I use it for target shooting on an authorized range. Every round is counted by the range marshal. Other than for the ones I fired on the day my place was raided, every bullet that gun has ever fired can be accounted for."

"Good. Do you sell guns?"

"No."

"Did you ever sell or move guns to other people by any means?"

"No."

"Handguns, machine guns, bazookas, artillery, grenades, mines, explosives—ordnance of any kind or description?"

"No."

"Never?"

"Never."

Randolph's answers were coming without hesitation or anger—just matter-of-fact—the way Ms. Tomlinson liked them. She smiled her approval.

"Were there any guns in your house, besides the one handgun you told me about, on the day of the raid or during the days shortly preceding it?"

"No."

"Will the ATF officers find evidence of the presence of guns in your house, in your basement, or buried in your backyard—like rifle crates, ammunition pouches, bullet casings, creosote?"

"Just some gun solvent and oil in the kitchen and on my little workbench in the basement where I usually take care of my pistol."

"Any criminal associations, friends, connections? Anybody suspicious in your background? Any skeletons in your closet that we need to deal with before the prosecutor springs somebody on us in the grand jury room?"

"Nope. Not in my family or Irene's family or anywhere in our circle of acquaintances."

"What about the guy who swore in an affidavit that you had guns and lots of other ordnance in your basement and that you were one of the main links in an international gun smuggling syndicate? Where did he come from?"

"Beats me. I don't have any idea who he—or she for that matter—is, or if he or she really exists even. I have never heard a name, have you, Mary?"

"No. I have a sneaking hunch that they have spirited him away to the WP program, and he's now farming in East Dust Bowl, North Dakota or some equally bovine place. They'll keep him there until the day of your trial and spring him on us then."

Mary had bitter feelings about the witness protection program that so conveniently allowed the government to obtain testimony from their witnesses without the witnesses ever being deposed or—all too frequently—even being subject to cross examination.

"Randy," she said earnestly, "You got anything at all—and I mean anything—you want to tell me? Now's the time, not when we get into court and are unprepared for a prosecution surprise."

Randolph reassured her that he did not. The two of them poured over the complaints filed against him and the brief summary of particulars from the federal prosecutors. After three hours of intense study, the effort was becoming obviously repetitious; and Mary called a lunch break.

"I think you're ready. I'll be out in the hall waiting for you. Don't let them wear you down. Stick with the truth and the famous old KISS principle: Keep It Simple, Stupid."

"Thanks for the vote of confidence in my mental powers," Randy said with a mock hurt expression.

Mary made a little face, as if saying, 'if the shoe fits…"

Margaret Thaler reported directly to the president on the case preparation for the grand jury in the matter of US vs Randolph Armstrong Kennedy. President Vantassa listened to the brief presentation without interrupting.

Her comment at the end was, "about all you have is an affidavit from the druggie snitch that there were arms in the guy's house. That sounds like a weak defense for the ATF and my drug war to end all wars program than it does an indictment of the accused. Do you agree, Margaret?"

"'Fraid so, Madam President."

"Then you'd better pray that the bumpkins on the grand jury—and after that the petit jury—love cops and think they can do no wrong. Maybe we can get an indictment, and the guy will roll over and accept a plea for a light sentence. If we don't get that indictment—even in our skewed system—do you think Kennedy is a loyal enough American to forego suing us?"

"This is the twenty-first century, Madam President. All of those kind of Americans died off before 1950, some sixty plus years ago. I don't feel that hopeful. But, you know the old saying is that a federal prosecutor can get a grand jury to indict a ham sandwich or something along that line."

"Nor do I think we can escape a civil case if the grand jury does not do its duty for queen and country. It's time to circle the wagons. Margaret, get someone good on a defense case for us on the presumptive worst case scenario that this Kennedy person gets no-billed by the grand jury and that he files suit against the motherland."

"I think that's wise and not really premature, President Vantassa. We can't afford to muff this one. For the life of me, I fail to see a defense for us except for the ole saw that we were doing the best we could with the information we had. I hope it flies."

CHAPTER SEVEN

Mary Tomlinson received a telephone call long after she went to bed on the night before Randolph Kennedy's grand jury appearance.

"Hullo?" she managed, her mind and speech viscous with sleep.

She looked at her digital alarm clock. It was just past two in the morning, an obscene hour in Mary's estimation.

"It's two o'clock. This better be important."

"Do you know who this is?"

Mary recognized the voice of Kerry Pageant, one of the assistant U.S. attorneys prosecuting the Kennedy case.

"Uh-huh," Mary muttered, trying to shake the cobwebs from her mind.

"Don't say it—my name, I mean—we need to talk, okay?"

"It's your dollar," Mary said.

For some reason, she remembered how her grandmother used to say, "it's your nickel." Now that was indicative of the times.

"Look, this is unofficial—off the record—but officially unofficial, if you get what I mean."

"Perfectly clear so far. Like I said, it's two in the night. This better get better."

"Your client, the Kennedy guy?"

Mary was alert now.

'What about him?"

"Look, I think we could work a deal, a plea. Maybe not even have to go to the grand jury. We offer him a slap on the wrists, probation; and he walks. No fuss or lost time for any of us. He doesn't hear from us, and we don't hear from him after that. Sound like something you'd like to consider?"

The plan that Pageant and the other three assistant U.S. attorneys had discussed with Margaret Thaler included another element. They elected to keep quiet a proviso in the contract that required absolute silence—and down the line a while—they would find a snitch who would get Kennedy to talk about the case, incriminate himself. They—the feds—could lock him up for a violation of parole. That way, everyone came out smelling good, with the possible exception of Randolph Kennedy who did not count in the equation.

"Let me see if I get this right. It sounds like you're proposing that we skip the grand jury and go right to sentencing on a guilty plea, that right?"

"That's it. I said this was officially unofficial. I think we can do that."

"On what charge?"

"Look, the AG—and you didn't hear me say that—is prepared to go down from premeditated murder of a federal officer to simple assault. The judge could be persuaded to adjust the sentence. The powers that be give their assurances."

"'Powers'…like the attorney general of the United States? Maybe even her boss?"

"You didn't hear that from me. Look, I can't stay here. I'm in a lousy pay phone, and I'm nervous about the neighborhood. We want to clear this thing up with no fanfare before the ten o'clock start of the grand jury session. Whatta you say, Mary? Are we gonna play ball?"

There was a moment of silence on the line and only their breathing could be heard.

Then, in a clearly enunciated voice—slightly raised but free of rancor—ACLU attorney, Mary Tomlinson said, "go piss up a rope, Pageant," and hung up.

Mary and Randolph seated themselves on a hard straight back bench outside the grand jury room at the federal building at quarter of ten. Randy's two guards removed his shackles and flanked him. Five minutes later, three U.S. attorneys and a coterie of aides whisked by them and entered the jury room. Kerry Pageant glanced at Mary but did not acknowledge her, and they scarcely made eye contact. Thirty-five minutes went by.

"What's going on, Mary? I thought I was supposed to testify at ten. I thought that's what this was all about," Randy said, betraying his nervousness.

"Take it easy, my friend. First of all, the grand jury runs on FST—that's Federal Standard Time for outsiders. They can be anything from five minutes to an hour slow. We're lucky to be first on the docket, and this isn't

Washington. Second, they're in there get in their licks, sort of rousing the jurors up to picture you as a slathering, smelly monster who sells bombs wholesale to terrorists for sheer love of destroying the jury's loved ones. Cheer up, Randolph, it's a nice day."

She delivered her message with a completely straight face.

He laughed. There was little else to do.

The jury door opened, and a bailiff stepped out into the hallway.

"Randolph Armstrong Kennedy," he called in a basso voice that was meant to intimidate and was successful.

"That's me, Randolph said.

He raised his hand like a school boy, then quickly dropped it, having serious second thoughts about his small attempt at levity.

"Follow me, sir," the bailiff ordered. "You're on to testify."

Randolph got up. Mary gave his hand a small squeeze as he left for the grand jury chamber.

"Break a leg," she whispered.

His two jail guards slipped quietly into line and followed the accused witness into the room. Randolph counted twenty-three people sitting in the jurors' section. The prosecutors and the presiding judge were arrayed on one side of the room, and the witness seat—a worn old wooden arm-chair—was situated in the center of the room opposite the jurors. The room was close and smelled faintly of sweat. To Randolph it was the smell of fear. If the smell was coming from him, he knew it was fear.

The bailiff swore him in.

Without any introductions or preamble, the presiding judge intoned his formal instructions to the jurors, who appeared bored. They had heard it all before, too many times since it was late in their terms of service. It was not even necessary for a judge to be present during the day to day proceedings, but the mutton-chop bewhiskered and wizened old jurist had been brought in as a rent-a-judge for the purpose of going through the twice a quarter ritual of swearing in the jury.

Judge Jendrassik's monotone voice recited, "Ladies and gentlemen of the grand jury of the United States of America, it is my duty to tell you that you are the accusatory body with the sole purpose of rendering judgment as to whether the accused—Randolph Armstrong Kennedy—has been shown to have committed a crime based on the evidence presented by the prosecution. If the evidence is unexplained or unrefuted by the prosecutor, you will tender a bill of indictment. If you do not believe the evidence sufficient, you will render no bill. You are to rely solely on the information provided by the prosecution, which may or may not include testimony by the accused. You will not hear from a defense attorney. There will be no examination of adverse witnesses or presentation of contrary evidence; there will be no tedious objections."

Having performed his brief duty, the judge became silent.

Randolph glanced nervously at the jurors. They seemed to him to be over-awed by the judge and by the large coterie of prosecutorial attorneys. The jurors—in turn—looked at Randolph as if they presumed that he could not be there unless he was guilty. At least that is what Randolph felt. He felt very small and very alone.

Assistant U.S. Attorney Geraldine Constant introduced herself, then asked, "Is there anything we can get you, Mr. Kennedy? Some water, perhaps?"

"Please," he answered gratefully.

He forced himself to calm down.

"The jury is considering the matter of US versus Kennedy. Perhaps your attorney informed you that the grand jury is less formal than that of a regular courtroom. The jurors are free to ask questions at any time. Why don't we start with your version of the events of August 11, last."

Judge Jendrassik quietly slipped out of the room as the prosecutor began to speak.

Randolph slowly and thoughtfully recounted everything he could recall about the day and night of the raid on his family by the ATF agents. He had had several weeks to collect his thoughts and to put the events in order. The jurors obviously liked his crisp and unembroidered delivery. He told his story in less than ten minutes.

"We have a sworn affidavit attesting to the fact that your house was full of lethal firearms and explosive ordnance, as recently as the day before the officers executed their search."

Randolph loved Constant's euphemism.

"Would you please tell the jurors how you disposed of that contraband before the officers arrived on the evening in question? They will be particularly interested in your informant, since it cannot be a coincidence that the arms disappeared only hours after the search warrant was prepared."

Randolph paused, considering his answer and making sure that he did not come across as angry. He looked at the jury. An older lady on the front row sat knitting without looking down at her work. Her eyes were fixed on him. Randolph thought of Madame Defarge and waited for the juror to drop a stitch.

"Mr. Kennedy?" Geraldine Constant insisted.

"Who signed the affidavit accusing me?" Randolph countered politely.

"I ask the questions, sir. That's how it's done here. Should I have the question read back?"

"No, ma'am, I remember it. I never had any arms in my house, ergo, I never disposed of any. I did not have any informant, unlike the ATF. And who was that, ma'am? I'd bet the jury would like to know that name and to hear from him or her."

"Again, I remind you that I do the questioning, and you do the answering."

"Well, I for one demand to know who this phantom informant accuser is!" called out one of the jurors, a florid-faced man in a checkered sports shirt and ill-matching tie, trousers and two-tone shoes.

"I'm afraid that I cannot divulge that information, Mr. Juror. First of all, I don't have it; and I understand the person is now in the witness protection program and beyond our reach for his own good. I'm sure you'll appreciate the implications of that, sir."

"I'd still like to hear him tell his story. Seems awful convenient to me," the juror groused.

As Mary Tomlinson had predicted in their preparation sessions, the U.S. attorney ran down all of the accusatory questions about drugs and guns. About the only crimes not attributed to Randolph thus far were trafficking in child pornography, wife-beating, and being the cause of the recent hurricane. He thought that they would likely get around to those charges as the day wore on and the attorneys' creativity increased.

"Did the cops find any evidence in this guy's house that he had been a dope dealer or a gun runner?" asked a lady juror, a portly African-American with a world-weary, untrusting face.

"There were several areas in the home where gun-cleaning chemical residue were found."

The juror snorted, "He already told us that he has a gun and that he keeps it clean. That's only sensible in this day and age. Everybody lives in a war zone, now. Need some protection," she said.

A scrubbed-faced athletic blond woman—no older than twenty-two or twenty-three—spoke up from the second row, "Did his gun check out? I mean, is he telling the truth about it being registered and all that?"

"Yes, so far," the assistant U.S. attorney replied, unable to keep a touch of reluctance out of her voice. "But the investigation is still ongoing."

The young woman juror spoke softly now, "Mr. Kennedy, your wife and baby were killed, isn't that what you told us?"

"Yes, ma'am."

Randolph's head drooped slightly. There was a short catch in his voice. He found it difficult to look up.

"I have one last question," she said. "I want to know exactly what evidence there is against this man. I want to know about something tangible, something we could see, or smell, or touch. I don't want to hear about a piece of paper that someone we can't even talk to signed. I want to hear some incriminating evidence, real things. I don't think I have yet."

"We have the testimony of a reliable police informant, a man who has assisted the police a number of times to bring criminals to justice. We have to protect these sensitive sources of ours from violent criminals like Mr. Kennedy sitting there. No one could deny the evidence of his having slaughtered five federal officers in the performance of their duties. He doesn't even deny that evidence—*real evidence*—of five dead bodies. This man is a cold-blooded skillful killer, ladies and gentlemen. Whatever evidence we may or may not have, Randolph Kennedy is a murderer. You heard Agents Drake and Bailey testify. The man was waiting in ambush for them, gun in hand. He ambushed and murdered those federal officers."

Constant was passionate now in contrast to her earlier controlled objectivity.

The jurors were quiet and thoughtful for a few minutes, mulling over what Ms. Constant had just told them.

The silence was broken by the juror in the ill fitting clothes, "So, as I see it, we're supposed to bring back a true bill on a man who was sitting in his home when a mob of men dressed in black and carrying heavy artillery busted down his doors and killed his wife and baby. Think he used them as bait, lady?"

"I'm not so sure that you aren't right. Mr. Kennedy certainly put them in harm's way," Constant replied, regaining her professional composure knowing it was more effective.

The juror snorted, "This Kennedy guy is either the ballsiest guy on the planet—sitting alone in his own house with nothing but a little pistol to lure a dozen highly trained and heavily armed federal agents in there to ambush them—or the rottenest—lets his own wife and daughter get killed while he cold-bloodedly picks off the agents. Or…he is the victim of the decade."

"I'm ready to retire to deliberate right now," blurted a white-haired elderly man wearing a toupee that had become slightly askew in his excitement.

He looked over thick glasses that had slipped down on his nose.

"Me too," several other jurors chimed in chorus—including Madame Defarge—who had desisted from her knitting without dropping a stitch.

"I have nothing more, ladies and gentlemen of the jury," concluded Geraldine Constant.

She had the distinctly uncomfortable feeling that she had lost control, and her ship was sinking. She kept that sentiment off her face with effort.

"The witness may be excused."

"I got one more real serious question, Madam U.S. Attorney," called out the juror with the mixed pattern outfit.

The man had been a thorn in her side for the full fourteen weeks that the jury had been sitting. She could scarcely wait until the next term would bring in a new set of jurors.

"What is it, Mr. Juror?" she sighed.

"Why are we here? Why is this man here? Way I see it, we oughta be sending him flowers and a sympathy card from the jurors, and a written apology from the government. We should be recommending him for a key to the city insteada treatin' him like he was a criminal. That's all I got to say."

It was more than Geraldine Constant could bring her self to do to thank the man for his contributions even for politeness sake. She had Randolph Kennedy escorted from the room and gave the jurors their charges.

"Push the button when you have reached your decision. The defendant will be waiting outside with his attorney unless it gets to be too long."

There were a few snorts of laughter from the jurors that Ms. Constant ignored.

"So, how'd it go, Randy?" asked Mary Tomlinson when he came back into the hallway waiting room and took his seat on the hard bench beside her.

His guards sat across the hall facing them. They appeared completely bored.

"Okay, I guess. Too soon to tell. Jury is out. Some of them didn't seem to be all that much against me," he said.

"Tell me what happened. I want to know everything."

"Well, it was like you said, same sorts of questions. Some of the jurors…"

The door to the jury room opened, and the bailiff walked out and motioned to Randolph.

"Mr. Kennedy, would you please step back inside the jury chambers?'

Randolph followed him obediently, accompanied by his shadowing guards. Mary Tomlinson was unprepared for so rapid a response from the grand jury. He had not been out of the grand jury room for five minutes. She gave him a thoroughly puzzled look as he disappeared into the jury room.

The twenty-three jurors, the presiding judge, and the prosecution team were all in their assigned places. The white-haired juror spoke as soon as Randolph was seated.

"I am the grand jury foreman, foreperson, or whatever," he said. "We the jury in the matter of U.S. v. Kennedy return no bill in this action against you, Mr. Kennedy. We all got together and wanted to say this to your face. We're sorry for what happened to you and your family. There was not a one of us that thought you are a criminal. Please accept our sympathy for your loss."

Randolph thought he saw Madame Defarge's knitting project to be perfect—no dropped stitches, no head to roll in this modern version of the Revolutionary Tribunal of Charles Dickens's, *Tale of Two Cities*. He simply nodded his thanks. He did not dare to speak. His eyes filled with tears.

"You're free to go, Mr. Kennedy," said a taciturn Geraldine Constant.

She and her aides gathered up their papers and attaché cases and left without further comment, a grim-faced quintet.

The funeral was a simple one, conducted by the local Mormon bishop, since Irene had become interested that rapidly growing church in recent months and had been considering converting. Randolph was the only family member present. Irene's widowed mother was too crippled with rheumatoid arthritis to make the trip from Indiana. Randolph had no family. He came to the Perpetual Rest Mortuary early and sat alone on the front pew of the small funeral chapel eyes fixed on the open casket bearing his wife and daughter. Tears scalded his eyes and embarrassed him.

The funeral director padded up beside Randolph and softly laid a well manicured hand on the bereft man's sagging shoulder.

"It's time, Mr. Kennedy; the others will be here in a moment," he murmured in the dulcet tones common to all funeral directors.

Randolph was in a trance. He stood beside the mortician and forced himself to approach the bier. The coffin was made of pine stained to simulate oak, the best he could afford and not nearly enough. He mourned.

His family lay still and cold and silent. He could not bear to touch the embalmed flesh again. He had been shocked by the unnatural cold and hardness of the once vibrant skin when he had kissed them the day of his release from the grand jury. He struggled for composure, wrestling with desire to throw his face into his hands and sob out the agony welling up in his heaving chest. Silent tears cascaded down his cheeks and dropped one by one on the satin of the casket.

He bowed his head, and softly said, "Irene, my dear, how can you leave me? I am all alone. God help me; I don't know what I'll do. Annie, my sweet baby girl; you are the light of my life, and the light has gone out."

He cried, "I hope you're in a better place, you two. I would give anything to believe that. I long to see you again."

Bitter acidic tears poured out of his eyes, and he could not stop them. It was just raw pain, not even cathartic.

He could not go on. He nodded to the funeral director who slowly closed the lid of the casket and secured the side locks. It was an act of such finality that Randolph felt as if fingers of cold stone had closed over his heart. He felt dead himself.

He was unseeing when the mortician led him back to his seat.

An auburn haired neatly dressed woman sat next to him and introduced herself to him as "Sister Maguire. I'm the Relief Society President—that's the women's organization."

Randolph nodded dumbly.

Ten or fifteen men and women filed into the small chapel's benches and silently took their seats. There were all in dark suits and best dresses.

"Members of the ward," Sister Maguire said. "That's what we call our congregations. They came to pay their respects to Sister Kennedy and baby Annie."

It was the kindest and most unselfish thing Randolph could remember happening to him in his recent life. He did not even know these people who had taken time from their busy lives to offer solace to him—the freely given kindness of strangers. The Relief Society president's use of the title "Sister" under other circumstances and at another time when his world was whole might have seemed antiquarian or quaint. Now, it struck him as warm and inclusive. He felt that his wife and child were not so alone and cold and dead. It seemed that there was a surrogate family present for this last painful tribute. Conspicuous by their absence were any of his former friends and co-workers. Randolph knew that he had become a leper to them.

An unseen pipe organ played "Beyond the Sunset." Randolph found himself crying again. No one seemed to notice, and he was not the only one. The Mormon bishop stood at the pulpit and introduced himself. Tears rolled down the man's wrinkled farmer face. He gave an unembroidered talk on the sanctity and continuity of life and on death and the resurrection, on hope through Christ of families coming together again beyond the sunset. He touched on the fact that Irene and Annie Kennedy had died at the hands of another.

"We are all sinners," he said, "all in need of the forgiveness of Christ and Heavenly Father. As difficult as it appears at this moment of farewell, we must all learn to forgive those who have trespassed against us so that we—in turn— can be granted forgiveness when we face the judgment throne."

Randolph did not think he was nearly ready for such a magnanimous act of pure Christianity. He still felt that those responsible had more penance coming.

The gravesite was ready to receive Randolph's family. The bishop, Relief Society president, and the faithful followed the hearse and the black Chrysler limousine to the cemetery. It was a brilliantly sunny day with birds singing in the trees and flitting by in curiosity. Randolph was too numb to be aware of them. Members of the congregation acted as pallbearers with Randolph. He insisted on doing that one last thing for his two girls himself. The bishop dedicated the grave, and the casket holding Randolph's entire family was low- ered to the bottom of the six foot deep rectangular hole. He and his ward members solemnly filed by, shook Randolph's hand one last time, expressed their condolences again, and left the man to his private grief.

He was still there when the sun began to set. A burly man in bib overalls walked tentatively up to Randolph and cleared his voice.

"Uh, buddy, I don't mean to be no problem. I'm the sexton, and me and my guys gotta get the work done. You mind?"

Randolph roused from his torpor.

"Oh," he said, "sorry. Sorry to keep you. I'll go. I know you have to cover her…them. I know."

The sexton recognized the profound sadness, the irretrievability of his work to cover the coffin with impersonal earth. He gave Randolph a moment. Randolph slowly stood up like an old man. He felt old and worn. He turned his back and walked away with a parting glance at the hallowed ground and caught the sexton's eye. The sexton felt a shiver pass through him. He had had a glimpse into the soul of a man, and that soul was filled with a frighteningly unfinished rage.

CHAPTER EIGHT

The president accepted the telephone receiver from her aide.

"Yes," she said into the receiver.

Vantassa listened, then said, "I see. Not too surprising. Kennedy's not a threat, anyway; but I have a concern about some of our people being called to answer for the mistake. And that's what it was, a mistake. I'd personally like to kick their butts up around their necks, but we need to keep our teams working together. We have to regard this as collateral damage. We are not going to let the simpering liberals break up our force just because some of the ATF agents were overzealous."

She stood nodding her head at the telephone.

Then she said, "Thanks, Margaret. Keep me posted."

President Vantassa wondered to herself how long it would be before the civil lawsuit in the Kennedy Affair was filed.

Mary Tomlinson did not do civil litigation; so, she referred Randy to Chuck Murow, the chief of litigation for a private firm in Richmond and a fire-breather. She had characterized Randolph's case as "a slam-dunk, Chuck. You need to get it filed and into the public's eye and mind as soon as possible."

She would have loved to have had the option to stay on in the number two spot on Randolph's legal team, but the ACLU did not condone participation of its attorneys in civil litigation following criminal actions.

Randolph stoically accepted that Mary had to step out of her role of advocating for him.

"I appreciate your work, Mary. It was too brief. I still feel my head spinning. I am grateful."

"Maybe we could stay on as friends. I'd like that," Mary said to Randolph as she shook his hand warmly.

"I could use a friend. The ones I used to have or thought I had seem to think I caught leprosy. Thanks for the offer. See you around."

It seemed abrupt, even to him, but he could not think of anything more graceful. He left the ACLU offices and bought himself a large filet mignon for a lonely celebration lunch.

Chuck Murow filed the suit in federal court the following day.

He called Mary from the firm's lunchroom and asked, "soon enough?" after telling her that the papers were all in. Now all they had to do for the time being was to sit back and watch for the fireworks to begin.

The government fired its first salvo with its usual artillery. As if by magic, informed sources were insinuating stories into newspapers, television, radio, and online. It was apparent to Chuck that the government had been prepared well in advance. They were geared up for a war—perhaps just a war of attrition, with the news media as the battlefield—as was the rule in federal and state cases where the government was the defendant. With real attention to the battle, the U.S. government could poison the air so effectively that it would be difficult to bordering on impossible to find an unbiased jury. There were no Marquis of Queensbury rules at this level of skirmish.

Chuck Murow had a serious conference with his partners. When they were finished, they were all convinced that they would reap an eight figure reward from the case. They voted a budget for the news blitz that exceeded anything they had ever approved in the past, but they were adamant that the budget could not be exceeded. If the government did their usual and kept up the media pressure until they had to cry uncle because the feds had more money than their little law firm could muster, then they would have no choice but to capitulate. The partners reminded Murow that they were in the justice business to turn a profit, just like everyone else.

Thus sobered, the first step was for Chuck to wangle himself an interview on the Terry Weiss show—the nation's unofficial prime time sounding board. There he announced a $50,000,000 wrongful death suit against the United States government, the Treasury Department and its Bureau of Alcohol, Tobacco, and

Firearms, and 25 John Does for good measure. Chuck included agents Drake and Bailey personally by name. The show served as a grand pulpit. Chuck was able to present his case unimpeded by input from the opposite side and with every rhetorical flourish a sympathetic host and audience could provide. The next day, Attorney General Margaret Thaler presented the government's case in the same venue with an equally sympathetic host, but to a noticeably less responsive studio audience and set of outside callers.

The assistant U.S. marshals were enlisted in the media campaign, and the U.S Marshal's Office sent high-ranking speakers out as its contingent. Randy spoke at the Rotary Club, on six talk shows, and agreed to an article in *Good Housekeeping*. The President's Task Force took the public high road and spoke out against the scourge of drugs and guns, only obliquely referring to the Randolph Kennedy Affair, as it was now popularly and semi-officially known.

Murow's firm fed a steady diet of factual information to online bloggers which paid off better than any other propaganda medium they employed. Everyone in the country under sixty-five had a computer, and all but a handful of them regarded the internet as more honest, accurate, and informative than the networks and newspapers.

Kennedy's name was linked subtly to Colombian interests, to the Provincale crime family of New York and New Jersey, to the Aryan People's Republic, and once—as an aside—to an information highway child pornography ring. The ACLU volunteered to help and appeared on the few remaining liberal talk show forums to decry the escalating brutality and trammeling of individual rights in the president's law and order crusade. The Randolph Kennedy affair ranked high on the discussion agendas of the thought-provoking shows and in nationally syndicated newspaper and news magazine editorials.

"It's only news for a week," Chuck reminded Randolph. "They'll be onto something else next week. With no national figure directly involved, the media will scent new blood by then. We've done our share. I think we'll be hearing from the disloyal opposition any time now."

The call came a week later. It was during working hours, and Randolph was present in Murow's office when it was received. Chuck put the call on the speaker phone.

"Hello, Mr. Murow," came the genial voice. "Kerry Pageant, assistant U.S. Attorney, here. How are you today?"

"Fine, thanks. You?"

"Couldn't be better."

Chuck smiled at Randolph.

"Hope I didn't catch you at a bad time."

"No problem. What's on your mind?"

"We—that is the people in the U.S. Attorney's Office—thought it would be a good time to talk about this Randolph Kennedy thing."

"You mean instead of continuing the expense of the media circus?"

"Ha, ha," Pageant laughed with the sincerity of a TV program laugh track. "Something like that. Perhaps we could do lunch and hash this thing over."

Randolph hated people who 'did lunch'. He knew he was not going to like Kerry Pageant one bit.

"What's wrong with the present. Uncle Sugar's paying the phone bill, no skin off you. Why not take the time and do business here and now?" Chuck pressed.

"Well, good, then. Fine. We—that is the people in the U.S. Attorney's Office—were hoping that something of an amicable settlement could be reached here. No use in seeing this thing blown out of proportion. I think there are some who feel badly about the poor woman and the kid. Maybe we could come to an agreement, something fair to both sides."

"Hasn't been all that amicable thus far, Mr. Pageant, I must say. Why the change of heart?"

"I'm not far enough up on the totem pole to make the big decisions, but I could guess that the AG or even the president want to get on with weightier matters of the law, to coin a phrase. They don't want the nation's attention diverted to this two-bit case."

"Fifty million, actually."

That canned laugh again, heartier this time It was as if Pageant had not heard Chuck otherwise.

"We are disposed to be fair. We can call on you and your client to do the right thing by the country and to let this matter subside. Think you could talk some sense into that dope?"

"We'll skip the characterizations. Maybe we should start with the definition of fair."

"Just between you, me, and the gate post," replied Pageant with a few snorts of self-deprecating laugh track because of his use of the trite phrase. "I have been authorized to offer a full $100,000 and a waiver against malicious suit prosecution."

Chuck rolled his eyes and mimicked Pageant's offer with a prissy pinched face. Instead of getting angry, Randolph smiled at the mockery.

"If the gate post is where the money is, maybe you'd better go back and try again," Murow said. "I'll presume that you were not trying to insult me with that offer. Let's get down to cases, Pageant. This is the easiest case to win I ever filed. My client wants—and I have to say, deserves—a pound of flesh, his choice of bodily locations, from the thugs who murdered his wife and baby—*murdered*, Mr. Pageant. Add that the financial havoc of the destruction of his home and his work, the loss of consortium and companionship, reputation, and emotional distress, I do the math for a sum of fifty million."

Pageant cleared his throat.

"Now we can handle this professionally. We are not in front of the media or a jury. Let's get right down to cases and arrive at a compromise figure."

"Let's not get too far down to cases," Chuck said acidly.

He nodded to Randolph.

"While I am not fully authorized to run the settlement up into the seven-figure bracket, I think I am on firm ground to offer a million and a quarter."

"Are you being serious? Let's talk forty-five million and begin our discussion there."

"Please, Mr. Murow, try and be reasonable. That figure wastes both our times. We will never see the conclusion of this case."

"Get someone with authority to talk to me, Pageant. You know my number. I have work to do."

Chuck's voice had taken on an acerbic edge, now. Randolph was liking this conversation better as time went by.

"Don't be hasty, now. Let's be reasonable. I'll try for two million, and get back to you. How does that real world figure sound to you?"

"Try for thirty-five, and I will try and get my client—the 'dope' who is listening on the speaker phone with me—to consider the offer, and we will get back to you. How does that sound?"

"Impossible, and un-American, for that matter, but I'll run it past my principles."

"Oh, and lest you think we are playing a lawyer game, you should know that the thirty-five mil is the final pre-trial offer. I am not even going to discuss a dime less with my client now or in the future. My offer expires at midnight tonight, then the ante goes back up to 50 mil. I will enjoy seeing you and yours have a squirmy day in court, counselor. Ta."

He hung up without giving Pageant the courtesy of a rebuttal or a good-by.

"How 'bout them apples, Randolph? We're barely a week into this and already they have come to us hat in hand. Not a bad week's work."

"Two million is a lot of money, Chuck. Aren't you leery that they'll call our bluff and hold out until we are outspent, and they can force us to settle for less? Especially in the anti-gun climate of the moment?"

Murow readily agreed in part, "Not 'of the moment', but of the past century," he said. "Guns have been as popular as a cobra in the governor's punch bowl in an increasing number of circles. I think that's how the old saying goes."

He smiled knowingly.

"Only a few die-hard enthusiasts still go to the effort of having guns at all now. You stand the chance of being cast as a violent dinosaur if this thing goes on long enough. Our best chance is to get a decent settlement from the government in the very near future while they're still smarting from all the bad publicity attendant on their raid on your home. They can stonewall us and make us spend ourselves into giving up if they apply their almost inexhaustible resources to a siege mentality. I wouldn't put it past the battle-axes in the Justice Department or the White House. We can't be coy too long. On the other hand, Vantassa is committed heart and soul to her FBG, and she has to be hating all the bad publicity. Her election to a second term may even be threatened. Elections have turned on less. We still have leverage; don't cave in yet."

"I'm sure you're right. I guess we just have to wait and see what Pageant has to offer next time."

It was a war of nerves and attrition. Two weeks later, with the media blitz still in force but seeming to lose force, Chuck submitted his list of witnesses. Out of sheer audacity, he noticed the deposition of Margaret Thaler, the attorney general of the United States.

"This ought to get their attention," he commented. "It's a new departure. Let's see how they counter."

The maneuver did get heavy media attention and sparked a national debate on the powers and responsibilities of the government. There was a tilt in Randolph's favor and a consensus that the level of attack and response had been elevated and that in sum the subpoena of the AG was a stroke of one-upmanship for the plaintiff.

CHAPTER NINE

Henry Drake and Jack Bailey were sitting in the Special Response Teams Office in the Treasury Department Building sipping old coffee and complaining of its bitterness. Drake had laced his with Old Turkey to make it palatable. He kept a packet of Sen-Sens readily available in his pocket and on his desk in case he needed to rid his breath of the telltale odor. Alcohol consumption was officially and socially taboo within the bureau and grounds for dismissal if used while on the job. The amber colored toxin was, nonetheless, frequently imbibed by the older agents with a wink-wink, nod-nod from everyone else.

Oliver Quatraine was the only African-American member of the remaining five Special Response Teams—there had been twenty-four in 1995 when John McGraw took over as chief, and in Drake's opinion, had gutted the bureau. But that was ancient history. Quatraine sat in the far side of the room at his computer. He remained on the job out of pure contrariness. All of the other African-Americans had left in disgust at the failure of the Treasury Department and the Congress to correct blatant bigotry within the ATF. Sometimes Quatraine thought that the only reason he stayed on was to bedevil the honkies on the teams. He sat alone as usual and separate from the other two men.

There was a knock on the door. Drake and Bailey looked at Quatraine. He remained placidly in his chair to their annoyance. Finally, Bailey, the lowest in seniority, begrudgingly answered the third and more insistent knock. A scrub-faced young marshal stepped in.

"Henry NMN Drake? John Fitzhugh Bailey?" he inquired.

"Who wants to know?" demanded Drake in his usual surly voice.

"U.S. Marshall's Office," the young man said in the same irksomely pleasant tone of voice he had used when calling out their names.

He smiled directly at Drake's glare and took in the senior agent's name tag on his uniform blouse.

"I'm Bailey, he's Drake," said Jack, wanting to get rid of the marshal.

"It's your lucky day, gentlemen," announced the marshal.

He handed each of the named men a sealed envelope.

"These are subpoenas. Consider yourselves served. Have a nice day now."

He left the room before either recipient could find an object to hurl. He ignored the two upraised fingers. He had seen that kind of gesture before in his line of work.

Quatraine smiled without taking precautions to cover his amusement.

"Where is Prince George County, Virginia?" asked Bailey scrutinizing his subpoena.

"Why Prince George County, Virginia and why a civil proceeding? Those are better questions," Drake asked.

Bailey came to it first.

"I'd bet my hat that's where Hopewell is—the Randolph Kennedy Affair."

Drake emitted a guttural groan, "That creep didn't waste any time, did he? So, let's go find out how we can get outta this. I'm too busy to go down South and explain the functions of the federal police to a bunch of rednecks and jigaboos."

Drake threw the last in for Quatraine's benefit. He was disappointed when he saw that the black agent was squinting at his modem paying no heed to him.

Henry Drake's deposition was held September 21, a Friday, in Chuck Murow's office conference room. He was represented by Angus Potter, an attorney in his first year out of law school. Potter was taken from the bureau legal pool by a drawing of names and commented that he had drawn a black bean. The confrontation between the ATF agent and Chuck Murow was acrimonious from the onset. Angus Potter felt as if he were just along for the ride.

"Tell me, please, Agent Drake, what planning led up to the raid on the home of the plaintiff, Mr. Randolph Kennedy?" Murow asked after half an hour of preliminaries and unproductive interchanges that had threatened to rival the U.S./NVA peace talks wrangling over the shape of the negotiation table.

Potter placed a restraining hand on Drake's forearm.

"That is confidential police business, sir. I cannot allow my client to answer. That information is privileged because of national security interests."

"I remind you, counselor," Murow snapped, "your client is here under subpoena. He is required to answer, *sir*."

Potter was unsure of himself. Murow came across as being so certain, an expert. Potter let it go.

Murow repeated his question, enunciating every syllable at Drake; so, he could not possibly be misunderstood.

Drake responded bitingly, "I'm not going to, so put that in your pipe. This deposition is out of bounds. I cannot give you what you ask."

"Do you plead your protections under the provisions of the fifth amendment of the Constitution, Mr. Drake?"

"No, like this kid here told you, I cannot answer for security reasons."

Angus Potter winced at how he was characterized.

"I must warn you that you will be held in contempt of court if you persist."

Angus Potter's education clicked in. Now he was sure of his ground.

"Easy, Mr. Murow. My Harvard education led me to believe that contempt is the prerogative of the judge."

He turned to Drake.

"Don't answer. The national security interests still apply."

Murow looked over his half-glasses.

"I can take care of that. We can do this now among reasonable men, or we can do it in front of Judge Pickens and the press. Your call."

"Let's try a rephrase of your question, counselor," Potter offered.

"Ah, I like the tenor of your suggestion, counselor," Murow responded. "Let's see…tell us the details of the planning of the raid on the residence of Mr. and Mrs. Randolph Kennedy and their little daughter."

"No."

"Counselor. Would you like to have a short conference with your client?"

Potter found that he did not like Drake any better than Murow did. He made an effort to keep an expression of professional detachment on his face.

He turned to Drake and said quietly, "What can that bit of information…"

Drake peremptorily held up his hand.

He faced Murow with an almost disinterested look and responded abruptly, "I'm not going to answer that question or any like it. Period. It is a matter of national security. As for the contempt threat, I stand warned."

He did not look the least bit cowed by the threat.

"Mark this, Mr. Potter, Your client will be called to answer one day. The protective shroud of national security is not going to sell in front of the judge and jury. On that day, disregarding the command will present the issue of contempt with teeth. Let's move on."

Drake looked anything but intimidated.

"Who was the police informant who signed the affidavit that led to the warrant used in this raid?" Murow asked next.

"I cannot tell you that. He is under the witness protection program."

"That, sir, is not a fact. He is missing. I have sworn documentation to that effect from the FBI. You can tell us what we must know."

"I cannot, and I will not."

"Down the line you'll stand liable for contempt of court to answer this question every bit as much as the previous one. We will have this information from you one way or another. I am asking you to be forthcoming.

"Mr. Potter, perhaps you would like to counsel your client."

Potter thought not. As much as he disliked Drake's abrasive personality, he had to admit that the agent was carrying the day so far. If the man got his butt in a sling later, it was no skin off Potter's. He held his peace.

Drake looked at the No Smoking sign at the far end of the room. He slowly and deliberately broke out a Marlboro and lit it, taking a satisfying drag.

Then he flung back at Murow, "I am not worried about all of that. I am a federal officer acting in the line of my sworn duty. I am not responsible to this penny-ante jurisdiction. You can take the matter up with the local justice of the peace, the secretary of the Treasury, and the attorney general, if you'd like."

Murow held his temper. He had dealt with recalcitrant deponents before. He wanted the questions on the record. He had given up on getting answers, civil or otherwise.

"Tell us, please, Agent Drake, what it was that the informant said that was so compelling that it led to the violent raid on Randolph Kennedy's home?"

"The place contained illegal weapons and was used as a regional trafficking center."

"What evidence did he present that was so convincing?"

"That I cannot divulge."

"Noted. Let the record clearly indicate that the witness refused to answer."

Drake cast the opposing attorney a look of bored disdain. He made a small show of pulling up his coat sleeve and checking his watch.

"Did you know this man? Let me be more specific. Had you ever communicated with him in anyway before the circumstances that led up to the raid?"

"No."

"That was a serious decision you made based on this person's report. What, if anything, did you do to verify it?"

"Had him check out the house the day before the raid by the Response Team."

"Again, what evidence was actually produced for you to see?"

"He saw the guns and ammo. You hard of hearing?"

"Agent Drake, that is not an answer to my question. You told me what the person said. That is mere hearsay. What evidence did he produce? Videos? Voice recordings? Written documents? What?"

"That is classified police business. I am not at liberty to discuss that."

"Classification is for national security matters. This information is a routine police matter and nothing to do with national security or with being classified. We're here on a civil matter. I request that you answer the question."

"No."

"You refuse?"

"What is it about 'no' you don't understand, Murow?"

"I'll try one last time, Agent Drake. Aside from the unverified communication from an informant about whom you knew nothing, vouched for by a policeman whom you had never before met, was there any evidence—any evidence at all—linking my client to any violation of federal statutes regarding alcohol, tobacco, firearms, or illicit chemicals? Or to any crime whatsoever, for that matter?"

"That is classified information."

"One last time, Agent Drake. We're going about this the hard way. You risk an eventual contempt citation. We can do this here today in the quiet of these offices, or we can do it in court in the glare of public scrutiny. Since you appear to represent the attorney general and the secretary of the Treasury in this matter, I will include them in my complaint to Judge Pickins. You can answer, and we can get on with it; but my patience is not infinite. My client and I are entitled to an answer."

"Cite anybody you guys wish," Drake said looking sleepy and unconcerned. "Knock yourself out. And a plague on both your houses."

Jack Bailey's deposition went the same, stonewalling all the way. Randolph was a silent observer in each of the legal interrogations, each of which was videotaped. He had difficulty understanding the process. He was not overly surprised that the two ATF agents appeared to consider themselves and their governmental agency to be above the law. He found it difficult to understand why his attorney was so unperturbed by the arrogance of the agents and the inability to obtain straight answers.

Chuck took Randolph aside and told him, "This is a process. They think it will end when they walk out of the deposition room. They are quite mistaken. This process is just beginning. They will give us the information we ask for, or they will have to settle with us on generous terms to avoid having the information become public. There is no way that the government will allow either of those two gentlemen on the witness stand. They will come across like they have all the moral fiber of Indian Thuggies. They would make the best witnesses our side could ever ask for even if they don't contribute an iota of information about the case. Be patient and let me wheel and deal. That's what I do best. You will see this testimony come back to haunt those two arrogant trigger happy bullies."

Chuck sent a videotape copy of the deposition to Attorney General Margaret Thaler, who received it with mounting moroseness. The following day she received notice of her own deposition. She ignored it, filed it with a stack that she received every month. The day after she failed to appear for the duly noticed deposition she received a formal contempt citation from Judge Pickins's court. The day after that she had an assistant call Charles Murow to tell him that she would be unable to testify within the next year due to the press of her important governmental business.

The next morning, AG Thaler read a verbatim transcript of ATF agents Drake and Baileys' testimonies in the *Los Angeles Times,* along with a copy of the contempt citations issued to her and the men of her task force. The article included a transcript of the telephone call from Thaler's office. The *Times* included a brief comment from the plaintiff's attorney about the nature of the civil case filed by his client and a statement that "such activity on the part of the government indicated at least that they had something in their conduct and records they felt they needed to bury deeply—something they do not want the American public to know. They obviously consider themselves to be above the law."

The reporter stated that the Attorney General's Office and the head of ATF and the Department of the Treasury all had refused to comment when he asked for a response to the allegations he was going to make public. When asked by electronic media reporters that night for her comments, she responded angrily at the unnecessary and invalid extrapolation by the reporter. The news anchor noted that her answer was a non sequitur; she would not address the questions put to her.

AG Thaler pondered the best time to contact President Vantassa. While she was vacillating, the president called her.

"Margaret, I suppose you have read the latest installment about the Randolph Kennedy Affair—the piece in the *LA Times*?"

"I'm afraid I have, Madam President. And I have had the dubious opportunity of an encounter with the media on the subject."

"Give me your spin on this, Margaret."

"The bad news is that we cannot produce that weasel, Ivan Slavich, who signed the fateful affidavit. The worse news is that we cannot produce a scintilla of other evidence against Kennedy, and we are just spinning our wheels spending the People's money. This is my studied opinion, President Vantassa: the agents acted in undue haste in this instance, and I cannot see any way to avoid having that fact become public knowledge."

"We can throw a couple of agents to the wolves, can we not? Looks like we need a scapegoat, to be blunt about it."

"Madam President, I am not certain this line is completely secure."

"Thanks, Margaret."

"And besides, Madam President, the resultant demoralization among the agents by such an executive action would undermine the effort of the FBG and could unravel the entire warp and woof of the fabric of law enforcement for drug and gun trafficking. We may well be derailed before we can get a meaningful start."

The president's end of the conversation was now quiet. Attorney General Thaler knew that her superior was deep in thought and speculated that the president was analyzing the effects on her standing in the polls, her capacity to lead in the drug eradication effort she promised during the election campaign, and about the effects on her plans for reelection.

"Settle," she said, speaking abruptly and mildly startling Thaler. "Get this infernal pipsqueak Randolph Kennedy Affair out of the public view *tout de suite*. We need to get back to the work of the country and to stop pursuing distractions. Make those two agents eat some public crow over this. By 'public', I mean within the Bureau and the Task Force. Somebody has to look like the village idiot in this matter, and I don't want it to be me or you or any other senior official. Make it happen soon, Margaret, for all our sakes. Maybe we can come up with something on the quiet to make Mr. Randolph Kennedy's life a little more complicated. See what you can do about that, too."

The president's voice had risen half an octave as it always did when she was angry or determined.

"Remember the line security, Madam President. I'll take care of the court considerations. None of us are going to like this, but it will blow over. Give it one news cycle."

"Thank you, Margaret."

CHAPTER TEN

The call from Assistant U.S. Prosecutor Kerry Pageant came the next day. Chuck Murow was brutally abrupt, "Mr. Pageant," he said, "you are not high enough in the pecking order. Have someone who is high enough call me when you folks want to do real business. Otherwise, we'll read about each other in the *New York* and *LA Times*, and we'll talk again in court."

He hung up.

Pageant had not even had a chance to deliver his superior's neatly phrased message. He was furious, but he shrugged and bumped the responsibility upstairs.

The undersecretary of Treasury telephoned Murow's office an hour later. After the minimum of telephone courtesies, the undersecretary cut directly to the chase.

"We want this case out of the center stage lights. We will give you $2,000,000. We require silence from you thereafter, no more footsie with the press. I'm here to tell you, Mr. Murow, that the secretary of the Treasury and the attorney general will never testify in your courtroom. They will only testify before Congress. This case of yours is not worth any more of our time. You won't get a better offer. I am giving you the official and final figure. We can have that sum in your hands by this very afternoon."

Murow knew that his case was not so strong, nor his resources so vast that he could last out against the traditional stonewall of the feds. He dared a bluff.

"Make it twenty, and we can complete this transaction by fax right now. I will have to run it past my client. I'll tell you this; we asked for fifty, and we meant it. This is it on our end. My client wants blood for blood and will only settle for an amount of money that you will notice."

There was a pause at the government end and a muffled scraping on the phone. Murow figured that the undersecretary had his palm over the transmitter and was conferring. Three full minutes passed.

Then the undersecretary's voice returned, "I am against this kind of extortion personally, but I was surprised to get a less absolute response from the secretary. He is calling the AG and the White House. It will take a while. I'll get back to you."

"Don't take too long. I have press deadlines to meet."

"And don't push your luck. Don't try to hold us up for more. We will just dig in our heels."

The undersecretary hung up his phone.

Murow called Randolph and gave him a short synopsis of his conversation and the pending discussions in Washington.

"Don't get your hopes up too high. I think we are likely to get a hardball return, and this time I think they'll be dead serious. I don't think we'll get a better offer than what comes today."

"Okay, I appreciate your efforts and your expertise. Cross your fingers."

At five minutes to five Murow's administrative assistant buzzed him.

"The undersecretary of Treasury is on the line."

"Hold him for two minutes, then put him through."

The devil made him do it.

His phone rang.

"Hello, Mr. undersecretary. I'm listening."

"You must have something big on the brass because they gave me a ceiling of fifteen million. I have to tell you that I argued for no more than two and a half. They evidently believe you are for real and are not about to fold. They also told me that if you reject this offer, all future decisions will be made by the judge and jury."

"I'll put you on hold and call my client."

Randolph was sitting by the phone.

When he heard the offer, he laconically said, "Yes."

"Mr. Undersecretary, we accept your offer. I will fax a notarized copy of the court settlement form after I put in the figure, Not that there isn't a strong bond of trust between us, but you will need to fax me simultaneously a signed promissory note and a certified copy of the check. The check must be in my hands by the close of business tomorrow, and it must be delivered by courier."

"First thing tomorrow morning."

"Nice doing business with you."

"Let's don't make it a habit. Good day."

Faxes were in the hands of the opposing parties in three minutes.

At eleven the next morning a FedEx courier walked into the offices of Casper, Dayton, and Murow and presented a U.S. Treasury check to Chuck in the amount of $15,000,000. Chuck faxed a copy of the notarized acceptance that Randy had signed two weeks previously in anticipation of this outcome. He sent the check for deposit to the firm account and instructed the bank to deliver a check drawn on that account in the amount of ten million dollars to Randolph Kennedy. The firm's standard fee on contingency cases was one-third.

Margaret Thaler stood to take charge of the FBG Task Force meeting. The president sat quietly aside.

"Madam President, gentlemen," the attorney general said, more formally than usual. "We have just had fifty-two rousing successes and one costly and humiliating failure. There has been a serious discussion by the public and in the halls of Congress regarding the removal of ATF from this task force as a result of the Key Stone Coppers performance by Agents Drake and Bailey. At the request of the president, those two agents are here; actually, they are waiting right outside. We intend to make an impression on them and on the other agents in this large force. We cannot tolerate such mistakes, and we will present the pair of them with a formal reprimand for their service jackets. Before we do that, the president has asked to say a few words on the subject."

"A very few," the president said. "Much as I would like to string the pair of them up by their pathetic external protuberances, we cannot afford any more negative publicity. We will keep this internal. We will keep the two agents in place, in view of their records up to this sorry Randolph Kennedy Affair. There has to be some hate and pain, and Drake and Bailey are going to be the ones to absorb it. Bring them in, Madam Attorney General."

Mrs. Thaler nodded to one of the Secret Service agents, who went to the door.

"Drake and Bailey, front and center," the Secret Service agent called peremptorily out the door.

The two ATF agents marched in and were suddenly cowed by the presence of so many senior officials and agents. The president of the United States was not twenty feet from them and was looking at them with a decidedly sour expression. The men swallowed involuntarily. Bailey self-consciously ran his forefinger under the collar of his shirt. His tie had suddenly become too tight, and there was an excess of sweat under the collar.

"Sit down," the attorney general commanded.

Drake and Bailey quickly looked about and took chairs. They turned their gazes to the attorney general as penitents towards the Grand Inquisitor.

Mrs. Thaler said, "You two are here to receive a formal reprimand, one that will be entered into your service jackets and will count against you for the remainder of your service careers. The Randolph Kennedy Affair was bungled by the two of you from the very first instant. Your investigation was shoddy; you did no surveillance; you rushed to judgment; you hatched an ill-conceived and ill-executed plan. Your poor work resulted in the unnecessary deaths of agents under your control. Finally, the aftermath of the debacle over which you presided has resulted in humiliation for this committee, the FBG, and for the president and has set back the noble work in which we are engaged by years. You have cost the government, and therefore the People of the United States, millions of dollars in legal judgments. You are both disgraces."

Both penitents felt like sniveling. Drake wanted to protest that he was hardly in a position to be as important as the AG was suggesting and that others had been as gullible as him. He knew intuitively that speaking out at this moment was a mistake; so, he kept his silence and nursed the wounds being inflicted on his ego. He fought to control his rising fury. Bailey had all he could do in his fight to avoid shedding tears.

Mrs. Thaler had not finished.

"There has been serious discussion in this room about summarily terminating your employment with the government."

The two men were seeing their jobs and pensions disappearing. Neither of them could continue to look the attorney general in her cold bureaucratic eyes.

After a brief pause, Mrs. Thaler continued, "However, the Task Force and the Bureau have decided, based on your fine records to date, that you can be retained in service. Therefore, each of you will be reduced in rank one level, and your pay will reflect the demotions retroactive to the date of the incident, August 11. Your paycheck will reflect a biweekly deduction to compensate the government for the amount you were overpaid from the time of the sorry Randolph Kennedy Affair until the present. You're lucky you are not being required to pay the government's losses."

She planned to order their immediate dismissal if they lodged a complaint. The two ATF agents studied their shoelaces and wore appropriate hangdog expressions. Mrs. Thaler liked what she saw and decided that the lesson was now sufficient.

"Now, go back and redeem yourselves."

Drake and Bailey recognized that they had been dismissed and were glad to have come out with their skins and their jobs, albeit both were scarred and reduced from the flaying. They stood up uneasily and slunk towards the door.

"One last thing," the president said.

It was a mild shock to everyone in the room. Her voice broke a very awkward silence.

"Drake, you and Bailey have good records. You can get out there and do the good work of which you are capable in bringing down the terrorists who plague our nation. You need to be more zealous in building your cases. Perhaps you should even go back and review the Kennedy Affair for the lessons it can teach. Who knows? Maybe you will come on to something that could change things in our understanding of that mess. You're dismissed."

The number of individuals who listed Randolph Armstrong Kennedy on their compilation of persons needing a death sentence had been increased by at least two that morning.

Chuck Murow called Randolph.

"Hi. I wanted to give you a heads up. I'm sending you a release form guaranteeing our silence as part of the settlement and also a copy of the official reprimand given to the two ATF agents involved in the raid that killed your wife and little girl. At least there has been some pain all around. You can't imagine how much it hurts guys like the two agents to have a reprimand like this placed permanently in their service jackets. If I know the government, those two will never rise above their current pay grade. That will sting."

"And my wife and baby are dead. Doesn't quite balance, in my reckoning."

"It may not be justice, my friend, Chuck said, "but this reprimand and the money are as near as we will ever get to it. 'Life is a bowl of Munichs,' Thurber or O Henry said. We could be bogged down in legal hassles from now to the end of the century. The U.S. is the world's greatest obfuscator if it wants to be. A piece of advice; take the money and enjoy it. If I were you, I would move, start fresh someplace where there aren't so many bad memories."

"Thanks for your work, Chuck. I know you did the best you could. Still, I think they got off light. What happened at my house was nothing short of state sponsored murder. Nobody even addressed that. It's a lot of money, but, I have to tell you, it doesn't quite do it for me."

"I know. I feel much the same. But you've got to get past this. Consider it lucky that you got anything and that you are alive."

CHAPTER ELEVEN

Henry Drake and Jack Bailey sat alone in the Special Response Team Office after their public dressing down and demotions. Bailey felt intimidated and beaten. He slumped in morose silence. Drake had—by now—recovered his skin color and famous temper.

"Fifteen million bucks he got. The director told me this morning before we went up for our ass-chewing. Kennedy—that murderer—comes out smelling like a rose, and we get the whole load dumped on us. Can't really blame the high kahunas on the Task Force; they aren't about to take the blame. It always rolls down hill; that's the American way. That Slavich creep sitting there enjoying the sun and sand in Florida or someplace thinks he is about the cleverest guy goin'. I swear that he's goin' to pay and pay hard. I am going to get a line on his WP status if it takes the rest of my life."

Drake's soliloquy was concluded with a low menacing growl.

Bailey perked up, lifting his head off his chest for the first time that day.

"I still think Kennedy is dirty, and it galls me no end that he gets to be a millionaire compliments of the taxpayers and us two schmucks take it in the shorts. I hate to think that he just gets away with this. It ain't right. It just ain't right."

He slumped again.

Oliver Quatraine walked in. He was ignored as usual.

Drake spoke in a low, foreboding snarl, "Maybe we can change all that, partner. He's gotta be dirty, and we're gonna keep on him until he makes his mistake. Then, we're gonna roast 'im. I'll see the day when they cart him out to Hart Island."

"Who's dirty?" asked Quatraine.

He had overheard the reference to the island in New York Harbor that served the city as its Potter's Field.

"What're you guys working on?"

"Nothing that's any of your business," snapped Drake.

Quatraine let it bead up and run off his ebony skin as usual.

CHAPTER TWELVE

Randolph's abdominal wall wound developed a minor stitch abscess that became a small but uncomfortable local infection from a resistant staphylococcus. His HMO health insurance would not permit hospitalization; so, he was required to undergo intravenous antibiotic therapy at home. He missed two weeks of work because of the treatment, in addition to the time he had already missed following the death of Irene and Annie and the necessary absences during the civil proceedings against the government. He knew that his superiors were unhappy with him, especially since he was relatively new at his job. He became concerned when Leo Sondregger—his immediate superior—called and asked if it would be all right for him to come out to see him. Randolph had perceived a certain level of strain with his neighbors since the incident, and especially since the civil verdict had come back in his favor. It was not quite suspicion, but certainly not the former easy trust he and the neighbors had once enjoyed with each other. Randolph had the vague sense that the neighbors felt that where there was smoke, there must be at least a little fire. He wondered if that attitude had anything to do with Leo's visit.

Randolph heard Leo's car pull into the driveway. He waited until the doorbell rang twice because he did not want to appear anxious or concerned.

"Hi, Leo. C'mon in," he said cheerily.

Leo was by nature a salesman. He looked like a salesman—right off the pages of *The Auto Sellers' Weekly*. Leo was portly, bluff, and red faced. He even had on white socks to go with his sensible crepe soled shoes and his dark pants. He did not own a suit. Today's sport coat was a tame version of his favorite plaid.

"How's the belly, Randy? I guess that was a pretty nasty wound, eh?"

"Not that bad. It's about all healed up. Just a flesh wound, as they used to say in the old cowboy movies. How are you and Vera?"

"Can't complain. She had a breast lump taken off—new laser surgery. It was benign, no big deal really, but we had to hold our breaths for a while. Scary business."

"I'll say. Glad it came out all right. Find a seat that doesn't have stuff on it. It's the maid's day off," Randolph smiled. "Can I get you something? A soda? Some decaf? I don't drink beer."

"No, nothing for me. I can't stay long. Have to get back to the grindstone. Actually, I have a golf date with the Mitsubishi four-wheeler division people—same thing as work. I hate the game myself. Did you know that golf is the only game allowed in heaven from what I've heard."

Leo always had a joke apropos to the moment, or he made his latest joke be apropos. His red face lit up as he started to laugh in anticipation of the punch line.

"I hadn't heard," Randolph responded as expected, willing to play the straight man.

"Yeah, they say it's just one eternal round up there."

He laughed uproariously at his own joke. He enjoyed the telling and retelling of his jokes more than his listeners did. It was his most endearing trait. Randolph laughed politely.

"I didn't come just to share that bit of spiritual wisdom, though," Leo said.

Randolph had already guessed that he hadn't.

"I mainly wanted to see for myself how you were getting along. Looks to me like you've been enjoying this too much. You're far too tanned to be a complete invalid," he said it with a smile that involved his whole face.

"I'll be back first of next week, barring more complications. It won't be a minute too soon. I'm getting a touch of cabin fever, as they say in Alaska."

"Oh, that reminds me," blurted Leo, his face revealing his delight at the perfect segue Randolph had afforded him.

He wiped the sweat from his pudgy hands on his mauve pants.

"There is an opening in one of our Alaska branches, a place called Wasilla. Larry saw it and thought about you. Thought maybe you'd like to get away and have a fresh start, so's to speak...I mean, after all that's happened"

"I don't know, Leo. Alaska. That's way up there. I've never thought about living in an isolated place like that."

"Look, there's a promotion in it—assistant manager. You deserve it; and—between you and me—and I hate to say it; but Larry is kind of ticked off about your missing so much time with tax season coming on. I got to tell you, he's getting kind of nervous about all the bad press, too. You know it's not that he isn't supportive, and all. But, Randy, it's a tough market. Larry wonders how much this might have hurt us. You being on the bad side of the cops and the federal government and all. You can see it from his viewpoint."

Larry was Leo's supervisor, the manager of the Prince George County branch of the Virginia division. Second only to the Virginia president, Larry had the most seniority and therefore the most power of any executive in the company that either man had anything to do with.

Behind the polite platitudes, Randolph knew that whatever Larry said was going to happen. He did not have to brain surgeon to figure out what Leo was telling him.

Randolph did not like to banter or to beat around a subject.

"Look, Leo, I hear you. What if I don't go?"

"You wanna know the truth? Inside a month your office'll be in the broom closet. Larry'll make you quit. He won't say a thing, but it will get bad enough that you will want out. I don't think anybody will try very hard to find you a place in that case. The Alaska thing won't be open for long."

"What have I done that is so terrible?"

Leo's eyes opened wider as he stressed his point. The fat around his eyes kept them perpetually slit-like otherwise.

"Doesn't matter. Larry sees you as a liability. And you are expendable for the noble cause of profit making. Between you and me and the fence post, I heard that some feds came by his office and maybe put a little bug in his ear. You didn't hear that from me, though. Larry would put his grandma on a floating ice block if that's what it took to keep his career on track. Your future or mine is nothing compared to that. Think he's gonna buck the feds who help butter his bread?"

He gave Randolph an insider's secret look.

"And look, I don't know how much bearing this has on the price of tea in Indonesia, but the union pres and veep from the Fraternal Order of Police were into Larry's office day before yesterday. You well know that they are one of our big accounts. Well, anyway, it might have been to get a donation; but I don't think so. Their yearly drive isn't until fall. You can put two and two together. An hour after they were in his office, he called me in to tell me to get you to take the

Alaska job. He didn't say it in so many words, but the FOP is very tight with the ATF. You can imagine where you rank on their social register."

"I can guess. The ATF just won't give it up, it appears. Doesn't take that much to imagine that our Larry came in for his share of pressure. Doesn't leave me much of a choice, does it?" Randolph said.

He had been around long enough to know how the company did things. It was not a matter just of Larry being Larry.

"Not really, but," and Leo brightened, "this job in Alaska really is a genuine promotion. Under the circumstances, you'd be crazy to pass it up. That is if you want to have a future with the company. Not with the glut of CPAs being turned out by the universities. Maybe it doesn't matter to you since you got some sort of award from your trial. You're the only one who knows if that'll be enough to keep you for the rest of your life. I know I'd go nuts without having a job, even if I was filthy rich."

Leo was insightful Randolph knew he needed the stability, the ordinariness of the job. His ten million was a fine cushion, but a man is his work was Randolph's philosophy. He needed his job; and he didn't need to be fired, to have a failure at this juncture.

"Okay, Leo, I'll give it real thought. I'm due to come back to work on Wednesday. I'll let you know before then."

"Thanks, Randolph. Give it some good thoughts. It's the best thing for you. Look, this is nothing to do with me, nothing personal or anything. I just work there. I can't afford to put Larry off, you know how he is. Anyway, give me a call. Got to rush now—big golf deal. See you."

Randolph had the distinct impression that Leo could hardly wait to get out of the door.

For two days Randolph moped, caught in indecision but mostly feeling sorry for himself. He had had more than his share for the past several months, and the ten million dollars from the court settlement had done almost nothing to assuage his melancholy. He knew that he had to go on with decision making, work, and developing some kind of a social life. He felt like a hermit and knew that should bother him, but it did not. He had settled into a mental torpor of bereavement. Grieving over his dead wife and baby had supplanted progressive thought or planning, and he was incapable of concentrating on his work or anything else. He had recurring nightmares in which his family was shot down over and over again in vivid detail.

He brooded and mourned. Sad songs and poems kept flashing into his subconscious. He had written a paper on Edgar Allen Poe in college. He had loved *Anna Bell Lee* so much that he memorized it, and portions now intruded on his reveries:

"I was a child and she was a child,
In this kingdom by the sea;
But we loved with a love that was more than love-
I and my Annabel Lee;
With a love that the winged seraphs of heaven
Coveted her and me.

"And this was the reason that, long ago,
In this kingdom by the sea,
A wind blew out of a cloud, chilling
"My beautiful Annabel Lee;
So that her highborn kinsman came
And bore her away from me,
To shut her up in a sepulchre
In this kingdom by the sea...

"But our love it was stronger by far than the love
Of those who were older than we-
Of many far wiser than we-
And neither the angels in heaven above,
Nor the demons down under the sea,
Can ever dissever my soul from the soul
Of the beautiful Annabel Lee.

"For the moon never beams without bringing me dreams
Of the beautiful Annabel Lee;
And the stars never rise but I feel the bright eyes
Of my darling, my darling, my life and my bride..."

Whenever *Annabel Lee* intruded, he cried; and he was angry at himself for being unable to control his emotions. In the night most nights, he awoke from an intense image of flash-bang explosives, the rattle of small arms fire, a raging inferno, and of his wife and daughter falling into the flames. In every dream Randy fought to get to them—failing night after night—with an attendant heavy burden of guilt that he was never able to shake, in or out of his nightmares. Each time he forced himself to climb up out of his tortured sleep in order to start anew an attempt to get rest. It was futile; he was like the mythological Greek King Sisyphus who punished by being compelled to roll an immense boulder up a hill, almost reaching the top, only to watch it roll back down, and to repeat this action forever.

He needed some advice. He could not go to anyone in the office; it would be humiliating and inimitable to any hope of success in his career. He could not talk to the competition; that would be regarded as disloyal by both companies; and Randolph would come out with the short end of the stick all the way around. About his only friend; and, in fact, he was only an acquaintance, was his range master at the Prince George County Shooting Range. Daryl Haslip, originally from Coalville, Utah—a red neck, a Democrat, a former special ops soldier, and a regional director of the National Rifle Association—was rumored to be part of one of the ill-considered state militia race-hate groups—the Christian Identity. Randolph was unsure about the rumors, and more unsure about whether he cared. He liked Daryl and trusted him and his down-to-earth common sense.

Randolph made himself get up and move. He drove out of the city and into the county. It was early enough that no one would be shooting yet. Daryl was outside on the rifle range, removing tattered targets and setting up new ones when Randolph arrived. Randolph walked out to where the ex-Delta Force soldier was working.

"Daryl," Randolph called from a safe distance.

Daryl Haslip was not the sort of man you wanted to startle.

Daryl turned suddenly.

"Hey, if it isn't the famous Randolph Kennedy," he said. "What brings you out so early?"

Daryl was a no-neck, no body fat, no scalp hair guy who nobody messed with. He was five feet eight inches tall and weighed two hundred even. His hair would have been red if he had any, and his face was nearly confluently freckled from his long hours in the sun. He had whitish sores on his twice bent nose and on his lower lip that even nonmedical people speculated about as being cancers. He wore a military issue olive drab tank top undershirt—known by cops as a wife beater—tattered denim shorts, and flip-flops, and no hat on his sun burnt shaved head.

Randolph walked over to where Daryl had set down a pile of old targets, his staple gun, and several metal upright target holders.

"Daryl, I came out to pick your brain about something."

"You might not find much there to pick on," Daryl said with a self-deprecating smile.

"I might have to go to Alaska for my company, change offices. I know you've got friends up there, some people in the NRA," Randolph said.

"And in the North Star State Militia," Daryl offered gratuitously.

He was careful to whom he spoke about his affiliation with the widespread militia network. He was the NRA representative to the local Virginia militia and the liaison officer to the other states' committees. That much was for limited public consumption. The NRA and the ATF were avowed enemies, and Randolph had become a national symbol of resistance to the ATF and a member of the NRA. Therefore, he was considered to be safe.

"So, tell me what it's like. Up in Alaska. I hear a lot of funny stuff," Randolph went on.

"And most of the stuff is true. They carry guns and because of the attacks by bears and crazy moose; they have been granted an exception to Vantassa's violation of the second amendment to the Constitution. They don't like the infringements on their rights and the fact that the WOMs in Washington ignore their legitimate requests and that they are treated like the stepchildren of the country. Since way back in the 1970s, the right-thinking people in Alaska have been putting up a proposition for secession into the state legislature.

In the past five years a lot of the tree huggers, bunny huggers, and gun control freaks have been leaving the state—don't like the attitude there—bless their bleeding little hearts. So, the secession movement is gaining real strength with each passing year. Looks like it won't be more than another five years before the state formally requests to be separated from the rest of the union. The big fear on the part of the Wise Old Men in Washington is that Hawaii and California and then Texas will want to do the same thing, but that's something for another day."

"What's the country really like, the weather and all?"

"The Alaskans have a standard joke that they only have two seasons up north there—this winter and last winter. That's an exaggeration. Anchorage and the area around it are pretty nice, not too different from the northeast states or Montana."

"Know anything about a place called Wasilla?"

"Yeah. It's by Anchorage. Nice city. It's the main headquarters of the North Star State Militia, the salt of the earth. Not a black skin or a kike in any of those organizations."

Randolph inwardly winced at the racist overtone of Daryl's suggestions and especially at the tacit presumption that he, too, was of that persuasion. While he, personally, was a great supporter of the second amendment and the right to use firearms, he felt like he had kept a distance between himself and the gun lovers of the far right wing with their racist, anti-Semitic, and tax rebel rhetoric. He knew better than to launch into an argument with the range master on such an emotional subject.

"You may or may not believe this, Randolph—given what you've been through—but you need protection from the ATF jackbooters. The people in the pipeline tell me that the thing between you and the ATF gang isn't over yet, not by a long shot. That's not the way they operate. You gotta watch your back from here on out. Being in Alaska where you can carry a weapon at all times is a good choice for you. They would just love to find you carrying iron down here; so, they can have an excuse to lock you up. The good Lord is looking out for you, Randolph. Better pay Him heed."

"I think the threat from the federal government is past. They made a mistake, admitted to it finally in court, and paid the price. They couldn't pay for the lives of my wife and baby; but at least under the law, they paid up. I think it's over; so, I don't want to feel like I have to go around like an old time cowboy defending against the Indians and bandits," Randolph said.

"Whatever you think," Daryl said, "it can't hurt to have a few of the right kind of friends. Alaska has a bunch of them's all I'm saying. Are you seriously thinking about moving up there?"

"I don't really have a choice when you get right down to it. The Fraternal Order of Police came around to my office and let them know that their account would be moved out if I stayed on. There has been some other pressure on me and on my office in Hopewell to leave because my actions against the government were unpopular. I can go to Alaska with a little promotion, or I can sit down here and feel bad because I have to look for a new job. They as much as told me so officially."

"And you still don't think the ATF is nursing a grudge and is out to get you? Man, what more do you need for a wake-up call? They are hand-in-glove with the FOP. Take the hint! At least, take advantage of the opportunity the Lord of the good white people is presenting. He takes care of the folks in the Movement."

"I guess I'll have to."

"I'll get on the e-mail and let the brothers and sisters up there in Wasilla know to expect you. You're a good man, if your shooting on the range and your coolness under fire are any indications. I'm presuming you're a God-fearing Protestant. That'll go a long way up there. They'll take you into the Movement and look out for you."

Randolph thought about protesting that he did not want to be in any movement, but it would not help. Maybe those people that Daryl knew could help. He did not have to get in too tight with them.

"Okay, Daryl, thanks for the good word. I could use a friend or two."

"You want to do a little shooting? Ease the tension?"

"As long as I'm here."

"I'll get you an M-16 and an Uzi. They should give enough action to relieve the stresses. I still have to charge you; I'll make it at our cost. And—you know how it is—I have to record the firing of every round under your name and certification number."

"No problem. I don't have anything to hide."

Randolph went through two thirty-round clips for each of the guns. It was expensive, but Daryl had been right; his feeling of stress and tension did dissipate. His mind cleared, and he made his decision to accept Leo's offer. He went straight home and faxed a letter accepting the offer and indicating that he would clear his desk at the Hopewell office and arrange to start in Wasilla, Alaska in two weeks.

CHAPTER THIRTEEN

Oliver Quatraine sorted through the mail and papers in his in-basket during a late Friday afternoon respite from the nearly constant round of Special Response Teams missions. The ATF and the FBI coordination had never been better since President Vantassa had established her Task Force. The teams' successes only served to underscore the salient fact that whatever they were doing, it was not enough. The more guns and drugs they confiscated, the more smugglers and terrorists they arrested and killed, the more weapons and chemicals there were out there.

The worst element of the huge illegal gun problem was the growing realization on the part of the men and women of the ATF and the officials on the President's Task Force in Washington that ordinary Americans regarded the official attacks on alcohol, tobacco, and firearms ownership as an intrusion on their personal liberties. The citizens of the country routinely failed to cooperate, squirreled away there own small stashes of guns and ammunition, and refused to turn in smugglers and distributors of firearms.

A growing majority of the common people throughout the country—like the NRA—were coming ever more frequently and deeply to view themselves as the natural enemies of a law enforcement bureau, the ATF.

Quatraine was dispirited. He had the official approbation of his department and ostensibly—at least—of the president of the United States. He knew that he ranked below several orders of criminals in the minds of the people he was supposed to be serving, that he was doing his best to serve. He held an important titular position on one of the elite Special Response Teams, but he also knew that he was the object of ongoing racial disrespect from his fellow agents. The racism in the ATF had deep historical roots and was inextricably woven into the fabric of the organization. Lip service was given to the high principles of equal opportunity, social equipoise, and to redress from harassment and ill-treatment. Oliver Quatraine, himself, was the daily recipient of race-based disrespect for which there was not real recourse. There no credible supporting witnesses. The offenses that annoyed Quatraine seemed petty, or at least he would appear to be petty if he complained about them. It was almost impossible to document the pervasive subtleties of the racism and abuse.

He thought about resigning as he shuffled through the papers. He knew he could not do it. He had worked too hard to get into his present position, no matter what the white agents said about affirmative action and how much it had benefited him and had taken from them. He would never be able to rise as high in any other organization. He was too old to start over. Besides, he liked his work and considered himself to be good at it. He believed in what he and the Bureau of Alcohol, Tobacco, and Firearms were doing. He believed in the FBG, and he did not want a bunch of rednecks to have the satisfaction of driving him out.

The forms for the monthly reports lay on top of the weapons inventories; and they, in turn, lay on top of the invoices for requisitioning of new supplies of ammunition. Those forms lay on top of the team's incident reports accounting for every round of ammunition fired on their raids. This pile of paper lay on top of committee reports, copies of the Federal Firearms Registration Act work manual for all agents and the applications for advancement or transfer of the agents on his team. There was an announcement for the upcoming ATF bureau wide family outing in Langley, a copy of the bureau's printout of fugitives from prosecution for gun violations, and the *Federal Minority Officers' Union Magazine*. Quatraine set aside the blank forms. He flipped through the work manual and the printout of fugitives disinterestedly, then perused the announcement of the upcoming social event.

In the past, Quatraine had made it a matter of determination to miss such affairs. They were dull fare, and there were always implied reminders of the omnipresent racism in the organization. The impromptu speakers always had an anti-black or stupid black joke or story, always prefaced by an apology that the speaker was not racist; this story had been told to him by one of his black buddies. There were snide references to Jim Crow, displays of Confederate flags, filled eating tables that made it almost impossible to avoid grouping with other African-Americans away from the white officers and their families. In his new position of authority, Quatraine had to attend. His absence would be conspicuous. The unwritten rules did not, however, decree that he had to like the outings.

Dutifully, Sylvia Quatraine accompanied her husband to the social affair. She was no more fond of the get-togethers than he was but did not take the little slights so much to heart. She had a masters in social work, a busy and satisfying career, and could let the certainties of ignorance and the backlashes of prejudice she saw be relegated to where they belonged—to the immaterial. The stupid, racially motivated comments served—in her mind—only to categorize the speakers among the unintelligent, uninformed, ill-bred, ignorant, and weak. She tried to get Oliver to ignore the discourtesies as nothing more than unimportant slights and to take the high road of tolerance—or alternatively—to fight through the system. His way of responding by chewing up the lining of his poor inflamed stomach seemed to her to be the worst choice of them all. She picked up their camera, a blanket, and a battery-lit Frisbee to try and have a good time.

Oliver and Sylvia walked down the path towards the sounds of activity already under way. They eyed a softball game and decided to play a little before getting something to eat.

"I have to use the Port-a-Potty, Oliver. I'll be just a sec," Sylvia said and trotted towards the two rented comfort stations.

When she came to the green plastic structures, she stopped to read the temporary signs on their front doors. One read "White Men" and the other "White Women". Both structures had permanent signs indicating the rental company that owned them and in large block yellow letters, "RENTED FOR APRIL 12, 2016 BY ATF. MUST BE RETURNED BEFORE TEN P.M." She gritted her teeth. On the side of the Port-a-Potty marked "White Men" was a sign that had been hastily scrawled and taped to the wall that read, "African-Americans and Monkeys use the bushes." These two buildings appeared to be the only toilet facilities for the entire party group. Sylvia took a moment to snap photos of the signs, then deliberately stepped into the portable toilet marked, "White Men".

In the meantime, Oliver had waited politely and impatiently to be invited to play on one or the other of the softball teams. He was angry when Sylvia rejoined him.

"They're just purposely ignoring me. Since I have been standing here, two white couples have come and joined teams. They might well have a "Whites Only" sign up. At least it would be more honest," he groused to his wife.

Sylvia told him about the toilets and their offensive signs. His only comment came when she told him about taking pictures.

"Let's go. I've had enough. I can prove I was here if anyone asks about my attendance."

On the drive home, Oliver and Sylvia could talk of nothing but the offenses they had suffered from departmental racism. They admitted that the federal government in general had improved to an almost color-blind status over the last thirty years or so; the ATF was the lone holdout in the twenty-first century. The ATF agents and their families reflected the divisiveness of the country as a whole. Ever since the initial civil rights euphoria of the 1960s, and despite the volumes of rhetoric in the ensuing decades, the de facto segregation of blacks and whites and of Hispanics had increased in an ever-widening divergent angle. Still—the African-American couple argued—it was not right; it was neither the letter nor the spirit of the law of their country. Certainly, they did not have to put up with such trash in the workplace when their workplace was the Department of the Treasury of the United States of America.

"You know, Sylvia, I have been the Uncle Tom in the ATF far too long. It's time to get on with doing something about it. Those pictures of yours—if they turn out—may just be the ammunition I've been looking for. I'm ready to give it a shot."

Sylvia thought before answering.

"I'm with you. Oliver. But you have to go into this with both eyes open. Whistle-blowers have a dismal history in this country. I guess I feel like every other black person who ever walked to the front of the bus or complained about unfair housing for the first time. It is going to change our lives, mark my word on that. We are going to have pain from this. How much, I don't know, or whether it will be worth it in the end. You need to be sure about how strongly you feel about this, Ol."

Oliver Quatraine's face radiated his certainty. Enough was enough, and now he was ready to fight. His first letter was to the director of the ATF.

Communications between Randolph Kennedy and the Hopewell office were handled in a curious hands-off way. There were no face-to-face discussions with Leo or Larry in the Hopewell or the Virginia offices higher up the line. Everything came via fax or in the mail or by e-mail. There were no farewell parties, glowing letters of transfer, not even a round of handshakes. Randolph received verification of his new position in a simple declaratory letter from the Anchorage office, easily sold his house to a couple eager to take over his loan because of its favorable interest, and went by the AAA center to get a set of Alaska maps and city maps of Anchorage and Wasilla. He decided that it was too expensive to move his furniture from Virginia to Wasilla, since his company did not offer to defray the costs. He found a used furniture rental company and sold the lot to it. He rented a Ryder truck, put in his few personal belongings, and set out for the north.

The Wasilla office was not expecting Randolph before the end of the month; so, he had a three week vacation to get from the eastern seaboard of the contiguous forty-eight states to the western coast of Alaska. He had the AAA prepare a triptik for a leisurely and circuitous meander through the northern tier of states, across the western Canadian provinces, then up through British Columbia, the Yukon Territory, and into Alaska on the Alaskan-Canadian highway. He stopped when he wanted, slept as late as he wanted, got up and left early for a long day's drive on a whim. It was a refreshing freedom from the constraints of his work and of society. The only contacts he made were with the townspeople in the small towns and cities where he stopped to eat, to sight see, and to spend the night. Randolph found that he liked talking to the citizens of rural America and Canada because of their easy candor, affability, and helpfulness. These superficial contacts were enough for him.

CHAPTER FOURTEEN

ATF agent Allen Heaps found Randolph's rambling passage across the country both interesting and potentially incriminating. He reported his regular surveillance to Henry Drake—his immediate superior—and on to the other members of the Special Response Team on a daily basis and received back reports from the FBI and other members of the FBG. In that way, Heaps had access to an assortment of files about the cities and individuals Randolph was seen talking to. He was observed in conversation with suspected members of the infamous Michigan Militia and again with a woman who resembled the wife of a member of the Minnesota Patriots Council. On one occasion in North Dakota, the subject was photographed in conversation with a man in bib overalls who was holding what looked like an illegal hunting rifle. The man resembled a composite drawing of a wanted Odinist. The subject Kennedy seemed to make no effort to conceal his activities; but rather, he flagrantly went about talking to apparent strangers—listed in Heaps' report as unsubs—and to the occasional known but unindicted gun owners.

Jack Bailey went over every report every day. He knew that Henry would be more interested in Allen Heaps' confidential information than anything else that came through.

"Henry, look, the perp's reaching out for a weapon. Looks like a sniper rifle...see the big scope?"

"Good likeness of him, ugly mug. Any with him holding the rifle, Jack?" asked Henry.

"Nope, sorry."

Henry riffled through the small stack of long distance photographs.

"Any ID on these guys? This older woman by the café?"

"No, sir, they're just listed as unknown subjects at this point."

"Anything else juicy in Allen's reports today?"

"Not really. At least there's nothing to put your finger on. He's obviously up there in the great wasteland making contact with the network. He's seen enough members of the Movement to establish that; you were absolutely right about that and the decision to shadow him, boss,"

Jack simply echoed the opinion that Drake was certain was a fact. He was also certain that the perp would make a mistake eventually, and then they would have him. It would take some patience to prove that and to make a strong case. This time, they could not take a chance on anything rash or that was unverified.

"Tell Allen he's doing good work and to keep it up until I tell him otherwise. Also, tell him he doesn't have to worry about the brass thinking this surveillance mission of his is a waste of time and money. We've got plenty of both."

"Who're you tracking, Henry?" asked Oliver Quatraine from his desk.

He couldn't help overhearing; and as the team leader, he had a right, even a responsibility to know.

Henry gave Oliver his usual look of annoyance at being interrupted.

"That Kennedy guy. Looks like we have him on a trip to contact the members of the Movement in those little out of the way burgs up north. He's talking to every black and Jew hater in the northeast and on to the coast. You ought to get involved. This guy is one of the worst closet bigots of the bunch."

"Sure. He's the guy you raided, and he killed some of our guys. Isn't that the one?"

"Yeah, the same one that was able to sue for police brutality, abuse of his rights—that sort of pinko minority civil rights drivel—no offense intended, Oliver."

"None taken. Count me in."

"You're in. Not much to do but to sit and wait for now. But we'll nail him. He's dirty. One of these days we'll see him nesting on a ton of contraband firearms, and we'll take him down. Don't think there'll be any ticker tap parades for him then."

Drake sent his first report to Margaret Thaler, fleshing out the meetings Randolph Kennedy had with the militiamen along his meandering route with details that had to be true; there could be no other explanation. The attorney general forwarded the report to President Vantassa with a marginal note that this was hopeful for vindication, but she recommended all due caution.

Randolph took a room at the Matsue Resort in Wasilla for a week and backed his Ryder truck up against a side wall of the building to keep thieves from getting in through the rear door. He went to Tony's Chevrolet and purchased a Range Rover painted in camouflage. The vehicle had been repossessed after only 3000 miles; and the price was further reduced because of the unappealing paint job, for which the dealer apologized. Randolph—on the contrary—liked it. It amused him that the former owner had so obviously done the painting himself, and it looked like he had used a regular house paint brush on some of the areas. There was no accounting for taste—not even his own—Randolph thought and smiled at himself. He paid cash.

He spent the remainder of the week finding a two room cabin for rent; they were scarce and expensive. Wasilla was the most expensive city Randolph had ever known. Now, he realized why he was slated to receive such a healthy raise in pay at the branch office of the accounting firm. He bought odds and ends of furniture to equip his rooms, only enough to get by.

He was astounded at the abundance of wildlife he encountered in his travels around the city. Most wild animals were only talked about in historical footnotes in the twenty-first century lower United States. In Anchorage, however, his car was stopped by an arrogant moose; he saw a small skulk of Arctic foxes flash through the underbrush within the city limits; and he watched a gam of Beluga whales migrate up Cook Sound. He sighted a sloth of grizzlies moving unconcernedly along a jogging path in a city park while the human interlopers moved swiftly away from the group of massive predators. He knew that he was going to love living in the last frontier of the modern world. After his first week in the state, Randolph knew full well why the locals all carried guns.

His final piece of business that week was to read the real estate ads and to find an agent. Randolph chose the agency he did for two reasons: the land described in Devlin O'Herligy's brochure suited Randolph best, and O'Herligy was the man Randolph had been referred to by Daryl Haslip, the range master in Hopewell.

Randolph walked into the two-story log building at the intersection of Parks Highway and Tammy Moe Street that sported four signs of equally bright color, grand size, and prominence of print: O'HERLIGY REAL ESTATE, REGIONAL HEADQUARTERS OF THE ALASKAN

SECESSIONIST LEAGUE, WASILLA OFFICE OF THE NATIONAL RIFLE ASSOCIATION, AND OFFICE OF THE COMMANDER OF THE NORTH STAR STATE MILITIA. The signs effectively obliterated all traces of the building's log construction on the front and both sides. The color scheme outdid the rainbow in both color range and intensity. The signs' garish print was in several different and clashing print fonts, and every letter was over sized. On the door was a life-sized heroic pose photograph of O'Herligy in mountain man attire with a Kentucky long rifle and powder horn in hand. In the background of the poster stood two huskies.

ATF Agent Allen Heaps reported Randolph's entrance into the O'Herligy building by cellular phone. Heaps was dressed in a lumber jack's red and black plaid shirt, new denim trousers with the cuffs rolled up, and new, uncomfortable hard-toed shoes. Sitting in the dented and worn Chevy pick-up in the late spring heat, he stood out like a hippie at a pow-wow.

Randolph was surprised to find the inside of the office building/store to be modern, neat, and business-like, for the most part.

"I would like to see Mr. O'Herligy," he told the receptionist.

"May I have your name, sir?" she asked politely.

"Randolph Kennedy."

"Let me check with Mr. O'Herligy, see if he can see you. Is your business about real estate, secession, guns, or the militia?"

"Yes," Randolph responded, and gave the young woman a small wry smile.

She flashed him a toothsome grin. She was a pleasant country girl—big, flaxen-haired, abundantly bosomed—a Wagnerian Gunnhilde in demure calico.

She headed into the inner office and was gone for a couple of minutes.

"Take a seat, Mr. Kennedy. He's expecting you. He's just finishing up another matter, then he can give you his full attention. He told me to tell you that."

Randolph found himself a seat on one of the anachronistic black watch plaid upholstered couches.

A workman in a red and black plaid shirt, fresh blue Wrangler jeans, and shiny new hard-toed boots that kalumped on the hardwood floor sauntered into the building and took a great interest in the real estate listings. He was young, tall, and powerful looking with a military-style severe bulldog haircut.

Randolph paid him no heed, even when the receptionist called out, "Anything I can help you with officer?" which caused the man to blush intensely.

He made no reply and shortly left the way he came in. Randolph thought it was odd, but dismissed the man from his mind.

Devlin O'Herligy strode out of his office and into the main room.

"ATFer was in here, boss. Looked like a cartoon lumber jack," Marge, the secretary, said almost as an aside.

"So what's new?" O'Herligy asked.

He was a large, bluff, red-faced, and had an unruly shock of red hair that— at a distance—looked either like a rosy halo or a clown wig, depending on one's predisposition.

"Hey, Kennedy," he shouted from the short distance across the room with unfeigned bonhomie.

Randolph looked at the man with a small start.

"C'mon over here. Let's you and me have a sit-down in my office. We got a lot to talk about."

Randolph walked over to where O'Herligy was standing, shook the man's hand, and introduced himself.

"Marge," O'Herligy called out, "no more appointments this a.m. And would you mind getting this man some sandwiches and pop? We'll be going out to see the Terwilliger property soon's we have a chat."

She nodded and flashed her boss a winning smile.

"Oh, and if that ATFer shows his face again, set the dogs on him."

Marge laughed and walked back to her reception desk.

"Have a seat, Randolph," O'Herligy said and pointed at a comfortable leather cushion chair once they were in his office, and he had closed the door. "Mind if I call you that, or do your friends call you Randy?"

"I like Randolph better."

Only Irene and his mother had called him by the diminutive, 'Randy', and he considered that to be reserved to the absent and still tender past.

"I'm having biscuits and red-eye gravy, want some?"

"What is it?"

"Man, you haven't lived until you taste some of Marge's red-eye gravy. You take the grease from fried country ham—none too lean—and a dollop of black coffee and some boiling water. Then you smother some biscuits. It's some kind of good eatin',"

He smacked his lips appreciatively.

"I'll wait for the sandwiches if that's all right."

Grease was beginning to run down O'Herligy's lower lip.

"Suit yourself," Devlin said and smiled. "I got an e-mail-o-gram from old Daryl Haslip from down below. He say's you're okay. Says you had a real nasty run-in with the ATFers and might not like them all that much. I gotta tell you, Randolph, anybody that's an enemy of the ATF is automatically a friend of mine. That Gestapo bunch watches my little sinecure like a bunch of buzzards. Marge says there was one right in the place while you were sitting out there waiting to see me. You'd think they would have something better to do with their time, wouldn't you?"

The image of the out-of-place short haired man in the red and black plaid shirt came quickly to Randolph's mind.

"I did have some problems with them, but that's behind me. I don't want to have anything to do with them from here on out. That's part of why I moved to Alaska," said Randolph. "Anyway, I thought I was being sent to Elba when my boss told me I was being transferred to Alaska, but I can see that I'm going to like it here."

"Don't know Elba; but the rest of Alaska is my turf; and I know you're goin' to like it here. And amen to you being able to avoid the ATF for the rest of your natural days. We got better things to think about. Maybe even jackbooted thugs can find some kinda life without putting their noses under the flaps of our tents. First things first. I take it you came by to get yourself some land, maybe a house. Am I right?"

"Yes, I'm in the market, looking around."

"You don't have to be coy with me, Randolph. I'm the only worthwhile game in town. I'll treat you right, and you can get a good start here. I'll give you a first-class price on property. I don't want to alienate you. I got other, bigger things in mind for you."

Randolph was not sure that he liked the sound of that, of the implication that he was being handled. He turned the subject back to his original purpose for coming to O'Herligy's.

"I am going to settle here permanently, so far as I know. I want property, maybe ten, twelve acres—private, isolated, and wooded if I can."

"And secure," O'Herligy declared as if he had clairvoyance when it came to Randolph's needs.

"I hadn't exactly thought of it that way, but yes. I had some real trouble back in Virginia, Devlin. I presume Daryl filled you in about that. I just don't want ever again to feel so vulnerable. I guess I'm not quite over the trauma."

Randolph felt self-conscious about confessing that bit of paranoia.

"It's probably silly in our day and age, but…you never know, as I am living witness," Randy added.

"I would say so. I know just the place. Exactly the place for you. I saved it for you as soon as Daryl called me up. It's perfect for your special needs. Had a lot of call on it, too, even from some of the brothers in the Militia. We'll go up and take a look at it in a minute or two. You're in the NRA, I take it?"

"Yes."

"We meet here Thursday nights. Like to have you."

"I'll try and come."

Again the feeling that he was being managed.

"Good. That's enough proselytizing for today. But be on your guard; I'll be after you to serve on the secession committee. One thing at a time."

Randolph thought waiting was a good idea. Secession—he wasn't quite ready for that yet, for sure.

O'Herligy flashed his patented winning smile. The light from the window of the office behind him illuminated the big man's hair making it look as if it might have caught fire. He was an impressive presence, Randolph had to admit.

The two men drove out on Highway 3 north beyond Wasilla city limits a distance of nearly thirty miles. They traveled along the Sustina River, gradually leaving behind the flat and fertile valley of Wasilla until they entered the foothill country of the Talkeetnas. As they drove, O'Herligy glanced occasionally into his rearview mirror and either smiled, sneered, or rolled his eyes at what he was seeing, depending on his mood at the moment. Randolph resisted the temptation to ask Devlin what he was seeing that caused the variety of reactions, but instead turned and looked back himself or glanced at the side mirror. All he could see was a beat up old truck that was kicking up dust behind them, evidently going the same way as he and Devlin.

They turned off at a *For Sale—Call O'Herligy Real Estate* sign and pulled into a narrow, winding, poorly kept dirt road. Deep, high, willow brush flanked the rutted roadway until they drove into a pine forest that fringed a bare knoll giving the property the appearance of a tonsured monk's pate from a distance. Immediately above the tree line, the road improved; and a zigzag buck pull fence appeared. It had once surrounded the entire bald knoll as a sturdy barrier, but had long since been trampled down in large sections by migrating moose which never let a little thing like a fence impede their progress. The vicissitudes of weather—this winter and last winter—had taken their toll as well.

Just below the crest of the knoll stood a thoroughly dilapidated one-room log cabin. The old building's roof had caved in, and the glassless two front windows looked like the vacant eyes of a bleaching skull, accentuating the empty lifelessness of the cabin. Shades of the House of Usher flitted through Randolph's mind. The view from the top of the hill by the cabin revealed a series of hills similar to the one on which the two men were traveling and the great mountains beyond to the north and west.

O'Herligy and Kennedy drove up to the cabin and alighted from O'Herligy's Jeep truck. They stretched their legs and aching backs.

"Nice, huh?" Devlin commented.

It was a measure of the likeness of their thinking that Randolph did not laugh out loud at the bedraggled appearance of the property's "improvements". Instead, he nodded and turned slowly to take in the panorama.

"Kind of a fixer-upper," Randolph said and smiled in amusement. "Nice view, great country, though."

He made a 360 degree inspection of the landscape before speaking again.

"Two important questions, Devlin: How far down there does the property extend? And how much does all of this cost?"

"There's the good news and the better news," Devlin responded with genuine pleasure.

He was looking down towards the road up which they had climbed. There was no sign of the beat-up truck that had dogged them all the way from Wasilla.

"You can have from the edge of the pine trees all around the hill, or you can take the whole parcel from where the dirt road turns in. Depends on how much you want to take on. That leads us into the piece of better news. The State of Alaska will let you have either section at $160 an acre if you will develop it for nonhunting, nonlogging purposes. The bunny huggers and tree huggers run the legislature right now. You have to make $10,000 worth of improvements a year for ten years or the whole Magilla at once, and then full title to the land is yours. You still have to agree not to run a hunting outfitters lodge, but you could call it a dude ranch or a photo-safari area, that kind of politically correct sort or thing. I have no personal knowledge, but I think I heard by the grapevine that a few people have fudged on the hunting part a little. This is a big country, hard to police it all against non crimes.

"You can take possession in the blink of an eyelash. All you have to do is to put down $10,000 for the first year—the good faith money—then pay the rest of the requirement at $1000 a month after the first year. The state isn't being penny ante; they just don't want a bunch of broke squatters on the land.

They've had that experience with the 59ers, and it took forever and a fortune to dislodge that bunch of squatters once they settled in. Also, you have to establish that you have a reasonable set of means. For the big section, that's more like something in the range of $100,000 in holdings and yearly income, and that you have a steady and substantial job in Alaska. You can get provisionary approval with the down payment and be meeting the other responsibilities, but you have to prove that your intentions are correct by staying a full year in Alaska. That isn't too bad for a section of this size, you know.

"After that first year—defined as from April to April—to make sure you spend most of the winter here, you become eligible for a surplus oil revenue share, something on the order of $20,000 for a single man as of last year. It's even more for kids. Any way you look at it, that's better'n a poke in the eye with a sharp stick."

Randolph had to agree with that. He had the minimum means by a long shot, but his pragmatic nature calculated some of the difficulties.

"I suppose I could come up with the earnest money, but I obviously couldn't do the work out here by myself and do my CPA job. Can I find good builders?" he asked—and as an afterthought, added—"at anywhere near an affordable cost?"

"Depends," replied Devlin. "You come up here like any cheechako, and you pay full union wages and get a slow-ball kind of work, maybe good quality, maybe not. That's just the way it is up here. This is an expensive place to live. On the other hand, you have friends—the right kind of friends—and things fall into place somewhat easier."

Devlin paused, looked directly into Randolph's eyes, and let Randolph digest his meaning.

"Tell me about friends," Randolph said.

He knew that they were coming to the punch line. The good-old-boy talk was about to end. This was the serious moment of the day.

"For the time being, I control this property. State of Alaska commissioned me to handle it and to get the right party on it. I swing a lot of pecker in this deal, even though I don't make much commission. It's good for us two to be friends, for one. The other is you got to widen your social circle with some choosy care. Maybe you should oughta join an organization or two, get to know the right folks."

Randolph thought about it briefly taking care to retain a bland expression.

"Like, maybe the NRA, the State Militia, and the secessionist movement, maybe?"

He was very careful to prevent even a hint of sardonicism from creeping into his tone of voice.

"A lot like that," Devlin answered, looking Randolph squarely and unabashedly in the eyes.

There was no more fencing between the two men; the parry and thrust niceties were over. Randolph had just heard the requirements; it was up to him now.

He took a long moment to look around. The place was perfect: beautiful, wild, remote, and easily protected. In his mind's imaginative eye, he could see a crusader's fort on the knoll. More realistically, he could envision a sturdy log house and out buildings, perimeter electrified fencing, well-laid out gardens and some animal pens. He didn't know Devlin, not really. How much of a problem could entanglement with O'Herligy and all of those touted friends become? He was obviously at odds with the ATF, and Randolph wanted nothing more than complete anonymity with that organization. He took a breath and considered the things he was sure that Devlin stood for and was involved in. They were not so far different than his own opinions, and he had to admit that he had changed since the ATF raid on his house in Virginia. His own ideas, like O'Herligy's were pretty libertarian although

Devlin had carried the concepts to a point further out than was comfortable to Randolph. In final analysis he wanted this piece of land and all it represented. He believed what Devlin had said—he would not be able to do what he wanted with the property without some greasing of the skids from Devlin. His initial plans were quite modest, and even they would be very difficult without a push in the right direction by the right guy. He presumed that Alaska was not so different from Virginia where it took generations of human networking to get things done efficiently. On his own, he was sure that the land would be long gone before he could get everything together by himself.

Randolph turned to look at Devlin. Devlin smiled and indicated no annoyance or discomfort at the long silent pause. His smile was comforting and inviting—the salesman with the deal clincher, and no longer the high pressure sales look. He wanted Randolph—not just for a good sale—for a profit. He wanted Randolph, and Randolph was well aware that he did. Devlin liked the slender young man.

Randolph drew in a long breath, his decision made.

"All right, Devlin. I'm in, in all the way. I want the whole thing; if I'm going to be in for a penny, I might just as well be in for a pound."

Devlin shook his hand solemnly.

"I knew you would. I read the papers, too. I didn't need good old Daryl Haslip to tell me about you. I knew this was to be your place as soon as he let me know that you might be coming up here. You won't regret this."

Randolph was less sure. However, at the moment, he could not see any great drawback; and the advantages and opportunities seemed dramatic. He was sure that he could maintain an arms' length relationship with the several pet project organizations of Devlin's.

He and Devlin walked the land in near silence, drinking in its size, grandeur, and calculating its potential. They found a natural spring about 100 yards from the tumble-down cabin. The water issued out of the ground from a natural sink-hole lined with stones. An aged wooden pipe led a small stream of crystal icy water about three feet and let it drop off in a miniature waterfall. All water in Alaska is clean and does not require chlorination. This water had a very faint woody taste that made it interesting but did not detract from the relish the men had for it. A blacktail deer darted into the pines ahead of them. Squirrels barked at the intrusion of the two men. The sun was warm, and the air was clean, dry, and fresh.

"It's not for the weak of heart in the winter, Randolph," observed Devlin conversationally as they clambered back into his four-wheeler, Got to take that into consideration."

"I hadn't expected it would be," replied Randolph. "I kind of like the idea of pitting myself against the real elements. "

"Spoken like a true Alaskan, Randolph. You're going to love it here."

They pulled back onto the main gravel road. Three miles closer to Wasilla both men again saw the same old truck moving along behind them, never moving closer, never getting further behind them. Randolph accepted Devlin's unspoken suspicions. Devlin O'Herligy had not seen a real coincidence in decades, and Randolph was beginning to learn from the teachers at street smart college.

CHAPTER FIFTEEN

There were two items on the agenda of the FBG Task Force meeting that captured and held the president's interest on that pleasant Washington spring day.

"Margaret," she said, "I won't be able to stay for the whole session today. Would you mind going over items two and eleven out of sequence?"

The attorney general had been sure that President Vantassa would find those two items to be of interest. She was well prepared to report.

"Item two," she said. "The final report on the racial harassment charges against the Bureau of Alcohol, Tobacco, and Firearms. I have reviewed them myself. I think Ike Petrovsky and his people have done a good, thorough, and I think, objective job on this. I'll let Ike handle it from here. Ike, just give us the highlights. That okay with you, Madam President?"

"I prefer it. I'll go over the whole report in my copious free time."

Petrovsky stood on cue.

"Mesdames President and Attorney General, thank you for the opportunity. I'll be brief. There have been complaints against the bureau going back more than fifty years. I inherited an organization with something of a reputation. This investigation—ordered by the two of you—gave me the opportunity to dig into the facts. The past reports have always been rather self-serving and exculpatory—but between the lines—there was more than a grain of truth about the allegations of racist behavior on the part of the Caucasian agents against minorities. Until the recent incident reported by one of our fine African-American agents, Oliver Quatraine, we could not lay out the unequivocal evidence; certainly, we couldn't lay blame on any ranking official. With your permission I will elaborate on the Quatraine case."

The FBG members had been waiting for this report. They expected a turning point in the government's attitude about enforcement of its own clearly defined race and gender rules which had long since ceased to be mere guidelines. The members presumed that the decisions made in the morning that day would affect their own departments, not just the ATF. President Vantassa gave an impatient little nod to Director Petrovsky to move on.

"Special Response Team Agent Oliver Quatraine and his wife, Sylvia—who is a registered social worker and considered a wholly reliable witness—were attendees at the annual ATF family outing sponsored officially by the Treasury Department and the Bureau. In direct charge of the event were co-chairpersons Angela Horowitz and Terence Scolpagni, both from the Washington office. Agent Quatraine and Mrs. Sylvia Quatraine were subjected to exclusionary tactics during a softball game. They were—in effect—not allowed to play on an all white pair of teams drawn supposedly by choosing up sides from all available agents and their family members. All comers except blacks were admitted to play. No blacks participated, and the races remained strictly segregated throughout the day. Perhaps that could be explained away. However, these photographs cannot."

Ike Petrovsky brought out poster sized photo enlargements of the pictures taken by Sylvia. They were of excellent quality, having not required any enhancement. Images of port-a-potties on which hang damning signs— *White Men, White Women,* and the crudest of them all, *African-Americans and Monkeys, Use the Bushes.*

There was silence in the room. On the Task Force leadership board were two African-Americans and two Hispanics. Their faces were like dark cold stones.

"Let me point out to you, ladies and gentlemen," Petrovsky said after the initial impact of the display had settled on each of the Task Force members, "There is no possibility that these photos were taken at some other place or time or at a function of some other organization…any other organization."

He pointed at the clear lettering on the port-a-potties' walls immediately below the name of the rental company, where it was unequivocally specified that the chemical toilets had been rented by the ATF for the day in question.

"The agent in immediate charge of the affair, Terence Scolpagni, has submitted a statement admitting his culpability. I have it here. More damning is his description of the pervasive character of racism that is rife in the bureau. He states that he was only following the protocol of many decades and the will of the majority of the agents. Unless you would like more details, that is about the sum and substance of the complaint and the investigation," said Petrovsky.

Seeing no questioners, he returned to his seat.

The eyes of the minority members on the Task Force fixed on President Vantassa. She knew full well that this was one of those "buck-stops-here" moments.

"Ike," she said quietly, "tell me what part you played in the outing."

Ike seemed to wither.

"Madam President, I had nothing to do with the planning or the execution of that function."

He hesitated for the briefest of seconds then met her eyes.

"I take responsibility as the captain of the ship."

"Yes," said the president.

Her eyes continued to fix the man uncomfortably like a pinned bug.

"Were you in attendance?"

The question was posed softly, almost gently, like a tentative probe with an ice pick.

"Yes, ma'am, I was. I did not see the offenses in question."

She looked at him with what could only pass for sadness.

"Why not?"

Petrovsky writhed inwardly and fought for composure. He knew full well what was at stake here. He felt compelled to say something and was determined no to grovel or to shame himself.

"I am responsible. I serve at the president's pleasure," he said with a shaky voice that made him angry at himself. "I will resign if you wish."

He watched his power, his perks, his great job, and his pension float away out of his reach.

"Yes," the president said calmly. "Tell me, Mr. Director, exactly which senior officials were involved or were present at that particular racist orgy?"

Her use of inflammatory language confirmed to Petrovsky that he was not only finished but was to be the scapegoat for the many decades of racism for which he was not responsible. He was only glad that it was not Japan where he would be expected to commit seppuku.

"I will have a complete list of both senior and junior officials who were responsible for or had guilty knowledge of this affair on your desk by morning," he said, hearing his voice as if it were coming from someone else.

There was along, awkward pause. The president was maddening with her meaningful pauses.

He finally gathered his courage for the inevitable, "And my resignation."

He looked down at the papers on his desk.

"Yes," said the president. "Thank you."

She looked away from Petrovsky as if he were no longer in the room.

"Now, Madam Attorney General and Mr. Secretary, I have a couple of questions for you. First, has any of this been made public? Second, have you a plan of containment, perhaps of appeasement? And finally and most important, is this disgraceful state of affairs going to be corrected once and for all?"

Gerald Buchanan, Secretary of the Treasury, answered, "Madam President, we are fortunate that Quatraine is a team player. He agreed not to breathe a word of this outside official channels until we have had a chance to act on the report presented to this committee. His wife has been mum as well. We do have an olive branch to extend to Agent Quatraine. We have promoted this fine agent to the position of assistant director of ATF and will include him on this Task Force."

Eyebrows raised surreptitiously all around the room.

"Finally, we are going to launch an educational program ATF wide—a racial awareness campaign—that will convey the sentiments of yourself and the attorney general regarding racism, the fine points of the law, and the consequences of breaking the law in future. We are not going to change the hearts of the people of America. Racism is unfortunately as American as apple pie; it is endemic in our society. What we can do is to accomplish what the navy did many years ago. Every officer and agent in the ATF will know that there will be no discrimination of even the slightest degree allowed throughout the bureau from this time forward. We will introduce, implement, and enforce a zero tolerance attitude. We intend to let them know that they may think anything they want to think; but if they express racist opinions in any form—either on or off the job—they will be summarily terminated and will lose their accrued benefits. Every person in the ATF will be required to affix their signature accompanied by an officer's signature as witness, to a notice that they have read and understood and agree to comply with the zero tolerance of bias regulations in the matter of race and gender. We propose that the new assistant director be put in charge."

"In agreement for his keeping this incident in house," observed the president.

"Substantially."

"Good. Margaret, I want you, Ted Coleman, and Secretary Buchanan to speak fact to face with Agent Quatraine and to come away with his signed agreement by noon tomorrow. Also—by that same time—I want each person in this room to submit one name for the directorship of the ATF.

Mr. Buchanan, contact the leader of each of the five Special Response Teams and each of the regional directors for their preference. And...I want every department represented on this Task Force to have an antiprejudice program that is direct and to the point and ready to be implemented on my desk by week's end. This is the last I expect to hear of this kind of thing during my administration."

"Yes, ma'am," the attorney general, secretary of the Treasury, and Ted Coleman, Director of the FBI answered almost in chorus.

"Now, item eleven," said the president.

"This is the matter of Randolph Kennedy," said Mrs. Thaler.

"Again?" The president raised her eyebrows in angry surprise. "I trust this is something new."

"It is. Quite incidental to other ongoing investigations."

The attorney general did not think a small stretch of the truth would hurt at this juncture.

"ATF has come across Kennedy again. Although we got egg on our faces the first time around, the agents remained convinced that he is dirty. They—and I, for that matter—think we simply underestimated the cunning and resourcefulness of the man in the first incident. He has been seen and photographed meeting across the country with known members of the Movement, people on the attorney general's list."

She laid out a spread of enlargements of Agent Allen Heaps' surveillance photographs. Some of them were grainy, obviously taken at considerable distance; but Kennedy's face was unmistakable in all of the photos.

"Any idea what transpired in those meetings?" asked the president.

"We do not have audio, Madam President, but there are two photos in which guns are seen. In this one," she used her extendible pointer, "it appears as if the rural terrorist is handing a weapon—presumably an illegal weapon—to Kennedy."

"But no direct evidence that he had anything directly to do with the weapon himself, nor that he was selling or smuggling firearms to the Militia, I take it."

"No, ma'am. Unfortunately, our agent could not get that exact shot and has yet to turn up any clear evidence of the transactions. We are treading very lightly as you might appreciate."

"And nothing less than convincing irrefutable evidence will do," the president said, and the attorney general interpreted her statement as an order.

"Absolutely. We will not make another mistake with this perpetrator. He is clever, and he is represented by the worst legal talent dirty money can buy."

There were appreciative chuckles through the Task Force.

"Have you more, pray?" President Vantassa said, indicating her obvious relish for anything that put Randolph Armstrong Kennedy in a bad light.

He had, after all, single-handedly done more to hurt her administration's most sacred project than all of the criminal forces with which they contended put together.

"Indeed we do, and better," the attorney general responded, her vocal inflection indicating her shared animus.

"I could use a little perking up, Margaret, do proceed."

"The subject as been traced to Wasilla, Alaska.

"Where, pray tell, is that?" asked Ted Coleman with his usual condescension for any place smaller or less urban than Chicago.

They all laughed.

"Anyway," she continued, "he was not there a day before he was in face-to-face contact with the leader of the Movement for Alaska, and a man who is known to be affiliated with the conspiracy nationwide. Name's O'Herligy, Devlin O'Herligy."

"Sounds like the old IRA," said FBI Director Coleman.

"I wouldn't put it past him. This guy is unbelievable. He is at the same time the head of the state's NRA office and some loony secessionist organization."

They all boo-hissed like patrons at a melodrama. There was laughter all around.

"The commander of the so-called North Star State Militia—their particular branch of the Movement—has been the spearhead of the drive to turn Alaska into its own all-white country, and I'm not referring to their winter snows."

"Boy, he takes the term 'fringe element' to a new status," muttered Coleman.

"And, incidentally, he sells real estate," added the attorney general as an after thought.

"The most unkindest cut of all," said the FBI SAC for Oregon who was known for his vigorous off-duty support of legislation in his home state to take all food producing land by eminent domain to preserve it for the people.

Accordingly, he was vehemently opposed by the realtor's lobby. He said it with mock severity and drew a hearty laugh from the group.

Mrs. Thaler went on, "Our subject spent a full day with O'Herligy evidently inspecting a large parcel of rural land with a commanding view and defensive position. Through O'Herligy, Kennedy was able to procure long-term tenancy with eventual full homestead rights for the property. Our agents have documented the beginning of construction of a fortress-like log structure on top of Kennedy's hill and what looks like above and below ground storage facilities that we presume will be used for a weapons cache. Kennedy has been active in NRA meetings—more so than when he lived in Virginia. We have one of our people in the organization there who confirms his activity. He appears to have joined the secessionist movement, and we presume that he has linked up with the militia there and also that he is able to continue his underground affiliation with the Movement in the lower forty-eight states. That's all we have at the moment."

"Good work, Margaret. Convey my kudos to the ATF intelligence teams, please."

"It will be my pleasure, Madam President."

"And keep me up to date, please. I want to relish every scintilla of evidence that leads to this Kennedy character's downfall."

CHAPTER SIXTEEN

Kennedy presented himself on Monday at the accountancy office to start work. He greeted the secretaries and introduced himself as the new assistant manager. They were appropriately deferential, as deferential as Alaskans know how to be. No person in the entire state viewed himself or herself to be anybody's inferior, let alone anybody's servant. He was introduced to his new office, a small room that needed redecorating in the worst way and then to Ian Laird—his supervisor—the statewide manager.

"Greetings and salutations, Randolph. Am I ever glad you're here. We didn't expect you for a week; so, this is a doubly glad day. We got ourselves up to our eyeballs with a new account. You probably don't know the organization that has secured our services, but it is a real plum. We will be doing all of the bookkeeping, taxes, payroll, and auditing for a big real estate typhoon. You'll hear about him—name's Devlin O'Herligy—one of the local characters—a funny sort of guy, likable, but a major mover-and-shaker hereabouts. You can't miss him—he's a real part of the local color. Specifically, we want you to get to like him and for him to like you. Consider that about as near to an order as we give around here. We want you to handle the account. It'll be your first and biggest account. It will take a big load off my mind to have you take over."

"I'll give it my best shot," Randolph said.

"Anything I can do to help you move in?"

"No, thanks, I'm pretty well underway."

"Just between the two of us, I wish you luck. O'Herligy's not my cup of tea—too brash, too political, too pushy. He'll take some handling."

Randolph was impressed and becoming a little concerned at the speed and thoroughness with which Devlin O'Herligy was insinuating himself so prominently into his life. He said nothing about his dealings with the real estate entrepreneur during the previous week. He was not much of a believer in coincidence, and the O'Herligy factor was looking more and more like a well-orchestrated involvement.

Laird said, "My wife wanted to have a little welcoming party end of this week, if that would be okay with you. We'll have the staff and some of the town's notables over for a BBQ. It's a good chance for me to do a little necessary schmoozing and for you to have a genuine chance to meet the rest of the movers-and-shakers of Wasilla. These will be the people that we need to keep in touch with. You know the company has set new quotas for business for the first of January, when the new CEO—Jed Carmichael—takes over. No more Mr. Nice Guy, apparently. It's even possible you might have a good time at the party anyway," he laughed.

Ian was an unaffectedly happy and personable man, hale and bluff, short and round. It was easy for Randolph to like him. Unlike his superiors in Virginia, there was no phoniness and no veiled threats. It was implicit in their first encounter that Randolph would be expected to be responsible for bringing in serious business and to deal with it well, and he did not have to be hit over the head to pay attention. Randolph like that sort of handling, and the meeting with Ian Laird reinforced his growing pleasure with his new place in life.

Having the O'Herligy account was magic for Randolph's career in Wasilla. The magic started during the welcoming party. The manager of Tony's Chevrolet, where he had bought his Range Rover, edged Randolph into a corner.

He said quietly, "I know you must hate guys who pry free information out of you, but I have a capital gains question. Devlin said I oughta talk to you about it. Down at the lot we had a great year. I don't mind telling you, it was a *great* year! That left us with surplus earnings. My tax guy said I had to roll it back into the business or risk having to give it up to those pork-barrel free-loadin' politicians in Washington. I don't want a bigger car business. I don't want to be forced by some idiot tax requirement to have to expand. First of all, this town's not big enough to handle more automobile inventory. Besides, I got a great life with fishin', huntin', and settin' around when I want to. I don't want to throw my money or my precious free time away for a federal boondoggle. Anyway I can avoid straight income tax on my good year or stave off the capital gains hit?"

"Mr. Carson…"

"Tony."

"Okay, Tony, I'm Randolph. Anyhow, I can't say without taking a good long look at your books. I would have to know how much you made, how you made it, and all of that. But, yes, you can defer taxes, tax-average, make a 401K, an IRA, or a Defined Benefits retirement program, buy tax-exempt municipal bonds, lots of things. What would be best for you could only be determined by an audit and some thoughtful looking into your business and your life by an experienced estate planner who would seek your input all along the way."

"My accountant never even mentioned half of that stuff. Think you could take a look at my books and how we did this year—on the sly? I don't want to hurt Greg, that's my tax guy, but I have to get serious. Maybe we could work a little something out, a consultation like."

"Tony, I would be happy to give you an overview. I think it would be better if you just let me do it as a goodwill gesture, sort of my way of getting introduced around rather than getting a consultation fee. Maybe you could put in a good word for me in the right ears. Maybe we could even have a business arrangement in the future, who knows?"

The barbecue welcoming dinner produced three solid new clients that week and introductions to half a dozen more of the principle business men and women of Wasilla. Tony Carson switched to Randolph's firm with Randolph handling his case before month's end and became his second largest account. Randolph had enough work produced on his own initiative to ensure his fledgling career in his new city. He was happy with himself and his situation after a little more than two weeks in Alaska. Still, he wondered just how much of a role the influence of Devlin O'Herligy had played. He could not knock it; everything was coming out in the plus column.

The small house Randolph rented was rapidly becoming too small. He began to collect tools, sets of plans, materials samples, and books for the building of his projected home in the wilds outside Wasilla. Devlin O'Herligy came by the rental house late on a Saturday afternoon, and—in his annoying fashion—walked into Randolph's house without knocking.

"Randolph, me boy," he called in his theatrical Irish brogue.

Devlin could not have been further removed from Ireland and its speech patterns if he had been a Cajun.

"Faith'n I've come bearing glad tidings. Top of the morning to ye!"

"And the rest of the day to you, Devlin," Randolph responded in kind but without the brogue.

He looked up from his study of log cabin construction in the *Foxfire Book*.

"Didn't your mama ever teach you to knock?"

He laughed in spite of himself at the audacious redhead.

"Nope. She taught me that friends don't even close their doors on friends… and that you don't open your doors at all to nobody else—might just be revenuers or some other gument buttinsky. Up here that buttinsky is like as not an ATFer."

He spat out the initials and sat down then put his feet up on Randolph's polished walnut coffee table. He lit a heavily chewed cigar that emitted a noxious cloud of burning tobacco mixed with some sort of fruit marinade. Randolph could feel the foul smoke infesting every little cranny in his house. He was a confirmed nonsmoker.

"Won't you sit down, please?" Randolph invited with exaggerated courtesy, ignoring the *fiat accompli*. "Make yourself at home."

Devlin nodded his acceptance of the offer, either missing or ignoring the irony.

"Have a drink?"

"Coors, thanks."

Randolph fetched three cold cans—two for Devlin—and took a seat beside the red-haired eccentric.

"Why have I come?" asked Devlin ingenuously.

"I give up, probably because you were run out of the parlors of polite society. Why?"

"I have found you a house, a big one. You can live and work out of there for a very modest monthly rent. Seems Harry McDonald is leaving for a round-the-world cruise for about three months and wants a house sitter. He and Tracy are good people, in the NRA and the Militia. They like to keep things in the family. I vouched for you."

"I appreciate that, Devlin."

"Last I checked, Harry was planning to take his niece—if you follow my meaning—on a month's Carnival cruise in the Caribbean; but Tracy got wind of it, and now it's a three month furs and diamonds, tux and ball gown Holland Line cruise around the world. I understand Tracy had to have a whole new wardrobe of furs, diamonds, and ball gowns to be able to fit in with the cruise crowd. Harry—the poor booger—has never worn a tie, let alone a tux. I would love to be a fly on the wall when he puts it on for the first time. This'll be a lesson he won't soon forget," Devlin laughed.

"His bad luck, my good," Randolph said.

"You should be able to get most of your house built before first snow and stay in Harry's house in comfort while you do the planning and general contracting. We need to truck on over to his place; so, I can show you how his alarm system works and what all needs to be done. Great place, full of gadgets. You'd need a PhD in electronic engineering to use the house, but luckily you have me."

Devlin laughed at himself, but was unabashed at his declaration of his valuable personal contributions.

The house turned out to be perfect; Devlin had understated the elegance and comfort of the mansion. Besides the great personal physical comforts it contained, there were three garages full of an impressive array of tools—electric saws and tile cutters, joiners, lathes, and drills. One three car garage was empty, ideal for storage of lumber and other supplies that Randolph needed to buy in the city and truck to the country.

The most fascinating things about the place were the building and perimeter security systems. The estate rivaled Fort Knox in sophistication. There were underground pressure and movement sensors, laser, electromagnetic, and infrared alarms. The edges of the property were protected by twelve foot high electrified elk wire fences topped with two rolls of razor wire. On the ground inside the high fence were two rolls of razor wire to provide distraction for anyone who made it over the elk fence somehow. The house windows were barred; the doors were made of case hardened steel with a triple dead bolt system that included both vertical and horizontal eight inch bolts—six above, six below each matching door, and six connecting the two doors to each other. The dead bolt system was integrated with the foundation and frame of the house. There was a reinforced concrete bomb shelter in the basement stocked with enough food, water, fuel, weapons, entertainment systems, and generators to have saved Carthage from Rome's last siege. Randolph was most taken with this special feature of the house. He took notes.

Devlin gave Randolph keys to the gun safes. There were four of them, one on each floor. In addition, there were small closet doors at intervals along the hallways that opened to small containers of loaded handguns and short barreled riot guns, and not a trigger lock in sight. The place was a fortress equipped with more fire power than many small countries possessed. Closed circuit television cameras monitored every entrance, hallway, and the grounds from the walls and foundations of the house to the farthest boundary of the property. The house could only be entered by keying in a twelve-digit entry code that could be changed with ease several times a day at the whim of the occupant.

Any entry error in the code resulted in immediate activation of the complete door and window lock system, and in one minute, if not corrected by inputting the master code, weapon lasers were activated across every window and door of the house. The signal that activated the lasers automatically contacted the armed guard who lived in a cottage at the rear of the grounds. He could disarm the system and get the dogs into their kennels, or the police could deactivate the electronics from their headquarters. The police department had standing orders to dispatch K-9 units whenever they answered a call at the McDonald residence. The chief of police was second in command in the Militia to Harry McDonald, and the police department considered it a priority to please their chief; while he, in turn, considered it a sacred duty to protect his general.

The eventuality that federal or state police organizations would disarm the connections between the impregnable fortress and the local police office had not escaped the McDonalds. Circuits they called anti-ATF devices had been put in place to prevent the friendly police connections from being disabled. The owners themselves kept a simple code to override police connections or disconnections. They simply dialed in F-R-E-E-D-O-M on a special pad. In that event, the electronics were overridden as desired, and an automatic SOS signal was delivered to the homes of ten Militiamen; all of whom were sworn to drop everything and proceed directly to the McDonalds in full battle dress. Randolph was prepared to be amused at such an extravagant display of paranoia, but remembered his own experience and tempered his judgment. O'Herligy told him that the system was only minimally to protect against criminal intruders; but rather, its main function was to protect Harry and Tracy McDonald and all of their records and secrets relating to the patriot movement from attacks from federal or state police.

After examining the McDonalds' elaborate systems and the premise behind the setup, Randolph concluded that he would spend the money necessary to have a system of his own built in with the smart-wire fiberoptic electrical wiring from the beginning. One thing he did not like about the McDonald arrangement was that so many people knew about it. Much as Randolph wanted to be able to trust O'Herligy, or the Militia, or the good old boys of the Movement; he determined to play it closer to his vest when he finally made his own defense system. It was the old gambler's creed: Trust everyone, but always cut the cards yourself.

As his plans and the early construction progressed, Randolph arranged to have his own generators as a backup to the city electricity. Rather than use any local security or alarm system company, he had all of the plans and work done by a company whose books he had done when he worked in Hopewell, Virginia. He did not connect to the local police department, nor did he inform them about his system. When the security devices were put into place, he took pains to camouflage them so that only he knew the nature and location of the monitoring equipment or weaponry.

At Devlin's persistent insistence, Randolph finally officially joined the North Star State Militia, and arranged for his security system to be linked with ten other Militiamen, a reciprocal arrangement. Beyond the fact of the hook-up, he did not share information with them. He installed pressure and movement sensors under his doors and windows and under all floors. With the exception of these upgrades, his system was comparable to the McDonalds'; but the circuitry was radically different, and could not be tampered with easily even with full knowledge of the arrangements at the large estate where Randolph was living during construction of his own place. The security devices were all in place and wired as the framing went up. The elaborate million dollar system was invisible to anyone except himself by the end of August when enough of his house was completed that he could move in and camp as the finish features were being built.

Attorney General Thaler sent ATF Agent Drake's latest report regarding Randolph Kennedy to the president through regular secure channels with copies to DFBI, DATF, DDEA, and DFBG. The copies were distributed to the authorized individuals in each of those departments and filed by their respective secretaries. Oliver Quatraine perused his copy:

> Subject terrorist, Randolph Kennedy, quartered in the fortress home of Harry and Tracy McDonald, known to have connections within the Movement. Elaborate security precautions in place and presumably being installed in the new building under construction by Kennedy. McDonalds out of Alaska and out of CONUS, suspected of being on a

mission to obtain and distribute illegal firearms. Kennedy's association with McDonalds considered highly suspicious. Surveillance continues.

Quatraine was mildly troubled about all of the effort being expended to track and document the activities of a man on whom there was such a scanty criminal activities record. It was more guilt by association than anything, and Quatraine knew a thing or two about that from personal experience. The documentation thus far included little of substance, even by the ATF's notably liberal interpretive standards, and nothing that would hold up in court certainly. He jotted a note in the margin of the memo to question the propriety of continuing to use limited federal resources on a project with such limited expectation of return.

CHAPTER SEVENTEEN

Working on his log house was heavy manual labor for Randolph personally. It was therapeutic, and there were days when he concentrated hard enough that he did not think of Irene and Annie for a stretch of an hour unlike the earliest days after they were killed. He still had regular dreams of them, still had flashes of near photographic exactness of his wife and daughter that unexpectedly filled his mind whenever he had an idle moment. The images were still so vivid that he felt that he could remember smells, sounds, and emotions associated with his girls. One small image kept invading his subconsciousness: Annie had made a small round happy face on which she had attempted to scribble her name, but the name was too large for her small unpracticed fingers. She had glued the little gift to Randolph's bathroom mirror with a small scribble at the bottom—"kv". He had shed a tear when he first saw the small contribution of his daughter, and now he could not control his tears whenever the image flashed into his mind. He began to make a concerted effort to keep the emotionally charged thought out of his mind.

For his own mental hygiene, Randolph forced himself to keep in view only one framed picture of the two of them in order to avoid his inclination to create a photographic shrine as he had seen other bereft spouses and parents do for their lost loved ones. He was determined to put his dreadful experience behind him or at least to go on with his life. His determination to put away his store of accumulated hate and anger and recrimination was less successful. He recognized the corrosive nature of such feelings, but he was unable to keep out fleeting ruminations of vendetta and vigilante justice. The Militia's unending diatribes against the ATF kept the hatred at a point just below boiling—the "water for chocolate" as an old movie put it.

Randolph joined the Militia for practical reasons—self-serving and perhaps somewhat ignoble reasons. He knew how much benefit his business and the building of his house derived from his association with Devlin O'Herligy. He would not have been able to get his house as near completion as it was without Militia involvement. The expense would have been tripled without the connections to the organization and to Devlin. It followed all too naturally for him to join up and to appear to be a believer. Despite what had happened to him in Virginia—and notwithstanding the fiery rhetoric of the Militia meetings—Randolph still maintained a basic faith in the American system and in the United States government. He worked on himself to be able to accept that men make mistakes—even policemen—and to let go of his personal pain and animosity and not to internalize the anti-government, tax revolt, secessionist rhetoric of the Militia meetings and publications. It was something of a difficult effort because Devlin and his Militia provided a safe haven and camaraderie for a very lonely man. Randolph's notions of forgiveness and faith in his country's basic goodness did not—however—dissuade him from the preparation of his defenses.

He stayed at the developing hilltop house now full time, leaving only for work at the firm. There was a measure of obsession in his activities, and he knew it; but he regarded the concentration on the house and its defenses as being rehabilitative. Part of the process involved an escalating effort at concealment on his part. He kept secrets from Devlin and the Militia; he still could not bring himself to trust them fully. There were some very squirrelly guys in the organization. If someone had questioned him about his secretiveness, Randolph would have been embarrassed and would have had little in the way of rationale to convey. If pressed, he would not have been able to provide an answer that was satisfactory even for himself. He was not asked, and he did not probe his own motives. He just knew that the security defenses had to be included in his house, and no one need be the wiser.

The ground at the location Randolph had selected for his reinforced log home was rocky and unyielding. The site was picked because it was immediately adjacent to the only spring on the knoll, a clear stream of pure mountain water that flowed out of a natural rocky crevice in both winter and summer under considerable force. Randolph hired an excavating company from among the Militia members and commenced work on a deep basement-bunker-storage room. It was only about a foot from the surface to bed rock, and most of the excavation had to be done by blasting. The products of excavation included very little dirt and tons of medium sized rocks which Randolph utilized to build a high perimeter wall around his house. He had a Virginia company put in the basement floor, walls, ceiling, and the rest of the foundation and did not share the details with the local builders. The room was imbedded in solid rock except for the ceiling and all of the concrete was reinforced with re-bar and steel mesh, well in excess of code. The spring water was piped into the bunker basement as well as the rest of the house using insulated pipes and shut-off valves. Upon completion of the foundation, there was no external evidence of the spring.

Without telling anyone about the spring as a source of water, Randolph hired Devlin O'Herligy's brother-in-law, Tad Winters, to drill a deep well. Devlin's brother, Sean, was a plumber who also owned a septic tank company. Randolph hired him for all the publicly acknowledged work. Randolph had Sean put in two separate tanks and plumbing systems, one for the main house, and one for the bunker basement. The basement was equipped with its own generator and was fitted out as an apartment separate and independent from the main house. It had its own heating and air-conditioning. There were gun port openings that were screened and barred but did afford some small view and a chance to hear what was going on outside. They were completely unidentifiable from the outside unless a person knew exactly where to look. Except for the builders, no one else was aware of the existence of the bunker basement apartment.

Unknown to the contractors referred to him by Devlin—and who were to commence their work in three weeks—Randolph acquired the services of Tecla Mining Company located near Point Hope, well to the north. He had them create a deep tunnel from the bunker to a rocky cliff located three-quarters of a mile away near the bottom of Randolph's knoll. One great advantage of using Tecla was that the crews were transient to any one area. A given individual miner seldom stayed at one job in Alaska for more than six months. By the time Randolph's fortress home was completed, none of the men who worked on his tunnel were still in the nation's largest state.

The exit opening of the tunnel was created at a forty-five degree oblique angle to the vertical surface of the cliff and could not be detected from either below or above at a distance of more than a hundred yards. Even looking straight on at the cliff, it was all but invisible until one stood directly in front of the opening. Randolph studied the old Vietnamese Cu Chi tunnels for ideas and used the natural terrain to maximum advantage. Like the Cu Chi tunnels, Randolph made several air holes and narrow escape exits. In order to get in or out of the exit opening, Randolph had to scale the difficult rock of the cliff walls or to rappel. He avoided electricity in the tunnel, but left a series of battery-operated lanterns at exact intervals along the length of the tunnel. He left small caches of storage food—mostly ready-to-eat military issue—and he left climbing and rappelling gear at the mouth of the tunnel. As a final—almost afterthought—he left a box of money, and credit cards, passports, and drivers licenses that he had had the Militia's forger create for him. He included an outfit of dress clothes and one for rugged back country traversing in his cache.

Access to the basement from the ground level of the main house was via an ingeniously concealed door that took up the middle of the main level bathroom floor. The door was tiled so carefully that its match with the remaining floor covering was indistinguishable. The handle for the basement door was concealed by having a brass towel rack base set in it. When the first persisting snowfall came in mid October, the basement bunker and the framing and insulation were finished and the rest of the house was framed, insulated, and inside and outside wall boards were in place. It had taken considerable overtime and overage on the costs. Randolph was able to set up a wing with a single bedroom, a bathroom, and a kitchen that was fully insulated, heated, and livable. The ferocity of the Alaskan winter set in before he was able to finish the rest of the home. It was just as well because his move to Alaska to date had cost in excess of two million dollars. Esthetics were of minimal consequence; Randolph's new home looked like thousands of other unfinished houses in Alaska.

"The meeting will come to order," announced Margaret Thaler after the federal departmental representatives and their staffs had taken their seats and had had a few moments for the necessary jurisdictional banter and chatting.

"The president will be along shortly, but she asked that we get started. Item one on the agenda is the failed raid on the downtown Trenton hotel site. Mr. Quatraine, will you bring the rest of us up to date? Be brief."

Quatraine shifted uneasily in his chair. He had not expected to be the one to give the report. Although he had been the senior field representative for the ATF, he had shared mission responsibility with DEA and the fibbies.

Because they had been senior to him in the field, he had been obliged to defer to their orders throughout the action. A short burst of anger-induced adrenaline coursed through him at the unfairness of being singled out. He looked around the room swiftly. The new DATF was there, as were the directors of DEA and FBI—all still senior to him. It did not take any kind of genius to realize why he had been chosen to give this onerous report.

He stood, feeling a little embarrassed because he did not know if that was customary.

"Madam Attorney General, thank you. In brief, acting on reports from usually reliable sources…" he thought he heard a slight groan from somewhere in the small audience, "a small force of FBI, DEA, and ATF units, acting under the authority of this Task Force, surveilled the Abernathy Crowne Hotel for three days. During that period of time, more than a dozen known weapons and drug law violators were seen and photographed entering and leaving. A large number of boxes were taken into the building. Our sources could not tell us exactly which room, or even which floor, was being used for illegal purposes; so, we had to obtain a search warrant for the entire hotel. On the night of September 14 last, a force of thirty-three officers and agents staged a full-scale raid on the hotel. The raid resulted in two arrests of drug pushers and the confiscation of three illegal weapons and $725 in cash."

He felt himself blushing furiously; he was glad no one could see the rise in color under his dark skin. The dope dealers had been nickel-and-dimers, losers found with less than $1000 worth of crack cocaine between them. The weapons confiscated had included a sawed-off shotgun that the hotel's night manager kept for protection, a Saturday night special, and a teen-ager's zip gun. Quatraine remembered thinking that zip guns had gone out with zoot suits, high button shoes, and flappers doing the Charleston. He had made Henry Drake do the report out of general spite.

"Impressive," said President Muriel Vantassa who had chosen this auspicious moment to make her entrance. She never seemed to miss a thing.

Oliver Quatraine loosed a heavy sigh to a background of suppressed chuckles.

"Please do continue," the president said pleasantly.

"There is not much more to report, Madam President and Madam Attorney General," Quatraine responded.

For him, the title, 'madam' had such connotations that, in his anxiousness, he had to suppress a creeping little nervous smile.

"Our post-mortem on the raid showed that we were in the right place at the right time. Apparently, our informants were wrong, and our analysis of the pre-raid surveillance was overly enthusiastic."

He sat down.

"Um hmm," muttered the president *soto voce*.

There was a pause—one of the president's famous pauses that made strong men quaver.

"And how much did this crime-busting adventure cost the good tax payers of our country?"

The newly appointed assistant director was unprepared for that question. Usually FBG members considered that they had financial carte blanche for their activities. He had to consult his notes. It made him more ill at ease than ever to fumble through his briefcase for his papers and his official mission notebook. There was an awkward interlude punctuated by the crackling of his papers.

"$35,000," he finally announced with a note of triumph in his voice for having been able to find the obscure information.

The president looked at him and let out an exasperated sigh. She shook her head.

"I am at a loss for words, at least for words that could be used here in polite society. And I hope I'm right—nobody was killed. This isn't another Kennedy Affair. Just send me a very detailed report, Mr. Quatraine."

Oliver was shocked out of his false sense of anonymity. The president knew his name, and that couldn't be good. His mouth was dry.

"Yes, ma'am," he replied briskly.

Quatraine was glad to slip back into obscurity for the moment while the reports were given on the next two items on the agenda. They were about a large and modestly successful pre-emptive raid on a farm house in northern Wisconsin associated—it was thought—with the Phineas Patriots and the apprehension of three kingpins of a guns-for-drugs syndicate working between Canada and the United States via motorcycles. One of the arrested kingpins was the leader of the Hell's Angels.

When his adrenaline and general anxiety level died down, Quatraine was once again able to think clearly. He was going to be the scapegoat for the Trenton thing. The WOMs had selected him—probably because of his skin color—but it would never be presented as that. It would sound paranoid even to voice such a thought. He rationalized that it was a pretty small matter and was unlikely to be a career threat. Maybe—he thought, instead of being angry and going around like an adolescent with hurt feelings—he should learn something from the experience. He made a resolution to get a mini-recorder to tape all important meetings, verbal orders, and field confrontations. If they could play the CYA game, so could he.

"Item number four," called Margaret Thaler.

Oliver was lost in his own thoughts and plans.

"Item number four!"

The emphasis in the attorney general's voice brought Oliver back from where his mind had been.

This was the report he had prepared and was champing at the bit to deliver. Henry Drake, Jack Bailey, and Allen Heaps had headed up a raid on a private residence on the outskirts of Ketchikan, Alaska. The informer—a frequently used RCI—had been wrong in his information. This time—miracle of miracles—the quasi-Reliable Confidential Informer had *under*estimated the magnitude of the cache of arms, the money involved, and the seniority of the gun and drug dealers involved.

Quatraine stood again, this time more confident.

"Madams President and Attorney General. The Ketchikan raid proceeded on information from a reliable source in that city that was funneled to the ATF from the office of the Fraternal Order of Police. One of their people thought it was big enough for the FBG to be involved. We ran surveillance for three days, and even sent in a couple of undercover agents to see what was going on for sure. They reported large supplies of guns, cash, heroin, marijuana, and cocaine. It looked to our undercover agents that a large-scale transfer was imminent. Acting on that intelligence, the Special Response Team decided to cut off the ongoing preliminary investigation in favor of going in with the information we had. Forty-one agents of the Task Force from all branches—including some local drug enforcement officers—staged a raid under the capable direction of Agent Henry Drake. We achieved total surprise. We placed eleven individuals—several of whom were foreign nationals—under arrest, confiscated a large collection of illegal fully automatic machine guns and machine pistols, grenades, old M-79 grenade launchers, LAW rockets and launchers, and antipersonnel mines."

"Sounds like preparations for a war," mused the president.

"It is, Madam President, you're right about that," complimented the attorney general.

There was a general agreement of head nods.

"This time, it appears that some of the warriors were Russians, part of one of their mafia organizations," she went on.

"There's more," Quatraine continued. "We brought in a large amount of cash money in hundred dollar denominations, the medium of exchange in the drug and gun smuggling world. Actually, it appears that there were several tons, *tons*," he emphasized, "of cash. We can only estimate the value of the money because we are leaving the shrink-wrapped pallets of currency as they are for use in the eventual criminal proceedings. Already, four or five of the lesser lights in this criminal enterprise have rolled over and are providing state's evidence against the rest and against as yet unindicted co-conspirators."

"Just for fun, try an estimate," asked the president.

"Ma'am?" Quatraine asked, not quite understanding that such a high level opinion was being asked of him, a lowly assistant director.

"Oh, c'mon, how much money? Don't be shy, just approximately. Is it on the order of a million, or ten million?"

"Considerably more, ma'am. Very considerably more. Something on the order of $200,000,000, and that is conservative. I have to admit that I am not all that versed in how much money weighs. I have never seen anything like that much money. Remember, I'm the son of a man who, if Cadillacs were ten cents a gross, he would not have been able to afford a radiator cap. Maybe there is as much as half or three-quarters of a billion."

He had to smile.

"It's a truck trailer load, that's all I can say with any accuracy."

He was thinking that the two raids had come out better than a wash.

"And it seems that Agent Drake has redeemed himself," the attorney general said. "Maybe it's time to redeem him and Jack Bailey and get them an office bigger than the broom closet we assigned them a while back. What do you think, Madam President?"

"Seems timely to me, Margaret. How does that strike you, Director Holdaway?"

The new director of the ATF looked up sharply, a little startled at this change of heart from two of his superiors. He had wanted to move Drake back up to a more senior position for some time, but had not dared to do so while the man remained a pariah.

Holdaway nodded, smiled, and replied, "I think that would be good for troop morale. I'll take care of it first thing, with your permission."

The president nodded.

Oliver Quatraine did not think that piece of personnel advancement would help his own morale; but then, who cared what he thought?

CHAPTER EIGHTEEN

The spring thaw in Alaska that year and its attendant break-up of the roads into mud was the most welcome period that Randolph could remember. Randolph's first Alaskan winter had dwarfed his total previous experience with weather: longer, colder, snowier, windier, darker, and more isolating than anything he had heretofore encountered. He had had to force himself to go out into the frigid landscape around his homestead. Devlin had warned him of the dangers of developing cabin fever or even of getting rickets from lack of exposure to the sun if he didn't get out and take advantage of the short daylight hours.

Devlin predicted that Randolph would give up on Alaska as hordes of other earnest one winter sojourners had done if he did not find things to do to enjoy the hard-biting country. He had to put chains on all four tires of his Range Rover just to get back and forth to work. On the average of one or two nights a week, he was unable to get back out to his home and had to stay in town. He learned to snowshoe and to ski cross country, to hunt arctic ptarmigan, to ice fish, and he bought a snowmobile to replace his Range Rover for the worst days. He took pride in getting to work almost every day and acting as nonchalant about his accomplishment as all of the other hardy workers in his office. Nonetheless, it was good to thaw out his bones and insides after the long cold siege.

Tax season came and went before truly good weather came again. The main advantage of the long winter had been that Randolph had hardly spent any money. It was too physically difficult to get out to waste money on frivolous things like entertainment or restaurant dining—fun things. He was not ready to date. His thoughts of Irene were still too vivid; going out with another woman seemed, irrationally, like an infidelity. He started back to work on his home as soon as the roads were passable.

"Devlin," Randolph said over the telephone, "I'm ready to get the whole megillah done. How about getting the crowd out here, and we can finish the job before next snowfall?"

"We don't even speak of the next snowfall at this time of year, lad," answered Devlin. "I'm with you, though. I'll get the plumbing and wiring guys out there tomorrow to finish up what they started. We'll hire a bunch of Indians and Inuits and start on the finish work of the main structure by the end of the week. I think we can have the painters and cabinet makers on the job by the last week in July at the latest. How does that grab you?"

"Great!" Randolph said, *"unheard of with any contractors I ever knew,"* he said to himself, *"and all I have to do is to pay for all of this."*

He was aware that his ten million was rapidly being sunk into the house and daily living expenses. He was glad he had a job as well as the cushion from the government.

"So, maybe you can stop fussing about this and get down into civilization and return a few favors," Devlin said cheerily.

Randolph knitted his brow at the telephone. He had been expecting this— you get nothing for nothing.

"Sure, give me a for instance," he said.

"I got a ton of work to do on secession. I think we have a real chance to bring the bill out onto the floor of the legislature this year for the first time, maybe even get a vote and on to the governor. It's going to be a real push. I need you with me, boy."

Randolph had not thought much about the secessionist movement, and what he did think was fairly negative. It seemed sort of un-American. On the other hand, maybe it was a good idea, and one whose time had come. He was not ready to be enthusiastic, certainly. No question about it, though, he owed Devlin.

"I'll be down there this afternoon. I have some free time from the office."

"I'll count on you. See you about one. That okay?"

"Fine,"

"Bye."

"Goodbye, Devlin, and thanks for the help on the house."

"It's nothing. We old sourdoughs and Militiamen have to stick together."

Randolph was in and out of O'Herligy's business office a dozen times that afternoon. He winced every time he looked at the library in Devlin's private office. The shelves were lined with antiestablishment magazines like *American Freedom, Media Bypass,* and *AntiShyster*—the tame ones. There were rows of Paladin Press, Boulder, Colorado books and videos. Randolph thought his office co-workers would be particularly enamored with the complete *How to Kill* series, *Ultimate Sniper: the Video,* two well thumbed copies of *Hitman,* and the CIA's *Psychological Operations in Guerrilla Warfare* by Tayacn from the 1980s.

Randolph considered the library to be representative of Devlin's harmless bravado; at least, he hoped that was the case. He defended his own involvement in an organization that espoused such things much like the Democrat who personally opposes abortion, but will fight for the right of a woman to choose. He eschewed that dark side of the Movement into which he was being inexorably drawn, but soothed his conscience with the conviction that he was above all that and would work on the positive issues; and there were plenty of them. His pesky conscience nagged at him for his failure to speak out against the racism and other excesses of the Movement, but he did not yet know how he would handle it.

He and an Inuit boy, Charlie, carried boxes of secessionist literature to supporters in Anchorage and Wasilla for general distribution over the upcoming two weeks. They hung posters on telephone poles and delivered billboard advertising materials to the agency. To make room for all of the secessionist advertising materials that came flooding into Devlin's place of business, Randolph carried out several boxes of guns and ammunition that got in the way. He took part of the weaponry to his boss, Ian Laird's, storage shed. Ian was a true believer. The bulk of the weapons and ammunition he took to Harry and Tracy McDonald's house for storage in the capacious garages.

Devlin had somehow arranged to become a certified and licensed federal weapons dealer many years ago before the great push had come to divest the citizenry of guns. Every weapon in the inventory was legal, a comforting thought for Randolph as he moved the highly visible and well marked boxes and crates. The last thing he wanted to do was to tweak the ATF tiger's tail and come to their attention. Devlin kept warning him to beware because the FBG had agents everywhere.

Allen Heaps watched Randolph's activities from the vantage point of his old truck and took four rolls of color photographs.

When everything was shipshape, Devlin caught Randolph and said, "Thanks, Randolph. I'm happy we had use of your nice muscles today."

He wore an expression of expectation that meant to Randolph that there was more to come.

"No problem, Devlin. Glad to be of help. I can come by tomorrow afternoon, too, if you need me."

"Well, thanks, but I have something more important for you to do for the cause."

Devlin looked and sounded like an old revolutionary planning the overthrow of the sitting government from his seedy loft overlooking the Seine.

"Such as?" Randolph asked cautiously.

Devlin laughed at Randolph's somber look.

"Nothing much, just a little public involvement."

"That sounds bad, Devlin. I'm not much of a public involvement sort of a guy, and besides, I am not fond of the idea of appearing on the ATF radar screen ever again."

"It's no big deal, just a little speech to like minded people. We've rented the gym at Wasilla High for a seminar on secession. We have a couple of lawyer guys from Anchorage to explain the ramifications. Steve Carter from the legislature and the lieutenant governor will be there."

"So, what do you need me for?"

"Don't be coy, Randolph. You are going to represent the local committee and the Militia. You're a real presentable fella, and it's time to get your feet wet."

There was a hint of good humor in Devlin's voice, but he wore a look of determination, of pay-back time. Randolph did not like it and felt manipulated, but he knew that he could only blame himself. He had allowed the favors to pile up into a backlog, and he knew that he owed Devlin. He also knew that Devlin had set out to enmesh him in the Movement web. He could not refuse with the retention of even a small modicum of grace. All of this was deeper and more public than he had ever wanted to go in the secession business. He admitted to himself that his reservations were due more to his own general shyness and his apolitical nature than to any heartfelt noble objections. Randolph Kennedy envisioned himself as a background guy, and this offer would definitely push him out of his comfort zone.

He was also a dedicatedly private man, and he was loathe to have the whole world presume that he was some sort of big-wig in the North Star State Militia and a secessionist. The very word conjured visions of some radical Southern slave-owner defending his despicable 'peculiar' institution. The only saving grace was that no one was really going to pay attention to a small town rally in favor of a piece of activism that most people would regard as cockamamie.

He took a breath.

"Oh, all right, I'll do it. Do I get to wear a wig and a trench coat?"

"Not on your life. This is pointedly about public exposure. We want to get our message out. This is not for the back rooms loonies; this is for Mom and Pop and the kids. They have to get behind us. We're set for Thursday at eight-thirty. Wear your best bib and tucker. You can get your speech out of old info letters, if you want. They're full of stats and facts. I figured that you would want to give that sort of thing in your talk. Don't make it too dry, bro; we want them awake through the whole program and able to get at their wallets at the end."

"Thanks for the vote of confidence, Devlin," Randolph said and grinned.

"You know what I mean. You whip up something that will knock 'em dead, you hear?"

"Yes, sir," Randolph answered and gave a little mock salute that belied his inner reluctance.

"Thursday night, brother Militiaman. It's Alaska out of the corrupt union and on to her destiny. This is an important first step. Don't underestimate what we're doing there that night. You might just make a little history. Now, get on outta here; do, I can do my work."

He gave a good natured wave.

Agent Allen Heaps had it all on tape. He had looked like a bumbler when he went into O'Herligy's establishment, but during one of his bumbles, he had placed a high quality bug, and it was working perfectly. He had spent long hours of surveillance that week and felt that his efforts were amply rewarded. In addition to the photographs that he obtained of Randolph Kennedy and a native carrying clearly marked—and presumably illegal—guns and ammunition crates, he collected an incriminating flyer for the rally that featured Randolph Kennedy's name and picture prominently. He stapled the flyer to his notes and photos of the activities of Devlin O'Herligy, the McDonalds, and Kennedy. Under a subheading, Heaps listed the identities of the visitors to O'Herligy's business. The list carried a short synopsis of the known activities of each listee—most of whom were members of the North Star State Militia or of other affiliated militias from the Movement down below. Heaps knew that he had preliminary evidence of a criminal conspiracy. He said as much in his dispatch to Henry Drake.

There was a good crowd at the high school on Thursday evening. The sound system was tested and worked well because the kid who was responsible for it took out his frustrated computer hacker's energies on the sound system. Alaskan flags—white stars in the form of the little dipper with a prominent north star at the end of the dipper handle on a navy blue background—flew everywhere. One large United States flag with its fifty-two stars hung near the podium that had been set up in the middle of the playing floor. Randolph was the third speaker, his contribution coming immediately after the large crowd took a rest break and sang the Alaska state song heartily and off key. They were noisy and rude as he stood. The background din made it difficult for him to speak and for the FBI and ATF agents interspersed with the crowd in the auditorium to record his speech.

Randolph was nervous. He did not want to be there, but he knew that it was payback time for Devlin. He had a serious implicit contract. He had his misgivings about that debt, but he was committed—in for a penny, in for a pound.

"Ladies and gentlemen," he started.

He knew from looking at the faces of his audience that he had started wrong.

"Fellow Alaskans."

That was better.

"Some of you were born here, some came here last week. Fifty years ago, less than 20 percent of us in this building would have been born in this state; now, that number approaches 70 percent. With our population of 1.75 million and growing, we are the state with the smallest and most disperse population of the 50 states. We few fortunate people have an incredibly large, rich, and blessed country. If we were independent, we would prosper; and we would do so in our own way."

A chorus of cheers and applause broke out in typical political rally fashion. Randolph was embarrassed.

"My small part on this program, speaking as a common citizen and a relative newcomer—and as a CPA—is to present a reasonable scenario, an objective estimate of what secession from the American union would likely mean to us individually—emotions aside. I spend my life dealing with estate planning problems and predictions for individuals and families, and I see this as such an estate planning project. We are individuals; it is true, but we are also a family—a special entity."

He was interrupted by applause.

"Must have had plenty of practice; he's good at this demagoguery," Allen Heaps whispered hoarsely into Henry Drake's ear.

Drake nodded his agreement.

"I won't take a lot of your valuable time tonight with a bunch of boring numbers, but let's look at the big picture. We have prepared a brochure that you can obtain at our offices or in shopping mall booths around the state. Let me just assure you that secession would be an unqualified advantage for each us and for us as family from a financial point of view. No longer would our state be subject to the expensive whims of the foreign federal government in Washington D.C., thus eliminating redundant, ill conceived, and pork-barrel programs that benefit special interest groups whose interests are not our own. Consider only one example. Currently, the U.S. serves as the world's policeman, often uninvited and at a staggering military expense. Alaska has no enemies; we have no need to provide any more military than is necessary for homeland defense. At least—after secession—the pork barrel programs would be our own; and we would be responsible for getting furious and for throwing the rascals out—our rascals."

The crowd roared with appreciative laughter. Allen Heaps laughed along with them until he caught the disapproving look from Henry Drake.

"After secession, you would immediately stop paying taxes. With oil demand and revenues as they are, we would be able to function like the Arab oil producing nations who have great national infrastructures for their peoples—all from the bounties of the earth—and without paying taxes, any taxes. You and I have gotten so used to paying confiscatory taxes to the IRS for One World Government schemes and to keep corrupt politicians producing unnecessary programs designed to keep them in office in perpetuity, that we have never even taken time to think about what we could do with all of the money we give them to waste. The average family in Alaska would experience an immediate pay increase of at least 30 percent, and more affluent families would see a pay raise of upwards of 65 percent."

The crowd whooped and whistled.

"Right on," they shouted.

The ATF and FBI infiltrators furiously scribbled notes, making every effort to look inconspicuous.

Heaps whispered, "Is that *true?*"

"Consider the source," Drake snapped irritably.

"We are a young, vigorous, fairly homogenous democracy here. As a nation we will not need to support a massive health care program in the beginning at least. Even Hillary Clinton—near the end of her administration—questioned the need for our involvement in other nations' military and internal affairs. Congress voted her down, but the idea has been gaining momentum in the lower forty-eight. We have the opportunity to learn from other nations' mistakes. One glaring example: we do not have to repeat the hugely inappropriate entitlements programs the U.S. finds itself mired in. We have oil, and young workers. We do not need—and by the independent prickly nature of our citizens—we don't want a welfare state. Just think how much we could benefit without one."

"Oh, yeah, right on man," shouted a bearded hunting guide.

He seemed to speak for the rest of the crowd, and they gave him a big round of applause.

"That is the good news, Now for the bad news…"

The audience groaned.

He paused for a full two minutes. The crowd grew silent, waiting for the other shoe to fall. Randolph scratched his head.

"I can't think of any bad news right now. Give me a while…"

The crowd laughed together, slapped their seatmates on the back, clapped and whistled. Randolph had had something of an epiphany with his study of the facts and had to admit that he was being swept up in his own oratory along with his audience. He was very nearly a full convert to the secessionist gospel.

"We are not alone," Randolph continued when the laughter died away. "Long before California split into two states, there was talk; and there were bills submitted to their assembly for secession. After North and South California were established and admitted separately into the union during Al Gore's administration, South California pursued the secessionist idea ever more vigorously. Last year the assembly agreed to put the question on their election ballot and it was defeated by a slim margin of three percent. South California is the fifth largest economy of any nation in the world, and this year again they are going to try to secede. It is not an idle saying that 'as California goes, so goes the nation.'

"The Puerto Ricans have regretted accepting statehood as the fifty-second state almost from the beginning. The citizens of PR discovered the burden of taxes and restrictive political correctness laws under the Clintons and the harsh radical environmental controls under Gore. They have chafed under the massive weight of social restructuring bills under Mrs. Clinton and Mrs. Vantassa. Puerto Rico has only been a state since 2010, and they want out altogether. They don't even want to go back to their territorial status—they are opting for full independence.

"Hawaii filed for secession immediately after the Supreme Court struck down that state's same-sex marriage law. The secessionists were narrowly defeated before they could go all the way, but they will keep trying.

"The southern quarters of South California, Arizona, New Mexico, and the southern halves of Texas and Colorado have strongly indicated their intention to form a new, more congenial nation with Mexican states of Baja California, Sonora, Chihuahua, Coahuila, Nuevo Leon, and Tamaulipas. Approval has been given in full by Mexico, and by the U.S. Senate for the creation of the new Hispanic nation which—with final U.S. approval—will be called Republica del Norte. Texas considers itself to be a captive nation and that inclusion in the United States was an illegal annexation just like our own situation here in Alaska. For a decade they have been harassing the federal government with suits based on that premise—and now ownership of many properties, because of the confiscation of original landowners' holdings under the nefarious Treaty of Guadalupe Hidalgo—is so clouded as to make ordinary business transactions impossibly difficult. Their tactics are working, and the feds are wearing down. The people of Texas are solidly behind the movement. They want to have the right to pursue their own destiny—half of them in the Republica del Norte—and they might well be out of the union in the next two or three years."

His mouth was dry. He took a small sip of water.

"My fellow Alaskans, we need to join these other secessionists. Those other people don't trust their government any longer. The government in Washington has broken its promises to them for more than a century just like here in Alaska. Our territory—like that of Texas—started out as a land of broken promises, nothing more than a cow to be milked by unscrupulous business and political cronies. It's time to turn that sorry situation around to our favor. America has dry rot related to its inability to stop feeding at the public trough. The standard of living in the country has been eroded seriously by governmental waste, intrusive social restructuring programs, and from ill-conceived foreign misadventures. We don't need to do that when we are a new country. We do not need to be lemmings and follow that once great and vital democracy over the cliff of its own making. Support secession!"

Randolph's voice had risen a decibel for the last sentence.

The crowd was cheering thunderously when he sat down. Devlin gave him a brief but heartfelt thumbs-up sign, a gesture that was not lost on ATF agents Drake and Heaps. Randolph thought that he had committed petit demagoguery; but all-in-all, he was not that displeased with his performance.

Drake and Heaps left the crowded and overheated meeting as soon as Randolph Kennedy finished his rantings. Agent Heaps, especially, felt chilled, felt as if he had been listening to a replay of the speech at Nuremberg by Adolph Hitler from a century earlier. There was the same demagogic intensity in the speaker, the charismatic crowd control so carefully nurtured. Heaps was sure he was witnessing the birth of a new Nazi führer, in this case even before the demagogue himself realized his own role. Randolph Kennedy was a dangerous man. Heaps knew that he was already involved in a movement that secretly smuggled the implements of war. The Movement undermined the federal government, and Kennedy effectively preached an insidious doctrine of rampant individuality which undermined the very core of cooperative social, financial, and foreign affairs control that came from the enlightened post Bush administrations. Heaps felt as if he were the only person around who recognized what a threat this lunatic, Kennedy, was to the orderly world that President Vantassa was working so hard to maintain.

The agent dispatched a long, thoughtful report to Henry Drake—his immediate superior—and sent copies to Oliver Quatraine and Roger Holdaway at ATF headquarters and to Margaret Thaler at Justice. Heaps was careful to include every bit of objective data he had. He stated at the onset that he knew there was not yet enough evidence to convict Kennedy or any of the Alaska separatists of a felony; but his thesis—as presented to the recipients of his dispatch—was that Kennedy, O'Herligy, McDonald, and a number of unnamed co-conspirators were engaged in sedition at the very least and were secretly conspiring to foment a revolution. He just had to get proof.

His concluding paragraph emphasized that salient observation, and he decided to take a step beyond his role as an undercover agent. He took the liberty of recommending that major action should be taken to stop the conspiracy before it could gain enough strength to be put into force. He reminded his readers of the conspiracy that resulted in the assassination of President John F. Kennedy in 1963 and the militia backed attempt of Vice-President Gore's life in 1998. Weapons violations had been the key then, and were the key once again.

Heaps' last sentence was: "It is incumbent on the FBG and the government to halt this movement, and particularly to prevent the full rise of this new Hitler—Randolph Kennedy—before their sedition can become revolution; and before this would-be neo-Nazi becomes a national rallying voice for armed revolution against the duly sworn officers of the United States."

He was pleased with his work and confident that history would acknowledge his prescience. He knew that it was too late in the day for timidity. ATF Agent Allen Heaps saw clearly that national security was threatened. He felt like the little Dutch boy with his finger in the hole in the dike. His real worry was whether or not he would be able to touch a responsive chord in someone who mattered in Washington. That concern became a crusade.

CHAPTER NINETEEN

When he got back to D.C. after his brief trip to the secessionist backwater, Henry Drake was galvanized by his subordinate's report, all the more so because he had been a witness to the events described by Heaps. He requested the opportunity to convey his field agent's report on the Alaska situation to the Task Force committee as a whole. The chain of command required that he first clear the request through the ATF Office of the Director. That request was granted because Holdaway recognized Randolph Kennedy's name and knew that it was anathema throughout his bureau and with the FBG. He did not want there to be the slightest suggestion that he had failed to act on information about an incipient insurrection. Director Holdaway thought the field agent's report was long on opinion and surmise and a bit short on objective evidence, but it was credible. It bothered him that the next link up the chain to the FBG governing committee was one of his underlings, a junior ATF officer, Oliver Quatraine; but Holdaway was a team player, and this was a team game.

It galled Henry Drake to have to get Quatraine's permission to forward the report up the chain of command. He resented Quatraine for having gotten the Task Force position that should have been Drake's only because he was the token black. Since his problems with the Task Force brass, he had kept a low profile; and he took great pains not to let his opinion of the token black show.

Quatraine thought Heaps' report was not only heavy on supposition but was somewhere between *Alice in Wonderland* and a pre-trial defense of the Salem witch hunt. Knowing which way the political winds were blowing, he nonetheless signed his agreement to the transmittal, confident that the wiser heads of the FBG would give the report a timely death.

Drake was anxious to complete his redemption with the FBG. It was more than fortuitous that his full redemption should derive from the very same case that had produced his public reprimand and demotion. Unlike the official decision, Henry Drake had never closed the Randolph Kennedy case. Although he was usually very reticent about speaking before groups—especially groups of senior officials—Henry was excited and enthusiastic about this presentation. The thought of getting back at Kennedy overcame any of his trepidations.

Agent Heaps' field report, with all of its documentation, commentary, and suggestions was item number two on the sparse agenda of the FBG Task Force meeting that Wednesday. Quatraine introduced the background of the case even though everyone in the room was familiar with the Randolph Kennedy Affair.

"I ask the president's permission to have Agent Heaps' immediate superior officer, Agent Drake, read the report. He can answer tactical questions if there are any."

"Granted," said the president brusquely. "Show the agent in."

"Agent Henry Drake, ladies and gentlemen."

Margaret Thaler smiled her frosty smile at Agent Drake.

"We are happy to see you here under more favorable circumstances that the last time you appeared. Incidentally, Agent, you and your teams are to be congratulated for your recent work in Ketchikan. That truly furthered our work, and a commendation has been forwarded to your service files.

"Thank you, Madam Attorney General," Drake responded and added a small head bow.

He was genuinely pleased and was on his best behavior.

"Please get right into the report, Agent."

"Yes, ma'am."

Drake read the report with the required objective monotone of an appointed court room reader. When he was finished, he signaled to Mrs. Thaler.

"Thank you, Agent Drake. Again, we have to compliment you and your team for your good work. Agent Heaps is one of your better people, I take it."

"That's right, ma'am."

"Convey our accolades for his work.'

"I'll do that."

"Any questions for Agent Drake?"

Quatraine waited. He was ready for this report to be round filed and was already preparing his commentary about item three, the last topic of the day. To Quatraine's surprise, President Vantassa came up with a question.

"Agent Drake, do you have evidence that will stand up in a court of law against this man, Kennedy?"

"No, Madam President, not yet."

"But you are convinced that he is—as you agents put it—dirty?"

"Without a doubt. We know he is, but it is another thing to be able to make the case in a court."

"Do you agree with your Agent Heaps that Kennedy is part of a conspiracy to overthrow the United States government? I mean, do you think he is a serious risk to national security? You are the one closest to the source here and have certainly had the most experience in dealing with this guy. Is he just a nut case, or do we have to protect the nation from him and his ilk?"

"I do agree with Allen Heaps, Madam President. We are dealing with a very smart, streetwise criminal who is part of an excellent information network. He was successfully warned of our raid the first time. I' m sure you recall that incident."

"How could I forget?"

"I underestimated how intelligent and well connected this man is. I won't do it again. What I think—after reviewing this case over time—is that we may never have nice, neat evidence. This man is part of a self-styled army, one with significant ordnance. We can't afford to underestimate him or them. It is unfortunate but true that these Movement people have substantial and helpful sympathy from the local populace wherever they have their headquarters. They have access to the latest information on explosives and firearms, established and effective networks for smuggling arms, and in many instances they have local policemen under their influence. We will have to use the rules of a knife fight to get this one, I'm afraid."

"And what are those rules, Agent," the president asked, not comfortable with street jargon.

"There are no rules, ma'am."

She nodded and responded with a knowing smile.

Quatraine listened with growing incredulity. The president of the United States was giving credence to this philippic from a little known agent in Alaska. She was being taken in by an agent who was patently biased and had proved himself a loose cannon before. Drake had obviously touched a raw nerve in the president, and she had suspended her judgment. He knew that she was a fighter and did not like to lose; Kennedy was an opponent who had bested her once. Quatraine realized that the time would come for the man to pay a dear price for that small victory. He could see it in her face. He fingered the controls on his concealed tape recorder and turned it on.

"Agent Drake, I want you to draw up a preliminary plan of attack on this man. We cannot let one person subvert the purposes of the American people and the American government. Ever since President Clinton in the close of the last century decided to cast aside important police methods in favor of a war footing with terrorists, we have seen results. This is the general plan I want you to follow: Do nothing overt for the time being. I want more convincing intelligence on the man," the president ordered. "We still have some time and time enough for him to hang himself."

She inclined her head towards Margaret Thaler to indicate that it was time to go to the next item on the day's agenda and time for Agent Drake to be about his work. He took the broad hint and made his exit. Oliver Quatraine turned off his hand held recorder; he doubted that history would need to record the upcoming item three—methodology of destruction of the masses of weapons being accumulated in ATF raids.

CHAPTER TWENTY

Wasilla Police Sergeant Alex Tolberg got the call from Militia headquarters thirty minutes before the end of his shift. A work gang of Militiamen was needed to help Randolph Kennedy with a project at his place up north. Kennedy had worked on every other project requested by the Militia; and by rights and common decency, he could not turn the man down. Besides, Alex liked and respected Randolph; they were becoming friends, as much as two loners could become friends.

"Yeah, Devlin, I'll be there. I had plans, and it'll take a bit to get out of them. I'll drive up as soon as I can."

"Good boy, Alex. I knew we could count on you. Say, did you get that step-up in grade yet?"

"Not yet. I passed the test, but it's a slow process—affirmative action, you know."

"I'll put in a good word with Commissioner Walker. The man and me go way back. He owes me a favor or two or three. Maybe I can pull in a mark on your behalf."

"Not too heavy-handed there, Devlin. You know the department's officially against the Militia. They call it the Movement, echoes of Washington D.C. I wouldn't last out the day if they knew I was a card carrying member."

"Not to worry, lad. I didn't just fall off the turnip truck. I'll move slow and around the point. Walker'll never know where this idea of his to promote you came from."

"Thanks, Devlin," Alex laughed.

The old red fox was famous for his ability to get things done for the Militiamen and the secessionists, who were just about one and the same. He knew from past experience that O'Herligy's intervention could only help. Alex felt rather good about going out to the Kennedy place to help even though it screwed up his weekend.

Randolph was supervising a gang of men working on two bulldozers and a grader. There were building a road from just over the top of the hill on the opposite side of where the house stood. That road did not connect to the road from the main county access to Randolph's main drive but simply stopped in a dead end. Alex Tolberg pitched in. It was a curious road, he thought. It seemed to go the long way and the hardest way—a sort of path of most resistance. It was set into the hill and ran through the trees and bushes in such a way that jt was almost invisible when looked at from the top or from the bottom of the hill. It had so many arbitrary curves that it was impossible to tell what lay beyond the next turn.

"Security," Randolph told him when he asked about the peculiarities.

The newly graveled road was of exceptional quality for a route that was unlikely to be used with any frequency. It ended beyond the bottom of the hill about fifty yards through the brush from the main road. With effort, one could drive a four-wheel drive truck from the end of Kennedy's seemingly pointless road and onto the main county road in a matter of minutes if you were not overly sensitive to dents and scratches on your vehicle. Even knowing that the road's end was in the vicinity, it was impossible to detect any part of it from the county artery.

"Security," Randolph reiterated.

The sun was still up, and the hill was bright with afternoon light at ten o'clock at night when Randolph called a halt.

"Thanks, men. C'mon up to the house. I have a good meal ready. I appreciate your work. I wanted you guys to do this part because I knew I could count on your discretion. You can't ever be sure about hired construction workers."

The men nodded their understanding. The house was altogether livable now. It lacked anything of a softening woman's touch, but Randolph had found a few pictures of bears and caribou, and had scrounged up bed spreads and throw rugs. It was comfortable in a masculine sort of way, full of modern conveniences and appliances, very utilitarian—something more than a man cave, but less than even an Alaskan woman would tolerate without a few changes here and there. Although he likely had another year of work to finish the interior, the fundamental structural work was done. The security system in the door yard and in the perimeter of the property was in and functional; it rivaled the McDonalds' in sophistication. Randolph had guns and ammunition located in strategic places and booby traps inside the house. He felt uneasy about installing lethal traps or mines anywhere outside. He had elected to depend on an array of completely hidden early warning sensors and monitors and to rely on his indoor arsenal as the final line of defense.

"C'mon in. We've got moose roast and pickled Dolly Varden. Help yourselves to the salad."

The men were starving, having used up about 3000 calories on the job. They ate as if they had been on a desert island for the past month. Randolph knew their favorite foods; they were a meat and potatoes bunch with not a scintilla of finickiness about red meat. They did not eat quiche. Randolph had acclimated to Alaska's customs and had left his gourmand's tastes behind. The parched workers downed a case of beer—no lite beer offered—while Randolph stuck to Diet Coke. He had not been able to acquire a taste for the bitter amber liquid.

Devlin O'Herligy showed up in time for the apple cobbler and ice cream dessert.

"Nice timing," the Militiamen chided him good naturedly.

"My mama didn't raise no fools," Devlin said. "That work stuff's for the ranks, not for us officers."

They all laughed. In the North Star State Militia there was one commander and several section chiefs for every hundred men. The officers were elected by the rank and file for indeterminate terms of office and could quit or be unelected at any time. There was no saluting, no rank insignia, and no perks of rank. Officers did the same work as any man in the outfit. Officers stood to take a good deal of ribbing and were in for frequent criticism. It went with the territory. However, every man in the Militia was committed to obey to his last breath the officer he had helped elect. Most of the men had been in the U.S. military—one branch of service or the other—and a majority had served under men or women for whom they had had no respect. They had obeyed orders while in the service out of legal obligation. They were all willing to obey orders from Devlin O'Herligy out of esteem for him and for the democratic process which they cherished. These men were true believers and unswerving zealots.

Devlin popped open a Moosehead beer and chugged down half of it before taking a seat.

"I'll take a dish of that cobbler if you've got any left," he requested of Randolph.

Randolph scooped up a huge dollop of the sweet concoction and put it in a fresh bowl. Devlin waved away Randolph's offer of ice cream. The men chatted for another fifteen minutes.

"Hold on for another minute," Devlin said as some of the men made ready to leave. "I want to run ad idea past you guys. You see I got all of the section chiefs up here. It wasn't no accident."

The men registered the fact and looked at Devlin for the reason. His coming out that late and going out of his way suggested that the reason was probably important.

"You know I have gotten a whole lot on my plate. I have ended up holding the bag for the secession movement when the McDonalds went on their mission. You guys elected me Militia commander, and I have a business to run; somebody's got to keep up with the bribes and protection money," he sighed.

They laughed.

"What I had in mind, if you guys were not averse, was to step back into the ranks and let another trooper be elected in my place. I think it's time for some new blood."

It was something of a shock. Many of the men had known only one commander during their time in the Militia. They pondered Devlin's announcement.

Alex Tolberg's mind moved one question faster than the others.

"Have anybody particular in mind, Devlin? We have a democracy as far as it goes, but a long time ago we decided that the mountain men and hayseeds weren't quite up to the task of picking out a good slate of candidates."

"Well, I didn't come all the way out *here* for nothing. I'll get right to it. I'd like to run the name past you and your men. I was thinking of Randolph— Randolph Kennedy."

Devlin did not look at Randolph when he dropped his name. He had never broached the subject with Randolph and had wanted the idea to come as much of a surprise to him as to the rest of the principle men. Randolph had been sleepy and peripheral to the conversation until then. His ears perked up fully when he heard his own name, and he had a sudden rush of adrenaline.

"*Me*!? was all Randolph could manage.

There was quiet in the room for a moment. Then there was a series of short animated conversations that went round-robin through the group of tired but now fully engaged men.

"How long's he been up here?"

"What's he know 'bout the brothers down below?"

"What do we really know about him?"

Devlin let the men talk themselves out. It took only about five minutes. Randolph kept himself aloof from the conversation. It was odd to have people discuss you as if you were not there. He had not decided whether or not the change would be a good idea for the Militia or for himself. It was sudden, and he needed time to adjust. It did not look as if there was going to be any such time for making up his mind, if he knew how Devlin functioned. He knew that he was less of a redneck than the rest—less bigoted—more of a cityslicker. He was not much of a "tractor and a trailer" as they jokingly referred to themselves. He wondered if he could change to be high profile; he knew himself to be a back ground dweller.

Randolph worried if he could use the position Devlin was requesting for him to soften some of the harshness of the white supremacy rhetoric that he sometimes heard, but he was enough of a realist to know that it was unlikely that anyone could. The Militia had good men and was based on a solid premise of thinking so far as Randolph was concerned, and the racism and opposition to any other religion than Christian evangelical Protestantism was a secondary concern. Like any other organization, the Militia was no better than the people in it for all of its fine aims and activities. Randolph made up his mind that he might well be able to make a difference—even a small one— if the Militiamen were to accept Devlin's request and elect him.

"We'll think on it, Devlin…Randolph. It's pretty sudden," Alex said.

He had become the de facto spokesman for the rest of the men in the room by some unspoken agreement.

"Nobody's opposed; we'll say that right now. But Randolph's pretty new. We'll have to think on it and run it by the rest of the guys. Give us maybe a week, okay?? We think you ought to stay out of it until them—both of you— but especially you, Devlin."

Alex grinned, and Devlin laughed.

"So, I'm an incurable buttinsky," Devlin said. "But I'll control myself. Give me a call long about Saturday, okay, Alex?"

"No problem. Now, we have to get on home or face a severe beating from their wives."

The men all left in short order, including Devlin.

The Militia had an efficient communication system, even though it was not obvious to outsiders. In a week the men and women of the North Star State Militia had voiced their democratic opinion. They did as they always did and elected the man proposed by the outgoing leader. They elected Randolph unanimously. The votes were repeated until they *were* unanimous in accordance with the Militia rule. In fact, the vote was more an affirmation of support than a true election. Afterwards, most of the men who stepped up to congratulate the new commander cited his secession speech as the deciding factor. Randolph had had time to think about taking the position during that election week—and when it was offered formally—he accepted with the appropriately modest proviso that someone who knew what was going on had to help. The word of that bit of humility quickly made it back to the rank and file, and it sat well with them. In another week FBI and ATF agents were in possession of the secret of the reorganization, and that news was in the hands of Henry Drake, Oliver Quatraine, and Margaret Thaler in Washington.

During O'Herligy's term of office, the Militia's equipment—including the weapons stored around the state—had been largely ignored and allowed to deteriorate. Randolph had noticed rust pits, grease, and dirt on several of the machine pistols and assault rifles hat had passed under his eye during times when he visited the former commander. He had not felt that he was in any position at that time to criticize; so, he kept his peace. Now that it was his responsibility, he ordered a general inventory and cleaning of every weapon in the entire state Militia arsenal.

There was a great deal of affable grumbling through the state because the order entailed considerable work. Many of the weapons were hidden in underground caches. Most of the weapons would have to be transported and taken care of in small numbers requiring multiple trips—almost always at night—and with all the effort that secretiveness required. However, no one in the Militia disagreed with the wisdom of the order; and, in fact, issuing it enhanced Randolph's esteem in the minds of his subordinates.

Randolph exercised every security precaution he could when moving or working on the weapons. He did most of his share of the work in his bunker basement and did it quickly and with only a few weapons at a time. On any given night, he was likely to have a row of combat shotguns—Chinese SKS assault rifles that had been altered to prevent automatic firing—and one or two old sniper rifles. Although he was sure that his predecessor in the office of Militia commander had handled illegal weaponry, Randolph was rigid in his refusal to have anything to do with them personally; his memory of the attack on his house by ATF agents who had only *thought* that he had illegal guns and ammunition was too vivid and horrifying. If they could wreak such destruction by mistake, he shivered inwardly to think of their capabilities if he actually had illegal guns in his possession. Every time the subject came to mind, Randolph saw images of his wife and child being killed by paramilitarists. He was far from over his great loss.

Lance Pederson from Anchorage called Saturday morning.

"Hey, Randolph," he blurted in his booming voice as soon as Randolph picked up the phone, "how's it hangin', bud?"

"Okay, Lance, what's up?"

"Have a shipment, man. I need to get it out of town. Too many feds."

"Are we talking legal or illegal things in that shipment, Lance? You know my stand on the law and weapons. As long as the Militia wants me in command, we all have to keep squeaky clean."

"No prob. I have clay pigeons, targets, a few old 12 gauge Ithaca 37s we can use for skeet guns, and some mint condition M-60s."

"Speaking of illegal," Randolph said tartly.

"No, chief. These pigs are gutted. No firing mechanism at all and the barrels have been plugged. We want 'em for the parade in Anchorage on the fourth. They look nifty; only we know they're impotent."

"Somebody's been teaching you big words, Lance," Randolph said, laughing as he calmed down from the fear that his section chief in the capital city had been trying to foist trouble on him.

"I know about words like 'impotent', Randolph, gimme a break."

Randolph paused meaningfully.

"Not personally," stammered Lance, "I mean, don't get no rumors goin'."

Randolph laughed.

"I'll borrow Devlin's truck and come into town first of next week and pick up the goods. That soon enough?"

"I guess so. They'll be in Henson's warehouse on fifth."

"I'll need a little help"

"They'll all be crated in good marked boxes. Make it noon on Monday, and I'll swing by and help you load 'em."

"Done," said Randolph. "See you Monday noon."

"Roger," Lance hung up.

Allen Heaps signaled to his electronics tech to set that tape aside. The taps on Militia members' phones was starting to pay off. His crew had had to listen to a lot of drivel from Lance Pedersen to his girl friends up to this point. They deserved this break. This was the first solid lead linking Kennedy to weapons smuggling and would add to the pile of evidence the man and his Alaskan terrorist group. He dialed Drake at ATF headquarters in Washington.

"Yeah," said Drake. "This is not a secure line."

"Heaps," Allen said.

"Important?"

"Yeah."

"Hang up. I'll call you on a good line."

Heaps laid the receiver back in its cradle.

In a few seconds the phone rang as promised.

"Drake?"

"Um hmm. What've you got?"

"Your favorite perp is picking up a load of crates next Monday."

"Illegal stuff?" Drake asked.

He was unable to keep the urgency out of his voice.

"Very strong maybe on that. I'll keep you posted."

"If it is, we'll have to move fast; so, we get him with it in his house."

"That's always a problem, Mr. Drake. Kennedy moves the stuff in and out of his house overnight. You can never count on what might or might not be on the premises."

"We'll have to be super cagey on this one, Heaps. There has to be evidence no matter what. Can't have this guy make us look like chimpanzees again."

"You got that right. Ever consider bringing a little insurance along on a raid, like the famous cops' drop gun sorta thing?"

"Funny thing you should ask, Heaps, my man. I would never think such a thing. But—on an unrelated subject—do you still have access to the evidence from the Ketchikan raid?"

"I could easily. There's a ton of it. Enough to spread around and aid the cause, seems to me."

"Let's have a good look at it when I come up there to the frozen north. I have a hunch it won't be all that long."

"Me neither."

"I don't need to say anything about keeping this just between us girls, right?"

"You don't. I'm a true believer. See you, boss."

"Yeah."

Oliver Quatraine made an early review of the evidence to be presented to the monthly meeting of President Vantassa's Task Force. Several hours of tapes of Randolph Kennedy's telephone conversations and videos of his comings and goings were in the prelim box along with the interagency investigative team tapes.

Quatraine ragged on the people in the technology section.

"I need a good condensation tape of the juicy stuff by Friday. I would rather have it the day before yesterday."

It seemed futile to give his review to the Task Force because none of the materials had yet been edited to remove the vast quantities of irrelevant conversation and background. Quatraine's new position gave him that bit of magic that gets things done in Washington—"The president has ordered…" The agents and copy editors grumbled and griped; but they set aside dozens of other pressing assignments and went over the evidence tapes, condensed them, and produced a single tape of relevant material and potential evidence by Friday quitting time.

Quatraine picked up a couple of the more recent raw tapes and planned to listen to enough to get a feel for what was coming in. Years ago, he had been assigned to analyze taped material and could still remember how the assignment had nearly driven him crazy. He was strictly a field man at heart. Even his present administrative slot was vexing to this man of action, tolerable only because of the extra money and the step up in grade it entailed.

He inserted a tape and thought about how much he had had to compromise to get his spot on the Task Force. A year before, he and two other African-American agents had started to organize a minority officers' cross-service coalition to combat the entrenched subtle bigotry that still permeated the federal law enforcement agencies—all sub rosa—but all effective in shutting out men like Quatraine. He had been looked upon as something of a Benedict Arnold to the other blacks and Hispanics when he backed out of the coalition after getting the appointment to the Task Force. No one had dared to whisper "Uncle Tom" to him—Oliver Quatraine was not a man to be trifled with by the men who called him brother—but he could read their minds.

Oliver listened to snatches of the recent tape. There were calls by Kennedy to his car dealer, from the county recorder's office to Kennedy about some glitch in his deed, from Kennedy to Devlin O'Herligy regarding the secession nonsense, and from Kennedy to a friend in Anchorage, a man called Lance. Quatraine heard mention of guns and began to listen more fully. The tape had nothing on it, just some arrangements to move a few dummy machine guns for one of their so-called Militia's meaningless parades. He listened to the entire conversation and judged it to be boring and put the tape back in the basket. Its case bore a note to see the intraagency tape marked with the same date. Quatraine checked his watch. He had time to listen a few minutes more before heading to the appropriations request committee's meeting.

The tape started with the unmistakable whir of a scrambling device. Quatraine presumed that he was going to waste his time hearing the buzzes and clicks of an electronically scrambled message. At least he was wrong there. The message had already been descrambled.

Oliver instantly recognized the two voices—Drake and his boy, Heaps.

It was Heaps' voice first: "Drake?"

"Um hmm, what've you got?" Drake's voice was so clear that Quatraine started a little.

"Your favorite perp is picking up a load of crates next Monday."

Quatraine knew that that could only be referring to Randolph Kennedy. Everyone in the bureau knew about Drake's fixation on the man who had killed his team and had gotten away with it.

"Illegal stuff?" Drake's voice again, more insistent now.

Now Heaps. "Very strong maybe. I'll keep you posted."

Quatraine listened further.

Drake again: "We'll have to be super cagey on this one. There has to be evidence, not matter what. Can't have this guy make us look like chimpanzees again."

There was a steely resolve in Drake's voice. Quatraine was familiar enough with Drake to know that he could be a good agent and a great friend to the members of his team so long as he wasn't required to include blacks or women. But he was an implacable bulldog of an enemy.

Heaps spoke again briefly.

Then Quatraine heard Drake say, "Funny you should ask, Heaps, my man. I would never think of such a thing. But—on an unrelated subject—do you still have access to the evidence from the Ketchikan raid?"

Heaps indicated that he did.

Drake then said cryptically, "Let's have a good look at it when I come up there to the frozen north. I have a hunch it won't be all that long.

Quatraine was particularly interested in a sort of oath of secrecy the two men agreed upon. They signed off, and the tape ended.

Oliver scratched his head, not completely sure what he had just heard. He played the tape again, then he replayed the conversation between Kennedy and Lance. By the time notations, the two tapes were obviously related. Quatraine wondered what Drake planned to do with this information, including the exculpatory statements by Kennedy. He decided that some changes might take place to the tapes' contents, or they might be discarded as immaterial so far as their use as evidence was concerned. He made up his mind. Oliver hurriedly picked up the two tapes and took them to the lab to be copied. He knew there would be a notation in the lab's daily log made of his dealings with the tapes. He also knew that it would be buried in the thousands of other notations in that log. He was not worried. He pocketed the copies and replaced the two original tapes where he had found them and went on to the allocations meeting.

Later in the week, Quatraine approved an entry on the Task Force agenda for its Friday meeting. He was curious to see how Drake would handle the information in his possession. At the meeting, the subject was relegated to the item number twelve position.

"Mr. Quatraine, I see that ATF has been doggedly tracking Randolph again," said Margaret Thaler by way of introducing item number twelve.

Quatraine ignored the implicit irony in her comment.

"Yes, ma'am. Agent Drake—whom you all may remember—has some new information. He has been invited to present it briefly."

Quatraine gestured to the guard, who left briefly and returned with Henry Drake.

"Proceed, Mr. Drake. What's new in the Kennedy affair?"

"Thank you, ma'am. We have taped telephone conversations, eyewitness accounts by our agent in the field, and videotape footage of Kennedy receiving illegal weapons. There's too much on the telephone tapes to present now; so, I have a summary tape. The film footage is only about fifteen minutes worth," he said smoothly.

"How adroit," thought Quatraine.

He wondered how Drake would react to hearing the whole tape played in this room.

The Task Force briefly heard the condensed auditory tape with Lance Pedersen saying, "Hey, Randolph, how's it hangin', bud?"

Kennedy said, "Okay, Lance, what's up?"

Pedersen: "Have a shipment, man. Need to get it out of town. Too many feds."

Task Force eyebrows raised and the members shared knowing looks.

Kennedy: "Are we talking legal or illegal things in that shipment, Lance?"

There was a very faint and brief hum; Quatraine presumed that he was the only one who caught it.

Pedersen: "I have..." slight static on the tape, "12 gauge Ithaca 37s..." more static, "and some mint condition M-60s."

The last phrase was crystal clear.

Almost immediately, Kennedy's voice came back on, "Speaking of illegal..."

His voice sounded hard and edgy, criminal. There was a slight hum of static again.

"I'll borrow Devlin's pick-up and come into town first of next week and pick up the goods. That soon enough?"

Pedersen: "I guess so. They'll be in Henson's warehouse on Fifth."

Pedersen's voice had an urgent note. To Quatraine it sounded like a man trying to get rid of something hot.

Kennedy: I'll need a little help."

Pedersen: "They'll all be in good…brief static…boxes. Make it noon on Monday, and I'll swing by and help you load 'em."

Kennedy: "Done. See you Monday noon."

Pedersen: "Roger."

The tape ended.

Drake motioned to Jack Bailey, who had accompanied him to the Task Force meeting and was sitting quietly in the back. Bailey turned off the room lights and started a video on the monitor sitting in front of the Task Force members. It was of professional television movie production quality. Image and sound were nearly perfect. The day was sunny and cloudless. A GMC pick-up, painted in camouflage colors—part of Devlin O'Herligy's small fleet—came down an industrial street and swung into the driveway of a warehouse. The driver was Randolph Kennedy. A second man came out from the corner of the warehouse building and opened the gate. Kennedy pulled the truck into the warehouse compound, and at the second man's direction, backed up to the hydraulic doors of a warehouse compartment. The doors lifted. Kennedy backed the truck partway into the opened enclosure. The two men talked, laughing and joking.

Their patter was inane—Kennedy had a joke about lawyers that the younger man could not understand, and the second man began telling Kennedy about the militia retreat in Kotzebue that past weekend. He chided Kennedy for missing it. The banter was good-natured, and the two men went about transferring fourteen slat board crates onto the bed of the pickup truck. The video zoomed in on the printing on one of the crates: "U.S. Army — M-60 SMGs — No. 15." The two men worked without further talk. They strained with the weight of the boxes. They shook hands.

"Have a good one, Lance," Kennedy said as he got into the truck cab. "Thanks for the help."

"It was nothin'," said the second man. "You comin' over to Hank Trepple's house raisin' this Saturday?"

"Can't wait," Kennedy replied.

Both men laughed. Kennedy drove out of the warehouse compound, and the second man swung the gate closed behind him and padlocked the gate.

Drake waited for the sound of the video to die down and for the lights to be put back on.

"That was Kennedy and Lance Pedersen, one of the local Movement functionaries in Anchorage, Alaska. Same two as on the telephone. Our agent followed the truck back to Kennedy's homestead some thirty miles northeast of Wasilla. He parked the truck outside in plain sight. Our agent got good shots of the truck with its crates and the house. The place is very distinctive, identifiable with ease. The next morning, a couple of other perps came up the hill to Kennedy's place and helped him carry the crates into the house. That was yesterday morning. Our agent assures me that the guns are still in that house."

Heads nodded. There were small, knowing smiles around the room.

The president spoke first, "Rather vindicating, eh, Mr. Drake?"

"I think so, Madam President. It would be hard to get anything better considering the sophistication and security consciousness of the Movement people."

"How about seeing the actual firearms...illegal firearms?" asked Margaret Thaler, ever the detail person, the ultimate careful pragmatist.

"Afraid not, Ma'am. Just the clearly marked gun crates."

Quatraine unconsciously fingered his pocket voice activated tape recorder. It was still running.

"Any way to get an undercover agent into the house to have a look, Drake?" Mrs. Thaler asked, her eyes more hopeful than her wary brain.

"I don't think so, ma'am. Too little time, too much security in those Movement houses. Those people are as thick as proverbial thieves. They are the most xenophobic lot I ever encountered. We have never been able to infiltrate a bona fide agent; they spot us every time. It's not for want of trying."

"I am very uneasy about this evidence, Agent Drake. What you have is circumstantial at best. I suppose you are here to suggest a raid. Any other helpful evidence? I would be a whole lot more comfortable if there were."

Quatraine leaned forward to catch Drake's reply. This would be the make-break moment of the decision making process regarding the future of the Randolph Kennedy affair. He checked his recorder—still running.

"I will guarantee that the evidence will be there, and it will stand up in court, ma'am. My job and my pension on it."

"Indeed," the president said archly.

"No more fiascoes. It would be 'off with their heads' for both you and me if we were to foul up on Kennedy a second time. The media would have a field day, a la the Monica Lewinsky Affair."

"I fully appreciate that, Madam President; believe me, I do. There won't be a screw-up—pardon my French—I absolutely guarantee it."

President Vantassa gave the man a wintry smile.

"You be certain that the evidence is there and that you go in with whatever you need to do the job. I don't want to hear that some more of my good agents have been hurt, and I will have a stroke if the Response Team comes back without credible evidence. Take care of it; make your guarantee happen. Do you get my drift?"

"I think so."

"Agent Drake, that's not good enough. Do you want me to spell it out?"

There was a quiet pause. The roomful of high ranking men and women collectively held their breaths.

"Well, ma'am, I guess I do. I can't be dangled out there alone. I act on your orders. If you want me to wait, to pass up this opportunity, okay. If you want me to salt it a little, I will."

The president let out an exasperated breath.

"For heaven's sake, man, drop an evidence gun if you have to. Do what is *necessary*."

She gave a little laugh and arched her eyebrows as if she had made a joke. The members of the Task Force laughed politely and nervously.

FBI Director, Ted Coleman leaned over to Oliver Quatraine and said quietly, "I hope this place is leak proof. That kind of little joke is the sort of thing to derail administrations. We don't even kid about planting evidence over at our patch."

Coleman shivered at the thought of facing his own OPR—the FBI internal disciplinary apparatus for the more than 11,000 professional agents. The Office of Professional Responsibility was notoriously unsympathetic to hints of impropriety, and completely conditioned against any concept that 'rank hath its privileges'. Both men knew that even hearing such suggestions and not reporting them made every person in the room an accessory before the fact.

Quatraine nodded in sympathy. The sounds in the room were reduced to the shuffling noises of the members exiting. It was only then that his recorder ran out of tape.

CHAPTER TWENTY-ONE

Randolph spent Thursday evening and all day Friday on a backhoe digging a series of staggered trenches and filling the bed of his huge old dump truck with the debris. Agent Allen Heaps sweltered a mile away taking long range videos. Mosquitos attacked in swarms. The two men had a long three-day weekend—Heaps had a partner now, Agent Terry Perrency.

"What's that weirdo doing?" Perrency asked Heaps, as much to pass the time as for information.

"Beats me," Heaps answered. "It's too hot to be out here at all. But it looks like busy work to me. The trenches he's digging don't even connect."

"At least it keeps him here and occupied while the Special Response Team gets into place. He don't look like he's in any rush."

The agents observed Randolph until he completed his series of trenches. The two watchers saw him carry wooden boxes into the trenches, work for about half an hour on each, then carry buckets of fresh concrete into the depths where they could not see. At eight, they broke off and went home, changing the guard with two fresh men, one on the road, and one in the trees where he could watch the house and be sure that Kennedy did not get those evidence boxes out of there. Randolph made it easy for them. He never left his property and puttered in the rough periphery of his land until after midnight. It was still light at that time. He moved fiberboard squares about, shifted more dirt, piled branches around in a haphazard fashion. To the watching agents, Kennedy's activities seemed pointless; but, no doubt, he was preparing to install some sort of piping—the purpose of which was unapparent. For all of the neatness in his work, the man was messy about clean-up.

He just bulldozed the pile of branches he had made back over the tops of the trenches. He would probably do brush removal another day, they concluded.

At their break, Agent Tucker told Agent Samuelson that it looked like a typical army job: dig a trench and fill it back up again. Pointless.

Randolph, on the other hand, was quite pleased with his Friday's work by the time he crumpled into his bed exhausted. In his mind, what he had done was a task neglected and long overdue.

In Washington, the ATF Special Response Team headed by Henry Drake was working feverishly to gather the full complement of men and women, to load its gear into the chartered 777 jet, and to complete the last minute paper work and round of meetings. Margaret Thaler met with the president three hours before the team was scheduled to leave. It was seven o'clock Saturday morning.

She was ushered into the Oval Office where the president was sitting pensively looking out at the Vietnamese gardeners working on the flower beds.

"Good morning, Margaret," the president said, "Please take a seat."

"Thank you for seeing me on short notice, Madam President. I wanted to clarify some things about the proposed Wasilla, Alaska raid."

"Thank you, Margaret. I'm glad you're here."

"I know you are aware that we are treading on thin ice here. Success is critical. It is more than the trite expression that came from the Apollo 13 crisis. Truly, failure is not an option. If the raid goes off well and Kennedy is exposed as a criminal; the previous disastrous raid will be vindicated,; the Task Force will receive a much needed boost in the public eye; and your administration will appear to be right on track on the crime-busting issue. We will likely have more public support for our efforts. On the other hand, if it is a failure, especially if there turns out to be insufficient evidence at the scene to warrant the raid, I think your popularity will hit an all time low, and with that unpopularity will come a serious difficulty in pushing the war to end drug trafficking…maybe worse."

"I couldn't agree more, Margaret. Do I understand from what you're saying that you have lost confidence in the team? In Henry Drake? Do you want to call it off? There's still time."

"No, somewhat, and no, but," Mrs. Thaler said with a self-deprecatory smile at her own attempt at humor. "I have not lost confidence in the Special

Response Team or the purpose it serves. I have to admit that Henry Drake makes me nervous. At best he is something of a loose cannon on deck at times; and at worst, he is ruled by his heart or other unnecessary organs and not by his head. He is not objective about this Kennedy thing. Frankly, I worry about whether he really has the evidence locked up. We cannot afford to gamble; we have to know about that evidence beyond the shadow of a doubt. I don't want to call it off, but I would feel a great deal better if we had another, cooler, head working directly with Drake in the field, someone who answers to you, not to Drake."

"Go ahead, whom do you have in mind?"

"Oliver Quatraine."

"Am I familiar with Agent Quatraine?"

"Yes, he's the black ATF agent on the Task Force representing the Special Response Teams."

The president nodded her recognition.

She said, "Good man, but a little prickly sometimes. I detect a black consciousness defensiveness, I think the pundits call it."

"That's him to a tee. But he's extremely careful, and can turn that defensiveness in our favor, Madam President. I think he's the man to rein in Drake's excesses. Drake doesn't like him because he's black, and Quatraine doesn't answer to Drake. I propose that he be the titular director of the action from a central team headquarters with final say, with outright veto power. Drake can handle the tactical operation on site. That sound all right with you?"

"Good idea. Will that make you comfortable enough about this mission? Remove the gamble?"

"It will go a long way. But in all frankness, Madam President, the answer, if I were pressed, is no. That does not put the required evidence on Kennedy's premises; it is just a tweaking of the administration of the mission."

She paused, her face a mask of indecision, unsure, finally, whether to go or to cancel.

After a full minute of silence between them, the attorney general said, "Pardon my asking, Madam President, but before I go on, would you tell me, please, if there is any kind of listening or recording device operative in this room?"

President Vantassa allowed a transitory trace of anger to pass over her countenance. She threw the AG a faintly disdainful look.

"I am neither a half-wit nor unaware of the lessons of history. There has not been a recording of so much as a syllable of speech in this office since poor neurotic Richard Nixon cut his own throat with the Watergate caper tapes."

"No offense intended, Madam President: I felt I had to know for sure."

"And none taken, Margaret. I understand the need for confidentially in its absolute sense. If the two of us cannot trust one another, there is no one we can, and we are sunk."

"Yes, ma'am. Then, I would like to tender a suggestion for our ears only. Agent Drake hinted at it in one of our meetings. He says that Kennedy is able to move contraband in and out of his place with amazing stealth. Even though we have good agents watching Kennedy, his confederates, and his property since this thing heated up; we cannot be sure that he has not used some of his old magic and has somehow hidden or moved the illegal weapons. The man is dirty, and he is clever. There is not a single person close to this case who is not convinced of that fact. Drake indicates that he has usable evidence that he can transport to the scene in case they draw a blank. At least I think his broad hint told us that. After the meeting, Holdaway, Coleman, and I met with him and he referred obliquely to the drugs and guns taken in the big raid in Ketchikan. That bunch was almost certainly connected with Kennedy's operations. It would be a way of having that arrogant smug criminal be hoist by his own petard to use that evidence against him."

"So, why doesn't Drake just do what he has to do? Why do we have to have this discussion?" the president asked calculatedly.

She thought she could see where this was headed.

"He's leery of us. You may recall that you and I administered a severe public dressing-down and demoted him for his failure in the first Kennedy raid. He fears—not without foundation—that he will take the full fall if anything goes wrong on this one. He wants the insurance of knowing that we approve of his plan, his fully insured plan."

"You can't know how much I want to get this Kennedy, Margaret."

The president's eyes burned with intensity and anger. Mrs. Thaler had come to recognize this look as the harbinger of implacability on her leader's part.

"In a funny sort of way, I consider it an honorable action since it is necessary in defense of this country. You might remember Patrick Henry of the Revolutionary War era. He was America's first spy, captured by the British at the age of twenty-one and sentenced to hang. Among his last words, he said, 'Every kind of service necessary to the public good becomes honorable by being necessary'. Well, Margaret, my office requires hard decisions necessary to the public good, and I deem this to be one such decision. Let Drake know that he has our blessing to go ahead. I won't lose any sleep over it."

"And pardon my bringing it up, but talk's cheap. We can tell him and still maintain plausible deniability for the sake of your presidency," Mrs. Thaler said in a conspiratorial voice.

"Yes," the president mused, "it's Machiavellian and ironic but that, too, is necessary."

Thaler contacted Henry Drake on the transport plane's secure line.

"Mr. Drake?"

"Yes, ma'am."

"Do you know who this is?"

"I do."

"Are you fully ready to proceed with the Wasilla raid?"

"We are finishing with the loading of the plane."

"Will the evidence be there when you go in? Not a shred of a possibility that you will turn up nothing again?

"Our intelligence is good, and we have been patient and but I can't absolutely guarantee that Kennedy won't be able to pull a rabbit out of his hat again, though."

"This has to be 100 percent. There cannot be a failure. In the interest of national security and for both of our jobs, the evidence has to be there for all to see. Do I make myself clear?"

"I am certainly in sympathy with your goal. It is obviously the same as mine. Still, I can't be absolute about what is in Kennedy's possession right now. He's tricky."

"Can't you make certain? Am I getting through to you?"

"Look, Madam Attorney General. I can see to it that there is evidence aplenty at the perp's stronghold. It wouldn't necessarily be kosher. Is it in the interest of national security to provide such insurance?"

"If you have to."

"Do I have assurances of protection for such...uh, above and beyond the call of duty activity, shall we call it?"

"I agree, and the president agrees. Do what you have to do to guarantee that presence of evidence of culpability at the scene, Drake. Are we clear on that now?"

"Pretty clear, ma'am, but this is serious business. I am putting my neck in a noose with this one, and I do not want there to be the slightest question about this just having been a wild hair of mine. This is a national security issue like you have been saying all along. I want to have you and the president order me, and I want a witness."

The attorney general seethed at her agent's impertinence. She spoke through her teeth.

"Listen, Drake, nobody's going to write you an order directing the commission of a technical felony. Suck it up and be a man."

Drake wanted to laugh. Two women telling him to be a man.

"I am not asking for a written order although personally, I would sure like to have one. In the greater interest, the less written on this affair, the better. I still want to meet eye-to-eye with the two of you. And I want a witness."

His voice was hard, almost challenging.

"You fly out in a couple of hours, I hardly need remind you."

She was trying to stall, and he knew it.

"Mrs. Thaler, all due respect, but without full assurance that the brass are behind me and the Team on this, and even at this late hour; I will cancel the raid. No one would go anyway. There is too much risk. Without the official sanction, I am left to twist in the wind with my men, and we don't deserve that."

"Is that some kind of a threat, Agent Drake?"

"No, ma'am, just common prudence."

She gritted her teeth once more. Time was wasting.

"I'll see what I can do."

She hung up and immediately called the president. She explained Drake's demand and was surprised to receive a brisk agreement to a meeting.

"Where?" the attorney general asked.

"Certainly not here. I don't want that man or any member of his team anywhere near the White House. We can meet in Senator Tomlinson's office. He will be willing to vacate the place for me for an hour. It's seven thirty-five now. Let's say that we have the meet in twenty minutes."

Margaret Thaler called Drake.

"Meet in the Senate office building at seven-fifty. Senator Tomlinson's office—Kentucky Tomlinson. Think you can make it?"

"I'll get a chopper. I know my way around the building. I'll be there."

"Good-bye, then."

"Good-bye, Madam Attorney General."

She thought she detected a note of gloating in Drake's voice. She did not like the man, but she had to admit that his ilk had their uses. He had better come through after all of this.

She next called Oliver Quatraine. His telephone rang three times before he picked it up.

"Hello," he said. "This is not a secure line."

"Get to one, and call me. Look my number up in the capitol directory."

Mrs. Thaler hung up before he could use her name.

Quatraine called her five minutes later.

"This is a secure line, ma'am. How can I be of service?"

"Your country needs a small, silent, sacrifice."

She let the description sink in. It had a theatrical ring, but she decided that—under the circumstances—she did not mind that. She quickly told him about her meeting with the president and the need for him to be able to leave almost immediately for Alaska. She then told him about the impending meeting in Senator Tomlinson's office and requested that he be there as an impartial witness. She admonished him against taking notes.

"I'll be there, ma'am. I'll have to break every speed law there is, but I'll be there. Anything else?"

"That's it, Agent Quatraine. You're a good soldier. I'm glad you're on the team. Good-bye."

"Good-bye."

He put down the receiver and rolled his eyes at the strange twist of circumstance that awaited. He was not at all sure what he was about to witness, but it had to be important if the president was going to go to that much trouble for secrecy. He put in a fresh tape in his voice-activated recorder and tested it. The performance was excellent. He taped the tiny device securely to the muscular medial upper thigh near his scrotum. Even a routine pat-down would miss it unless a real red-hot did the patting. He put on fresh Aqua Velva and sped to the Senate offices.

The hallway where Senator Tomlinson's office was located was deserted of regular people who had been replaced by a small army of grey suited men and women whispering into handset radios. The Secret Service agents were trying to look unobtrusive. Quatraine chuckled to himself when he looked down the stretch of the hall. If anonymity and secrecy were the purposes of coming to this place, then the choice was a droll one. The only things lacking were the throng of the press and a live marine band playing *Hail to the Chief*. A secret service agent gave Oliver the once-over and asked him to step into a janitorial room a few doors away from Senator Tomlinson's office.

"Mind if we check you for weapons or recording devices?"

As if they cared whether he minded.

The agent patted the muscular black ATF officer down thoroughly; but, as Quatraine had predicted, stayed away from his crotch and missed the small voice-activated recorder. Except in a real security threat situation, men did not grope around other men's scrotums.

"He's clean," the Secret Service Agent announced to his fellow agents. "Sorry to have inconvenienced you, sir. Just routine, you understand."

"Sure, just doing your job. Thanks for the way you are handling things."

"I'll take you to Madam Butterfly now," the agent told Quatraine.

Seeing his eyebrows lift in a question, the agent hastened to add, "Just our code name for Her Majesty."

Quatraine knew that he was in; the president's agents felt comfortable enough to share an in-house joke.

He and Henry Drake were escorted into Tomlinson's office together. It was eight sharp. Mrs. Thaler was all business and wasted no time on small talk or introductions.

"All right Drake. The president has your orders."

President Vantassa looked tired, bored, and out of sorts. She did not have time for this penny-ante meeting, and her face and demeanor spoke volumes.

"Agent Drake, you are involved in a matter of national security. Invoking the executive powers vested in me by," she glanced at a note card, "the McGrath-Hoover Internal Security Act of 1948 and more precisely by the Program for Apprehension and Detention of Persons Considered Potentially Dangerous to the National Defense and Public Safety of the United States— Senate Intelligence Committee hearings, 1952, volume 6, page 427, I hereby order you to carry out a raid on the premises of one Randolph Armstrong Kennedy in Wasilla, Alaska. Because of the extraordinary sensitivity of this case, I order you to place evidence at the scene if necessary and as much as necessary to obtain a conviction in the criminal case and to expedite the removal of this man from his threatening status as rapidly and as certainly as can be done. You are authorized to use deadly force if necessary."

She nodded to Margaret Thaler and started for the door.

Thaler said to Drake, "That's it. You have your orders. Time to get back to your job."

Drake said flatly, "You know the evidence we plan to use; I'd like to hear that in the order."

The president did not look back. She walked out the door and into the hallway where she was whisked away by her coterie of Secret Service agents.

"Don't press your luck, Drake. You have your orders and more than you should reasonably have expected from the president. Enough is enough."

She gestured towards the exit door, and as he left, she handed him a sealed envelope of orders explaining Quatraine's superior position in the mission.

Oliver Quatraine had been silent throughout the meeting. He had to work to keep his jaw from dropping open. He had just witnessed the president of the United States ordering the commission of a felony. The recording device irritated his scrotum, and he had to make an effort to walk normally. He was unsure whether he would have a quality sound reproduction on the tape given the unlikely hot and sweaty location of the device. He had no idea what he would do with this tape if it did turn out to be audible. He questioned himself about why he had gotten the recording as he left the Senate Building for Andrews Air Force Base where the Team was ready for the flight to Anchorage. What he did know was that he was carrying the most explosive piece of information about an American president since Nixon's famous missing fourteen minute office tape.

CHAPTER TWENTY-TWO

Randolph Kennedy's telephone jangled him awake at six o'clock in the morning on Monday.

"Hello," he said dully, still sleep stupid. "This had better be good news."

"Yes, sir, it is. You and me are going hunting for moose today. Got to fill up the larders. Don't say another thing; just be in your hunting stuff and ready to go. I and some friends will be there to pick you up shortly. You got to call in sick."

It was Devlin O'Herligy. Prudence indicated to Randolph not to mention names or to say anything the feds might find incriminating. He had been sure that his telephone was being tapped for some time now.

"Okay, if you insist," he said.

"Good man. See you inside forty-five minutes."

The telephone clicked dead.

Devlin was not given to theatrics in matters of importance. Randolph decided that this was important, and got ready for a hunt. It took him forty minutes to round up his stuff and to get dressed in tough hunting clothes. A few minutes later, two pick-up truck loads of men drove noisily up Randolph's road and clattered to a stop in front of his lawn. They yelled and punched each other like a bunch of adolescent boys going on an outing unsupervised by adults. They were clearly trying to direct attention to themselves.

The noisy camaraderie continued until Randolph let the men into his Devlin whispered, "Look, my friend, there are federal agents watching your place. Couple right out in your trees to the north, can't say how many others there may be. I think they plan to pay you an uninvited visit, a very noisy visit.

Probably to do with those crates of guns you brought up from Anchorage this past week."

"They're legal; most of them are plugged model M-60s incapable of being fired, don't even have a firing mechanism," Randolph protested.

"Doesn't matter. The crates look like standard military issue, and the press will have a field day. We don't need that kind of publicity. And you recall your incident in Virginia—they don't need much of an excuse—the feds or the press."

"So, what do you have in mind?"

"These two yahoos carry the crates out the back way and hide them in the woods. That's the best I can think of right now. The rest of us make the big noise and do all the male bonding crap and go off on a hunt. I don't think the feds will be sure of their count of us, and one or two more or less won't be obvious. They would have to use the fingers of more than one hand, and they don't go in for higher math that much," he grinned as he said it.

"Won't work. If my previous experience is anything of an indicator, they will hunt this hillside over until every crevice and cranny has been searched. I have a better plan."

"That's a relief. I didn't much like mine, but I couldn't for the life of me think of anything better on the spur of the moment."

"C'mon down to my basement. I have something to show you. This is for you guys; eyes only, okay?"

They all nodded, and Randolph took them into his bathroom. He let them look around for a moment, then he removed the towel rack, lifted the ring latch for the trap door and opened the way into the fortress basement.

"I'm impressed," said Devlin.

"You're missing the best part," said Randolph, after allowing his friends a few minutes to look around the basement.

"All right, you guys, find an exit."

They set about looking like a group of children playing hide-and-seek. None of them could find another way out other than back up into the main floor bathroom. Randolph stepped to the rack of skis and poles. He unlatched the second to the last ski on the rack, set the ski aside, and twisted the rubber ski holder counter-clockwise. The portion of the pinewood lined wall holding the ski rack eased away from the adjacent segments of the wall, and the men saw a cleverly constructed door open into a cavernous area beyond the wall. Randolph found the newly installed light switch on the vestibule of the secret tunnel and turned it on. A single bright light flashed on, illuminating 50 feet down the tunnel.

Randolph said, "There are battery operated lamps every fifty feet beyond the electric light. You can see the next one from the last lamp turned on. You can turn of each light in its turn and go to the next. No one will ever be able to figure out how to light the tunnel except with flashlights which will take them precious time.

"I'll be...exclaimed Kevin Wirthlin, one of the Militiamen.

"That's the best hidey hole I ever seen," added Derrin Crump. "It'd take the feds a year to find you in there."

All eight men had a rollicking laugh. Happiness—by definition—was annoying the feds.

"Longer than that," said Randolph. "In the interest of time, let me tell you that this tunnel leads down to an opening on the cliff south of the house— about a mile away. You guys can carry the crates of guns out of here and down to the main road. Bear to your left when you come out, and you can avoid the driveway onto my land. You ought to be able to drive off with the crates without anyone being the wiser. My old dump truck and back hoe're down at the bottom. Remember to bring it back. I figure it won't be all that long before I need it on the sly."

The seven visitors shook their heads in admiration.

"Okay," said Devlin, "Let's get outta here before the federales get suspicious."

Randolph showed the two men who were going to stay how to close the door to the basement bunker and to the tunnel so that no trace could be seen that a doorway existed. Then he and the hunters walked out the front door making as much noise as possible and milling about with frequent and rapid changes of position to interfere with the ATF agents' head count.

Allen Heaps quickly radioed along the line as soon as Randolph appeared outside.

"My count is five...no, six. Anyway, I think there may be a couple of them still in the house. Number three and number four, follow the trucks when they hit the main road. The rest of you stay put. I'm going to get some orders. Right now, I don't think it's wise to make any kind of significant move, over."

Four navy blue clad men with bright yellow block letter "ATF AGENT" signs on their backs started down the hillside on the double.

'Heaps' walkie-talkie crackled.

"Number one," he said quietly.

"Number two, over."

"Go ahead, Perrency."

"Maybe we can't do anything, but how about just going up to have a peek inside?"

Heaps thought about it and couldn't see any harm.

"Okay, you and Swensen go up. No noise, no chances. Understood?"

"Roger that. And willco. Out."

"Out," Heaps said to the now dead receiver.

Thirty minutes later Heaps' walkie-talkie squawked again.

"Number one," he answered.

"Number two, here. Quiet as a tomb in there. I'm sure nobody's up there. Want to go in now and secure the place, boss?"

"No. Repeat, no way. We want the perps more than the guns. Sit tight. I'll call Drake down in Wasilla."

Heaps called the number for the ATF mobile headquarters.

"Yeah?" came Drake's brusque voice.

"Suspect has vacated the premises. Looks like he's goin' huntin' with a few of his backwoods buddies. Request instructions."

"Do nothing. Sit on your hands. Nobody goes near that house without I'm there. I want Kennedy. We'll wait a week if we have to. He'll come back. You copy that loud and clear?"

"Loud and clear."

Drake rang off.

Quatraine waited until Drake completed the call before resuming his argument with him.

"Look, every evidence says the perp has crates of illegal guns inside. We don't have to drop any evidence."

"I'm a belt and suspenders kind of guy, Quatraine. I'm also a team player—you could take a lesson. You heard the Pres. and AG; we nail this guy whatever way we have to. That's it. Now, go get on somebody else's case and leave me be."

Quatraine sighed and shrugged. He might as well have been speaking Sanskrit to his dog for all the good this conversation with Drake was doing him.

"Okay, don't forget that I warned you. This is hokey, too hokey. But I'll shut up on the subject. Show me the evidence you're going to drop."

Drake rolled his eyes.

"If it'll get you off my back."

He gestured for Quatraine to follow him. They walked into the backyard of the old house they had rented to use as headquarters. Nearly twenty ATF agents were in the yard having a barbecue. Drake put his forefinger to his lips.

"Loose lips sink ships," he muttered through his teeth.

The two men walked into a side yard where an outsized decrepit old Dodge Ram II delivery van stood. It was huge, a sickly white in color, and looked as if it may have been a commercial milk truck or a bakery wagon at one time. Its paint was peeling, and it was covered with a myriad of old dents, scratches, and rusty gouge marks indicative of a long life of heavy use. A long, tall trailer covered with a tarpaulin was attached to a hitch on the back of the van.

Drake looked around to be sure that no one was paying attention to them, then he unlocked the padlock on the large van's rear doors. He pulled open the doors quickly and stepped into the interior. He motioned for Oliver to follow him. He drew the doors as nearly closed as possible and turned on his flashlight. On the floor in front of them and making entrance into the trailer difficult were several large bags of ammonium nitrate fertilizer. Quatraine did not think it necessary to wonder if this van load represented a large scale gardening project. There was enough raw chemical there to make bombs capable of taking out the White House and six city blocks.

Next forward stood boxes full of chopped leaves densely packed into ziplock baggies, and five kilo bags of white powder, hundreds of them. Lying on the floor in front of the drugs were six wooden crates of guns standing upright. Quatraine guessed that the street value of the powder, either cocaine or heroin, had to be in the multi-millions; and the munitions had to be of nearly equal value.

"Pardon me if I don't open the crates. Take my word," said Drake, pleased with Quatraine's stunned expression. "You're looking at two crates each of LAWs, M-72 grenade launchers, and Roadblockers, and one each of Czech Vz.58s, AK-47s, and 9mm Parabellum Tokagypts."

Quatraine ached to have a look at the famous Vz.58s, the terrorist's choice of automatic rifles, and especially at the 10 gauge shotgun that held only three rounds, known as a Roadblocker because it was an accurate description of the power of the weapon. He controlled his curiosity and resisted examining the crates further.

"Man, the world would be a worse place if those ever fell into the wrong hands," he said as an understatement.

"They were, and they won't again. The ATF is on the job," Drake said smugly.

Quatraine shook his head unconvinced.

"I'd hate to be in our shoes if anything ever does happen to those things. The perps'll be better armed than a Response Team."

"Stop being such an old lady, Quatraine. This is the majors. Suit up and get in the game."

Drake's voice carried an intentional sting.

Quatraine ignored the implication as he did with most of the white agents' snide remarks toward him and his fellow minority agents.

"Let's have a look in the trailer," he said.

The windows on the rear doors had been painted over. He opened the large cargo doors, and Drake pushed aside one row of the "New & Brite Fax Paper" boxes that stood against them and set aside the loading ramps. It was pitch black behind the rearmost row of boxes.

"Look, and weep," said Drake, and shined his light into the depths of the trailer.

Oliver took an involuntary breath and hissed it out through his teeth.

"Geez, is that what I think it is?"

There were three rows of pallets stacked two high all the way to the front of the trailer. On each of the pallets were bundles of tightly packed currency secured to the pallet with plastic shrink wrap. The money was pressed into the compartment floor to ceiling and wall to wall. It was not possible to tell the denominations, but even if they were all ones, it was a staggering amount of money. Quatraine remembered a silly fact from a boyhood visit to Washington D.C. where he had taken the standard tour of the Bureau of Printing and Engraving. A stack of ones a mile high was fourteen and a half million dollars. This looked like a hundred miles of money—a fortune large enough to rival Croesus. It was breath taking.

"Is that real?" he choked out.

"All hundreds. Uncle Sugar's finest. All used, unmarked, no purple dyes, no newspaper cuttings in the center of the stacks. No ringers. All stacks are at random, no serialized bills. We have never monkeyed with that little fortune since it came our way from the raid in Ketchikan. And it's all evidence. Don't think of it as money."

That was said with genuine jocularity.

Quatraine could only stare for a few minutes. It made him feel all warm and good inside just to stand near so much money. He shook his head to bring himself back. It was not a dream. That was real money and more than he had ever imagined, let alone seen.

"Any idea how much there is total?" he managed.

Drake laughed out loud.

"Don't get any thoughts, Quatraine. This stuff is going back into the impound vault where it came from as soon as this case is over. As long as I have a say, not one bill of that stack is going to find its way into the wrong hands, perp or copper."

Oliver thought for a moment; his analytical side showed itself as usual. He had a nagging thought which he now expressed aloud.

"If this is the Ketchikan loot and constitutes the main evidence from that raid, how can it be used twice? I mean, once the Ketchikan trial is over, it will be distributed to the federal agencies. It won't be available for this case, will it?"

His face showed serious concern. He was sure he had discovered the fatal flaw in the whole phantasmagorical plan.

"Don't give it a second thought, Ollie, my boy," Drake taunted gleefully. "Uncle Henry has all of that under control. Don't worry your pretty little burr head about that inconsequential problem. Your Uncle Henry will take care to see that that never becomes a problem."

There was a hard, nasty edge in his gruff voice. That part of the plan had escaped Quatraine; and he thought maybe it was better if he did not know everything; but he could not avoid the chill that raised the hairs on his neck. He ignored the mockery.

"Back to my question, Drake. How much do you think is there?" he asked, changing the subject.

"I don't honestly know. I'd say that you could put three kids through Harvard and give them each a house with one of those little bundles out of one of those stacks. Whole thing? Maybe four, five hundred mill, maybe more."

He tossed it off as if he were describing the kids' lunch money.

Quatraine felt numb and distinctly uncomfortable standing there before all that money and all the implications of its presence. Drake's cocksureness failed to assuage Oliver's misgivings. No need to worry, to concern himself? Fat chance. Quatraine was a worrier, and he was vividly aware of the hazards of using the arms and money to frame a suspect—even one as reprehensible as Kennedy—compounded by the audacious plan to use that same evidence twice. The deeper realization that the Response Team was going to stage a raid that had no intention of resulting in a post-raid trial in a court of law made Oliver Quatraine—the letter of the law straight shooter federal agent— shudder at his own involvement, even at his guilty knowledge. Oliver was now immensely glad that he was recording everything. He walked away from Henry and surreptitiously switched the recorder off, reminding himself to get some new tapes.

—2—

Randolph shot a large bull moose late Tuesday afternoon. He, Devlin, and Tom Bradshaw had been hunting the easy way, from a small river boat on the Mulchatna River. By the luck of the draw of straws, Randolph had been the one to shoot the first animal. In the distance they saw a fine bull with an estimated sixty inch spread of his airplane propeller antlers. The men silently glided to within a mile of the big black beast, beached their boat, and crept up on it slowly keeping downwind. Randolph put two rounds from his .338 into the kill zone, and the beast dropped and was still after a slow twenty yard run. It was well after dark before they had skinned and field dressed the carcass and loaded all of the meat, the expertly caped hide, and the skull and horns into the boat. As it turned out, Randolph was the only one of the hunters to get a shot. The meat was all that mattered to the rest of the men; they had trophies aplenty. When they divided up the 1900 pound animal, there was more than enough deboned meat to provide a winter's supply for all of their families.

Randolph was ready to head back home Wednesday night, but Devlin cautioned him, "I think the feds will get tired of watching your place given another day. Or you might only annoy them. Either way is a plus. Let's wait until tomorrow. I look for them to be gone by then; and you can get back to living like a regular American citizen—one who doesn't have the special protection of federal officers watching him and his property all the time."

Devlin could not speak of 'federal officers' except with a hard edge.

"All right, Devlin. I have a ton to do, and my boss just might get on my case if I don't get back to work there before too long."

"Don't worry, friend, Ian Laird knows it's the moose hunt. No real man would begrudge a man his inalienable right to the moose hunt, right? Besides, your position as head of the Militia covers a lot of sins; I ought to know."

"Right," agreed Randolph, amused.

He liked Devlin's spurious logic even though most of the time it was at the level of an adolescent boy's rationalizations.

CHAPTER TWENTY-THREE

Tuesday night at 2300, the two ATF agents watching the house reported in to the headquarters house in Wasilla: "Subject has not returned. No sign of activity."

Drake stormed at Allen Heaps as if it were a matter of the younger agent's perfidy that their quarry was no longer available. Heaps was a calm man, used to Drake's outbursts. He did not really mind serving as the foil for the senior agent's reactions to stress. He kept his voice understated.

"Look, Henry, this is an advantage, not a problem. There is every indication that the man simply went hunting, and we don't have to read anything more into it. Nobody saw anything that suggested a plan for flight. The airports, bus terminals, and borders have not reported him passing through. Relax. He'll be back. This gives us the golden opportunity to set up a raid at his place undetected. I would like to suggest…" and here he grinned boyishly, "in my humble way…" He turned his eyes down and did a Stepinfetchit foot shuffle, "that we head out to the house in force tonight."

Drake laughed in spite of himself. He liked Heaps. The younger agent always seemed to understand the right turn of phrase or logical construct to move aside Drake's anger. He knew that he always expressed his strain with outbursts of anger. He was always severely stressed immediately before a raid. He made a mental note to recommend a promotion for Heaps when the mission was completed.

"You're right, Heaps. I need some action. Sitting around is driving me nuts. I need to get the force out into the field before we all lose our edge, even if we can't launch quite yet. Get Jack Bailey for me, will you?"

"Sure, boss," Heaps said and left Drake's makeshift office, glad to get away from the volatile and irascible man. Drake was good under fire, but unbearable in the period leading up to action.

Heaps ran into Oliver Quatraine as he was leaving Drake's office.

"What's the big rush, Heaps?" asked the black agent.

"I'm after Bailey. Drake has a bug in his bonnet. I think he wants to set up the raid tonight."

Quatraine groaned. He was tired from his day's work; and if they moved now, it would mean an all-nighter. On the other hand—he reasoned—it put him one day closer to being quit of Drake and his Action Response Team. So, the idea was not all bad. Heaps moved on past Quatraine in the narrow hallway.

Distracted, Heaps left Drake's door open. Drake was too busy to notice. Jack Bailey sauntered back to Drake's office. He was tired, too.

"Heaps said you needed me, boss," he said to the seated man.

"Yeah. I've decided to set up tonight. I want our guys in place and let them get thoroughly out of sight. Let the fibbies and the local cops know what's up. When the perp gets back, we will be ready. I want him inside the house. It won't be any good if we don't catch him with his hand in the cookie jar. I don't think we'll have to wait more'n a day or two at the outside."

Oliver Quatraine was curious. He wanted to know if it was going to be a go that night or if he could hope for a short sleep in his motel room. He took a nonchalant walk past the open office door. Heaps was down the hall, and Drake and Bailey were in the office. Otherwise, no one else was in the temporary headquarters building.

"How do you want to deal with the perp when we go?" Bailey's voice was asking.

Quatraine's interest was piqued enough to switch on his recorder.

"He was killed resisting arrest," came Drake's quiet, chilling voice. "Someone has to have the *attempted* apprehension of this armed and dangerous fugitive as his main if not sole purpose during this raid."

Drake was not one to mince words.

"And if by some miracle he gets by our little army again—or if any of his little play soldier friends think to set up business in his hilltop fort again—I've got this."

He showed Heaps a glass stoppered vial containing a clear liquid.

"I give up, boss; what is it?" Heaps asked.

Drake's voice dropped a couple of decibels and became conspiratorial, almost a whisper. Quatraine—listening at the door—could hear everything, but he was not sure the recording device was up to this.

"Sodium fluoro acetate, most deadly water poison there is. It is going into Kennedy's well after he meets his untimely end while attempting to escape lawful arrest.

"It's illegal just to have that stuff, not so?" Heaps asked, concerned.

"A technicality. This is the case of the end justifying the means. I have my ways of coming up with the means that you don't need to know. National security, understand?"

For his own good, Heaps did not even want to know, but he admired Drakes bull dogged chutzpah.

Quatraine hurried away from the door when it appeared that the conversation was about at an end. He definitely did not want either speaker to realize that he had heard the damning conversation. It was more than his life was worth—he was sure—if they found out about the recording. He mulled over in his mind what he had heard and what he might do about it. Confrontation was out; neither man would admit anything; and neither man would be likely to alter the plan. It was too convenient for everyone concerned to have the plan work, except—of course—for Kennedy.

Quatraine had corroborating evidence that he could use to defame the complicit agents and the government, but he was well aware of the dismal fate of most whistle blowers. It occurred to him to call Washington; but he was painfully aware that the attorney general and the president—herself— had sanctioned the raid and it's irregularities. He was sure that he would be told that this was war; and he needed to suck it up and be a good soldier, a team player, for a change. War justified a plentitude of "irregularities" in Washington-eze.

He pondered the idea of warning Kennedy thereby becoming a traitor to his team mates and his country. Was Kennedy's life worth the risk to Quatraine? It was a dilemma that Oliver had never encountered before. But the more he thought about it, the better that alternative seemed. He had a conscience, and he would never have peace within himself if he failed to save Kennedy. He was a bad guy, but Quatraine thought it was way overboard to...what?... execute him? A nonjudicial execution? He began working on himself to drive out the idea that he was some sort of a traitor if he called Kennedy. It took some time for Oliver to make up his mind.

He walked out onto the deserted Wasilla back street. He looked around for a telephone booth—found one two blocks away—and fingered through the worn telephone book for Kennedy's number. Luck was with him; he even had a pocket full of coins from the agents' endless poker game. He dialed Kennedy's number. Four rings.

"Hello, I'm not able to come to the phone right now. Your message is important to me. Please give a message at the tone, and I will get back to you as soon as I can."

It was a canned message, not even Kennedy's voice. It was annoying. Right then Oliver Quatraine hated answering machines. He slammed the receiver back on its hook with a satisfying jar of the booth's flimsy walls and splintered off another small piece of Ma Bell's plastic equipment. Quatraine had tried; it was frustrating not to have gotten to Kennedy—but he had at least tried—and at no small risk to himself. It was all he could do.

He hurried back into the headquarters. Men were rubbing sleep from their eyes. They had been asleep in makeshift cot beds spread around the building. They started to carry boxes, gun cases, bullet proof vests, tear gas and flash bang launchers, packages of plastique, gas masks, and bullhorns out to the three black pick-ups parked behind the building. Quatraine hoisted a heavy box of ammo and joined them. Drake and Bailey were running down a list of inventory.

When the gear was stowed, Drake looked around with a practiced eye and then waved his arm above his head in a circling motion, ending with a theatrical forward pointing.

"Head 'em up; roll 'em out," he yelled like a wagon boss. The agents clambered aboard the three trucks. Bailey brought up the rear in the oversized white delivery truck towing the expensive trailer.

After three trips that cost them two days work, Steve Maloney and Dick Trentham arduously moved the last of the gun crates out of the tunnel exit to Randolph's house. They shoved them into the dump truck they had originally found parked within sight of the entrance to the property. The day was still light, despite the lateness of the hour. The two men were drenched in sweat and exhausted from a set of labors that had taken them four hours to complete.

"I'm whipped," declared Steve, panting.

"Me, too," responded Dick from where he lay draped over the hood of the truck, unable to move to a more comfortable resting spot. "And I have a horrible thought."

Chapter Twenty-Three

"I don't want to hear bad news after two days of this," said Steve.

"Did you close up the exits in the commander's house?"

"I thought that was your job."

Both men groaned inwardly. With unspoken shrugs of resignation, they trudged back up the hill, climbed the low cliff, and hiked back through the tunnel.

"I'll close up the entrance to the basement," Steve offered.

It took him less than half a minute.

"All sealed and invisible," he said.

The two men drew the tunnel door closed behind them and heard the satisfying crunch of the metal edges that sealed the exit from view and now closed them off from the house. They were in the truck in another thirty minutes.

"This playing at war is getting to be real work," breathed Dick when they were able to settle into their uncomfortable worn seats.

"Isn't it, though?" agreed Steve. "Let's get this stuff out of here and get on home. I've gotta have a little shut-eye; I'm a growing boy."

Dick leaned over and patted his friend's beer belly and laughed.

"More truth in that than you'd like to admit."

Steve growled.

Dick drove. The cumbersome old dump truck lacked power steering or comfort shocks. The terrain was rough. He had to dodge boulders and bushes and had to stay off the edge of several inclines. He wormed the truck over a serpentine course until it finally pulled out onto the county road and shortly onto Highway 3 and headed south back to Wasilla.

"What are we going to do with these crates?"

Dick said, "Leave 'em in the truck, at least overnight. They're covered with a tarp. Nobody's interested in this old heap. We can decide where to stash the lot tomorrow. Right now, I'm bushed."

"Heaven forbid that my job should interfere with all this glorious Militia stuff," Steve groused good-naturedly.

"I know what you mean," agreed his partner.

By then, it was midnight—nearly as bright as day—but still the middle of the night. Just outside of Nancy, they passed three black pick-ups and a white Dodge Ram II van pulling a trailer headed north. The two Militiamen could see large numbers of short-haired, fit-looking young men and women in the vehicles.

"Feds," they said at the same time.

"Care to guess where they're headed?" asked Steve.

"How many guesses do I get?"

"Three, and the first two don't count."

The vehicles roared past their dump truck paying no attention to the two rural Alaskans.

"Makes you wonder what Randolph ever did to be so popular with the Feds, don't it?" asked Dick. "Glad I'm just a common grunt in our little old army."

"Me, too, bro. Amen to that."

"It'd be a good thing to give Randolph a jingle soon's he gets back," Dick said.

He gave his head a perplexed little scratch.

"Can't be done," Steve pointed out, reading his friend's mind. "Man's phone's been tapped for sure, and nobody's gonna get up that road once the ATFers are set up. I'm afraid he's gonna have to go it alone, unless the Militia plans to take on the U.S. Marines."

Dick did not have an answer.

Steve had his usual response to knotty social problems.

"We'll tell Devlin, he can figure out what to do. That's why the big brass make the big bucks."

He laughed. The Militiamen all made the same salary—zero per hour. Participation in the all volunteer outfit was a costly drain on the men's money.

Both watchers on Kennedy's hill called in to report that nothing had changed on their shifts. Aside from a truck or two on the main county road, there had been no traffic; no one entered or left the property. It was boring, but comforting. When were their replacements coming?

Drake wheeled his black Ford pick-up off Highway 3 and onto the county road, kicking up a cloud of dust on his followers.

"Eat that," he snickered.

A short time later, he pulled onto the obscure roadway that entered the Kennedy property.

The other three vehicles pulled in behind him and parked beside Drake's truck with their lights off. It was beginning to get dusky, as dark as Alaska gets that time of year.

"Pull those trucks a full mile away from here. Go on down this road and find a place to hide them. I don't want any yokels coming by and getting suspicious. They all work for the Movement. I want you back here in ten to fifteen minutes, no more."

"What about the van?" Jack Bailey asked quietly of Drake after the other men left.

"Let's find a spot reasonably nearby to hide it. I want it to be available on a moment's notice. When I signal for the assault to begin, let the guys start for the house, then you move the van over here; so, we can get it up the hill during the confusion of the break-in. I want it to be sitting beside the house when the crime scene and media photos are taken. I also want ATF agents and fibbies or local county Mounties to discover the evidence, not one of us two. You'll play head's up ball and drive it up there while we're inside."

Bailey nodded. The two men roamed around the lower property for twenty minutes before selecting an out-of-the-way place where the van and the trailer could fit. It turned out to be no more than ten yards from the three black Ford pick-ups. Drake fretted over that, but knew that Bailey could be trusted to move the evidence carriers at the right time. Bailey faded into the growing darkness, and Drake headed back to the rendezvous point in time to meet up with the other twenty-eight agents, all of them sweaty and breathing heard. They were so quiet that Drake had not been able to see them before they were almost upon him.

"Nice quiet work, ladies and gentlemen," he said in a loud whisper.

The agents smiled at the bestowal of a morsel of praise. Drake had the fleeting thought that his agents responded so well to a little commendation that he might try it more often. He quickly put it out of his mind as sissy. The agents dispersed among the trees. Drake snapped his fingers with the sudden memory that he had not reminded Bailey to wipe of his prints in the van, but he knew that his deputy would do that on his own initiative.

"Give me a fix on your location and progress in an hour. Don't anybody leave his or her spot unless I tell you to," Drake instructed them as they began to settle in.

He assigned each team of two agents a number from 2 to 15 as he learned their positions relative to one another. Number 2 was to the north, and number 15 was to the south. He and Bailey were number 1. The teams called in and identified themselves with their number once an hour. He knew that Bailey was close to the van. He placed himself a distance of a three minute run from the vehicles and set-up a small field headquarters. Once everyone was in place, he called back to the unit's official headquarters in Wasilla. Quatraine picked up the phone on the first ring.

"All's quiet," reported Drake. "Nobody here, yet. We'll wait him out. Over."

"Okay," Quatraine responded tersely. "Routine reports every four hours until the perp returns, then every two until you strike, then every fifteen minutes. If you fail to report three times in succession, I will send out an army of reinforcements. Let's don't have that happen; this is an ATF operation."

"Check. Out."

It rained for two hours on Wednesday night, and most of the two person teams' calls were laced with invectives against the vicissitudes. Morale stayed high despite or perhaps because of the venting provided by the good-natured griping. The Team, as a whole, was primed for action; and the rain only made them the more determined. To a man or woman, they believed in the righteousness of the raid; Randolph Armstrong Kennedy was a dangerous man who was intent on bringing down the fundamental freedoms of Americans, and the FBG members—as represented by this Action Response Team—were the designated representatives of America. The man had to be stopped once and for all.

There was a drizzle for five hours on Thursday. Not a rain, more like a heavy mist. As the soggy hours dragged on, the reports became more full of gripes with less joking about the inclemency.

"They're getting edgy," Bailey said after one reporting session. "We need action."

"And we could do without this rotten rain," muttered Drake. "Only good thing about it is that it is a lot harder to see us in this fog than it would be in the clear. Works for us, I guess; but I hope it clears before we have to go in. It's a mess trying to slog into a house with six inches of slick mud on your boots holding a slippery gun. Can't see decent either in this kind of muck."

He was not sure if Bailey even heard him. He was just passing the time anyway.

Bailey—from his vantage point—was the first to spot the small caravan of trucks that pulled into the entrance road late Thursday afternoon. The hunters moved right along. They were obviously determined to get in without delay. They were boisterous, probably drunk.

"Heads up," he squawked into the mike with the all-channels button on. "Enemies on the way in."

He turned to Drake, "Want to engage?"

"Don't be a jerk," Drake snapped.

Sometimes he wondered how Bailey got his shoes tied in the morning.

"The bunch of them won't stay. Watch."

The hunters had spent Thursday driving home in the rain over slick roads and delivering meat to their respective houses or to the local meat markets for butchering. It was well after six before Randolph and the other two truck loads of men drove to his house and hauled his meat and gear inside. The Militiamen helped their commander put his meat in the freezer.

"Devlin was right; no more feds, that's a nice small favor," Randolph said to himself.

The other five hunters left immediately to attend to all the chores and honey-dos that they had neglected until reality—i.e. life beyond hunting— intruded back into their lives. They had all had enough male bonding.

Randolph did his routine round of checks on his alarm system and the ready availability of his weapons, made sure that the entrances and exits of his house and especially his basement were secured, and got himself ready for bed. Dick and Steve were good troopers. They had missed the hunt and had done a good job of getting rid of the incriminating evidence. There was no trace that gun crates had ever been in the house. The basement was as tidy as he had left it, except that a Disney video had been left out on the coffee table. It seemed to give such a touch of innocence to the stark room that Randolph decided to leave the video where it lay. It reminded him of Annie, and he had a twinge of sadness when he looked at it. The video itself was probably a holdover from the small film library that he and Irene had maintained for their little girl. The nostalgic thought tugged briefly at his emotions before he went to sleep.

CHAPTER TWENTY-FOUR

"Signal Wasilla," Drake ordered Bailey as soon as the last truck load of hunters cleared Kennedy's property line.

The line opened.

Bailey said, "Bogeyman is back. Alone. Don't think he sighted officers. Over."

"Two-hour reporting schedule until kickoff, then as needed. Over," Quatraine reminded Bailey.

Bailey informed the dispersed teams of the perp's status. Their spirits were immeasurably buoyed up at the prospect of getting moving. Together, he and Drake went over the map dotted with pushpins marking the two-person teams' locations.

"A little skimpy on the far side, boss. Want to shuffle a couple of teams back there?"

"Naw," replied Drake. "I'd rather concentrate our force on a frontal assault and count on full surprise. He won't be getting out the back."

He smiled knowingly at Bailey. Bailey acknowledged the implication with a nod.

"No question he's in there. I saw every face that came out. He's in his house," said Drake, over the closed line to Heaps as much to reassure himself as to communicate to Bailey and Heaps.

"That's a true fact, boss. I made sure of that, too. He never came out. We have him. The raid'll be an anti-climax," Heaps responded to Drake's message.

"Ya know, this thing is planned so well—and the perp is so important—I wouldn't be at all surprised if what we do here didn't become a study at the academy," Bailey said earnestly.

"Flattery will get you everywhere," Drake thought, but he was pleased with his young partner's enthusiasm.

From Wasilla, Quatraine called Washington. He spoke directly to DATF Holdaway.

"Quatraine here. Sorry to call you so late, but the field team has Kennedy surrounded in his house. Every evidence is that the goods are still there."

It was pro forma, but Quatraine had to ask, "How do you want to proceed?"

"What's the situation look like? Is the guy armed like a small army as everybody says? Is he alone?" responded the DATF.

"He's undoubtedly heavily armed, but every indication is that he's alone. None of us has tried talking to him. That would be too novel of an idea," said Quatraine, the irony showing through more than he intended.

"The sarcasm is noted, Agent Quatraine. Despite that, I still believe in letting the field agent have his head. Drake can handle it. He's a good head. I do have an order. It's one none of you are going to like. Comes down to us mortals from the politicals on high. A *Washington Post* and a *New York Times* reporter have arrived in Wasilla. Vantassa wants them embedded with the troops to cover the scene. It was a compromise—those two getting the play-by-play or an army of undisciplined reporters. Somehow hints of this leaked out, and the media sharks are ready for a feeding frenzy."

"You've got to be kidding!"

"Nope. And you have to be nice to them. And, Quatraine..."

"Yes?"

"You will be serving your country in someplace like Heber, Utah, population 2000 if one of those two reporters so much as breaks a finger nail. Orders from the exalteds' offices."

"Where is that?"

"What?"

"Heber?"

"You got my point? Good," said Holdaway. "Now, go pick those two civilians up at the courthouse and take them to your HQ. They have instructions to stay there and wait. I don't want them doing their own poking around. And, Quatraine, give them a good song-and-dance, dog-and-pony show while you tell them next to noting. Think you can handle that?"

"Aye-aye, sir. But with prejudice," Quatraine said briskly.

"That's the old ATF spirit. My best to the boys and girls in the trenches. Keep me informed."

"*Great,*" muttered Quatraine as he hung up on the director. "That's what we need, a couple of nosy reporters to coddle. Drake'll have a fit. As an afterthought, he smiled and said aloud, "*So, it can't be all bad.*"

Then he anguished for a few moments about the next call. Ethics was a strange and inconvenient business when the situation is part of the real world and not a class exercise. It was ordinary ethics—even morality—to let the intended "presumed innocent" victim know that he was marked, to try in some small way to help him protect himself.

If he were a truly brave man, Quatraine knew that the logical extension of that argument was to stop the raid and protect the man for real. He had the authority to do that. But Oliver knew that he wasn't that kind of personal career destroying brave. He was an organization man. He knew what would happen to him if he interfered overtly. So—in his abbreviated scenario—he would do the right thing and be a semi-traitor to his organization; but he would do it from an undetected place. Or, he could elect not to call at all and be the good team player he was expected to be. He could let that criminal—Kennedy—get what he no doubt really had coming to him; and no one would ever be the wiser. Be a traitor to Kennedy. It was the moral equivalent of shinnying across a razor blade.

He looked up Randolph Kennedy again in the white pages. He hurried out to the phone booth, put in fifty cents for a local, less-than-three minute call, and dialed quickly before he changed his mind. Oliver looked about furtively to be certain—absolutely certain—that he was not being observed. The phone rang three times.

"Hello," came a tired voice.

"You don't know me, and you don't need to," Quatraine said rapidly and curtly.

He was angry with himself and the situation, but all Kennedy could know on the other end of the line was that his caller was angry.

"What do you want?" Randolph asked irritably.

He had been asleep, and this sounded like a crank call. He was about to hang up.

"Shut up and listen," said the ATF agent quickly and sharply.

He had to get this over with.

"Your place is going to be attacked tonight. Soon. And by real serious people. Get out of there if you can or hide…whatever."

"Who is this?" Randolph insisted, now wide awake.

"Never mind. Just listen. The people who are coming are going to kill you, even if you surrender. Don't give them a chance to see you or to get anywhere near you. Get out of there and hide someplace."

Click.

The line went dead.

Quatraine put down the receiver and walked as fast as he could back to the headquarters without drawing unwanted attention to himself. He went to the communications room, put on his suit jacket, and headed for the court house. The two reporters he was supposed to pick up stood out like beacon lights.

The *Washington Post* reporter was a lanky, tousle-headed tweedy sort, a truly homely man whose clothes looked as if he had deliberately mismatched colors and patterns and sizes. His face was pocked with old acne scars, and he had an asymmetrical pugilist's nose. The *New York Times* reporter was the diametric opposite—a tall, leggy, buxom blond woman of thirty who seemed confined into a close fitting suit and beige blouse, all coordinated and precise. She had an icily handsome high cheek boned Norwegian face without a trace of nonsense or intentional femininity about it. Her eyes were intense and curious, ice berg blue. She had a slightly *retroussé* nose, and if she wore any makeup, Quatraine could not see it.

Every other person in the open vestibule of the court house's first floor was dressed casually in denims, boots, plaids, or brush popper shirts. Their hair was long; they had scruffy beards; and they were loud. The two reporters looked every bit like city people and as out of place as Barbie and Ken in Dog Patch.

Quatraine strode directly to where the two reporters were standing and making idle conversation. They watched him with practiced observant eyes as he came towards them.

"Hello," he said, and stretched out his hand to shake that of the woman first. "I am Oliver Quatraine, Agent of the Bureau of Alcohol, Tobacco, and Firearms."

He shook her hand—a cool, firm hand—and opened his credential wallet for them to see.

The man extended his hand as well, and Quatraine shook it. He showed the second reporter his cred-pack.

Brocklin Phelps, *Washington Post,*" the reporter said.

"Gwen Chambers, *New York Times*," the woman offered, more crisply.

The two reporters proffered their business cards and exchanged them for one of Oliver's.

"*She's a cold one,*" Quatraine thought, but it was none of his concern. "Shall we go?" he said.

"How did you know that we were the reporters?" Phelps asked with a growing twinkle in his eye.

Quatraine nodded his head to indicate the locals all around the large room. They all laughed at the unspoken comparison.

In the car Oliver explained the rules of embedment for them vis-à-vis the federal agents in the assault team. They offered perfunctory protests, but they were there with mandates of exclusivity only because they had agreed to the rules beforehand. Quatrain's recitation of the rules came as no surprise. It was suppression of the press—and they knew it—but it was better than nothing. Both reporters reluctantly voiced their willingness to comply.

Quatraine ensconced the reporters in the two most comfortable chairs in the temporary headquarters building, which was not saying much. He left them to their own entertainment and went to call Drake. He could not put off this call much as he wished not to make it.

Jack Bailey answered.

"Command."

"Get me Drake It's important," Quatraine said in a flat voice.

"It better be. We're just about to start up the cavalry."

"Just get him and stand back a few feet from the receiver," Quatraine said mirthlessly.

"One of those kind of things, huh? I'll get the man."

Jack was gone for three minutes. He was out of breath when he returned to the line.

"Quatraine?"

"I'm still here."

"Henry'll be here in a minute. Everything all right down there?"

"In a manner of speaking. How about with you guys?"

"We're in good shape, ready to go. Don't tell me you have a stop order," Jack pled.

"Okay, Jack, I won't tell you."

Neither man said anything for several minutes. Then Henry Drake's rough voice came on.

"What is it, Quatraine? We're a bit busy up here."

It suited Quatraine to speak exasperatingly slowly. He effected a black Southerner's drawl.

"And ya'll are goin' ta get a heap busier, Agent Drake."

He could hear Drake breathing into his end of the line.

"Ah have a surprise foah y'all

"Get on with it, Quatraine. Quit with the hillbilly crap."

"There are two reporters here in the office that are going to be where you are *before* you go in, compliments of the Director of Alcohol, Tobacco, and Firearms, Roger Holdaway."

"You got to be kidding."

"Do I sound like I'm kidding? And incidentally, I used exactly the same words when DATF gave me the orders."

"Does he have a wild hair stuck up somewhere?"

"I am given to understand that it is not his idea. Definitely not. Two ladies in positions superior to his nibs have sent down the official decree."

Drake's voice became quiet. Then, for one and a half minutes he cursed, never uttering the same profane or obscene or scatological phrase twice. Evidently, it made the man feel better. Quatraine certainly did; he was laughing until tears ran down his cheeks.

When it seemed that Drake had finished rhapsodizing, Quatraine ventured to speak again.

"Hearing how much it pleases you, I will bring the two purveyors of truth out to you. Have somebody on the road. I don't suppose it would do to drive up the driveway at this particular time."

"I don't suppose so. What am I expected to do with these civvies? Can you answer me that, *Mister* Quatraine?"

"Indeed, I can. You are ordered by the WOMs not to get them killed, maimed, injured in the slightest, frightened, or offended. Not so much as a scratch or being subject to harsh words. That order was put through by himself, the director."

"So, I'm supposed to nursemaid them, like I don't have anything else to do out here in the wilderness. You can call Holdaway and tell him where he can put the next idea he gets that compares to this dud."

He slammed down his receiver.

Oliver said, to no one in particular, "*That was worth the rest of the day's aggravation. Who said cop work can't be fun?*"

He was in a much improved mood all the way out to the turnoff into the Kennedy place. Jack Bailey emerged out of the cover of nearby trees to assume control. He was as sweet as saccharine to the pair of reporters, but the bitter aftertaste was not lost on them. Quatraine turned around and headed back to Wasilla, glad to be quit of the scene of impending action. He felt a little cleaner that way.

As soon as Randolph put down his phone from the mysterious caller, he became wide awake and galvanized into action. He thought—as never before about his defenses—about how alone he was. If it was a crank call intended to rattle him, the caller was fully successful. Randolph took several deep breaths and forced himself to calm down and to think rationally. He could feel fear oozing out onto his skin. His brow was damp with it. His mouth was dry.

He knew that his stashes of house protection guns were intact—loaded and with chambered rounds—and all of them were off safety. He had plenty of ammunition for each weapon. Randolph knew instinctively that it was too dangerous to attempt to escape through the upper level doors or even out through the tunnel Even a successful escape at this time would only lead to a next time. He had to have a better plan. He wracked his brain as he sped about collecting his security and escape necessities. Maybe his mystery caller was setting him up to try to sneak out of his fortress and into a fusillade. If the mysterious caller was right, the hillside must be crawling with agents. He would fall into their hands. He hurried around the house from spot to spot where his traps waited to be set.

The stairway to the upper floor stood directly in front of the main entrance to the house. Randolph pulled down the shotgun from the stairwell and set it in its holder. It was trained neck high at the doorway. A trip wire was set so that when the front door opened wide, it would go off. At that range it would spread about four feet in diameter removing any organic matter that happened into its path.

Randolph went to the back door and removed a garland of hand grenades that sat in a kitchen cabinet drawer. He pulled the pins on them all and inserted a stay rod in their mechanisms to prevent them from going off prematurely. He very gingerly hung the deadly garland over the doorknob. He knew that a sudden jar of the door or the knob would jerk the stay rod loose, and ten feet of the back wall of his house would disappear, leaving a crater where the porch had once been six or eight feet deep. Anyone within fifty feet of the door would be haphazardly filleted into proteinaceous confetti. The booby trap setups brought to mind a vague sense of the Rube Goldberg; but he was sure that they would be effective, nonetheless.

He hung a second garland of grenades on the inside sill of his bedroom window on the second floor and camouflaged it with a nondescript piece of army blanket as covering. Twin shotguns were mounted on the sides of the only other upstairs window. An intruder who attempted to step into the room through the window would depress an inconspicuous net suspended a foot beneath the inside sill. When the full weight of the intruder pressed the net down, both shotguns would go off simultaneously, catching the intruder in a deadly crossfire. The effect would be to leave a vacant space nearly a cubic foot in volume where the intruder's legs joined his or her pelvis. He tripped the disabling switch to all of the lights in the house and carried a large MagLite to find his way.

During the period of building his house, Randolph had made up his mind to hold out in his basement bunker. He was no soldier and knew that he did not stand a chance against the small army that would burst into his house en masse and with overwhelming organization and firepower. He could do them a great deal of harm, but he was a realist. In the end, they would take him—or as the mystery caller had warned—they would kill him. His best hope was to lower the odds against him and create doubt and confusion among his enemies. In the confusion while the marauders were reeling from his unmanned traps, he hoped to be able to make his escape. That was the plan. He had his doubts, but he was sure that his life depended on making his plan work.

He looked anxiously out of his windows and saw no one. He hurriedly lifted up his hallway runner carpets and installed two Claymore antipersonnel mines in each hallway in depressions laid in the flooring during construction. There was no visible evidence of the Claymores' presence once the carpets were replaced. Randolph had been working for thirty-five minutes since he received the call and knew that if the information was correct, he was living on borrowed time and not much of it. He was sweating lightly, but the hurried pace of his work had proceeded according to plan, and the work had served to dissipate his previous anxiety and fear induced paralysis. He took one more rapid look out of every window. No one.

It occurred to him that—more likely than not—he was the victim of an elaborate hoax, and that all of these preparations were a waste of time and effort; or worse, made him look like a paranoid looney. At the very worst, he would blow himself up when he finally decided to dismantle his security weapons. Paranoia bordering on lunacy was the very impression that the majority of Americans had about the state militias.

His analytical mind won out. He decided that the consequences of his failing to prepare for an imminent small war far outweighed any minor inconvenience or feeling of embarrassment he might experience from a false alarm. He would be alive, and the caller would never know whether or not he had induced panic in the commander of the North Star State Militia. Maybe he could eventually have a quiet little laugh at himself.

What a disconnect all of this was from his life compared to two years ago before the Hopewell raid. How strange it would look to his old friends in Virginia and to his clients. He was an accountant—for heaven's sake—contented to be dull, methodical, colorless, nonviolent, nonconfrontational. Now he was planning to take on the United States government in armed conflict all by himself. How strange was that? How different from his real self? Maybe he *was* nuts. Maybe this was all a nightmare. However, he was awake, and his mind was functioning and when he considered the alternative that an impending armed attack was real; it spurred him to rapid and methodical action.

Randolph prodded himself into even faster and more thorough action. He could sit around and contemplate another day. He ran back up upstairs and turned the light on in his bed room. He found the control boxes and shut off the electricity for the rest of the house except the basement. Using his flashlight he made his way to the first floor bathroom and opened the trap door. He laid a Claymore mine under the rug in front of the shower then climbed down in to the bunker basement. He made sure that the trap door closed securely and virtually invisibly when he descended into the basement.

Randolph assisted his situation and plans thus far. As another level of security—and on the spur of the moment's paranoia—he suspended a concussion grenade immediately beneath the basement ceiling door, set to go off when the next person lifted the hatch. He would be able to disarm it with ease should the whole episode prove to be a pipe dream. He deeply hoped that it was a hoax, but the evidence told him that violence was about to strike the home he had come to love and which had cost him a small fortune. Until he knew for sure, he continued on with his preparations. He set up his last stand in the far corner of the basement. He had bullet-proof barriers that he purchased from a Fraternal Order of Police fund-raiser. His Kevlar helmet and body suit were close at hand along with a chemical protection mask and suit that fit under his helmet and over his clothing. The protective garb was too hot to put on except when it was certain that it was necessary. He examined his last stand weapons.

There were several layers of grenades stacked on the empty shelves of a small bookcase he had kept by his favorite easy chair. His principle weapon for the upcoming battle, if it transpired—if it penetrated into his bunker—was to be an Israeli Galil SAR carbine, the shorter version of their combat ARM assault rifle. It was his only out-and-out illegal weapon. He had chosen the weapon for its 35 round magazine and tremendous muzzle velocity—3,215 feet per second. He kept in reserve a Heckler & Koch MP5 that had once been made legal by removing the automatic firing mechanism. Devlin O'Herligy had taken the gun from Randolph and converted it back to its original deadly automatic status. Devlin called it a "Hockler".

"You never know when it might come in handy," Devlin had said at the time. He was right, you never know.

There six full boxes of ammunition for each gun—several thousand rounds.

Randolph had a web belt to which were attached holsters for a 9mm Parabellum Tokagypt Firebird pistol that had made it to Alaska by way of Europe, where a surplus had been created when the U.S. rescinded import licenses in the last push to expand the 1990s Brady bill into an all encompassing antigun action. It was not strictly illegal to have one because licensure could be defended under a grandfather clause. The other holster held a bulky .357 Magnum—a blockbuster that, like all other revolvers—was incapable of being put on safety. The guns were cleaned and oiled; the ammunition was at hand. Randolph's last preparatory duty was to lay Semtex charges all around his weapons cache in anticipation of going into the tunnel and disposing of all evidence in the bunker. He had a throwaway cell phone to close the circuit on the ignition apparatus.

He was ready—prepared to repel boarders—he told himself ruefully. He sat back and began to relax. He had been at his preparations for nearly and hour and fifteen minutes and nothing untoward had happened from the outside world. It was like waiting for lightening to strike in the same spot. His mind drifted to Irene and Annie while he sat in the semi-darkness. Waiting.

CHAPTER TWENTY-FIVE

"All right, people, listen up," Drake said on the open channel. "We go in at 0315. Synchronize."

He waited a few seconds for the agents to make any necessary chronometer adjustments. He had turned up the timetable by an hour and a half because of the arrival of the reporters. It would not do for them to snoop around and ask the wrong questions. Idle minds are the devil's workshop, especially tonight. He particularly did not want them to fumble around freely enough to find that precious white van and its trailer and to open questions about them.

"I figure we can all be outside the house at 0345; that should be enough time even for you, Rogers. Report in to me when you are in position. Get your artillery ready now. Remember, this one is a major gun supplier, and knows how to use every piece of ordnance you ever heard of. Be careful, people. Out."

Heaps wondered how Drake knew all that about Kennedy, how the perp was so adept with the use of firearms. It was more than he had learned in all the months he had been watching the man.

The crackling transmitters quickly grew silent. In ten minutes the Action Response Team would begin to move. Every man and woman on the line was glad to be doing something at last. Their muscles were cramped and sore, and their nerves were edgy from the overly long wait. They had not had enough sleep in the last several days in anticipation of this night which made it hard to focus. They were veterans and used to trying conditions. Once the action started, it would soon be over; and they could get back to Anchorage for steaks, beer, and soft beds. Their moods began to lighten even as they tensed for the beginning.

The ten minutes crept by at a nerve-wracking slug's pace. Gwen Chambers from the *Times* positioned herself next to Henry Drake because he was going to have the whole perspective of the operation. She wisely held her questions during this tense phase and won a grudging bit of acceptance from the team leader. Brocklin Phelps attached himself to Jack Bailey and pestered him with questions just to get him used to the presence of a reporter and to soften him into a habit of conveying information if only to damp down the chatter. Part of the reason that each of the two reporters had been chosen by their peers from the press pool was because of their opposite styles that—in combination—produced great results. This was especially the case when the two of them were reporting from the same place at the same time. At the insistence of Drake, the two reporters were burdened down with protective gear. Gwen found it hard to see because she was sweating inside her helmet and fogging the Kevlar lenses.

"Okay, Senior Agent Drake barked, startling everyone out of their sleepy reveries. "It's 0315. Let's go. It's a jungle out there. Watch your backs. Watch your partners' backs. Let's all go home safe. It's time to take this gangster down."

"Yeah!" and "hoo-ah" came the reply from fifteen listening posts.

The enthusiasm rattled across the air waves. Fifteen teams of two agents each began to move carefully but with dispatch up the hill towards Randolph Kennedy's arsenal of illegal guns and probably of drugs as well. In an hour they would carve another figurative notch on their gun butts, and another repository of evil would be removed from the ongoing competition. The green vision of their night goggles made the going easier, but the way was strewn with an unforgiving tangle of brambles. Thirty crusaders made their way towards the illegal arms storehouse. The only complainers at the sound of the go signal were the unlucky three men who drew short straws and had to stay behind with the trucks.

Jack Bailey slipped over to Henry Drake's side.

"You want to give me some kind of obvious signal when to go back and get the van?", he whispered.

"Yeah, if you are not around after we first blast our way in, I'll fire a flare. I want that thing brought up while there's still action and confusion up at the house."

"No fail, boss."

Drake turned to the reporter who was staying annoyingly close.

"Let's go. You follow me, Ms. Chambers."

She was definitely a Ms.

"Do not let yourself get out of sight of me. And no matter what, you keep away from the action zone. No closer than the edge of the perp's lawn. I think Agent Bailey filled you in on the type of criminal we are up against. We don't want violence; but frankly, I don't think he is amenable to any kind of civilized discourse. We will go in unannounced and get control of him, then you can come in if you want. I think there's going to be shooting; so, wait for my signal."

"All right," Gwen said quietly.

She was not altogether keen on being in the first line entering the house. She hated to admit it, but she was getting scared.

Drake knew her type. She thought he was all macho and no brains—that she was a civilian not under his orders—and was probably going to do what she pleased anyway. It was how she did her work, he presumed. As they had been waiting, he had her know that this Kennedy guy was the John Dillinger, Pretty Boy Floyd, and the Symbionese Liberation Army of the twenty-first century. She would turn to mush when the shooting started and would be glad to have every protection afforded by his small army.

Bailey conveyed the same message to his reporter tail. Phelps agreed out loud although Bailey distrusted him. Bailey was convinced that the reporter would try to take advantage of the upcoming confusion to get inside with his camcorder and tape the action while it was still taking place. Bailey made a mental note to prevent that eventuality when the time finally came.

The four of them started up the road, keeping well behind the vanguard. Drake had Bailey call Quatraine back in Wasilla to let him know that they were underway. It was up to Quatraine to let the Wasilla PD and the Alaska state troopers know.

The waiting was getting on Randolph's nerves. He had been tired and muscle sore when he went to bed, had been awakened out of a deep sleep by his mysterious caller, and he had enjoyed a powerful adrenaline rush. That was fading away rapidly, leaving him fighting an insistent need to sleep. The telephone rang. It was so incongruous with the tense situation that Randolph felt a sudden violent rush of hot excitement course through him. He stared at the telephone uncomprehendingly at first.

It rang again. This time it seemed intrusive. Randolph picked up the receiver. He did not speak.

"Do you know who this is?" came the distant whispered voice.

It was Alex Tolberg of the Wasilla PD.

'Um hmmh."

"Never mind saying anything. Your place is going to be attacked in a matter of minutes. You are surrounded. I don't think they mean to take any prisoners from what I could read between the lines. I got a call about half a minute ago. Protect yourself—and good luck—brother. I'll do what I can."

The line clicked dead.

Two calls. He trusted Alex. The Wasilla police sergeant must have taken a terrible risk to warn him. No mistake. He had to believe that they were coming. He tensed—wide awake, acutely ready. Frightened. His bladder felt loose.

He strained himself to hear anything coming from the outside through his barred basement gun ports. Nothing.

Bailey called Drake from ten feet away.

"Six units in place in the brush by the lawn. No one in front or on the north yet. We have three casualties. They got zapped by a high voltage electric perimeter fence; one dead—Sam Wellsely—the other two will be all right, but they're out of commission for the rest of this party. They got some pretty nasty burns. We underestimated this Kennedy guy. Put out the word to be extra careful. Who knows what else he's got going for him. Over."

"Keep me posted. Out."

No emotions for the downed officers. Drake was overwhelmingly excited. He had been waiting for this moment for two years. He could hardly contain the testosterone rush that was surging through his veins. The loss of three agents was a nuisance, but this was a war.

"Are you going to announce yourselves, Agent Drake?" Gwen Chambers asked in a low, husky voice.

Drake jumped at the unexpected voice practically in his ear.

"Geez, lady, don't you know when to shut up? I do the cop work; you write about it. This isn't the time or the place for a chat. Just follow me."

It stung like a slap in the face. Gwen flushed involuntarily. She gritted her teeth to hold back a retort to the unnecessary bit of nastiness from the arrogant chauvinist throwback. It would take real effort not to cast this guy as a thug in uniform when she filed her piece to the *Times*.

Then, coming from a quarter of a mile away, she heard a blood chilling scream of agony.

Sitting in the darkness of his basement cradling his Galil SAR, sweating and straining his ears, Randolph heard the unmistakable sound of a man screaming. The horrific cries went on for several minutes. Like nothing before in this entire surrealistic scenario, that sound brought reality to center stage. Randolph felt blood surge behind his eyes. Pure animal instincts were flooding him.

Bill Slider had been walking up the hill, moving quietly around downed branches and ensnaring clumps of willows. It was a warm moonlit night, and he was enjoying being out of doors and on the move. He was an inveterate backpacker in his spare time. He jumped over a large rotting tree trunk. The full weight of his heavy muscular body landed on the opposite side of the trunk. With sudden exhilaration, Slider felt himself shoot straight down into the ground feet first. Branches snapped beneath him. Before his mind could question what was happening, he felt a searing pain in his feet. He glanced down and saw, to his unspeakable horror, a large spike growing out of the top of each shoe. The pain was both excruciating and terrifying. He began to scream involuntarily, a primeval sound. He could not dislodge his feet. He thought it was the worst pain he could imagine. Then he lost his balance and fell backwards, tearing his feet to shreds and impaled his buttocks and scrotum on still more of the vicious spikes. Now, he *knew* the worst pain that could be imagined. He began screaming like a pig being slowly slaughtered until he mercifully blacked out five minutes later.

"What was that?" Gwen quavered. "What on earth happened?"

She felt faint, so sick that she did not care if anyone could see it in her face.

Drake cringed. He banged on the squawker on his phone.

"What was that?" he demanded of Bailey.

"Dunno. Maybe a booby trap. I'll check."

As if the first terrible sounds coming in the dark were not enough, another hideous scream, a woman's voice. This screaming came from below them. It had a gurgling character to it. It was short-lived.

Agent Mary O'Leary had turned to look in the direction of the man's terrible screams and was still looking when the ground gave way under her feet. She pitched forward and impaled her right groin on a punji stick. She screamed when she saw the gouts of blood pumping and spurting around the huge spike sticking in her femoral triangle. O'Leary was a bull fighting aficionado who had seen both men and women gored in the groin in the rings of Mexico. Her last thought was that she had been gored. She lost all muscle strength, fell forward facedown, and drove a spike through her eye and into her brain. Another spike punctured her left lung. Her last sound before dying was a brief, high pitched, gurgling scream.

Gwen and Henry both swiveled their heads in the direction of the latest outcry. The silence that now prevailed was almost worse. They could only imagine the degree of tragedy. Drake pounded on his telephone, opening all channels to all units.

"Booby traps!" he yelled. "Use a walking stick. Step lightly. Might be mined!"

Another heart-rending scream issued from a point no more than fifteen yards to their right.

"He's killing us all!" Drake shouted. "I am going to see Kennedy on a slab if it's the last thing I do!"

His voice was wild, murderous. Gwen Chambers cringed in the face of such hatred. She had descended into the ninth circle of hell.

Drake detoured in the direction of the nearest and most recent screams that had now degenerated into guttural mewling. He broke his own rules when he got to the edge of an opening in the earth. He shined his Mag-Lite into the depths of the hole. Gwen Chambers leaned against the agent's hard shoulder and peered in with him. Instantly, she wished she hadn't. Kurt Erickson lay face up, spread-eagled on the floor of a bed of spikes held upright in cement.

He was struggling feebly with his right hand to extract the point of a spike that was showing through the middle of his lower abdomen just above the pubis. Blood and urine were spreading over his shirt and pants. His right arm and both legs were pinned to the cement floor by spikes; there were two spikes in his left leg. Another spike had grazed a deep cut on the right side of his neck. He was pale white from blood loss, as pallid as the victim of a vampire attack. He emitted pitiful little weeping sounds, much like a little girl's cry. Gwen vomited over the edge of the pit, totally unexpectedly, and spattered the unfortunate victim.

"Thanks, jerk," snapped Drake, beyond any control of civility.

Gwen tried to speak, to apologize, but the burning bile and vomitus choked off sound. She retched again, this time spilling the remaining contents of her stomach on the ground. Dan Kupfurer, Erickson's partner, looked in at his friend writhing in agony and involuntarily emptied his bladder in his pants. He looked down at the spreading black stain with surprise and consternation.

Drake realized that something had to be done to salvage the operation. He opened the telephone channels and barked a general order.

"Everyone not at the house stop where you are; turn around and retrace your steps. We'll all go up the road. No exceptions."

It was 0345. In half an hour there were at least two dead and four severely wounded out of an ATF Action Response Team of thirty. They had not so much as laid eyes on their criminal quarry, and twenty percent of the force was out of commission. It was evident that if they continued in the direction they were taking, the unit would be decimated. This operation was turning into a spherical disaster—a catastrophe no matter which way you looked at it. Drake's worst imaginations and fears were being realized.

"This is not going to happen!" he screamed out into the night.

At ten to four in the morning, Randolph heard one more terrible scream and knew that his punji stake trap had claimed one more of his enemies. He could not be glad about it. He held to the Judeo-Christian concepts of mercy and kindness and the sanctity of life. But he had not brought this on. The lost men and women had only fallen victim to their own unprovoked attack. He could not bring himself to feel particularly badly about it. He envisioned his dead wife, Irene, and their baby, Annette. These were the same monsters who had done that. Randolph gripped his gun stock and steeled himself against the weakening feelings of compassion for his fellow men. He knew that he had crossed a personal Rubicon, and he would never be able to come back.

Drake sent two teams to bring in the wounded and dead if they could find them. He authorized the use of lights. The element of surprise had been severely compromised anyway. They came back with Mary O'Leary and

Jensen Roylance's bodies and badly wounded Kurt Erickson and Bill Slider on stretchers. The two survivors were more dead than alive. Morale was at a nadir for the completely shaken remainder of the Action Response Team.

Drake dispatched two of the trucks to take the wounded into Wasilla. He called Quatraine, explained the dire circumstances in the field, and requested back-up. Quatraine called the FBI and asked for the DEST—Domestic Emergency Support Team—counterterrorism officers. Then Drake called 911 and arranged for ambulances to bring in the other agents wounded earlier on the electrified fence. He had Allen Heaps and Terry Perrency set the three bodies under blankets in a grove of trees where he hoped it would stay shady if this pathetic disaster of a raid continued into the daylight hours.

Wasilla PD sent three units to the scene; it took ten minutes. They had been waiting at the junction of Highway 3 and the county road that led to the turnoff into Kennedy's land. They had been in place to prevent any escapee from coming back down the road toward Wasilla. Oliver Quatraine came behind them, and shortly two highway patrol units pulled in as well. It looked like a circus with the intermingled dancing lights of the police vehicles adding to the noise and confusion. Drake moaned to himself.

Gwen Chambers watched the team leader crumbling. Drake could see her growing distrust of his management; he was sure she was making mental notes about the escalating disaster and his part in it. Drake knew he was becoming paranoid. There was nothing he could do about her opinion; she could write what she wanted. He only hoped that she could develop her own powerful emotion of hate for the criminal terrorist locked up there in the house laughing at them. Only then could she understand what moved those violent men arrayed against him and tailor her article accordingly.

Brocklin Phelps walked up to her.

"Gwen," he said, "I'm sorry for what you saw. It was terrible. We haven't had a real war for quite a while; so, none of us is a combat reporter. I'm not altogether up to it myself."

She searched his face for signs of male chauvinistic condescension. There were none. He was quite open and genuine.

"Thanks, Brocklin. I guess my distress shows. Not very professional, huh?"

"Join the club, Gwen—the human club. Look, we still have business to do. My guy, Agent Bailey, tells me they are ready to go up again. They're going to go straight up the road and attack in force, no more attempt at surprise. One of us has to stay down here and find out what everybody else is doing and thinking. We need to be split into two clones each, but since that's not going to happen, I'll flip you for who goes, and who stays."

Gwen looked wan and done in. She knew her limits.

"You know, Brocklin, I wouldn't want this to get out; but if you would take the attack part and leave me here, I would be most grateful."

Brocklin knew that Gwen had made a wrenching admission. He respected her candor and had no intention of betraying her or humiliating her. For all her apparent toughness and professionalism, Gwen Chambers was a sensitive girl.

"Okay, partner, keep your eyes and ears open."

The signal went out. A complement of forty able-bodied officers from several jurisdictions and departments swept up the road behind Oliver Quatraine, who had officially wrenched control of the operation from Drake and earned the volatile agent's undying enmity. There were no casualties in the approach to the house. In ten minutes Quatraine had all forces lined up and surrounding the entire house.

In the bunker basement, Randolph could hear the occasional soft crunch of footfalls on gravel. It was now 0440 and was becoming as light out as early morning in the lower forty-eight.

A remarkable display of firepower bristled around the man's home. Quatraine was constantly on the phone with one unit or another. He wanted to saturate the entrances with an all-out overwhelming attack so that Kennedy would not have time to respond to any one threat. That way, Quatraine hoped to be able to stun Kennedy into submission without having to kill him or to have his own Response Team suffer any further casualties.

Drake walked up to Quatraine, accompanied by Jack Bailey, and announced bellicosely, "I'm going in the front door. You can't keep me out of the action."

Quatraine saw the almost boyish earnestness in Drake's face for all of its overt pugnacity.

"Sure," he said disarmingly, ignoring all of Drake's bombast.

"Thanks," said a subdued Drake.

Quatraine allowed the two men time to take their places on either side of the door.

"Go!" Quatraine shouted into his phone. It was 0444.

In his place in the basement bunker—unsure of what was going on, only that he knew that a serious armed force was out there and after him—Randolph waited with mounting anxiety. He glanced at his watch. It was almost quarter to five. He wondered idly—probably more hopefully—if they would call the whole thing off now that it was daylight. He presumed that the ATF liked to carry out their work under cover of darkness.

With a sound like Gabriel's trump at the beginning of the battle of Armageddon, Randolph's world turned into an explosion. When his adrenaline permitted, he knew that the blast of the front door shotgun booby trap had fired. It was followed in a fraction of a second by simultaneous earth-rocking explosions from the rear and south side of the house, presumably from the grenade traps. The foundations of the house groaned, and he felt the ceiling of the basement fortress shudder. The cacophony lasted about three seconds before a few human noises could be distinguished. Outside the house he heard the shrieks of wounded and the cries of violently angry men shouting dozens of imprecations and frenzied orders.

He readied his Galil and sat in the darkness waiting for the inevitable attack down the basement stairs.

Upstairs, pandemonium reigned. Jack Bailey had knocked the front door off its hinges to lead the charge into the house. A shotgun blast blew his head off. His compatriots were spellbound by the horror of blood fountaining out of the stumps of his carotid arteries. Drake was liberally splashed with his partner's blood, but was otherwise unhurt. The man on Drake's right took a pellet in his left eye and dropped to the cement of the porch, both hands clutching his face. The FBI agent on Drake's left swept in and led the charge down the hallway, guns blazing. He set off the first of the Claymore mines, and the lower two-thirds of his body disintegrated into a bloody pulp. Drake felt the sensation of being stabbed by a hot knife under his Kevlar vest. In a fraction of a second, there was no more pain. He felt nothing below his navel. A piece of random shrapnel had sped through his abdomen nicking one fold of small intestine and lodging squarely in the terminus of his spinal cord at the level of the second lumbar vertebral body. He crumpled to the floor, bemused at the nothingness in his legs and genitalia. All he could feel was a growing wet spot in his shirt pocket where the vial of sodium fluoro acetate had been so carefully protected. It seemed so unfair.

Terry Perrency was the first man through the side door into the kitchen. He became part of an eight foot deep crater where the kitchen porch had been. A hole large enough to drive a semi truck through had taken the place of the door and the wall. The two men immediately behind Perrency were shredded into chunks, their protective attire having afforded no attenuation of the blast.

Alex Tolberg had volunteered to enter Randolph's house through the rear window opposite Tom Perrish, one of the state troopers. Alex wanted desperately to get to Randolph to save him if the faintest possibility still existed. He and the trooper burst into the upstairs bedrooms at the same moment and with the same lithe athleticism. Alex never heard the blast from the layered grenades beneath him, all exploding at once. His body flew like a man blasted from a cannon and hung akimbo from the branches of a handsome old fir tree in the backyard. The state trooper took a shotgun blast in the neck and was dead a half a second later without it ever registering in his brain that he had been hit. Agents, policemen, and troopers poured into the gaping holes in the walls of what was left of Randolph's house. Quatraine shouted for them to stay out of the hallways. They somehow heard him over the din and obeyed instantly. No more of them were hurt during the initial entrance. The dust and the debris stopped flying around, and an eerie terrible calm of indecision and bewilderment settled on the officers. All of that carnage, and still not the first sign of the terrorist.

The officers of the law all were beginning to have the sickening feeling that all of this may well have been for a building whose occupant was not there.

Quatraine walked sadly into the entryway of the house and surveyed the nearly unbelievable amount of damage. The walls were splotched with blood and pocked with blast holes.

"Drake, you did everything you could, everything anybody could have done. It's over for you. You're hurt, and we have to get you out of here. We'll get him. Mark my solemn oath on that."

"He's mine," Drake protested feebly, clawing at his impotent legs demanding that they respond.

Then he turned his head to the side, no longer able to face Quatraine.

"Medic!" shouted Quatraine.

The ambulance crew quickly and efficiently loaded Drake into a Wasilla Community Hospital ambulance along with three other wounded and wheeled out of the war zone.

Quatraine felt very much alone now that the full impact of his responsibility registered in his psyche. Before, he had had Drake who was the on site leader. Now he, Oliver Quatraine, was the man.

He turned to the ATF agent standing next to him, squinted at his name tag and ordered, "Jacobsen, you get Al Necco and organize two teams. Get the wounded collected and comfortable over there by the big pine east of the garage."

Jacobsen was glad to have something useful to do. He made a sharp about face and set out to find Agent Necco.

Quatraine felt ill and afraid. He knew he could not betray weakness now; so, he sucked it up, entered the cordite smoke filled house and personally walked into every room, terrified all the while of the possibility of another booby trap. ATF agents who had regained the ability to think and to react had torn up the hall rugs and had dismantled the remaining Claymores. Quatraine found nothing himself and organized teams to search the premises, what was left of them, for any sign of the terrorist or of any more traps.

"Everybody else out," he called. "We'll go back in when we have some better idea what's going on."

In the basement Randolph was sweltering in his protective clothing. He felt emotionally drained and physically exhausted. He had done nothing; but he was so tired, so spent from nervous exhaustion, that he knew that he would not be able to do anything effective against a force coming down into the basement after him. He figured that they must be furious over the injuries they had to have suffered. It was hard to think, hard to know what to do. He slapped himself in an effort to force his mind out of its torpor.

It was very quiet now. Nothing seemed to be happening. Randolph reached up and grabbed a bottle of water and a Diet Coke and downed them with great gulping swallows. He had been parched and realized that he was dehydrated. He had not been aware of the insensible water loss from all of his sweating under his gear. The fluids revived him. He could not even hear the sounds of people walking or of their voices from the outside or from the floors above him. He knew it was only a matter of time before the entrance to the basement was discovered, and he would be directly involved. They would kill him. He knew that with a clarity that bordered on the clairvoyant.

He got up and walked to his well-stocked refrigerator and took out another icy Diet Coke and chugged it down almost in one swallow. The double dose of caffeine hit him quickly, and he began to feel sharper. He realized that almost every asset the police forces in Alaska could muster was at his house. He had a flash of insight borne of desperation. It was very unlikely that anyone would be watching the exit of his tunnel a mile away. Maybe it was wishful thinking, but it was his only chance.

CHAPTER TWENTY-SIX

Gwen Chambers was furious with herself. Once she calmed down, she castigated herself for thinking and acting like a school girl and for allowing herself to miss out on one of the great stories of the decade. This was probably as near to a war that the nation would have the rest of this century, and she had wimped out on the story. Brocklin Phelps would do the right thing—and he would share with her—but she would always know that she had not had the right stuff. She kicked herself again for good measure. A man had gotten her story for her; that was the worst part. She imagined what Brocklin must be thinking about her down at the bottom of the hill swathed in a cocoon of safety. She was filled with self-loathing.

Gwen heard the series of dreadful explosions over a few seconds duration, then nothing. She started determinedly up the road but turned back, knowing that she would only get in the way now that the action was underway. That would be the worst cut of all, to be an impediment. She shook her head.

What an action it must be, her mind's eye constructed. The explosions had been like a major bomb going off. More than one bomb. She shuddered and had to admit that it was nice to be down here out of harm's way.

Gwen had a full bladder. She attributed it to nervousness, but it was insistent nonetheless. The men were all gone, and she could relieve herself without embarrassment now, whereas later it would be awkward. Maybe it was silly, but she had not yet become enough of a feminist to do it in front of men. Gwen walked off into the trees, getting deep enough into the copse so that no one would be able to see her.

She relieved herself and sighed with the pleasure of it. She looked to her right, saw something slab-walled, white, and curious, walked to it. She found a very large, very beat-up old Dodge Ram II van to which was attached a large semi-trailer partially covered with a blue tarp. The covering was out of place in the picture, being new. Odd place to park the thing, and an odd vehicle to have at this battle scene. She presumed the vehicle and trailer contained police equipment, and after a casual effort to open the doors failed, she moved on.

In his hiding place in the claustrophobic basement, Randolph made up his mind. It had not been three minutes since the last blast and flurry of activity. The cops had to be mulling around and reconnoitering up there. The last thing they would be thinking about would be points a mile away. He shrugged out of his protective gear and walked to the hidden tunnel entrance. He was now armed with two hand guns and an automatic rifle. He would be a formidable opponent, he thought. Then he laughed at his own hubris. The reality was, that outside of his little fortress, he would be nothing more than a target for the determined officers. Since he could not be invisible, his only chance was to look harmless or even to appear to be part of the hyperactive scene if he ran into witnesses. He reasoned that he could blend in and be relatively safe if he gave no provocation. That would be his back-up plan if he could not just sneak away. He did not feel altogether confident about his theory, but he concluded that he had to give it a try.

Randolph quickly shed all of his weapons. They would be incriminating evidence against him, and not enough to stave off a determined attack if he were spotted outside. Also, they were too heavy. He forced himself to think. He had booby-trapped the basement entry door with an antipersonnel mine. The rest of the ordnance might as well blow up with that expected blast. He set to work feverishly now. He hauled two ladders from the basement storeroom and laid the coffee table across their paint can platforms with its legs sticking up in the air like a dead cow. He hurriedly stacked all of the remaining grenades, guns, and ammunition on the under surface of the tabletop, taking care to avoid any noise or overburdening of the aluminum ladders. The lethal cache of explosives was now located a mere three feet from the mine attached to the trap door leading from his first floor bathroom into the basement. He very gingerly dangled a string of grenades from the door latch, undid the clips, and taped them; so, they would not go off until they were jarred. But then…he vividly envisioned the disintegration of his basement and the first floor of his house. There was a brief pang of regret for all of the work and expense that now counted for nothing. He also knew that even if he escaped, he would never be able to touch any of his own money, and it was most sobering to contemplate life as a fugitive and a penniless one at that. He shook himself to regain the immediacy of reality. All of those other concerns belonged to the past or to the future and were irrelevant for the here-and-now. Satisfied with his final preparations, he opened the exit door into the tunnel. He had done everything he could possibly do and stepped into the opening of the tunnel.

He entered the tunnel vestibule and turned on the row of ceiling lights near the entrance. He remembered to close and lock the huge door behind him with its large dead bolt system. To this he added two six by six oak crossbeams. It was cool, almost clammy in the tunnel in contrast to the cloying atmosphere of the basement. Air seemed sparse, but that was only an over working of his imagination due to his claustrophobia. He had made air shafts, and the quality of the air when he tested it was fine. He guessed that he should permit himself a few jitters. He trotted briskly down towards the end of the tunnel, lighting each battery operated lantern as he went.

Oliver Quatraine was in control now. The situation was clarifying. Ambulances were on the way for the wounded. For the time being, the injured officers were being treated in the garage. They had moved Kennedy's car out; so, they were sure that the terrorist was still inside somewhere, probably dead. When the search teams reported finding nothing in their search for the arms dealer or any more booby traps, Quatraine came to the conclusion that either there had to be a basement bunker arrangement—even though no one had seen so much as a trace of any entrance—or Kennedy had somehow escaped out of the back of his house before the onset of action. Or—maybe—he had left with his hunter friends; and the observers had missed his departure. That seemed most unlikely. Every evidence and cop's intuition indicated that he must still be there holed up in a bomb shelter.

A group of FBI agents gathered around him. It was amusing how the fibbies always want to take over and be in charge and to get all of the media attention and glory when it was a safe bet. Except this time. To a man, they were all more than happy to have Quatraine be the man in the heat of the spotlight. That little fact was a pithy statement on this raid.

"Lamar," he said, turning to the senior man from the Wasilla PD squad who was standing nearby, "You guys got a bomb squad?"

Lamar gave a prideful smile.

"Bet your booty, Oliver, my friend. What kinda rinky-dink outfit do you think we're running up here?"'

Oliver did not think he was a pot that was in any position to call any kettle black.

"Great. They have a chance to excel. Can you get them on the horn and bring get them here with everything they've got? I think our perp is holed up in a basement bunker. We are going to find the entrance, and we are going to protect ourselves from any kind of bomb he may have planted there. I suppose he's willing to go up in the explosion."

"Wilco," said Lamar, glad his department could make a real contribution.

The loss of Alex Tolberg was contribution enough, maybe, but Lamar wanted the Wasilla PD to be able to do something that would make Alex's death seem less of a waste. Maybe it was a little about vengeance. He gave a short salute and walked away to do his telephoning.

"I have a job for the FBI, if you would like to help some more, Oscar?" Oliver said to the lead special agent, SAC Oscar DeLentigo.

"Name it. We're here to help. We lost an agent, too. We've got a stake in this."

DeLentigo's mouth was set in a tense line.

"Thanks. Organize your DEST people and comb that house with the highest index of suspicion you can manage and find us an opening into a bomb shelter. There has to be one. It'll likely be booby trapped so leave it alone if or when you do come up with a likely prospect. I've got the Wasilla bomb squad on its way for when we do locate it."

"Okay. Wish us luck, Oliver. We don't need any more casualties."

"You got that right. Godspeed, Oscar: Godspeed."

The FBI agent nodded and went to gather and to instruct his Domestic Emergency Support Team.

Nick Scarlotti and Allen Heaps were the only two ATF Action Response Team members that Oliver knew personally who were still on the hill. He called them to him and gave them instructions.

"It's pretty decent light now. Scarlotti, I want you to take a team and disable the electric fences and check the perimeter and the grounds for any more booby traps. Remember about those pits. Get some evidence photos then blow them up. Allen remembers seeing our perp digging trenches with a backhoe but didn't know what was going on at the time. There are probably more. Let's find them and make this place safe for decent people to work around in."

It was 0550.

"Okay, boss. I'm on it."

He left and gathered ten assistants from the several different branches of law enforcement clustered about on the grounds doing nothing.

Quatraine then looked at Allen.

"Heaps, you get a team and go over the immediate grounds with a fine-toothed comb. I want anything that can be useful as evidence, and I want anything that looks like a hidden entrance to a bomb shelter anywhere near the house. Go out quarter of a mile if you have to. Any doubts in your mind that he might not still be here?"

"He's here. I'd bet my pension and the money I've saved for my kids' tuition on it. I just want to be the first one to find him. I want to have two minutes alone with him."

"I share your Sentiments; but, between you and me, that is the kind of thinking that got us where we are right now. We have got to get calm and to start acting like professionals. No more emotional overdrives. For one thing, this guy is not one for us to underestimate. He is as bad of an opponent as we've any of us seen. I somehow don't think it is over yet."

"You're right, boss, I didn't mean anything by that. Still, I am asking your authorization to be the first one into the bomb shelter. I owe the guys that much.

"You've got it, and no problem with my confidence in your profession-alism. Let's get on with it."

Quatraine liked Heap's new attitude; it was refreshing after all the belli-cosity of Drake and Bailey. He did not like to speak ill of the dead; but Bailey had been wrong; and Drake might well end up as a KIA whose own arrogance had lead to his downfall. How like Greek tragedy, he reflected.

Heaps set off to gather his team. In under a minute they were fanning out in two man teams and were beginning to inspect methodically every foot of ground around the battered house. They were working outward in concentric centrifugal circles.

"*Last but not least*," Quatraine said to himself, "*the necessities of life.*"

He called to an ATF agent who did not seem to have anything else to do and sent him off into town for food, tents, sleeping bags, and soda pop—the necessities. It was an acknowledgement that this was going to be a long term deal, more a siege than the slam-bam-thank-ya-ma'am affair that was originally envisioned.

Randolph cautiously peered out of the tunnel exit. As he had hoped, no one was in sight. It was quiet; the animals and birds had all gone to ground during the humans' war on the hilltop. He sidled out—keeping low—dressed in camo. He brought along a change of clothes to a regular casual street outfit. Before advancing further, he had a good long look around. It was clear; so, he made his way down the cliff side along the rock track with which he was familiar from dozens of previous ascents and descents. He looked about frantically for his old dump truck and realized that Steve Maloney and Dick Trentham must have been unable to return it because of the law enforcement presence. He fought back panic. He had to have a ride out of the area and soon. The feds would figure out that he had gotten away and would institute a dragnet. He simply had to find a vehicle. He fantasized about how valuable it would be if he could become the invisible man for the next hour or so.

He decided to be brave and began walking towards his entrance road. He heard a noise in the brush on the far side of the entrance road and froze. He looked hard in that direction and caught the glint of noonday sun on blond hair. It was an agent. She had her back to him, and her blue tee shirt had ATF embroidered on the back. She had to be part of the garrison guard. Randolph's mind raced. He could not go out through the woods on foot and hitchhike. He was going to have to use his wits, and he was going to have to do it right now.

He knew he would stand out in camo, but it would be worse in his dressy casual second outfit of clothes. He made up his mind and walked purposefully out of the trees. Gwen Chambers was standing in the road squinting in the direction of the house. The young woman actually seemed glad to see him, and she paid no attention to his clothing. He presumed she was waiting for some information about all the hullabaloo at the house.

"Hi," she said as he walked up to her.

"Hi, yourself. You holding down the fort?" he asked and smiled affably, presenting an infinitely more relaxed façade than his inner turmoil might have betrayed.

He sincerely hoped that his was an Oscar winning performance.

"Yup," she said, "the one and only at this point." She smiled. "Actually, I'm Gwen Chambers. I'm with the *New York Times*. Don't hold that against me."

"Uh…Glen…Glen Rogers," he stammered and mentally kicked himself. "Nice to meet you."

He extended his hand, and they shook. Randolph worked to control himself. She seemed to be buying his bona fides, even with the camo clothes.

"How come you're back down here? Are they done up there?" she asked casually.

"Not by a long shot. The terrorist is still at large. We'll get him though. Don't worry," he answered. "Oh, I was sent down to get some supplies in town. You know which one of these trucks I can use?"

"No idea. I suppose you can take any one with the keys in it."

He nodded.

"Okay. Nice talking to you. I have to run, or Drake will get on my tail… no pun intended."

He smiled sheepishly. She seemed to react favorably to his boyish bumbling. That was a plus.

Randolph made a hurried inspection of the ignition switches of the five trucks parked by the road. Every one of them had a key in the ignition which simplified matters.

Gwen was walking away, but turned back and asked, "Don't the white truck and trailer have what you need?"

"I dunno; nobody said anything about them."

"C'mon, I'll show you."

"Thanks."

A series of small explosions took place up at the house. Randolph knew they had not been part of his defense system; he figured the officers were blowing up his punji stake booby traps.

Gwen said, "I better go up a ways and be a reporter. Wonder what that was?"

Randolph shrugged. She smiled at him then turned and trotted in the general direction of the house. As she was leaving a truck pulled into the entrance driveway pulling a trailer with what looked like a black cement mixer on it. Randolph recognized the equipment as a mobile bomb ignition chamber. That further piqued Gwen's curiosity.

She called back, "Have a good time in town. I gotta get to work."

"You have a nice day," he called inanely, but at least she had been out of range of his voice.

He was alone. He was curious; so, he looked under the tarp covering the old van. He pulled open the rear doors and quickly inspected the contents.

There were an assortment of bags and boxes, and next in line were large bags of ammonium nitrate fertilizer.

"Fertilizer?" he asked himself.

Closer inspection revealed the larger bags to be filled with what looked at first glance like chopped alfalfa. He was not into the drug scene, but he was not so naïve as to be unable to make the obvious conclusion that he was looking at marijuana.

"Marijuana?" he asked out loud, incredulous.

He knew he had to hurry away, but now his curiosity was so strong that he had to know more. Anyway, he could not use this truck. He envisioned a fluke where a speed cop stopped his vehicle and burned him for having drugs. His whole plan would be dead.

"Why the drugs and why the fertilizer? He made the connection between the raid and the fertilizer. It had to be the makings of a bomb. Weird. Why bring this stuff up here? And why bring drugs? He began to get a sick feeling. Nobody was going to smoke pot, and nobody needed to make a crude bomb when they had the most sophisticated explosives money could by. They were going to frame him. His heart took a dive. He did not have a Chinaman's chance in the system. He almost bolted right then.

He pulled himself further into the back of the van and found the cache of guns and ammunition-crates and boxes of them. He recognized some of the names: Vz.58s, 9mm Parabellum Tokagypts, AK-47s, enough to conduct a small sustained war. Since it wasn't up at the house and did not look like regular governmental issue, Randolph made the 2 + 2 + 2 summation that this was the ATF version of a frame-up. It was more than elaborate; it would work.

The scales of his remaining illusions dropped from Randolph Kennedy's eyes presenting his opponent's plan in full cold relief. The government of the United States of America to which he had pledged his allegiance all of his life, the law enforcement agencies of his own country which had commanded his respect, the very institutions and people who had represented the law and stability and the repository of correct behavior had brought a truck load of false evidence to convict him wrongly. What had Alex Tolberg said? Something about them wanting him dead. That's what the mystery caller had said at the very first. He stifled a scream of outrage.

He had to think. He had to make sense, or he was going down. He was in a war, and he had to do better than his enemies, or he would not live out the day. At best, he would spend the rest of his days in a jail cell. He shuddered at either option.

Chapter Twenty-Six

He decided to look into the trailer. What more did they have in mind?

He opened the doors and saw stacks of New and Brite FAX Paper. It didn't make sense. He climbed up into the small space between the boxes and peered in towards the front of the trailer. He pushed the boxes aside. The sun was shining in and afforded enough light for him to make out the contents. To his consternation and amazement he made out pallets stacked high with money, millions and millions of dollars, if it was the real thing. He pushed himself forward and slit an opening in the shrink wrap on the nearest pallet. He struggled a little, but succeeded in pulling out a small handful of hundred dollar bills. It certainly looked like the real thing. It was a panicky feeling to be in the presence of so much money, even if some of it was counterfeit or even outright padding.

His mind quickly returned. He tore off his shirt and assiduously wiped off the boxes and the shrink wrap. He hurried out to do the same to the door handles on the van and the trailer. He sweated and wracked his brain. Were those the only places he had touched? He calmed down and decided that he had not put his hands anywhere else. He turned to run out of there, get in one of the black pickups, and put as much distance between himself and his former home, his former state, as he could do and as fast as he could possibly do it.

He trotted back to the line of trucks. Off to the side of the road was something he had not seen before. A row of blanket covered bodies. He got an idea. He ran to them, lifted each blanket and found one uniformed corpse that was near his size, maybe a little bigger. He clumsily stripped the body and himself and switched clothes. The shirt had dried blood and two jagged holes in it, but that would not be seen unless a cop leaned right into the cab of the truck he would be driving. He re-covered the body. Then he realized that the naked corpse would be an instant giveaway. He pushed himself to think. The only thing he could come up with was to hide the body and allow it to become part of the confusion. He dragged the corpse as quickly as he could, straining for all he was worth. He located the ancient rubbish pile left by the original owners and shoved the corpse under layers of old moose and elk hides, and an assortment of decaying organic matter. There was no sign of the body, and the eventual smell would not attract any attention because it would only mingle with the already almost overpowering scents emanating from the dump.

Time was wasting, and he knew that he had to get going. He bade himself calm down; he was just adding insurance, the cover-up he had to have to make his disappearance be a mystery and not just another step in his eventual capture.

He finished his trek to the trucks. They were identical, all black, all Fords, all with trailer hitches. Trailer hitches! A serendipitous idea took shape. He started up a Ford 380 dualie. Its powerful engine leaped into life. He backed up and headed to the trailer. He parked his truck, found a pair of leather driving gloves on the seat, put them on, wiped off the steering wheel, and got out. He got into the van and backed it up to where he could switch his truck for the van. He had no intention of taking the drugs and guns and getting caught with them. He would take his chances with the trailer full of money. He quickly set the park brake on the trailer and twirled the release lever to separate the van and the trailer. It was simple and quick. He drove the van further into the woods and parked it taking care not to touch anything in the van. He backed his Ford pick-up to the trailer tongue and attached it to the ball of the pick-up's trailer hitch. It was necessary to back up some distance into a clearing in order to negotiate the turn back to his entrance road.

Gwen Chambers, the attractive blond reporter, was standing on the gravel entrance road. She put up her hand in a traffic cop's stopping signal. Randolph paused at the verge of his road getting ready to run her down and to storm out onto the county road if necessary. He steeled himself. Then three trucks sped past, obviously on errands relating to the action on the hill. The drivers waved to him—the camaraderie of fellow officers—and Randolph waved back, an informal friendly salute. When the dust died down, he managed a dry swallow and pulled onto his road. He was trembling. The reporter had taken refuge from the passing dust in a clump of trees; she waved good-by to him as he pulled out towards the county road.

Just ahead of him, he saw the dust of the three trucks that had preceded him. He turned in the same direction, glad for the obscuration provided by the billowing dust. He had not yet had time to savor his *nouveau riche* status especially since it could easily prove to be a very short lived experience.

CHAPTER TWENTY-SEVEN

The bomb squad trucks pulled in front of the devastated house with their impressive array of equipment, every bit as modern as New York City's. The need for antiterrorist teams like the FBI's DEST, dangerous chemical units like the Energy Department's CEST, bomb squads, SWAT units, and intelligence departments was universal in the United States after the turn of the new millennium. The Arab and even home grown terrorists were everywhere—it seemed—and the battle against terrorist crime had become a war of attrition being fought in the cities and towns throughout the country. No place was too remote or too small to be safe, and Wasilla was no exception. Lamar Willets greeted the men from his department and introduced them to Oliver Quatraine and Allen Heaps.

"Glad to have you guys up here," Heaps said. "We've found a bunch of mines around the house. We were just lucky not to set them off. I think we have a big one waiting for us when we find Kennedy's basement or bomb shelter. FBI are looking now."

Allen Heaps and his team of agents had done a good job of finding the antipersonnel mines dug in around the near perimeter of the house. They had dug them out of the ground using the techniques from the military manual they brought along. Heaps had been pleased with his men and women and promised them a beer bust when this was all over. There had not been a single casualty. He was buoyed up at being able to make that report to Quatraine.

SAC Oscar DeLentigo came trotting out of the house. A few paces behind him followed his ASAC and their contingent of FBI agents. From the look on their faces, they also had a positive report. Two pieces of good news in one day; Quatraine did not know if his heart would hold up under the strain.

"Hey, Quatraine, we got good tidings. I am pretty sure we have your door to the basement. If not, this guy had funny ideas about how to build a bathroom floor. We need to get the bomb guys in there to have a look. Our agents treated the place like porcupines making love."

"Good, good work. I knew the fibbies could find the door if it was findable!" Quatraine said.

Things were finally beginning to look up.

"Look, Quatraine, I know you don't mean any offense, but we kinda don't like being called fibbies. It's a sort of derogatory term...mostly it's used by the criminal element. We don't have to be real formal out here; names are all right. I mean, you don't have to call us special agent exactly; but maybe you could kind of watch it."

"I knew you'd understand. All right, chief, the FBI stands ready for a new assignment."

"Okay, Oscar. Whey don't you clear everybody back from the house...well back. I'm going to send the bomb squad in. Hopefully, we can blow any booby traps and avoid casualties. Might be a big one. And I'm sorry if I offended your sensibilities. I meant the term 'fibbies' in a joking way, a means of lightening things up a bit and to get us to work together as friends."

DeLentigo nodded his okay.

"We'll do as you asked. One thing, Quatraine. Do you want to call in a warning to the perp first. Just thought I'd ask, sort of a pro forma gesture to him. It's your show all the way," DeLentigo said.

"*Thanks a million for dumping the whole mess on me,*" Quatraine thought. "*I only hope some small thing good comes of this fiasco; so, you sensitive fibbies can take credit when it comes to press time.*"

He hoped his sense of scorn did not show on his face.

He said out loud, "No, I think it's a little late in the day for niceties or daintiness. This is a war, and our side has taken fatal casualties. We'll just finish it like that."

"My sentiments exactly," said the SAC.

He set off to marshal the forces away from the site of the next potential explosion. The crowd of officers was so large by now that it took nearly forty-five minutes to clear everyone out of the immediate danger zone.

Quatraine spoke to the ATF agent standing nearby without anything to do.

"Hey, Agent..."

"Parker, Willard Parker. Were you calling me, sir?"

"Yes Parker, think you could round up Allen Heaps for me? The ATF has a role to play in the next few minutes."

"Sure will, sir. Give me a minute."

True to his word, Parker had Allen Heaps standing before their boss in almost exactly one minute.

"Present and accounted for, chief," barked Heaps in mock military fashion.

Quatraine wondered how anybody could be enthusiastic and jovial this late in the day. Still, he appreciated Heaps' unquestioning willingness. It was one less hassle in a long, nasty day.

"Heaps, I want you to get together the best guys we have for an assault on the basement. Maybe six total. Load 'em up with grenades, .357s or 9mms and three or four Model 870s. When the smoke clears after the bomb squad blows the door, I want you and your team to go get medals."

The implications were apparent to Heaps. He and his men got to be the heroes that dropped into the basement and faced the perp, if there was anything left of him to face. He determined to be the one carrying the Remington 870P shotgun. The ATF agents kept a supply of special short barreled Secret Service models with pistol grips and folding metal stocks as standard arms. It was a reliable street sweeper, and this was a street that needed swept.

"Okay, Mr. Quatraine, I'll get on it. We wait out here until after the blow?"

"Yeah. The whole floor of the house may go down. The whole house may implode for that matter. I don't want anybody more hurt. Between you and me—and just you and me—this is not exactly a prisoner taking exercise."

Quatraine was angry at Randolph Kennedy. The man had been warned to get out to save his life, and as repayment for Quatraine's generosity of forewarning him; the man had let the federal agents be murdered. It had been preventable, and now Kennedy had to pay.

"Gotcha there, boss. That is a thought that never crossed my mind."

He turned and left to select his team. In the confused milling about status of the law enforcement officers, it took nearly thirty minutes to round up the men he wanted.

Quatraine conferenced with Lamar Willets and the bomb squad sergeant, Harold Philips. The bomb squad organized itself and deployed into the house with all due caution. For twenty minutes there was silence from inside the house while Philips and his men and one woman examined the bathroom floor and convinced themselves that it was indeed most likely a trap door opening they were seeing. Philips came back out to Quatraine.

"Looks like an entrance," he announced. "No evidence of a device on the top side, but I am not going to take any chances on opening that door, even a crack, I want my guys and everybody else well away from the site, and we'll blow it with a remote crew-serving detonator. Sorry about messing up the evidence that might be down there. It'll be hot enough to melt cement. Can't be helped."

Quatraine agreed.

"Can't be helped. Let's get on with it."

Philips sent his second in command, Sandra Lakewood, to the squad truck for a box of fresh plastic explosives, fuses, blasting cord, and detonators. Two of his men strung wires from a crew-served detonator box and set up their position well into the woods. The crew laid a string of small charges all around the house to clear all of the land mines. Philips had Quatraine and his people back everyone else up two hundred yards away from the house. He went back in and supervised the placement of the packets of plastique all around the seams of the trap door and connected ribbons of the explosive clay to a central pocket of dynamite in the middle of the tiled door. Twenty more minutes elapsed. Quatraine thought he would go crazy with frustration at how long all of this was taking. He could only imagine the tension Kennedy must be under as he waited in his loneliness in the basement.

"You ready?" Philips asked Quatraine, DeLentigo, Willets, and Heaps.

"Let her blow," Quatraine said, speaking for everyone else.

Gwen Chambers thought it odd that the ATF agent was pulling the large van *away* from the site. She had to admit that there was a great deal she did not understand about this operation. She decided that she must be tired because she was focusing on trivia when the reportable action was on the hill. She turned to trudge up there and see what was happening.

Suddenly an explosion of fire and incredible noise blew smoke, debris, and flames two hundred feet into the air. Even in the wars she had covered, she had never seen an explosion of that magnitude. The effect was as if two or three 2000 pound bombs—maybe more—had gone off at once. The cataclysmic explosion caused the young reporter to take an involuntary step back and to cover her face. She was sure that the entire house was gone, and she worried that more officers might have been injured or killed. A searing thought gripped her: maybe all of the policemen and women had been killed. She instantly became a reporter again, threw out all of her idle fears and squeamishness, and ran up the road towards the action. This had to be the story of her lifetime. Maybe she would be the only one to tell it.

Randolph was at the crossroads when the explosion occurred. He reacted with a start. He turned and watched the entire hilltop blow—his house, two years of work, all of his possessions—gone in an instant. He felt the ground shudder beneath him like a minor earthquake. He presumed that the blast was from the improvised bomb of his making, and he had a pang of conscience that he may have been responsible for even more deaths of police officers. The blast seemed out of proportion to the ordnance he had planted, but he was no expert.

He snapped back out of the near trance the blast had caused in him. It was not a time for rumination. He had to get going. He had to think. It was clear that any remaining officers would soon know that he was not in the house; so, they would come to the realization that he had fled; and they would come after him in force.

His mind raced, and he came up with an idea for a delaying tactic. He stopped the truck, left it running and sprinted back to the other pick-ups. He jumped in the first one and drove it to the narrow portion of his road that was closely lined with trees on both sides. He stopped the vehicle against trees on the right side at right angles to the road. He jumped out and jammed his knife into all four tires. He ran back to the next truck and placed in against the trees on the left side, punctured all four tires, and repeated the effort with the remaining two trucks. The result was a barrier of all but immovable trucks completely blocking the only exit from the house to the county road. Only a tank could plow through the barricade. He was satisfied with his work, and now he had to get out of there. He knew that he was on borrowed time, and had no clear idea of how much head start he had given himself.

He pulled out onto Highway 3 and hurried away. The truck was powerful, even pulling the trailer, and he made good time. His main concern was to keep near the speed limit—the standard five miles over rule. It was a nervous strain to go at a speed that seemed so terribly slow to him. He wanted to put the truck into Mexican overdrive (throw all the Mexicans out). Going the speed limit was a strain on a human system already taxed near its limit.

The gas gauge read quarter full. Wouldn't it be his luck to have gone through all he had only to run out of gas in the middle of the highway where he would have to wait for the cops or try and run, an absurd option. He hated to have to take time to do it, but he pulled into the Mobil station at the busy Nancy Lakes campground. He filled the truck's large tank with 85 octane and automatically pulled out his VISA card to pay the young man in the store. He caught himself before making a stupid mistake. He was now in enough of a criminal frame of mind to recognize that the police would be tracing his credit cards. He also recognized that he had to keep his wits about him *all* of the time. He certainly had plenty of cash. He gave the pimply teenager a hundred dollar bill and received a fish eye back along with the change.

He moved smoothly through Wasilla on the Parks Highway paralleling the railroad as rapidly as he dared, past Jacobsen Lake, past the Alternative School, past both malls, and, with trepidation, past the city hall and the Police Department Building. He never saw a single law officer, and he presumed that every cop in the region had to be out at his place. He drove on out of town and down to Anchorage. He felt paranoid. He must have looked out of his rearview mirror three-quarters of the time he was driving, but he saw nothing to fuel his suspicions. As he drove, he thought. Plans came into his mind, were mulled over, modified, accepted or rejected. By the time he was in the heart of the capital city, he had a fairly cohesive plan in mind.

CHAPTER TWENTY-EIGHT

Gwen was a runner, lean and in superb physical condition. It felt good to exercise and to get sweaty after her nerve-wracking night and morning. She ran into the cleared area around Randolph's house, what was left of it. The grounds immediately adjacent to the house were changed to heaps of excavation, the obvious result of a string of explosive devices. The back and south end of the house were missing, just not there. Flames engulfed the remaining portion of the house, and it was apparent that the building would soon be reduced to a pile of charred rubble. She saw many officers standing and gazing at the inferno and was relieved that they had made it. She headed towards Quatraine whose dark mahogany face stood out from among the men around him. The other agents were drawing in towards the African-American agent eager to find out what was next on the agenda. There seemed to be an air of morbid fascination on the faces of the officers as they observed the destruction.

"Ms. Chambers," Quatraine said, "Getting your story?"

He had been unaware that she had been absent from the scene of action for several hours.

"Yes, sir, thank you. Any evidence for where Kennedy is now? I mean, did you find a body or anything?"

She looked up, presuming that the terrorist was somewhere up there in the mushroom of smoke that was slowly drifting south with the prevailing winds.

"Not yet. The Special Response Team is getting ready to go in now."

"In?"

"The basement. We think the terrorist may still be holed up in the basement. It looks like quite a sturdy structure pretty much separate from the house. Most of its roof—that doubled as the floor of the house—is still intact as incredible as that may seem. Only the center and northern part blew out. It is within the range of possibility that he could have survived down in there. We are getting ready for a potential firefight."

She looked around for a moment, then had a sudden fright.

"Where's Brocklin Phelps?

Quatraine gave her a blank look.

"The *Post* reporter."

"I know who," he said, "I just don't know where."

He shook his head. He was embarrassed to have forgotten about the guest who was supposed to be so well protected, whom he had been commissioned to protect. He had a sinking feeling.

"I'm sorry, Ms. Chambers; I've been busy and haven't seen him."

"He was with Agent Bailey."

"Bailey bought it," Quatraine said as gently as he could. "I thought you knew that."

"No," she said.

She was shaken. She looked down hardly daring to ask.

"And Phelps?" she managed.

"I guess we have to consider him unaccounted for—MIA—right now. I'll assign a couple of agents to help, and you can try and locate him. Please report back to me, if you would, Ms. Chambers."

"Yes, sir," said a much subdued Gwen Chambers.

She spoke briefly to a pair of ATF agents who were looking at the building. They were glad to have something constructive to do. The three of them set off in search of Brocklin Phelps.

Heaps led his team to the gaping hole in the cement floor where the trap door had once been. It was smoky pitch black down there.

"Nothing could have survived that blast," he said. "But play head's-up ball anyway."

He gestured to one of the agents, who sprang forward and dropped a nylon rope ladder into the depths of the basement. A second agent directed large halogen lights into the gloomy interior.

No shots were fired at the lights; that was a small but welcome sign.

"Let's go down," Heaps said. "Me first."

He descended the ladder, pausing occasionally to swing his shotgun in a 360 degree arc. No response came from the interior. He dropped onto the rubble-strewn floor and did a hurried visual check with his MagLite.

"Send down the lights," he called up to the men above.

Now there were three men in the basement. The lights were set up and illuminated most of the area, cutting through the muck in the air.

"Set up the machine guns," Heaps ordered, and the two agents sprang to the task.

Heaps waited a few more minutes. It was quiet except for the steady roar of the flames as they continued to eat away at the house's frame. The air was dusty and sooty. The walls were seared and coated with a fine dusting of greasy soot.

"The rest of you get down here," he called up to the remaining agents on his team.

They were all leaning into the hole in the basement's ceiling. At Heaps' command they descended rapidly.

"Careful of traps. Watch your every step. Two agents head to each corner. Report to me when you get there," Heaps ordered.

He and Jane Tankton manned the guns in the center of the large cement room, standing back to back and slowly revolving to detect the slightest hostile movement. The subterranean bunker's walls were homogeneous shiny grey-black from the melting heat except in the patches where the layer of soot did not adhere. They were pocked with myriad and variably sized blast cavities, but were entirely structurally sound. In the periphery of the room some furniture was still intact, remarkable as it seemed. It was remotely possible that a man could have survived the blast, Heaps had to admit reluctantly. The agent who was sent to the far south corner reported that everything was intact and unmarked there, and there was no sign of a perp living or dead.

"C'mon back," Heaps told the crew. "Anybody see anything that looked like a piece of a body?"

"Nothing," was the consensus.

"I found a gun stock and a plate that might have been part of a Claymore," one man offered.

Another agent volunteered that she had seen a twisted gun barrel and a pile of metal clips that looked like they had come from hand grenades and several brass casings, probably 5.56mm.

"No trip wires?"

The agents shook their heads. There were broken wires dangling like spider webs all around the room, especially from the ceiling. Nothing looked like it could be attached to a booby trap.

"Spread out at will. Let's give this place a combing," said Heaps. "And, Jane?"

"Yes, sir?"

"Go up and give Quatraine a preliminary report. Looks like a dud."

She scaled the flexible nylon ladder with strong lithe movements and was gone.

The agents scoured the room for twenty minutes and found nothing. The blast had melted the paint, wall coverings, and even the surface of the concrete effectively obliterating all traces of the seams where the tunnel doors abutted the walls. The doors themselves had been rendered inoperable for eternity. The uniformly blackened walls of the basement presented such a homogeneous surface that there was no suggestion of an outline of the door edges.

"Do it again," Heaps insisted over the groans of his teammates. "Look at every crevice in the walls. I want to see if there is an escape hatch we've missed."

"How James Bondy that would be," muttered one of the agents.

They all did what they were told, their personal opinions notwithstanding. The men and women methodically ran their fingers along the sooty walls probing for defects and did so with a high index of suspicion.

"Nary a sign, chief. How about we go back up into the world and get some clean air?" asked one of the agents, speaking for all the rest.

Heaps shook his head in defeat and pointed up at the hole in the ceiling above them. They hit the ladder and went out they way they had come in.

In what had once been the backyard of Randolph Kennedy's mountain retreat home, Gwen Chambers found portions of a charred notebook. Its cover contained remnants of writing: Brok...lps. Near the notebook, half submerged in rocks and dirt was a boot. Gwen asked one of the agents to look at the boot for her; she was just not up to it.

"Sorry, ma'am, there's a foot in it...wearing argyle socks."

Brocklin Phelps always wore argyle socks; it was one of his little trademarks. In town he wore blue serge suits and white shirts with a club tie. In rougher country he sometimes dressed down to the look of a tweed and plaid professor. Gwen wanted to cry. She knew it was his shoe and his foot. There was no immediate sign of the rest of him.

"What an awful day," she moaned. "And for what?"

It was intended rhetorically, but one of her helper agents responded.

"I don't know, ma'am. We have not found a single thing that could pass as evidence. We didn't see, let alone arrest or kill the terrorist, if he was ever even here. There's going to be hell to pay."

Gwen looked at the grim reminder of the once vital reporter, her friend.

"There already has," she said, "there already has been."

She looked around, distraught, and was at a loss for words—a professional wordsmith unable to articulate.

"He was Jewish, I think," she said after a moment. "Maybe somebody could say something."

Quatraine looked stricken when Heaps informed him of the paucity of his team's findings.

"Nothing?" he asked, unbelieving. "No arms cache, no body, no exit? I'm asking you, Heaps, are you sure that guy was in here?" Is this even his place?" Don't tell me we've blown up some other poor schmuck's house by mistake."

Heaps could do little but shrug. He was completely bemused by the lack of findings. He would have staked his life on Kennedy still being in that house, and he had no explanation for his absence. Maybe he could not even believe what he had seen, but he would swear to the end on the proverbial stack of bibles that he had personally watched Randolph Armstrong Kennedy—in the flesh—carry crates of guns into that house, that he had seen Kennedy enter and never again leave that house the night before the raid. Kennedy was a bad guy, better off dead; but Heaps did not believe in demons that could materialize in and out of solid walls…until now. But on this unholy day, he was willing to question anything he had ever seen or believed in.

Oscar DeLentigo walked up to Quatraine when Heaps finished his report.

"Bad news, I take it?"

Quatraine nodded, as much in perplexity as in answer to the FBI SAC's query.

"I'm not sure what all of this has been about, Quatraine; but I am sure that there will have to be some explaining done."

The two men's attentions were diverted to a crash of uprights and joists burned through and falling among the smoldering debris on the floor of the house. Several sparking beams pitched through the gaping hole and into the basement. Other larger ones piled over the opening, obscuring it from view.

"Probably so," Quatraine said wearily, "And when it stops rolling downhill, it's going to stop right on top of me."

SAC DeLentigo nodded sympathetically. The FBI could only look good in comparison.

"I think it's time to call it a day, Oliver," he said gently. "Let forensics people and graves registration techs do their work. I'll get the crime scene ribbon up, if you want."

Quatraine nodded in resignation.

"You've got your work cut out for you just letting your bosses, Thaler, and the president know about this," the senior FBI special agent added in a supportive tone.

"To say nothing of the next of kin," sighed Quatraine.

That would be the worst part of the whole ordeal.

"I'd appreciate it, Oscar, if you would set out the yellow tape, and I'll mop up otherwise. I'll call in the APB."

"Okay, we'll get on it."

"I am going to move right along; I have to get to the hospital. They must be about ready to name a new wing for us by now."

"I hate to have to say it, Oliver, but you know that I will have to submit an independent investigative report from start to finish, get the LAFO involved. I'm sorry—nothing personal—just business. You know the drill."

"I know, Oscar. Give us the benefit of the doubt. It'll be like tying to paint a turd, but try."

LAFO—the Los Angeles Field Office explosives laboratory—located in the Hoover FBI Building in Washington, D.C., was as impersonal and as unforgiving an organization as existed on earth, and Quatraine knew he had next to no chance of them cutting him or the ATF any slack.

The FBI agents quickly and efficiently put up a large rectangle of yellow crime scene tape around the entire scene of the action. They were overly generous on the distances, extending a quarter of a mile out from the house site in all directions. They could not have known that by concentrating the great resources of the federal government into the quarter mile square restricted zone that they would effectively cancel out the possibility of ever finding the entrance to Randolph's tunnel. It was never located.

It was quiet on the hill now. An ATF man, holding up Brocklin Phelp's boot sang in a mellifluous practiced baritone voice the *Mourner's Kaddish*, the prayer for the dead.

"*Yisgadal ve yiskadash shmei rabooh…*" [Oh, Lord and King, who art full of compassion. Receive in thy great loving kindness, the soul of Brocklin Phelps who has been gathered unto his people.]

Gwen Chambers stood with her head bowed not caring that anyone could see a river of tears flooding down her cheeks.

CHAPTER TWENTY-NINE

Randolph drove directly to the Eagle Self Storage Company in the southeast corner of Anchorage. It was old, established, busy, and nondescript. He got out of the truck and went into the office. Ian "Jake" Jacobsen was sitting drowsily in his chair on its two back legs with his feet crossed on the utilitarian gun metal grey desk. He set aside his quart bottle of Revel wine.

"Help ya?" he asked as Randolph strode in trying to be as nonchalant as his tired and frazzled psyche would allow.

Jake was dirty, sweat stained, and malodorous. He fit into the present surroundings quite well.

"Yes, sir, I'd like to rent a big storage unit."

"This is your lucky day. That's what we do here," Jake replied and flashed a gap-toothed smile.

"How much?" asked Randolph as if it mattered.

The only thing that did matter was to be quick about it. He wanted to scream at the dilatory activity of the old man.

"How big?"

"What sizes do you have?"

He was speaking rapidly, hoping to urge the old man into a more accelerated pace.

Jake Jacobsen had only one pace. He paused to think for a minute.

"Eight by eight, eight by twelve, and ten by twenty. That's it, 'less you want a two-car one."

Randolph was too flustered to do any calculating; so he said, "Give me the biggest one you've got."

"See what I've got."

He thumbed through a worn map of the storage compartments.

"Don't have no eight by twelves," Jake announced indicating by his demeanor that it was impossible to accommodate Randolph.

"I'd rather have the two car one anyway," Randolph urged the old man on. "How much?"

"By the week, by the month, six months, or a full year. Depends."

Randolph was going crazy. The tell tale trailer was out in front of the storage facility for every cop who happened by to see. What did he care about the price?

"Give it to me for a year."

Jake looked at the man to see if he might be just funnin' him; lotta guys did that. He did not have to take that from nobody, especially on his last day of work for that Scrooge, Harry McDonald. He decided that the guy was probably okay.

$769 plus tax for the year. Includes insurance—rats, fire, flood, acts a God, the whole schmear."

"Such a bargain. I'll take it."

"Got to fill in the form. Everythin; legal. Protects you as much as it does us, ya know," Jake told Randolph perfunctorily.

Randolph scooped up the form. It asked a hundred or more questions about his address, work, income, holdings, the nature of his storage items. Bold letters emphasized the prohibition against storing flammables, dangerous chemicals, and illegal substances. The truth would have the cops here in a matter of hours and putting down even one fragment of the truth was out of the question. Randolph knew Harry McDonald and knew neither that he nor anyone in his business would ever look at this stupid form. He thoughtfully lied on every line. The name under which it was to be rented was "F. Delano Roosevelt." Randolph had no idea where he came up with that. The stored items were "household effects". The entire form was filled out in good blah prevarications, and done with Randolph's left hand.

He paid cash. That brought the first smile of the day to the wizened old man. And—as Randolph had presumed—Jake put the form in a large cluttered filing drawer without looking at it. Randolph watched as he did it; the form was filed with the "Hs".

Jake handed Randolph the key.

"Don't go losin' it, young fella. You got one, and we got one. None to spare. And it's against Alaska law to duplicate this here key. You bear that in mind. Now, I'll say it again. Keep aholt of this key. I won't be workin' here no more after today, so's no one will be here that ever remembers you. I'm goin' to live with my daughter in Florida, and I ain't never gonna be cold another daya my life."

"Yes, sir."

It couldn't have turned out better if he had planned it. The old man wouldn't even be here, let alone be able to remember him if ever the cops came snooping by.

"You got a fork lift I could use, Mr...?"

"Jacobsen. And yeah, but it'll cost ya."

"Okay. How much?"

"Hunnert for the day. Wanna good strong lock?"

"Please."

"At's another eight bucks."

Randolph paid him cash. It was like having all the Monopoly money he could ever want. Free at last, Randolph rushed to his storage unit—number 7304—out of sight of old Jake. The unit was on the end and its entry door was unobstructed by adjoining units. Randolph opened the sliding metal door, backed the trailer near the entry into the space, and went to fetch the fork lift. He put down the trailer's loading ramps and gingerly drove the fork lift into the back of the large container. He had a little difficulty figuring out which knobs, gears, and switches did what and initially made something of a mess of the first pallets.

Shortly, with concentration borne of necessity, he got the hang of it; and was soon able to move the pallets of money out of the trailer and into neat stacks in the unit. He worked for twenty minutes or so, then had to pull the truck forward ten feet to get the next set of pallets stacked in the back. Finally, he emptied the trailer and pulled it out onto the storage facility's driveway. He took pains to stack the New and Brite FAX paper boxes in front of the stacks of money; so, at least the casual observer would not see the main contents immediately. He cut into the shrink wrap covering a stack of money and removed as much as he could carry. He locked the storage compartment door, then he returned the fork lift to where he had found it. He hopped into his newly acquired truck and pulled out of the main gait of the storage facility and onto the back road that led to it. Jake was sound asleep with his head on his desk when Randolph passed the office.

He found a dead end side road strewn with trash and drove to the end of it. He wheeled the empty trailer off into a small ravine and unhooked it. As soon as he did, the large trailer lurched backward, gained momentum, and after hitting a derelict freezer, turned over and lay nearly unseen on its side.

"Things are going pretty well," Randolph said to himself. "It's better to be lucky than good."

He drove the Ford pick-up to the Alaskan Gentleman's Outfitter's store and bought a pair of khaki slacks, a white dress shirt, and a nondescript tie, a standard issue blue blazer, penny loafers, and two large sturdy suitcases. He picked up a kit with all the shaving and grooming necessities, and threw in the first bottle of men's cologne he came across. He assumed that he would be flying soon if his luck held and would have to check in the suitcases. He was not sure how x-ray would view the cases full of nothing but money; so, he bought an assortment of belts, metal combs, cigar holders, and a pair of shoes with metal caps on the toes. It was no matter that the shoes were two sizes too small for him. He threw in a gaudy Hawaiian sports shirt that he would not have buried his cat in. But, it had silver and gold metal thread running all through it. That ought to solve the airport x-ray problem, he hoped.

He wore the new clothing out of the store and dropped his old clothes—the ATF uniform—into a trash can on the street on the way back to the truck. He drove into an alley and made sure that no one was watching. He jammed the suitcases full of the loose packets of money he had extracted from the pallet and scattered the pile of travel accessories over the top of the money. It was all he could do to get the suitcases closed even by sitting on them with his full weight. He had overestimated how much of the money he could get into the cases. They weighed a ton. He could scarcely muscle them around.

The feds—maybe even the local police—had to be on to him by now. He had to move, and he had to get rid of the incriminating truck. His tension was almost palpable. He was shaking, partly from exhaustion and partly from stress. He was going to cave in soon without food, drink, and rest. He determined that his next two projects had to be to get rid of the truck and find a place to hide. How he was going to do that was not coming to him.

Quatraine and six other ATF agents walked dejectedly together down the steep dusty road to where their trucks had been parked. None of them had anything left in them to hurry.

"We better only take two of the units. Leave the other transport for the rest of our guys," Oliver said.

He was lugubrious, and his dirge like mood infected his fellow agents. They headed for the trucks like cattle at evening feeding time headed for the barn.

Quatraine led them to where the pick-ups had been parked. Funny, they were not there. Maybe he was mistaken about the parking area. The wooded areas all looked pretty much the same. He moved on fifty yards to the left, then turned and came back and went fifty yards to the right. Something was not right. Maybe some of the cops had taken the trucks to get back and left the rest stranded, the jerks. He was getting angry. He knew where the van and trailer were parked; so, reluctantly, he moved in that direction. The other agents followed him like puppies. The van and the trailer were not there. The tire track impressions were clearly indented in the grass, and the tracks showed that a circular turn had been made.

"Guys, something is off here. Let's go down towards the main road. I'm hoping somebody moved our units to another area although I can't for the life of me figure why they would. Sorry about this."

The agents trooped on down the road, somewhat more disheartened. They came to the narrow and wooded section of the road. They saw the four pick-ups parked at right angles to the road effectively blocking future traffic completely when the bulk of the vehicles began to move out. This was beyond odd, but Quatraine could not focus in on what it meant.

"Maybe it's some idiot's idea of a joke," Jeff Stoner said.

He was angry. This was no day for a joke.

"Straighten these units up, and let's get the flock out of here," Quatraine ordered, equally put out.

Without any of them making a careful observation, four of the men hopped into the trucks, turned over the engines and jerked to an abrupt halt on their trucks' four flat tires. Every agent looked aghast at the flat tires and the stranded trucks. They all knew that this was intentional, and somehow serious.

Quatraine knew more than they did, and he felt a sudden wrenching of his guts.

"Jeff, come with me. Everybody else sit here and wait. I think I know what's going on."

Stoner ran behind Quatraine as they returned to where the van and trailer had been parked. There was a set of tracks heading straight ahead into the woods. They ran forward, made a small turn to the left and almost ran bodily into the van.

"What is this old crate doing here?" Jeff asked.

Quatraine looked at the van in undisguised horror. He had forgotten about it and its incriminating contents. It was like the Ghost of Christmas Past come back to haunt him. He could only pray that it was empty. He somehow knew without looking inside that that was too much to hope for. He had a pretty good idea now about what had become of the big trailer—the trailer that only he, of the men left standing—knew what it contained.

Jeff moved to the van immediately and checked the cab. Nothing special. Quatraine made a feeble attempt to distract him, but Stoner wasn't having it. He marched purposefully to the rear of the vehicle and flung open the doors. He jumped into the back and in a matter of seconds discovered the bomb making materials and the cache of sophisticated weapons.

He jumped back down, looked quizzically at Quatraine, then yelled for the other agents.

"Get up here everyone of you. Got something for you to see. On the double!"

The other five agents ran up the incline to where Stoner and Quatraine were standing.

"Back here," Jeff called.

Quatraine remained quiet while Stoner showed the other agents the evidence in the truck.

"What do you make of this, boss?" Jeff asked, a little afraid of what the answer might be.

"I haven't a clue, Jeff. I guess it's either the perp's stash or maybe it's even something Drake or somebody in law enforcement brought up here."

The keys were in the ignition. One of the men attempted to start the van, but got no response when he turned the key. Jeff checked under the hood. Every wire under the hood had been torn off or cut. It would be like moving a small tank to get this thing out of here.

Jeff shrugged and said, "I guess we just let CSI have it and figure out what's going on. And, I just had a serious thought. We're contaminating the crime scene. Every one of us has put his fingerprints on the vehicle. We'd better back off, don't you think, boss?"

"Absolutely. Let's get ourselves into town somehow, then we can come back in the morning and see what we can do. Get on your radios and find us some wheels. We need somebody from town to get out here and give us a ride back to Wasilla."

"Or better, out of this whole state," one of the men muttered.

Quatraine could not have agreed more with that sentiment. He was afraid he was going to vomit or hyperventilate. It was as clear as a mountain stream that someone—maybe Kennedy, maybe somebody in the Militia—had slashed the truck tires to slow the cops down and made off with the fortune. It was impossible that Kennedy had gotten the trailer. There were cops all over the place. He wouldn't have a chance of moving that cumbersome thing without being caught. Besides, there was no evidence that the man had been anywhere near his place when the raid took place. He reluctantly ruled out Kennedy. Oliver had the terrible feeling that one of the law enforcement officers had discovered the money and had succumbed to the overwhelming temptation. It was a sickening thought.

"What do you think this is all about?" asked one of the agents.

"I do not have the slightest idea, Fred, not the slightest," Quatraine lied.

At least he was telling the truth about one thing. He had no idea how that stupid van and trailer had been moved, and certainly, he had no explanation for the missing trailer. He kept any mention of that thing to himself. Even his knowledge of the existence of the trailer could land him in Leavenworth.

"*Where is all that money? That evidence?*" Oliver's frayed mind screamed.

"Hey," Jeff Stoner said after the men had made there calls and were waiting for their rides. "We never saw any perp. I personally never saw one scintilla of evidence which says that he was here, or he is the smartest dude we ever came up against. Either way, this van full of drugs, bomb making materials, and crated weapons seems way out of place. I had a flash a minute ago. I think I remember seeing a description of this stuff someplace. Can't remember where."

Fred Hicken said, "I think I remember. I had to do the inventory in Ketchikan. Let me have another look."

He went back to the van, spent five minutes, then came back grim faced to where the agents had moved.

"Gentlemen, those gun crates and the ammonium nitrate came from the evidence locker in Anchorage. That stuff is or *was* the evidence our guys picked up in the Ketchikan raid."

The reality of what it all meant descended upon each of the agents like a cloud of poison fumes.

"Somebody's dirty. Kennedy had no access to this stuff. Only cops, guys— only ATF agents—had any access to this. We have a bad cop among us and the brown stuff is going to hit the fan in very short order," Jeff said out loud, confirming every agent's worst opinion.

When they got back to where the four black Ford pick-ups had been left, nearly twenty vehicles were backed up behind them. Three times that many agents and officers were milling about. There was an angry accusatory atmosphere.

Men were openly speculating about the lack of evidence, about the possibility that they had hit the wrong house, about the absence of a perpetrator, and now this apparently deliberate sabotage.

"I'm tellin' you there never was a perp, and he did not do this to the trucks. I don't know what went down here—but something is rotten in Denmark—and I think ATF is the Denmark of choice," one FBI special agent said to another.

Two ATF agents bristled and walked towards the FBI agents menacingly. Cooler heads intervened before there could be a fight, one that might just result in a mini-cop riot.

Stoner said to Quatraine as they moved quietly past the angry collection of cops, "Can you imagine the mood if they had seen what we have? And, thank all the saints, that the money from that Ketchikan raid didn't get out here. Can you even imagine what that would stir up? First thing I do tomorrow is to check into that evidence locker."

"Now, more than any time I can ever remember, we have to band together," Quatraine said in deadly earnest to his small team, "It's us against them, and we look bad. One of us *is* bad, it appears. We have to let them—CSI and the fibbies—have a field day by speculating about what that van is doing here. We don't have to help them speculate. I'm for calling it a day and getting out of here."

"Amen," the other six men chorused, but they were a severely chastened and quiet team by the time they were deposited in their motels in Wasilla.

Before he settled in, Quatraine drove his rental car directly to Wasilla Community Hospital. He showed his credentials and asked where his team members were.

"ICU", answered the desk receptionist laconically.

Quatraine used the elevator; he was too done in to climb stairs.

He chatted briefly with four agents—wishing each of them well—and expressing gratitude that they had not been hurt any worse than they had. It was scant reassurance, because he and every one of the men knew that their injuries were serious and would be maiming. It seemed a little strange to him, but none of the agents inquired about the operation. Out of it and safe, they no longer cared; or they did not want to have to cope with any more bad news that terrible day.

Henry Drake was asleep with two IVs running, a foley catheter leading out of his bladder and into a urine filled bag hanging on his bed rail. Another tube came out of his abdomen and connected to a second bag on the rail. That one had nasty looking brown liquid in it. He had no covers on, and Quatraine was struck with how little external damage there seemed to be on the man aside from the narrow bandage covering an obvious mid-line abdominal incision. Quatraine tapped Drake gently on his arm; he did not want to have to return to the hospital until after he had had some rest and had made his report to the higher-ups.

Drake groggily opened his eyes and waited for them to focus.

"Quatraine?"

"In the flesh."

"Did you get Kennedy?"

Not, "glad you made it" or how are the other guys?" or "how did it all turn out?" Drake's eyes burned through his narcotic induced fog with intensity.

Quatraine shook his head.

Drake rolled his eyes back in his head in a gesture of ultimate despair.

After a few moments of silence, he asked softly, "Bailey?"

"Dead."

"How many?"

"I'm not sure, at least eight or nine. Too much mess up there to be able to get a good fix on any part of the raid. I'm pretty sure that the *Post* reporter... Phelps...bought it. We'll get an accurate head count tomorrow. Everybody is too done in to do anything more today."

"How much evidence did you find?"

"Nothing there that couldn't arguably have been part of the raiding party's stuff."

"How much of the armament did you haul up there that we could use against him?"

Quatraine was quiet for a minute.

"Gimmee ballpark numbers."

Quatraine sympathized with Drake, but he could not forget the racist denigrations he had had to suffer at the man's hands; so, he felt no great urge to protect the corrupt agent's feelings.

Quatraine's facial features tightened; and his lips flattened as he growled, "Nada, nichts, zilch, zippo, crapola, nothing."

Drake's face drained of all color. He was nearly the same shade as the sheets under him.

"The van?" whispered the beaten man in the bed.

"Weird."

"We have to have weird, too? What kind of weird?"

Drake's voice was almost plaintive.

"I don't know quite what to make out of it but the worst," Oliver said, tired of holding anything back from anyone. "Anyway, the van with all of its wonderful contents was found in some trees a little ways beyond where it was left. Several of our guys saw it—all of it—and by noon tomorrow an investigating team will see it, too."

"Get back up there and move it out. It can't be found there with the evidence still inside it."

"I can't. Whoever moved it punctured all of the tires. It would be like pygmies trying to move an elephant carcass."

"Who?"

"Beats me. The best case scenario would be that some of our guys did it as a joke; or the fibbies did it for spite; and maybe they won't get too serious or thoughtful about it."

"You didn't say anything about the trailer. Tell me it's there someplace. Incriminating would not be as bad as missing."

"Missing," Quatraine said bluntly.

"Who did it? Some cop? Kennedy? although that has to be impossible. He must have been long gone, and he would stand out like a light house driving around towing that thing. I can't believe that scenario, and that leaves us with a thieving cop. He has to be an idiot, and he'll get caught. It won't take a brain surgeon to guess where that particular trailer load of money came from."

"It was my guess that it was a cop, too, and all my guys independently came up with the same supposition."

"We're cooked," sighed Drake.

He was ashen, and he seemed to have diminished in the bed.

"*Who's 'we', paleface? This was your doing,*" Quatraine thought, saying it to himself over and over. "*You get to pay the piper; I've got insurance. I've got tapes. I'll get a reprimand, maybe even dismissal, but you are going to be hung out in the wind,*" he thought.

Oliver couldn't bring himself to broach that subject with the nearly helpless Drake. There would be plenty of time to throw stones in self-protection later when it hit the fan.

"So, what'd they do to you?" Quatraine asked, shifting the subject to one that was the lesser of evils, at least, for him.

"Did what they call a laminectomy…some surgery on my back. The doc opened my spinal canal and took out a couple of pieces of shrapnel, and the general surgeon patched up my gut. They had to stick it on the outside of my belly—a colostidy or something like that."

"You going to be okay?"

"The operation went all right, so far as that goes. The neurosurgeon seemed like a good guy, had to come up from Anchorage. Too early to tell about the spinal cord function yet, he says."

"But, you'll be able to walk, right?"

It was a stupid question. Quatraine knew it, but it just came out. He was glad he hadn't asked about the future of the man's sex life.

Drake turned his head to the side.

"Don't know. Too soon."

Then he closed his eyes and shut Oliver out.

CHAPTER THIRTY

After filling his suitcases with the emergency cash and the odds and ends he had purchased to convince airport security of the benignity of their contents and securing the locks, Randolph removed the license plates from the Ford pick-up and threw them into a Dempsty Dumster in the alley.

He walked out of the alley and looked around. The streets were nearly devoid of activity. At midday, everyone was at work; their cars clogged the curbs nearly bumper to bumper on both sides of every road Randolph could see. He stepped between two cars and swiftly removed two license plates, one from each vehicle. No one saw him, he was sure of that. He attached the nonmatching new plates to the pick-up and got into the driver's side again. He edged out of the alley and onto the street. He was distracted by the noise of some children screaming at each other over a sand-lot touch football game. He almost turned right into a police car coming from his right, the only other vehicle in motion in the town, as far as he could tell. He broke into a nervous sweat.

The police officer flashed a broad smile and waggled a finger at him in mock sternness. Randolph waved back with a *mea culpa* sort of gesture. He expected the worst—to be stopped and questioned—but it did not happen—to his immense relief. He slapped his forehead to punish himself for his lack of attention, and drove on. His armpits had a pungent aroma of fear wafting from them.

Randolph drove directly to the Anchorage Federal Building. His newly developed criminal's logic led him to conclude that the last place the police would look for their missing truck was at their own headquarters; and if they found it there, they would have a devil of a time explaining who brought

265

it there and the odd license plates. He found the most distant and obscure parking spot he could and stepped out of the cab with his suitcases. As he headed for the street, he encountered secretaries, lawyers, and even the occasional uniformed police officer. In his paranoid state Randolph fantasized that all eyes were on him; every brain was calculating about who he was. In truth, they just wanted to go home at the end of their day's shift.

Randolph was shaking with exhaustion and nervousness by the time he reached the street, and he knew that he had to go to ground pronto. He did not want to draw attention to himself by making a vigorous show of hailing a cab; so, he found a phone booth across the street. He headed towards it, lugging his super heavy suitcases and trying to appear as if they were not great anchors. He set them down in front of the phone booth—took a breath—and allowed the blood to recirculate into his arms and hands.

He stepped into the filthy phone booth and looked for a *Yellow Pages* for the listing for cab companies. The book had been torn from its anchoring chain, and the chain dangled impotently to taunt Randolph Kennedy. Nothing was going very well at this point after a series of good fortunes earlier on. He had to call the operator for the number of the taxi company. For that he needed two quarters or a fifty cent piece. He searched his pockets knowing before he started that he did not have any coins. Hundred dollar bills? He had a plethora of them, but nary a coin…for the want of a nail, the shoe was lost…

A woman hastened past the phone booth. Randolph hurriedly jerked the booth door opened and called to her. She jumped in surprise and rushed away from him with a look of fear. Such was life in the city. He didn't have time to make a placard announcing that he was not a rapist, a thug, or any kind of monster. He vowed to try again, this time more adroitly.

An African-American man came across the street in the direction of Randolph's phone booth. Randolph forced a bland expression and concentrated on how to fake being friendly and at ease.

"Pardon me, sir, Do you have a fifty cent piece? I need to use the phone and haven't got a coin."

The black man looked at him with naked suspicion. He was a city man to his bones and he had not gotten to be seventy-two without taking due care. Randolph kept his hands in plain sight.

It was just past midday on a busy street in front of the United States Federal Building. He kept a distance of five feet between himself and the upscale looking white man. Although he was hesitant, he reached into his pocket and fished out four or five coins. Their jingling was music to Randolph.

"Yeah, I got one. Here you go, brother," he said.

Seeing the look of profound relief on Randolph's face—out of proportion to the situation, it seemed to him—the pleasant African American gentleman relaxed and grinned broadly.

Randolph returned the smile and it was a genuine expression complete with teeth showing. He pulled out a ten dollar bill, part of the change from the Mobil station and offered it to his benefactor.

"Got change?" Randolph asked, not caring a whit about anymore money, but he presumed it was expected.

"I don't, mister. It's all right. You need that coin a whole lot more than I do, looks like."

No truer words were ever uttered. Randolph debated about whether to offer the other man a hundred; he was feeling intense gratitude. He finally decided against the pressing the gesture—afraid it might insult his Good Samaritan—or give him reason to remember the transitory encounter. He made a perfunctory offer.

"Sorry, this is all I have right now. Why don't you take this and have a dinner on me? We can both consider it lucky we met."

"Naw," the man said and shook his head vigorously to emphasize his refusal. "I don't want it. Just doing a good Christian turn. You accept the help as a brother, all right?"

"All right. Thanks, my friend. You really saved my day."

There was an awkward pause. Randolph wanted to get into the phone booth. The Good Samaritan wanted to chat.

"My name's Ezekial Barnes Washington," he said and extended his hand.

Would this never end? Randolph wanted to flee. But he shook Ezekial's hand warmly.

"I'm, uh...Delano Roosevelt."

It sounded so hokey that he could not bring himself to look the man in the eyes.

"Hey, Del, glad to meet you. I see you're in a hurry. I won't keep you. Godspeed."

A perceptive Good Samaritan. Randolph could see a flicker of hope.

"Thanks again, Ezekial. You have a good day now. I won't forget that I ran into a real Christian on the streets of Anchorage of all places."

Ezekial laughed out loud. His laughter was self-deprecatory, but it pleased him no end to have someone recognize his practical faith.

"Go with God, brother," he said in parting.

Randolph all but leaped back into the phone booth as soon as Ezekial turned and started to walk away. He used his fifty cent piece to get the information operator. She gave him the number for Yellow Cab, the only name he could come up with on short notice. Then it dawned on him that he would need to get another coin to make the call. He was getting too tired to think clearly, and this phoning process was developing into a slow-motion nightmare. He felt on the verge of panic, and it was over such a small thing.

"Please, operator, don't hang up. I don't have another coin, and I can't get one. I'm going to miss my flight at the airport. Could you please dial the number for me?"

"That would be highly irregular, sir. I'm sorry, company policy won't permit me to do that. Sorry."

He could feel her about to cut him off.

"Please, I'm desperate. Won't you help a poor guy in distress? I could leave a bill in the phone booth to cover the charge of the call. I have money; I just don't have a coin. Please?"

He could almost hear the wheels turning in her head in the silence that ensued.

"You really would leave a bill in the booth?"

He knew he had her.

"Tell you what I'll do. I will make it worth your while; that's a promise. I'll hide it in the corner under an old piece of newspaper; so, only you will know where it is. You should come pretty soon; so, nobody else can get it."

"Maybe. You calling from the booth in front of the Federal Building?"

"That's the one. Please make the call."

Another pause. This was like pulling teeth. He wanted to scream, but he knew that he could not betray the least bit of displeasure. He saw police officers moving up and down the street. He was certain they were looking for him. He was going to be captured ignominiously standing out in front of the federal law enforcement center. What a dummy! He castigated himself for having allowed himself to get into this predicament. In the pause, he ran over the several options he should have taken.

"I'll do it. I'm not supposed to, but you sound so upset. I hope you won't make me regret this."

"You won't. Please call the cab company. And, thanks a lot."

It was a major step for her, and it would be the end of her trust in mankind if he failed to do right by her. It was a heavy responsibility.

"You won't tell, will you?"

"Of course I won't. You're the Good Samaritan, just like in the Bible."

That seemed to be the clincher.

"I'll just tell them where you are. Now calm down and enjoy your trip. God bless you."

She had given in entirely to the rapture of her act of Christian compassion. He set down the receiver and placed a $100 bill under the yellowing newspaper on the dirty ground. What the heck, he could afford to give her a little thrill, show her that that Christian stuff really worked.

He hardly had time to get himself out of the phone booth and to the street corner with his bags when a new, undented Yellow Cab pulled up to the curb. It was indeed a day for miracles.

"You thee party in a roosh to thee hairport," the cabbie asked in heavily accented English.

He was only obeying the rule that cab drivers must be from a foreign country.

"That's me," Randolph said. "I have to make a quick stop at the bank on the way."

"Then jou hop in. It's my especiality to make roosh trips to hairport. That's when I'm not going around hobeying my fare's orders to 'follow thata cabbie.'"

He laughed heartily at his joke, one from the cab drivers' handbook.

Randolph's tension eased a trace now that he was not standing out on the street for all to see. He laughed at the corny joke.

"Any particular bank jou gotta stop at, baas?"

"No, the first one that we see will do. Let's pull into one with a drive-through."

They pulled into the drive-through entry of a Bank of America branch. Randolph changed $3000 worth of hundreds into more usable fives, tens, and twenties. He knew enough to keep his transaction below the $10,000 threshold of interest by the authorities. It would not do to have to fill out the Federal Large Cash Transfer Form. In less than five minutes, he had his cash. It was bulky, but would probably come in handy.

The cabbie hurried—broke speed laws all the way—and somehow avoided getting a ticket. Randolph was on the sidewalk of the airport twenty minutes from the time he got away from the bank. Randy overpaid him as was his habit of late, and thanked him for hurrying. Together, they struggled to get the suitcases out of the trunk.

"Jou got goldt in them begs, mister?" the cabbie asked, puffing.

"I wish," Randolph answered, returning the man's friendly smile. "Just samples. I represent a book company."

"Haf a good trip, mister."

"Thanks."

The Skycab porter caught his attention.

"You want to check in your bags here, Sir?"

"I don't have a ticket yet. Maybe you could help me get them into the terminal and help me find Delta."

Randolph looked around for a police presence. He knew that he could only be a little in head of the APB that had to be going out soon—as soon as someone up on his hill figured out that he was missing, and the trailer with him. If he could get on the plane early, he might be safe.

"Good as done, Mr…" the Skycabbie shrugged when no name was forthcoming.

He hefted the heavy bags onto his dolly with ease born of long practice. The two men walked briskly in to the terminal. The Skycabbie threaded his way through the crowd, and Randolph followed in his wake. Hunters with their moose and caribou antlers and waxy yellow boxes of meat clogged the way. Most of them were more than a little under the influence, Randolph noted. It took a few minutes to get to the Delta ticket counter. Luckily, there were only two people ahead of him. Randolph paid his porter a ten spot, making another friend.

"What flight would you like, sir?" asked the counter attendant when it was his turn.

"The next flight to San Francisco, please."

"That would be at two-ten." She turned and looked at the wall clock. "Twenty minutes to take-off, I'm not sure you can make it."

"Let's try; it's real important to me, please."

She looked disappointed after checking her computer modem. He felt his heart sinking.

"I'm afraid that we only have a first class accommodation left, sir."

His clothing suggested that he might not be first-class passenger material.

"Fine," he said without hesitation, surprising her. "How much will that be?"

"One way or return?"

He thought it would be the smarter thing to do to get a round trip ticket. He was already likely to arouse suspicion by paying cash. He knew the inevitable question about his photo-ID was coming.

"Return," he said.

"That will be $1896, please. Which card would you like to use?"

"Is cash all right? I have maxed out my card."

"It's a little irregular, but no real problem, especially for our first-class passengers."

Randolph reached into his jacket pocket and extracted a large stack of bills. As unobtrusively as possible, he counted out nineteen hundred dollar bills.

He hated flashing all of that money, but the young lady did not seem perturbed or even overly interested. She gave him his change. It was not her job to wonder; she worked the computer, answered the patron's questions, and toadied to the first class passengers. There were not a lot of those in the current Delta financial crisis.

"Thank you, sir. May I have your name?"

Franklin Delano Roosevelt flashed immediately to mind by force of recent habit. He did not think it wise to use the same pseudonym for the flight that he had used with the cabbie coming out from the city and at the storage place. She looked at him curiously when it took him more than expected to come up with his own name. He was behaving a little suspiciously, and he knew he was not handling things well. It was going to take him a while to get the hang of this new life as a criminal. He was doing pretty well as a liar thus far, he prided himself.

"Richard Lindstrom," he blurted out without really thinking.

It was ridiculous. Richard Lindstrom was the ambassador to the Court of St. James and had been in the news frequently because some sort of minor sex scandal. He was relieved not to see a flicker of recognition of the name in the attendant's face. She did not seem like one to follow the news.

"Oh, dear, Mr. Lindstrom, we really have to hurry."

"Yes, looks like I'll just barely make it."

"Photo ID, please."

"I showed it to the Skycabbie already."

"Oh, that's right. I saw that," she said.

Apparently improvisation was a two way affair, Randolph thought. Another small miracle.

"Three B, sir. How many bags?"

"Two, please."

He hoisted them onto the scales. The weight was just under the maximum for each bag, and Randolph shed yet another worry. He would be most relieved to sink into his plane seat for a few hours of pampering. The attendant grunted a little as she moved them onto the baggage conveyor belt. She gave him a little smile anyway.

"Hurry, Mr. Lindstrom. You'll just make it. I'll call ahead. Thanks for traveling with Delta."

"Thank you. I'll put in a good word about your extra help, Miss…?"

"Pendleton. Jackie Pendleton."

"Got it. Bye now."

He looked around carefully and saw no one paying any attention to him. There were no security officers of policemen in view. Everything seemed to be going smoothly. He couldn't exactly feel relaxed, but he was calming down. His VIP status as a first class passenger and the fact that he was moving through the security gate with a horde of boisterous post hunt drunks, helped him get through the last hurdle.

He knew he had to present a photo ID here, and there would be no exceptions or excuses. He handed the TSA officer, a harried trainee, his boarding pass, fumbled a moment for his own driver's license, and handed it to her upside down.

"Please move right along, sir; you can see that we are a bit crowded."

A burly red-faced man in camo clothes bumped into Randolph's back, and he bumped into the security agent. She smiled indulgently at him and handed back his pass and his drivers license. She had looked at it, and presumably saw that the picture matched his face, but she was too rushed to verify the name on the ID with that on the boarding pass.

He quickly shed his shoes, wallet, and belt and stepped through the metal detector. Nothing about him or his belongings attracted attention, and he breezed through. He ran along side several other late arrivers and got to the check-in counter with less than a minute to spare.

"Thank goodness you made it, Mister Lindstrom. Go right on. Have a great flight and a nice stay in San Francisco."

Randolph collapsed into his seat and gratefully accepted a nice glass of orange juice from the attractive late middle-aged woman attendant whose only apparent purpose in life was to afford the gentleman in 3B the maximum comfort on his journey. He heard the hubbub back in the steerage section and wondered how the poor people ever tolerated such privation. He was asleep before take off and did not stir until landing. It had been a long, nearly forty hour day.

DeLentigo made the call to the Wasilla PD. It was clocked in at 1426, sixteen minutes after Delta Flight 206 took off for San Francisco.

"Wasilla Police Department, how may I direct your call?"

"This is Special Agent in Charge DeLentigo of the Anchorage FBI office. I want an immediate all-points bulletin put out on one Randolph Armstrong

Kennedy for unlawful flight to avoid arrest, violation of federal firearms and drug statutes, and murder. He is to be considered armed and extremely dangerous. We need to seal off every possible exit from this city and the state. Make him a priority one and red alert with an all-precautions label."

He was telling his fellow officers to shoot first if there was the slightest suggestion that Kennedy was not going to surrender like a lamb. That understanding would never be written down.

The desk sergeant input the information into the network computer, and within ten seconds, it was appearing on the modem screens of police departments throughout the state and in every federal office in Alaska. Sergeant Carl Thompson, a member of the North Star State Militia and fifteen year veteran of the Wasilla PD, got the assignment for their department.

"Randolph Kennedy!? You sure? I know the guy. He's just an accountant, a citizen type. I'd about as soon think my grandma was a terrorist," he said to the watch officer who handed him the message.

What he didn't say was that he knew that Kennedy was the commander of the Militia, and had access to a massive arsenal of weaponry, and almost certainly knew how to use them. He also didn't say that he had no intention of pushing the man's capture any too hard.

"Where've you been, Carl? On Mars? This is the guy the feds and most of this department have been having a war with for the past day and a half. Lives up above Nancy on some hill in a fort. Killed a bunch of feds. I got news that he killed Alex Tolberg. This guy's public enemy number one, and all of the stops have been pulled to catch this cop killer. Between you and me, he's about as likely to get away or get a cell as a snowball has of staying hard packed in hell."

"I been fishin' up on the Wulik River—Dolly Vardens. Haven't heard a thing. You say Alex Tolberg bought it? That's terrible. He's got a nice little family, real shame. I'll get right on it…Randolph Kennedy…whooda thunk?"

"I'm not one to put my nose into other people's business, Carl, but this militia stuff is getting out of hand altogether it seems to me. Maybe you oughta give your membership in it a second thought. I know there's some guys in the department that's members, and the scuttlebutt has it that you're one of them. It's against policy, and after this, I don't think there's gonna be any more nod-nod, wink-wink about it. Members of the Militia are gonna be about as popular as a whore in church from now on. A word to the wise."

"Thanks, Abe. I'm with you," said Carl. "I've been having second thoughts for a couple of years. I really don't like the secession stuff or the racism, I have to tell you. We're all Americans, and I guess it's time to cut my ties with them. I've always considered it pretty tame stuff—a lot of gas—but it don't look like a guy will have a chance to go up in rank if he's got a militia background. That's just the way it is, and a guy oughta look out for himself. It's probably time for the Militia to fade away."

Abe nodded and went back to his paperwork accumulated from the collar of the "Midnight Rambler", the B&E crook who had been behaving as if he had been given a free pass for over a year.

Sergeant Thompson moved efficiently. He called Devlin O'Herligy in Wasilla, and Dick Trentham and Steve Maloney in Anchorage. His message was simple and quick.

"Listen up. There's big time trouble for the commander. Something outlandish went down out to his house, and some cops got killed. I don't know the details, but I have to put out an APB on him. Do what you can."

He did not wait for a reply.

At 14:48, thirty-two minutes into Flight 206, Thompson figured he had stalled as long as he dared and set in motion the communications network. At 14:59, a force of uniformed and plainclothes officers—local, state, and federal—swept into Anchorage International Airport, the downtown Greyhound terminals in Wasilla and Anchorage, and into every charter flight office in operation in the region. No one had a photograph of the fugitive yet. Every ticket counter attendant, porter, check-in attendant and restaurant waitress was canvassed over the next two hours.

The Skycab porter who had been over tipped was off shift and on his way home. The ground attendant who ticketed Richard Lindstrom for his flight to San Francisco was on break and was not available when her fellow counter attendants were questioned. None of the attendants at any of the ten gates for six airlines that had had flights out that day recognized anyone of that description—which, after all—was no more than the description of John Q Public—mister average man. The woman who had checked first class Richard Lindstrom onto his flight was put off by the brusque manner in which she was questioned and was disinclined to be helpful.

While officers began the tedious grunt work of interviewing flight and ground personnel, taxi records, bus station workers, porters, and charter flight services, Sergeant Carl Thompson phoned his preliminary report to his lieutenant. He gave essentially the same message to the state police, FBI, ATF, and the DEA.

"Lou? Carl Thompson here. Out at the airport. We got nothing on the Kennedy APB. We sealed the place up tight as a spinster's thighs. I ordered all flights cancelled. No manifest today had his name on it. I can only guarantee that he won't get out of this state from this point on, but I can't do anything about the possibility that he left earlier. Time frame seems wrong, though. No evidence that he got by—nobody seen or heard a thing, and his name hasn't appeared anywhere. I got people checking phone logs on the usual suspects and on the lookout for Kennedy's credit card. So far as we know, he only has one; that simplifies matters."

"Keep on it, Carl. The feds are having a hissy. This guy is like Hitler, Manson, and Dillinger rolled into one and on the loose. They really got the hots for him like nothing I ever seen before. We got a score to settle ourselves—Alex Tolberg, one of our own. I'm here to tell you that you have nothin' better to do than follow this case. I'll reassign your whole plateful. You find him, Carl."

"I will. He's still here; I can feel it in my bones. I'll get on the Militia people and the secessionists like warts on a toad. Somebody must be hidin' him. I'll sweat 'em until we get a lead. He's here. We'll find him."

"You do that. Keep me up-to-date, hear, Carl?"

"I hear you, boss."

CHAPTER THIRTY-ONE

D elta Flight 206 landed in San Francisco thirty minutes early. They had encountered a strong tail wind, and United Flight 818 from Hong Kong encountered mechanical difficulties and had to be diverted to Hawaii. This afforded 206 an unexpected opening in the landing pattern.

Randolph and his seat mate—an elderly Chinese woman—commented that the age of miracles had not ceased.

She said, "This is very good joss. We will both have profitable days."

Randolph thought he could use one. He waited fifteen minutes for his baggage. The two large bags came off the carousal in the middle of the pile. He drew no attention to himself in the general scramble to dislodge his bags in the company of four other frustrated dislodgers. He put five dollars in the slot and rented a baggage cart, muttering that the price had certainly gone up. He showed his luggage checks to the airport security guard and made his way through a throng of travelers and greeters. He went directly to the hotel courtesy desk.

"May I be of service?" the attractive young African American woman inquired.

"Yes, please, I'd like to get a room at the St. Francis."

"Going first class today, I see. Great place," she said with a broad affable smile, her white teeth almost luminescent. "I'll see what I can do. May be tough. Big computer convention in town. Hang on."

She picked up her red phone and pushed a button on the panel of hotel photographs on the screen in front of her.

"Marilyn Paget from the airport courtesy desk. We need a room for one gentleman. Queen sized bed, please, no smoking."

She raised her eyebrows at Randolph for his approval, and he nodded.

"I know you're busy, but please try. He seems very nice."

Marilyn flashed Randolph an infectious grin and rolled her eyes. He laughed.

"I knew you could do it, brother. I'll ask."

She looked at Randolph.

"You want one of their limos for the ride into town?"

"Please," he replied.

"Of course," Marilyn said to the hotel desk agent. "We have a first class guy here; what were you thinking?"

She laughed into the receiver, "Name? Uh oh, I forgot to ask."

She turned to Randolph.

"Name, sir?"

He had forgotten to think up a new fake name, and for a second, the question stopped him.

"Uh…"

A cart full of deli supplies passed behind him. Out of the corner of his eye, he caught the lettering: ORLANDO'S PRIME DELI. Randolph did not hesitate nor fumble.

"Orlando," he said to Marilyn, "Ralph Orlando."

It was possible that Randolph was influenced by the packages headed for the deli that prominently read, RALPH'S GROCERIES.

It had been a fairly long pause.

Marilyn said, "That was a tough one, eh?" and laughed.

It was obvious that she made nothing of his hesitation; so, he didn't either.

Marilyn gave the hotel receptionist the name.

"I'll ask him. How come I have to do all your work for nothing?"

Her smile remained intact throughout.

"He wants to know if you'll be using a card?"

"Tell him yes."

He fished into his wallet for his VISA card. He read off the number, transposing two of the numerals in each of the three sets of four numbers, then faked the expiration date.

"Thank you."

She put down the receiver.

"All done, sir," she said to Randolph. "The limo will be right out front, maybe five minutes. Have a good stay in San Francisco."

"Thank you. I appreciate your help and efficiency," Randolph said and handed her a ten dollar bill, part of the change from the ticket transaction at the Anchorage airport.

"That's all right, Mr. Orlando. You don't need to do that. We're really not supposed to take tips."

"I'd like to do it, Miss…"

He looked at the ID tag hanging from a chain around her neck.

"Paget."

"Well, if you insist. Thanks. I really could use it. You're a nice guy."

She looked at him, trying to guess what he was like in anticipation of her next joking comment.

"For a honky."

She gave him a doe-eyed look, and he laughed out loud.

"Have a good day," he said.

"You, too," she said as he started away from her desk.

The ride into the heart of the city from the airport was excruciatingly slow, with the traffic on the 101 looking more like the world's longest eight lane parking lot than a major traffic artery. It served him right for having arrived at early rush hour.

It was one of those rare glorious sunny days in San Francisco. The morning fog had cleared off early. As always when a truly nice day occurred, every San Franciscan who could get out of his or her house or could invent some excuse to leave work went out doors. The sidewalks and cafes were crowded; the parks were jammed with families and show-off Frisbee players; and the surface streets as well as the freeways were congested nearly to the point of gridlock. The limo driver was a bluff old Irishman who considered it his duty to give Randolph the grand tour spiel about the city since they had to stop so frequently.

The limo pulled onto Market Street.

"That's the Prudential Building. That's the Mission District—fulla bums. Cryin' shame. See the juggler. Pays big bucks to work that corner. I knew a hot dog vendor who clears a quarter mil on a corner by the convention center. See them guys—spics lookin' for work? Illegals. Nothin' stops 'em. I can show you a corner where you can get a real driver's license, green card, birth certificate, social security number from them wetbacks—the whole schmear. Them guys can have a new ID in half a day that checks out. Gives the immigration people fits."

He turned north onto Powell. Randolph had been largely ignoring the garrulous driver, but the Mission District exposition had piqued his practical interest.

"This is the Powell-Mason cable car route."

The crowds were as heavy as in Time's Square New York on New Year's Eve.

"Now we're gettin' into the nice parta town. That bit 'o green's Union Square. And that's the St. Francis across the street. Been here 150 years, maybe more. Class from the beginning. You ever stayed there before?"

"No."

"You'll love it. Best service you ever saw. They wash and iron your money for you. That's a service I wouldn't be a needin'. It's not for us workin' stiffs. But you might find it nice."

He pulled into the main entrance between Geary and Post Streets.

"Okay, sir, this is it. You just leave your bags with me. I'll see that the bell boys get them to your room. If you wanted to leave a tip, I'd be glad to pass it on to the boys."

Randolph withdrew a ten and a twenty from his inside jacket pocket.

"Here's the tip for the bellmen."

He handed the driver the two bills.

"And here's a little something for you."

The change money was gone. Randolph had only hundred dollar bills left.

"Hey, thanks, Mr…Now, I can buy me wee ones some shoes," he laughed roguishly, but was obviously very pleased with the extravagant tip.

Randolph laughed with him.

"I've heard a lot about San Francisco. I'm a free lancer for *Time Magazine,* and I'm writing an article on the great cities of the country. I have to get a hook for each city, you know, something different, not the usual travelogue stuff. Tell me where those illegal aliens, the ones who make the new identities, hang out. It would be worth a column."

The driver threw a quick suspicious glance at Randolph.

Randolph said, "Maybe I could include you and your limo company as part of the local color."

The driver changed his expression to one of it's-no-skin-off-my-back.

He already had a hundred bucks, and the guy looked clean cut. What the heck? he thought.

"Sure, that'd be interestin'. Any morning before seven, you go down south of Mission by the Santa Fe Depot. Mission and Third or Minna and Third, one of those two corners. You nose around a bit, and you'll find one 'o them spics that can put you on to the ID operation. It's flagrant as can be. I don't see why the cops don't shut it down. Like as not, they get a little back rub outta the deal, if you catch my meanin'."

"Got any sources I could use for that?" Randolph asked as if he were seriously interested. "That would be a great little addition to my piece."

"Naw, just speculatin'."

"Well, thanks. Maybe I'll look into it, if I can free up some time. Might be interesting. See you around."

"Yeah," said the driver, and returned to his limo.

He had another airport call coming in.

Randolph watched the limousine pull away from the St. Francis. His bags were inside the hotel now. He made a quick detour to two banks around the corner and cashed in hundreds for $6400 in smaller denominations. He cashed $3200 at each bank to keep his transactions beneath the radar screen of bank or federal scrutiny.

He walked back to the cool marble interior of the venerable old San Francisco landmark and strode quickly to the mahogany reception desk.

"Orlando," he said. "I called ahead from the airport."

"Ah, yes, Mr. Orlando. If you'll just fill in the registration form," the handsome Eurasian receptionist said.

Randolph quickly filled in a set of lies on the form for his address, telephone number and the name and address of his business. He was becoming quit facile with lying, but it occurred to him that he would pretty soon have to make some notes to keep track of all of the phony information he was leaving to avoid being tripped up. He had been working on an emergency basis thus far, and soon he would have to be able to show ID and look a lot more like a normal citizen. Only not now.

"May I see your VISA card, sir?" the mildly effeminate desk clerk asked.

"I've changed my mind. I'll pay cash. Do you want an advance?"

"I apologize, sir, but with cash we like to have a two day advance on the daily rate. If it wouldn't be that inconvenient?"

Not that it would matter if it were inconvenient.

"No problem. What do you need for the two days?"

"That's $550 a night, $1100 for the two. That doesn't include the city and state VAT and the twenty percent service fee. We can add that in later, if you want."

Randolph shook his head slightly. Hotel accommodations had become so expensive in the last few years that he had hardly ever stayed in one. It was a shock whenever he did. The prices escalated every year, keeping pace with the galloping inflation and taxes that were trying to stave off the apparently imminent bankruptcy of the United States. The 17 trillion dollar national deficit had to be paid somehow. He counted out the $1100.

"I hear you clean your guest's money. That true?"

"Yes, sir. Have done for 165 years. Have it for you in the morning, if you want to leave us some."

"How much cash would be appropriate for that service?"

"We have a limit of $10,000.

"I'll bring by a packet tomorrow morning."

"Here is your room entry device. It's keyed to your thumb print, of course." Of course.

"Just press your right thumb firmly on the marked square. Put that end into the door slot, and you're in. Nobody else has that unique entry information, not even the hotel; so, don't lose your device, whatever you do. Have a nice stay at the St. Francis and enjoy your time in the city. If there is anything we can do for you, don't hesitate to ask. The concierge desk is open 24/7."

"Great, thanks. My bags?"

"Bellman already has them in your room. He e-mailed his thanks for the tip on the in-house system. Oh, I forgot to ask, how long will you expect to stay?"

"A week."

"Fine. Is there anything else I can do for you today?"

"That's about it. I'm bushed. I'll go collapse. Thank you for all your help."

"Don't mention it."

Randolph found his bags on the luggage cots and his bed turned down. There was a chocolate Italian truffle on a Wedgewood dessert plate on his pillow. He was famished and almost swallowed it whole. He stripped naked and fell on the starched sheets and slept the sleep of the dead.

Sergeant Carl Thompson waited two hours for any word about any sighting of Randolph Kennedy at any of the bus or plane disembarkation locations anywhere in the state. There were no cruise ships due in or out of Alaskan waters for three days. Nothing came in from any of his sources. He had left wanted persons information everywhere in case Randolph holed up then left later in the week. There was no activity from the state highway patrol checks of the border crossing below Norway Junction. The common remote trails into the Yukon territory of Canada were checked, and everyone came up with a zero. The US Marshall's Fugitive Apprehension service had a BOLO out with a full description and a good picture of Randolph.

It was possible that the Militia had secreted him out of the state in one of their vehicles since they knew the state better than anyone else—every road, trail, and river in and out of the state that is five times larger than Texas. They would prove to be dangerous if apprehended with the fugitive. The more he investigated and received reports, the more likely it seemed to him that Randolph had escaped via the Militia's underground network. He knew he might be complicit after his call to O'Herligy, but he was sure his secret was safe.

Over the past two hours, Thompson made a point of interviewing men and women who had been at the site of the ATF assault. He came away with the disturbing sense that there was something very off about that affair, but no one could give him a precise or satisfying explanation. None of the Wasilla PD men and women had seen the slightest sign of Kennedy the whole night and day, and many frankly scoffed at the idea that he had been there at all. There was no evidence of any arms or drug cache on the property, except for a big old van parked off in the boonies that was full of contraband arms. One of the ATF men openly suggested that the van had been loaded with materiel removed from the Ketchikan Evidence Locker. Thompson would have to look into that. The hilltop site was now sealed off by the FBI, and none of the other law enforcement agencies were allowed in there.

He sighed. It would do no good to bother the airport and bus people again. They were competent, and he had to rely on them—no use antagonizing allies. He could not just sit there; so, he called the federal building.

"Oscar DeLentigo, FBI, please," he asked when the Federal Building operator came on the line.

"Just a moment," she said. I'll connect you to his voice mail."

As instructed, he pressed the four button on his phone.

"Hello," came the syrupy female federal voice.

They all sounded the same, about as sincere as an expert in snake oil. It was little short of a miracle that it was a human voice and not a recording; so, Thompson didn't complain.

"Carl Thompson, Wasilla PD. I need to talk to the boss, please. It's urgent."

Everything was urgent. This was the FBI, after all. She stifled a yawn.

"He's in conference. May I take your number?"

"Get him out of conference. This won't wait."

It was worth a try. The man probably only came out of conference for a call from Director Ted Coleman, the attorney general, or the president. Then again, he might only be in the can.

"DeLentigo, here. What can I do for you, Sergeant Thompson?"

Carl was pleased that the latter of his alternatives had evidently been correct.

"The Kennedy case. I'm in charge for Wasilla PD. We have zilch so far. Can you give us anything?"

"On the case?"

"Not so much that, although I do have a couple of questions. But I need everything you've got or have done towards apprehension of the perp: so, we don't bump heads.

"We are participating in the APB, and we have our own BOLO out. We forwarded it to Scotland Yard, the *Sûreté* in France, the *Carabinieri, Arma dei Carabinieri*, the *Polizia di Stato* all the *Polizia Provinciales*, and *Polizia Municipales* in Italy. We got the BOLO to the German *Bundeskriminalamt* or *BKA* and to their regional and local police. Essentially we have been in contact with every European police agency, and to Interpol. Everything we get will be sent to you as the central data base. So far, we don't have a thing."

"Look, Mr. DeLentigo, I gotta ask. Are you convinced that he was ever up on that hill during the time of the assault? We are all going to look pretty dumb if we turn over every rock between here and the border and find out belatedly that Randolph Kennedy was innocently sipping mint juleps with the Militia boys someplace."

"Part of our investigation centers on that very question. It's preliminary; so, I can't give you any very good answers. I do think we have enough credible witnesses to put him at the site that evening, and no evidence that he ever left. However, as you know, there's also no actual evidence that he was, in fact, in the house during the raid. It's a mystery. We have cadaver dogs sniffing for remains. We did find portions of the *Post* reporter, otherwise nothing. We have the coroner going over the place with a luminal light. We haven't so much as located a bitty piece of him. We've pulled out all the stops. He needs to be regarded as a fugitive from justice until we can sort all of this out."

Arson and explosion investigators from Wasilla PD, aided by the LAPO—the forensics laboratory of the FBI—were still sifting through the fragmented rubble at Kennedy's former home. They had been on the scene in time to detect any lingering petroleum-based accelerants. There were none. The "sniffer"—a portable vapor detector—had turned up nothing. Kapak Corporation polyester-polyolefin bags were being filled with debris by the hundreds as a matter of course for future chromatography, infrared spectophotometry, and x-ray diffraction.

DeLentigo went on, "They did find residues of military ordnance—TNT, PETN, and RDX, confirming the presumption that C-4 had been present. There were AFNO explosives made up of ammonium nitrate soaked in fuel oil and primers: lead azide, lead styphnate, and mercury fulminate. We have trace evidence of magnetic and fluorescent taggant chips using magnetic instruments and ultraviolet light."

Taggants are tiny color coded chips, the size of sand grains, which are added to commercial explosives during their manufacture to lead investigators to the manufacturer and through the distribution chain to the final legal possessor.

"Randolph Kennedy's supply of tagged explosives had come from Tecla Mining Company and was traceable only as far as the warehouse where Devlin O'Herligy had obtained them sans paperwork. He evidently got the explosives from a Tecla man who was a Militia member and who had long ago left the state. We are looking for him, but the most recent location for him, was somewhere in Saudi Arabia. We know that our fugitive used explosives to blast out his foundation, and I doubt that we will be able to make anything criminal stick. Even O'Herligy can plead guilty to having a sloppy secretary and will get nothing more than a reprimand he can file with all the rest of the official scoldings from the federal government.

"I have to tell you that the only unexplainable findings thus far from the investigating team are what was *not* found: the remains of the terrorist, gun runner, drug dealer, and deranged secessionist, Randolph Armstrong Kennedy, and not a single shred of evidence of illegal weaponry on the property unless you include that van we found just off the highway. The investigators turned up no indication that a non law enforcement individual or reporter had perished in the gunfire, explosion, and holocaust in that house. That includes the basement. All other charred and shattered bodies could be accounted for among the missing police officers and the *Washington Post* reporter found well outside the house itself. All told, we are charging Kennedy for nine murders, but that may be wishful thinking judicially. Peter Batchelder, FBI agent stationed in Ketchikan and Juneau, was seconded to this operation. He was one of the wounded taken out early in the morning. DNA testing on the organic fragments found thus far exclude Kennedy.

"What we have here is a Sherlock Holmesian story of an escape from a locked basement under the watchful eyes of an army of law enforcement officials. We also have a ringer—a van full of illegal weapons that do not belong to Kennedy. Unfortunately that is a proved fact. There are ATF fingerprints and DNA all over the thing, and not the smallest print from our star suspect. Two ATF agents have identified the contents of the van as having come from the Ketchikan Evidence Locker. That needs some investigation. When we have time, we are going to have a field day at the Locker. Want to come?"

"Very much. Let me know when. That is going to take a lot of sorting out whatever we find, or don't find. We are getting nowhere in our search for evidence that he has escaped the confines of our fair state. I'm afraid it's time to expand our APB to the rest of the country. It can't hurt to get all of CONUS involved, to ask for Canadian help, and alert the Mexicans. While we're at it, we probably ought to hit up the airports that run international flights from Alaska and around the country. If we don't get him here, we will have to get Interpol involved. What do you think, Mr. DeLentigo?"

"Sure, it looks inevitable. Go ahead and start it in motion. My office will issue the formal APB. It may result in us getting egg on our faces, but being perceived as overzealous would pale in comparison to being not thorough enough and having this loony turn up someplace like Chicago and carry on his version of World War III there. We are entering a lose-lose arrangement, but we have to keep on trooping anyway.

"This has been such a fiasco here, why not make it a 'spread misere'—as DanMcGrew would say—all the way across the country, why not the whole world? But, no matter what, we have to catch this guy. You work your end, and I'll work mine. I don't want...I *hate* to advertise our 'shortcomings'. I suppose is the world the bureau publicists will use. But, I have to, and so do you. Let's get it done," DeLentigo said glumly.

"Keep me posted, Mr. DeLentigo. I'll do the same."

"Thanks for the call."

They hung up. DeLentigo composed the text for a nation-wide all points bulletin.

Chapter Thirty-One

APB
WANTED: MAXIMUM PRIORITY
20 June

RANDOLPH ARMSTRONG KENNEDY
Age: 34, Height: 6'3", Weight: 210, Race: Caucasian
Hair: blond, Eyes: blue, No identifying marks or scars.

Wanted by FBI, ATF, State of Alaska and City of Wasilla for questioning in the death of nine federal agents, for suspicion of interstate trafficking in illegal armaments, interstate trafficking in illegal chemical substances as a drug lord, conspiracy to mount armed insurrection, RICO statute violations, and illegal flight to avoid arrest.

Presumed to be armed and extremely dangerous, bur agencies strongly desire that subject be taken into custody for questioning. PDD-39 may be invoked if necessary.

Approach only with extreme caution, and if possible, with group armed force.

If sighted, contact SAC Oscar A. DeLentigo, FBI, Federal Office Building, Anchorage, Alaska. Tel: (907) 349-8159, Fax: (907) 349-0034.

The message went to the NCIC [National Crime Information Center] operated jointly by the FBI and the states to provide information to 19,000 agencies controlling 24,000,000 law enforcement records. In addition to the U.S. nationwide dragnet that he set in motion, DeLentigo sent the directive OCONUS. DeLentigo considered Kennedy to be an international terrorist under the 1984 Act to Control International Terrorism. He was serious about even the harshest provisions—including, if necessary—application of PDD-39, a Clinton presidential administrative directive that contained a pugnacious paragraph. "If we do not receive adequate cooperation from a state that harbors a terrorist whose extradition we are seeking, we shall take appropriate measures to induce cooperation. Return of suspects by force may be effected without the cooperation of the host government."

For U.S. agencies outside the continental United States, DeLentigo forwarded the all-points bulletin to all foreign FBI offices through Department C-3—the International Counterterrorism arm of the bureau—and to the

Central Intelligence Agency with the request that the communiqué be sent WW SB—to all agency stations and bases world wide.

For non-U.S. agencies, he dispatched the information to Interpol and to the Middle-East terrorist hotline that ran television advertisements featuring Charles Bronson and Charlie Steen, despite their relative lack of significance on the U.S. national entertainment scene. As an afterthought, DeLentigo placed a call to the America's Most Wanted Hotline. Randolph Kennedy's description would be presented to all reward seekers who dialed the 1-800-HEROES-1 call-in line. The callers would be treated to a recorded narration by the former actor and former president of the NRA, Charlton Heston. That bit of irony was not lost on the FBI agent.

Satisfied with his thoroughness, DeLentigo then called his second in command, Denny Lathrop, into his office.

"Denny, I want you to head this up yourself. We have to get this guy. I think he's still here, so go after the Militia, the secessionists, and their families with everything we've got. Get someone on a search of every airport that received an airplane flight from Anchorage, Fairbanks, Juneau, Ketchikan, or Sitka between ten o'clock last night and ten o'clock tonight. Circulate the man's picture everywhere. We need every passenger manifest from every flight. Find out the name and whereabouts of every person who paid cash. Check for credit card matches. This is full priority and urgent; so, move in anyone you need. Use every snitch in the state. Get in touch with the RCMP. Finally, give me reports as needed but at least twice a day."

"Okay, Mr. DeLentigo, but you know that's a lot of man hours of work, a lot of overtime on the books. We aren't going to show results any time soon unless we break somebody down or have a bona fide miracle."

"So, let's get on it and work out a miracle."

Lathrop gave a little salute and attempted an about-face turn, but he had been out of the army for too many years, and he tottered, making both men laugh.

"Good luck, Denny," DeLentigo said earnestly.

"I don't much believe in luck, sir. You can wish me success."

"I do that, fervently."

Lathrop left the SAC's office and set his program in motion. DeLentigo called Special Agent Cynthia Gaffin. He had to wait three minutes for her.

"Out for an early lunch, Cynthia?" DeLentigo chided in a mock reprimanding tone.

"Oh, no, sir," she said in her little girl voice, "I forgot to sign in on the pee register. Won't happen again, sir."

He laughed. She was as tough as any of the men and was the best investigation leader in Alaska. He thought of her as the best female agent in the country since the department first accepted women in 1972.

"We'll keep this blemish off your record. But you'll owe me," he said, continuing their habitual banter.

"Wait just a second while I get my recorder on. This sounds like one more count of sexual harassment to me."

"You wish. Look, Cyndy, we've got a big time problem investigation on our hands. I'm not comfortable discussing this over the phone. How about coming over to my office; so, I can tell you about it."

"Still sounds like sexual harassment. I'll be over as fast as I can."

She gave a little mm-mm sound as if contemplating good food. He laughed and was once again grateful that the WOMs in Washington kept her in Alaska.

"Hi, boss," she said when she entered his office ten minutes later. "What's up?"

"I'm not altogether sure. Sit down and relax; it's a long story. I know you've heard about the Kennedy fiasco, but you need to be in the loop for all of the details.

DeLentigo gave her as much as he knew of the history of Kennedy and his problems with the ATF and with the President's Task Force, the plans and execution of the raid outside Wasilla last night and today. He carefully told her about the van and the sketchy hints about a trailer—their contents—and the possible alternative implications of their temporary presence at the scene and about the absence of the trailer.

"That's about it, Cyndy. I want a super careful and hush-hush investigation and report. Anything you turn up is to remain strictly between you and me until this thing is all sorted out. If there is anything hinky in all of this, I am not sure how far up the ladder it may lead; and I do not want to do anything precipitous. I certainly don't want a media circus, understand?"

"Sure I do. The SOS. I understand the same old political BS went on back when Hoover was the director. How come I think I am likely to get my sweet little patootie in a grinder before this is over?"

"Because you're perceptive. Look, I don't like this either. My tushy will be right there with yours if it hits the fan. Keep me posted."

"Okay. And boss?"

"Yes, Cyndy?"

"I love it when you talk dirty."

"Get out of here."

"Yassa, boss, on my way."

In an hour, special agents of the FBI and local law enforcement officials in twelve U.S. and six foreign cities were distributing clear photographs of Randolph Kennedy around the airports. The photograph they used came from the cover photo on the secessionist brochure. Passenger manifests were beginning to come in on the Alaska FBI fax machine and were copied and forwarded on to Carl Thompson of the Wasilla PD. San Francisco, Seattle, Salt Lake City, Chicago, New York, Dallas, Honolulu, and Denver were given the highest priority. Preliminary reports began to pour in two hours later and were uniformly disappointing, although that was a pretty routine happening at that stage of the game.

Despite wholesale arrests and threats against the Militia, no one admitted to having seen Randolph Kennedy in weeks. There was not a single admission of anyone having been at Kennedy's house for the past fourteen days, and no confession regarding any movement of guns in or out of Kennedy's property at any time. Coincidentally, there appeared to be an inordinate number of Militia on vacation just now—most of the plans having been made very recently.

Ian Laird, Kennedy's boss, was out of the country, and Kennedy's fellow employees were sketchy about when he was last in the office. He liked to do much of his work from his home computer, they said. Steve Maloney and Dick Trentham—who were reported to have been in Kennedy's house by watchers of the ATF—and Lance Pedersen—an Anchorage carpenter who was alleged to have helped carry crates of guns to the Kennedy place from Anchorage—were among the vacationers, their whereabouts unknown. Randolph Armstrong Kennedy seemed to have been swallowed up by the earth.

CHAPTER THIRTY-TWO

Gwen Chambers finished her article about the Wasilla shootout on her laptop on the flight back to New York. She arrived at midnight and printed her article off the computer the following morning at eight o'clock. She was in editor William Fitzgerald's office by ten after.

"Thanks for seeing me so early, Mr. Fitzgerald."

"My pleasure, Gwen. How did it go up there in the frozen north?"

"It was hot. How it went is something we ought to talk about."

"That sounds ominous. It's your nickel, shoot."

"I'm sure you know by now that Brocklin Phelps was killed in the explosion that occurred up there. That's for starters," Gwen said.

Her voice skipped an almost imperceptible beat.

He sat looking at her solemnly. Fitzgerald had a good habit of hearing his reporters out if they had his respect, and Gwen did. If they did not come up to his standards, they never made it into his office.

"It was a war, a sort of a war. Except, it was rather one-sided. Nobody up there ever saw the criminal—Randolph Kennedy—during the entire raid. Police intelligence—and in this instance that may well be a real oxymoron—had it that he was seen entering his house; the house was surrounded while he was in there; so, he could not possibly escape. He was never seen leaving. The place was blown to pieces along with more than a half a dozen cops and Brocklin, and the pieces were gone over in minute detail. Not a single trace was found of the man. Furthermore—to date—the FBI and the ATF have not found any convincing evidence that he had illegal guns, etcetera in his place. The scene was so contaminated with the residue of the government's explosives and firearms, that it looks like they will never be able to make a case against Kennedy if or when he might be found."

"He's the guy that is a member of one of those white supremacist hate groups, no?" Fitzgerald asked. "The Order of the Viper Militia, or some such Nazi bunch, isn't that right?"

"I guess you could say that. The government says that. The liberals all say that, and I am sure almost every media outlet in the country is going to say that. Incidentally, it is the North Star State Militia. I must say that I don't have enough information about that bunch that he is a member of—in fact, is the head of—or about the secessionist movement up there. He's certainly involved, gave one rousing speech thus far; at least that's what I've been able to glean on short notice. I didn't run onto anything that's all that incriminating, nothing like plotting or advocating sedition or armed insurrection.

"The locals complain that it is interesting how the most extreme left-winger is always portrayed sympathetically in the press—including especially our shop—and their organizations and opinions are demonized.

"There's more than a grain of truth in this instance, I think. The nuttiest lefty theories are given a hearing—especially if they emanate from some victim group—and particularly if that group happens to be the latest favorite oppressed minority. We excuse the most heinous acts—the good folks up there in the hinterlands say—as long as their activities have something to do with minority rage, reaction to the patriarchy, or against right-wing extremists. They point out—accurately, I must agree—that the aspirations, attitudes, and activities of the right wingers get very short shrift when it comes to any discussion of their point of view."

He raised an eyebrow at her.

"And your point?"

"Look, Mr. Fitzgerald, I don't think we've dug deeply enough into this affair. You know, the real story may well not be that some right wing fanatic ran afoul of the law. There may be something rotten in Denmark—that part of Denmark nearer the capital and the centers of power—is all I'm saying. There are a couple of puzzling aspects about this story. First of all, where is he? Where *was* he? Did he kill those agents, or did they do themselves in with friendly fire? Secondly, an odd thing happened. I went out to the woods for a moment of private contemplation."

He laughed, envisioning that deep personal moment and not presuming that it was a la Thoreau at Walden Pond.

"And I stumbled onto a big white van with an attached trailer hidden in the trees. I got a small chance look inside the van myself, but…before I cleared off that hill, the FBI found it and it had been moved into a hiding place further into the trees, than when I saw it; and the trailer was gone. Maybe they don't even know about the trailer, for all I know. Give a little guess what was inside it."

"I give up. The terrorist?"

"Alleged terrorist. And no-o, it was jammed full of guns, stuff to make bombs, and heroin and cocaine as near as I could make out."

"Which would be confirmatory evidence of the terrorist's possession of dangerous illegal weaponry, it would seem to me," the editor opined.

"I don't think so. The cops all seemed pretty pershimmered over its presence—not the heartfelt joy at discovery of the 'smoking gun' that one might have expected. For one thing, it was certainly in a peculiar location. For another, it got moved by a person or persons unknown. I can't even imagine this Kennedy character taking time to futz around with a van when it would have been all he could do to get his heiny out of there. And I do know that the FBI is going to run a quiet investigation of the whole affair with considerable emphasis on the van and maybe the trailer—the missing trailer. I think we should research what that stuff was and where it came from and how it got there before we rush to judgment in an article that leaves us with egg on our faces like that old news disaster, the Ruby Ridge incident years ago."

"Gwen, I know you reporters have to maintain a high index of suspicion; but as I listen to your description, I come away with the best theory being that Kennedy hid weapons, and they were found."

"Maybe, but it was certainly in a peculiar location, and one of the agents towed the big trailer away. I watched him do it. So far, the trailer isn't part of the crime scene. I don't know what to make of that, but it points me away from Kennedy. The fibbies closed off the entire hill as a crime scene and have kept everybody—and I mean everybody including other law enforcement officers—away. I would give a month's salary to know why, and to find out what they learn about the whole business. Aren't you curious about whose fingerprints are in the van? Wouldn't it be a twist if Kennedy's were *not* there?"

"That would be the interesting story in all of this, and I think you ought to stay on it. But don't get over anxious or overzealous. You have a back page story of a spectacular police raid—a pretty mundane story—right now. If you can pry some info out of the FBI about the investigation or about Kennedy, that will add to your story; and we can move it up to page three. Find something that clearly demonstrates planted evidence or some such chicanery on the part of the cops, and you'll see your byline on the front page. I am telling you right now, Gwen, I will not allow one word of speculation about that in the *Times*. We would be sued for everything the paper owns, and it's not going to happen on my watch."

Gwen looked hurt; she felt hurt; but she knew he was right. She would have to get to somebody, and she would have to come up with something solid before she cast any aspersions on the great ones of the land.

She turned to Fitzgerald.

"I'll get it. I'll go back to Alaska and pester the FBI agents there. I deserve a break after everything I went through and after Brock died for this story."

She was not angling for sympathy, and she knew that William Fitzgerald—the man with a stone heart and printer's ink for blood—would not be handing out any. She went back to her office and sent her article on for publication the next day. She informed the copy staff that Fitzgerald had ordered it to be featured on page 3 with pictures. The imp in her made her fib to keep it off the back page. She would have liked to expand the lie and get the article placed as the front page headline and to take up the whole right column. Gwen—however—was a pragmatist and did not relish having to find a new job; so, she settled for a token bit of insubordination. She shut down her computer then called the FBI office in the Anchorage Federal Building.

It was nearly noon when Randolph awakened in his comfortable king size St. Francis Hotel bed. He was stiff, and his hands were asleep where he had lain on them without hardly moving the entire night. He yawned, stretched, and luxuriated. It took him several minutes to remember where he was and why he was there. That part he would have liked to forget, but he turned the TV on to the Fox News Channel, and watched the national news. The first item was about the first forest fire of the new season, presumed to be an arsonist involved blaze. The next item caught Randolph's full attention.

"Officials close to the abortive raid on the hate group in Alaska yesterday have informed CNN that the FBI is now investigating suspected irregularities in the raid. They have launched a dragnet nationwide—indeed—worldwide, for the white supremacist hate group leader, Randolph Kennedy. His whereabouts are unknown; but the FBI, working with a number of other law enforcement agencies has several strong leads, and expect an arrest soon, according to the Special Agent in Charge in Wasilla, Alaska, Oscar DeLentigo. He would give no details. The supremacist leader is considered to be a fugitive and is presumed to be armed and very dangerous. These are recent photographs taken of the wanted man; the first is a mug shot from Hopewell, Virginia where Kennedy was arrested two years ago on terrorism charges. The second photo comes from a hate literature brochure published by a white supremacist Militia and secessionist group in Alaska. Mr. DeLentigo cautions all our viewers to avoid taking any actions yourself if you should see the fugitive. Simply contact local law enforcement officials or the nearest office of the Federal Bureau of Investigation.

"It is suspected that Kennedy—a ranking official in the hate group—is being harbored by members of his organization. The network of survivalist, anti-tax, anti-government, minority hating paramilitarists is known to be very sophisticated and has tentacles worldwide. As a result, the hunt is being conducted on every continent."

Randolph was treated to a motion picture of himself taken in front of Devlin O'Herligy's gaudy store front. He was dressed in camouflage clothing. That short video clip faded into another short video, this one featuring a bearded, partially toothless, camouflage dressed moron pacing nervously around a campfire. He was carrying an M-16 and brandishing it at the shadows outside the light of the campfire. The man's arms were covered with crude tattoos, and the video camera zoomed in on one forearm to show clearly the simple black tattoo—a typical prison tattoo—that read: "Jesus Loves White People".

Randolph ground his teeth both at the overdrawn linkage of him to white supremacy fanaticism and to the inaccurate juxtaposition of the camo moron tape to the pictures of himself. He knew that the viewers would not be able to separate the two.

"And, ladies and gentlemen, after a word from our sponsors—Seagrams and RJR—we'll be back with the latest on the NBA point shaving scandal."

It was something of a shock to see himself so vividly and negatively portrayed to a three hundred million viewer television audience. He should have expected it—of course—but that did not lessen the impact. He was wide awake now, and he knew fully that he would have to be extremely careful that day, and he would somehow have to contrive a disguise when he left the safety of his cocoon in the hotel. He showered and shaved and called down to order room service for breakfast. He left a tip on the dresser and stayed in the bathroom until the room service waiter arranged his breakfast tray and left. Although it seemed a feeble attempt, he only fluffed out his curly hair instead of brushing and combing it into his usual neat coif. He looked in the mirror—there was a somewhat aging hippie looking back at him, but the change in his appearance was short of dramatic.

Randolph knew that he needed new clothes—things that did not look like the old Randolph. He checked out the hotel's exclusive boutiques and shops and selected a men's shop where no TV was in sight. He made the clerk's day by purchasing several shirts and a suit, shoes, and a floppy wide brimmed foppish European girly man hat and large Italian sunglasses. In his new get-up he felt like a transvestite, but his appearance was significantly enough altered to give him confidence to go out in public. This was San Francisco, after all.

He got in the first cab in the queue in front of the St. Francis and told the driver, a Chinese woman who could scarcely see over the steering wheel, "Corner of Mission and Fourth, please."

She was a pleasure. She never spoke a word from the St. Francis until she let him out below the Santa Fe bus station.

"Ten dollar, fifty-two cent," she said tersely in strongly accented English.

He gave her two tens. She gave him back a five and began to search for the rest of the change.

"Keep the rest," he said.

"Thanks you," she said and was gone.

Randolph looked around. A few stragglers, a homeless man lying on the sidewalk, threadbare women purposefully walking past. The buildings were old and uninviting, many of them windowless. They were uniformly grimy. There were no doors on the street, and the entrances were located down trash strewn alleys. He wondered idly where all those women could all be going in such a concentrated frame of mind. He saw no Mexicans anywhere.

He walked down a block to Minna Street. On the corner stood a dozen or so obviously Hispanic men in work clothing. They held gloves and lunch pails and made motions toward the street every time a vehicle went past. Randolph was uncomfortable out in public and felt only partially protected by his new costume. He comforted himself that the men on the street did not look like they spent much time watching CNN. He sauntered up to the nearest group of workmen as nonchalantly as he knew how.

"Do any of you speak English?" he asked tentatively.

He was afraid that he might scare them off. He hoped he did not look like an immigration officer but was pretty sure that no self-respecting INS officer would be caught dead in a hat like the one he had on.

They were reticent; most moved away slightly and cast quick glances around the area. Randolph assumed that they were either looking for additional officers or were calculating their best route of escape. He knew how they felt.

A powerfully built man with skin like bronze and an Aztec warrior's face said quietly, "I do, a leetle beet."

"Thanks. I need some information. I'm not a cop, not from immigration, and I'm not a reporter. I need some special information for myself."

The Aztec warrior scrutinized Randolph from head to toe with penetrating black button eyes.

"Let me see jour wallet," he said laconically.

Randolph flinched, but guessed that he had no choice. He handed it to the man.

"Pleny money, Anglo. What you do? Rob *un banco*?"

"Maybe," Randolph said and smiled, at ease.

He did not feel threatened by them. Rather, he felt a sort of kinship, the camaraderie of those looking from the outside in at society. He was ripe for some kind of kinship and was in no position to be choosy.

Now, the man began to look at Randolph more seriously.

"Maybe jou tell me what you want, and I can help jou do some beesiness."

He was drawing Randolph gradually away from the other men who were beginning to lose interest in the Anglo interloper.

"I want some new ID."

"Jou got ID, good ones. I seen jour wallet."

"I want *different* ID papers and cards, and I want them today. I am willing to pay for good quality. If you can help, I'll make it worth your while. If not, I'll go find another man."

"Not getting hasty, *señor*, a man has to be careful. Like maybe jou are the law. Jou know what I'm talking about?"

"I do. I have more to lose than you do. Now, can we do business? And I don't mean out here in the street."

"Jess."

The Aztec warrior wrote his name: 'Guillermo Perez' and an address: '736 Minna, apartment number 330, by the Greyhound bus station' on a piece of notepaper and handed it to Randolph.

"Jou be there in fifteen minutes. I gotta see a man. *Adios*."

He turned abruptly and walked down 4th Street towards Natoma.

Randolph let him get out of sight then sauntered west on Minna, checking his watch to be sure he was precise about his arrival at the place of assignation. From time to time, he casually turned around to satisfy himself that he was not being followed. The area was badly run down. The side walk was cracked and covered with litter, the walls of nearby buildings with gang graffiti. There enough signs in Spanish that—along with the litter—he could have been in a backwater Mexican city instead of the American 'City by the Sea'. There were few people on the street, and those few were sullen and unresponsive to him. It was a perfect place for him to be, he realized. He paused in a Korean grocery which gave him a chance to look all around—still no sign of police or of anyone interested in him.

Randolph passed the old U.S. Mint on 5th and the post office on 7th. He was becoming accustomed to paying attention to his surroundings and to the people in them. Did he see the same person more than once? He could not afford to write anything off to coincidence. He was rapidly developing criminal reflexes. Just across 7th, behind the bus station, he found the address Guillermo had given him. A strung-out none-to-clean middle aged African-American woman in a hot pink mini-mini skirt and a tank top that was struggling to contain her approached him while he was killing time waiting for Guillermo's deadline.

"Lonely, dearie?" she asked.

He shook his head.

"Wanna party?"

"No, thanks."

"You like what you see, sailor?"

"Not really," Randolph said, "I'm gay."

He was learning to think quickly as the situation demanded.

"Oh, nuthin' wrong with that, bro. No offense meant."

Randolph smiled and nodded. She gave her Afro a little flaunce and sashayed away intent on finding a more likely prospect.

There was still several minutes left, and Randolph was afraid that he would draw attention to himself by standing around. He meandered around the block on the mean streets of the Mission District. Only when it was the agreed upon time for the meeting did he cross the street and approach the door of number 736. The number Guillermo had written down—330— belonged to a door on the third floor of a dilapidated walk-up apartment building. The bathroom was in the middle of the hall to provide equal access for all the tenants. There were smells of cooking beans, tortillas, saffron, cilantro, and chilies. Women shouted in Spanish; babies and children cried, laughed, and shouted in the same exuberant language generating a steady stream cacophony and all behind closed doors. He knocked on the heavy door of 330.

He heard several dead bolts and chain locks being unlocked.

"*Venga*," came Guillermo's now familiar voice from behind the still closed door.

Presuming that meant something like, 'come in', Randolph twisted the knob and pushed the door. When it was open, he stepped inside and found himself facing two determined men with short-barreled shot-guns pointed at his midsection.

"What is this?" he demanded cursing himself that he had allowed himself to be set up to be robbed or even killed.

He was so tense that he thought he was going to begin to tremble and to shame himself in front of these men.

"I came to do business. Is this how you do business?"

"Shut up."

The command came from the man with Guillermo—the man he had evidently gone to see. He was older than Guillermo, better groomed, and fat. He wore a black suit, black tie, and gray silk dress shirt entirely reminiscent of old mustachio-Pete mafia gangsters of the prohibition era. His face was the color of walnut wood, and he wore a pencil-line mustache. Guillermo gave him deference which the man accepted as his due. There was no rancor in the man's voice, just authority. Fear prickled the back of Randolph's neck, but it was partly assuaged by seeing the trappings of a photographic studio and a small printing press in one corner of the sparsely furnished room.

The older man looked Randolph over carefully for several minutes before speaking.

"Freesk heem, Guillermo," he ordered.

Guillermo moved with alacrity to do the fat man's bidding. Guillermo was very thorough.

"Nothing, *compadre*."

"*Bueno*. Now, *señor*, you get one minute to tell us if jou are any kina cop," the fat one said in a controlled but threatening monotone.

"We fine out later jou are, and…"

He passed his index finger slowly across his throat from ear to ear and mouthed a convincing slitting sound. No words were necessary. The portly man in the gangster suit squinted at Randolph, sizing him up for what seemed to Randolph like just short of eternity.

Randolph broke the awkward silence, "I'm not a cop. I don't want to have anything to do with cops. That's why I'm here. I really don't even want to go back out on the street until I absolutely have to."

A shadow seemed to pass away from the authoritarian man's face.

"I yam Pancho. Pancho Hernandez de la Riva. Who are jou?"

"You don't need to know that. Can you make me new ID documents and cards that will pass or not?"

"Of course…eef I want to. Can jou pay? Cash?"

"Yes…if I want to. I will want to for good quality stuff. I want the work done today. I don't want to be on the streets without the proper papers even one more day."

He knew he was throwing away his bargaining chips by showing these men that he was anxious, but it was a fact that he needed to have the documents and could not wait. He only knew to say it in so many words and to take his chances with these criminals. He hoped for honor among thieves.

"I beleef jou," said Pancho, having made up his mind and to the relief of Randolph.

In another time or place, maybe in a better world, Randolph would have laughed at himself for being so eager to attain the approval of such men. That attitude was from another life.

"Now, jou say what jou want. Hexactly."

"Birth certificate, social security card, driver's license, passport, maybe a Teamster's or UAW card and all three major credit cards. Come to think of it, I want three separate identities. Maybe a green card for one of them."

"That all?"

Pancho's voice dripped with friendly sarcasm as if Randolph was the fisherman's wife who had just asked for the sun, the moon, and the stars.

"Not quite. I need to change my appearance for two of the three new identities, and I need to have all of them done today."

"Wheew," whistled Pancho and Guillermo. "Jou don' wan much, do you Señor No-Name? What jou ask; no ees possible. No in only one day, señor."

"I can pay."

"I hope so, because eet weel cos' you pleny," said Pancho. "But ees no the money. These things they take a leetle time to do right. I jam arteest you know."

He smiled with pride and without a hint of irony or self-deprecation.

"How long is the fastest you can work and do your artistic best?"

"Three days."

Randolph's heart sank. What was he going to do for three days?

Chapter Thirty-Two

Guillermo sensed his need.

"I don' know what you deed, *pero* I theenk jou are all right. Jou can stay weeth me and my Maria while Don Pancho does hees work. That hokay weet jou?"

Randolph was surprised, pleasantly so.

"It would be an honor and a pleasure, Don Guillermo."

No one had ever used an honorific with Guillermo. It warmed him.

"Hokay, we are poor people. Jou can pay $100 a night, *amigo*?"

Randolph would willingly pay a $1000.

"A deal," he said.

He extended his hand, and he and Guillermo shook hands like old friends.

"All of these weel cos' jou about 4000 American, *señor*. Can jou handle that?"

Randolph took a small gulp. This fugitive status was an expensive business.

"Yes," he said with meekness and reluctance.

What else could he do?

"Hokay, we get started. Take the *fotographias* first. I theenk one weeth jou just like jou are, then one weeth a *rubio* beard."

Pancho walked to an old theater trunk in the corner of the room and picked out a very well made blond beard and a pair of round spectacle frames without lenses. He held them up to Randolph and muttered his satisfaction.

"*Mañana*, we fine jou a black beard, dye jour hair, and get jou some temporary tattoos. Jou won' know jour own self."

Randolph sat for two sets of photographs, one with himself in a smooth face, pomaded hair, shirt, tie, and jacket. The other was a frowsy, light-bearded professor in a gray turtleneck sweater and tweed jacket. In that picture he wore round, wire-rimmed glasses. Only with effort could even Randolph have told that the two pictured men were one and the same, and neither was the old Randolph.

After dark, Randolph left the Mexicans and returned to the St. Francis to check out. He picked up his washed and ironed money and smiled his amusement.

"Looks like you made it in your basement," he said to the cashier.

"We do, sir. Just part of the service," the cashier replied with a naughty twinkle in her eye.

Randolph had his bags taken to the curb, and the doorman hailed a cab.

"To the Greyhound bus station," Randolph requested when he was seated in the back seat.

The cabby looked at him with curiosity. Guests leaving the St. Francis never— but never—traveled on the bus. He shrugged. It was none of his business.

"Would you help me with the bags, please?" Randolph asked when they stopped in the cab stand by the Greyhound station.

"Sure, Mac."

Randolph gave him a twenty for a five dollar ride. The cabby became enthusiastic about helping him. The doorman and the cabbie made themselves indispensable until he and his overweight bags were deposited Randolph and his overweight bags at the ticket counter.

"Have a nice day, buddy," said the cabby when he took his leave.

"You, too," said Randolph.

He bought a round-trip ticket in the name of Peter Gordon to San Diego with the return to be within the month. He paid cash as was his new and obligatory habit. Randolph moved away from the ticket booth and into the teeming crowd in the large bus terminal—into oblivion, so far as the ticket seller was concerned. He lugged his suitcases to a wall of lockers and squeezed one suitcase into each of two lockers. He kept the money from the St. Francis in his suit coat pocket.

He was nervous and sweaty when he knocked on the second floor flat that Guillermo, Maria, and their four children occupied. It was immediately below Pancho Hernandez de la Riva's photographic and makeover studio. Maria was a short round little woman with a red-brown berry toned Mayan face and hair the color of India ink. She wore a pullover cotton dress with vividly colored Southwest patterned stripes and flash accents. She had been expecting him.

"*Venga conmigo, Señor,*" she said, self-conscious and shy about her lack of English.

She let him into a small bedroom that smelled faintly of urine and messy diapers. Obviously one or more of her children had had to vacate their bedroom to accommodate him.

"*Gracias,*" he said exhausting his minimal Spanish.

She bowed and blushed. He lay on the bed, paced the floor, or sat on the rocking chair after she left him alone in the room. The rocking chair was the only piece of furniture in the bedroom outside the bed. He spent the night and most of the next day in the room.

That evening, Maria invited him to *la cena*. Supper was simple and good— vegetables strongly seasoned with *poblano verde* chilies and *empañadas* with *picadillo*. As if the spicy meat filling was not hot enough, Maria made sure that Randolph had his own bottle of four-chili rated Endorphin Rush Beyond Hot Sauce, a portion the size of a pencil lead being strong enough for a gallon of chili for the unwary gringo. The table cloth was starched and brilliantly clean and white though frayed in places. The utensils and dishes were chipped and of the cheapest manufacture, but also spotlessly clean. The children were uncomfortable in their Sunday best clothing, their black hair shining and squeaky clean in his honor. They were too timid to speak, but flashed warm shy smiles each time Randolph looked at them. There were so charming that he could not help but smile all of the time he was around them. His obvious spontaneous affection for the children was infectious for their mother and for them. It was the best he had felt since he had last sat down to a greasy fast-food supper with his wife and his little girl.

In the late evening, he heard a low knock on the main apartment door. He sat up on the bed—nervous and overly attentive—concerned that he had been betrayed for some reward money of which he was unaware, and that he was trapped in this tiny room. Muffled men's voices came from the doorway heightening his sense of alarm. He eased the door open and saw Pancho and Guillermo talking. Guillermo saw him and bade Randolph come. Pancho had more "peechers" to take.

He and Pancho walked up the flight of stairs to the third floor, and Randolph followed the Mexican into his studio. There was another person in the room, a large, very muscular Mexican Indian woman.

"We change jou now. Jour own mama weel not know her own son."

That was a relief. Randolph had grown tense and jittery during the last two days whenever he met someone new and at the very thought of going back outside with all those photographs of himself floating around. The woman had him sit in a chair in the middle of the room, and then she proceeded to give him a bulldog hair cut with a square top, something out of the previous century, the 1950s. He checked himself out in the mirror when he could and was shocked at the difference the change in his hair-do had wrought. His regular hair style had grown long through mild neglect, and he had begun to comb it over his ears and down to the nape of his neck. Now he looked like an aging mercenary soldier on leave.

"Deeferent, no?" Pancho laughed.

"Different, yes. It's good," Randolph answered, obviously pleased.

"We jus' started. Angelina, she will make jou: so, even *jou* won't know yourself."

True to Pancho's word, the big strong, affable Mexican woman dyed Randolph's hair coal black, including his eyebrows. Randolph looked at himself in the mirror and once again was astounded at the transformation. It was amazing, and confidence building. He would defy anyone to pick him out of a crowd by comparing his new look to the old photo being shown by the police.

"Steel no' done, amigo," said Pancho.

He was enjoying himself at Randolph's expense. He was no longer the least bit apprehensive about the gringo who was now regarded as a good client. Angelina opened a small bag she had set down in one corner of the utilitarian room.

"Take hoff jour clothes, amigo. Hall off them."

Pancho was laughing at Randolph's discomfiture. Randolph looked at the fat man with incredulity.

"Ees hokay, amigo. I weel protect jou from these wild *mujer*!"

He was now laughing so hard that he had to sit down. Randolph was pressed to find the humor in the situation. He was naturally reticent and even shy around women, and taking off his clothing in front of the behemoth Mexican woman was a hard pill to swallow. Angelina extended her hand and showed him a tube of brownish cream. He inspected it. "Chemical Formulation, temporary tanning cream".

He understood and knew he was being silly. Angelina had no doubt seen better specimens than him. Randolph took off his clothes quickly. Angelina smiled broadly in appreciation of the gringo's trim and muscular body which made poor Pancho break down again into hysterical laughter, his jowls shaking. Randolph looked so ludicrous to himself standing there as the one naked man in the room that he began to laugh as well. It was a minor cathartic laugh, the first time he had felt that he could still manage such a vocal response in many days. Angelina's usually stern peasant face was creased with affectionate smile lines.

She kept him standing and began to rub his back with the browning cream. He took dollops in his hands and rubbed the areas that would have been best for shy Angelina to avoid, Randolph decided. She even covered his face, including expertly coating his eyelids and the curving ridges and valleys of his ears. When Randolph next looked in the mirror, he was an entirely new person, a tough Mexican field worker, thin, sinewy, muscular, and dark brown.

The transition was incomplete as it turned out. He was now directed to sit down in the chair again. This time, the versatile Angelina reached into her magic plastic bag and withdrew an electric tattooing machine and set out three patterns of typical Mexican tattoos for Randolph's approval. At this, Randolph balked.

"I don't want some permanent marking. I'll take my chances; and I'm confident that I will get out of this mess someday, and I don't want to have a tattoo disfiguring me then. I am going to want my own skin back someday."

"No *tienes preocupado, mi amigo*. Ees no' *permanente*. Weel go away, maybe *tres meses*. Never know jou had them."

Randolph looked dubious.

"Three months," explained Pancho.

Randolph agreed to submit. What on earth had he gotten himself into? He longed for his old life as a boring, plain vanilla CPA back again. He was nervous; and it hurt as Angelina tat-tat-tatted away on his skin, pausing frequently to wipe away the small accumulations of blood. After what seemed like an all night torture session, Angelina signaled that she was done. Randolph Armstrong Kennedy, erstwhile unremarkable American WASP CPA, now sported three south-of-the-border tattoos. His right forearm had Jesus on a cross with a prominent Catholic bleeding heart and the words, "*Santa Maria Dame Socorro*". The fingers of his left hand had crude letters on them, "*Mal Parido*" In the middle of his back, Randolph displayed the major work of Angelina's art—a large, vividly colored diamond-back rattlesnake in a sombrero about to strike a gringo in a suit lying terrorized beneath him. A small Mexican flag was incongruously stuck in the ground near the menacing snake.

Randolph could only shake his head when the two Mexicans held up mirrors; so, he could scrutinize the artwork.

Pancho opened his own plastic bag and handed Randolph a new set of clothes: a black Harley Davidson tank top, black, tight-fitting jeans with a wide black leather belt with a silver buckle from Tasco, and rough black boots with steel buckles.

Randolph's face must have framed a question, because Pancho said, "They was jus' worn for a leetle time by the previous owners."

He handed Randolph a black motorcycle helmet and heavy black motorcycle gloves. When Randolph had finished putting on the motorcycle regalia at Pancho's insistence, the transition was complete indeed. Not only would his mother—rest her soul—not recognize him; she would not have wanted to. With the jacket zipped up all the way and the black visor of the helmet pulled down, his facial features were as obscure as Darth Vader's.

Randolph did not know whether to laugh or to cry. But he did know that the real artistry of Pancho and Angelina were going to make him safe for some time to come, and that was a cause for celebration.

Angelina gave him an extra supply of the deeply staining tanning cream and instructions about the frequency of application. The dye on his skin had matured into a sun burnt deep bronze color, as natural as the color of the two other people in the room. Even under his careful scrutiny, Randolph could not detect even a hint of his Nordic origins. Angelina smiled at him and left. It was well after midnight.

"Now, back to Guillermo and his Maria before they send the *policia* out to find jou," said Pancho.

When Randolph awakened and dressed the next morning and ventured into the family areas, Pancho and Guillermo were at the breakfast table eating salsa and beans on fresh tortillas. Randolph had showered and shaved and the color had remained as deep as when Angelina applied it. He was impressed with her work. The children looked at him with unabashed curiosity. Although they knew from his voice that he was the same man who had sat down to *la cena* with them the previous night, he might as well have been a different person—probably a mean *pachuco*. His eyes revealed his affection for them, and they soon responded in kind. The initial curiosity and trepidation of the children vanished and shortly the two men, Maria, and the four children were enjoying a noisy, laughing meal.

"Time for business?" Randolph asked the two men.

Maria shooed the children into the other room.

"Eef jou are ready, *Señor*," said Pancho with courtly courtesy.

"I haf an itemized beel for jou," said Guillermo.

It was much like a visit to the doctor's office with the settling of the professional fee.

Randolph inspected the carefully hand lettered bill without great interest. The total was $4,210. Pancho handed Randolph three separate packets of documents. There were appropriate and apparently genuine driver's licenses, birth certificates, passports, union cards, and social security cards for each of the new identities. The new men lived in different states, had different jobs, and had completely dissimilar faces and modes of dress. At will, Randolph could become Jaime Hidalgo Cortez', a legal alien from Guaymas, Mexico, or he could assume the identity of Dr. Gerald Packer Wertz of the California Institute of Technology living in Carmel. He could also change to Dan Spencer, a long haul truck driver from Murray, Utah. Dan had an LDS temple recommend; Jaime had a glossy credit card sized painting of Our Lady of Guadalupe, and Dr. Wertz had a Unitarian Church membership card to complete the authenticity of the documentation. For the time being, the only choice Randolph had was to be the nut brown—betattooed Mexican—Jaime Cortez'.

He left the two Mexicans and went to his room. His wallet—full of cash— was sitting where he had left it. The family could have taken tens of thousands of dollars from it or from his suit jacket pocket, but not a *centavo* had been touched. He brought out $5,000 in crisp $100 bills and set them in a pile on the table. Pancho counted it very swiftly and expertly.

"Too much," he said when he was done.

"I want something more…two things more," Randolph told them. "First, I want you to forget that you ever saw me, ever did anything for me."

"For who?" asked Guillermo.

Randolph smiled.

"Secondly, I want you to buy me a used Harley and a couple of panniers. Maybe you can show me how to operate it. I'll give you the cash."

"Done," said Pancho.

CHAPTER THIRTY-THREE

After a fruitless week, Carl Thompson called his boss, Lieutenant Bradley. "Nothing, Lou. Either he's holed up somewhere, and nobody's going to tell us where, or he's flown the coop. Either way, this is a waste of time. I say we pull back and put it on the back burner."

Carl Thompson was known as a bulldog but a pragmatic one. When he said there was nothing to go on, there was nothing to go on. Bradley agreed.

"I'll call the fibbies. You pick up your old neglected cases. This guy isn't worth three-quarters of our department working full time for another week."

Bradley did not have to call DeLentigo. The special agent in charge of the Anchorage office called him.

"This is DeLentigo, Lieutenant Bradley. I put in a call to Carl Thompson who's in charge of the Kennedy case in your jurisdiction, but he was out for the moment. The secretary referred me to you, okay?"

"Sure, whatta you have?"

"It's what I don't have that I'm calling you about. I don't have clue one where Randolph Kennedy is. Your department and mine have been running redundant investigations, and near as I can tell we are no place. We have talked to every snitch, rousted every Militiaman, stirred up every nest of them and have zilch. Threw a bunch of them in the lockup on one old charge or another, some pretty flimsy. Nothing. Nothing shook out of those trees no matter how hard we tried. We have sent people into all the airports we could rationally think of in the lower forty-eight where he could have gotten out. We had the full cooperation of the RCMP. Nothing. Nobody has the slightest inkling of where the man could have crossed a border, taken a flight, or traveled with someone in his movement without us being able to turn up some witness or some suggestive document. My investigator, Lathrop, is good. I have heard nothing but good things about your guy, Thompson. And our combined efforts have come up with nothing. Maybe Kennedy was never there. I think it more likely that he was; but now he's been able to skip, maybe even to Europe or South America. We're gonna pull back our horns for now. Maybe you folks will want to do the same."

"We came to the same conclusion just before you called, Mr. DeLentigo. I'd like to know what you're coming up with on the investigation at the crime scene. We lost a very good man up there. We want to know why."

"Don't blame you. I have a fine agent working on it. She's very meticulous and slow. Drive you nuts, but her work always stands up. We're all going to have to be patient. I'll tell you frankly, Bradley, I may have to keep some of the material we turn up confidential. There is something about this case that doesn't pass the smell test; and if I get bad news, I won't be able to share it, I'm afraid. I'll tell you that up front. Sorry, that's the way it is."

"That's the way it always is," said Lieutenant Bradley unable to contain his pent-up anger at the way the FBI had dealt with his department over the years. "It's a give and take world; the local cops give, and the fibbies take... the credit. SOS. But in this case, it sounds to me like even more than that. Your attitude smacks of cover-up. I am going to run my own evaluation of that raid, and I'm going to tell you up front that I won't allow anyone to get off the hook just because he or she is a high muckity-muck among the feds. I guess we are about to start a game of hard ball."

"Now, Lieutenant, don't take offense. I'll let you know what I can. You understand; I'm just doing my job."

"Umm-hmm."

There was an awkward silence.

Finally, DeLentigo said, "Bye."

Bradley just hung up his receiver. He was steamed.

SAC DeLentigo drummed his fingertips on his desktop. Cynthia Gaffin was good, but she *was* exasperating. He had no choice but to call her. She never called him a report. He dialed her office extension.

"Special Agent Cynthia Gaffin's office," came the secretary's melodious but mechanical voice.

"This is DeLentigo. I need to speak to her."

"To whom?"

Now whose office had he just called? To whom, indeed.

"To Ms. Gaffin," he said, working to be civil.

"I'll ring her."

There was a brief pause.

"Hi, boss. I was meaning to call you."

"*Sure you were*," he thought.

She continued, "I have some prelim material."

Everything was always 'prelim' to her. She always saw that more could be done. Cynthia hated to hand in a report for fear that there would be the slightest morsel that could have been missed.

"Let's hear it," he requested.

"Are you sitting down, boss?"

"That bad, huh?"

He felt a little chill.

"Two things. First, the fingerprints. We went over every millimeter of that van. There was not a single print of Randolph Kennedy's or of any other secessionist or Militia freak anywhere. Nothing had been wiped off, either."

DeLentigo was shaking his head at his phone.

"There were beaucoup prints otherwise. Guess whose?'

"Ted Coleman and Roger Holdaway," DeLentigo said sourly.

"Almost, but you're on the right track. There were prints from a dozen or so ATF agents, many of whom were involved in the shootout."

"And some who were not?"

"That's very perceptive of you, boss. We'll make a first class detective out of you yet." She laughed. "Indeed, some who were not. The extra prints are from ATF evidence impound personnel in the Ketchikan Federal Building."

DeLentigo felt a little light headed. He was letting himself get several steps ahead of his investigator.

When he said nothing for a few moments, she returned with, "And that's the good news."

"I hope that's just a figure of speech," the SAC said. "It would be hard for me to figure what could be worse than the implications of that."

"How about the fact that every scrap of the contents of that van came from the Ketchikan ATF raid—the one where they confiscated the huge cache of loot for evidence, lots of guns and money; and I mean lots of money."

"Oh, brother," he moaned, and leaned his forehead on the heel of his hand and closed his eyes. "You're right, that's worse."

"This is sort of one of those times when there's a choice of worse, and worse than that. Ready for the worse than that?"

She paused for effect.

DeLentigo was sure he was going to faint. What had he ever done to the Gods of Justice to be placed in the middle of this one?

"No," he said, quietly. "I'll just sit here and cut my wrists with my car keys instead."

"Glad to be of service, and I take it that I have your attention?"

"Go on, Cyndy, give me the whole thing," he said with resignation.

"Glad to oblige, boss. Anyway, the last factoid that we have been able to establish—and you need to know—is that there was a truly huge amount of cash money in that impound locker. The money had not even been fully counted, but it was measured by the semi-truck load—something like five hundred mil or more. No one really knows how much."

"I noted the use of the past tense."

"Past perfect tense, to be picky. But maybe they didn't teach that kind of technicality at community college night school."

She regularly took delight on picking at the fact that he had been educated at NYU whereas she graduated with honors from Harvard.

"And, yes, I purposefully used a past tense…can you believe that?"

"By now, I'd believe anything. I don't remember hearing you mention money as being among the evidence found in the van at Kennedy's place."

"No, it was not at Kennedy's place—not a dime. At least I can't establish that it was there for a fact, yet. There are whisperings that there was a big semi-trailer on the property at some point during the raid; but the agents directly involved are either dead, or not talking. I have not had a chance to question Henry Drake since he's recuperating from surgery. He's going to be paraplegic."

"Do the impound logs reflect the chain of custody of the weapons, the bomb making materials, and the money?"

"Funny you should bring that up. There are clear records, duly signatur-ized, for the discovery of the evidence at the Ketchikan crime scene and for its delivery into the impound locker. There is not so much as a pencil mark concerning any disposition beyond that point. So far as the records reflect, it didn't happen. The records do clearly show that the mountain of money shared a big bin right along side the weapons and the bomb materials. That was attested by the U.S. attorney who was to handle the prosecution in the Ketchikan case."

"There's that past tense again," DeLentigo sighed.

"Right at this moment, none of the evidence is where it is supposed to be. I have custody of everything listed except the money, and its whereabouts are completely unknown and only a matter of speculation. Suffice it to say, the chain of custody of the Ketchikan evidence has been compromised."

"You are the mistress of understatement, Agent Gaffin."

"And it's not my place to draw conclusions, of course, boss. And, besides, it's all preliminary."

DeLentigo rolled his eyes.

"Give me a break, Cyndy. Is there any other information about the money's present whereabouts—even a scrap—we can use to start tracking it? Are there any other possible suspects in its disappearance?"

"You mean, other than cops?"

"Yeah."

"No, and no," Gaffin answered laconically. "Maybe you have reference to a certain homeowner on whose property some of the contraband was discovered and whose presence during the period in question is in doubt and problematic, and whose present whereabouts is a mystery?"

"Any evidence that could implicate that nice man so as to narrow down my list of possible participants."

DeLentigo released a long, heavy sigh. The burdens of being the special agent in charge bore heavily on him that day.

"You know what all of this means to the Ketchikan case."

It was a statement. They both knew the answer to the implied question.

Agent Gaffin replied for both of them, "The only question is when those south Alaskan terrorists will get their free passes out of jail. There is no longer a legal case."

"I know who I'm talking to; but are you absolutely certain about all of this, Cyndy?" DeLentigo asked in one last effort to shy away from the bald truth.

"What I have reported can be registered as fact. I am working on establishing other findings and lack of findings as facts, but I'm not ready for that part of the report yet. Although it's all preliminary, you can take the information I have given you to the bank."

"So, you're not ready to tell me for a fact that Kennedy was or was not present during the raid, I take it. That would be a salient part of this puzzle."

"It's too preliminary."

She could be exasperating.

"Then, I get to be the one to call the Ketchikan federal prosecution team, and they will have the most fun of all. They get to tell the terrorists' shysters that their clients will be released this very day…great."

"That's why they gave you such a big badge and so much money, boss. Comes with the job…and such big shoulders, I might add. I don't envy you your task," she said gently.

He appreciated the brief surcease from their usual well intentioned banter.

"Thanks, Cyndy. Good work. Keep it up. I'll catch you later. I don't need to say how important it is to keep all of this under your hat."

"I'm on your team, boss. Bye."

"Good bye."

DeLentigo put down the receiver and contemplated what he ought to do about the explosive information now that it was beyond the rumor-mill stage. Unfortunately, there was—of necessity—a growing number of people in the know. It could not be kept under wraps forever. The automatic and probably the safest response would be to kick it upstairs and wash his hands of the mess. He pondered his conscience. How far 'upstairs' might this conspiracy go? As he sat thinking, his secretary with the mechanical voice buzzed him.

"Call from the *New York Times* reporter who was at the Kennedy scene. Gwen Chambers is her name. She doesn't seem the type to take 'no' or 'maybe' for an answer. Are you in?"

Talking to a reporter was about the last thing he wanted to do right now; but she and Phelps—the reporter from the *Washington Post*—had been selected from a pool of journalist sharks to hold down the extent of the media feeding frenzy. It was still important to have a modicum of control; so, DeLentigo had to concede that an interview with Chambers now was the lesser of evils.

"Put her on."

"This is Gwen Chambers."

"Special Agent in Charge DeLentigo," he said when he found the right line after three tries. "What can I do for you?"

"I have some questions about that raid outside Wasilla, Special Agent DeLentigo, some loose ends before I send in the final draft of my pool report to *Reuters*, the *AP*, and the *Times*. What was that big Dodge Ram delivery van doing parked on Kennedy's homestead, and why all the hush-hush about it?"

Worst fears realized.

CHAPTER THIRTY-FOUR

It was nearly noon before Pancho and Guillermo arrived back at Guillermo and Maria's apartment with the keys to a Harley Davidson Heritage Softail II. The two men presented Randolph with the keys and excitedly led him towards the door; so, they could show him how to operate the motorcycle. The three men, Maria, and the children stood in the small, trash littered back alley and marveled at the sleek powerful machine. Guillermo's middle daughter tugged on Randolph's finger for a good-bye hug. He leaned down to accommodate her, looking at the pretty little girl's face with affection.

She suddenly began to laugh, a little girl's unaffected tinkling bell laugh.

"*Los ojos son azules. Mama, venga verlos!*" she called excitedly.

Maria Perez was embarrassed by her daughter's personal comments about their guest, and she started to whisk the little girl away for a scolding.

"No, please, *Señora* Perez. What did she say? What was so funny about me?" He was amused and concerned at the same time. Out of the mouth of babes...

Maria looked at the floor and shook her head. She spoke no English and was worried that her daughter's misbehavior would reflect poorly on her as a mother.

Randolph turned to Guillermo, "What? What is it?"

"Oh, is nothing, amigo. She only say that jou have blue eyes. Is funny in a brown-skin man. Is all. She deed not mean any harm," Guillermo said defensively.

Randolph stepped back to look at himself in the handle bar mirror of the Harley. He saw a tall, lean, brush cut Latino, a biker with deep brown skin. And he also saw the incongruity. Out of that native brown face, under the jet black hair, burned a pair of exotic, piercing Nordic blue eyes. He laughed and winked at the little girl and eased everyone's tensions.

"I'll have to get brown contact lenses," Randolph said, glad the oversight had been detected early on. "Maria, I am glad that the little one found my blue eyes. It will help me. Thank you."

Maria smiled in relief.

"Now we teach jou how to ride thee hog," said Pancho.

The two Mexican men explained the intricacies of the 710 pound motorcycle with its 1340 cubic centimeter evolution engine and the various dangers of riding in the city and on and off the highway. Randolph had never been on a motorcycle before and considered them the personification of personal risk taking. He was reluctant to mount the bike at first; but when he was finally seated on the powerful machine; he had to admit to himself that he was feeling a surge of virility. He started the engine and felt the tingle of it through the seat and heard it rumble out its patented roar. He eased the gear and moved slowly up and down the alley several times. Then, he got brave and went around the block a few times. He was an obvious beginner—a learner—and the neighborhood filtered out onto the sidewalks to cheer him on. It was exhilarating.

Randolph stopped back in the alley by the Mexicans.

"Not too bad for a beginner, eh?"

"Not bad for a gringo," Pancho said.

They all laughed. Randolph shook hands with the men and Maria and gave each child a hug and a peck on the forehead.

"How much did this thing cost, amigos?" Randolph asked.

The two Mexicans looked down.

"More than you gave us…twenty-two thousand," Guillermo said softly.

Randolph had given them twenty thousand for the purchase because that was their estimate. While they were out, he called on Guillermo's apartment phone and talked to a Harley dealer he picked out of the Yellow Pages. He was ready for their announcement. They must have haggled—it was in their blood—because the dealer had told him twenty-four.

"Here is what I owe you."

He peeled twenty hundred dollar bills and handed them to Pancho since he seemed to be the senior of the two. He paused for a moment, then extracted another forty bills and pressed them into both men's hands. They looked quizzically at him, but did not hasten to give back any of the money.

"Consider this a tip, maybe a gift. It makes us square. I want you to remember this money from your friend. If someone comes to talk to you—or if you should see a picture of me and you become tempted—remember my gift to you. You don't know me, and you don't know what I've done. More importantly, you can't guess what I would do if you were to betray me."

He let the implicit warning sink in, then he mounted the hog, shook each man's hand again, and eased out of the alley. Guillermo and Pancho gave each other serious looks.

"We will not have anything to say about this man. I fear him. You make sure that Maria and the kids know that they don't speak of him either," Pancho said emphatically.

It went without saying for Guillermo. Despite *Señor* No-Name's overt kindness, generosity, and civility, Guillermo was sure there lived within a very dangerous man.

Randolph drove first to the bus station and removed his suitcases from the two lockers. Then he drove up Taylor Street through Russian Hill and into North Beach. He turned east on Union Street and rode all the way to the Embarcadero, where he found a shady spot to park. There were tourists all around him, but no one paid him the least attention. He looked around very carefully, then removed the suit cases from the panniers, and transferred the money from the suitcases into the empty panniers. He replenished his personal supply of cash—putting bills in every pocket—some six thousand dollars worth.

He walked a block to a nice men's store and bought a wallet and credit card case for forty dollars. Next door was a convenience store where—with the change—he bought four three minute phone cards at ten dollars a card. They would give him the chance to communicate anonymously since they were untraceable. He also found brown tinted nonprescription throw away soft contact lenses and put one pair in his eyes. He was surprised at how comfortable they were.

He located a phone booth, took out his little black address book, and dialed 1-804-541-1849.

"Prince George County Shooting Range, Haslip speaking," came the familiar voice.

"Daryl, I think you know who this is, remember me? Let's not use names."

"Sure, long time no see. You went way up there and settled in, I hear. Made yourself a reputation. The news and the grapevine has it that you are in a heap of trouble. That right?"

"I'm afraid so. I hate to impose on you, but I can't talk long on this phone card. I need some real help. I have to stay out of the way of every law enforcement person in the entire country, even the whole world. That obviously limits where I can go and what I can do pretty severely."

"I'd guess so. Where are you now?" He paused. "That's a dumb question. Don't answer. Just tell me whether you are east or west."

"Let's do this; you give me any info you can about either the east or the west, and I can choose. That way, you can't be pressured to divulge something you don't know."

"Okay, my friend, give me an hour; then call back. I can have something for you by then."

"Thanks, my friend," Randolph said, then hung up.

He killed time walking down the Embarcadero to Fisherman's Wharf and watched the throngs of tourists ogling each other. Girls on roller skates wearing next to nothing floated by in fluid abandon. Hucksters inveigled the unwary. Iranian rug merchants recounted the tremendous bargains they had to offer in their perpetual going-out-of business sales. The smells of raw shrimp and frying oysters mingled with a dozen *grande monde parfums* wafting from the pampered bodies of passing elegant women. Catcalls, imprecations, sales pitches, and oohs and aahs of conversations in a multilingual Babel filled the air around him. Anonymity was the easiest thing in the world for him to achieve.

When his hour's wait was up, Randolph found another phone booth amidst the swirl of humanity and inserted his calling card that still had two and a half minutes left on it.

"Haslip here."

"How did you do?"

"Worked it out. I got in touch with some people I know in the Movement. Good, solid, white people. I have a number for you. Go to a little burg named Heber in Utah—mountain country. Call the number, and they'll see you get help. Keep your head down boy. I checked my sources, and you are considered public enemy number one in some circles. I can't say for sure, but seems they've got a shoot-on-sight order out."

"I will. I'm new at this sort of thing and probably not very good at it. It will be a decided comfort to be able to go to ground. So, what's the number?"

"(435) 654-1052. Don't use names on the phone, including mine. You can't ever tell when one of the brothers and sisters is bugged. And a bit of advice to the wise—the folks I'm sending you to are old friends from when I was a kid. I know them personally and trust them. There are spies for the FBG and traitors in the Movement, I'm sorry to say—whores for the ATF and the FBI. Be real choosy about who you trust and what information you give out. Always know a back way as an escape route. Put some money in phony names in banks around the country; so, you can get to one of them when the need comes up. Now, get on your way before some fed who might have tapped the lines of your old friends and acquaintances uses this call to trace you. Good luck; go with God; and keep in touch."

"Thanks, you're a real friend."

They hung up at the same time. Randolph bought a substantial lunch from an assortment of street vendors. He placed it in the rear luggage compartment over the neatly layered packages of cash. He bought a California and a U.S. map and a full tank of gas at a Conoco station. He paid the four dollars a gallon bill and moved his Harley into the throbbing noontime traffic. He turned onto I-80 headed east, crossed the Oakland Bay Bridge and set out for Utah.

DeLentigo thought about his next call very carefully. He had no requirement to tell the ATF anything since they were not in the same club, and he did not particularly care for the ATF way of doing things. They seemed sloppy, bordering on brutish, most of the time. He knew that he should—by rights—contact Director Ted Coleman at the Hoover Building and leave the investigation in his hands. However, that nuisance that plagued him and was not really useful to a good obedient soldier, cop, or lawyer—his conscience— was nagging at him again. He presumed that the assault on Kennedy had to have come from the President's Final Battle in the War on Drugs and Illegal Weapons Task Force. Every top federal officer in law enforcement was on that committee; and potentially, any or even all of them were compromised by guilty foreknowledge, or might be culpable at least.

He thought about his next promotion, now somewhat overdue. He would be able to choose among the top cities to be the SAC—New York, Chicago, Dallas, Los Angeles, or San Francisco—they were all his for the choosing as long as he stayed the good obedient soldier, did his job without asking questions, and did not make waves. That was the problem with having a conscience. It might feel the least bit good to do the right thing, but the pain he and his wife would suffer by his so doing would be a high price.

DeLentigo let his conscience get the better of him against his practical judgment. He dialed Assistant FBI Director Phil Craig's number in Washington at the WMFO, more commonly known by insiders as "Buzzard Point". The name derived from the uninviting spit of land on which the Washington Field Office—second largest in the country after New York City—was located. DeLentigo had known Phil Craig since the academy—and unlike most academy friendships—theirs had endured; and they had kept up over the years. He trusted Phil which was more than he could say of any of his other high ranking FBI acquaintances.

"Washington Metropolitan Field Office, Federal Bureau of Investigation, Mr. Craig's office," the administrative assistant's stock telephone reply answered.

"May I speak to the assistant director, please? This is SAC Oscar DeLentigo from Alaska."

When Craig came on the line, DeLentigo came right to the point after the briefest of courtesies.

"Phil, this is Oscar."

"Hi, Oscar, how's the fishing up there?"

"Just okay, Phil. Been too heavily fished to be all that good any more. How goes the political war from Buzzard's Point?"

"Same as always. I keep one step ahead…some days."

"Look, I called about a real thorny problem. I hate to involve you, but I have nowhere else to turn."

Phil dropped his bantering tone immediately. He knew his friend.

"Sounds like a political problem, how can I help?"

He stayed mostly quiet during the remainder of the thirty minute telephone call while DeLentigo went over everything he knew about the Randolph Kennedy affair. Occasionally, Craig would interrupt for a brief clarification of some detail, but then allowed Oscar to continue his narrative. Oscar concluded with a cautious suggestion of his suspicions about the President's Task Force.

"It's a Pandora's box," he said, "It's got to be opened, and a lot of evil is going to escape when we do. That's what I mean by hating to involve you, Phil. You are a straight shooter, and that's what this case needs. It is a bit late to get started on the injection of honesty, but here we are."

There was a thoughtful silence between the two men at the opposite ends of the United States.

Craig broke the silence, "We don't have to draw any final conclusions, yet. I agree that we need to keep this between us and as few others as have to be in the know. Lock up your evidence in your personal safe, preferably well away from the federal building. Maybe we will be lucky and find out that no one but that ATF agent, Drake—I think you said—was involved, or it was just the actions of a criminal, that Kennedy fellow. Do you remember what was left after Pandora opened her box and let fly all the world's evil?"

"My study of classical mythology didn't get that far, Phil. I thought I was doing well to remember Pandora. I'll have to defer to your night school education."

"It was hope, my friend, hope. We can still hope. But while we do, I'll set a tiptoe investigation in motion through our people in C-1 and maybe even C-3. Hang in there, Oscar. Bye, now."

"Bye, Phil. I appreciate being able to count on you."

Phil Craig pondered what he had heard and its implications for a few minutes. Oscar was right about the need for secrecy. If any member of the President's Task Force got wind of what was suspected, the investigation would be scuttled from on high. That meant that he would have to keep this away from DFBI Ted Coleman, at least for the short term. He knew with perfect clarity that it was worth his job if his clandestine investigation were to be found out. On the other hand, if Coleman was eventually and convincingly demonstrated to have been an accessory before the fact, he would be out of his director's chair in a matter of minutes.

Craig, as ADFBI, made no secret of his ambition. He wanted to clean up the FBI from top to bottom to make it efficient and transparent. In order to accomplish anything, he would have to be the director. If his political appointee superior and rival were to be toppled for a crime, he stood a real chance of being appointed to the top post. He was an ambitious man, and this was the closest that he would ever come to getting the chance to be the nation's top cop. It was worth some risks.

He needed the best investigator he could have, and more importantly, one that he could trust. It took him a while because he was ever mindful of his need to be careful in the extreme. He had to have someone who would be enough of a maverick to be willing to bypass all other links in the chain of command and to deal solely with him. He or she was going to have to be an effective liar, a skill that was sure to come in handy during the course of this tricky investigation.

He came up with the name of Nancy Delgado from special investigations. Nancy was a misfit in the bureau: an agent entirely devoid of ambition, incorruptible, unimpressed with the great, powerful, and famous. She was a thorough going skeptic when it came to the poobahs—the persons in high places. All of these traits had thus far prevented her from making strong allegiances or from finding a rabbi or a fairy godmother who would move her up the hierarchal ladder—a quest of every other agent he had ever known. Special Agent Delgado was smart and tough, dogged, sometimes abrasive and apparently insubordinate, and always discerning—all qualities that earned her degrees of enmity from her peers and her superiors, but which made her an investigator par excellence. Not the least of the things that persuaded Phil Craig that he should have Nancy Delgado was that she was not associated with either C-1 or C-3. It did not take an organizational genius to know that the DFBI Ted Coleman would have the ambitious chiefs of C-1 and C-3 in his pocket. When he came right down to it, Nancy Delgado was perfect. He called her on his secure line.

Special Agent Delgado listened to the entire scenario from Assistant Director Craig. The assignment was to find Randolph Kennedy before anyone else—keep the man from being killed or from killing her—and to unearth any criminal conspiracy related to the man originating or executing from the FBG. Craig told her about the work of Agents Lathrop and Gaffin in Alaska; they should provide a good place to start. She was given to understand that she would need to get close to some of the lower ranking officers of the FBG to see if they would cooperate with an investigation that could sully one of the WOMs with whom they worked and upon whom they relied for advancement. It was a tall order.

Delgado hated the sound of it. She had spent a career avoiding the rampant political machinations that abounded within the Bureau. She had been content to let her good works shine through. For ten years she had been assigned away from the Hoover Building with all of its political step-ups and snares. She had worked in relative obscurity at the Washington Field Office, hating the ugly 12 story building on the banks of the Anacostia River in one of D.C.'s worst ghettoes. But she reveled in its low-profile opportunity to do real work. She knew—as a result of her choices—that she would never gain high rank; but she could hope for respect from those whom she respected. It had been enough for her. Now this.

Nancy had never married. It was trite to say but true in effect, that she was wed to the Bureau in something of a dysfunctional marriage. She had no close relationships; and she took it personally whenever her spouse—the Federal Bureau of Investigation—came under attack, from within or without. She respected Phil Craig more than anyone else she had known in the Bureau for his honesty and his competence. He was too ambitious by half for her liking; but she was convinced that he would never compromise the Bureau; and it was beneath him to frame a superior for the sake of blind ambition. When he finished his discussion of all of the ramifications and possibilities of the case—including the possible eventual pain of confronting even the White House—Nancy made up her mind.

"I'll do it, Phil. There're a couple of conditions. I have full charge of the investigation and decision making power over the final report. Nobody gets to bury it if it's bad, and nobody gets to use it if the facts are not established. This can't be a white wash, and it can't turn into a witch hunt."

"Granted."

"I get a *letter de marque* from you."

That would be an explosive document against him if ever she was cornered and forced to save herself at the expense of his career. He did not hesitate, however.

"You'll have it. You will be able to go anywhere I can, do anything I can do, get the cooperation of anyone who will follow my lead. I hardly need tell you the critical importance of discretion on your part. One misstep or one miscalculation about the integrity of an agent we choose to trust, and the two of us will be twisting in the wind."

"I'll have to dump a few things I'm doing. I should be able to get on it in three days."

"Good luck, Nancy."

"I'll probably need it. I don't think I'll thank you for the job. Bye."

"Bye."

CHAPTER THIRTY-FIVE

Gwen Chambers's article was sent out through *Reuters* and the *Associated Press*. *The New York Times* printed it on page three just as William Fitzgerald had said. It was a little more than a ho-hum description of a bloody raid on a terrorist fortress in Alaska with connections to the nefarious Movement. The only concession she was allowed from her questions posed to the SAC in Alaska about possible improprieties on the part of law enforcement agencies was to conclude her piece with the harmless sentence, "Investigations into all aspects of the raid are continuing, according to ranking FBI and ATF officials."

Towards the end of following up on her quest for more incriminating material, Gwen importuned Fitzgerald for an expense account to return to Alaska. She had some ideas for leads that would prove to be very useful if they panned out. He was interested enough in the project to grant her that, but with a short leash and a stingy stipend.

"Don't push your luck with first class, Gwen. I will have a hard enough time justifying this junket."

"Right on, boss. You know thrifty little me," she told him.

She was exuberant at the chance to dig her teeth into a really meaty story, may even get a Pulitzer. Travel and accommodations were incidentals; she could make do or do without—as her mother used to say—for quite some time if she had to.

Gwen's first stop in Alaska was at the FBI office of Oscar DeLentigo in Anchorage. She was somewhat surprised to find him evasive, however naïve that seemed even to her.

"I tried to tell you during our telephone conversation, Ms Chambers. I have nothing new or of interest to report. I'm afraid you've wasted a trip here."

"You have the report on the raid on the Kennedy place, the straight information on the role of the several law enforcement agencies, the strange white van," she said, irked at his recalcitrance.

"Surely you must know that I can't comment on an ongoing investigation in a criminal case, Ms Chambers."

"But just as surely, the incident at the hill is finished. I fail to see any reason why you can't divulge the results of the raid. It can't be part of the Kennedy investigation at this late date. I presume he has left your jurisdiction."

"I'm truly sorry that I can't be of further assistance, ma'am. That is really all I have to discuss with you. I hope you will be able to take in some of the sights in our grand state before you head back to the big city."

"*It's 'ma'am' now, is it?*" she thought. "*I have really gotten under his skin.*"

"Thank you for your time, Special Agent DeLentigo," she said frostily. "You have convinced me that somebody up here somewhere has something to hide. It is my job and my best skill to ferret out what people are hiding, especially dirty little secrets. See you around."

He started to rise from his chair.

"Don't trouble yourself. I can see myself out."

He gave her a dismissive gesture and bent over his desk ignoring her.

"*Yoo-ul be so-orr-ry!*" Gwen thought to herself.

She was actually rather glad that she would not have the cooperation of the FBI. She would not have to play by any confining rules. Gwen was not particularly angry at the stone wall that had been thrown up before her. She had half expected it. It would just be harder work, she thought. She took a taxi to the airport an arranged to be on the earliest Alaskan Airways flight to Ketchikan. She had a hunch she wanted to play.

In Ketchikan Gwen caught a cab in front of the airport.

"Take me to the Federal Building, please."

"Jess, madam. I vill be heppy to," the cabby said briskly.

He was a nondescript exotic foreign person, one of the quintessential taxicab drivers of the world. It could have been in Singapore, New York, or Lisbon. He drove directly to the building and flashed a crooked toothed grin.

"A safe and honest ride."

She could not resist; she tipped him handsomely, partly to avoid having to hear about his sick wife and their unfortunate children.

Gwen was unsure if this was the right place, but she marched in as if it were the most routine thing in her day. She walked up to the information desk.

"Impound lockers, please?"

The indifferent woman at the desk did not even deign to look up. Her *Cosmopolitan* was open to a particularly compelling advertisement for casual loafers.

The bored woman asked, "FBI, DEA, or ATF?"

"I'll need both FBI and ATF. Let's start with ATF."

"Subbasement one. That's two floors down. You'll have to go through a wire mesh gate, then it's the third door on the right."

It was a little hard to understand the woman's speech impeded as it was by the two-stick Double-mint gum wad that occupied so much of her attention.

"Thank you," Gwen said with saccharine sweetness.

The receptionist went back to devouring the captivating shoe ad.

"Have your clearance?" she called after Gwen had turned and started for the elevators.

"Of course, and thanks," Gwen responded matter-of-factly.

Small problem: she had no clearance. They probably wanted a badge. Her mind raced. She had her original letter from Special Agent in Charge Oscar DeLentigo. It authorized full cooperation to the journalist bearing this letter in the Randolph Kennedy case. It failed to specify a cut-off date or a location. Her main concern was that someone would think to call DeLentigo for confirmation.

She found the room. The directions—though terse—were accurate. The area was clean, scrupulously neat, and entirely utilitarian. She rapped on the steel door. A buzzer sounded; but she reacted too late; and the door lock reengaged. She knocked loudly a second time and stood back at the ready. In a few moments the door opened. A portly, florid faced man in a police uniform motioned here to come in. He had a telltale beer belly and rheumy eyes, all of the stigmata of alcoholism with incipient liver failure.

Gwen stepped into what was the anteroom of the impound section. In front of her was a cage door with a slot for handing through items like printed requests, Gwen thought, trying not to panic.

The officer walked through the cage door and closed it behind him.

He sat down in his chair and asked, "What?"

"The evidence from the Kennedy case...from Wasilla. I'm Gwen Chambers with the *New York Times*. Here's my letter of approval."

She looked at him with full confidence, as if there were not the slightest question of her bona fides to see that evidence. He scrutinized her, then gave the letter a cursory once over. She was sure that he was about to give her a hassle; and most likely, she would come away empty handed. Or he would have the good sense to call DeLentigo.

"Sorry, lady," he said finally, and her heart dropped. "This is a no take away case. You see it here or not at all."

His porcine face was very stern. She could have kissed him. He obviously had been impressed by the letter from the SAC. She wanted to shout for joy—taking anything was the last thing on her mind. There were still guardian angels who made a miracle to let her get to see the evidence. She did not believe in God, but she still believed in the Catholic Church from which she had lapsed. Maybe that was what had produced the mini-miracle.

"And…" he said.

"*Uh oh,*" she thought.

"You can't touch nothing. Order of the presiding judge, chief marshal, and DeLentigo himself," he announced grandiosely, quite taken with the august authority of his position.

He took three or four breaths from the exertion of his short speech.

"No problem," said Gwen demurely, careful to be on her best behavior.

The impound officer sat briefly catching his breath and gathering strength for the upcoming exertions.

"*Today!*" she pleaded in an inward scream.

"If you'll just come this way."

He heaved himself out of his creaking chair. Gwen followed the impound officer down a labyrinthine set of corridors lined floor to ceiling with envelopes, plastic bags full of assorted items, and locked cages with larger pieces of evidence. There seemed to be no chronological, alphabetical, or case type logic to explain the location of evidence for any given case. He took her to the very end of the spacious room next to a large vertical roll door. She figured the door opened onto a ramp that permitted the trucking in of large items or quantities of evidence as in the Kennedy or the Ketchikan shootout cases.

"This here's it," the officer announced and gave a few short puffs from his exertion.

The door was flagged: *Randolph Kennedy, ATF seizure, 26 June.* Below it, a hand scrawled sign added: *Refer to ATF drug/guns raid of 21 April.*.

"I gotta stay right here. Orders, you know. Nobody is to put their fingerprints on nothing."

He fiddled with the padlock and opened the cage door for her. Gwen inspected the gun crates, bales of marijuana, bags of heroin and cocaine, and the sacks of ammonium nitrate. She scribbled quick notes in her own short-hand and strained to get down sizes and numbers. She wrote as fast as she could to get down the kinds of guns listed on the sides of the wooden slat cases. She was certain that it was the same stuff she had seen in the white van on Kennedy's property.

"*Something is missing here*," she thought to herself.

She had seen evidence from drug busts before, and there stuck in her mind something about them that she was not seeing in this collection of evidence. She shook her head trying to drag up what that was.

"That it, missy? I gotta get back to the front desk."

"Thanks, I guess so."

Something nagged at her. She turned to leave the cramped cubicle taking elaborate care to keep her hands well away from any of the evidence. She felt the heft of her purse swinging as she executed the movement. That was it! Every other time she had seen evidence, there were bags and boxes of cash. The illegal drug and guns business was on a cash-and-carry basis. As one crusty old criminal had explained it to her once, in a parody of the motto on the dollar bill, "In God we trust, all others pay cash."

"Where's the money from the raid, I mean from the Ketchikan raid? The sign ties the two raids together. Where did it go? It's supposed to be with this lot, isn't it?" she blurted.

It was a calculated risk in a day of long shots. She did not have a scintilla of evidence about any money, but it seemed so logical. It was well worth taking a flyer.

"Don't know about that, ma'am. That happened on the other shift. I never checked none of it out, none of it. All I knows is that the money and all of this stuff got checked out, and the money never come back. Way the fat boys incorporated is actin', somebody's butt is gonna be in a sling. They're just tryin' to figure out whose."

He was speaking in a low conspiratorial voice, presuming that Gwen was one of the insiders. He seemed most anxious to assure one and all that he had not been responsible. He likely should have known that he was not supposed to be talking about this, but his self-protective instincts overruled his sense of duty. No anatomical part of his was going to be in any sling over this, nosiree.

Gwen restrained her mad desire to sing and shout and dance a victory jig. She had just gotten at the nut of this case and had a fabulous quote. She made a strong mental note to remember his exact words. This was exactly what she had come to Alaska for, and it had been handed to her on an engraved silver platter. She calmed herself, told herself to be patient.

"Thank you, officer. You have been most helpful. I'll let Mr. DeLentigo know how efficient you were."

She smiled seductively at the rheumy old alcoholic. He blushed and shuffled his feet.

"Next," she said, "we need to go see the Ketchikan evidence."

It was a leap. Even her outdated letter from DeLentigo, that had been the excuse for admitting her to the locker, did not permit her to see that evidence. However, she was sure that the officer had given the letter no more than a cursory glance.

"Okay," he said, "but we gotta make it quick. I hafta be back at that front desk PDQ."

He led her around the corridors of the labyrinth to a very large wire cage locker. It was almost empty. There were a few boxes of papers and an assortment of household items, but no gun or ammunition crates, bags of contraband drugs, and most conspicuous by its absence: no money.

She looked at the impound officer with a question on her face. He shrugged. It was an unspoken denial of complicity.

"Okay, missy, I think you seen it all."

"Oh, thanks," she said, "Hey, I've got one more little question."

She smiled coquettishly and turned her shapely body to its best angle.

"I suppose that awful Kennedy terrorist got away with the money, huh?"

"Nobody can say, ma'am. Just between us two, I heard that they never found any of his fingerprints on the truck or on the evidence. They don't know squat about whether or not the money was ever really at his place or if he got away with it or if somebody that had no business having that dough trucked it off, if you get my meanin'?"

"Whose *did* they find?" she asked reflexively.

He was unguarded with her now; something he would undoubtedly regret a little later when he reviewed the meeting with her. His brain was so chronically sodden with alcohol that he might not even remember her coming in.

"Nobody's sayin'. I kinda think it's gonna hit the fan when they do say."

He clamped his lips shut and drew an index finger to indicate that his lips were sealed.

She could have laughed.

"Well, this is all I needed to see. Thanks again so much for all your help."

Gwen actually batted her eyes, embarrassing herself. It seemed to work. She made a mental note of his name from his tag: Sergeant Harold Proxmire.

Gwen signed the roster of visitors then left the impound locker and exited the subbasement the way she came in. She poked around the federal building until she found a pay phone on the second floor. She put in a fifty-cent piece, the only coin that worked in the few remaining U.S. pay phones. It seemed smart to Gwen, who used pay phones all of the time. Her cell phone battery always seemed to be dead for some reason. She consulted her notes then dialed the Wasilla Police Department. She wanted another corroborative interview, and she thought she knew where to get it.

"Lamar Willets," she requested when the receptionist answered and asked how she could be of help.

"Willets," a man's voice answered resignedly a few minutes later.

"Mr. Willets, this is Gwen Chambers from the *New York Times*. I don't know if you remember me, and I'm sorry to bother you. I was present at the Kennedy place incident. I'm trying to tie up some loose ends for my story. I wonder if I might be able to talk with you? In person."

"When? I mean, when did you have in mind, Ms. Chambers?"

"How about tomorrow? How would ten be?"

"Can't then. Tell you the truth, I'm going fishing. I leave at five tomorrow morning."

"I know this would be a great imposition, but what about tonight? I would be happy to buy you dinner, and we could talk over a good steak."

He seemed like a good steak kind of guy.

He mulled the thought.

"I promised my wife…"

"Bring her. My treat. We'll make it kind of a party, a three way date."

He was hesitating.

"Please, Officer Willets, it's important; or I wouldn't bug you about it."

"Okay, how about eight? That a deal?" he asked.

"Wonderful. You pick the place. I'll be staying at the Sheffield House on Seventh West and Fifth Street. Maybe you could come by and pick me up?"

"We know the hotel and know the perfect place to eat. We'll be there with bells on. See you then. Hope your paper has a generous expense account."

"No problem. Until then, bye."

An Alaskan Airlines commuter flight was scheduled to leave within the hour. It was maddening to Gwen to have to endure the stops in every dinky hamlet from Ketchikan to Anchorage, but it was far better than nothing which was her other alternative. Gwen saw a great deal more of Alaska than she wanted to before she was able to deplane in the seaside city. It was seventhirty in the evening by the time she was finally deposited at the Sheffield House Hotel lobby by the hotel's shuttle. There was not enough time to clean up. She was sweaty and had rank armpits. Nobody was perfect all of the time.

She pulled off her blouse, did a quick spit bath on her arm pits, applied deodorant, and found a new blouse just in time to be presentable when the knock came on the door.

"Typical man," she grumbled, "he came on time."

"Hi," she said as cheerily as she could muster, "come in please. You must be Officer Willets, and you are Mrs. Willets, I presume."

"It's Sergeant Willets," said the attractive brown haired woman firmly but with an ingenuous smile.

She looked fondly at her husband.

"I'm Carol Willets."

"Gwen Chambers. I am pleased to meet both of you. I hope this doesn't interfere with important plans. Take a seat; I'll just be a minute. I only got in from delivering the mail from every little town between here and Ketchikan ten minutes ago. I need to freshen up a bit. I still glow, as they say."

Sergeant Willets laughed.

"Glow?" asked Carol.

Gwen laughed, "You know, 'horses sweat, men perspire, and ladies glow'."

"Oh, that kind of glow. Take your time."

Gwen decided that the police officer and his wife were calm enough and pleased enough by the offer of the steak dinner that they could be patient for a few minutes. She did her quickest clean up job: shower, leg and armpit shave, and put on a new face, underclothes, and dress. She felt like she could take on the world now.

"I'm starved. I hope you guys are. Take me to the best steak house in town. The *New York Times* is feeling generous tonight."

The threesome had an excellent dinner at The Captain Cook Steak House overlooking Cook Inlet. Gwen carefully avoided the subject of Randolph Kennedy, the ATF, and the white van while they shared seasoning stuffed Chateaubriand, herbed potatoes, and fresh asparagus tips, a good Apennines Chianti, and a flambé bread pudding. Gwen and the couple were talking like old friends when she finally broached the subject.

"Sergeant, there are a couple of things that concern me about the ATF raid on Randolph Kennedy's house outside of Wasilla."

Chapter Thirty-Five

"Such as what?" he asked.

"I was up there through the whole affair. I tried to listen to any and everyone I could, and I tried to see in the house and all around the grounds. I never heard or saw anything that indicated that Kennedy fired at the law officers or was even there during the raid. Apparently, someone from the federal end said that the terrorist went into the house the afternoon before the raid and never came out again. I guess my question is, did all of you guys make war on a man's house?"

"Gwen, I knew nothing about the ATF investigation before the very day of the raid; in fact, not until things went south. I was there soon after the ATF started up the hill and well before the FBI arrived on the scene. I personally never saw hide nor hair of Kennedy or anybody else in that house. I know Randolph on sight. He was not there."

"How about evidence of criminal activity—illegal guns, bomb making lab, drugs…anything?" she asked, her eyes fixed on his.

"Nothing up at the house or on the grounds. We went over the place very, very carefully before we left, and the fibbies did it all again after everyone else cleared out. It's their baby now, you know. And you called Kennedy a terrorist which is the term being bandied around by lots of people who don't know what they're talking about. Maybe you and your colleagues ought to check your facts before you continue to use a liberal news media label so freely. Maybe you ought to see if the charges have foundation, is all I say."

He seemed a little embarrassed at his emphatic declaration.

"Well placed criticism, Sergeant. I'll try to be more objective. To tell you the truth, I'm about the only reporter interested in this story. I have been having a devil of a time trying to get information about the reason for the raid, the findings after the raid, and where the heck the van found on his land came from to say nothing of where the man was or is now."

"Then I hope you get it right. Remember way back in the 1990s, the Ruby Ridge thing. A guy named Weaver and his family lived someplace in the hinterlands of Montana. Or maybe it was northern Idaho, no matter. Feds got the idea that they were some kind of big-time criminals way up there in the woods, that little family. The feds went up there like Hollywood gangbusters and shot the crap out of his place, killed his boy, his wife, even his dog. Ends up that it was all so much baloney. He sued them and won beaucoup bucks. Anyway, what I'm getting at is that for months before and for about two years afterwards, the liberal press swallowed what the feds told them about the affair hook, line, and sinker. The media never bothered to do any investigating, any real reporter work on their own. They just passed on the government's line as they were told like it was the gospel. The story got sent along mouth-to- mouth, and pen-to-pen over several years about how Weaver made war on the poor defenseless feds and was such a violent racist hate monger.

"Only after the civil trial did the FBI and the press have to admit grudgingly that the truth was quite something else. The feds were the bad guys, no question about it. The liberal press mentioned that little fact as briefly and obscurely as possible and went on after other conservative targets. I never saw a corruption scandal about a liberal darling like the entitlement programs, but let the military have some sort of scandal; and the *New York Times*, the *LA Times*, and that rag, the *Madison Capitol Times*, are all over it for weeks; and they never back down until they have milked it for everything possible, even if they know their facts are wrong. All I'm saying is that maybe you ought to step back and find out if Kennedy really is a racist, hate crimes fomenting, dope smuggling, gun runner or not before you hang that 'terrorist' label on him permanently—not that your paper would ever print anything positive about this so-called right-wing supremacist."

Gwen hoped Willets felt better after that extensive venting. She knew there was more than a grain of truth in what he was saying.

"Point well taken," Gwen said.

She saw the wisdom of the country police sergeant's observations as confirmatory of her own suspicions and of her unspoken criticism of the paper for which she worked. Admittedly, she had been largely blind to the possibilities that Kennedy was anything but what the government said he was. She determined to find out as much as possible about Randolph Kennedy before another article appeared under her byline.

Carol Willets was aware of the serious turn in the conversation. She was the self-appointed guardian of her husband's status and career.

"Honey, maybe it would be better if you spoke…how do they say, 'off the record'."

"No, Carol, it's okay. There's been too much 'off the record' in this case. Gwen, I'm not sure what went on up there. I mean, what led up to the raid. To give the ATFers the benefit of the doubt, maybe illegal arms and ammunition blew up in the explosions and fire. I can't say about that, and I don't think anyone is ever going to be able to prove a case one way or the other what with all of that destruction. I can say for a fact that there was no great store of illegal ordnance in Kennedy's house. There was no evidence for anything like that at all.

"It was just weird. It was not evident when we first went in except for that cock-eyed white van. Everybody up there is talking about the arms and ammo in it—like was it Kennedy's or not? Maybe you heard about a trailer that was supposed to have been there. Nobody that I talked to ever saw that. And even if it was there, how did it get out of there? Did a bogeyman just fly it away? I don't think so. It's a puzzle. I have a feeling that some cops are going to have a lot of explaining to do."

"Where's Kennedy?"

"No idea, and neither does anybody in law enforcement. He's probably out of the state, maybe out of the country. He could have been there, wherever that is, well before the raid ever started. I just don't know that."

"Any idea who might know? I mean, I know you've investigated; but maybe there's somebody who would not talk to a cop, but might talk to me."

"The guy who knows Kennedy best and in fact knows about everything that goes on around here is a kind of Wasilla town character named, Devlin O'Herligy. He has a store and real estate office on Main Street. If you're interested, you can't miss his place—gaudiest thing you ever saw—huge signs with stuff about Alaska's secession, the North Star Militia. O'Herligy plays the buffoon much of the time…you know, loud and acts about half drunk. But he is as sharp as they come. If anyone up here knows where Randolph Kennedy is or where he was around the time of the raid, he does. And he's not going to talk to the police."

"Thanks, I'll talk to him. Some more dessert?"

Carol looked at her husband and down at her midriff that was just begin-ning to widen, indicative of a long losing battle. She cast a jealous eye at Gwen's trim nulliparous body.

"Sure, why not? Carol asked. "What's another pound on the gut of a woman with four children and has to spend another two weeks on hard workouts? I envy your figure, Gwen. It's the reward for not having babies."

They all laughed and ordered chocolate mousse and espresso.

Although it was well past eleven that night when Gwen was able to be alone in her room in the Sheffield House, she looked up Devlin O'Herligy's number and dared a call. There was an answer after the third ring. The man's voice sounded fully awake and alert.

"Hello, are you Devlin O'Herligy?"

"That's me. Who're you?"

"My name is Gwen Chambers. I'm a reporter from the *New York Times*. I hope I didn't wake you. I'm covering the Randolph Kennedy story. My infor-mants referred me to you as the best source on Kennedy and whatever else important is going on in the state. Have I got the right man?"

She had to suppress her smile as she ladled it on thick.

"You have, and flattery will get you everywhere. What is it you want…exactly?"

"I'd like to talk to you in person tomorrow. I am too tired to think right now. Would that be all right with you?"

He waited a moment.

"What the hay? Why not? Let's do lunch, as the flits in the lower forty-eight like to say."

"When and where?"

"I have to come into the big city in the morning. How about we have halibut at Phyllis's Café and Salmon Bake? It's on D Street between Fourth and Fifth. Ask anybody where it is. Straight up noon?"

"Thanks, Mr. O'Herligy, that'll be fine. I'll be there. Sorry if I woke you up."

"Missy, it's early yet. I still have some hearty partyin' to do. I'll whip myself into some kind of shape by midday tomorrow and see you then."

"Good-bye, Mr. O'Herligy."

"Good-bye, Gwen."

So, it was already Mr. O'Herligy and Gwen. She could do without the 'missy' that seemed to be such a popular form of address up here in the mountains.

Gwen ate a skimpy continental breakfast in the hotel coffee shop as repentance for her overindulgence the previous night. She spent the morning seeing the sights of Anchorage: the Fort Richardson Wildlife Museum, Earthquake Park, Alaska Native Crafts Cooperative, the Arctic Valley Road Lookout, and Captain Cook's monument. It was dull fare for the jaded New Yorker; but the air was bracing; and it was a gorgeous day to be out. She had forgotten that air you couldn't taste could be that pleasant.

At noon, she took a Checker cab to Phyllis's Café. It was a simple, inviting, hole-in-the-wall sort of place with a small patio for outside service that was unusable nine months of the year owing to the weather. She had never seen nor met Devlin O'Herligy, but there was no doubt who he was when she did. He was sitting at the center table in the restaurant holding court when Gwen entered. She heard him before she saw him—raucous laughter at his own jokes, unsolicited advice shouted louder than would be have been necessary in a deaf-mute colony. His hands were moving in a personalized sign language, and his arms gesticulated broadly as he drove home his points at any and all comers in the restaurant. And the man had the most incredible shock of flaming red hair that Gwen had ever seen outside a Looney-Tunes cartoon.

"Mr. O'Herligy, I presume?" Gwen asked when she was able to wedge her way up to his table.

"In the flesh. Have a seat. Don't get mad if I started without you. I am the classic biblical natural man when it comes to my appetites. I couldn't wait."

He was well into a Caesar's salad and had already decimated a small loaf of bread.

"Don't let me interfere. I'll just join in," Gwen said and took her seat.

The waitress stepped to her side.

Gwen said, "Give me whatever he's having."

Gwen and Devlin both laughed when the poker-faced waitress returned with three bottles of beer as her appetizer.

"I hate to shorten this delightful meeting with you, Gwen, but I have promises to keep and miles to go before I sleep, to quote Wordsworth."

She didn't think it would be adroit of her to tell the man that the quote was from Robert Frost.

"Anyhow, I have another appointment. Mind if we talk with our mouths full?"

As if it would matter that a gentile New York lady was present.

She smiled, "Not at all. I get some of my best stuff that way."

"Now, what is it a country bumpkin like me can tell you and the famous *New York Times* newspaper?

It was clear that he was not a great fan of the world's greatest newspaper. His halibut came, and he began forking off large flaky white chunks with animated gusto.

"I always liked halibut the best. Maybe I can't bear to eat them poor salmon. You know what they say about their being born orphans and dying childless."

He chuckled at his rendition of the old Alaskan joke.

She smiled her appreciation.

"Where's Randolph Kennedy?" she asked without preamble as much to disarm him as anything.

"My, aren't you the direct one? Sorry, Ms. Chambers,"—no longer 'Gwen'—I don't know. You are a Mizz, are you not?"

It was drawn out like the buzzing of an insect.

"Yes. Do you know who does know where he is, or how I can get hold of the man?"

"No."

He began concentrating on his baked potato, a complicated process of adding butter, sour cream, chives, bacon bits, grated American cheese, and salt and pepper and thoroughly mixing them into the steaming white meat of the Russet potato the size of a Pop Warner league football.

"Do you know whether or not he was in his house on the twenty-sixth of June?"

"Is that when the armed forces of the United States feloniously and with malice aforethought attacked and destroyed that innocent man's property without due process or adequate cause?"

"In a manner of speaking."

"The answer is yes."

She watched and waited while he killed another Moosehead beer. He was disinclined to elaborate on his rather Delphian answer without prodding.

"Would you mind sharing with me what 'yes' means?"

"You'll have to ask old President Clinton about that one," he answered and guffawed at the cleverness of his riposte.

She laughed dutifully.

"I wouldn't mind sharing with you, not at all."

He said it with a little leer.

"You asked if I know whether or not Kennedy was in his house. I do know that. He was not in his house. In fact, he was not in his house for the better part of a week before that nefarious and unprovoked raid. I know that for a fact."

"Do you know where he was...exactly?"

"I do know that. He was with me, hunting."

His face remained dispassionate and absorbed in his gourmand activities. If he was a liar, Gwen decided, he was an altogether convincing one. She did not want to play poker with the man. He would make a terrific witness, unless, of course, one favored the government's case. Then he would be a formidable opponent.

"The whole week?" Gwen pressed.

"Better part of it. You kind of a picky eater? You haven't touched you halibut. Great stuff."

"Oh, I was distracted by our conversation."

She ate a few bits, but her mind was busy digesting the information from O'Herligy. She recognized that the food was good; and she was hungry; but she could not focus on both things, unlike O'Herligy.

He watched her for a few moments as she turned her food over with her fork.

"You gonna eat that fish? If not, I'll make the sacrifice and take it off your hands. Can't have waste, not with all those starving Armenians, right?"

She moved her plate to his side. He ate her halibut from her plate with her fork without the slightest hint of self-consciousness or germ consciousness.

"Guess they don't do that sort of thing in New York City, huh? But this is such great stuff. Even good for the figure. I think it's on the approved list for all you mizzes, even."

He smiled broadly at her, and strings of halibut meat showed in the cracks between his teeth.

"Mr. O'Herligy," she started.

"Call me Devlin."

He paused to drink his entire glass of ice water with a satisfying chug-a-lug sound.

"Devlin, then, please put me in touch with him. I am a professional journalist. I never—and I mean never—betray my sources."

"Everybody betrays, missy. The price just has to be right and in the right currency. You can verify that bit of wisdom by a quick browse through ATF records. Nevertheless—even if I were inclined to rat out my friend—I couldn't do it. I really don't know where he is."

"And you wouldn't tell me if you did know, would you?"

He never faltered in the rhythm of his fork movements.

"And, I wouldn't tell you if I did."

"Thanks for your time. Here's my card if you ever change your mind."

She beckoned the waitress who sniffed at all the good food left on her plate, and Gwen paid the bill for both of them.

"I have to be off now."

He nodded and said, "Me, too. I hope we meet again. Here's to golden days and purple nights."

It was obtuse like most of his comments. He raised an eyebrow and squinted a little, the look and the phrase giving him the expression of a corpulent *bon vivant* Irish roué, by his own reckoning. Gwen thought of him as antediluvian and more than a little peculiar. He also knew more than he was telling.

"Hey, Phyl, how 'bout some of that fine lemon meringue pie for which you are justifiably famous?" he was yelling as she walked away.

If he was aware that she had gone, it was not evident to her or to any casual onlooker.

She got a cab back to the hotel and had the driver wait while she collected her bags and checked out. He took her to the airport. She studied the departure board and found the next flight out to New York. She was in luck. A United flight was leaving in an hour, but it made three intermediate stops and did not serve a meal. The Delta flight an hour after that was nonstop and was scheduled to arrive in the city a full two hours before the United milk run trip. She bought a first-class ticket after finding out that that was the only one available to stand-by flyers. She hid out in the VIP lounge and composed her notes.

CHAPTER THIRTY-SIX

Randolph flew over I-80, from San Francisco to Sacramento—on his two-wheeled rocket—averaging nearly 120 miles an hour. He kept a very wary eye out for cops of all stripes, and saw none. He also noted that he was not traveling all that much faster than the general traffic flow. On the eastern outskirts of California's capital city Randolph was irritated to have to slow down to 80 and sometimes less between Sacramento and Reno and to have to lose his liberating sense of exhilaration. The traffic was unbearable, with hordes of Californians entering and exiting the national traffic artery at every little town: Citrus Heights, Loomis, Auburn, Colfax, Gold Run, Emigrant Gap, Verdi. The worst point was a section of the freeway under construction. The concrete lane dividers on both sides gave the stretch a luge-like character that intimidated the timid and slowed all of traffic down to a ten mile an hour crawl. Time passed with annoying deliberateness and a deepening sense of exposure.

He was grateful to cross the Nevada line and onto the greatly improved and enlarged highway. There was no speed limit across the northern Nevada portion of the Mojave Desert, and Randolph was able to crank the powerful machine to its maximum cruising speed of 200 miles per hour at times. It had taken two decades for the citizens of the western United States to learn to accept the concept of traveling in a traffic lane appropriate to their chosen speed. Randolph, in the so-called "autobahn" lane—the inside fast track— fairly flew past the more land bound of his fellow travelers. It was exhilarating and liberating. He was totally anonymous in his helmet with the opaque facial wind screen and felt a relaxation that he had not enjoyed since the day of the first raid on his house.

The fugitive was not paying attention when he passed through Wendover, Nevada and did not recognize that he had crossed over the line into Wendover, Utah. That brought him back into the world of enforced speed limits, speed traps, and avaricious cities for whom speeders were the life's blood of their sickly economies. He was enjoying himself so much, that he never saw the 80 miles per hour speed limit sign. He was doing in excess of 150 at a point sixty miles east of Wendover along the Dwight D. Eisenhower expressway portion of Utah I-80 when he was radar and laser clocked by the UHP. Far to the rear, Randolph saw the flashing blue, yellow, and white lights, and only then looked down at his speedometer. He reflexively slowed to 100 like a good law-abiding citizen, but he knew he was too late.

Randolph had read the AAA booklet reports on Utah speed traps and had ignored the warnings in his pre-occupation with putting distance between himself and San Francisco. He kicked himself for the risk he had taken, for his inattention at a time when he had to be on guard constantly. The police car was approaching. He began to run his options through his mind. He could outrun the cop, but he knew that he could not outrun the officer's radio. He could stop and try to bluff his way through, but he knew from past experience that almost every traffic violation was used as a pretext to permit a search of the driver's vehicle, and he could not let that happen. Finally, he could act the part of the fugitive he was, jump the policeman in total surprise, and escape. Realistically, even if he were to be successful in subduing the cop, that would leave a witness, and there would be a bulletin out for a dark skinned Mexican on a souped up Harley. No, looked at soberly, being stopped meant that he was going to have to kill the cop. All he could hope for was that he or she had not called in a description of his motorcycle. It might prove difficult to assault a trained police officer and to succeed in killing the man or woman. And, there was the small factor of his conscience.

The slowing process took nearly 70 miles until the police car finally drew up behind Randolph close enough to call him on a bullhorn.

"You on the Harley, pull over."

Randolph had been slowing down enough to keep the cop from getting excited and calling in help. When he heard the bullhorn, he decided on his option, and pulled over immediately. Now, he sat sweating, steeling himself for what he knew he had to do.

"Good afternoon, sir," the highway patrolwoman said with exaggerated politeness. "Please step down and away from the motorcycle."

Randolph complied. The patrolwoman stepped to the Harley but never took her eyes off him.

"This your vehicle?"

"Yes, ma'am."

"Where's the registration?"

She seemed rather slight for a policewoman. He calculated his chances against her. She was armed, and he was not. He would have the advantage of surprise, but the distance between them loomed large. He was unsure whether he could bridge the gap before she could draw her gun and shoot him. There was no choice. He had gone through too much to be captured almost by accident by some woman cop in the middle of a Podunk state for a stupid traffic ticket. There was too much at stake. His blood pressure and pulse rate went up. He tensed himself to spring.

"In the leather case in front of the gas tank lid," he said.

He made an effort not to look at the side pannier holders crammed with cash. He thanked his guardian angel that he had not put his wallet and the registration in one of the panniers.

She kept an eye on him while she opened the leather flap and extracted the papers. She looked from them to him and back again before she was satisfied. The desert sun beat down mercilessly. The two of them were sweating. Wavy heat mirages distorted the horizon in all directions. She put the papers back in the leather box, then looked at his wallet, checking the driver's license photo. That evidently satisfied her as well.

"What's in those holders?"

He forced an easy smile, belying the tiger instinct to snarl and to spring.

"My stuff. You know, clothes, shaving things, some books."

'You a tourist?"

"Not really. I'm moving."

"To Utah?"

"No. I was thinking of going to North Dakota. I heard there are jobs around Fargo."

"You don't have much of an accent for a Mexican, Mr. Cortez. How is that?"

She looked at him with unfeigned suspicion.

"I spent most of my childhood and early teens in Corpus Christi. I went to school there. I learned to speak English without an accent to get along with the kids, and to speak Spanish to please my parents."

"What sort of work do you do, Mr. Cortez?"

"I'm a mechanic."

He glanced at his hands and hoped that she would not notice that they were free of grease stains and calluses of any consequence. He looked at the motorcycle.

"A motorcycle mechanic."

A whirling wind blew up a dust devil around them. Grains of sand and small pebbles whipped at them.

"I have to give you a ticket, Mr. Cortez. I'm sure you realize that you were exceeding the speed limit by a considerable margin, nearly 100 miles an hour *over*. You have the option of paying me here or accompanying me into Salt Lake City to appear before a magistrate. That usually takes six to eight hours."

She said it blandly; but he knew he was being robbed; and he had no choice. 'How much will the fine be, officer?"

"A dollar fifty per mile over the limit. That's $150 here. I'll tell you this; it would be $250 through the court because you have to pay court costs over and above the fine. But it's your choice."

It was all so matter-of-fact—so business-as-usual—this bit of highway robbery.

"All right, I think it would be best for me to pay you here."

"I'm sorry, sir, but it has to be cash. State can't accept checks, too many rip-offs. Can't use cards; I can't carry the stamping apparatus."

Of course it does.

She looked coolly at him. He pulled out his wallet from his coat pocket and extracted $200. He knew that she had made a quick wallet check when she searched the contents of his side box. He was sure she was hooked into a little shakedown. He handed over the money. She accepted it, gave him change— which surprised him—and wrote out a legible receipt, which surprised him even more.

"Looks like a shakedown, doesn't it? Like your federales in Mexico."

He nodded almost imperceptibly, afraid to do more for fear of antagonizing her.

"It's not. This is just the way we do it here. Most of the Western states do it this way. Wyoming has been doing it this way for half a century. It will all be recorded in the national drivers' computer and points will be issued against your license. All very proper. You can check once you get to Salt Lake City. My name and unit number are on the ticket. Have a good day, sir; and try and hold it down. Utah still has a sensible set of speed laws, and we intend to enforce them."

"Thank you, officer," he said perfunctorily, for what he was not sure.

He had made his decision to kill her if she forced his hand be requiring him to open his panniers. The wind was now quite fierce, blowing heat and dust like a giant sand blaster making the two of them shield their eyes with their forearms.

"I should check your vehicle; I usually do. But I guess this is your lucky day. This wind would blow everything to kingdom come. Even I'm not that mean. And besides, I don't want to take all of the time to help you retrieve your stuff that blows away. Take off now, and take it easy."

For the first time since he had heard the siren behind him, Randolph began to relax. He felt the strength drain out of him as the troopers cruiser pulled away. He breathed a heavy sigh of relief that he had not had to commit murder. He had been altogether too close—biblically too close. He knew he was going to have to find another option besides murder to extract himself from this kind of situation when it arose again.

He was just not cut out for that sort of thing. His bothersome conscience was going to get him into trouble, but it was part of him. He felt a wave of profound relief that he had not had to make such a final choice that day. He also vowed on all that was holy to him that he would obey the law henceforth. This had been a stark lesson, and the next time it would be worse. And, incidentally, he made a resolution to drive the speed limit, like any good illegal Mexican, for the rest of his life.

CHAPTER THIRTY-SEVEN

The president, attorney general, secretary of Homeland Security, directors of the FBI, ATF, DEA, and the commander of the coast guard and their aides were all in their places at 0900 when the business of the President's Final Battle in the War on Drugs and Illegal Weapons Task Force commenced. There was one item on the agenda: The Randolph Kennedy Affair.

DFBI Ted Coleman leaned to whisper to DATF Roger Holdaway, "You know, this Kennedy thing keeps coming back like a bad case of Falciparim malaria. We ought to do something permanent about him, get him off the streets once and for all."

Holdaway nodded his amen.

Margaret Thaler, the Attorney General, banged the gavel to signal the start.

"I am pleased to announce one major piece of good news…The meeting is going to start on time today with 100 percent attendance—two firsts."

There was a ripple of understanding laughter.

She went on, "We have one nagging item to deal with today, and I thought it important enough to dedicate the entire meeting to that problem alone. We have a fugitive, Randolph Kennedy, whose at large, spit-in-your-face status stands as a symbol of failure in our otherwise virtually perfect record. The regular media paints the man accurately as a criminal—a terrorist—but some of the conservative talk shows and bloggers are beginning to make him out to be some kind of cult hero, a modern day Robin Hood. I find that unacceptable. This agenda item can be divided into two parts. First, how are we going to bring this terrorist to justice—how are we going to capture him? And second, who is responsible for the abortive disastrous raid on Kennedy's fortress in

Alaska and for the dismal state of the evidence against this criminal. Ted has listed Kennedy officially as public enemy number one, and nobody knows the least thing about where he is or what he is doing."

There was some squirming in the seats of the ATF contingent. Oliver Quatraine refused to look nervous or chagrined. It took effort.

"Ted Coleman from the FBI will address the first question," Thaler continued. Director Coleman stood.

"Ladies and gentlemen, to date we have very little to go on. As near as I can determine, Kennedy is out of Alaska, and probably out of the country. We have mounted an extensive manhunt, but the press of our many responsibilities and the lack of a designated budget to field a unit of FBI professionals hampers us. We need a team that can travel extensively, at will, and at a moment's notice. The team will need the resources to deal with violent confrontations, and will have to be professional enough to maintain the necessary low profile. So—thus far—our success has been limited. We need for this committee to provide the funding. FBI will provide the DEST investigational and capture unit; and other federal, state, and local law enforcement personnel will act as backup."

Roger Holdaway from ATF, the DDEA, and the coast guard rear admiral shared a quick communication of eye rolling. Even among insiders, the DFBI still felt the need for elaborate aggrandizement for his Bureau. It was a new verse of an old song—the FBI is responsible; the FBI fails; the FBI blames lack of money for its failure; and the FBI gets a new infusion of taxpayer money and builds its base and reputation.

"How big a unit?" asked the president.

"A modest proposal, ma'am. We would like to have ten hand-picked senior people," replied Coleman, making it obvious that he had his plans ready to be set into motion. "And their best troops."

"I take it you have thought of a leader?"

"Yes, ma'am. Gerald Silberberg, head of the Bureau's C-3 Department including all COINTELPRO. That's the Counterintelligence Programs. He is a highly experienced counterterrorism expert, an organizational genius, and a practical street cop. We'll include VICAP people; and if the need arises, we will bring in special weapons and tactics units as soldiers. Randolph Kennedy may be thoroughgoing Dantonesque, but Silberberg is his match. He has a group of special agents with whom he was worked for years, often enough on an undercover basis. Violent Criminal Apprehension Program members are enthusiastic to throw in their resources. I see no need to involve anyone else except on a standby basis at this stage. The fewer people who know the makeup of the unit, the less likely it is that there will be leaks. It goes without saying that any of the extensive resources of the Bureau or our brother enforcement partners will—would—be at Silberberg's disposal."

DATF Holdaway tugged Oliver Quatraine's shoulder and whispered, "What does 'Dantonesque' mean, pray tell. Coleman's big words give me a pain."

Quatraine nodded in amusement.

"I think Danton was some kind of very clever French Revolutionary in the late 1700s. He had a reputation of thwarting the royal government and its police efforts. Not a bad comparison, don't you think?"

Holdaway nodded.

It was well known that Silberberg had Coleman's ear more than did anyone else in the Bureau and was—therefore—the expected choice. For one thing, he had a reputation for getting things done even if he had to bend the rules. For another, he was generally acknowledged to be brilliant. The rank and file thought he ought to be the DFBI, and that he served Coleman as the *l'Éminence Grise* to Coleman's *l'Éminence Rouge,* an allusion to Silberberg's undue influence. And this by men and women whose grasp of history— especially French history—did not go back beyond the introduction of the mini-skirt in 1965.

Oliver Quatraine, with his educational minor in French history and the French language, knew the underpinnings of the reference. Cardinal Richelieu (*Rouge*) was the supposed power behind the throne of Louis XIII, and Richelieu's secretary and confessor, the grey cloaked, Pere Joseph de Trembley, (*Grise*) was the advisor and presumably the power behind Richelieu.

"Any dissenters?" asked the president.

There was a unanimous shaking of heads around the conference table. President Vantassa looked over at Attorney General Thaler and nodded.

"Consider it done, then, Mr. Coleman," Thaler announced. "We will work out the financial arrangements after this meeting, but I foresee no real difficulties."

She looked back to the president, who gave another small nod of approval.

"We'll make it a war, then. Perhaps a war of attrition; but Americans are used to wars, even wearying wars. We will wear away our enemy's support system until he stands alone with only his own meager defenses. I don't think it will be quick, but it will happen. You can take that to the bank," Thaler emphasized, her voice rising to a speechy enthusiasm.

Quatraine wondered how well this committee would do against the wily Randolph Kennedy after so much high-profile failure in the past. He had kept abreast of as many reports and details about the search for Kennedy as he could get his hands on. As far as he could tell, the hunt had been extensive and thorough, and had yielded nothing—not even leads for future searches.

"I would like to have Roger Holdaway recount for us the information at his disposal giving responsibility for the Alaska raid that resulted in the deaths of so many good people and at so much dollar cost, and with so little retrieval of useful evidence," Mrs. Thaler said, turning to the second part of the agenda item.

"I have a considerable interest in that, as well. Director Holdaway. Please elaborate," the president ordered.

Roger Holdaway stood up, and Oliver Quatraine reached into his front trouser pocket and surreptitiously switched his voice activated recorder to the 'on' position.

"Madam President, Madam Attorney General, ladies and gentlemen, the ATF has conducted its own internal investigation and has obtained information the FBI has agreed to release."

The DFBI flashed the DATF a scowl.

"This data is contained in an extensive report, a copy of which is in front of each of you. I will hit the high points, and you can study the full document at your leisure. There is evidence to indicate that the terrorist, Randolph Kennedy, transferred crates of M-60 machine guns from a warehouse in Anchorage to his house in Wasilla. The actual guns were not seen, but we have clearly incriminating videotape evidence of the crates themselves being handled by the perpetrator and being taken into his house. There is no evidence of them having ever been removed, and we had trained ATF observers watching the man's house constantly for a week prior to and during the raid of June 26.

"ATF agent Henry Drake was in direct charge of field operations including planning, until he was injured in the line of duty. Agent Oliver Quatraine, who sits on this committee, was in overall command of the operation and assumed field command when Drake was put out of action. As near as can be determined, only those two men were in full knowledge of the available evidence and were essentially the sole planners from start to finish. Our final report details a number of errors of planning and execution by these two agents."

Quatraine stiffened, caught unawares. He had had no warning that this public criticism was being hatched. It was a sucker punch, and it made him furious. He strained forward to see if he was going to be the official public scapegoat. Roger Holdaway made a determined effort to avoid Quatraine's gaze.

"The errors committed by these men that are most pertinent to the question before us today have to do with the collection and preservation of evidence. Heavy fire power was used in the raid. The FBI found fragments of grenades and an assortment of weapon parts. One problem for this investigation is sorting out whether the weapons were Kennedy's or whether they were brought in to the location by law enforcement agents. Records on the ordnance Drake had brought in are skimpy and—in some instances—contradictory. One plausible scenario is that the government's armaments and explosives were detonated and destroyed in the uncoordinated mad rush on the house that ended in a veritable holocaust.

"In the aftermath, we can not determine with any certainty that any one weapon or piece of ordnance or the preponderance of them were there before the raid. The videotapes of the crates being brought into Kennedy's property do not correspond to the types of ordnance found. The other scenario—considered the most probable—is that the destruction was so complete, that the weaponry Kennedy had—and therefore the evidence against him—was obliterated. Without more corroborative evidence, it would appear that we can not make a case that will hold up, not even in the most generous federal court. In short, the case against Randolph Kennedy as been bungled, and the responsibility for that lies with the man in charge."

Quatraine felt all eyes in the room turn to him. At least, Holdaway had had the decency not to identify him by name. He felt blood rising in his face, and he had to fight to maintain composure.

"And, Madam President and Madam Attorney General, I'm afraid that that is not even the worst part of this report. FBI investigators found a large white Dodge Ram delivery van on the premises and have looked into rumors that there was also a semi-trailer there as well. The van was filled with illegal guns, ammunition, drugs, and bomb making materials—millions of dollars worth. Because only federal agents' fingerprints were found on the vehicle, the only conclusion to be drawn is that agents brought the van to the site, not Kennedy. It appears to have been deliberately left where it would be found and could pass for evidence—a plant."

The room fell silent. The president and attorney general wore newly grim expressions of shock and dismay.

"The FBI report indicates a very extensive search of the vehicle for prints. Kennedy's prints are on file from his previous encounter with the ATF, and there were no matches among the dozens of altogether clear, 10 and fifteen point prints found. The prints that were found include those of Agents

Quatraine and Drake—and even more damning—there were clear prints on the truck and its contents belonging to impound personnel from the federal evidence storage facility in Ketchikan, Alaska. The implications are too clear to ignore."

Quatraine was aware of his teeth grinding against one another and of his clenching jaws. He hoped that he did not look as guilty as Holdaway's description indicated.

Holdaway took a breath and went on, "With a notable omission, the contraband in that van tallied exactly with the inventory from the Ketchikan facility that originated as evidence seized in a successful raid on a terrorist location in Ketchikan last April. Henry Drake signed his name to the inventory list which—in addition to the drugs and weapons—included a semi-trailer load of baled cash. That cash is nowhere to be found. If we can believe the rumors— and that is all that they are—the trailer was also temporarily on Kennedy's property then disappeared. The details of any of that remain a mystery.

There are no records indicating that the money or any of the evidence material was ever officially and legally removed from Ketchikan. The armaments were returned to the impound facility by the ATF under FBI orders after the abortive raid. Suspicion obviously falls on Drake, and maybe Quatraine— certainly for the improper removal of the materials and possibly for the grand theft of the money. At this point, the FBI's thorough search has not yielded a scrap of evidence that directly links either man to the money—either before or after the raid—but they remain persons of interest."

Quatraine felt as if he had been struck with a board. He had gotten up that morning feeling fit and content with his world. This was the first inkling he had received that he—that *he*—might be under consideration as a bungler, let alone a *thief!* He was nauseated.

"The conclusion in part two of the agenda item is that Henry Drake—with the possible collusion of Oliver Quatraine—caused the evidence from the Ketchikan raid to be removed illegally from the evidence impound center and to be used as planted evidence against Randolph Kennedy. Since there is no possible way that Kennedy could have come into possession of the money or even known about it—for that matter—it must be presumed that Drake—or Quatraine—or some other co-conspirators within law enforcement stole the cash. What they might have done with the huge volume of money is problematical and bespeaks very careful advance planning."

Now everyone turned a frankly hostile look at Quatraine. He knew that the bee was on him; he was the fall guy—the single catchment fool at the bottom of the hill as the stuff ran down—with Drake out of commission. He was raging inside, but continued to stare straight ahead tight lipped, almost without blinking as he was being roasted by the angry scrutiny of his peers.

For more than a minute, no one spoke. No one could. The AG broke the silence.

"What is the ATF going to do about this, Director?"

"Henry Drake is recuperating in a rehab hospital associated with the University of Washington Medical School. He was rendered paraplegic by a bomb or shotgun booby trap and is reportedly profoundly depressed—to the point that he is unable to participate in questioning. While we deem him responsible for the on-the-scene blunders, we will require more results of FBI investigation before instituting criminal proceedings. With your permission, Madam President and Madam Attorney General, ATF internal affairs officers in conjunction with the FBI, would like to have the opportunity to detain and to question Agent Quatraine regarding his involvement. Hopefully, we can secure enough cooperation that we can avoid some major public fallout that would attend a sensational trial."

Margaret Thaler glanced at President Vantassa for approval, received the nod, and said, "Go ahead. Keep me posted. We may yet have to put the agent on trial to demonstrate to the public that while we may have a rotten apple in the Task Force, it is not the way we intend to do business. Director Holdaway, do your duty."

She gazed at Quatraine with steely, unforgiving eyes.

Roger Holdaway pushed his chair aside and stood over Quatraine. Holdaway wore a disheartened expression, a genuinely sorrowful countenance.

"Oliver Quatraine, I place you under arrest for the crime of misuse of evidence under the color of authority, for complicity in the deaths of your fellow federal officers, for conspiracy, and for racketeering. You are hereby relieved of your position and duties in the ATF. You will be confined in the Bureau's holding cells until final disposition has been determined. You have the right to remain silent; if you give up that right, anything you say can and will be used against you in a court of law. You have the right to have an attorney present during questioning. If you desire to have an attorney and cannot afford one, the government will provide a defender at no cost to you. Do you understand these rights as I have read them to you?"

Quatraine angrily nodded his head. He was too humiliated to speak. He robotically extended his hands to be handcuffed.

Holdaway said, "I don't think that will be necessary. Let's don't make this any more difficult than it already is. And, Oliver, it's nothing personal. I hate to have to do this; I hope you realize that."

He led Quatraine from the room and placed him in the custody of two stolid faced ATF agents. When Holdaway returned to the Task Force conference room and closed the door, the guards roughly clamped handcuffs on Oliver's wrists.

So far as he was concerned, the life of Oliver Quatraine had just ended.

CHAPTER THIRTY-EIGHT

Randolph scrupulously minded the speed limits after his ticket out on the Utah desert. He bought a map of the state in a Stinker station, a humorously advertised gasoline dealership on the western edge of Salt Lake City. He charted his route, even to the point of learning the speed limits all the way to the little city of Heber, population 20,000. He drove in the right hand lane most of the way, an almost humiliating experience—being a fugitive had several decided drawbacks. Randolph was rewarded for his newly adopted practice of obeying traffic laws by being able to drive safely past several dozen speed traps; Utah lived up to its reputation as *the* speed trap capital of the country. He traveled the entire remaining distance into Utah's Wasatch Mountains without event. He followed I-80 past I-15, which had been upgraded to a fine, but now significantly overcrowded freeway, for the 2002 Winter Olympics. He drove sedately on the broad highway over Parley's canyon, and stopped at the Lodge at Parley's Summit for his first meal of the day.

He was gratified to see that no one was interested in him. The vacationers, the lodge employees, and the locals seemed to be a live-and-let-live bunch which suited him perfectly. The last leg of the trip took him onto the I-40 cutoff east of Park City, the famous ski resort area. What had once been windswept hills and a broad valley was now becoming a megalopolis of cheap and cute houses. What had some time ago been an isolated enclave of polygamists near the U.S. 40 Silver Creek Junction was now a nearly completely filled in indistinguishable conglomerate of cheap cottage homes stretching as far as Randolph could see.

Randolph moved along the four-lane freeway at 80 miles per hour, feeling as if he were creeping. The teeming tourist activity and people moving in and out of the bedroom and recreational community of Greater Jordanelle slowed him even further. At last, he began the descent into the beautiful—and now becoming over-populated—Heber Valley. The mountain tops were still majestic and spoke of the beauty that had greeted the Mormon pioneers of the area and had been the proud possession of their descendents for its first 140 sleepy years. Californians exiting the pestilential wasteland they had created in their state had invaded the valley after the creation of the second of two recreational reservoirs and changed the character of the valley irretrievably.

Now, the valley floor was becoming filled with cheap houses that were already beginning to show the decay reminiscent of California's San Fernando Valley. Where there once were farmer's pastures and meandering creeks, there were now parking lots, amusement parks, big box stores, an expanded regional airport, and a ground cover of asphalt and concrete. The hillsides and low elevation knolls were dotted with cheap imitations of Swiss villages. The developers had long since raked in their fortunes and had moved on to more remote valleys. The city and its environs had settled into a Californicated landscape and drab society. It was the perfect place for Randolph to hide in anonymity.

Randolph pulled into a phone booth park and set his Harley down on its kickstand in the shade of one of the artificial trees placed there by the city fathers in an attempt to recreate an illusion of the foliage of yesteryear with an inexpensive ornament that did not consume precious water resources. He bought a local phone card from the automatic vendor and dialed the number Daryl Haslip had given him.

'Yeah," came the gruff response.

"Daryl Haslip told me to call. Said you'd be expecting me."

"You the guy on the motorcycle?"—the man pronounced it 'sicle'.

"Yes."

"Where are you at right now?"

"In the city park south of the old pioneer city office building, the one with the clock standing in front of it."

'I know where it is," the gruff voice said. "What do you look like?"

"Mexican. All in black. You can't miss me."

"One a my boys'll be down there inside atwenny minutes. You just be a short dog in the high grass until he gets there. Don't talk to nobody or attract any attention. My boy'll be in a red BMW pickup. You follow him outta there and up to my place."

So much for low visibility, thought Randolph when he contemplated what a red BMW pickup truck was going to look like among the dozens of drab colored trucks belonging to the locals. He was hardly in a position to complain, to criticize, or to look a gift horse in the mouth.

"Okay, I'll be watching."

The other end of the phone clicked and went dead. Randolph replaced his receiver on its cradle and went about the business of looking obscure.

It was not until forty-five minutes later that a blazing metallic red—almost luminescent—pickup rolled noisily into the parking lot of the phone park. Without looking to one side or the other, the driver—a boy dressed in camouflage denims—wheeled past Randolph and headed straight for the exit. Randolph had to scurry to get on his Harley before the BMW truck was out of sight. He caught a flash of the gleaming red car making a right turn onto Center Street headed east. He followed as fast as he dared. The flame colored and racing striped truck slowed down as they passed out of the main city center and past red stone hills with their housing developments that constituted the Red Ledges, Beaufontaine, and Greenerhills suburbs of the city. The truck—with Randolph following closely behind—wound up the road into the heavily housed hills and turned right into the city of Timberlakes, a gated and guarded enclave of the valley's richest citizens. That surprised Randolph, but he was getting used to surprises.

So far as he could tell, no one had followed them. The traffic was so heavy that he could not be sure, however. The blaze colored pickup led Randolph to the uppermost tier of houses. The mountain had divided into serried ranks of housing developments, each one more exclusive and expensive than the last as the altitude and steepness of the hillsides increased. They pulled into the concrete driveway of an elegant but misplaced stucco mansion that looked as if it had been transported from Santa Fe by administrative mistake. The driveway circled to the rear of the property and ended in a line of spacious two-car garages. The truck pulled into one of the garages, and the boy beckoned for Randolph to follow him. Randolph felt the safest he had been in three days when the garage door shut, but he retained a measure of wariness as he trotted along behind the boy and into the rear of the house.

ADFBI Phil Craig called Special Agent Nancy Delgado at her small operations headquarters in Ballwin, Missouri. She had set up her clandestine center in that small suburb of St. Louis to keep her activities out of the public limelight; and, for that purpose, Ballwin was a choice well made. Besides—for Nancy—it was refreshing to be away from the bleak, gray-carpeted Buzzard Point office—in reality, only a cubicle separated from other squads, 640 other agents—by six-foot tall carpeted office baffles. She and her two assistants—Romaine Terrife, and David Bendell—had been busy for a week evaluating passenger records for several score of flights that had started or terminated in Alaska or could have been a leg of one of the flights.

"Hello, Nancy, how goes the war?" Craig asked.

"Same-o, same-o. Lots of flatfoot work, nothing much to show for it yet, sorry boss."

"No problem. I have some news you'll appreciate. Coleman has been given the overall authority by the president to get this guy, Kennedy, as the number one priority of the Bureau. Coleman assigned Gerald Silberberg and his whole team with an unlimited budget as the investigators. They are going to operate with top media exposure as a strategy. You'll begin to see TV, newspapers, and magazine pictures and articles about this terrorist. Kennedy has been named public enemy number one officially; so, the hype will spill over onto every little police station in the country, onto the TV talk shows, and on the prime time cop shows."

"Sounds like that's that for our little operation. That about it, boss?" Nancy asked pragmatically.

"No. I've given this a lot of thought. I learned that in the last Task Force meeting, Oliver Quatraine—the Special Response Team chief for ATF—was chosen to take the whole fall for the Kennedy disaster in Alaska. I have a good hunch that no hint of upper level involvement is ever going to surface with the FBG running the show. Sort of the foxes in charge of the hen house, and that naturally rankles me. I still think something is rotten in Denmark and I want you to stay on it quietly. I will feed you everything I learn from Silberberg's work product, and I will try and arrange for you to get to Henry Drake and to this guy, Oliver Quatraine, before they can completely sequester them."

"Whatever you say, Mr. Craig. But I'll tell you, I am nervous. I have to trust you won't leave me or my guys out there to twist in the wind at the first hint of trouble from Coleman. Promise me that."

"Cross my heart and hope to die," Craig answered completely seriously.

"Okay, here's to the confusion of our enemies," Nancy said. "I'll be in touch."

Chapter Thirty-Eight

They needed a break. Badly.

"Look," Nancy said to Romaine and David as soon as she was off the phone, "we have to get out there and make ourselves some luck. I'm going stir-crazy. I have a hunch."

Both men gave theatrical groans, the type reserved for men hearing a new feminine intuition. Actually, they tended to trust her hunches, but neither of them could let her know that.

"I'm up for anything that means getting out of here of a while," David told her. "Let's hear your hunch."

"I think old Kennedy came out of Alaska very early in this caper. I also think that the most likely places for him to go and get lost were Seattle and San Francisco. He would have had to change his appearance almost as soon as he got there. So, my hunch is that we should go to San Francisco first since the time frame for the flights out of Alaska fits best. We should concentrate initially on the characters there who specialize in creating new identities, driver's licenses, phony passports, stuff like that. What do you guys think?"

"Needle in a haystack," David said.

"Has merit," replied Romaine in his characteristic laconic way.

"I think Romaine's response indicates his superior intelligence. Let's consider the decision of the group to be an enthusiastic yes and get our butts in gear," Nancy said throwing a smile in David's direction.

"Sure," said David. "I hear they have been getting in some abalone again. I would love to have abalone; it's been twenty years."

"We're on our way," said Nancy.

She closed her pile of computer printouts and stretched luxuriously. She was looking forward to a field contest with a cunning quarry. It was what passed for fun with her.

Special Agent Gerald Silberberg addressed his troops—112 of them—the morning following his assignment to capture Randolph Kennedy. His thin, nervous, ferret face was animated.

"Agents, we have a straightforward task—not necessarily easy or quick—but at least it is simple in concept. We have the responsibility of a manhunt, the thing the Bureau has historically done the best. It is not our problem to collect evidence or to mount a case except as information is collected secondary to our mandate: find, then catch Randolph Kennedy, public enemy number one—we will focus on that with all of our energies. I am assured that we will not only have the considerable resources of the Bureau to use as we see fit, but I have it on good authority that we may exercise certain extraordinary powers since this case has been officially listed as a matter of national security. We will divide into fifty regional teams with an additional team operating out of Washington to collate information and to move players as needed."

The gathered agents smiled and nodded their affirmation. These were the best of the best in the Bureau—the best disciplined, the best groomed, and they were as loyal to Silberberg as early agents had been to J. Edgar Hoover. They knew that Silberberg was the Grand Vizier behind the silk screen whispering to Sultan Coleman and that Silberberg's star was in the ascendancy. They had every intention of rising along with their boss, and their smiles reflected that confidence.

"No one knows where Kennedy is, or where he has been," Silberberg went on, 'however, I think it is reasonable to the point of being glaringly apparent that the man has been swallowed up into the underground network operated by the Movement. Our COINTELPRO files are full of locations, descriptions of personnel, lists of their assets, and documentation of their activities. We will start with them.

We want a high-profile news media saturation attack on those vermin where the live. Move in with haste and force. Arrest them, detain them, interrogate them, threaten them. They've had a free ride long enough. Let them know loud and clear that harboring Randolph Kennedy is what brought this unwanted attention upon them, and that giving him up is prudent if they want to see us go away. These people are essentially simple folks—Luddites and feudalists. I see them capitulating early in the game; so, they can go back to their comfortable bovine existences, playing at protest and making elaborate and inconsequential plans for guerilla warfare against the minorities.

"I do not fail in my assignments, ladies and gentlemen. I will not tolerate failure in this mission—it is not an option for you to contemplate. It goes without saying that only your best will be acceptable. Any questions?"

There were none. The agents all knew how Silberberg worked. He was methodical to a fault in his planning, organization and execution. They were ready for the planning and organization meetings that would take place that day and fully expected to be ready to travel to their first assignments to launch the dragnet.

"We'll need a little clarification on the methodology," mentioned one of the younger agents to a seasoned team member of Silberberg's.

"I have the sense that we've seen the dawn of a new day," replied the agent seated nest to the young man. "We are going to trample a few toes, tap a few lines, bend a few civil rights. We are going to do what it takes to get this job done. About time; nobody cares a fraction of a whit for all of those race-hater loonies. Any complaints are going to be shuffled by the brass and round-filed by the public at large. John Q. Public is sick of these hate groups and all of the time and effort that has gone into making sure that their civil rights are protected down to the last jot and tittle while they flaunt the law at every turn. That's the methodology I'm hearing. And I predict that we aren't going to be hearing from the ACLU or the liberal talking heads about this. If we were going after some liberal hippie bunch, we would catch a barrage of verbiage, but the survivalist superpatriots don't come under the definition of victim groups to the libs."

CHAPTER THIRTY-NINE

G wen Chambers wrote another short article for the *Times*, and this time her editor, William Fitzgerald, put it on the front page under her byline after insisting that she trim it of anything she could not prove in a court of law.

"Mr. Fitzgerald, I suppose we have to run this past the attorneys."

"No, run it as we made the last revision. I'm comfortable with that. I'll take the heat."

The first paragraph of the new article read:

> The manhunt for suspected terrorist, Randolph Kennedy, one of the officers of the shadowy 'Movement—a loose-knit organization of eccentrics, race and religious bigots, purveyors of hate, right-wing Christian religious fundamentalists, and criminals— is accelerating. According to FBI sources, Special Agent Gerald Silberberg—who is in charge of the Bureau's elite Counterterrorism division—was recently appointed to head up the force charged with bringing Kennedy to justice. Even as the manhunt heats up, this reporter has learned that certain significant irregularities in the investigation of Kennedy's alleged crimes that led to the assault on his Alaskan mountain fortress-like home are being evaluated. Informed sources close to the government's case are suggesting that there may be problems with evidence and with the strict adherence to federal guidelines for search and seizure.

The next three paragraphs outlined the plan of attack on Kennedy's actual and potential supporters, the history of the first raid on Kennedy's home when his wife and child were killed; and the wrongful death suit that came in the aftermath of the raid. Chambers included a very carefully worded description of the findings in the large white Dodge Ram II delivery van and made mention of the possible sighting of a trailer that cast something of a cloud over the certainty of Kennedy's actual crimes. She mentioned in passing the evidence linking federal officers in the transfer of the evidence including the arrest of a prominent FBG Task Force officer related to the matter. She took pains to allow the readers to draw their own conclusions about the implications of the federal officers' activities. Gwen referred only briefly and obliquely to the possibly mishandled money since that part of the story had the weakest evidence trail.

After putting her article into the paper's publications computer pipeline, Gwen began a long day of calling FBI and ATF agents for their comments on her story and for any news about the progress of their investigations. That part of her day was not fruitful.

The boy who had driven the fire engine colored pickup led Randolph Kennedy from the complex of garages at the rear of the groomed portion of the property to the side entrance of the Southwest style sunset pink stucco mansion, misplaced there amid the natural alpine oak brush, dark cedars and pines, and quaking aspen trees.

Inside the house, the boy led Randolph past a series of women's bedrooms, each with a double bed covered with its own unique 19th century appliquéd quilt, and on into a large family sitting room with a huge double pane window looking out over the valley below. The view of the majestic Mount Timpanogas—dotted and scarred with its movie location villages and cabins with their contrived rusticity created by Robert Redford—the erstwhile publicity hound environmentalist and movie mogul—was still suggestive of the magnificence of the range of mountains in their pristine state.

A hard-faced, full bearded Old Testament patriarch sat in an oversized leather chair contemplating his domain. Beside him on an antique side table, sat several packages marked "Nitro-pak Preparedness Center, Heber, Utah".

"This is the guy on the motorcycle, Dad," the boy said.

When his father nodded, the boy turned and left Randolph alone with the taciturn man. The older man was dressed in comfortable worn western attire.

"Set yourself."

Randolph pulled an arm chair to where he could face the speaker and sat on it.

"You got a name we can use? Mine's Nephi. Nephi McDonald."

"Jaime Cortez, Guaymus Mexico."

He extended his hand, and Nephi stood and took it, dwarfing Randolph's. The force of Nephi's grip made the handshake a minor contest that Randolph promptly lost. Randolph could now see Nephi's impressive belt buckle—silver studded with semiprecious stones, bear claws, and turquoise was the size of a small dinner plate. He wore a silver and mother-of-pearl bolo tie slide.

"That's good enough for me. Daryl Haslip told me somethin' about your difficulties, enough for me to know what's needed, and not enough to be able to tattle. That's a good practice. I understand that you're hidin' from the feds; they burnt your house and killed your family, somethin' like that. You got my sympathies. Anybody who is on the run from the ATF can't be all bad."

His lips pressed together in what Randolph took to be a sort of smile and responded in kind.

"I don't know how hot I am, but I gather that there is considerable interest in me, Mr. McDonald," Randolph said.

"I like first names, Jaime. Okay with you?"

"Sure."

"All you gotta do is look at the evenin' news, local or national. You'll get a pretty good idea of just how popular you are with the fibbies. I take the *New York Times* and the *LA Times* just to keep up with the communists in the cities, and the *Salt Lake Tribune* to get the local news and the opinions of the local liberals. They all got your story. New article in the *New York Times* just today. You ought to give it a read."

"Thanks, I've been out of touch," Randolph said.

"Where's my manners? You must be starvin'."

Randolph nodded. It had been a long time since he had had a decent meal.

"Sarai!" Nephi yelled, startling Randolph.

In a few minutes, an attractive young woman in a floor length calico print dress, a good twenty years younger than Nephi, entered the room quietly.

"Yes, husband?" she asked with a pleasant demure smile.

"My dear, would you be good enough to fetch our guest some lunch? He's famished. You know he's the one we spoke of in family council day before yesterday.

She inclined her head in recognition of Randolph's presence.

Randolph stood and offered her his hand. She shook it with strong fingers and a callused palm.

"Sarai McDonald, Mr…?"

"Cortez, ma'am."

"Glad to have you here," she said genuinely.

"I'm honored to be your guest. Thanks for having me. I hope it won't be too much of an imposition."

"Nothing is an imposition for a fellow Movement member. We offer our home to you."

She smiled and went in the direction of the kitchen.

"One of my wives, Jaime. Just to keep things straight between us, I got five of 'em. That bother you?"

Randolph had to admit that it was an adjustment but—after thinking about it for a second or two—he could not see any reason why it should bother him. For that matter, he was in no position to be picky on social issues.

"Not at all. You Mormons?"

"Nope. The Mormons don't hold with us polygs, haven't acknowledged the sanctity of plural marriage for more'n 120 years. We don't have much truck with the dominant religion hereabouts, nor them with us. That way we get along fine. They think we're quaint or pretty eccentric. We think they took the wrong road and caved into the feds all them years ago. The arrangement keeps them from pryin' into our affairs. Also helps keep attention off of our guests. I presume that's good for you."

Randolph nodded.

"I gotta go into town to finalize a land deal. Make yourself to home. Read the paper; watch the tube if you can stand it. You probably gonna be with us for a good spell. Might's well settle in early and get comfortable. He moved his bulk out of the chair. The man was not fat, just big. When he stood up fully, it was like looking at a tree trunk in cowboy clothes.

Randolph stood again.

"Thanks, Nephi. I'll be great to relax."

"Do the best you can. This here used to be a great place with honest friendly people that minded their own business. It's been Californicated, mostly ruined, but I think you'll like it around Fort McDonald here."

The big man grinned.

Nephi took his leave, and Sarai returned to the spacious room with a good lunch of home made whole wheat bread, cheese, an elk meat sandwich, and fresh, unpasteurized milk that had the faint aroma of cow manure. At the side of the platter lay copies of the *New York Times, Los Angeles Times* and *Backwoods Home Magazine.*

"Thanks. I'd like to be able to help around the place, sort of earn my keep. Give a thought about finding me some chores, please, Mrs. McDonald," he requested.

"Call me Sarai. And I'll do that. Men don't like sittin' around. Makes 'em mean. Can't have you gettin' mean on us, now."

She flashed him a toothsome grin.

He was feeling much more at home now.

Sarai left him alone with his newspapers, the magazine, and his lunch. He ate the sandwich and drank half of his milk before his eyes settled on the article by Gwen Chambers. He skimmed it once, then read it intently, word for word. Several phrases jumped out at him—"manhunt", "suspected terrorist", "Movement", "irregularities with the investigation", "problems with the evidence".

He tried to envision the writer. Maybe it was the young woman reporter whom he had encountered near his road during the ATF raid on the twenty-sixth. The more he thought about it, the more sure he was that he had seen this woman. He felt a little like he knew her. The article was even-handed, he thought. He also thought that there was more between the lines than Gwen Chambers was telling. He made a mental note to commit her name to memory.

Nephi returned as Randolph finished the last morsel of his meal.

"Care for some coffee, Jaime? Ain't got any fancy cappuccino, just plain store bought Java. For all its growth, Heber Valley's old timers like me still got a sodbuster mentality, and I like bein' a redneck with the rest of 'em."

"Thanks," said Randolph. "I'd enjoy a cup of regular country coffee. Lots of cream and sugar, if that's all right."

Nancy Delgado sat with her two aides in the lounge of the Mark Hopkins Hotel making a last minute review of the interrogation reports of San Francisco hotel personnel from the day of the Wasilla raid to a time three days later. It had been a busy week in the San Francisco tourism business. People from all over the world had entered and left the hotels making the likelihood of getting any kind of a lead on Randolph Kennedy an unlikely chance. There were hundreds of unusual looking and suspicious acting men using hotels and restaurants: Arabs sneaking out to porno parlors, black sports figures squiring more than one white woman, a crew cut Mexican biker, a traveling bus of homosexual AIDs volunteer workers wearing fluorescent chartreuse jump suits, and a bearded street preacher with enough money to rent the bridal suite of the Meridien Hotel, among the many that attracted some attention from Delgado's investigators. No one had seen anyone who looked remotely like the photograph of Randolph Kennedy.

Undaunted, Nancy said, "Okay, you guys, let's go find out where you buy a new identity in this town."

It was eight o'clock in the morning. Outside, it was a typical midsummer day in San Francisco—cold and shrouded in sea fog. The three FBI agents had the hotel valet drive their olive drab government issue Chevrolet sedan out from the basement parking facility—tipped him less than he thought was his due—and drove down to the Mission District to act on a tip. Their informant told them the obvious; they should be able to find the ID makers somewhere around Mission and 4th and 5th or on Minna Street. All they had to do was to locate the illegal itinerant Mexican workers gathered in that area every morning looking for day labor jobs.

It was early. Drunks and dopeheads still lay asleep in the streets. Liberal San Francisco city governments had wrestled with the problem of the homeless for more than three-quarters of a century. They were no further ahead than they had been in the 1970s, much to the anger of the working population of the city. The three FBI agents walked along nonchalantly, making an effort to blend in with the foot traffic but knowing that their cause of anonymity was lost. They stood out like liveried waiters at a luau. Mexican laborers gave them suspicious glances and moved slowly away and off into adjacent alleys as the three approached.

"This isn't going to work," Romaine told Nancy. "They know we're the fuzz. Might as well be official and see what we can shake out of the tree."

"I agree," declared Nancy. "Let's roust the two guys by the drink machine who seem to be doing some kind of business rather than waiting for labor work. Maybe they would like to share information with us."

"In a pig's eye," David said, "but here goes."

He made a sudden turn and laid his hand on the arm of portly Pancho Hernandez de la Riva who was totally unsuspecting of any action. Romaine collared the other man, Guillermo Perez.

"Hey, man, what ees these? What jou theenk jou doing?" demanded Pancho when the initial shock wore off.

He knew it was a cop; and he knew it would go worse for him if he struggled.

"FBI," said David, and flipped open his badge wallet.

"So, Whatta jou want weeth me?" Pancho asked.

"Better me than the immigrations," David said harshly. "Let me see your ID."

"Why?"

"Because I said, and I am the law. We are looking for people who make fake IDs for illegals and for fugitives, maybe people like you."

"Hey, man, I'm legal. See. See my green card, all legal."

"Looks perfect, like you made it yesterday. Nice work."

Pancho glared at the FBI agent but held his tongue.

Only the two Mexican men remained; the rest had scattered. Romaine held the arm of Guillermo so tightly that it hurt, and he squirmed.

"Jou got no right," Guillermo protested.

"ID," demanded Romaine.

Guillermo shrugged and looked down at the hand on his arm. Romaine released his grip. Guillermo rubbed the hand print indentation out of his arm, then pulled out his wallet and ID—valid California driver's license, green card, and Farmworker's Union card.

Romaine made an elaborate display of examining the identification documents.

"Phonies," he declared, as if he knew that for a fact.

In truth, they looked perfectly genuine to him. He was watching Guillermo's face and was rewarded by seeing an unconcealed nervous twitch and a blanching of the man's skin. Guillermo was looking down.

"Tell you what, wetback. I need some information. You get that for me, and I don't turn you over to the immigrations, and I don't bust you for counterfeiting."

Guillermo looked hopeful, like a rat that could see an escape route.

"What jou want from me?"

Romaine produced a 5 by 7 glossy of Randolph Kennedy.

"You see this guy before?"

The shock that registered on Guillermo's face was the answer Romaine needed. Pancho saw it as well. They were both good at telling lies, and at telling when other people were lying.

"*Silencio!*" snapped Pancho.

David jerked him to one side. Guillermo looked confused, then afraid.

Romaine shoved the photograph into Guillermo's face.

"Where? When? You tell me quick, or I take you to the immigrations so fast your feet won't touch the ground. You don't get to make any telephone calls to that little family of yours."

He had a vice grip on Guillermo's arm.

Nancy Delgado stepped up to Pancho and said in dulcet tones, "Let's take this one in now. He's dirty."

David started walking him up the street. The machismo in Pancho's round face began to fade rapidly.

"I done notheeng!" he pleaded. "Why jou doing thees to me?"

"Move him out," ordered Special Agent Delgado.

"Wait a meenute. Maybe we can talk," Pancho said as he was being rushed away. "Maybe I know sometheeing to help jou officers."

David slowed down just a little. Pancho and Guillermo looked at each other meaningfully.

"Pancho," Guillermo said, "Hee's no worth eet. We make a deal for ourselves and our *familias*. No Anglo ees worth eet!"

He spat out the word 'Anglo' while looking at Romaine.

Pancho wavered. His face was contorted with pain and indecision. It was against his innermost code to sell out a customer who had paid him fairly. It was part of what they paid him for—his *silencio*. But a jail term, then deportation? He would never be able to get back in. He couldn't go back to Jalisco and grub out an existence as a farm hand. He wouldn't last a week. Guillermo was right; no Anglo was worth that.

David reinforced his pain, "I promise you that I will personally see you go to jail, and then I will be around to haul you to the border. No doubt there's a jail waiting in old Mexico for you, too. I don't like wetback crooks."

He started pushing Pancho up the street again.

"Hey, gringo, maybe jou show *me* that peecture. Maybe we could make a deal," Pancho said somewhat breathlessly as the two men began to increase their walking pace.

David's expression mellowed to something approaching that of a sympathetic executioner.

"Sure. You have a look. Maybe this would jar your memory."

Pancho reluctantly took the photograph and made a big thing about studying it.

"Yeah, maybe I seen that one. Can't be sure."

"You better be sure. You better give us some information that helps, or you buy yourself a free ride to Immigration Court and to Sonora."

"Pancho, we both tell heem. Hey cop. Jou let us go, leave us be, if we help jou?" Guillermo called out, first to his friend, then to the FBI agents.

"Give us something good, and you walk," said Nancy.

She knew they were on to something important here. She did not want to appear overeager, but it was the first time in her memory that she had run onto something useful with the first interrogation of a canvass.

"Jou promise to let us go?"

"Show me something worth it," Nancy said coldly.

"Hokay, hokay. Look," said Guillermo with a guilty side glance at Pancho who gave him a resigned nod, "I think we seen this guy. Maybe two, tree days ago, maybe four. Maybe he had some ID made; maybe he paid cash."

"*Maybe?*" Agent Delgado asked angrily.

"Hokay, I mean we know," Guillermo confessed and gave the agents a pleading look.

David and Romaine's expressions had softened to avuncular, a little short of kind, and forgiving. Nancy shifted her expression to neutral.

"I'm listening," Special Agent Delgado prodded.

"Give us a name, something we can use; and you walk away. We forget all about you," said David.

"Can't geeve jou no name, lady and mans. Don't have no record of that, but we bought heem some wheels. We tell jou about that."

Nancy's heart quickened. For the first time in the case, it looked as if they were about to get a little break. In fact, they already had one. They had confirmation that Kennedy was alive and had been right here not more than a couple or three days ago, if they could believe these squirming little crooks.

"What kind of wheels?" Romaine demanded.

"Harley."

"Motorcycle?"

"Jess, a beeg one. Call Heritage kind of seekle. Heritage *Dos*."

"What color?"

"*Negro.*"

"Black," translated Romaine.

"Not enough," pushed Nancy. "We need a name. You know a name because you made fake IDs. Give us a name, and you are out of here. I won't let you go until you do."

With a guileless face, Pancho protested, "We deen't. We don' make no illegal IDs. Don' got no name. But we can tell jou what he look like."

"You let us go, *then*, lady cop?" asked Guillermo, anxious to clinch a deal before divulging anything more and risking losing their trump card.

"Yes," she declared flatly.

"He look like a Mexican hombre, 'cept he got very short haircut. He got *moreno* skin, thee *negro* hair, even thee *moreno* eyes. He go away een *negro* biker clothes…that's eet. Now jou let me and my friend go. We got a deal. No more hassle?"

Nancy studied the men's faces. She thought they probably knew more, but were unlikely to give up a name without a prolonged interrogation, and even then the answers would more likely than not be lies.

"You go after you tell a police artist what he looks like. You get us a good drawing of his face, and you are free men."

The two men groaned at the addition of one more requirement, and reluctantly said, "*Si.*"

The trio of FBI agents took Pancho and Guillermo to San Francisco PD headquarters, where they produced a photo after prolonged deliberations between the men that led to a computer enhanced drawing.

Pancho and Guillermo declared, "is heem! Hexactly!"

The agents chose the local law enforcement agency over their own office to avoid word getting into the FBI grapevine about the success of their ongoing investigation. The use of SFPD services circumvented the need even to admit to the existence of their team.

Nancy marched the two Mexicans to the front door of the police building and said, "Okay, you can go now. Keep quiet about this. If I learn that you have contacted this man, I will come back here and put you in prison and throw away the key."

"How about jou geef us a ride back home?" Pancho asked, not relishing exercise.

"Don't push your luck. Get out of here."

Special Agent Delgado called Assistant Director Phil Craig at home.

"Bingo," she said by way of greeting.

CHAPTER FORTY

News of the dragnet out for Randolph Kennedy and of the FBI's involvement in it was an item in the media every day for over a week. Nephi McDonald took a rather relaxed, often amused attitude at first.

"Like to see themselves on the tube, don't they?" he said to Randolph as they watched the six o'clock *CNN Headline News* together on the tenth night that Randolph had sheltered under Nephi's roof.

FBI agents were shown dragging Movement members out of their dilapidated mountain shacks; the camcorder zoomed in on caches of weapons and boxes of hate literature.

"Gerald Silberberg—special agent in charge of the investigation and of the field raids—reports another success for the FBI and for President Vantassa's FBG Task Force. Mr. Silberberg, could we have a statement, please?" the CNN correspondent was asking.

Silberberg turned from his discussion with two men, clearly identified as FBI agents by the yellow block lettering on their black Tee shirts, and smiled for the camera.

"Happy to," he said pleasantly. "The FBI has scored another victory for the people here today. After months of painstaking work and surveillance, we have brought in another major link in the chain of Militia Movement terrorists. It is safe to say that being a terrorist today is decidedly more difficult than it was a year ago, or even a month ago."

"Thank you, Special Agent Silberberg. We have heard it rumored that you are being considered for the number two spot in the Bureau. Care to comment?"

"Thanks, Kent, but I can't make any comment on that story now. All I can say is that; so far as I know, Assistant Director Phil Craig is doing a fine job in that position; and I have heard no official information to the contrary or that his job is about become vacant."

There was a five minute break for commercials—a whiskey ad, plugs for a new wrinkle erasing cream for man and women, a revolutionary new armpit deodorant, an Olympic gold medalist touting CNA Insurance because it kept its rates low by stamping out fraud, and a syndicated law firm that was willing to give a written guarantee that it would get accident victims a higher award than they could obtain by working directly with the insurance company. The reporter and Special Agent Silberberg faded back in to view.

"Another question, Agent Silberberg. Can you tell us anything about this particular hate group's tie in to Randolph Kennedy? Are you any closer to apprehending the terrorist?"

"I'm afraid that information would jeopardize our investigation, Kent. I can only say that we are much closer. It is only a matter of time now."

He turned to give the camera a broad smile.

"Those guys do their best work in front of a news camera," observed Randolph, in response to a question from Nephi. "I guess we can hope that he spends a lot more time being in the limelight. I sure like to see a man enjoying himself."

"Too good to be true, I'm afraid," said Nephi, now serious. "Heard they were snooping around Heber a couple of days ago asking questions about the Militia here abouts. Travis Mair had a coupla agents by his place asking a few questions. 'Fraid it's only a matter of time before they get out this way."

"Can you tell us whom the FBI will be targeting, Agent Silberberg?" asked the familiar television anchorman, adjusting himself into a slightly greater left profile, his best photo angle.

"That I can tell you, at least in broad terms, Kent," replied the smiling Agent Silberberg. "Let this message go out to all of the antigovernment factions out there. We will be paying visits to all segments of the Movement: the obvious virulent hate merchants like the Skinheads, Aryan Nations, White Nationalists, the KKK, the White Tribalists, the Mountaineer Militia, and their ilk."

Randolph wryly noted that it was apparently not polite to mention hate groups involving brown skin people like the Nation of Islam or to risk the sacrosanct Jewish vote by including the radical Zionist movements.

374

"Then there are the ostensibly less violent secessionists from Hawaii, Alaska, Puerto Rico, California, and Texas. In this grouping are such diverse organizations as land use and property rights advocates. The ones we will target are those who reject the role of government at all levels to enforce environmental and other land use laws, the tax revoltors, the ultra fundamentalists of all persuasions, the paramilitary marching militias, super patriot organizations, and groups of radicals advocating nonviolent racial separation."

"Anything new for our TV audience, Agent Silberberg? Anything they might be on the lookout for in the Kennedy Case."

"Yes, Kent, I'm pleased to report that San Francisco Police Department officers have found evidence that Kennedy is still alive, and that he has been in San Francisco within the last three days. We have a composite picture of him as he looks now."

The sketch photo flashed on the screen to Silberberg's left and revealed a dark skinned, Mexican looking man dressed in black with a short cropped crew cut of black hair. The image filled the screen, and Silberberg's voice over came as the audio.

"We do have an important new lead that just came in this morning, Kent. One of our fine investigative team members learned that the man pictured on your screen was riding a large black Harley Davidson motorcycle. We have a picture of that vehicle for you which was supplied to law enforcement by the Harley Company which has cooperated fully with our investigators, and we are grateful."

Kennedy's disguise-face faded, and the picture quickly changed into a full-frame view of a Heritage II motorcycle.

"We ask the good citizens of the country to be on the lookout for such a motorcycle. Report to the nearest FBI office. Take no action on your own. Kennedy is known to be armed and will not hesitate to inflict harm. He is—after all—behind the deaths of nine of our officers."

"Thanks for the warning, Special Agent Silberberg. We are glad you and your team are on the case. We, here at CNN, wish you Godspeed."

The series of five advertisements intruded again. Nephi switched the set off.

"We oughta tune in to WWCR outta Nashville, get the rest of the real news, the stuff the One-World press leaves out," commented Nephi half-heartedly.

The 100,000 watt station's transmitters beamed the unabridged commentaries of Movement sympathizers, Militia members, and survivalists from all over the country. The station took pride in serving the "left-wing" commentators, defined as any nonviolent ultra-nationalist, government-hating organization. The principle groups covered in this "left-wing" category were the NRA and The Coalition of Arizona/New Mexico Counties for Stable Economic Growth. The station's main emphasis was on "right thinkers" like the readers from the Library of a White Tribalist and the representatives of Skinheads, U.S.A.

Randolph did not indicate his need to listen to WWCR and was enjoying the silence. He hoped that he could do without another harangue from The Aryan Nations or a presentation from the Ku Klux home page on the internet.

"How could they know about the Harley?" Randolph asked almost rhetorically.

"It's a mistake to underestimate them, Jaime. Them fibbies are not the ATF stumblebums, and they are nowheres near as dumb as the WWCR commentators make them out to be. They are efficient and every bit as ruthless and willing to tromp on folks's rights as the ATFers. You know this means that the Harley has to go."

"Yeah, I think I put about 800 miles on the thing. Shame. Another item is that I have to look different. My Mexican look is going to be on the news every half hour for a month. I couldn't step off your property without being spotted. While I'm at it, I need to get some less noticeable spending cash. I have almost nothing but hundreds."

"No question about any of that. I think we better get you ready for a move. Might have to get outta here with no notice."

He smiled at Randolph who could almost see a thought forming in the big man's mind.

"What?" asked Randolph when he saw Nephi's expression.

"Oh, nothing. I was just wondering how you'd look bald and with a beard."

Randolph's heart sank. Although he was not a particularly vain man, he was of the opinion that 'bald' was for old guys, and he detested the image that sprang to his mind.

"Hey, Sarai, c'mon in here fer a minute, please," Nephi called in the direction of the large kitchen.

Randolph had seen the patriarch to be unfailingly polite and respectful of his wives during the time he had stayed in their mountaintop home.

"Yes, husband," Sarai said when she came into the study.

"We need a beautician. I should say that our guest here does."

Sarai recognized Randolph as the terrorist of recent television fame. It did not take much thought on her part to agree that the man needed a radical change in appearance.

"I'll get Rebecca Bingerly. She's discreet, and her and Lemuel are good Movement people," Sarai said.

She smiled as she turned away from the men.

Rebecca had lived in Wasatch County—most of the time in Heber—her entire life. She was born in the area that was locally known as Center Creek—'crick' to the locals—an unincorporated village near the foothills of the Wasatch Range of the Rocky Mountains. The citizens of that sector kept their individualism. She had never been as far as Salt Lake City, and no one in her family had ever been out of the state of Utah.

She assessed the situation and Randolph quickly.

"Needs a change. Only question is a beautician's change or a plastic surgeon. Sarai?"

"Nothing drastic, I think. Do something artistic, Rebecca. This is a man worth saving from the One Worlders."

It was discomforting to Randolph to hear himself being discussed as if he were not there.

"I have some creative ideas," Rebecca said with a mischievous grin.

Randolph was beyond discomfiture. He was getting right down nervous, but he submitted docilely. The two women were joined by Abigail—Nephi's second wife, a handsome fiftyish woman—and the three of them giggled and gossiped as Rebecca did her work with razor and scissors. When he was—at last—able to see himself in a mirror, Randolph was astonished. He scarcely recognized his new self having gotten acclimated to the Jaime Cortez look. His hair had been clipped very short and dyed grey. The hairline on his forehead had been shaved back to the point that he had a bald pate with a monk's tonsure remnant of his hair on the sides and back. His side burns remained intact. The artificially dark skin would have had to be retouched at this point because it had faded to a light tan, a rather unhealthy café au lait pallor which suited the new look perfectly. With the ministrations of the enthusiastic women, he had aged twenty or more years.

Nephi produced a pair of old two dollar magnifying half glasses. When he put them on, Randolph knew that he would be able to walk through a crowd of onlookers holding the FBI photograph in their hands and not be recognized. He hated the change, but loved the security it promised.

Abigail took his biker clothes out to the perpetually burning fifty gallon trash incinerator back of the house and disposed of them. Nephi's seventh son—a strapping trucker—hauled the Harley to Las Vegas and sold it to Hell's Angels in the Naked City—Meadows Village—area of Las Vegas behind the

Stratosphere Tower on the corner of Wyoming and Commerce streets. He reported back about his experience.

"Took a beatin', as you might imagine, only got somethin' like ten thou for it, sorry. But the whole gang of them rode out that day for a cross country trip to eastern Canada. That oughta spin a few fibbies heads."

Randolph handed over $100,000 in $100 bills to Nephi's fourth wife, Rachel, and four days later Nephi presented Randolph with a box of used fives, tens, twenties, and a few fifties.

"You can count it," the patriarch said.

"I wouldn't dream of it," Randolph told him.

Nephi's lips pressed together in that expression that the family recognized as a smile.

"How did you change that much money so fast, Nephi?" Randolph asked.

"Simple. We just capitalized on the sins of the world," he laughed.

Randolph looked at him quizzically.

"Sent my twenty-two year old boy to Lost Wages, Nevada. He just went around to a buncha hotels and casinos and cashed a few hundred at each place until he had the whole thing in small bills. Only took him a day. Got the idea from the sin tube. Hate to admit that to a God fearin' man."

Randolph and the family had some great laughs at the mental images conjured up by the inexperienced and proper young man's activities.

The fugitive now wore coarse grey work shirts and pants and an old leather belt. His feet where clad with scuffed and run down at the heels work boots. He learned to effect the posture and a small rotational hip limp of an old man until he did it almost absent-mindedly.

Nephi used his Movement contacts to get a new set of IDs for Randolph while they waited for further developments. Developments were slow enough in coming that Randolph was able to get a good start on a beard. His naturally blond beard lent itself easily to a change of color to silver-grey.

He transferred his large reserve of cash that had once been in the motorcycle's panniers to a set of empty Rubber Maid tool boxes. He was now ready to go at a moment's notice. The change in appearance made it possible for him to walk out onto the winding roads of the hillside community and occasionally onto the main thoroughfare, Lake Creek Road.

ADFBI Phil Craig waited almost ten days after receiving the information about Randolph Kennedy's motorcycle before he gave SFPD the go ahead to convey the information to the nationwide network of law enforcement agencies. He made no effort to give the information directly to Agent Silberberg; and in fact, had SFPD take all credit for finding the information. The source of the information and when it had been obtained remained vague. During the interim ten day period, Delgado, Terrife, and Bendell worked feverishly to capitalize on their exclusive.

The resources of the Bureau were put into high gear to interrogate the owners of motorcycle sales and repair shops, biker gangs, yuppie motorcycle club members, the extensive network of American Harley Owners United, service station attendants and restaurant employees on all major highways leading from San Francisco in all directions. The agents concentrated on the personnel who maintained the roads and policed the traffic in California, Nevada, Utah, Colorado, Wyoming, New Mexico, Arizona, and Idaho. It was that latter effort that finally came to the attention of Gerald Silberberg and thereby to Director Ted Coleman.

ADFBI Craig had a stormy session with his director for withholding evidence and for being involved at all. He defended himself by saying that his informants were unreliable, and his few agents had happened onto the information accidentally during the course of another investigation. They were casually doing some checking; that was all. It sounded lame, but Coleman and Silberberg could not prove that Craig was lying.

In retaliation Coleman leaked the story to CNN that Craig's job was in jeopardy. Being a dogged personality, Silberberg simply added the motorcycle and the physical description to his fixation on the Movement community and began using the possession of a motorcycle of any make or description as an additional item of probable cause for search and seizure operations. This increased the heat on the isolated survivalist, antitax, antifederal court system, antigovernment groups.

Delgado had a full seven day head start on her Bureau competitor, and no one was aware of her involvement. The Salt Lake City office reported to Romaine Terrife that a woman UHP officer had stopped a Mexican man who fit the description for speeding on a huge and expensive Heritage II Harley several days previously. She had given the man a ticket and had obtained an address and a telephone number.

"Check it out, Romaine," she requested of her subordinate.

She now had a direction, and wanted the concentration to be on I-80 East, but to include as quickly as possible the lesser highways that cut off the main interstate through way.

"Tall request, Madam Special Agent. I would estimate a three-month effort."

Delgado thought about it and knew that he was right. They had to find a means of narrowing the search.

"I know that, Romaine. So work mostly along the interstate and don't go beyond the eastern edge of Wyoming for the time being."

He nodded.

"David, I want you to look into every record of Movement communities in Utah, Southern Idaho, Wyoming, and Southern Montana."

"Piece of cake," Special Agent Bendell said.

He planned to access the Bureau's computer files and those of the Southeast Poverty Law Center in Montgomery, Alabama for the information.

The break came in two day's time. David Bendell moved quickly through the towns of the state of Utah from north to south. Midway through the state—in the town of that name—he met with one of the Bureau's planted informers in the Movement. Midway was only five miles from Heber, and the two cities had been involved in a multigenerational feud over population and environmental protection issues. The informant was only too happy to steer Bendell in the direction of Heber's Militia contingent...and away from Midway's. His enthusiasm was assisted by a generous gratuity from the FBI agent.

Acting on the information—and after letting Delgado know of his intentions—Bendell took a room in the new Wasatch Motel because his considerable physical size required a low profile exposure. Using that room as his office, he began to canvass main street store owners, service station attendants, and courthouse workers as inconspicuously as he could manage. Bendell struck useful pay dirt when he began to dig for information from the employees of the city's pay phone company.

Special Agent Bendell, wearing western clothes, knowing that his three piece grey seersucker suit, white button down collar shirt, and nondescript tie—the FBI uniform—would make him stand out like a tuxedoed bronc rider, sauntered insouciantly up to a high school dropout who was making some repairs on one of the pay phones.

"Hello, young man, could you take a minute to talk to me?"

"Sure, what kinda cop are you?"

So much for fitting in with the crowd.

"Good call. FBI, actually. I'm looking for a terrorist, a bomber. I need to know if you've seen this man."

Bendell showed his glossy of the computer generated photo of Randolph Kennedy.

"Sure," the red-haired teenager responded without hesitation.

Bendell's heart did a small leap.

"Here in Heber City? When?"

"Nope. On the boob tube, man. Seen his picture ever' day for a month, seem's like."

Bendell was crestfallen; but since he had gone to the bother to walk along Main Street checking out every pay phone along the way, he produced his photo of the large Harley motorcycle. The boy scrutinized the photograph of the testosterone generating vehicle with undisguised lust.

"Ever seen anybody with a scooter like that?" Bendell asked, not expecting all that much.

"*Scooter*," thought the young attendant, "*what kind of a dork is this guy? Must be an easterner.*"

He said, "Don't see many the like that one. I'd give a nut for a ride on one."

He continued to drool over the picture.

Bendell reached out to take back his photograph. He was ready to get on down the street. It was a waste of time pandering to the boy's fantasies.

"Hey, man, I seen a guy in here. Funny thing, he set here better part of a hour, waitin' for somebody. And it was the guy on TV. I never though nothin' about it at the time, but now you go and show me the picture of this sweet thing, I had a brain flash. It was him awright."

Bendell's heart soared again, this time for real.

"You certain? It's important."

"I'm sure, fer sure," the attendant said, and chuckled at his little joke.

"I seen that terrorist guy right here in little old Heber, if you can believe that."

"What about the person he met? Did you get a chance to see him or her?"

"Him. Yeah, sorta. I'm havin' another brain flash only a littler one."

"Sorta?"

"Yeah. I seen his truck, I mean. The one that come in here after the terrorist guy. The truck was cool, a fire engine red pickup. Was a Beamer."

"Really?" Bendell did not know that BMW made pickups. "Did you see his face?"

"Maybe, I don't pay that much attention to faces when a coupla setsa wheels like those ones are in the place."

"Recognize the truck?"

"Me? You gotta be kiddin'. I go around with the four and five year old Chevy and Jimmy club types. No BMWs in my set. No way."

"Get a license plate number, by any chance?"

"Gimmie a brake. I got work to do. Think I got time to go around memorizing a bunch of license plates? Might's well memorize the phone book in my spare time, geez."

"That's okay. I'll need your name and address and telephone number."

"Think I'll get on TV like you FBIs?"

"You might. You well might. Here, write down your particulars."

The attendant scribbled in his personal information. David pocketed the notepaper.

"Hope so," the attendant said eagerly, "don't forget about the TV."

The homely young man flashed a somewhat crooked smile. One of his lower incisors was missing.

Bendell telephoned Nancy Delgado. She started the system working and tracking the fire engine red BMW pickup truck and called Romaine and his assistants back from their fruitless investigation of the business along I-80. They had made it as far as Rawlins, Wyoming.

CHAPTER FORTY-ONE

Gerald Silberberg confronted the West Virginia Mountaineer Militia leader himself after Silberberg's agents had interrogated the man for several hours without success. The FBI raid had occurred just as the so-called "leaderless resistance" group was beginning its observance of the twin holy days of the Movement: the day of the Oklahoma City McMurrin Federal Building bombing, and the ATF/FBI raid on the Waco Davidian compound.

"You like the forests and rivers and lakes up here in West Virginia, Elmer?" he asked benignly.

There was an impassive cruelty in the agent's face and voice. At the best of times, Silberberg had to work to look friendly; and more frequently, like this time, he could not pull it off.

"Told you, FBI man, name's not Elmer. It's Elvin. I know you think you and your city folks are so superior to us country clods that you can make fun of our names and all. But as long as you want to play the game, I'll play. But for the record it's E-L-V-I-N."

"No offense, Elvin. Just making conversation. Anyway, you like being free out here in the woods, I take it?"

The senior agent's agate eyes honed into the mountain man, making him progressively uncomfortable.

"Sure I do. Ain't a block from the opera house, but we kin make do anyways."

"I can see how you would, Elvin. It's very pretty up here…and peaceful," said Silberberg with a vague menace.

"Was 'till you fabulous boys got here and started botherin' us for no reason. We ain't done nothin' to attract your attention."

"What I was getting at, Elvin, was that there are a couple of ways we can go about this. You can give up Randolph Kennedy nice and easy, and we just go away. Or, we can take you and your hippie play soldiers into the city and start a very long round of legal procedures. Cost you a fortune and a ton of time. We have recovered lots and lots of evidence, Elvin. It'll be a slow process, and it'll dig up all that old stuff about how you used to plan bombings. All of this will take place in the city, in rooms without windows. Who knows what'll become of your little commune out here while you're in a nine by twelve for the rest of your life? I like things to be easy. Personally, I only want Kennedy. I get him, and you can romp around these hills chasing innocent sheep and looking for eight year old virgins. You can play army to your heart's content without ever seeing the likes of me again. Of course, you will have to give up on all of the chemical weapons."

Silberberg's speech had the chill of threat and a cruel streak of condescension, neither of which was lost on Elvin Hunsaker. Nor did it escape him that the FBI man somehow knew about the chemical grenades that were the most closely held secret of his Mountaineer Militia.

"You ain't been listenin' I don't know where this Kennedy—Rudolph Kennedy—is. I don't even know who he is. You can't squeeze blood out of a turnip. I can't give you somethin' I don't have. Now leave us be," Elvin Hunsaker said insistently but with less self-assurance than before.

Special Agent Silberberg exhaled a theatrically heavy sigh, a harbinger of pain to come.

"I wish you hadn't said that, Elmer. I truly do. I thought we could have a cooperation of sorts—man to man—a way to save this quaint subculture of yours."

Silberberg meaningfully patted the copies of *The Anarchist Handbook*, Richard Mack's book, *From My Cold Dead Fingers: Why America Needs Guns*, *American Survival Guide: The Magazine of Self-Reliance*, *The Turner Diaries*, the 32 page Montana Militia catalogue *God, Guts, and Guns*, the 169 page *Terrorist's Handbook* that documented with detailed instructions how to make chemical weapons and explosives, and the *CIA Psy-Ops Operations in Guerilla Warfare*, all of which were found in Hunsaker's house.

The raid would be worth a lead-off on the night's television news. Silberberg had been careful to bring along Bureau cameramen to record significantly more damning evidence than the anarchist literature. The pictures would show bags of ammonium nitrate, vials of prussic acid, packages of sodium cyanide, nitric acid, and diisopropyl fluorophosphates, the components of nerve gas. There were small containers with Japanese kanji lettering that would be confirmed to hold Sarin. The cameras zoomed in on bags of castor beans, flasks of salt water and solvents—the components of ricin, a poison 6,000 times more toxic than cyanide with no known antidote. A hand written recipe was taped to one of the castor bean sacks: "Blend salt water and solvents with c. beans, 4 oz. acetone. Shake it up nice". One box contained propanethiol, a chemical used in utilities in miniscule quantities to give naturally odorless natural gas its characteristic smell. In large quantities it caused a terrible nose burning stench and was a favorite harassment tactic of the Movement. Mere possession of these chemicals was sufficient to send the mountaineers to prison until they were too old to be a threat any longer.

The special agent adopted a pensive look allowing a pause for the mountain man to relent his obstinacy.

"Draper," Silberberg snapped when Hunsaker stood by quietly. "Take 'em in. Take the whole porcine lot of 'em to the federal lockup. Take the scenic route. No hurry about any of this."

There was an undercurrent of seething anger just beneath Silberberg's surface calm. He was determined to break the Movement in any way necessary to get at Kennedy. Because he and his agents had found such a treasure trove of illegal substances, this particular enclave of the Movement would serve as the example to the rest of them. Even if this bunch did not know where Kennedy was hidden, the lesson from this group's experience with the wrath of the law would loosen scores of lips. Silberberg was going to see that every news outlet in the nation had a five day supply of news worthy material. It was going to be a saturation bombing operation.

Elvin Hunsaker looked back wistfully at his rude forest cabin as he and the other men, women, and children were herded into prison buses. As the caravan slowly wound its way into the last curve of the rutted gravel road leaving the mountain, Elvin looked back to see inky smoke pluming up over the horizon of treetops from about the spot where his clearing lay. Van loads of news media rushed by and camcorders recorded his misery.

Kurt McDonald, Nephi's third son, rushed into the noontime meal, breathless and excited. He whispered anxiously to his father.

Nephi stood up and calmly gave a series of orders.

"Sarai, you and the wives gather the children and head up the back way towards Wolf Creek. Plan to camp three days. Take two packhorses and the tents. Live off the land. There's not enough time to pack food. Kurt, you and your two brothers stand at the lower gate and obstruct the federals for as long as you can. Make as much commotion as you can without actually assaulting any of those legal thugs. Don't give them an excuse to arrest you or to shoot you. Randolph, you take the Jimmy pickup and get out of here, now. You know where you're headed."

Plans had been made well in advance of this moment for Randolph to go to the Movement community in upper Michigan headed by Doug Yancy. It would be a long, slow trip in the old Jimmy. He was going to miss the Harley. Since its sale in Las Vegas, Randolph's expensive Heritage II Harley Davidson motorcycle had been repainted a glossy orange and was presently the proud communal possession of a brigade of Hell's Angels somewhere near Mojave, California.

The kitchen came alive. Everyone moved. Breakfast foods lay uneaten on plates. One of the wives remembered at the last minute to turn off the stove. Randolph moved swiftly to his room and dragged his three Rubbermaid tool-boxes down the polished stairs, across the flagstone entry level, and loaded them into the cluttered pickup bed. In his enforced isolation and to kill time, he had counted his money—almost $600,000 in $100 bills remaining despite his free spending from the time he stepped off the plane in San Francisco.

He could hear angry voices echoing up the hillside from the front gate. He presumed that the federal officers were demanding entrance to the McDonald property and were encountering unwanted interference. He started up the old truck's engine and drove slowly around the house and onto the primitive back road. It was nearly a mile straight up the hill to the upper McDonald gate over a poorly kept—and better—a poorly visible, dirt track. Quaking aspen fringed the sides of the road in a nearly impenetrable phalanx. Lake Creek Road was empty and quiet when Randolph stopped to let down the old farmer's barbed wire gate. He drove through the gate, then turned back down the main road and proceeded—heart in mouth—towards the scene of animated activity he knew was in progress at the lower entrance.

There were three officers in one nondescript—typically FBI black Suburban—slowly entering the gate as Randolph clattered past. He hardly rated a glance from any of them. The three McDonald boys were loudly protesting, attempting to close the entrance gates, and were obstructing the ongoing federal vehicle. The FBI agents moved doggedly forward at a snail's pace, determined not to run anyone over, but equally determined not to be thwarted. Head down and concentrating on the street in front of his dusty, nearly opaque dirty windshield, Randolph Kennedy drove on past, down Timberlake Hill, past Lindsay's Hill, past The Red Ledges Golf Course, down Heber's Center Street, and turned north on Main Street headed towards I-80 twenty miles away. Neither his passage nor his absence was noted.

Nephi McDonald stood outside his front porch screen door, arms crossed over his broad chest. He was the picture of calm determination. Nancy Delgado strode purposefully across the flagstones, up the porch stairs, and found her way blocked by Mr. McDonald.

"You Nephi McDonald?" she asked unnecessarily.

"Who wants to know?" he asked deliberately and without menace.

"Federal officers with a warrant. I am Special Agent Nancy Delgado," she replied authoritatively.

Nephi took his time.

"Have ID?" he asked.

Nancy produced her badge and photo ID in her cred-pack.

"Well, Special Agent Nancy Delgado, what is it that you want with our humble property?"

"Randolph Kennedy. We have it on good authority that he is being harbored here."

"Who?"

"Randolph Kennedy. Fugitive from justice. Terrorist. Surely you watch the news, Mr. McDonald?"

She knew perfectly well that this obstinate man towering over her knew about Kennedy and was harboring the fugitive for that matter. It was a pain to have to go along with this charade, but she could not let McDonald win the war of nerves.

"No, ma'am. Work of the devil that TV. My good wife bought us a set in her innocence. But once I became familiar with the lascivious, worldly, and socialist nature of the programs, I wouldn't allow the devil's own device to be turned on. We hold to a more sure iron rod of truth, Agent Delgado, the word of God from His holy scriptures. We occupy our minds with the truths of the gospel, not with the transitory things of the earth, and surely not with the trash that spews out of the television set."

Delgado rolled her eyes and did not bother to hide her incredulity from the big man who was shoveling it on so deeply. Bendell and Terrife standing behind her stifled their laughter at her predicament.

"That's all very nice, Mr. McDonald."

"Call me Nephi," the powerfully built patriarch standing on the top step of the porch stairs said.

"Well, Nephi, much as I would enjoy discussing all of those fascinating topics with you at length, I came here to find Randolph Kennedy. You can direct me to him, or I can search the place, give it a good toss. Your choice."

Delgado looked McDonald squarely in the eyes, no more intimidated by his large stature and physical superiority than he was of her badge. Nephi smiled disarmingly. He paused and waited. Inside the house his two sons were frantically removing all traces of Randolph's stay. They made sure that there were only four places at the breakfast table. Each of the wives had quickly made up hers and her children's rooms so that no one could tell when they had last been occupied.

"Well, Mr. McDonald…?"

There was mounting exasperation in Delgado's voice.

"Nephi."

"Look Nephi, no more horsing around. You tell us where Kennedy is. If you don't, and we obtain evidence of his whereabouts being on this property or otherwise that you have assisted him, we will charge you with aiding and abetting a fugitive of a felony after the fact. That is a felony, sir."

Nephi did not flinch at what Nancy had been hoping would be taken as a verbal coup de grace. His lined face remained impassive, pleasant, and implacable.

"You say you got a warrant, officer?"

"I did say that," she said testily.

Nephi paused again. The sense of frustration on the faces of the federal officers was giving him considerable pleasure. The heat of their mounting anger was about to smoke the ozone.

"Show me," he asked deliberately.

She did. Now, her patience was exhausted.

"Take down the door and toss the place, gentlemen. This man is obstructing justice. You may arrest him if he puts up any further resistance."

Bendell and Terrife advanced up the stairs, wary of trouble.

"Stand aside," Nancy ordered.

"Go around," Nephi said.

He said it matter-of-factly, neither defiantly nor angrily, and certainly without fear. He was just there, and his message was that he intended to remain there. Nancy shrugged and went around him.

While Nephi watched impassively, Bendell and Terrife kicked in the ornate paneled front door. It took multiple forceful blows. The search was thorough, quick, and fruitless. The three older boys kept their mouths shut as they sat like statues at the breakfast table, outwardly unperturbed by the heedlessly careless searchers.

The place was a shambles when Romaine finally said, "Nothing, Nancy. Let's move on. We know he was here; we just can't prove it. He can't be far, and we're wasting time. Let's get out and beat the bushes some more."

"I hate to admit defeat to that smug hillbilly out there," Nancy groused, well within earshot of Nephi's sons.

David gave her a chiding look. She nodded her understanding.

Outside, she stopped her two subordinates and fumed, "Think we should drop a LAW or a grenade somewhere and use that as a pretext to drag the bunch of liars and felonious confederates in?"

"You mean like Silberberg and COINTELPRO would handle it?" asked David archly.

"Point well taken," Nancy responded, momentarily chastened.

She had not been serious, and they all knew that; but all three agents had run the thought through their brains for a moment or two.

"Let's set the dogs loose around the house, and the three of us can scout out the town."

The three agents left the property under the baleful eye of Nephi McDonald, still in his place on his porch. His three sons were inside laughing themselves silly.

Delgado ordered the full court press: mail interception, phone taps, and minicamera plants by the shadowy Surreptitious Entry agents, IRS file review, examination of confidential employment records, canvass of the neighbors, and 24-hour stakeout, known in the Bureau's parlance as "the dogs"—on the McDonald place. She knew that she and her men were that close.

David made the calls by cellular phone before they had arrived back on Heber's Main Street. Obtaining permission for the surveillance was simplicity itself. One call to the secretary of the secret panel of seven federal judges who oversaw electronic surveillance, a brief explanation of the case, and approval was granted. The formal approval was faxed in five minutes.

The agents parked in the six story parking garage located on what had once been the site of the high school, then a city park that had gone the way of the dinosaur with all of the other city parks in the nation when liability insurance rates skyrocketed due to the relentlessly litigious fervor of the society served by an army of underemployed attorneys in the latter years of the twentieth century. They walked north past the old yellow stone Carnegie Library, now a museum, and took their place in line for lunch at an old museum piece of a café called Chick's. The place retained its nineteenth century look and put out the best chicken fried steak in the country as it had been doing for the past seventy-five years.

The two men ate massive plates of hot roast beef sandwiches, and Nancy had the chicken fried steak and mashed potatoes special. Each order included a massive bronze colored scone dripping with half a cube of butter and six ounces of local honey. They were all eating lemon meringue pie when the local sheriff's deputy found them and delivered the McDonald's stack of mail that had been accumulating in the post office for the past week. Nephi McDonald did not allow federal officials—including postmen and women—on his property and had to come to town to pick up his mail himself.

"Thanks, Sheriff," Nancy said between bites of the tart tasting pie. "Anything up at the McDonald place?"

"Nope, and there isn't gonna be, neither," the deputy answered with the surety of long experience with the local Movement people. "We're roustin' the other members of the Wasatch County Militia Coalition, but they genuinely don't seem to know anything about this Kennedy person. Don't want you to think that I'm tellin' you how to run your business—you being FBI and all—but you're barkin' up the wrong tree. I know you got a two billion dollar budget and can afford to waste a whole lot more than we can, but it'll still be a waste in the end.

Nancy was tired and feeling down.

"I think you're probably right, Sheriff. We are pretty sure he was up there, but he sure doesn't appear to be here now. We'll go over this mail, then start over again someplace else."

The prospect was a grim one.

The three federal agents spread out the mail on the cleared café table in front of them. They began to sort through mail order catalogues, utility bills, a notice from the library, two obvious wedding announcements, a pile of first class envelopes containing political candidates' final pleas before the imminent election, and three letters bearing a return address for Doug Yancy, Rural Route #3, Chippewa County, Mich. Those three letters captured the FBI agents' attention. Each one tore open a letter with no attempt at subtlety; someone else could explain the tattered and obviously violated contents some other time.

Placed in chronological order and deleting the homey news, the messages read:

- Dear Brother,

Happy to help a brother in need. We can accommodate your friend's requirements at our place or at one of the brothers' places around Sault Ste. Marie.

• Brother Nephi,
Have the package sent right to my house. Best place for it.

• Bro. Nephi,
FBI Gestapo agents here. No time to write a long letter. Cancel parcel. Don't let parcel be delivered here.

The brief notes were all signed with initials, D.Y.
"What do you make of that?" Nancy asked.
"Same thing you do," David said, smelling blood again.
"Think he knows that Silberberg put the Michigan bunch in the hoosegaw?"
"I doubt it. These letters have never been picked up. Let's take a trip to Sault Ste. Marie," Romaine said.
He pronounced it salt.
The deputy was standing by dutifully.
"Go up there and arrest Nephi McDonald and his three sons on charges of harboring a fugitive. Whatever you do, don't let any of them near a phone for the next week, that clear?" Nancy asked the deputy pointedly.
"Yes, ma'am. Should we suspend all of their Miranda and habeas corpus rights?" he asked sarcastically.
"No, Deputy…just delay them. We have to get to Michigan before those Movement freaks can squirrel Randolph Kennedy away again."
Nancy gritted her teeth in an effort not to lash out at the Mayberry Mountie.

CHAPTER FORTY-TWO

Three days later at two o'clock in the morning, Gwen Chambers was dreaming about riding in a canoe with a gay blade in a straw boater and barbershop quartet striped shirt. In her dream all was languid with warm sun, fluffy clouds hanging in a friendly azure sky, and the sound of oars gently shipping the water. The bedside telephone rang and ruined the soothing fantasy.

"It's two a.m. This better be important," she growled.

Gwen was not her best in the middle of the night.

"It might be," said the caller. "This is Rudy Lorcher at the *Times* night desk. I had a guy on the line who says he's the man you met in Wasilla, Alaska, the one they're looking for. Said you'd know what he was talking about and that it was urgent. He refused to wait. Said he'd call back in fifteen minutes. I can tell him to bug off if you want. Thought I'd take a chance."

She was awake now.

"Rudy, not Randolph Kennedy?" she asked.

"*Couldn't be, Naw!*" she thought.

There was a pause while she collected herself.

"Ms. Chambers?"

He thought she'd fallen back asleep.

"I'm here. I'm also awake," she said using her womanly telepathy. "You might as well put him on."

"I told you that he said that he would call back. You want me to ring you?"

"Most definitely, and as fast as you can."

Twelve minutes later, her nightstand phone rang again.

"Rudy?"

"It's me. I have the guy. Want me to patch him through?"

"Yes, please."

There was a definite click as the night clerk put down his receiver, but the line remained open.

"Do you know who this is?" came the husky male voice. "Don't say my name if you do know."

"I think so. Are you really the guy that every cop in the country is after?"

"That's me. Look, I didn't call to chat. Your phone may be bugged. I am in trouble and that's an understatement. There's another side to this whole story, and I think maybe you are one who might be willing to listen. No one else is. I'd like to get to talk to you if you'll listen and won't bring the cops."

Gwen got more than her fair share of crank calls in the night, even though she had an unlisted telephone number; and her calls at night all had to go through the *New York Times* reporter pool—the NYTRPL, or *New York Times* Reporters' Protective League—as those involved called it. A night officer or secretary screened all calls, and for the most part, did a great job of preventing the craziest of New York's denizens from disturbing the dreams of its best reporters. Still, a few got through with convincing preambles. This could be one of them—probably was—she cautioned herself. With only a moment's hesitation, however, she answered.

"It's your nickel, I'll listen."

"Can't do that, not on the phone. Don't trust telephones anymore. I can't afford the possibility of your somehow tracing this call to my location. No...I want a personal meeting...in a public place. How about in the lobby of the Chicago Hilton on Saturday...say eleven-thirty?"

"Hey, buddy, I'm in New York. I can't just drop everything and head out west to the hinterlands."

It was a measure of her New York hubris that Gwen still thought of Chicago as the west and the west as being beyond the Pale—populated by congenital morons, the products of incestuous liaisons. This was an opinion she shared with he majority of her fellow citizens in the Northeast. It did not occur to her that her opinion might be offensive.

"Then, I picked the wrong reporter. Sorry to bother you. Good-bye."

"Hey, take it easy. Can't we compromise?"

"Nope, I'm through making concessions. Do you want to talk to me or not?"

"About what?"

"An exclusive. Yes or no, and right now."

"Yes."

"Chicago Hilton, eleven-thirty on Saturday in front of the main restaurant."

"All right. How will I recognize you?"

"You won't, and don't even try. Come alone, or you'll never see me. I can smell cops a mile away. Wear a red business suit."

"A red business suit?! Nobody would be caught dead in one."

It was a silly bit of style consciousness in view of what was at stake; but Gwen was a woman after all, and it just came out.

"Except you, if you want to meet me."

"Oh, all right, as long as I don't have to wear a fake white beard."

"And another thing. I'm calling from a phone booth. I'll be long gone if you do trace this call. The people I was supposed to stay with here have all been caught up in the FBI dragnet. Innocent people. I saw at least three FBI agents in the town here. I am ahead of them, and I intend to stay there. I will be on the move. It will be a waste of time to try and find me."

He hung up.

"But, I don't even know where I can find a decent red suit. Nobody wears that kind of thing," she exclaimed in petulant exasperation at the idea of someone else being in control of her manner of dressing.

She realized that the line was dead, but she had to vent. It was two o'clock in the morning.

"I wonder if I can write off a stupid red suit to the *Times* as a business expense?" she asked herself thoughtfully, still talking to the inert phone.

"Are you Agent Henry Drake of the Bureau of Alcohol, Tobacco, and Firearms?" a woman's voice broke into Drakes midday siesta startling him.

Her voice was crisp with authority, and it immediately announced itself as 'cop' and set his teeth on edge.

He had been sunning himself in his wheelchair in the solar room of the National Rehabilitation Hospital off Irving Street in the Bloomingdale section of Northwest Washington D.C. He did not look up—presuming it was more likely a hard-nosed rehab nurse—and he was just being paranoid. More than likely the battleaxe was there to take him for another torture session in PT. He had been hiding in the relative obscurity of the plants in the solar room to avoid his afternoon appointment.

"Yeah," he said after a pause. "This's too early; give a man a chance to rest."

The young woman moved around in front of Drake. She was attired in an all-business suit and was carrying a briefcase. She showed him a flip-wallet with ID and a badge—Special Agent Cynthia Gaffin, Anchorage, Alaska. Drake was fully awake and hyper-alert now, no more concerns about PT. This could not be good. Fibbies did not make social calls or get well visits to ATFers, not even to a wheelchair ridden hero.

"I am Cynthia Gaffin of the Anchorage, Alaska office of the Federal Bureau of Investigation. Are you Henry Drake?"

The formality was daunting.

"Yes," he said tersely.

He was determined to keep his mouth shut otherwise—name, rank, and serial number—that's all.

"I have a federal warrant for your arrest, Agent Drake."

She began reading from a copy of FD 395, "You have the right to remain silent. If you give up that right, any and everything you say can and will be recorded and can be used against you in a court of law. Do you understand that right as I have explained it to you, sir?"

"Yeah, yeah, I ought to," he growled, "I administered the Miranda oath plenty enough times. You don't need to run through the whole litany."

She did it anyway and with a recording machine on as she did. Then she took out a pair of handcuffs.

"You don't need to do that."

His voice was almost pleading. He looked around to see how many vets or other patients or hospital personnel—his new little world of acquaintances—might be there to see his humiliation.

"Yes, sir, I do. Just following regulations. You wouldn't be considering giving me any trouble, would you, sir?"

"No," he said.

He dutifully—albeit reluctantly—held out his wrists. He was angry and had to struggle to keep the anger out of his voice and demeanor. She applied the handcuffs.

"Hey, what's this all about?" he asked lamely.

"The arson of a private residence in Wasilla, Alaska, in June of this year. You are also accused of falsifying evidence at a crime scene, falsifying an official ATF report, theft of evidence of a crime that was in the custody of the federal court in Ketchikan, Alaska. The evidence was valued at over six million dollars. Additional charges filed against you include theft of monies from the federal court under the color of authority, official corruption, willful and wanton endangerment of officers under your command, dereliction of duty and conspiracy. Charges of murder are being investigated, and it is my duty to inform you that you may well face formal charges—possibly for capital murder—once the investigation by the FBI is complete."

Special Agent Gaffin recited the list of damning charges with all the feeling of the voice in an automatic teller machine.

"Can't we talk? I got an explanation," Drake exclaimed with no more of his usual tough-guy rumble in his voice.

"You'll have all the time in the world for explanation, Agent Drake. You are going to talk yourself into laryngitis before this is over."

Cyndy Gaffin said it with all of the disdain that she had accumulated during her two month long investigation of the events surrounding the ATF raid on Randolph Kennedy's home in Alaska and from the airtight case that had been developed against the federal police officer. She despised rotten cops and did not care that he knew it.

He recognized the uncompromising, unfeeling tone; it was exactly like the one he usually employed when he addressed a skellum. He felt like he was about to be roasted on his own spit.

"I'm not gonna whimper and say I never did anything wrong in that case. I'll tell you something, thought, dearie, I'm not gonna go down alone. You tell your bosses that I'll sing like a canary, name names that'll curl your hair. You tell 'em."

He was pleased to see that Agent Gaffin was assiduously taking notes and that her recorder was whirring.

Item #7 on the Task Force agenda was "The Kennedy Affair". Director Ted Coleman gave a brief report.

"FBI agents have been systematically tracing leads regarding the whereabouts of the terrorist, Randolph Kennedy. All leads point to member communities of the Militia Movement, and we have been moving vigorously against them. We know for a fact that Kennedy has been in San Francisco and have evidence for his having stayed in a little place called Heber City in Utah. He was briefly in and around Sault Ste. Marie, Michigan. We have verified sightings of him riding a large motorcycle, and have good evidence of at least one house where he was harbored in Ohio. At this point we are unsure where he is, but the net is tightening, and it is just a matter of time."

President Vantassa interrupted him, "I'll assume my prerogative as chair and bring up a mounting concern. I assume that all of you read the *Washington Post* editorial three days ago? The question produced both nods and shakes of heads.

"I'll read portions: 'The Randolph Kennedy Affair never seems to go away. It is not the hottest item in this election cycle, neither can the coals of controversy be entirely put out. Kennedy is the object of a nationwide man hunt as a domestic terrorist and purveyor of deadly weapons. *Washington Post* sources inform us that the hunted man may also be the victim of—for lack of daintier terminology—a government frame-up. As in most cases such as this one, there seems to be more smoke than fire on the frame-up issue. The White House insists that it is no more than Republican dirty politics as usual.

The Democratic president has pointedly refused to comment publicly on the Kennedy Affair, citing the now lame excuse that the administration cannot comment on a case under investigation as if that ever stopped this president or any other from holding forth when he or she could benefit from the release of information.

"'No, we at the *Post* think it is time posthumous for the president to convey to the nation what she knows. Did the government of the United States of America fabricate evidence? Could it be that this is more than Republican election rhetoric?'"

The president looked sharply around the room at the assembled officers.

"Is there a leak here?" she demanded in a sudden loud, accusatory voice.

The officers all jumped a little.

"Is there *evidence* of a frame-up? I want the FBI to tell me everything there is to know on that specific subject, and I want the report in no more than a week."

She drilled Ted Coleman with laser look.

He dropped his gaze after a moment, not strong enough to win the staring contest.

"Yes, ma'am," he said.

"He has disappeared, gone completely to ground," concluded Gerald Silberberg in his formal report to the DFBI.

The report was delivered in person to Coleman in the director's office in the Hoover FBI Building. There had been no verifiable sign of Kennedy for a month. There were reported sightings aplenty. The reward seekers, paranoiacs, and looney confessors had run Silberberg's COINTELPRO officers from Elk on the wild Mendocino coast of California to a sure sighting at an illegal cockfight in Beaver Dam, Arizona to the Separatist Homeland, Republica, in the Nantahala National Forest of Tennessee.

He had been seen in the company of such diverse fringe groups as God's Covenant People, the Church Militant, the Minnesota Patriot's Council, the Army of God, the Odinists, and even the Provisional Communist Party. One report had him in the company of body guards from The Nation of Islam. The official newspapers of the suspect organizations such as The *New Daily Worker* and the *Remnant Report* made claims of solidarity with the "True American Patriot", Randolph Armstrong Kennedy. His middle name had been made into an icon that looked a great deal like the *Arm and Hammer* product logo.

Incredible numbers of overtime man hours had been expended investigating every report—however ludicrous it seemed—and every lead proved futile. Even the crazies were in a decrescendo reporting phase after such a long futile spell. Silberberg was showing the wear and tear of yet another fruitless week of searching for the elusive fugitive.

"Keep on it, Gerald. He has to come up for air some time soon. The rats he lives with will have to start giving him up. They can't tolerate the pressure we're putting on them forever. Their daily lives are being disrupted, and their communities are beginning to go bankrupt and to fragment. Someone will crack," the DFBI told his subordinate, although with less conviction than formerly.

In the assistant director's office Nancy Delgado was giving her report to Phil Craig who had his chin in his hands as he listened.

"Boss, we were this close to the guy," she said using her thumb and index finger to demonstrate just how close. "We missed him by minutes in Sault Ste. Marie, I am positive of that. But part of the problem at this point is the perception in the Militia Movement community that Silberberg's unit is operating above the law and has suspended all civil rights. They are all furious with the government and have circled their wagons with a vengeance. We can't get one iota of cooperation anywhere, not even from our RCIs. We will have to come up with something new. I think the way to get him is for the man to believe that it is in his best interests to come in out of the cold. We have to have a way to communicate with him while he feels perfectly safe. If we could get across to him that the investigation of the ATF agents has spread enough suspicion over the government's case that he can expect a sympathetic ear or at least some modicum of even-handedness if he comes in. At the moment, I don't know how to communicate that to Kennedy; but I am going to make it priority number one.

Randolph sat quietly in one of the great soft chairs across the Hilton's lobby from the entrance to the restaurant. He had a pair of opera glasses—and as unobtrusively as possible—used them at brief intervals to check and recheck Gwen Chambers as she stood nervously by the door to the restaurant and checked her watch. He was fifteen minutes late for their meeting. In the half hour during which he had observed her and the other people coming and going in the large hotel registration area, he had seen no one who looked like a policeman in or out of uniform. No one seemed to be paying the slightest attention to him or to Ms. Chambers.

Randolph did a final quick scan of the large room, then nonchalantly got up and sauntered around its periphery in slow narrowing concentric circles in the general direction of the reporter. His senses were as keen as a tiger's in the dark.

Gwen was ready to give up. She took another look at her watch. She had the vaguest recollection of a slim, blond, young man at the Wasilla crime scene and wondered if that was the man who had telephoned her. At any rate, she had not seen anyone in the hotel who looked the least like that young man; she was convinced of that.

An unhealthy gray-faced elderly man tapped her on the shoulder and asked, "Miss Chambers, I presume?"

She almost lost control of her bladder. The man and the voice had materialized from nowhere.

CHAPTER FORTY-THREE

"A y!" she exclaimed, "You scared me!"

She laughed nervously.

"Are you Gwen Chambers from the *New York Times?*" the old man asked again, his voice raspy and muffled.

"Yes, yes, I am," she said, "I'm waiting for someone. Is there something you needed?"

She looked at him quizzically.

"I'm Randolph Kennedy," he told her.

She looked at him in bemusement.

"Bit of theatrics, I'm afraid. Kind of a disguise."

She continued to look wonderingly at him, still unsure. But, as she studied his face, her mind's eye removed the very convincing makeup and revealed his youth and vigor. He had a strong mouth, a chiseled, aquiline nose, and the most penetrating, most cerulean, eyes she had ever seen.

"Please come with me. This is no place for a serious conversation."

Presuming her interest in him as a story, Randolph began to walk slowly away towards the bank of elevators with his old man him limping walk. She looked around, and seeing no one paying her the least bit of attention, followed him into an elevator.

A well-dressed, portly, middle-aged woman started to enter with them, and Randolph announced with authority, "This elevator is taken. You'll have to wait for the next one."

The woman backed out promptly and said that she was sorry.

"Sheep," he observed. "People are sheep."

She laughed at his arrogant audacity.

"Where are we going?" she ventured, now becoming cautious again.

"My room, m'dear," Randolph said, and cackled with a mischievously lecherous twinkle.

Gwen shook her head.

"I guess I'm safe with the nation's public enemy number one, the terrorist par excellence. You wouldn't hurt me, would you?"

Her statement was facetious, but her question was completely in earnest. She and the rest of the country were fully aware that the Justice Department's UCR-Uniform Crime Report-listed the man as a mass cop-killer, a kingpin drug dealer, and a major honcho in the shadowy, violent, anti-government Movement. And here she was, about to go into a hotel room with him. How stupid could she be?

It hurt him to see that she was afraid of him.

"I have never hurt anyone in my life, anyone who was not out to kill me imminently," Randolph said.

He was now standing at his full height, back straight, and speaking in his usual conversational voice. The disparity between his appearance and his firm voice and lithe movements was striking. It did nothing to assuage her fears. But Gwen was fascinated.

The door opened onto the eleventh floor. Randolph looked out into the hall, and finding it empty, stepped out and beckoned to Gwen. She followed him, figuring that she was now committed. For some silly reason, her overly tense mind dredged up the old saw that defined involvement versus commitment. 'Consider eggs and ham. Eggs are an involvement for the chicken, but ham is a commitment on the part of the pig.' She knew that she was violating every safety dictum put out by the newspaper for its reporters. It was a judgment call of the first order.

Randolph inserted his magnetic card key in the slot, then opened the door to 1154. The fugitive and the big city reporter entered together as if they were old friends.

"Have a seat. Can I get you anything? Booze? A Coke? Some nasty candy? Wanna watch a feelthy movie?" he asked and tilted his eyebrows towards the TV set.

He was successfully breaking the ice.

"No, no, and especially no," she answered.

She was feeling very much more at ease, and the objective and wary part of her mind found that odd.

"I was never very good at small talk, Ms. Chambers. I have become even less so in the last few months. Please forgive me if I seem to be rushing you, but I would like to get right down to brass tacks and get out of here."

"Go right ahead. I am you captive audience. Mind if I record our conversation. That way I can concentrate on listening fully without having to take notes."

He had not anticipated that. He was unfamiliar with talking to reporters. He knew about being on and off the record. He guessed that anything he had to say might as well be on the record, and a tape would be a more sure way of achieving accuracy.

"No," he said, "but before we go any further, I have to set down some conditions."

She wrinkled her brow, dubious, afraid that he was getting cold feet at the last minute.

"I have to be able to trust you that you will not tell anyone where or when you met with me. Is that agreeable?"

"Sure, no problem."

"And nothing I say about where I've been or where I might be going can be divulged. I am going to try to avoid speaking of such things, but my guard may be down, and I might let slip some of that kind of information."

"Agreed."

He nodded, and she turned her recorder on.

"This is Gwen Chambers of the *New York Times*. I am in the presence of Randolph Kennedy at his request. I am not permitted to state where we are meeting nor when. My first question, Mr. Kennedy, is: have I or my paper had anything to do with helping you maintain your fugitive status or in any other way been involved in any criminal activity with you?"

"No. We are meeting for the first time. All of the arrangements are mine and will continue to be so in the future."

"You said that you had a side to the story—stories—about you in the media that allege that you are a terrorist, a gun runner, and a drug trafficker. Why don't you start from the beginning and tell me and the recorder all about it. I won't promise to print everything you tell me; but I will promise not to distort anything you say; and to the best of my ability, I'll try not to leave out anything important in anything I write."

"Fine. Let's get to work," Randolph said.

He settled down in his overstuffed chair, put his feet on the ottoman, and began to tell his story in a very careful, unemotional, and succinct manner, ever the accountant. His presentation was long—two and a half hours long—full of facts, names, dates, and places, and did not seem to leave anything out.

He did not spare himself when it came to his involvement with the Alaskan separatist and gun groups, nor did he hold back about his planning and setting up of the booby trap system at his house. This was done even though—as he told Gwen—he knew that setting the traps was a felony. He denied emphatically that he had ever dealt with illegal guns or sold drugs. He stated flatly that he was not a criminal, at least in the dimensions that the press and the federal officers painted him. That was a contrivance of the FBI and the ATF. He laid the blame for the entire miserable affair squarely on the shoulders of ATF Agent Henry Drake whom Gwen determined was Randolph's nemesis from the beginning.

Gwen was a good listener, only interrupting occasionally to have something clarified or to probe into an area that seemed to have been treated superficially. Randolph left out all names or evidence that might possibly lead to his capture or to the incrimination of the many people in the Movement's underground railroad. He left out any reference to the money in the trailer, even when Gwen pressed him about it. He told only one lie, and that was about how he got in and out of his house at the time of the raid, and exactly when he did it.

"I just climbed out the back bathroom window the night before the assault. I was wearing black clothes. No one saw me. I knew they were out there, but I was able to walk around them and down to the road. I hitchhiked down to Anchorage, caught a flight to San Francisco, and then started on the run. I was not there during the actual attack on my house. I wasn't even in Alaska."

Randolph paused for a time, trying to recall anything he had left out.

"I think that's about it. Any more questions?"

"Sure," Gwen answered. "I have all kinds of questions about the money, for example. But you have told me in no uncertain terms that you are not going to say anything more about money. I have questions about why on earth some obscure ATF agent would want to hurt you. What are you to him?"

It was rhetorical. Randolph did not respond.

"Then, I guess that's about it for now," she said and turned off her recording machine. "Now, off the record, what do you want me to do? What do you expect of me?"

"Nothing more than to print my side accurately. Even if you don't believe me and choose to write negative comments or conclusions, just promise me that you will convey what I said; so, at least sometime, somewhere, my side will be presented to the public."

"I promise that I'll do that. I want you to promise in return that you will keep me as an exclusive. That is not as self-serving as you think. For your own protection, I don't think you will benefit from involving anyone else from the press."

"I took my one chance with you."

"I guess it's presumptuous, but I'm going to make a couple of suggestions. When we first walked in here," she said, "I mean after I got over my fear that you were going to beat me up, torture me, rape me, and kill me, I was determined to convince you to give yourself up. That's what a good citizen would do. After all, we have the vaunted American system of laws. You are presumed innocent until proved guilty. You are safe in the hands of the law.

After listening to you for more than two hours, I think there is some credence to your fears about the federal police. I have another suggestion to make now instead of you giving yourself up. Let me get you a lawyer, a good one. I know just the man. You can talk to him safely. He can give you the straight skinny on your status—what laws you might really have broken—and what defense there may be. He can speak to mitigating circumstances. You and he—and me, of course—can come in together when the time is right. I think that would guarantee your safety—having the full floodlight of the media shining on you the whole way."

Randolph said nothing.

"I'll tell you some things I've learned that maybe will throw some light on this strange case," she went on, "I think there are important people in high places that may be involved—however tangentially—that may well prefer to have you and me keep quiet and would be willing to go to extremes to prevent your talking. After I print my story, I am going to ground. Those people with powerful influence may well be willing to do a heck of a lot of bargaining about charges and punishments if they can't get at you on their terms. This much I learned while I was in Alaska."

Still off the record, Gwen filled Randolph in on the events in Anchorage and Ketchikan that she had experienced or learned about on her own. Again Henry Drake came across as the number one culprit in the entire scenario, no matter from what angle it was viewed.

Randolph gave Gwen the same courtesy she had given him. He did not interrupt.

When she signaled that she was finished, he asked, "How long will it take you to contact the attorney?"

"A week, no more, provided he's in the city. I haven't had much to do with him recently."

Randolph thought that statement cloaked a multitude of hurts. It was none of his business, and he let it slide.

"I'll call you in your office Monday after next. I will use a name that will correspond to the case, but I won't tell you what it is until then."

"Don't want to tempt a nice girl like me, eh?" she asked, a little hurt.

She had thought that she and Randolph had achieved good rapport. Rationally, she realized that he had eluded the whole nation's police for these past several months by trusting no one and by being cautious about just about everything and everybody.

"Something like that," he replied with a touch of sadness in his voice.

She could see in his face how desperately the man needed to trust someone, and how little he dared.

"Okay, buy a copy of the *Times* every day. I should have the article in there tomorrow or the next day."

He nodded his compliance. They did not speak again. He left first. In five minutes, she left the room. There was no sign of Kennedy anywhere. He had melted back into the forest.

Agent Henry Drake had been treated with a disabled hero's deference from the time he had first entered the hospital in Anchorage on the day of the attack on Kennedy's house until he was transferred to the Veteran's Center in Washington and then to the National Rehab Center. Nothing had been too good for the injured hero of the nation's war on its criminals. No expense was spared; no demand of his was too great. All of that came to an abrupt halt on the day Special Agent Cynthia Gaffin moved him out of the Rehab Center to the Boling Air Force Base Brig.

To limit the number of people with knowledge of this aspect of the Kennedy Affair, Anchorage, Alaska SAC Oscar DeLentigo was transferred on temporary duty away from Anchorage to head up the interrogation; and Drake never saw anyone but the two Alaska agents, DeLentigo and Gaffin for the next month. It was a long, drawn-out game of give and get, divulge and verify, promise and demonstrate felicity. The results were meager for all of that.

DeLentigo was nearing the end of his forbearance.

"Look, Drake, we've been patient. We've checked out all of your suggestions. We come up with zip except for you. This is the deal. You deliver one of the higher-ups you keep talking about or you are going to take the fall for the whole mess, which is probably a capital case. You gave us a few names who helped—flunkies. They'll go down, maybe, so what? You know more than you're telling. You can be the good soldier and take the flack for your bosses, or you can just be convicted for all the felonies because you are guilty; and the prosecution's case against you is the best I ever saw. If you want something from us, you gotta give up someone important and back up the charge with verifiable evidence. And you will do it today, or else we will just wrap it up and present our evidence to the U.S. Attorneys for the grand jury."

The look on DeLentigo's face clearly convinced Drake that he meant what he said.

"You got some question of me moving evidence," Drake said. "I have the right—the duty even—of dealing with that evidence. It was my case, in case you don't recall. You got some question of me planting evidence at that perp, Kennedy's, based on the observation of some officers who saw a white van and a trailer. Pretty flimsy stuff. Save yourself some grief, DeLentigo. Check with your boss, Teddy Coleman. Check with Margaret Thaler, herself, even the president. There's not going to be an indictment of me or anybody else. You'll get more mileage out of busting that darky, Quatraine's, chops than you will outta me. Even then you are never gonna see any ATF guys do time for that raid. You check; we're the heroes," he said with the same confidence as when he had first stated the same litany of defense a month previously.

Drake was unbreakable, unbendable. He exuded self-confidence even from his wheel-chair. He shifted to relieve the strain on his back, a chronic complaint since the injury.

Oscar DeLentigo reluctantly reported his lack of progress by way of a secure courier and a "Top Secret" envelope to Ted Coleman. The director read the brief message, put down the report, and took off his glasses. With his thumb and forefinger, he rubbed the bridge of his nose as he habitually did when he was weighing an important decision. He made up his mind and dialed Margaret Thaler's private phone in the Attorney General's Office.

"Office of the Attorney General. This is her private line, limited to authorized personnel only. This is a secure line," an all-business middle-aged woman's voice said.

"This is the director of the FBI," Coleman told the administrative assistant.

"Do you have a time-slot scheduled for this call, sir?" the assistant asked.

"No. Tell her it's important, for her personal program."

"Please remain on the line. I will give the attorney general your message."

Coleman twiddled his thumbs. He was used to being treated with deference and to having his messages go through without the slightest delay, even to and from the president. He did not like being kept waiting, and it aggravated his tension.

"The attorney general will speak to you now."

"Hello, Ted, what can I do for you?" Margaret Thaler said coming across like a marine general as usual.

"Hello, Madam Attorney General."

Thaler did not like to be addressed by her first name, no matter how familiarly she treated her underlings. Almost the only person who used her first name was the president, whom Thaler always referred to as "Madam President". She was a stickler for formal protocol.

Coleman went on, "I need to run something past you. My agent in charge in Anchorage has just finished interrogating ATF Agent Henry Drake, who is under arrest for improper actions surrounding the Kennedy Affair. Drake is playing the good soldier, not saying anything about the Task Force or anyone in authority over him."

"So, what's the bad news?"

"He expects to be no-billed on this. In fact, he expects someone in command to quash his arrest now and to expunge his record. That's what DeLentigo told me in his call to my office this morning. I have to tell you that SAC DeLentigo and his number two, Cynthia Gaffin, are good solid officers and excellent interrogators. They are not going to get any more information from Drake. The agents have accumulated a very tight case against Drake and the ATF in this matter. They seem to think there are disturbing indications of involvement by the highest officers in the nation and that there may well be a cover-up comparable to the Watergate Affair in progress."

"I see. What do you expect from me?"

"I'm not sure. Do you want to give Drake what he wants—let him walk? That would save a lot of finger-pointing that might prove embarrassing."

"What's the downside of that?" Mrs. Thaler asked.

She had a pretty good idea of the possible repercussions of a decision to let the man go free. There was that reporter from the *Times* who seemed to know all about Drake's criminal involvement. She asked the question just to see if the downside was as obvious to the DFBI as it was to her.

"My two agents sense a conspiracy to conceal material evidence of a felony, of malfeasance in office on the part of any number of government officials. The woman in charge of the investigation thus far, Cyndy Gaffin, is a bulldog. She's bucking for sainthood—totally incorruptible—and dedicated to the cause of truth and justice. She'll never let him be let off quietly. And there's Gwen Chambers, the pool reporter who was at the scene and has been bird dogging me ever since. She seems to have inside information."

"Oh, spare me the Joans of Arc," the AG muttered, "can these two agents be convinced to be team players, if for no other reason that to save their jobs? Can the two of them be controlled, bumped up as a reward, sent into obscurity, fired, compromised, anything?"

"Not really. Short of killing them, they could speak out even if they were out of the Bureau or the *Times*. They are a rarity—truly honest and committed to the cause of finding out the truth and seeing to it that it is used in court. No, I think you can forget any manipulations; they're too tough and too bright. Neither one of them seems to care much about money or overmuch about promotion."

"And, if we let Drake take the fall, will he be the good soldier and keep his mouth shut?"

"What do you think? Is there anyone out there that would do that? You remember back in history to Nixon's Watergate scandal. Some of his people kept the faith, even went to prison for the president. Others spilled their guts on national TV. It seems like a horrific risk to me to make Drake our fall guy. You know as well as I do that he received instructions from you and me, much as I hate to say it. And there was a roomful of witnesses. It is beyond reality to hope that everyone there will keep mum when threatened."

"You said you hated to say it; then don't say it again, ever. No one else will verify that. All we have to do is to keep calm and to hang tough, and we're going to be okay. The president will be able to stay above it. At worst it would be the word of this pip-squeak ATF agent against the word of the most important and trusted leaders in the free world. In the final analysis, whom do you think the public and the courts are going to believe, Drake or you and me and the president?"

"I suppose you're right. I certainly hope so, for all our sakes. I guess my advice would be to let him go and to face the week's worth of criticism from the media. I think it would be easier to deal with the media and my two agents than with Drake. He is considered to be a loose cannon by his ATF cronies at his best. I hate to imagine his response when he sees that he has been deserted, and his back is up against the proverbial wall."

"You have heard my decision." The attorney general said. "Run the 'good-soldier' ideal past him; do it in person. Get Roger Holdaway over at Treasury to meet with him, too. Give him some rah-rah about sacrifice for king and country—*pro patria mori*—that kind of crap. Get him to go to the firing squad defiantly and without a blind fold smoking a last cigarette like a real man. Keep in touch. I won't bother the president about this unless you give me some follow-up that is worth disturbing her about."

She hung up on the DFBI without the traditional courtesy of a 'good-bye'.

Coleman arranged with the DATF to accompany him to visit Drake in person. That ought to be enough to inspire even the weakest liver in his army, he thought as he and Holdaway sat in the FBI director's limo on the way up South Capitol Street towards Boling Air Force Base where Drake was still being held.

Cyndy Gaffin escorted the two directors to Drake's cell.

"Leave us," Coleman ordered Gaffin.

She looked surprised—even a little insulted—but she obeyed without hesitation. She did not bother—however—to turn off the recording system that kept a record of every syllable uttered by the defendant.

"How are they treating you, Drake?" asked Roger Holdaway solicitously.

"Not too bad, considering."

Drake gestured around the bare cell and down at his useless legs, with an expansive swing of his right arm. He gave the two directors a wry smile.

"I had no idea this was going on. You have my word that you will be moved to better quarters immediately after we finish our visit," Ted Coleman lied, as if he were truly amazed about finding Drake in the deplorable conditions that he, himself, had ordered.

"That would be a help," Drake said. "I don't suppose you two came all the way down here on Christian compassionate impulses, though. To what do I owe the honor of an audience with the two of you?" he asked, getting right to the heart of the matter.

His face was impassive, indicating that the camaraderie had not entirely convinced him.

"I like a man who gets right to the point, a professional," said Coleman. "We came to talk to you about the Kennedy case, a talk among professionals."

The DFBI smiled broadly, showing expensively capped teeth. Drake thought the director would have made a great used car salesman.

"This Kennedy thing has the potential to hurt our service, Henry," said Holdaway, "You don't mind if I call you, Henry?"

Drake shook his head.

Holdaway continued, "We need to get this affair contained."

"And what role do I get to play in all of this containment?" asked Drake.

The other two men looked at him to see if he was being sarcastic.

"There is no way that this thing is going to go away, Henry. I think you know that. If the plan had worked the way you laid it out, we wouldn't be here. As it is, Pandora's Box has been opened, and we can't get all the snakes and spiders back in the box. The two agents who have been interrogating you, the officers at the Ketchikan Federal Office Building evidence impound room, and some *New York Times* reporter, all know about it. There are too many people in the know. We can do…nothing about it," the DATF said.

Holdaway was looking earnestly at his agent sitting in his wheelchair. His look was pleading.

"So, the crip takes the fall, that the idea?"

The two directors squirmed. Ted Coleman took a breath.

"That's part of it, I'm afraid. We are asking you to be a good soldier, the Oliver North of this misadventure—fall on the grenade for the rest of your squad."

"And a few other overused euphemisms," Drake said, the anger rising in his voice.

Coleman looked embarrassed. This was exactly how he had expected the meeting with Drake to go. He knew that Drake would have to be nuts to accept their proposal. He knew he had to sweeten the deal, or see his career and a score of others go down to ruination. He gritted his teeth and elected to go beyond his mandate from the attorney general.

"I give you my personal word that we will get the charges reduced to the minimum. We'll get you off for time served or on probation or after a minis-cule token bit of jail time. When things calm down—and you are out of the news—we'll walk you out, save your pension; and we will all forget this mess ever happened. If it is allowed to hit the fan, you'll get far worse; there won't be any way for us to intervene."

"You think about specifics, Mr. Coleman. I think I could live with some of that provided you do the right thing by me. And it will have to be in writing—secret if you insist—but written with a copy in my possession."

Drake looked long and hard into Coleman's eyes. When he was sure that what he had demanded had registered fully, he shifted his gaze to Holdaway—who looked embarrassed—as if he understood it all too well.

"I think your…uh, disability, deserves not only consideration in all of this, but also some compensation," Holdaway said, and the sentence seemed to catch in his larynx.

"Um hmm," Drake said, "I have given this a bit of thought while I have been being abused here for the past month. I figured you would see it my way eventually. I took the liberty of having my attorney come out to the base to stand by if I thought I needed him…I think I need him."

He swiftly maneuvered his wheel chair to the bars on the brig cell door and began to bang on the bars with his breakfast tray.

"You want him now?" the guard called from down the hall.

"Yeah, thanks, Jake."

"I don't really see what benefit a lawyer could contribute, Henry," stammered Holdaway, who was obviously unprepared for this eventuality.

Drake smiled at his boss's discomfiture.

"Funny, seems obvious to me."

He felt that he had scored a coup that gave him the upper hand for the moment, and it was the first good feeling he had had since being brought to Boling.

A young Iranian man in an expensively cut, perfectly tailored three-piece grey suit came hurrying down the corridor. The uniformed air force MP followed behind him at a less anxious pace. The Iranian banged impatiently on the bars, causing the several gold chains on his wrist to jangle dully against one another until the guard strode up and unlocked the cell door. The attorney moved inside quickly. All of his movements were nervous and energetic.

"Ali Mahmood Ajami, Esquire," he announced with a flashing, affable grin.

He offered his well manicured hand to all present. The two agency directors introduced themselves and traded business cards with the attorney.

"Let's sit, if you please?" Ajami requested.

He did not seem impressed to be in the presence of or with the rank of the men in the room, but was almost habitually servile in his efforts at courtesy to everyone.

"Now," he said, directing his attention to his client, "what offer have we on the table?"

He had learned that westerners prized directness to the point of being abrupt, unlike the course of negotiations in his old country.

"Yes, Mr. Director," Drake said, looking at Coleman, "please make the offer formally and with this witness, who is an officer of the court."

Coleman felt a little dizzy. Control of the situation seemed to have been wrested from him; he felt that he was no long directing events, contrary to his original plan of operation.

"Well, uh…let me see, how did I phrase it?"

Drake was amused to imagine the cogs and wheels whirring in the FBI director's head. No one offered to help the man. Drake knew he had made a counter-move to block the director from reneging in the future as those guys always did once they had squeezed what they wanted out of the defendant. Drake was enjoying the turning of the tables.

Coleman composed himself.

"I believe the offer was for Mr. Drake to plead guilty to a minimal charge and for our agencies to argue strongly for a light sentence—minimal jail time at worst or probation or even time served at best."

"And when things calm down?" Drake prodded Coleman's memory.

"Oh, yes. We will quietly move Mr. Drake out of confinement and into more comfortable quarters," Coleman added.

"And?" Drake pressed.

Coleman had to work to remember.

"And, we get Mr. Drake out of custody and back home as soon as it can be done discreetly."

There was a pause while the men in the room digested the communication from the DFBI. Ajami sat quietly, his smile still in place as if it had been placed there permanently by plastic surgery. His eyes moved intently from speaker to speaker, but he did not enter the conversation.

The pause lengthened. Coleman's forehead and eyebrows knitted. He was forgetting something; it occurred to him that his memory problem must be Freudian. What was it he did not want to bring up?

"And our bureaus will seek to preserve Mr. Drake's pension and will make every effort to find a source of compensation for his disability as an addition."

He was sweating; but he knew—even then—he had not covered everything he had promised, as painful as it was to him personally and professionally to have to make such promises in front of the oily little attorney.

Ajami looked at all of the men, a question on his expressive brown face. The other three men acknowledged his prerogative to speak.

"Mr. Drake, is that about as you understand the offers made to you?"

"About."

"And do you agree with them in principle?"

"I guess so. Depends in the final wording."

"Indeed. The reason for my presence, gentlemen; I have a few questions. First, do you have any objection to having this agreement memorialized in a written, signed document? A formal plea bargain, as it were?"

He held up his hand as Coleman started to answer.

"Let me finish all of my questions before you answer. I believe the situation will become much clearer if you will."

Ajami smiled ingratiatingly.

"Second, let us be specific about the charges to which my client will plead. The plea will be *nolo contendre*, incidentally. I always think that sounds nicer, don't you?"

The directors nodded unenthusiastically.

"The charge should be mishandling of government evidence. That might even be a misdemeanor."

Again Coleman moved as if to protest. Ajami ignored him and continued.

"The sentence must be probated or for community service only. We cannot have our wheelchair ridden officer going to prison, not even for a short stay. Think how that would reflect on the sensitivities of the administration. And we shall need a commitment—on paper, of course—of the amount of compensation for our wounded hero. I believe a million dollars would be the minimum range to start."

Ajami nodded that he was finished speaking. He reached into his suit coat pocket and withdrew two pieces of folded heavy bond paper and handed them to Coleman. The director saw at a first glance that Drake had already signed them, and that the ATF agent's signature had been notarized. The documents were a monument to the hubris of the agent and his attorney.

"If you will examine these documents just now, I am sure that you will find them to be in order," Ajami smiled collegially.

The pair of documents were identical. Coleman handed one to Holdaway. There was a space for each of their signatures to be affixed on the documents and room for the new signatures to be notarized. The text was brief and communicated in crisp, correct legal English. The terms of the plea bargain deal as set forth by Ajami were all included and spelled out in precise detail, leaving no detail unattended to and no wiggle room.

Coleman and Holdaway had the distinct feeling that they had been set up and were now only acting out their minor roles in a play.

"We'll have to run this by our superiors," Coleman said lamely, more as a stalling technique than anything.

He had not come mentally prepared to sign an incriminating document. He was a political animal; and politicians learn early to leave themselves an escape by having underlings put their signature—or better, having no signatures at all—on documents that could later prove to be uncomfortable.

Ajami smiled broadly, almost obsequiously.

"Ah, my esteemed directors. I am under the impression that you *are* the superiors. Certainly you possess the requisite power to authorize a simple plea bargain. I was also under the impression that you wished to avoid involving powerful members of the administration. Am I wrong in that?"

Holdaway answered for himself and Coleman, "I, we, still think it would be best for our superiors to give the final say."

Ajami looked hard at Holdaway.

"Perhaps that would be best."

His voice no longer had the tenor of obsequiousness.

"I believe you might want to have the president of the United States make a formal agreement to grant a full pardon to our law enforcement hero. Perhaps that would be better than the agreement we have so reasonably negotiated heretofore. And, gentlemen, if you should venture to leave without affixing your esteemed signatures—the pardon, a very public acknowledgment—will be the minimum we shall seek. As you western poker players would say it, we will up the ante."

"Now wait a minute, we're getting out of our depths now with that."

"Ah, the difficulty of having choices. I have always thought that to be one of the more distressing aspects of American life. How disturbing. The more I think about it, the more I like the prospects of great President Vantassa granting the pardon. Indeed, the vindication that would demonstrate would be most satisfactory."

"We can't."

"Or perhaps you would prefer to reconsider the value of our original patently equitable agreement among gentlemen."

The two government officials gave each other quick nervous glances.

Coleman winced, "No, you're right, we'll sign it."

He pulled out a gold Cross pen from the pen pocket inside his suit jacket.

"Please, Mr. Director, if you could help in a small matter. Lest there be any question as to proper procedure in the future, would you be so kind as to sign in the presence of a notary?" Ajami asked in his most syrupy voice.

Holdaway shrugged. He knew when he had been outmaneuvered, and Ajami had foreseen every eventuality in his preparation. The man must have an auxiliary office in the brig building. Coleman was getting angry and was working not to show it, but was not very successful. He knew he was being forced into a corner.

"We'll have to take these documents back to the Bureau to have them notarized," he said with a note of one-up-manship in his voice.

He needed to win a small battle even if he was losing the war to this slick little Persian.

"Ah, my esteemed colleagues, I believe I can accommodate you. It seems that the Air Force, in its efficiency, has such persons available. Readily available," Ajami said, a twinkle now present in his eyes.

Drake moved to the bars and jangled everyone's nerves by banging his metal food tray on the unyielding steel of the cell door. The MP returned.

"What now, Drake? This isn't the country club, you know."

"Just one small thing. The directors of the FBI and the ATF request the services of a notary public," Drake said smugly.

The guard looked at the directors, who gave him resigned nods of concurrence.

In a few minutes a notary, a staff sergeant, joined the crowd in the small cell and witnessed the round of signatures. The notary's seal was crimped on the paper, leaving the official embossment.

"Good day, gentlemen," said Ajami when the formalities were completed, "Now, if that concludes our business, please excuse me while I confer with my client."

The two directors considered themselves to have been dismissed and followed the notary public Air Force sergeant out into the brig corridor.

Drake called after them, "Don't forget the move to better quarters, Director Coleman, Director Holdaway. Put in a good word for a TV, too."

The two bureau chiefs looked straight ahead and walked very briskly out of the brig building.

CHAPTER FORTY-FOUR

Monday dragged on. It was a quiet news day. Gwen Chambers waited all day with one ear tuned towards her telephone hoping to hear Randolph Kennedy's voice on the other end. Three o'clock, four o'clock, four forty-five crawled by and none of the more than two dozen calls came from Kennedy.

Gwen fretted that she had lost him and her exclusive. Her article about the meeting with Kennedy had gotten her fulfillment of a lifetime dream—a front page, above the fold, right column exclusive, and the headline. It had also produced a firestorm of communication with the FBI laced with veiled threats. She had held her ground; and the FBI agents seemed—after a while—to dismiss her information, suggesting that it was either fabricated or overly dramatized. She wanted to rub their noses in it with another exclusive.

She had kept her promise to Kennedy. She had gotten hold of Hartley Proctor, the thirty-year nemesis of Washington prosecutors—an attorney who knew the ins and outs of the District and its euphemistically termed justice system better than anyone else in the country. He had been delighted to accept Gwen's offer contingent on Kennedy's agreement. Gwen had even talked her editor into agreeing to foot Proctor's outlandish fees in return for the exclusive. It now required only the call from Randolph Kennedy to complete a perfect week.

The call finally came five minutes before quitting time. Her pulse quickened. It was the last time he would be able to get through the switchboard.

"Chambers here," she answered.

"Do you recognize my voice, Ms. Chambers?"

It was Randolph Kennedy. He had a characteristic softness to his voice as if he were in the early stages of developing laryngitis.

"Yes."

"Are you recording this?"

"Yes. Is that okay? All of the reporters' calls are recorded. You know how the liability world is."

"Okay. We have an agreement that you won't make any attempt to trace my call, right?"

"That's right."

"I'll be brief. Did you find the attorney you wanted?"

"Yes. He is the best there is—a real tiger—and a very smart one. He knows how to talk Washingonese and has been in D.C. longer than anyone who will oppose us."

"Good," he said.

Randolph like her use of the concept of 'we'.

"Even better. If you will agree to complete exclusivity for your story for our paper, the *New York Times* will handle your defense. I'm presuming that you don't have any money. The feds have probably frozen your assets."

"I am sure they have frozen my assets."

'You need to meet with the attorney; his name's Hartley Proctor."

Like most Americans, Randolph was thoroughly familiar with the eminent attorney's name and reputation.

"Agree," he said. "I'd like to tell you when and where. I've given this some thought. I'm sorry, but I do not feel the least bit safe anywhere near Washington or New York. And for that matter, I can't be sure that this phone is not being tapped. Go to the nearest pay phone in your building. Call me at this number."

He read a ten digit telephone number to her.

"I will be here for three minutes. Then, I'll give you another number to call."

It struck Gwen as paranoid and overly dramatic, but then she was not the one on the run for her life. She had to admit that she might see things differently if she were.

"Okay," she said, "I'll do my best."

She rushed to the floor below and found an unoccupied pay phone in the hallway in front of the bathrooms. She rang. He answered immediately and gave her a second number. Following his instructions, she went to still another pay phone and called him again at the new number.

He spoke rapidly, "There is a vacation spot in a place near Midway, Utah that I saw on my recent travels about the country. It's owned by a Militia man whom I trust by the name of Dastrup. It's called the Dastrup Mountain Spa. The two of you should book a week's worth of vacation there—enjoy the natural hot mineral water in a beautiful little Swiss village resort. I'll find a way to run into you there. Can you swing that?"

"Randolph are you trying to get me fired? My editor is already on my case for my trip to…anyway, the last trip."

She just caught herself in time. Then she flushed as she realized that she had used his name. She felt like kicking herself.

"No names," he said sharply. "You have to be careful, on your guard all the time. See you and this Proctor in Utah in two weeks. Nobody else, or the deal's off. I won't be there until I am convinced it's safe. I have friends who will let me know if they see any cops or feds. They will know, believe me. I will not be messed with again."

His voice was hard and edgy. He clicked off the connection.

Randolph now faced his greatest crisis since he first learned that the ATF were massing outside his home in Alaska to attack him. He had become a professional fugitive and had grown accustomed if not truly comfortable with his status. At least as a fugitive he knew that he could not trust anyone fully and that he was entirely on his own. Now, he had come abruptly up against the threat of an idea; he could trust someone enough to give them a meeting place in advance. If Chambers and Procter proved trustworthy, he could surrender with the help of the attorney and have a chance to fight within the system instead of outside and against the faceless, soulless system. The inherent risks were obvious and daunting. He was unsure how to proceed. If he gave in to the idea of surrender, he would be wholly in the care and keeping of this man, Procter, a person he had never met and one he did not know that he could trust. He decided to risk a call to Devlin. The leader of the Movement—the number one freeman and patriot—always seemed to know what to do.

It was six in the morning for Randolph and one a.m. for Devlin in Anchorage when Randolph called using a prepaid phone card.

"O'Herligy here."

"Devlin, do you recognize my voice?"

Devlin had been settling off to sleep after an evening of watching old movies with his wife. As soon as he recognized that it was Randolph, he became instantly and completely awake.

"Yeah," he said.

Randolph spoke rapidly telling Devlin of his proposal that he surrender to the FBI with the anticipated legal protection that would be provided by the prominent attorney and by the public exposure of the event in the media sponsored by the *New York Times*. He soberly acknowledged that his main purpose in all of that was to prevent him being conveniently "shot while attempting to escape" or some other pretext.

Devlin's response was immediate and succinct, "No attorneys, Randolph. They are the government, improperly so, but it's the way it is nonetheless. You cannot get justice with a lawyer pleading your case against other lawyers in front of a lawyer judge for breaking laws made up by lawyers. It's as simple and terrible as that."

"I can't keep on the run forever, Devlin. Some trigger-happy cop is going to make a notch on his gun handle of me eventually. I can't use my money or my education, and I can't think of a way to get a job without the risk of exposure. I have been on the run for a long time, and I have come to the conclusion that I have to fight this thing out within the system somehow."

"I agree with that concept, Randolph…more or less. The patriots in the Movement have skilled law readers—no attorneys, no esquires—who can help you defend yourself. Us freemen take the position that the courts have no jurisdiction over you because they are manned by lawyers, an illegal profession. Your case is the perfect, high-profile one to test our ideas. You would do the Movement a great deal of good by following this route of defense."

"I'm afraid I'm not following, Devlin. What do you mean, lawyers are in an illegal profession? They've been around since before the Constitution was framed."

"True enough, and we've put up with them long enough. You familiar with the 13th Article to the Bill or Rights?"

"Not specifically. What can that have to do with me?"

Randolph was no Constitutional scholar, but even he knew that there were only ten articles—the first ten amendments to the Constitution.

"You need a history lesson, son. Hear my information and follow its logic."

"All right, I'm listening."

"In 1819 a 13th Article to the Bill of Rights was ratified by three quarters of the states; but then mysteriously—and by no accident—the lawyers and autocrats in power quietly removed the article from the Constitution during the upheaval of the Civil War. The purpose of this stolen amendment was to prohibit lawyers from serving in government."

"I've never heard of such a thing, Devlin. You sure about this?"

"Give me a sec, I'll read the text to you," Devlin rifled through the Freeman Legal Policies file that he kept at his bedside. "Here it is: 'If any citizen of the United States shall accept, claim, receive, or retain any title of nobility or honor, or shall, without the consent of Congress, accept and retain any present, pension, office or emolument of any kind whatever from any emperor, king, prince, or foreign power, such person shall cease to be a citizen of the United States, and shall be incapable of holding any office of trust or profit under them, or either of them.'"

"I'm dense, I guess," Randolph said, "but I didn't hear a mention of lawyers anywhere in that article. That is to say nothing about the fact that that article did not make it to be a part of the Constitution."

"Look, son, the freemen of the Movement interpret the term 'title of nobility or honor' to include lawyers by the simplest of straightforward reasoning. Lawyers are given the title 'Esquire' after their names. The term originated in the British system of peerage. Knights were squires, and the people who carried the knights' shields were esquires. Likewise, judges—also illegal—are given special titles of honor. They are referred to as 'Your Honor,' in strict violation of the 13th Article to the Bill of Rights."

Randolph was quiet for a moment, reconsidering the wisdom of calling on members of the Movement for advice.

"Look, Devlin, I have to get off the line and get away from where I am. The feds are probably busy tracing this call even now. I'll give your advice some serious thought."

"Be sure you do that. The Freemen care about you. The Movement needs you as their poster boy if for nothing else. Stay strong, my friend."

"I will, Dev. Thanks; I'll be in touch."

Randolph had been willing to accept or at least to tolerate some Movement rhetoric and logic that seemed to be rather well off the wall. He had consistently refused to go along with the racist espousals of the majority, and this current bit of advice seemed nothing short of cockamamie to him. Besides, the advice was self-serving on Devlin's part with Randolph becoming the martyr to the cause. He rejected it without further reflection and made up his mind to accept the inherent but reasonable risks of being defended by the eminent mainstream attorney.

CHAPTER FORTY-FIVE

Romaine Terrife sighed, "We have nothing minus. We need a new lead. My spies tell me that old devil, Silberberg, has come up with zip for all of his crunching of the Bill of Rights of the mountain folk. What about going to see that *Times* reporter—whatshername?—in person and trying to work with her? I don't think she was all that impressed with your phone call after her article about meeting him in person came out. You know, Nancy, she had to have gotten calls from two or more special agents a day there for a while. Reporters always know more than they're telling."

"Great minds run in the same direction," Delgado said.

She was bored and frustrated. Romaine was entirely right; they had nothing. The only consolation was that the opposition—Silberberg's unit—was no better off.

"I'll give her a call and set up a meet."

David Bendell offered, "Hey, maybe that's not such a great idea. I like the element of surprise. I kinda think she'll do a stall on us if we forewarn her. What do you think about confronting her in the street outside of the *Times* office, or better, by her apartment?"

Romaine nodded.

Nancy said, "I'll get a file photo of her. We can get her address, too. Let's call it a day. T.G.I.F. I'll get the file info together tomorrow morning, and we can plan our roll first thing Monday."

The three agents were staked out in their taupe-colored Dodge across the street from the address in New York City that the files had yielded for Gwen

Chambers. It was five o'clock Monday morning, humid, and already starting to get hot.

"I bet she doesn't go to work until noon tomorrow," Romaine grumbled, "It's just a small torture to have Bureau policy require surveillance starting at four o'clock in the night."

"If she's here at all," David added, "She might be making the two-backed monster somewhere else for all we know."

He had the hardest time of the three getting up for early morning stake-outs. He was perpetually jittery from the punch bowl full of coffee he consumed trying to become human by nine.

The team consumed McBreakfasts, glue pies that might have been apple, a dozen of yesterday's doughnuts, and corn chips with salsa made in New York City while they waited for their quarry. They were all dyspeptic, of an equally bilious disposition, and a trifle dizzy when Gwen finally walked out of her building.

"I hate her," Nancy grumbled as they watched the athletic young beauty trip lightly down the stairs of her brownstone and skip to where she kept her bicycle chained. Her face was wreathed in smiles as she greeted the new day, one that was apparently made for her. The world was her oyster.

"Disgusting," Nancy added.

Gwen worked on the two hardened tungsten steel chains and four padlocks that secured the crossbeams and each of the wheels of her bike to huge stone screw rings cemented into the side of the building. The three FBI agents got quietly out of their car. Romaine belched uncomfortably, and Nancy shushed him. They ambled to where Gwen was now standing, putting her bicycle seat in place. She kept the seat in her capacious purse since it was detachable, and nothing detachable remained in one's possession more than an hour or two if left in sight of the unfortunate and misunderstood of the city.

"I beg your pardon, Ms. Chambers," Nancy announced.

She walked up to Gwen, showing her badge and ID. Romaine and David spread out, one on the side nearest the building steps and the other a short distance away along the sidewalk. They left no place to where Gwen could retreat should she bolt—just standard FBI confrontation technique.

"I called you Friday about your article on Randolph Kennedy."

Gwen looked at Nancy suspiciously.

"What more do you want of me? I answered all of your questions then," Gwen asked, annoyed at the interruption of her routine.

If they kept her long enough, she would have to drive her car instead of riding her bike, and that was a real hassle.

"Just a few more questions. Please, let's talk. We mean you no harm. In fact, we mean Mr. Kennedy no harm. If you know where he is, if you even have an idea where, it would help us immeasurably, and would serve to protect him."

"I don't," Gwen answered as if she were in a deposition, contributing nothing more than what she was directly asked.

"You know we'll get him eventually. Right now, he hasn't been forced to hurt anyone to keep on the run so far as we know. That means there's hope for the guy. Maybe there're extenuating circumstances. Maybe he can get through a trial and be acquitted. But, I'm telling you, Ms. Chambers, one of these days a trigger happy cop someplace out there is going to shoot first and ask questions later. Maybe you don't believe this, but we actually want to help the man."

"Like the ATF and the rest of the agents in Alaska?" Gwen retorted sarcastically.

"No, not like that. I want to help him, to keep him away from the shooters. I can't do that if he remains a fugitive. Look, give me the benefit of the doubt. If you know how to reach him, tell him about me. Let him come in out of the cold to me. Agents Terrife and Bendell and I will protect him. Our mandate comes directly from the assistant director of the FBI, Phil Craig. We are not part of the team to collect evidence against him. All we want to do is to get him into safe custody as soon as possible."

Gwen was not responsive.

"At least take my card. Here's Phil Craig's. Call one or the other of us if you hear from him. Please. You and he have to trust someone. Make it me. I know that we don't know one another, but try and believe in what I'm saying. Like you, I think he's in danger. He needs to get to where the system can handle him in the bright light of public scrutiny. That's all I'm offering. Think about it."

Gwen defrosted a little.

"Look, you're acting as if I'm hiding the guy, like I know where he is. I don't know any better or any more than you do, believe me. If I hear from him again, I'll tell him what you said. I have nothing to do with his flight or any of his activities. I only report the news. If he uses me as a conduit—that's news—and I'll be involved to that limited extent. I hope you're sincere about helping him, Agent Delgado. I think there's a lot more in this than has come out, and he deserves to be heard. Like any American, he deserves a fair trial. I don't make any excuses for what he did. I guess he's really a terrorist, but even terrorists have constitutional rights in our country last time I heard—such as the presumption of innocence."

Nancy, David, and Romaine thanked Gwen for her courtesy and allowed her to speed off on her bike. She looked beautiful, firm, and fit—all curves without angles or sides. Nancy felt pangs of jealousy and bemoaned all the doughnuts she had been forced to eat on stakeouts. The two men had some pangs of their own.

Margaret Thaler read and reread the document Ted Coleman, Roger Holdaway, and Henry Drake had signed. She was thoughtful. Her hard face was lined with concern, and she was working a decision around in her mind.

"Mr. Coleman…"

He did not like that formal beginning. She usually called him Ted.

"This is not what we agreed on. This goes well beyond my instructions. I'm not quite sure what to think about it. Maybe this defuses the issue; maybe it just leaves it for a greater mess later on. I'm going to run this past the president. I think it is eventually going to impinge on her, and she will want to have the final say. You went too far with that criminal. Now, we have to see what to do about it."

Thaler pushed the button that summoned her administrative assistant. The trim gray haired woman dressed in a perfectly tailored deep maroon business suit entered the inner office almost immediately.

"Kerri-Jane, please make an appointment with the president for this afternoon if at all possible. Tell her it's the Kennedy Affair again. Something new."

"Yes, ma'am."

She glanced briefly at Coleman who appeared downcast, thinking he looked like a man on the hot seat. She made the appointment and entered it into the attorney general's electronic day planner.

The appointment was originally for three, but the president had a cancellation, and Thaler was forced to rearrange her schedule and to appear at the Oval Office at nine in the morning.

"Good morning, Margaret. Good of you to change your day and come early," President Vantassa said from her chair.

Only on the rarest of occasions did the president ever rise to greet a visitor and never for a rank as low as the attorney general. There was no egalitarian hypocrisy about this president.

"No problem. I have a brief concern to present to you, but one that may have significant political repercussions."

"I might well have guessed. The Kennedy Affair again, Kerri-Jane said. When is that pip-squeak little nuisance going to go away for good? While we're on the subject, when are your people going to bring that insignificant thorn in my shoe to justice?" the president asked irritably.

"I don't know the answer to the question of when he is going to be apprehended. He seems to be a very professional terrorist with adequate resources in the underground to protect him from detection for a prolonged period of time. We will eventually get him. I have something else that relates to the case that I think is even more important for you, Madam President."

"Oh?"

The president raised an eyebrow. This was not something she wanted to hear, undoubtedly.

"I have here a signed plea bargain agreement with that ATF agent Henry Drake, letting him off with what amounts to a patty-cake on the wrist for stealing federal evidence to use as false evidence in the Kennedy case. At the least he has probably torpedoed the case against that terrorist. Worse, in my opinion, making a very generous plea bargain agreement sends a message that your administration, and especially your Task Force, is soft on crime, at least if it comes relates to a government agent. You could come across as having a taint of corruption since the criminal in this particular facet of the case is an officer acting directly for the Task Force, which you head."

"Why won't it just go away with this guy getting his wrist slapped and passing off into the sunset? Tell me that."

"Because there are too many overly zealous *honest* people involved. These things can never be contained. The history of every presidency confirms that."

"Whatever became of the cardinal virtue of loyalty, Margaret?"

"Went out with FDR as near as I can tell. Nobody ever made his extramarital affairs or even his paraplegia public. Ever since then a president can't handle a national security crisis without someone making a scandal, a cause célèbre, out of it. It comes with the territory, I'm afraid. At any rate, we do have a potential problem here. On the one hand, this ATF thug is threatening to expose you and me as the instigators of that stupid Kennedy raid, and more pointedly, as ordering him to plant false evidence."

The president's face turned purple, but she waited until her attorney general finished.

"On the other hand, waiting in the wings are the so-called loyal soldiers—a set of FBI agents—waiting to expose the administration for corruption and favoritism if Drake is treated leniently. It doesn't jibe with your get-tough stance on crime, and I don't think anyone is going to cut you any slack on this. The termites and the maggots will have a field day."

"The who?"

"Justice Department parlance for the members of the media who gnaw away at the fiber of our country—at our Bureaus and departments—until they find something they can expose—those are the termites. The maggots are the ones that don't do any of the dirty work themselves. They just follow along behind the termites and keep the whole situation messy."

President Vantassa scowled. Thaler shrank back in her chair a little. The president suddenly and inexplicably laughed.

"Don't cower, Margaret. I won't have the bearer of bad tidings killed. I guess this is about the buck stopping here as old Harry T. was so fond of saying in this room. Damned if I do, and damned if I don't. That seems like a standard presidential problem. I've come too far on the crime issue to back down because some dirty little blackmailer thinks he can hold me for ransom. It has never happened before, and I am not about to start buckling under now. Tell Ted Coleman to take that plea bargain back to Agent Drake and let him know where he can put it."

The president's jaw was set, clenched. Her eyes were flashing.

"I was hoping you would say that, Madam President. It was my original call which got subverted by Coleman when he met up with Drake and his slick lawyer. I don't think there is a shred of evidence that can link you or anyone in the administration to that raid. I'm all in favor of letting Drake twist on a gibbet. His accusations will come. We'll give them a one news cycle treatment. You'll lose five percentage points for a week, and it will all blow over."

"Give me a follow-up at the next Task Force meeting, all right, Margaret?"

"Be happy to, Madam President."

The president was already back at work on the pile of papers in her in-box. The attorney general showed herself out.

Coleman took the outcome of the president's decision philosophically. He was a good soldier, and he would deliver the fateful message. It was out of his control. He had a quick image of himself calling for a bowl of water to wash his hands in front of witnesses. He directed his administrative assistant to call Ali Mahmood Ajami, Esquire.

The respective secretaries connected the two attorneys.

"A very good morning, Mr. Director," came Ajami's cheery voice with its Iranian flavor.

"Yes, Mr. Ajami. Good morning to you as well," responded Director Coleman with considerably less warmth.

"How can I be of service to the esteemed director of the Federal Bureau of Investigation on this fine day?"

"I'll come right to the point, Mr. Ajami. My superiors have reviewed the potential of a plea bargain with your client and have decided against it," Coleman said and paused for a reply; there was silence. "We will not enforce the tentative agreement arrived at the other day. The government intends to prosecute Mr. Drake to the full extent of the law; to do less would be to send the wrong message to the criminal community. We want it known that we will even prosecute federal officers who engage in criminal behavior."

Coleman could hear Ajami's quiet breathing which assured him that the Iranian lawyer was still on the line. He waited for a response, half fearing an explosion of stereotypical Middle Eastern temper.

"Is that the end of your message, Mr. Director?" Ajami asked levelly, breaking the silence.

"Yes, I'm afraid so. If your client chooses not to plead guilty as he should, then we will see you and him in court. You will be hearing from the U.S. Attorney's Office."

"Mr. Director…I never make threats. However, I wish you to know that one day you will reflect on this telephone conversation with profound regret. My client has no other recourse except to…involve—shall we say—the government. For one thing, we do have a formal and notarized plea bargain document signed by your illustrious self. Perhaps you would like to reconsider?"

Ajami's voice was low, educated, soft-spoken, and hard as flint.

"No, sir. That is the decision of the government by its highest officers. Be prepared to back up any threats. I personally, and I am certain any others in the government who are libeled, will take legal action over and above the criminal charges. Furthermore, we will be acutely sensitive to instances of perjury. This is not an idle comment, sir."

Coleman felt his voice rising and quickening, unlike Ajami's. He wished he had the same degree of aplomb, the *savoir faire*, that he was hearing from the

Iranian attorney. But perhaps the intensity of his delivery would underscore the firmness of the government's resolve.

"I am well aware of my adversaries, Mr. Director. You will find me to be a man of caution, but you will also find that Mr. Drake has a most compelling case. It will be long, unpleasant, and very public. I believe that the outcome will be most disagreeable for your side. '*Mene mene tekel u-pharsin*.'"

Coleman asked, effecting a bored tone, "I presume that is Farsi. What is it supposed to mean?"

"Actually, esteemed colleague, it is Aramaic—the Hebrew prophet Daniel's interpretation of the handwriting on the wall seen by the great and wicked King Belshazzar. *Mene, mene* means, 'God has numbered the days of your kingdom, and has brought it to an end'. *Tekel* means 'you have been measured in the balance and have been found wanting'. *U-pharsin* means, 'and your kingdom will be divided and given in equal measure to the Medes and the Persians'. You will recall from your Jewish Bible, Mr. Director, that the impious king was slain that very night. Good-bye."

He hung up on the DFBI.

Director Coleman felt an evanescent flush of anger followed by a sense of unease. However, he had more pressing things on his agenda than to brood over some nonsense about handwriting on the wall that came as an example of a camel jockey's rudeness.

CHAPTER FORTY-SIX

Randolph paused in his seemingly eternal odyssey in Tabernash, Colorado on the Fraser River. He was headed south and east on old Highway 40 towards a promised long term safe house in Virginia Beach. From the town's one telephone booth, he contacted the Bock brothers, who were number one and number two in the Colorado Militia and co-Grand Wizards of the Knights of the Ku Klux Klan, Mountain Region. The two men were cordial to a point.

Lincoln Bock told Randolph succinctly, "Look, man, we're glad to help a brother in the Militia, especially one who is being dogged by the One Worlders; but, man, times are a mite difficult. We can't make a move, can't have a meeting, can't hardly go to the john without an ATFer, a Fat Boy Inc., or a Southern Poverty Center geek checkin' us out. We gotta ask you to move on outta here soon's we take care of your immediate needs. I'm sorry, Randy, but it's simple self preservation—hope you understand."

"It's all I would ask. Now this is what I'll be needing," Randolph said and gave them a small shopping list.

He indicated the need for a safe house in Colorado just for the morning.

"I want to head out before noon. I have a long jaunt before me," he told the brothers.

"Where're you goin', if you don't mind me a askin'?" Junior Bock asked, just making polite conversation.

Contrary to Randolph's personal law that no one was to know his destination, he had a momentary lapse of vigilance and told Junior his destination. The long standing rule of the underground railroad was that not even the current benefactors or the kind Militia people along the way should have that information for everyone's protection. Randolph was lonely, and it was natural to want conversation.

"Virginia Beach," he said, inadvertently, and regretted having spoken as soon as he said it.

"With the Tate's?" Junior prodded, making more innocent conversation.

He referred to a well known Movement family, Arch and Mattie Tate and their eleven indoctrinated children from Florida who owned a string of apartment buildings throughout the South. Those apartments had been used regularly in the Movement's underground railroad. They were the last remnant of a once powerful Florida and Virginia Klan before the splinter group, the Knights of the KKK, had overwhelmed the parent group. The parent organization had been forced into bankruptcy by the Southern Poverty Center lawyers ten years ago and thereafter faded into obscurity in the Movement.

"Yeah," said Randolph half under his breath, knowing he was getting himself in deeper.

Seeing that Randolph was reluctant to continue that line of conversation, Junior let it go.

He said, "Me'n Linc'll be getting' your things. Hang tight here. Don't go outside, okay?"

"Not to worry," Randolph said.

He did not think he had to be told to avoid unnecessary exposure by the Tabernash contingent of the Movement. He said no more for fear that his irritability from the fatigue and stress of his long flight from the law would make him say something that would result in his failing to get the help he needed. Or, worse, he feared letting down his guard and divulging even more of his plans than the Bock brothers should know. He had already compromised himself; but the brothers seemed to be good old boys; and he did not need to worry so much.

The Bocks were gone less than an hour. Randolph left Tabernash at eleven-fifteen in a plaid long-sleeved work shirt, bib overalls, and worn work boots. The clothing was artfully padded to create the image of a corpulent and muscular farmer fresh in from the sticks, even to the manure on his boots. Randolph now wore a full-face, salt and pepper beard and topped off his sartorial ensemble with a Ferguson Tractor, Co. billed cap.

"Hey, man, you'll be just in time for the South Klan Kongress in Virginia next week. Give our regards to Arch and Mattie," said Junior as Randolph began to pull away from the Bock's humble mountain cabin.

432

"I'll do it," Randolph called back.

"*Lucky me,*" he thought when the image of himself at the Klan Kongress came to mind.

Lincoln and Junior Bock breathed easier when Randolph's pickup passed out of sight.

Randolph drove the 132 miles directly from Tabernash into Deer Trail, a tiny hamlet located a short distance south of I-70, and parked in the customer parking lot behind Donna's Motel and Café. He paid cash for a room for three days, although he intended to stay only for one night. He selected the small off-highway town for its obscurity and because no one, not even Movement members, had any knowledge that he planned to stay there. He was more wary now after his slip of the tongue with Junior Bock.

Over time, Randolph had grown habitually cautious and professionally distrustful of even chance encounters. His index of suspicion was constantly set on high. He had learned to avoid public places; and this afternoon, he decided to forego the dubious pleasure of eating unadulterated lipids in Donna's Café or of dining in either of the town's other two eating establishments. He decided to have a solitary in-room picnic with supplies that he could buy for himself. He had a choice of two local general stores—the Deer Trail Merc or the Conoco Quick Service Food Center. He selected the Merc because it was closer and less frequented.

He was very wary now, mostly by force of habit rather than from any sense of the presence of the law or of prying eyes. He had no premonitions, and the hair on the back of his neck did not stand up. He was just at his usual ill-at-ease state. His greatest fear was that he would be recognized, even in his elaborate disguise, by some yokel who matched him up with a memory of a face seen on TV. The town was lazily quiet as Randolph stepped out of his room and looked nonchalantly in a 360 degree arc that—by now—was almost instinctual. He was confident that all was clear before he descended the three steps of the stoop. It was a brilliantly sunny day; the air was clear, high, and dry; and Randolph felt good to be able to stretch his legs.

He walked the two blocks to the Merc, checking over his shoulder every now and again to see if he could detect any undue attention directed his way. Randolph's gait was slightly awkward owing to the bulky padding under his clothing. There was no one on the gravel street, let alone anyone interested in him.

A set of small cowbells over the door to the Merc jangled noisily overhead as he entered, twanging his taut nerves.

"Hi, there," called out the owner as Randolph stepped inside.

The interior was dimly lit and not air-conditioned. It took Randolph a moment for his eyes to adjust to the subdued light before he could see the source of the voice.

"You just passing through, Mister?"

"Yeah," Randolph replied and busied himself behind an aisle barrier with his search for provisions.

He kept his face away from the storekeeper as much as he could without being obvious. He filled a basket with a six-pack of Cokes and a couple of Red Bulls, a package of Fig Newtons, packages of bologna and cheese, and some Wonder bread. He hated the soft, gooey white bread, preferring firm multigrain types that his wife and little girl had called "cardboard bread". He was stuck with gooey; it was the only brand available. He pulled a half gallon of 2% milk out of the refrigerator, settling on the compromise from among the gallons of whole and skim milk. He knew he should drink skim milk; Irene used to nag him about it. He could not take the chalk water that he deemed skim milk to be, and he knew that his arteries could not tolerate the sludgy lipids in whole milk.

An assortment of paper plates, cups and toy plastic forks finished off the basket.

As he made his way back towards the cash register, he passed a display of Twinkies. On impulse he grabbed two packages and muttered, "Only the rocks live forever."

His purposeful stride towards the register was interrupted by the clanging of the cowbells over the Merc's door. In walked the town's deputy marshal in a severely starched and creased khaki uniform with an American flag decal on the right shoulder. The deputy carried a long barrel .44 pistol that seemed oversized for the holster attached to his Sam Browne belt. The gun was over-sized for any purpose, Randolph thought.

"Hi, Bill, how's it hangin'? Long time no see," the shopkeeper greeted as the deputy entered.

Randolph took a sudden great interest in the stack of Legg's women's panty hose and the nearby display of condoms. The variety of the latter was mind-boggling. Gazing at the displays of merchandise required that Randolph keep his back to the deputy.

"They're hangin' okay, Don, and it was all of yesterday since I was in here. How 'bout you? Any more trouble with those little punks from Denver?"

"Haven't been back since you ran them off."

"Gimme a call if they do. Got any fresh cherry pies in?"

Chapter Forty-Six

"Just apple."

"The missus doesn't like apple. I'll just pick up some doughnuts."

Don smiled.

"Don't make any cracks about cops and doughnuts, or I'll move my trade over to the Conoco Quick Stop," said Deputy Bradshaw with a broad smile.

It was an old joke between the two men.

"Hey," Don asked, "you picked up any Most Wanteds this week, Bill?"

He could not suppress a soft horse laugh at the deputy's pretentiousness.

"You laugh, but if someone comes in here that's on that list, I'll recognize him. I have been studying those guys for the past year. I'll know one of them even in disguise. That'll get me out of this hick burg, and you'll lose your best customer."

Randolph's muscles tightened, and he felt a surge of fight or flight adrenaline surge through him. His eyes dilated, and he began to sweat. The deputy brushed past him on the way to the doughnuts. Their eyes met. Randolph forced himself to smile and nodded his head by way of greeting.

"Hot enough for you, officer?" he asked.

"It's that all right," he said and gave Randolph the once over. "I'm Deputy Bill Bradshaw. You new here?"

The conversational tone was entirely casual, but the deputy's inquisitive eyes seemed to be drilling a hole in Randolph's forehead.

"Just passin' through," Randolph answered. "Got my trip munchies."

"Where to?"

"California," Randolph lied spontaneously.

His life as a fugitive had made him a quick and facile liar. He felt a slight hesitation trying to remember which ID he was carrying and which license plate was on his car.

"Heading home?"

"Yep, got to get back to work."

The deputy eyed Randolph for a second. It seemed longer to Randolph.

"Have a good trip, then. Don't get too sleepy driving."

"Thanks, I won't. I'm stocked up with plenty of caffeine. Besides, I'm in no hurry; I'll take it easy."

"You do that," Bradshaw gave Randolph a stiff parting smile.

Randolph forced himself not to rush. He worked to appear to be at ease. He paid cash for his purchases as usual and moved deliberately but without obvious haste through the cowbells and out of the Deer Trail Merc. He was trembling slightly and found that he had been holding his breath. He looked over his shoulder more frequently now as he walked directly back to his motel room. He was sure the town cop had not recognized him. After all, he was a national, not a local item, and he was in an effective disguise. He hoped.

Almost by instinct—and with no concentrated effort at decision—Randolph grabbed up his bag where it lay on the bed and threw it into the backseat of the truck with the groceries. He took a brief second to note that his license plate was a Utah designer plate with the red rock arch, not a California one. He shrugged it off, got into the driver's seat, and pulled out of the small parking lot. At the junction of I-70, he headed east.

He had not gone a quarter of the 24 mile distance to the next town, Agate, when he saw a police car approaching. He slowed to five miles below the speed limit and set his cruise control; so, there would be no replay of his mistake coming across the Utah desert. The police car's blue and white flashing lights came on. Randolph began to consider his options. He racked his brain for a reason for the cop to be stopping him, other than the obvious worry. The cop pulled up behind him so quickly that there was nothing to do but to stop. His old truck was no match for the average low-budget car let alone a high powered police vehicle. He pulled to the edge of the freeway near the turnoff to a ranch exit.

He recognized Deputy Bradshaw from their brief encounter in the general store, and alarm bells sounded inside his head. This time the hairs on the back of his neck actually did stand up. The deputy had his hand on his gun but was not making any sign that he intended to unholster it. He strode up to Randolph's driver's side door in no hurry. His face did not suggest any special interest or malice.

"Hello again," the deputy said through Randolph's open side window.

"What's the problem, officer?" Randolph asked politely.

"Pretty routine. Seems your left taillight is out."

Randolph knew for a fact that all of his lights were in perfect order because he had made it a point to obviate that cause for a pullover by an observant highway patrolman. The mental alarm bells had become blaring klaxons.

"Sorry, officer. I'll get it replaced in Agate. Do they have a parts store there?"

"They do. Say, I thought I understood you to say you were from California and were on your way home."

Randolph winced knowing he had been caught in his lie. He tried to improvise more lies to fit the fact that he was headed east in a truck with Utah license plates.

"That's right. I borrowed this old wreck from my brother who lives in Salt Lake City. I have to pick up some applications for the elk season in Limon before I turn around and head back west."

Randolph knew it sounded worse than lame. He should have rehearsed a better set of lies as soon as he met the deputy marshal in the Merc. He realized that he had given the officer incorrect information. It was clumsy of him, and now he was about to face the consequences of his poor preparation. He could only hope that the stereotype of a dumb local cop would be borne out in his favor.

"Would you mind stepping out of the car, sir? I'd like to check your registration and have a look around the interior, if you don't mind?"

So much for the county mountie being a dullard. Randolph's worst fears were being realized. He fought to think of a way out of this. Bradshaw stepped back away from the car door, moving in the direction of the front bumper to let Randolph out. Randolph made an instant decision. He exploded out through the open door hurling it into the astonished and unprepared police officer. Bradshaw was knocked off his feet; and before he could gather his wits to reach for his gun, Randolph was on top of him. In his excitement, Randolph pounded the hapless officer's face to a pulp, venting his pent-up stress and latent fury. With each blow, the deputy marshal's head bounced against the hard pea gravel of the freeway shoulder. The blood screen behind Randolph's eyes diluted enough for him to realize that the policeman was unconscious and luckily before he was dead. From somewhere deep in his psyche came a stop notice.

Randolph's chest was heaving from his exertions and his blood lust. His pulse rate was off the monitor. He fought to be able to think with his cerebral cortex instead of his limbic system. First, he looked up and down I-70 for cars or trucks that might have been witness to the attack. There was no traffic in either direction to Randolph's profound relief. He rolled his victim over on his abdomen and removed the man's two sets of handcuffs. He secured Bradshaw's arms behind his back with one set and placed the other in his pocket. He dragged the inert cop to the trunk of the police vehicle and laid him on the roadside while he found the car keys and opened the trunk lid.

Bradshaw was not a big man, and Randolph was able to hoist his inert body into the trunk with reasonable effort. He climbed into the driver's seat, adjusted it for his longer legs, and made a U turn. There were still no vehicles to be seen on the freeway. Randolph squealed rubber off the tires as he accelerated towards the ranch road exit. He turned off and followed the paved road for two miles before it turned to gravel and then to dirt. He found what he wanted—an obscure side road that curved away from the main track and out of sight.

It took some maneuvering to get over the deep ruts and exposed boulders without high centering in a vehicle manifestly not constructed for such abuse. Finally, Randolph judged that he had gone in far enough out of sight. He stopped the police car—got out—and looked around. The terrain was hilly with occasional copses of trees standing out against otherwise sandy, sagebrush covered hills. A long neglected ditch ran alongside the road and into the nearest patch of aspen trees. He could make out a pile of old trash laying next to the trees. Rusting hulks of 1930s cars, antiquarian ruined refrigerators, lengths of snarled baling wire, and rotting cardboard boxes had been left as litter by uncaring ranch owners decades before. There was no evidence of recent deposits or activity. Randolph found several likely tethering places.

He opened the trunk lid and looked into the awake and panic-stricken eyes of Deputy Marshal Bill Bradshaw. The police officer appeared dazed and clearly impaired but alive. His skin was cyanotic from lack of oxygen which gave Randolph considerable concern, but he said a little prayer of thanks that he had not left the helpless policeman in the trunk long enough to have killed him. He would not have been able to get over having committed a murder; serious aggravated assault on a sworn police officer in the line of duty was plenty on his plate. He dragged the enfeebled man out of the trunk and over to the trash pile.

"You're not going to kill me, are you?" Bradshaw begged plaintively.

"I will if you give me any trouble," Randolph answered malignantly. "You cooperate with me; and I'll call in your whereabouts; and you won't starve or be eaten by coyotes or cougars."

"I got a wife and kids. Have pity…please. Please don't kill me," Bradshaw pleaded.

All traces of his former swaggering panache and machismo were gone. His starched uniform was completely disreputable, torn and smudged with dirt and blood.

"Shut up," Randolph ordered.

He jerked the officer, who was now crying unashamedly, up to his feet and dog trotted him on his unsteady legs over to the hulk of an old Ford.

"Lie down here with your feet up by the door handle."

Bradshaw moved as if he could not comply fast enough to please the monster who now had life and death control over him.

"Just don't kill me. Don't leave me to die. Have mercy!" he pleaded over and over in a mantra of terror.

Randolph steeled himself to ignore the pleas and took out the second set of handcuffs from his shirt pocket. He secured one ankle in the handcuff, and the other side of the cuff he attached to the old window frame. Bradshaw was in a miserable position, his arms trussed behind him and lying on his face with his leg stretched out to reach the window frame above him.

"I cooperated, right? I did. You don't have to kill me. You promised. I want to live. Please!"

Bradshaw was pleading piteously. He began to pray, calling on sweet Jesus to help him.

Randolph's face softened a little.

"I'm not going to kill you. Take it easy. Once I'm safe, I'll call in where you are. It won't be too long."

Bradshaw was sobbing loudly and could hardly hear the soft spoken voice of his tormentor. Randolph was unsure whether the crying was from relief at hearing of his reprieve from a death sentence, or because of his continuing fear and physical misery. He turned and walked away without further talk, ignoring the growing stridence in the pleas from the marshal. He paused long enough to disable the police car in as many ways as he could think of and to wipe down anyplace that where he might have touched. He set a pace faster than a jog back to his truck still sitting on the road side of I-70. He cranked up the old truck to 120 miles an hour, surprised at the old vehicle's vigor. He made sure that he kept under the speed limit.

Deputy Marshal William C. Bradshaw—the "C" was for Cody, a fact that Bill would never allow to be known—had loved his job up until this terrible day. His aspirations had transcended the town for which he worked. He had been studying for the Colorado State Trooper examination every minute of his spare time since he had already failed the tests twice. He had developed a consuming ambition to make a spectacular collar that would bring him the favorable attention he needed to get out of his hick town. Now, he was going to rot in this place—this garbage dump—or almost as bad, if he did get out of his present humiliating fix, he would wither away as the joke cop in a Podunk town. He was the most miserable of men, too exhausted and sore and hungry to be able to feel the great fear and anguish he had known when he first woke up from his beating. Now, all he had was anger; he would live to see Randolph Armstrong Kennedy dead.

Kennedy waited until late that night before making a call. He stopped beside freeway phone booth 247 outside of Evansville, Indiana and placed a call to Illinois State Police. He gave the precise location of the hapless policeman in Colorado—precise to within two feet, based on the GPS unit in the police vehicle. The Illinois dispatcher was seriously confused and doubtful since Randolph would not give even the slightest explanation of how Deputy Bill Bradshaw had come to be in such lamentable circumstances. He made sure the dubious Illinois officer had received and understood his message, then abruptly hung up, knowing that the location of his call had been recorded.

It took an hour to find a different car in Evansville in which the trusting owner had conveniently left the keys, then Randolph headed east again. He pulled off the road and into a farmer's corn field for a three-hour sleep. He drove the remainder of the way to Virginia Beach without incident. The Tates had been expecting him for a couple of days.

CHAPTER FORTY-SEVEN

After the director of the FBI hung up, Ali Mahmood Ajami stared at the telephone for a few minutes lost in thought. It was a formidable task that he had before him, taking on the U.S. government. He did not altogether trust his client, but Drake's claim of having been acting under the order of higher officials—even for ostensibly felonious activity—had a ring of truth; and besides, it was all he had to go on. Ajami had read the FBI evidence against his client and knew that there was no defense against the resulting charges. The federal agents had his client cold.

He moved himself out of his reverie and pushed the button on his desk console to summon his secretary. She was a blond woman. Ajami had dreamt of coming to America and being surrounded by blond women, and it was one of his personal measures of success that he could now command one of the distant Christian beauties.

"Yes, Mr. Ajami?"

"Arrange a meeting with Henry Drake in the Boling Air Force Base brig as soon as possible."

"Yes, sir," she said.

The Nordic woman was all legs and enticing curves. It always gave him pleasure to watch her turn and leave his office to do his bidding.

In a few minutes a red light flashed on his console. He picked up the receiver.

"Yes?"

"Mr. Drake on the line, sir."

"Leave us."

"Yes, sir."

"I want your permission to contact some people I know to begin our campaign in your defense. I want to get you to the U.S. Marshal's Office or the U.S. Attorney's Office. I am going to send your story to the newspaper. I think that Chambers woman from the *New York Times* has had the most involvement, even seems to have interviewed Kennedy. Do you agree?"

He said it without preamble or explanation and without so much as a greeting to his client.

"I take it the DFBI and DATF reneged?"

"Indeed so."

"Thanks for sharing."

"What is your response to my query, Mr. Drake?"

"It's a 'yes'. But we do have a signed paper by the renegers. I mean, doesn't that count for something?"

"It could, but it would be expensive to pursue and a drawn out process that will keep you in your cell much longer. I favor our more active approach."

"Okay."

"Good. I will first contact a government official of my acquaintance. He has a reputation for honesty, and I think he is none too fond of Theodore Coleman. That can't hurt, and, as Americans are fond of saying, 'he owes me one'."

"Gotcha, boss. Don't forget, I want out of here ASAP. I am bored out of my skull."

"Patience. I will be in touch soon."

"I have to ask you again, Mr. Drake: is it a fact that you were ordered to plant false evidence in the raid on the Kennedy residence? And…can you produce those witnesses you allege, or do you have other tangible forms of proof of having received that order?"

"The president and the attorney general were both present in the private meeting. The whole Task Force was present when the raid was discussed. Records were kept including recordings. The idea of planting evidence was at least alluded to pretty broadly. It was an obvious consensus that we had to bring that perp, Kennedy, down whatever we had to do to accomplish his fall. The president herself even cited some obscure national security policy."

"I will need to have you prepare a comprehensive list of everyone who heard conversations about the raid, especially persons in positions of authority. You also need to work on your story for the Chambers woman "

"No prob. Good-bye, Ajami. Thanks for the efforts. Let's bring down Ted Coleman!"

"Indeed, and at least. Good-bye, Mr. Drake."

Ajami pulled the government telephone directory out of the second drawer of his ornate Philippine mahogany desk. He found Federal Bureau of Investigation, moved his index finger down to "Assistant Director, Phillip Craig", and dialed.

"Mr. Craig's office."

"Is the assistant director in, please?" Ajami inquired politely.

"He is in conference. Do you have an appointment?"

"No, but I do have crucial information about his biggest case."

"May I ask your name and the nature of your communication?"

"My name is Ali Mahmood Ajami, Esquire. The information I have is for the assistant director's ears only. It is quite serious, and quite urgent. Please do disturb him. I apologize for any inconvenience."

Phil Craig had just gotten off the phone with Nancy Delgado. She had given him a thumbnail sketch about her current progress in the Kennedy case. Aside from waiting for a possible communication from some newspaper reporter, there were no prospects in sight, no leads, not even a good theory. Craig was depressed. It did not look as if this Kennedy thing was going to provide the all-important leg up he needed to get into the director's chair.

The speaker phone squawked, "Mr. Craig?"

"Here."

"I have a gentleman, a Mr. Ajami, on the line. He says that he has urgent and crucial information on your most important case—the Kennedy Affair, I presume."

Craig felt a small jolt of alarm.

"How on earth did he find out about me?"

"He didn't say. Insists that he will only speak to you, sir."

Craig knew that Ajami was part puffery, but he had never known him to over dramatize on an important issue.

"What have I got to lose? Put him on."

"Hello, Mr. Director."

The smooth accented voice was mildly foreign; it could even have been Japanese.

"This is Phil Craig. What can I do for you, Mr. Asami?"

"It is Ajami, sir. Ali Mahmood Ajami, Esquire. You may recall me from the Wilson scandal. I represented Speaker Wilson and was able to supply you with certain information about inappropriate activities on the part of his accusers. Currently, I am the advocate for an ATF agent involved in the

Kennedy Affair, a Mr. Henry Drake. Perhaps his name is already familiar to you. I have news of considerable interest and would like to run it past you. Perhaps you would then be so kind as to advise me where to turn next."

"I'll do my best," Craig replied, becoming intrigued.

"I trust this is a secure line, sir?"

"It is."

"I am sure you would not remember such as me; but, besides our professional interchange, you and I met privately at a season's end party for our boys' soccer league. Your son and mine were on different teams that were quite competitive with one another. They both played on the all-star team in the post season. We talked on several occasions. I remember you as being one who struck me as candid and forthright. It is for that reason that I thought to contact you rather than some others I might have. I am hoping that you are one who would not be inclined to sweep a rather delicate matter under the rug—as they say—just because it involves senior FBI officials and even more important governmental officials."

Craig remembered Ajami's habitual flowery speech habits and his lengthy round abouts to get to the point. But he also remembered that the Iranian attorney always ended up with clear logic and valuable information.

He said, "I'm not afraid to confront anyone as long as I have the evidence. Convince me."

That was exactly what Ajami wanted to hear. The astute attorney launched into a long and detailed account of Agent Drake's involvement in the Kennedy Affair, not sparing his client's admissions of having been directly involved in the commission of felonies. That alone was convincing to Craig. The possibility that Ted Coleman might be tarred with the same brush was tantalizing. He had a tingle of a thrill at the prospect of being on the side of the angels in a nationwide scandal that involved the directors of the FBI and the ATF and might well include the attorney general—his direct superior—and perhaps even the president, herself.

"Have I piqued your interest, Mr. Assistant Director? I hope I have not conveyed my very frank message to the wrong person and that you might betray my confidence. I hope you don't mind me saying so; but these are perilous times for me; and Washington is a devious place full of unseen traps."

"You are right, Mr. Ajami. And, yes, you picked the right man. Did you know of my involvement in the case?"

"No, I simply assumed that the assistant director would be privy to what was going on. I presumed on our brief but pleasant relationship to unburden myself to you."

"Let me think about this for a moment, if you don't mind. I'll put you on hold and concentrate fully. Don't hang up. I won't betray you. It is not in my best interests to do so," Craig said.

"Go right ahead. I am in favor of thinking,"

He began to hear Muzak. Ajami disliked Western music at its best, and Muzak was to music what rice puffs were to food. He drummed his fingers on the mirror finish of his desktop while he waited.

Craig considered his options and mulled them around in his head. He could back away and save himself confrontations and grief; but he had to admit that he enjoyed confrontations, especially when the other guy was made to sweat. The image of Ted Coleman tugging at his shirt collar, red-faced and angry, was particularly appealing. He could handle Mr. Ajami and his client himself and limit the spread of credit for an exposure of potentially gargantuan proportions. On the other hand, if this business backfired, he would eat a full plate of crow and would do so while reading the want ads.

Craig settled on the idea of referring Ajami to another office. He briefly considered Justice, but Margaret Thaler was the head and would put this matter so far on the bottom of the pile that they would all be pensioners before it ever found its way out of the last drawer. The U.S. Marshal's Office was a little too close to Justice for Craig to feel fully comfortable; the FBI was out of the question. He decided on the U.S. Attorney's Office. Even though the hundred or so U.S. attorneys were under the nominal control of Justice, Craig knew that they pretty much did as they pleased, a fact that had troubled administrations for nearly two hundred years.

"Mr. Ajami, are you still there?"

"I remain your humble servant."

"Forgive me for the delay. I don't want to give you a wrong steer. I, personally, am not the one to handle this. It is my opinion that the matter should be referred to the U.S. Attorney's Office."

"Are you giving me—how is it said—the brush off?"

"No. Not at all. If you will be patient a little while longer, I will get through to an assistant U.S. attorney I know and put you two together. His name is Daniel Hernandez. He's an Apache Indian—mean, honest, and a very thorough prosecutor. He is incorruptible; so, nobody likes him. I think he's perfect."

"Thank you for your courtesy, Mr. Assistant Director. I will try and be patient."

"Good. Shouldn't be more than five more minutes."

More Muzak. More finger drumming.

"Mr. Ajami?"

"I'm still here."

"I have been lucky enough to get hold of Mr. Hernandez, himself. We'll make this a conference call."

Craig pressed the conference button on his receiver.

"Hello, this is Daniel Hernandez. Mr. Ajami?"

"I am on the line, sir."

"The assistant director has outlined your information for me. I am definitely interested. Here's what I think we need to do. First, I will arrange to have your client moved to a secure location where he will not be subject to FBI or other federal interrogation except with our agreement. Second, I don't want you to discuss this matter with anyone except me. No news media, no cops, no politicians. That clear?"

"Yes, however, I retain the option to pursue this matter fully in the news media in the defense of my client if that becomes necessary."

"I will even help you when the time comes. I am stepping out on a limb, Mr. Ajami; but if your client's information proves to be credible, we will probably be willing to entertain an offer of complete immunity from prosecution and even enrollment in the Witness Protection Program. I will put the transfer of Mr. Drake in motion as soon as we hang up. Would tomorrow at ten be too early for us to meet?"

"No, that would be fine."

"Do we have an agreement until then?"

"Yes, you can count on me."

"Until ten, good-bye."

"Good-bye, and thank you. Good-bye to you, Mr. Craig as well."

"Don't mention it. I mean, don't mention it. Keep me informed as best you can."

"I will do my best. Good-bye."

Ajami had been impressed with Phil Craig and Daniel Hernandez from the conference call and considered himself to be a good judge of character, even after only a telephone conversation. He was not about to rely fully on the word of two government agents, however. His long history of dealing with governments, both in the U.S. and in his native Islamic Republic of Iran, had left him with more innate caution than that. He always required a back-up. He next dialed The *New York Times*.

It took some persuading, but Ajami was able to get Gwen Chambers on her beeper. She responded by cellular phone with Ajami's office twenty minutes later.

"Gwen Chambers here."

"Pardon me, Ms. Chambers. You do not know me, but I have an important story for you. I read that you have been involved in the Kennedy Affair from the beginning and have even spoken face-to-face with the fugitive."

"That's right. Do you have information on Kennedy?"

Her heart quickened.

"On a related matter. I cannot discuss this on the telephone; and in fact, I cannot divulge full details now. I am willing to promise you an exclusive in this matter if you would be willing to be patient for a time. I am the attorney of record for ATF Agent Henry Drake; perhaps you are familiar with his name?"

"I am that. What do you have in mind, Mr. Ajami?"

"My client and I are meeting in secret tomorrow morning with a high ranking law enforcement officer; so, my client can present evidence of his own and other members of the government's wrong doing. The matter bears directly on Randolph Kennedy. Like my client, I am a bit skittish when it comes to dealing with the federal government—and for good reasons—I might add. I regret that I cannot give you details, but I am sworn to secrecy for the time being."

"Then, what do you want of me?" Gwen asked, not seeing a connection to her.

"I am asking if you would accompany me to the meeting and act as a witness. You will have to promise not to publish anything that comes of the meeting until we are given a green light by the officer. Would you be willing to do that?"

"I might. When and where is the meeting?"

"That I cannot say. I am asking you to trust me. I will pick you up wherever you say tomorrow. The meeting is at ten in Washington. If it would be of comfort to you, I can bring along my wife."

"That would be a comfort; please do bring her."

Gwen's mind raced through her feminine and professional intuitions on both sides of the issue—personal security versus the opportunity for a journalistic coup. It took her a moment to commit herself.

"All right, I'll come," she said, "Pick me up in the lobby of the Shoreham. I'll be waiting there at nine a.m."

"Thank you, Ms. Chambers. I am sure that the effort will prove to be most worth your while. Have a pleasant day."

"Thank you."

"Until nine tomorrow, then?"

"Yes, good-bye."

Gwen felt exhilarated. She now had three potential exclusives on a related story in one week! She seemed to have stumbled onto the King Solomon's mine of journalism and was going to mine it for all it was worth, maybe even a Pulitzer. She was excited but not giddy. Her next call was to the paper's research department for any and all information available on Ajami. She was rewarded with a comforting resumé of a reputable attorney. She relaxed on the security issue.

As for Ali Mahmood Ajami, Esquire, it had been a good morning's work. He had his administrative assistant make copies of his interrogation of Henry Drake and to assemble his work-product notes. He looked forward to the meeting at the U.S. Attorney's Office with anticipation.

CHAPTER FORTY-EIGHT

Oliver Quatraine was now a house husband and had been for three months since having been placed on indefinite suspension without pay pending completion of the investigation of his role in the Kennedy Affair. He was bitter and frightened and humiliated. His wife was now the family's sole bread winner. Oliver was confined to his house except under special circumstances when he could receive permission from the head of ATF Internal Affairs to go out on errands. Quatraine seldom asked for and half of the time was refused permission for such errands. He knew that the adverse rulings were just for spite. His appetite was poor; the taste of bile in his throat was too vivid. He and Sylvia had not made love since the day Roger Holdaway had had handcuffs clamped on his wrists. He could not bring himself to do useful work around the house; he did not call his friends; he was sliding into a deep depression; and he did not seem to be able to do anything about it.

After the big show in the Task Force meeting that day, Oliver had been questioned for several hours in the ATF office by Internal Security. He told them everything he knew about the preparations for and the execution of the raid on Randolph Kennedy's house in Wasilla, Alaska. He held back the fact that he had made tapes of meetings of the Task Force as a potential bargaining chip for later.

Oliver knew that his career was ruined no matter what the outcome of the investigation. Now, his main aim was to save his sorry skin from prison. Strangely—after the intense session of questioning—he had been allowed to go home under house arrest with a leg band monitor and had not been contacted since. It was like finding a handful of grenades with their clips removed and trying to keep control of them with greasy hands. He got ever more tense each day.

The phone rang just after four in the afternoon. Oliver let it ring six rings. The answering machine kicked in. Before the automatic cutoff to take a recorded message, a deep authoritarian baritone voice cut in.

"Hey, if you're there, Mr. Quatraine, I need to talk to you. This is U.S. Attorney Daniel Hernandez."

That sounded important and stirred Oliver out of his torpor. He picked up the receiver with trepidation.

"Quatraine here."

"Very good, Agent Quatraine. I am a deputy U.S. attorney in charge of an investigation into charges of improprieties at the ATF, especially with regards to the Kennedy Affair. You name has come up."

"*Has it now?*" Quatraine thought, "*what a surprise.*"

"I want you to meet with me tomorrow about eleven o'clock at the Justice Department Building. Understand that this is not just a request."

"Fine," said Oliver. "You know this places me squarely on the horns of a dilemma. I am under house arrest and can't leave without permission from ATF IAD. That permission is extremely unlikely to be given if past experience is any indication. Tell me what to do."

"I'll fix it with IA. You don't even have to contact them. Come to the meeting and don't talk to anyone, even ATF—especially ATF—about it. Don't be too surprised if it appears that authorization for the meeting and clearance with your people came from some other agency. I have my reasons."

"Okay," Oliver said resignedly, "if you say so. I'll be there."

He had become a pawn without the ability to control his own life. He sank deeper into his depression, deep enough that he did not even mention to Sylvia that he would be leaving the house when she went to work.

He left early the next morning, and it took him half an hour in the city to find the U.S. Attorney's Office on 555 4th Street, NW. It should have been easy but he floundered.

"*I'm pershimmered*", he thought, "*this is as obvious as it gets, and I can't function.*"

Fortunately for his psyche, he cleared his torpor fogged mind and—after two passes—found the building. He was not late having left himself enough time to find parking in the impossible city and to spend some lost time before locating the office; there were offices for 360 assistant United States attorneys and over 350 support personnel. It was SOP when coming into the District if one did not know the exact location of an office.

When he arrived in Hernandez's office, he found no secretary. Daniel Hernandez, himself, greeted Oliver and led him into a utilitarian but comfortable inner office.

"Take a load off," said Hernandez after introducing himself. "I am going to be straight with you, Agent Quatraine, and I want the same from you. First off, I will repeat my admonition of yesterday on the phone. Don't talk about this meeting with anyone, not even your wife—for her own safety. You understand that I am dead serious about that?"

"You have made that perfectly clear."

"Second, I am going to tell you that you need a lawyer, a good one. You have truly stepped in it this time, and you need all the help you can get. I just got out of a meeting with one Henry Drake. I believe you know the man. He seems to know you. He laid some heavy stuff on you."

"He's a prince," Quatraine said.

"My sentiments as well. However, Mr. Quatraine, he is, or was, your colleague, not mine. The Spanish have an apt proverb: *Si duermes con los perros te levantes con pulgas.* Loosely translated: Lie down with dogs and you get up with fleas."

Quatraine's Spanish was good enough that he did not need the translation. It certainly fit him and his relationship with that cur, Drake. Quatraine nodded his understanding and agreement.

"He credits you as the mastermind of the whole caper—from planning to planting of evidence to the fiasco of execution. It appears that there is enough evidence to put you away for a long, long time, my man."

Hernandez paused to let the grimness of the statement sink in.

Quatraine was afraid that he was going to disgrace himself and cry.

"There is another side to all of this," he managed. "For one thing, Drake is the one who planned it. He just roped me in at the last."

"It may interest you to know that I have granted Henry Drake complete immunity from prosecution."

Oliver was stunned and felt completely defeated. He looked at Hernandez in bemusement.

"What!?" he exclaimed.

"You see, there seems to be more to this case than meets the eye. Drake convinced me in the presence of his lawyer and a *New York Times* reporter that he can clear up the disturbing details of the case that have been obscure up to this point in time. He mentioned the names of two of the highest officers in the United States government as being directly involved in a conspiracy in this affair, and gave me the names and titles of a host of others who were co-conspirators. Some only had guilty knowledge before the fact of plans for a felony—make that felonies, multiple. These alleged felonies were to be accomplished under the cloak of authority. He made so much out of your involvement as a heavy that I got to wondering if anyone could be as bad as all that who was so low on the Task Force totem pole. You see, I have done my homework. I want to give you a chance to explain in detail every little bit that you know."

"Just make a confession and take the whole rap? That about it?" Quatraine said ruefully. "How dumb do I appear to be?"

Oliver was more angry than depressed now, and that was clarifying for the function of his brain.

Hernandez continued to look completely unperturbed.

"You handle this anyway you want, Agent Quatraine. I'll tell you, though, if you help me fry bigger fish, I will see to it that you get a sweetheart deal. The catch is that you have to 'fess up to every detail—nothing left out—and before my deadline. I am going to have a general meeting in one month with all participants; and you will have to give me your answer well before then; let's say in two weeks."

Quatraine opened his mouth to speak.

"Don't," said Hernandez. "Not another word from you until you have a proper lawyer with you. You call me between now and two weeks from now with what I need to hear, and I will make a deal with you as good as your help warrants."

He gazed quietly and penetratingly into Quatraine's black eyes.

Oliver was constrained to believe him.

"Okay, you'll hear from me."

"I was sure I would. Now, I am going to repeat myself. Say nothing to anyone but your attorney about our dealings. If you do, it's all off, and you stand the gaff alone. I want you to enter the Witness Protection Program as of now. You may be able to get out after this whole mess clears up, but I want you protected and in my control until then. Agreed?"

Quatraine gulped. He felt like he was being pulled down by quicksand.

"What about my wife?"

"She'll have to come in too. I know this is disruptive, but the people we are about to challenge are quintessential Hegelians—what is useful to them must be good. They play for keeps."

Quatraine nodded his understanding. His depression deepened because from this day onward, his life was not his own.

Nancy Delgado was asleep in her own bed, which was unusual for her despite her celibate life. She had had three straight nights of bliss because nothing was happening in her case. Phil Craig continued to urge her to stay on, but her frustration was mounting. The bedside telephone rang, shaking the whole room. She had to remember to turn down the ring volume. She fumbled for it; stupid thing was hidden. There, under yesterday's *Washington Post* for some unknown reason. Four rings.

"Hello," she said dully.

The phone felt funny. She turned it the other way around. That seemed better.

"Hello," she said, this time into the speaker end.

"Nancy, wake up! Sorry to call you at this hour. Phil Craig calling. Look there's been a big breakthrough!"

Nancy transformed into an awake person instantly. She felt a powerful surge of adrenaline warm through her leaden limbs and vacant head.

"What is it? Is this for real?"

"Yeah. I was informed routinely because I am in the chain of command. Silberberg's team got a call from a snitch in the Movement. A man fitting Kennedy's description is holed up in an apartment building in Virginia Beach."

Craig gave her the address.

"He apparently doesn't know that he's been ratted out. I don't know if it's possible for you to do anything, but go down there with your guys and see if there is anything you can pick up. Kennedy is pretty resourceful. Maybe you can be in the right place at the right time for a change. Silberberg is mobilizing his team as we speak. They are going to fly out of Andrews."

"I'll give it my best shot," Nancy said and hung up.

She punched her telephone's speed dial for a conference call with Terrife and Bendell and told them what had transpired.

Terrife checked his watch.

"My ex lives in Norfolk. I use to go there all the time. I'm pretty sure there's a United red-eye flight that leaves Dulles about three-thirty. It's two-twenty now. If we hump, we can make it."

"That's our only chance. We will be persona non grata at Andrews. You hear all of that, David?"

"Yep, Bendell said.

He was the easiest of the three to wake up. He was already throwing on his clothes.

"See you guys at the United ticket counter at Dulles in half an hour. Red lights and sirens."

They made it with time to spare—about five minutes. They had to be forceful to get their weapons into the cargo hold, but their FBI IDs worked small miracles. Throughout the flight, the three agents urged the plane along, prayed for a tailwind, put a hex on all other airplanes in the sky; so, they could not interfere with United 132. Their luggage had been handled as VIP priority to avoid waiting at either end.

David rushed over to the Budget Car Rental booth and secured a mid-size sedan with his FBI Express card while the other two agents hauled the heavy luggage out to the sidewalk. The suitcases were packed with ordnance and were skimpy on clothes and toiletries. None of the three had bothered to bring a change of clothing. They forced the bags into the car's trunk, and the team broke every traffic law on the books getting to the address in Virginia Beach that Phil Craig had given them. It was peculiar; there was not a cop anywhere, just like in the movies.

"Can you believe this? I think we beat Silberberg and his COINTELPRO Nazis. I don't see a soul," Nancy said ebulliently.

Her adrenaline had plateaued at about ten times maximum output. She did not dare drink a cup of coffee for fear of going into orbit.

The apartment complex was a squat, angular, unlovely set of four preformed concrete slab buildings reminiscent of the USSR city of Leningrad, now St. Petersburg. They were all painted a peculiar shade of light gray-blue-green known locally as "haint blue" because the owner, R.M. Tate, was originally from the low country of South Carolina and Georgia, where the early inhabitants had insisted on using that particular color for its accepted property of warding of "haints" and other spooks that might try and enter a good Christian building. Tate had ordered three broad stripes of accent color to alleviate the depressing haint blue. The stripes encircled all four buildings in their upper thirds. The enlivening colors were aquamarine, chartreuse, and turquoise. The apartment complex was in need of reapplication of the flaking haint blue.

"Then let's us move in and grab the glory," Romaine said in a shouted whisper.

David was out of the car and opening the trunk. He did not have to be told twice. He had not come to chitchat. The three agents threw on flak jackets and helmets under blue FBI windbreakers. They looked official enough.

Randolph Kennedy's radio alarm had gone off, and he was trying to ignore the drone of Chuck Harder's voice, a recording of a tape of the Florida based talk show popular with the separatist-survivalist community. Subliminally, over the monotonous radio voice that was explaining a complicated facet of the globulist conspiracy theory, Randolph heard the FBI car pull up outside his building. In the midst of the radio and the background hum of morning street noises, the sleepy fugitive paid the sound of the FBI vehicle no particular mind. He had a full bladder and groaned at being awakened even partially to have to go and empty it. He gave a cursory look out the window—a pattern of habit he had unconsciously developed along with the habit of sleeping with one eye half open—since becoming a fugitive. Despite his habit, he had never seen anything; and he did not expect to see anything now. Since his hasty retreat from Timberlake Estates in Utah and his exit from Deer Trail, Colorado, he had not even had a close call. The nearest he had come to trouble was when a county mountie in Greenville, Mississippi had stopped him for having a brake light out. The people with whom he stayed in Greenville had admonished him for that.

"Y'all gotta 'spect that kinda thing in Missy Pissy. Be moah careful, ya heah?"

There was something out there. Randolph did a double take. He looked again. Three agents in clearly emblazoned FBI jackets carrying enough armament to stage a small war of their own were advancing up the sidewalk towards the entrance to the far south building in his complex. His urge to urinate vanished. His blood pressure and pulse rate climbed to full fight and flight status.

Randolph had always slept naked. Now, he jumped into his clothes, cursed his slip-on shoes for folding under at the heels. He left all of his clothes in the room and made a last very cursory look to see if he had left anything incriminating or of real value to his use as a fugitive, a fleeing fugitive. He bolted for the basement garage. He kept his money in the old truck, and the old truck was always ready to go for just such an emergency.

Four new truckloads of agents pulled up to the apartment complex. The man in charge of this new contingent, Gerald Silberberg—easily recognized by Randolph from his frequent television appearances—dispatched his teams to the several doors and a unit to cover the back of the building complex. He whispered orders into his walkie-talkie and made quick decisions.

Randolph watched the FBI agents' progress with morbid fascination from a basement window. He judged that they would all be preoccupied with their search inside and would not be prepared for what he had planned. He revved up the old truck's engine and hurtled up the parking structure's ramp and out of the building barely keeping four wheels on the pavement. The agents on the first floor heard the truck and rushed outside in time to see the battered vehicle roar full throttle down the street. The truck was out of sight before the first agent could get inside the first FBI vehicle.

"I just figured out the building layout, boss lady," Romaine was saying as the excitement began.

The three agents were standing on the second floor of Building 2. Suddenly, they became aware of the commotion starting outside. David looked out the window.

"Old pickup tearing outta here!"

The implication was obvious. Before any of the three could react, David reported that the entirety of Silberberg's teams were sprinting out of the apartment complex and streaking for their vehicles.

"You want us to join the cops and robbers chase, Nancy?"

"Too late," she said resignedly. "We'll just announce ourselves for nothing."

Silberberg's agents were piling into the four vehicles in a disorganized frenzy—the Keystone Kops scenario. All four vehicles were pointing in the direction opposite to that in which the old pickup had taken flight. The FBI trucks spun in an about face with the doors still closing on stragglers. The entourage roared up the street in hot pursuit looking at that moment like an old Laurel and Hardy movie sequence.

"So, Silberberg wins," David sighed.

"We'll see," Nancy said. "Kennedy has been pretty slick so far. Maybe he'll live to fight another day. What do you say to going to his hidey hole and getting a free peek."

"I'm all for getting first peeks, and I know where his pad is now. As I was saying when we were so rudely interrupted, I have figured out the layout of the place," Romaine repeated to his two colleagues.

The three agents walked directly to Building 4, following Agent Terrife's lead.

David banged on the door that corresponded to the number that Phil Craig had given them. There was no answer, and none was expected. He banged again, reaching his fist out from his position on the left side of the door. The other two agents were on the right side.

"Kick it down, Romaine," whispered Nancy.

"Ever consider trying the knob," whispered David back.

"Novel idea, but not standard practice. The manual is clear on the subject, and you definitely did not learn such a technique at the academy," she whisper-growled and wrinkled up her nose at him.

He reached out and tried the knob.

"*Voila!*" he said and laughed.

The door opened easily and noiselessly.

"I'm reporting this. The Bureau has no room for nonconformists," said Nancy with mock severity.

Romaine advanced into the room, both hands on his gun and his legs in the standard academy shooting stance. Nancy went in next, going to Romaine's left and assuming the same stance. Both agents kept in constant motion and looked about hurriedly. David brought up the rear. In less than a minute, they verified what they might have taken for granted; the fugitive was gone.

"All clear," Nancy said.

The Spartan two-room apartment was all but empty. There was nothing in the rear of the two rooms, the bed room. The main room contained a cot with a sleeping bag on it, a small table with a few dirty dishes, an unopened bottle of All Collection Grappa Di Moscata d'Arti still sitting on top, and a bill from the Checca Lodge on Islamarada in the Keys. On the floor were some newspapers and a AAA map."

"Not much help here," David said.

Nancy knelt down and picked up the map. She kicked the newspapers to see if there was anything else under them. There was nothing.

"Give them a quick look, you guys. I'll check the map," Nancy ordered, already unfolding it.

"I'm telling," said David with comic seriousness. "Let's see, interference with an official FBI investigation, tampering with evidence…"

"Removing evidence," Nancy added. "Look, he's traced his route here, has little circles on some areas, presumably where he stayed."

She refolded the map and put it into her inside jacket pocket.

"Nothing in the papers; thanks for your help," Romaine groused good naturedly turning a critical glance at David, who was too busy being funny.

"I suggest we beat a judicious retreat before Henrich Himmler Silberberg and his Gestapo agents decide to come back and finally figure out how to find this place," Nancy said.

She was already halfway to the door. Her antithesis towards Silberberg went way back. It had started at a cocktail party shortly after she graduated from the academy when she was having a glass of port wine. Silberberg characterized it as a "sissy drink" and intimated that she and the other female special agents should be relegated to keep company with the "don't ask, don't tell" sissies. He categorized Nancy into what he called the "pixies".

"You really don't like the guy, do you, Nancy?" Romaine asked.

"I really don't," she answered matter-of-factly.

Randolph never slowed down or went more than a single block without turning. He knew the cops were in hot pursuit of him, but he had not seen one of their vehicles anywhere since he bolted from the apartment complex. He was zigzagging a northerly trail in the general direction of Cape Henry and on around west towards Newport News. He could hear sirens in the distance, obviously coming in from several directions. He figured the town police and state highway patrol would block off 58—the straight shot to Norfolk— immediately. His only hope was to get to Newport News and Hampton; so, he could head out west on I-64 to Richmond or back down south to Norfolk and Portsmouth and get on 58 and 460 going west to Emporia.

He knew the truck's description would be going out to every law enforcement officer in a 100 mile radius, and it was only a matter of time before he was stopped. He looked around frantically for a place to hide or for a car to steal. He figured it was futile to try and hide; the cops would cordon off the area and close in on him. But he had no idea how to hot-wire a car. His criminal skills were only in the nascent stage of development. A vengeful thought flashed through his mind regarding the Tates—who owned the apartment complex—and about the Bock brothers of Tabernash, Colorado, who had to have betrayed him; but it was fleeting. He had too much else to think about.

Silberberg was in the second car.

"Get up front, you dummy," he yelled at the driver.

The driver honked his horn in a constant staccato while his chief punched his walkie-talkie trying to communicate with the car in front. The other vehicle finally got the message and pulled to the side to let Silberberg pass.

"Any signs of the perp?" the senior agent asked.

"No, sir," the driver answered.

"Any idea where he's going?"

"Not really. Probably up towards 58 would be my guess. That's the shortest route out of here. I would think the last thing he'd want would be to be to get cornered in Virginia Beach. It would only be a matter of time before we closed in on him."

"In the meantime, we are playing around in a Chinese fire drill," Silberberg complained.

He calmed himself down and began to work his radio-phone efficiently. He found the police band and ordered an all-points bulletin giving Kennedy's and his truck's description, a best estimate of his whereabouts, and his likely route of escape. It seemed pointless to wander around in the area of short blocks.

"Let's get to the highway. Maybe we can beat them there," he ordered.

The four-vehicle caravan—sirens blaring and red lights flashing—roared through the residential streets scattering children and dogs.

White Magnolia Street was run-down with old cars, pink plastic flamingoes on lawns, and trash on the driveways and in the gutters. The neighborhood was staggeringly colorful. Viewed from a distance the houses looked like so many M&Ms strung out like beads. It seemed deserted which suited Randolph perfectly. The day was too hot for even the children to be out. Randolph looked into his rearview mirror for perhaps the thousandth time and convinced himself that he had eluded his pursuers for the time being. The sirens seemed to be growing more distant. He looked nervously up and down the street and could not see a soul.

There was a line of garishly painted four wheel drive trucks with oversized wheels on the right side of the street with two more in the driveway. One of those had a partially finished design of flames and a naked girl in the process of being emblazoned on the driver's side cab door. It was a cottage industry car painting establishment. No one seemed to be around.

Randolph parked behind one of the trucks. He waited for a few seconds. No one appeared. He got out and casually walked up the line of trucks like a scrutinizing and admiring customer. It was like criminal Christmas. All four trucks had keys in the ignition. Even the gas gauges read full. Randolph was going to have to have one of those souped-up and garish trucks by subterfuge if possible, or by main strength and awkwardness if necessary.

He figured that the latter option would attract a maelstrom of attention, and he would have a city full of Latino hotheads on his tail as he roared off with the cops following close behind. He was more afraid of them than of the FBI, knowing about their legendary driving skills. The other option—that of subterfuge—had more to offer, he thought. He planned to knock; and if no one responded, he would brazen it out and simply drive off in the lead truck. If someone was home, he would leave a deposit and go for a drive from which he would never return; or he could even pay cash for the best of the lot and leave behind a beautiful and unexciting memory. He walked purposefully up to the door of the house and knocked vigorously.

"Jess?" someone called from inside.

"I am interested in buying one of your trucks," Randolph yelled.

He prayed that the voice would open the door shortly; so, he could get out of the open.

He heard a lumbering set of steps advancing towards the door. Just his luck, King Kong. The door opened and a gargantuan dark-skinned man filled the doorway. His face was a huge, even white-toothed smile.

"Helloo, brother," boomed the loudest, most affable voice Randolph had ever heard. "You come for the truck?"

Randolph laughed to himself at this little stroke of dumb luck.

"Yes," he said. "I take it this is the right place. I had a little trouble finding you."

"Hey, I know how it is. You gotta be in the Tongan network to find any of us, and we all look alike. Anyhoo, brother, let's go have a look. Just finished it yesterday. It's a work of art, if you don't mind me bragging a little."

He beamed. Randolph found himself grinning, too. It was infectious and seemed the thing to do. He still kept looking over his shoulder for FBI cars.

"Looka this," the huge Tongan said, pride showing all over his face and in his body language.

It was the second truck in line, a brilliant metallic blue with some sort of sea god throwing flaming spears along the sides of the bed and cab. The hood was emblazoned with a huge Medusa head in magentas, flame oranges, and luminescent whites and multiple shades of red. It was a vision of loveliness. Randolph had to suppress a laugh; now here was just the thing to ensure anonymity.

"Great!" Randolph exulted as if he really did like the nightmare truck.

Part of him did not want to hurt the enthusiastic giant's feelings.

"Okay if I take it now? I can't wait to get in and gun it."

"Know how you feel, and that's the agreement. You brought the rest of the bread?"

"Yeah. How much for the final damages?"

The huge Tongan looked at him carefully for signs of guile or signs that he was going to renege on the deal. Maybe the Anglo was developing the early stages of Alzheimer's.

"You're not tryin' to do no bargainin' this late date, are you bro?"

There was just a hint of new darkness in the powerfully built man's eyes. He was wearing a muscle shirt that seemed two sizes too small. Randolph watched the muscles bulge and ripple.

"Nope. I have the cash. I just forgot the exact final cost."

"You gave us five hundred earnest money, man. You owe $3,500 balance."

The man was all business and made his account statement as if he were explaining to a four year old.

Four thousand dollars for a paint job!? Randolph kept his face bland.

"I'll go out to my truck and get it."

He went back to the beat up old truck for the box of money. Thankfully, the Tongan stayed by his handsome creation. Randolph tried not to hurry, but he moved right along. He counted out $4,500 in hundreds, having had a flash of inspiration.

"I really like what you did for me, man. It's real art."

The Tongan smiled shyly.

"I would like you to do my old clunker up exactly the same way. I want an exact twin. I'm gonna get it done for my wife as a surprise for her birthday."

"Bon idea," said the Tongan who, evidently, was able to conceive in his mind's eye the magnificence of such a creation even from such a challenging piece of junk. "You wanna put down a down payment?"

"Here's the thirty-five hundred for this one. And here's a thou for the old one. Looks like you'll need to do more body work to get that one ready. Give me a call when you have the final estimate, okay?"

"You got a deal. And you got yourself an Unga Mobile. We be famous in all the Tidewater area. You see. People from all around gonna step up and ask how you got the Ungas to make you a masterpiece."

He smiled broadly. His whole body showed his pride and gladness. It did Randolph's heart good just to see such pleasure, and to have actually contributed to it was little short of sublime.

"Mind helping me move the boxes out of my truck bed? I'll have to get going. Have a great day, Mr. Unga."

"Call me Matthew," the big man said.

He was the personification of the hospitality for which Tongans are famous. Randolph could hardly believe his good fortune. He felt like he was due a piece of good luck after his hair-raising morning. It just seemed right that his turn had come due. Matthew Unga helped transfer Randolph's precious cargo.

"I be takin' this heap aroun' the back. Might give the place a bad name," he laughed. "You have yourself a fine day, y'hear? Fine ting doin' business with you. Gimme call in say week…no, ten day. That cool?"

"That's cool," Randolph said. "I'll be out of town for maybe three weeks. I don't need it 'till then. The wife's birthday isn't for more'n a month."

Matthew drove the old truck around the back of his house and out of sight of the street. Randolph drove slowly away trying not to jerk the gears that were unfamiliar to him. He would have liked to stay around and see what happened when the real owner/customer came by to pick up his Unga Mobile. His conscience bothered him enough to leave an additional $30,000 cash in the old truck's glove compartment to pay for a new truck. He also thought that the gesture would keep the Tongans from running to the police any time soon.

Besides the money that had been left in the truck in case of a hasty departure, Randolph had picked up his bag of handy disguises as he fled the apartment complex. Now, he stopped in a Chevron station and took the bag into the station's rest room. He did a credible job of making himself into a bearded hippie or gypsy, even adding an earring on the right ear. Someone had told him that gays wore earrings on the left if they wished to convey the message that they were available, and Randolph could do without any further complications. He sucked in a deep breath and drove off in his brilliantly decorated Unga Mobile. At the approach to highway 58, there was a police road block with traffic backed up behind it for half a mile. Tempers were fraying in the bake oven heat and humidity. Randolph kept on north along the seashore to miss it.

Between Seashore State Park and the Cape Henry Memorial, he came to an unavoidable road block. He was intensely nervous. His bladder felt urgent again. He was afraid that he might humiliate himself before his turn to be inspected by the cop arrived. He was sweating. He felt blaringly conspicuous and knew that he looked like a kid caught with his hand in the cookie jar. He worked on his facial muscles to get rid of his panicked expression.

The Virginia State patrolman was approaching, and he looked bored, hot, tired, and annoyed. Randolph saw the trooper smile at the archetypal Virginia tawdriness of his truck.

"Good morning, sir. May I see your driver's license and the vehicle's registration?"

Chapter Forty-Eight

"What's going on, officer?"

"Just routine."

Randolph handed him his phony driver's license. The trooper looked carefully at the picture. It was the same beard, at least. Randolph had had to rummage hard to find the right driver's license. It was a Utah license. Nobody was perfect.

"The registration, please."

Randolph felt a sharp pang of panic. He had not thought of that. The registration would not be in his name. He did not even know what name or other information would be on the registration certificate or even if there was a registration in the truck. He was now sweating profusely.

"Hot day," Randolph said, and mopped his brow.

He leaned over and popped open the glove compartment. A plastic cover containing all of the vehicle's documents was in prominent sight. The real owner was a neat freak, Randolph observed. That was a small favor. He picked up the packet and fished out the registration. Perez Hidalgo Villaneuva, it read.

"This your truck, sir?" the trooper asked.

Behind him several cars began to honk their horns. The trooper gave them an angry glance over his shoulder. The horns stopped except one. That one kept on persistently, creating a loud and disconcerting interruption.

The trooper frowned, handed Randolph back his registration materials, and said, "Wait here. The moron back there better have something wrong with his horn, or he picked the wrong guy to annoy."

He gave Randolph a smile of resignation over the shortcomings of mankind that Randolph returned in sympathy, and strode back to the offending car.

Randolph watched him walk away then stop three cars behind Randolph's Unga Mobile. The honking stopped. In his rearview mirror, Randolph watched with satisfaction as the trooper stood back from the car. The driver got out complaining at the top of his lungs. The trooper made the angry driver assume the position, spread his legs, and began a methodical and thorough body search. Randolph slowly pulled out onto the asphalt and drove away. He expected a hail of bullets to come through his back window, the wail of a dozen sirens, and a bunch of cop cars to come at him from every direction.

None of that happened. Randolph laughed a little at his overheated imagination. He looked in his rearview mirror and saw the trooper at the window of the next car in line, doing his routine check. The fugitive hoped that he had been forgotten in the press of angry motorists abusing the law officer.

CHAPTER FORTY-NINE

Nancy Delgado studied the map she had purloined from Randolph's apartment hiding place. It was a triple A map of the whole U.S.A. There were routes highlighted in fluorescent chartreuse from San Francisco, California to Heber, Utah to Sault Ste. Marie, Michigan to Frankfort, Kentucky to Pineville, West Virginia, to Greenville, Mississippi to Islamorada, Florida, and to Virginia Beach, Virginia. There was also a direct fuchsia highlight from Virginia Beach up to Richmond on I-64 with an X there that Nancy interpreted as a stopover. The fuchsia continued up into West Virginia and followed I-81 to Knoxville, Tennessee where there was an other X. The line began again and went along I-40 all the way across the country with Xs at Jackson, Mississippi, Lonoke, Arkansas, El Reno, Oklahoma and Stanley, New Mexico. The fuchsia line ended there, but there were pencil lines going up Arizona 285 to Denver and on to Cheyenne, both of which had Xs and question marks. Another pencil line went towards the west on I-40. That line ended in an arrow point somewhere in the Mojave Desert near Ludlow, California with a question mark above the arrow point. There were disconnected pencil lines along I-80 from Cheyenne towards Salt Lake City and along old Highway 40 through Rabbit Ears Pass, Colorado and into eastern Utah. That dotted line ended in Vernal, Utah. There was a double flange on that arrow.

The three agents cruised along the main streets of Virginia Beach listening to the police band on their scanner. It was full of nothing but Randolph Kennedy, his old pickup truck, the status of the many roadblocks, the progress of setting up surveillance in the bus stations and airports, and the recruitment of ever more officers. It was the biggest manhunt in Virginia's history. An hour had passed since the old truck had careened out of the apartment house, and no sign of the elusive fugitive had been picked up. Even the confession and conspiracy loonies were silent.

"Let's go into Norfolk," Nancy said. "We can wait there. I need to call Craig. I think our rabbit squeezed under the fence."

Delgado, Terrife, and Bendell spent the long day monitoring the police frequencies and calling back and forth to Phil Craig's office. By dusk it was obvious that they were not going to find him. Nancy felt a grudging admiration for the resourceful amateur out there eluding the army of professionals. She was more than secretly pleased that Silberberg had not been able to reap the glory on TV.

The following morning the three agents ate their breakfasts at the Norfolk Sizzler. The eggs were watery; the toast was tasteless Wonder Bread; and the coffee was insipid.

"Brings back memories, doesn't it?" cracked David.

"No wonder they had to consider Chapter 11," said Romaine.

"Now what, boss lady?" David asked after downing his second orange juice.

At least they had been able to follow the directions on the concentrate can.

"We go back to Utah. I think it's time to lean on that McDonald guy with the funny first name again. The map gets pretty fuzzy over there, but it's obvious that Kennedy's headed in that general direction. I've been sure all along that that old polygamist knows more than he's telling."

"You ever think this might be a plant? Old Kennedy seems to be a pretty devious character. I wouldn't put it past him, would you?" asked Romaine.

He had shoved the remainder of his breakfast aside mostly uneaten.

"It occurred to me, Romaine, but it's all we've got. I would happily entertain a better idea," Nancy answered.

"How about home and a two day sleep?" David said dryly.

"How about a more productive idea, gentlemen?"

"Utah again. Good old plain vanilla bovine Utah. If we have to sit on our cans in one of those hick towns without even being able to buy a beer for another couple of weeks, somebody's gonna have to put me in a straight jacket," David muttered.

"We can go to a hoedown or a rodeo," Romaine said, pronouncing it road-a-o, like an over educated easterner. "Or we can watch a quilting bee or some other kind of bee. I hear there's lots of bees out there."

He laughed and the mood of all three agents began to lighten.

466

When Gwen Chambers first broached the subject of going to someplace called Midway, Utah to a resort called Dastrup's Mountain Spa to her editor, William Fitzgerald, he laughed.

"This better be a joke," he said.

"No, quite serious, sir."

She explained the meetings and calls with Randolph Kennedy and attorney Hartley Proctor. Fitzgerald remained dubious but finally gave in.

Proctor was more difficult. It took thirty minutes of persuading and a guarantee that the *New York Times* would pay for first class travel expenses and five hundred dollars a day to cover his extremely valuable time away from his practice. This had to be guaranteed by contract even if the venture proved fruitless. Everyone involved was becoming edgy. Randolph Kennedy had that effect on people.

They were pleasantly surprised when Gwen and Proctor saw what a beautiful resort it was and in such a magnificent setting. The Mountain Spa sat on the edge of a low rise in the middle of the Midway portion of Heber Valley. It had a 360 degree panorama of the Wasatch Range of the Rocky Mountains which seemed to leap out of the earth and into the clean blue sky. The grounds were lush green, and the buildings were right out of Switzerland. Gwen and Proctor took rooms in separate buildings and began a busy schedule of sunning, swimming, golfing, horseback riding, and stewing in the warm brown mineral water tubs while they waited for Randolph Kennedy to make his clandestine appearance. It was nasty work, but someone had to do it.

Gerald Silberberg gave up after two weeks of exhaustive search and two score arrests of suspected Militia Movement members and neighbors who were in the same apartment complex from which Randolph Kennedy had escaped. The unit's search of the apartment where the fugitive had stayed revealed nothing; no trace of the escape truck turned up; and Silberberg was infuriated.

He was now convinced that the answer was to offer a substantial reward that would tempt an apostle into Judashood. The President's Task Force was persuaded to put up an offer of one million dollars, tax exempt, for information leading to the arrest and conviction of the notorious fugitive. The offer was trumpeted on every news program, talk show, police drama, and as paid advertisements on PBS. With nothing better to do, Silberberg and his 112 man strong unit returned to Washington to wait.

Ted Coleman summoned the ranking officials of the Bureau to a conference regarding public enemy number one. Phillip Craig received notification of the impending meeting and told Nancy Delgado to be there with him. It was not in Gerald Silberberg's nature to accept a defeat gracefully or philosophically, much less to eat a portion of crow. He displayed his anger in the meeting.

"Someone tipped the perp off that we were on our way or when we arrived at the apartment complex in Virginia Beach. I will know who that was before this case is closed. I have my suspicions."

He looked at Nancy Delgado pointedly.

"For the time being, I need a bigger budget and more agents to get Kennedy."

It was the time-honored FBI response to failure once again: there had not been enough money; therefore we were unable to accomplish the mission; ergo, we need more money. It was hardly the first time the people in that room had heard the litany, but no one hinted at an objection.

Nancy sat still and refused to allow her facial muscles to betray any acknowledgment of the near truth of Silberberg's accusation. She was sure that he could not know that she had been there, but her coming to the meeting was a mistake calculated to add fuel to his suspicions. Phil Craig seldom made political blunders, but this was one of them.

Silberberg was well aware of the overt competition between the director—his liege lord—and the assistant director—Nancy Delgado's object of allegiance. His natural paranoia coupled with his refusal to look inward for a cause for failure had led him to the conclusion that somehow Nancy Delgado had sabotaged him.

He was looking at her when he said, "The man obviously has resources well beyond what we might have originally presumed. The Movement network is more extensive and efficient than we gave them credit for. Kennedy has demonstrated twice now that he has no intention of being taken alive. The ante has been raised a full measure. The man appears to be issuing a challenge to the government of the United States comparable to the historical Whiskey Rebellion, one that we have to meet. We cannot allow a publicized scofflaw to persist. Next time out, we will be more definitive."

His eyes narrowed into a lupine penetrating threat directed at Nancy as well as at Randolph Kennedy, or, at least, she saw it that way. She shivered inwardly for Randolph Kennedy and knew that the longevity of her career would be determined by the Kennedy Affair.

Oliver Quatraine had no money. More accurately, he had no access to his money. His savings were nothing great, but they would have allowed him to hire a reasonable attorney. The Witness Protection Program had its inefficiencies; and one of them was that the money to establish a new life—even a temporary one—lagged well behind the physical move into a new situation. The ability to remove an individual from an old life and into a new one was the very picture of speed and efficiency. Having accepted the choice of entering the WPP, he and Sylvia were virtual prisoners in a luxury hotel room. His efforts to find an attorney were futile because the second sentence in his conversation with the prospective attorney was always, "How are you going to pay me, Mr. Quatraine?" in one form or another, addressed to one pseudonym or another. Oliver had no answer.

He broke down and called Daniel Hernandez at the number in the U.S. Attorney's headquarters in the Justice Building.

"This is Oliver Quatraine," he announced as soon as Hernandez came on the line. "You said that I couldn't talk seriously with you until I had a lawyer. That is a catch-22. You put me in the WPP, and I can't touch my money. Lawyers don't talk to people who have no money. What am I supposed to do?"

He was angry and frightened. It made Daniel Hernandez smile at his telephone.

"Thought you'd never ask. This is becoming a contest of considerable proportions, Agent Quatraine. I will use my good offices to get you an attorney who is up to the task. Remember that stuff in the Miranda rights? We take it quite seriously here at the U.S. Attorney's Office. Sit tight, I'll have an attorney knocking on your door tomorrow or the next day at the latest.

"Thanks, I guess," said Quatraine.

He knew that he had been overtaken by a master manipulator.

"Don't thank me, Quatraine. And don't forget for a second that you and I are on opposite sides in this encounter. You will find me fair. Don't let that cause you to lower your guard. Good-bye."

CHAPTER FIFTY

Nancy Delgado and her two fellow FBI agents were given the broad okay from Phil Craig to keep on after Kennedy and to try their luck in Utah again. Craig agreed with Delgado that that was as likely a spot as any for him to be found. As soon as they disembarked from their plane in Salt Lake City, the three agents headed south and east to Heber, intent on seeing Nephi McDonald.

The gate to Fort McDonald was locked and barred as usual. David rang the intercom buzzer.

"Who is it?" came a soft female voice.

"Federal agents to see Mr. McDonald. We just came to talk. Please open the gates."

"Just a moment, I'll check."

In a few minutes, Nephi McDonald himself came walking down the driveway. He was dressed in bib overalls and held his hands palm up in front of him.

Delgado said, "Gentlemen, let us respond in like fashion."

She took off her shoulder holster and stepped out of the car.

"What can I do for you federal agents?" Nephi said from across the bars of the gate.

"We need to talk, Mr. McDonald. How about letting us in for a face-to-face talk like ladies and gentlemen?"

Nephi's response was abrupt in contrast to Nancy's courteous request.

"I'm busy. Say what you have to say through the gate, and we can all get back to our business."

His voice was as cold as flint.

Nancy sighed, "Mr. McDonald, we mean you no harm, not even ill will."

"You're from the government, and you've come to help," he sneered.

"In the present case, that is a fact, despite your sarcasm. Look, we want to protect Randolph Kennedy. We can only do that with him in custody. There are others—lots of others—who won't be so dainty. They won't hesitate to kill him on sight. They regard him as a mass murderer. Perhaps more importantly, he beat up that Colorado policeman, Wild Bill Cody something or other. I'm sure you are aware of that. He is a marked man."

"What do you think of this whole affair, Missy?"

"It's Special Agent Nancy Delgado, Mr. McDonald. And I don't know what to think about his guilt or innocence. That's for a legitimate court of law to decide. But I do know that he is in grave danger if he does not give himself up to the three of us and soon. Is he here?"

"No."

"I want to believe you."

"Believe whatever you want."

"Would you tell me if he were here? Will you tell me if he does come back?"

"No to both questions. No personal offense, Special Agent Delgado, but I don't trust you. That's a generic mistrust, mind you, but it includes the lot of you just the same."

"You can confirm all of this with Phil Craig. He's the assistant director of the Bureau. Here's his extension at FBI headquarters."

She wrote it on the back of her card.

"Would you at least give Kennedy the message?"

"I might if I should ever hear from the man. Depends."

"Fair enough. Here's my card with Craig's extension written on the back. Get Randolph to call me. Tell him he can give himself up to me and to my associates here and that we will protect him. No one else is going to give him a chance, I feel sure of that. Just tell him to call me. What can that much hurt?"

"I'll see what I can do," the taciturn man said, "I'm not saying that I'm in contact with the man—fugitive, you say?"

He turned slowly around and went back up the road towards his house.

"Likeable guy," David said.

"Now, what?" Romaine asked.

"Let's go into town. I hear they're having the state high school rodeo finals tonight. Ought to be great."

Both men—city born and reared—groaned.

Back in the house, Nephi dialed Niels Dastrup's insurance office on Heber's Old Mill Road. Niels was an eccentric. He depended on his secretary of twenty-seven years completely when he was out of the office. She could run the place every bit as well as he could. But when he was in the office in person, he insisted on answering the phone himself despite the office chaos that usually ensued.

"Dastrup."

"This is a mountain friend," Nephi said.

"I'm listening," Niels said.

"You got a guest coming in to the Mountain Spa. He's in a heap of trouble. There's a fibbie—a woman—who wants to see him. She asked polite. I think you should tell the man. He may need some help from her and her two toadies. This sounds real to me. You and I both know that he can't stay out forever. You got a pencil and some paper?"

"Go ahead."

Nephi gave him Special Agent Delgado's message, including the invitation to confirm her offer with the Assistant Director Phil Craig and hung up.

If it was important enough for Nephi McDonald to call about, it was worth Niels Dastrup's time to drive over to Midway and give the message.

He told his secretary to "hold down the fort and try not to screw things up too bad until I can get back and salvage the operation."

She stuck out her tongue at him. He fortified himself with a homeopathic pill from a brightly colored box labeled with fluorescent lettering: *Cell Tech Super Blue-Green. Super fuel for your Brain and Body.*

It took Niels thirty-five minutes to drive the five miles from Heber to Midway because Midway Lane was under construction—again! Niels mused that there were only two seasons in Utah—winter and construction. He cursed and complained every foot of the way. The traffic was incredible. Twenty-five years previously, the citizens of Heber had had to all but start a war to get their first traffic light. Now it was traffic lights and four lanes everywhere until you got to the lane. Even the old south fields were being developed to further ensnarl the traffic of the twenty-five year old residential development with no arterial thoroughfare. The state of Utah had refused to expand the road system preferring to expend precious UDOT resources on more politically important Wasatch Front megalopolises. It was a nightmare to get through now that the state had finally gotten around to making some improvements.

Niels parked his pink caddie—a restored 2002 Brougham, pre-electric cars model—that was his pride and joy and worth a good laugh to most of his friends. The caddie's bumper sported three stickers: "Have you cleaned your assault rifle today?", "Honk if you Hate Congress, the People's enemy number one.", and "Ready to try Leaderless Resistance? Ask me". He had a reserved spot—hallowed ground—at his resort. God save anyone who had the temerity to park in it. He looked around to see if he had attracted any attention. No one paid him any mind; he was a fixture at the resort. It was his, after all. He walked down Dumpf Noodle Strassa between the village bakery and the tobacconist's shop and hurried into the main stables at the end of Alte Strassa. The stables were spacious, painted bright colors—even the floor—and were cleaner than most people's homes. You could not have Easterners or Californians—whom he considered to be the same ilk—thinking that horses smelled bad or made messes. It was bad for business, and he had to do business even with those liberals.

Niels walked past small groups of cleaning people, grooms, and stable workers calling out to each of them by name. In the back, he climbed up a sturdy ladder into the loft. There was a small office in the middle of the loft, surrounded by bales of hay and sacks of reinforced oats. He knocked on the office door.

"It's Dastrup," he said.

The door opened a crack, then widely.

"What brings you here?"

It was Randolph Kennedy.

"Got a message from our much married mutual friend."

Niels had long ago adopted the presumption that the walls had ears, and that concern had intensified since Kennedy's arrival a couple of days before. He would be able to rest a whole lot easier when the wanted man decided to leave.

"Seems he had a visit from a fibbi named Nancy Delgado. She gave him her card. Here's the info. I guess she all but begged him to tell you to give yourself up to her. And to do it soon. She more'n hinted that there might be some bad fibbies out there with evil designs on your person."

He wore a theatrically astonished face, like he had never heard of such a thing before.

"You could knock me over with a feather as well," Randolph laughed.

He took the paper with Delgado's information on it.

"Makes me uncomfortable that the fibbies are this close. How did they figure it out so fast? I stopped believing in coincidences this year."

"Don't underestimate them. They are vain and media glory hogs, but they're very efficient. And you can buy anybody, you just have to have the right price," Dastrup said.

"Sadly, I'm learning that's true. I think the net is tightening. It's only a matter of time. Look, Niels, I'll be out of here by tomorrow night. I have a couple of things I need to do, then I just might take the lady fibbi up on her offer. Thanks for your help. Hang in there for one more day."

Randolph went to his cache of money and brought out $30,000.

"Here, please get me an untraceable used car, one that no one will take a second look at, and one that's up to some hard travel. I have to have it in a couple of days. I won't ask you anything more. You've been a prince."

He held out his hand and the two men shook.

Gwen Chambers executed a perfect half-gainer into the Mountain Spa pool by moonlight. She cut through the pool water with scarcely a ripple and glided underwater to the far end of the pool. When she came up at the shallow end, Randolph Kennedy was kneeling above her on the pool deck.

"Greetings," he said. "That was very nice. Looks like you're having fun. Could you spare a little time for me?"

She climbed immediately out of the resort's pool, and he handed her a fluffy white towel.

He said, "Meet me in room 212 as soon as you dry off and change. Call Mr. Proctor for the meeting. It will have to be brief, and I will have to leave immediately after."

"Okay," she said.

It was approaching midnight, and she was not sure how Hartley Proctor would respond to being awakened and summoned peremptorily to a clandestine meeting.

In her room Gwen toweled off briskly, bringing a flush to her skin. She put on a pair of sweats and called Proctor.

"Hello," came his sleepy voice.

'It's Gwen. He's here."

Proctor was suddenly wide awake.

"Where?"

"Room 212. He wants us to meet him there right now. There seems to be some urgency. I think he feels pressured to get away tonight."

"I'll be there in five minutes."

He hung up.

The reporter and the lawyer met in the hallway outside 212. Proctor tapped lightly on the door, and Randolph opened it after taking a look through the security peep hole.

"C'mon in, Ms. Chambers. I presume this is Mr. Proctor."

"Yes, Randolph, Hartley Proctor."

Gwen closed the door while the two men shook hands.

"Sorry for all the cloak and dagger. Things are getting a little more hairy all the time."

"I need to hear all about it, Mr. Kennedy," said Proctor. "I am presuming that you are willing to have me represent you, is that correct?"

"Yes. I need to trust someone. So far Ms. Chambers has done all right by me, and you come highly recommended by her and her paper. Why don't we get started?"

"This will be attorney-client privileged, Mr. Kennedy. I suggest that Ms. Chambers wait in the other room during our discussion, then the three of us can plot strategy."

The attorney looked apologetically at Gwen, who merely shrugged.

"I can take a hint," she said.

She smiled and left the two men alone in the kitchen.

"Start from the beginning and don't leave out anything, even if you think it incriminates you. I can't work with inadequate information, especially when the other side might possess that missing information. No matter what you've done, I want you to hold back nothing from me. I assure you that it will go no further than me."

Randolph told Proctor every detail—except once again—he withheld the fact of having the vast sum of cash. It seemed to him to be his last most vital protection.

It was two-thirty in the morning when Randolph finished. He and Proctor stretched and had coffee.

"Let's include Gwen, all right? For what I have in mind, we'll need her," Proctor said.

Gwen was asleep on Randolph's bed. She awakened and was ready to listen as soon as Randolph and Hartley Proctor came into the room.

"Here's what I have in mind," Hartley began. "It will seem a bit audacious, but hear me out. First, as soon as I get back to New York, I will file a lawsuit against the FBI, ATF, and the President's Task Force for willful and wrongful destruction of Mr. Kennedy's property, for endangering his life, for malicious prosecution, for use of stolen government evidence to incriminate Mr.

Kennedy wrongfully under the color of federal authority—a breach of his constitutional rights. I propose to ask for the outlandish sum of $100,000,000.

"I expect that will get their attention. Gwen, you have your story. Make it as public as possible. Get yourself on the talk show circuit, and I will do the same. Also, I would like you to do one other thing. You were approached by the same Agent Delgado who left a message for Randolph to give himself up to her and her two fellow agents. I think we should take her up on her offer. Randolph has agreed. He asked that the meeting be in a month or so because he has some things to do before he gives himself up. Get Delgado to include her boss, Phil Craig. I know him, and I will be able to negotiate sensibly with him. If you discount his blatant personal ambition, he is about the only honest cop left in the federal system.

"I will contact the U.S. Attorney's Office as Randolph's lawyer and coordinate a meeting with them on all issues at the time of your surrender."

Proctor looked over at Randolph for a gesture of agreement. Randolph inclined his head.

"We will do the surrender in the U.S. Attorney's Office in front of all kinds of credible witnesses. That should ensure Randolph's safety. I have in mind a rather dramatic meeting if I can swing it. I hope we can strike a compromise in that meeting that will serve your interests, Randolph, and give you the biggest exclusive of your career, Gwen. Publicity will be of the utmost value. Questions?"

There remained only the arrangements for future communications. Randolph left the room first. It was still dark outside.

CHAPTER FIFTY-ONE

Randolph walked a mile and a half west across the winding lanes of Midway Valley in the direction of Wasatch Mountain and the old Homestead Resort, the erstwhile competitor of Dastrup's Mountain Spa. He had taken the precaution of having the used car Niels had bought for him—with the cache of money in the trunk—be parked in the Homestead's parking lot. He started his walk as soon as he left Ms. Chambers and Mr. Proctor; so, it was still fully dark out on a moonless night. Nonetheless, Randolph frequently looked back over his shoulder and listened intently for foreign sounds as he moved swiftly along the quiet rural streets. He was dressed in dark clothing; and although no one could have seen him unless they came within fifteen feet of him, he remained his usual paranoid self. He saw no one, and there were no car lights. This section of town was largely inhabited by farmers who went to bed early, got up early, and worked hard. They had no truck with late night carousing.

When he reached the Homestead parking lot, he made sure there was no one around before he approached the car. He circled the lot staying in the fringe of trees or along the fence or in the umbra of the large conical limestone geothermal hot pot on the north. When he was certain that there was no one there to pay attention to him, he moved quickly to the car and drove away.

The car was a nondescript Ford—the best characteristic of the make—so far as Randolph was concerned. It was nearly ten years old, but Niels had assured him that it was in excellent running condition. He had had Niels arrange to turn in his brilliant blue and flame-decorated truck for the sedate four door sedan at Herb's High Klass Kars in Amarillo, Texas. Herb was a fellow member of the Movement. Herb's son, Freddie, had driven the vehicle to Heber as a favor to Niels and without requiring an explanation for the hurry. Along the way, Freddie had stopped by three airport long-term parking lots and expropriated sets of license plates from an assortment of different automobiles from several different states so that Randolph would be able to substitute the plates from time to time as necessity required, or his paranoia dictated.

Now, Randolph headed down Provo Canyon on 189 to I-15. When he was convinced that no one had followed him, he turned north. He figured to arrive in Anchorage in four or five days of hard driving up the Alaskan-Canadian Highway.

FBI Director Ted Coleman put in a call to Phil Craig.

"Yes, Mr. Director," Craig answered after noting his caller ID digital readout.

"I have some questions about one of the agents who seems to think that she works for you exclusively."

"And who would that be?"

"Special Agent Nancy Delgado."

"What about her?"

"Agents on assigned duty in a little town of Heber, Utah report seeing her and her two subordinates, Terrife and Bendell, there. The agents on official assigned duty were part of Gerald Silberberg's OPINTELPRO team on the hunt for Randolph Kennedy. I want to know what Delgado, Terrife, and Bendell are doing there."

For a moment, Craig thought about lying or denying. He did not know exactly what his three agents might have told the others; so, he hedged.

"They were following up on a lead from a confidential source regarding Kennedy. I did not know whether or not it would pan out; so, I thought it ought to be checked out before I troubled Silberberg. I know he's been working his tail off on that case, and I didn't want to pass on a false avenue for him to follow. He seems to be doing great work and needs all the help he can get."

"Um-hmm."

There was a period of quiet on the line.

"And have you anything to pass on to me, Phil?"

His voice had a distinctly peremptory tone, one of the many things Phil Craig disliked about Ted Coleman. He did not care at all to have anyone talk down to him.

Delgado had given him a report the previous day. She and her agents were almost certain that Kennedy had been in Utah's Wasatch County area very recently and was perhaps still there. They had received a tip from one of the ATF agents working undercover in the Mountain Militia that an important transient package was being moved through their area, and they were nervous about it. The exact words of a communiqué that had been circulated, according to the ATF agent were: "Brothers of the Mountain tops, give assistance to the brother in need of our help. The One-World Government Conspiracy is after him. He is a symbol of the resistance of Patriotic Americans. He may need wheels, money, or means of defense. Be prepared for a call." Delgado and her men were concentrating on the town of Midway, where the informant had heard that Kennedy was being harbored.

"Very little, Mr. Director," Craig told his boss, "Apparently there are four little towns in this Wasatch County, all in a cloistered valley. The latest report—unverified—was that our man was seen in a cabin in rural Wallsburg at the south end of the valley. I was about to call you, but it doesn't look like anything of a great lead. It's something at least."

He kept his voice neutral and objective. Lying to Coleman was becoming easier as it was becoming habitual. Besides, everything he said was true; it was just that he omitted some truth.

"Thanks for the tip, Phil. I'll be in touch."

Director Coleman's voice dripped with sarcasm.

"Let me know how it turns out," Craig replied.

Gwen e-mailed her article to William Fitzgerald at the *Times* editors' desk. She broke the news of a second meeting with Kennedy and of his defense case having been accepted by none other than Hartley Proctor. She quoted Proctor as announcing that he was filing a $100,000,000 law suit against the U.S. government and its chief officers based on recently obtained evidence of fraud, conspiracy, lies to Congress and the American people, and theft of government property with the express design to frame Kennedy—all done with malice aforethought. She did not reveal the location nor the time of the meeting.

The Chambers article was greeted with varying degrees of apprehension by the principles, ranging from distress on the parts of the heads of the several federal law enforcement agencies as represented on the President's Task Force to near apoplexy on the part of Attorney General Margaret Thaler. The president responded with what might be termed as wonderment. Daniel Hernandez felt the same and was taken aback by the evident one-upmanship. The Militia Movement across the country had the article shellacked and framed and hung it on their cabin walls. The American newspaper reading public was largely inured by information regarding governmental malfeasance and would have paid scant attention to the news had it not been for the mention of the colossal sum of $100,000,000.

President Vantassa called Margaret Thaler at her office in Justice.

"Margaret, I want something done. Tell your FBI agents in the field that I want them to come back with that criminal within two weeks, or they can effectively forget about their shields and their jobs. It is more than their jobs are worth to fail any longer and that includes Coleman and Silberberg. Between you and me, if we have not made any real progress by then, we'll have to negotiate with that dreadful Hartley Proctor to bring an end to this nonsense. It is the kind of thing that prompts Congress to think of appointing special counsels to investigate the executive branch—the kiss of death to an effective presidency, and I won't have it. I have too much to do to become embroiled in a stupid and complicated scandal, the likes of which brought down Dick Nixon and did away with Bill Clinton's effectiveness as a president. The paternity scandal turned Jesse Jackson into a lame duck during his second year in office."

"I'm already on it, Madam President. My personal interests as well as my professional ones are riding on this case, much as I wish that were not so. It has mushroomed out of all proportions, and I think it is time to rein it in."

When the president had ventilated sufficiently and had rung off, Mrs. Thaler called Ted Coleman at J. Edgar Hoover FBI Headquarters. The director was looking out across E Street in the direction of Ford's Theater when he received her call. He often thought afterwards of the appropriateness of that view as a symbol of the Kennedy Affair.

"Ted, this is the attorney general. Is this a secure line?"

"No, I'll switch my scrambler on."

He did that and also activated his telephone system recorder. He had become as paranoid as everyone else and was now fully self-protective in every aspect of the Kennedy Affair.

Chapter Fifty-One

In a moment he was back.

"Go ahead, Madam Attorney General."

"I'll come right to the point, Ted. It is rather late in the day for any daintiness. I want Randolph Kennedy, and I want him now. Pull out all of the stops, whatever it takes. Bring him in through his attorney, or have him give himself up to some hick county sheriff, or bring his head on a pike. But get him. Your job and mine are riding on this as never before. I have an ultimatum from the president. You have a month. If he is not in custody or dead, tender your resignation then. I will be obliged to do the same. Am I making myself clear?"

"Perfectly. We will deal with him with no quarter."

"Whatever it takes, Ted. Do it. The top is about to blow off the teapot."

Coleman immediately called Gerald Silberberg, who was—at that time— operating out of the Wasatch County Courthouse in Heber, Utah.

"Hello, boss, to what do I owe the pleasure?" asked Silberberg, knowing full well that a call from Ted Coleman at this juncture was neither routine nor social.

He had just put down his copies of the *New York Times* and the *Wasatch Wave*.

"We'll skip the pleasantries, Silberberg."

"That bad, huh?"

"Worse. We have a month to have that monkey, Kennedy, looking at us from behind bars or pushing up daisies—word from on high. If you haven't already, read the *New York Times* front page today. Then extrapolate to the future if Kennedy is able to work the press for another little while. From the way things are going, he's likely to get the Key to the City, and we will all be lucky if the worst thing that happens to us is to lose our jobs. That is no longer a potential threat. We have to shut him up. Either his civil suit goes away for some reason, or we will have to make a deal. You work on getting him. I'll be calling Hartley Proctor, hat in hand."

"You mean for us to go as far as a general edict for maximum prejudice?"

"Spare me the details, Silberberg. Just do your job. 'Pull out all the stops,' as someone up in that rarefied atmosphere just said to me. And look, for what it's worth, Craig told me that he had some information that the perp was in Wallsburg or some such name as that."

"There is a Wallsburg. I'll get right on it. You'll back me?"

"You know I will. Do the job right."

"What about Phil Craig and his stooges?"

"Do the job right; and in less than a month, and you can have Phil Craig's job. Plow Delgado and her men under if you have to. Thaler told me that if the man is not put down within the month, Vantassa is going to sack the lot of us, including you."

Silberberg did not trust Coleman. This was Washington—after all—and he knew that the worst stuff still ran downhill. He presumed that he understood what Coleman would not say directly. He determined to finish this investigation definitively. As soon as he hung up the phone, he called in his top five.

"Bring in the four leaders of the local Militia and sweat 'em hard. I know Kennedy is in this county. I do not want him to get away from us again. Fail, and I'll send you to Point Barrow to investigate Eskimo interstate pornography rings. Get me a dozen men. I have a tip that Kennedy is in Wallsburg. I doubt it, but I'll drive over and see. You get information from the Militia leaders."

His reptilian eyes flashed with merciless determination.

Randolph Kennedy was pulling into William's Lake, British Columbia, when Niels Dastrup broke under questioning. Special Agent Tom Fields showed him the FBI dossier collected on him including his IRS discrepancies. Fields had patiently and completely recounted the list of felonies the Bureau intended to charge him with. Dastrup was given the stark option of providing information on his fellow Militiamen—including Randolph Kennedy—or facing arrest, disgrace, confiscation of his money and property, and prison. Fields read the RICO statutes to Dastrup verbatim, and Niels was impressed down to his core.

Once he caved in, Dastrup released a symphony of information. He told about meeting Randolph Kennedy two days ago at his resort and predicted that Kennedy would still be there, probably with Hartley Proctor or Gwen Chambers. Niels Dastrup on that day became an RCI—Registered Confidential Informant—and sold his soul to the devil in the form of the United States government which—in his eyes by that time—was the lesser of the evils he faced.

Fields called Silberberg in Wallsburg, and the senior agent wheeled out of the little mountain enclave and roared back along the lakeside highway, sirens blaring and lights blazing. Fields was directed to continue to eviscerate Dastrup. Silberberg summoned every agent in the valley to converge on Dastrup's Mountain Spa Resort. He did not think to involve the local police.

Special Agent Gary Malders spent a thoroughly frustrating and unsuccessful morning using the same tactics to break Nephi McDonald. The mountain man was impervious to threat; "prove it." was his standard reply. Malders locked the large patriarch in the city jail for spite while he combed the Bureau's records for sufficient cause to work up an indictment on the recalcitrant polygamist.

An hour before all of that, when Kennedy was traveling past 100 Mile House on the Caribou Highway; and Niels Dastrup was still enjoying a wine-soaked Havana cigar, Gwen Chambers and Hartley Proctor shared a Mountain Spa limousine ride to the Salt Lake City International Airport. They missed the congregation of FBI agents at the sleepy resort by an hour and a half. They were in the air enjoying impeccable first-class Delta Airline service and cuisine when Special Agent in Charge Gerald Silberberg declared it a dry run, and had a screaming session about the FBI being too late again.

He procrastinated the rest of the morning before conveying the bad news to Ted Coleman. His road blocks had resulted only in disruption of the morning's commute. By that time, Randolph Kennedy was nearly to Hazelton in Northern British Columbia and was trying to decide whether or not to take the time to see Nizga's Memorial Lava Bed Provincial Park. Gwen Chambers was reporting in person to William Fitzgerald in New York, and Hartley Proctor was directing the formal preparation of a $100,000,000 law suit from his comfortable swivel chair in Washington, D.C.

Randolph changed license plates, driver's licenses, and passports and crossed into Alaska two days later. Despite his fugitive status, he had been able to enjoy the stupendous scenery of the Alaskan-Canadian Highway but was tired and longed for an undisturbed rest. Despite his fatigue, he pushed on towards Anchorage and found himself a musty room in a seedy motel in Ekulna, twenty miles north of Anchorage. The place was a no-tell motel which suited Randolph's main need perfectly. It was two o'clock in the morning when his head finally hit the pillow.

He awakened to blinding sunlight streaming in through the curtainless and blindless motel window. He was famished. It took him a few minutes to orient. He looked at his watch—three o'clock. How could it be that bright at three o'clock in the morning? He felt like he had slept all night. How could it have been only an hour? He took another few moments to establish to his satisfaction that it—in fact—was mid-afternoon. He had slept thirteen hours. The life of a fugitive was not all bad, he smiled to himself.

After cleaning up, he called Devlin O'Herligy at his business in Wasilla using a telephone card for its anonymity.

"Mr. O'Herligy's private office," said a cheery young woman's voice after one ring.

Randolph could picture the busty secretary and took a little pleasure in the memory.

"Is Mr. O'Herligy in?"

"Whom is calling?" the secretary asked, careful to remember to use the good English that she had been taught in her night school secretarial course.

"Tell him it's a friend who hasn't seen him for four months. He'll know."

"Yes, sir," she said. "I'll get him."

She reasoned that if he knew Mr. O'Herligy's private number, he must be all right. She did not think any of those nasty federal people had that information.

Devlin answered immediately. He must have been sitting on his phone or had the secretary on his lap.

"O'Herligy speaking."

"Devlin. You know who this is. I need to talk."

"At least. Meet me where we used to eat pan fried catfish and grits in an hour, okay? Know the place?"

"Yes."

It was the Lake Lucille Inn, a Best Western. Eating catfish there was from another life.

CHAPTER FIFTY-TWO

Randolph watched O'Herligy drive in and park in Wasilla's Lucille Inn parking lot. Devlin was driving a HummVee Special, a new, customized model. It probably cost a small fortune, but had a low enough physical profile that it was a good choice for this clandestine meeting. O'Herligy stayed in the Hummer for a full five minutes. Neither man got out of his vehicle, approached, or in any way signaled the other. They both looked hard at every vehicle that entered or left the parking lot until they were satisfied that Devlin had not been followed.

Then Devlin backed slowly out of his parking space and drove sedately out of the lot and onto the streets of Wasilla. Randolph waited a decent interval and followed him. He watched Devlin waving at passersby unnoticeable by his very customary conspicuousness. The Hummer honked at the students at the Alternative School, at the shoppers leaving the mall at Crussey Street, and Devlin whistled at a pretty young woman wheeling her Chevy Blazer out of Tony's Chevrolet dealership at the southern edge of town. Randolph found himself grinning at the man's panache and insouciance and wished he could feel the way Devlin acted under pressure.

They drove down the Glenn Highway and turned north onto Davis Highway, then west on Hubbell Road, which became Anchorage's Second Street, then moved onto Juniper drive. There were enough slow-downs, speedups, turns, and irrational decisions that had they been followed, it would have been obvious. There was not even a hint of police surveillance. The two men stopped their vehicles at the guard post at the entrance into Elmendorf Air Force Base. Randolph became very nervous. It occurred to him that Devlin might be betraying him. He could not run now. He would only draw attention to himself. The MP waved them through, and Randolph followed the HummVee with growing trepidation. Once inside the security fence, there was no escape if he was being setup. The recent experience trusting the Bock brothers was too vivid a memory for Randolph to be trusting. He had developed a light sweat.

Devlin led him to the large base movie theater parking lot. He got out of the Hummer and walked slowly away from Randolph in the direction of the senior officers' quarters. Randolph parked twenty cars away, got out, and started in the same direction. He did not look back to see if he were being followed; it was too late for that. Devlin never looked back at Randolph either. Randolph saw Devlin pull out his cell phone and speak briefly into it. He was now more afraid than ever that his old friend was signaling law enforcement. He began to look around frantically for a route of escape. When he returned his focus to Devlin, he saw his friend enter the front door of a large two-story officer's house.

Randolph shrugged, took a deep breath, and followed. He opened the tidy gate on the well-kept white picket fence. On the edge of the lawn was a sign reading, "Quarters—Colonel Mark Hathaway". He knocked on the front door where he had seen Devlin enter.

The door opened partially.

"Come right in. We're glad to have you," a crew-cut fit man in civilian attire greeted him and pulled Randolph inside with a handshake that enveloped Randolph's smaller hand.

Devlin was standing behind the tall white man, who did not need his uniform to announce that he was the colonel.

"Thanks," Randolph said, aware that he was sweating.

He felt profound relief at not running into a roomful of FBI agents.

The colonel excused himself.

"I am superfluous here. No need to know. I'll leave you two gentlemen. Please make sure the door is locked when you leave."

He gave a small, friendly salute and retreated towards the kitchen.

Devlin said, "Come in and sit down. You don't look all that much the worse for wear, but I'm sure it has been rough. I'm glad to see you alive after they nuked your house and from all I see on the news."

"Did seem like overkill, didn't it?"

"You always were the master of understatement. So what on earth are you doing back here? You a glutton for punishment? Have a death wish?"

"No, neither. This very temporary. I need to collect some possessions, and I'll need a little help to do it. It's important. When I leave, I'll need a big covered truck—like a semi—to haul some stuff to the airport."

"Where're you going, if I might make bold to ask?"

Randolph smiled a little sheepishly, but he had learned his lesson in dealing with the Bock brothers.

"To tell the truth, I haven't thought that out completely. I thought maybe Switzerland. The stuff I am going to take needs to go to a place like that."

"Could that stuff be green and measure about 2.61 by 8.14 inches?" Devlin laughed conspiratorially.

"How on earth would you know such an arcane fact, Devlin? You must be the only person in Alaska who knows such measurements."

"I just love the stuff."

"Well, yes, that's the kind of stuff I need to move."

Randolph kept his face inexpressive, even though he had an urge to laugh out loud at Devlin's obvious consternation.

"Whew!" Devlin whistled, having made all the right deductions. "We heard rumors that there had been a lot of money out there, but nothing on the order you're suggesting. Do you know how much is involved?"

"No, not really. Enough to tempt even the best of people."

Devlin looked at Randolph to see if he had been insulted.

"I need your help. There is no one else I can trust," Randolph said in answer to the look.

Devlin looked genuinely relieved.

"And you were thinking of shipping that money to Switzerland?"

"Something like that," Randolph told him, looking sheepish again.

He knew he was sounding woefully amateurish, but it was as far as his knowledge went.

"You need a little lesson in international finance. What you are going to learn is about offshore banking and the U.S. interference in the affairs of commerce of various countries, my friend. To begin with, you have come to the right shop. We have had to be very, very careful with money in the Movement. You know that the feds are on us like mean on an ATFer. We can't have a regular bank arrangement because they will find some pretext to freeze or appropriate our assets. So, I have had to become something of a financial expert."

He was relaxed and settled into his exposition.

"First off, you can forget about Switzerland, or Luxembourg, or Liechtenstein, or any of the old popular, so-called 'safe' places. They all have commercial extradition treaties with the U.S. government and several of its branches—DEA, President's Task Force, IRS, CIA, and several Defense Intelligence services. If the service can present evidence of a crime or that an ongoing investigation is in place, then those countries turn themselves inside out to kowtow to Uncle Sugar. Uncle pays the banks a hefty fee for the information; so, everybody is happy—with the possible exception of the depositor. The Cayman Islands and Aruba used to be pretty good for squirreling away funds—but with effort—the U.S. can penetrate them as well. They are very spooky about dealing with cash."

It sounded hopeless, and Randolph felt a sense of impending defeat.

"So, I take it that I just have to bury the stash and dig it up as needed? Great."

"Not at all. I told you that you had come to the right shop. You didn't let me finish. There is Vanuatu, the only secret banking system left in the world."

"Where, or even what, is Vanuatu?"

"Southwestern Pacific Ocean, about 1000 miles or so from Australia. There are several islands in the republic, all just specks. The speck that's of interest to you is called Êfaté Island—the capital city of Vila—to be exact. It is the commercial center. Believe it or not, there may well be as much money on the books in that little city as in New York or London. But no one knows. They are locked up tighter than an old spinster in spasm. Vanuatu doesn't share banking information with anyone—and I mean—*anyone*. Their law calls for very long prison terms for any communication of information about any account without the account owner's express permission. That includes the seller or giver of the information and the buyer or recipient of unauthorized bank account data.

"And they mean it! Prisons there are like Dante's ninth ring, I'm told. It is virtually unheard of for anyone to divulge anything. To sweeten the secrecy arrangement, everyone is very well paid to keep them free of the temptation for outside filthy lucre. The U.S. has offered foreign aid of preposterous level, has threatened them with withdrawal of all foreign aid, and finally with a financial blockade. Didn't phase them.

"They said, 'take your aid and stick it.' They are very sophisticated, able to handle all kinds of wire transfers, have telecommunication links with every bank in the world—and best of all—they handle cash. They love cash. If you can get it there, they can turn it into a ledger number you can work with. It becomes legitimate usable bank money transferable to any legal bank in the world, and no one can prove anything illegal about the money."

"And you have Secession Committee and Militia money there?"

"And only there. And lots of it. Wouldn't have it anywhere else. We don't dare. When Alaska goes her own way, Uncle Sam is going to punish our fair citizens something awful. We expect a freeze on all assets—personal and commercial—held in the lower forty-eight. If our money isn't in some safe—and here, I mean non U.S. place—when the time comes, we might as well have a big bonfire."

"And you can set me up with Vanuatu?"

"This very day. First on the to-do list is to put the cash into non obvious containers for shipping. Second is to forget about going passenger. We ship by air freight only. When it's important, we accompany our shipments in person. I've been to Vanuatu six or eight times. I'm an old island hand. Nice place. It's kind of fun to go there, really. Big adventure."

`"I'll share with the Militia."

"That's good of you. It won't come cheap. For the kind of secrecy we're after, we'll have to pay some form of baksheesh at every step. They take something on the order of ten percent for cash transactions in Vanuatu—take it or leave it."

"They ought to like me, then," Randolph offered.

"It's probably money well spent. They know how to take care of you. Once you are on their soil, you can stop worrying about the future handling of your money. You have real security, and you have the time to make any arrangements you need to. Oh, and they are scrupulously upfront and honest."

"Let's get to work," Randolph said.

His look of chronic concern had changed to one of determination. He had made up his mind to trust Devlin O'Herligy and the Militia under his control come what may. For better or for worse, he shucked away the husks of his doubts.

"We'll need the truck and the boxes—a real big truck, and lots of boxes that one man can lift. I presume you have some sort of connection for that, Devlin?"

"You bet."

"I want this to be just you and me, Devlin. When one person knows something, it's a secret. When two know, it's a party line, and when more than two know, it's news."

"I agree. I hope I don't have a heart attack lifting all of that money."

Devlin gave a little theatrical sigh of worry

"But what a way to go," laughed Randolph. "Here's the place where the money is being stored."

Randolph gave Devlin one of his Eagle Self Storage Company cards. He quickly scribbled "Unit 7304". The only things he held back was a key—he had two of them—and the name under which he had rented the unit—Delano Roosevelt.

"Like you said, 'let's get to work.'" Devlin said. "You leave first and go straight to the storage place. I think I know where it is. I'll get the truck and find boxes...You're welcome."

"Thank you," Randolph said, feeling that he was a little late.

He gave his friend an affectionate and relaxed smile. He had not felt such a release of tension in as long as he could remember. As he was leaving, he could hear Devlin already on his cell phone with one or another Militia member arranging to get a truck and asking about boxes.

Randolph drove into the dusty gravel road of the Eagle Storage Company. A pimply-faced teenager came to the gate, clipboard and attached papers in hand.

"Name and number?" the boy asked distractedly."

He seemed to lack full gusto for his work.

"Roosevelt, Delano Roosevelt. Number 7304."

The boy ran a grimy nail bitten finger down his list.

"Yep," he said. "Paid up to next July."

He undid the padlock on the main gate and admitted Randolph.

The key worked well despite the length of time since it had last been opened. The money sat there just as Randolph had left it. He took a few minutes to appreciate the scenery in the storage locker, laughed in adolescent pleasure, then went to let the teenager know to admit a man in a semi.

It was a forty-five minute wait in the storage unit before his friend came into the dusty compound. Randolph went out to greet him and helped Devlin back the large semi up to the open door of the unit. He opened the rear doors as Devlin alighted from the cab and walked around. Randolph saw the flat, factory fresh Gerber Baby Food boxes at the same time Devlin saw the mighty hoard of money. The two men guffawed in appreciation.

"You're as rich as Croesus!" Devlin exclaimed. "I think I brought the right size truck!"

"And I'm the baby food king," Randolph responded, sounding like an annoying television commercial. The two men had another laugh before starting to work.

The first task was to unload all of the boxes, rolls of clear packaging tape, and magic markers into the storage unit. There was barely enough room for the boxes, for the bales of cash, and for the two men to work. They took turns putting together boxes and loading neat packets of hundred dollar bills, conveniently joined into six inch bundles with heavy rubber bands. Devlin had thought of everything.

The Gerber Baby Food boxes measured 12 by 12 by 14 inches. There were 490 bills to the pound, and each box was firmly filled with thirty pounds of cash—$1,470,000—and securely taped closed. In a full thirty-six hours of work with only a few minutes pause for food and bathroom, the men filled 340 boxes—5.1 tons of cash—that occupied 101 cubic yards of truck space when they were finally packed into the semi. It was three a.m. on the second day when the exhausted men finished.

"Close to half a billion bucks, has to be," Devlin marveled as he packed the last packet of bills into the last box.

There were three packed boxes that had yet to be taped, and one box that was only one third full.

"Let's keep this out for incidental expenses," Randolph said, gesturing to the four boxes.

Devlin laughed giddily.

"I can't even imagine that kind of incidentals. I'll try to adjust though. I have to say that I could get to like this."

"The three full boxes are yours, Devlin. Do what ever you want with them."

Devlin clasped Randolph's hand.

"You don't have to give me a thing, but this will really help. You're a prince, Randolph."

"That makes two of us, then, my friend," said Randolph with genuine affection.

"We oughta get going before we attract attention," Devlin said yawning.

"What do we do with the truck, now?"

"Uh-oh, hadn't thought of that. We sleep in it; that's one thing," Devlin said seriously.

Randolph nodded his agreement. For lack of a better place, they drove the laden truck to the approach road to the city dump and sat up asleep in the cab for the rest of the night.

"You take off for Hawaii at nine-thirty," Devlin said when they roused in the morning. "This is the bill of lading. They'll have to check it out and bill you. They think it's legit, and you can't let on for a second that it's not a cargo of baby food. Apparently, all of those South Sea Islands are starving for good quality baby food; so, it looks like a regular import-export business deal. I don't think you'll have any trouble. People take advantage of the extra space and hop a ride with their goods all the time. Probably no one will question you about any of it, but get ready to give an Academy Award performance if you have to. Guys have had their throats cut for a millionth of what you're carrying."

"Hey, Devlin, how did you arrange all of this in such a short time?"

"I got contacts. In this case, I did the simplest thing. I called my travel agent and had her arrange for the shipment of the boxes. I really didn't do a thing."

Randolph shook his head in wonderment once more at the breadth of Devlin O'Herligy's resourcefulness. For his part, Randolph accepted the seriousness of his undertaking. It was not that much different in terms of adversity or danger from the vicissitudes he had endured as he fled Alaska for San Francisco four months ago.

At the freight section of the Anchorage International Airport, Randolph paid the freight to Hawaii and paid for a union gang to transfer the load from the truck to the cargo hold of the plane. Anchorage was a union town; and there was no possibility of moving the boxes himself, even if there had been time. No one questioned the load or the payment in cash—happened all the time. No boxes were dropped or broken to reveal the stacks of cash. Randolph made a display of insisting on a receipt. He had to pay a nominal $100 for the privilege of boarding the cargo plane as a passenger. At nine-fifteen, he said good-by to Devlin.

Devlin smiled solicitously and offered, "Have some fun with some of that money along the way. Never can tell what might come your way, and you can't take it with you, I'm told. We Irish have a saying, 'There are no pockets in a shroud.'"

"Thanks," Randolph said. "I needed cheering up."

They shook hands. The plane departed at exactly nine-thirty.

Randolph spent an uncomfortable cold day in the rough interior of the big aircraft. There was a hammock to lie and sit on and a hole in the floor of the back of the cargo hold that served as a rude toilet. He was starved because he had not thought to bring along food.

Randolph, acting on Devlin's advice, had not told the airline anything about the final destination of his boxes. He had made separate arrangements to move the goods from the Hawaii-bound plane to one going to Fiji before leaving Anchorage. He used different names and destinations to make tracking his precious boxes and their paper trail as difficult as possible.

Once in Honolulu, he had the cargo set aside in a short-term warehouse on a side street off the airport property under a different assumed name. He immediately arranged his next flight by Air Pacific to Nandi International

Airport in Fiji for the following morning. Next, he secured a labor gang from the union and prepaid to ensure that the work of transfer would get done smoothly. Lastly, he bought a bag of hamburgers and French fries and two large chocolate milk shakes. He wheedled permission to stay with his cargo overnight. The cargo handlers and watchmen were used to the penny-pinching paranoiac characters who shipped through their facilities and paid him no mind. Randolph slept uncomfortably but soundly atop his boxes that night. The greasy food did not sit well, and he spent most of his waking moments in the warehouse's dirty bathroom.

The ground crew in Fiji was remarkably efficient. The men—most of whom were dressed in skirts—met him at the terminal. He paid them for their work based on their undisputed and grossly inflated estimate, and his goods were in a second Air Pacific cargo hold in two hours. He had time to eat a big meal of Indian food that was remarkably good and to read the *Fiji Times* from front to back before setting off on the last leg to Vanuatu some 500 miles to the west.

It was a brilliant sunny day as the Air Pacific cargo plane moved in from the south and west over the chain of islands towards the main island of Êfaté. The cargo hand—speaking a mixture of English and Tok Pisin, the Melanesian pidgin language—pointed out the sights.

"You con see forever here, mon! Lookee see Mount Tabwémasana, 1900 kilometers, mon!"

They were looking north toward Espiritu Santo far in the distance. There were dots of islands moving swiftly out of sight beneath them. The islands appeared to be lush and forested with evidence of tiny hamlets here and there on the larger of them. Several of the islands were obviously volcanoes.

The large cargo plane settled out of the hot moist air onto the tarmac at Bauerfield Airport in Vila. The temperature was surprisingly cool, and there was a dry southeast trade wind blowing. Randolph accompanied his innocuously labeled boxes from the cargo hold of the freight plane into the airport short-term holding hanger. He signed the necessary paperwork including the customs declarations and walked up a flight of steel stairs into the main public area of the airport. There, he saw a black skinned man—who appeared to be from the Indian subcontinent—in an incongruous dark suit, white suit, and silk tie, patiently standing outside the restricted immigration area. He held a card board placard reading: "Mr. Gerald Werts-Vanuatu Copra Producers Bank". It took a few minutes for it to register in Randolph's mind that Werts was the name he had used on the last leg of his trip and in his communications with the bank from Fiji. O'Herligy had given him the name of the bank and of a bank officer named Rodriguez, the man with whom Devlin did business. He was tired, and it took a moment for it to dawn on him that the institution where he planned to do business was the Vanuatu Copra Producers Bank.

He waited patiently in the immigration line, showed his phony passport and stamped declaration cards, and passed through with a green light indicating that his personal luggage did not need to be searched. He walked directly up to the placard bearer.

"I am Gerald Werts."

The diminutive Indian man's face lit up with a sustained flash of even, snow-white perfect teeth contrasted against the ebony black of his skin, hair, and irises.

"I am so glad you have arrived safely. I do hope that your trip was no too onerous."

Randolph had expected more pidgin and was taken aback by the sophisticated greeting and the exaggeratedly clipped upper crust Etonian accent.

He returned the friendly Indian's smile and said, "nothing that a bath in gasoline and a wire brush and a beer won't cure."

The Indian laughed uproariously and genuinely.

"That's a good one. I'll have to remember that. Permit me to introduce myself, Mr. Werts. I am Jorge Joachim Rodriguez, at your service."

He gave a slight deferential bow and a click of the heels of his mirror-polished black wing tip shoes. Randolph thought the man looked more appropriately dressed for a boardroom in London or New Delhi than for the tropics. It was intriguing.

"It is very nice of you to meet me at the airport, Mr. Rodriguez."

"My pleasure, be assured. Now, let us get out of the heat and find some refreshment. We are ready at the bank if you would wish to accompany me there now. Or perhaps you would prefer to attend to your personal needs at the hotel first?"

"Let's go to the bank. I can sleep later," Randolph said. "What about the money I brought in?"

"If you will permit me to attend to it, we can have it delivered to the bank's storage area, counted, and vaulted in the next several hours. We were given to understand that it is a fairly...bulky shipment. Am I not correct?"

"That is entirely correct."

"Let us make arrangements, then."

He led Randolph to the airport security office. There he held a brief discussion with an officer in Bislama, the national language—an English based pidgin. Randolph picked up words and phrases enough to know that negotiations were underway to protect, store, and to deliver—under army guard—Randolph's cargo.

"And that is that," Rodriguez explained in satisfaction when they left the security office.

The airport was bustling with an international clientele, largely expensively dressed in western business suits, Arabic robes, and a United Nations General Assembly of other national costumes. They spoke a dizzying polyglot of tongues. Only the porters and taxi drivers seemed to be peasants and to dress in casual or work clothing. The city was clean and neat, but still looked like it had not yet fully awakened from the torpor of its colonial history. Randolph was swept along in a Mercedes limousine with a liveried Melanesian driver. Rodriguez allowed Randolph the courtesy of quiet.

It was Randolph who interrupted the stillness.

"I'm curious, Mr. Rodriguez, if you don't mind. You speak Oxford English; you look Indian, and your name is Spanish. You are an executive in a South Pacific Island bank. How does one like you happen?"

Rodriguez laughed delightedly.

"You are observant, Mr. Werts. I *am* something of a puzzle, I'll have to admit."

He was smiling, eager to communicate and not the least offended by the personal question.

"I am Indian through and through. A Caucasian—as are nearly all Indians—and a Brahmin. My native language is Marathi. I also speak Hindi and English as well as the local language here. My family originated in Portuguese Goa and migrated along the island chains four generations ago following the trade routes. We have been on this island for three generations and are full-fledged citizens of the Ripablik Blong Vanuatu, and proud to be.

"My father was the first to enter the banking business, and I followed in his able footsteps. We have accumulated more than sixty years of service to the Copra Producers Bank between us. My name is Portuguese, that of an adventurer in these parts from as far back as the days of the spice trade. As for the accent, it is Oxford. I was educated at Eton and went on to Oxford, and I have a masters from the London School of Economics. I am a Roman Catholic."

"I'm impressed. You—like your country—are fascinating. I have a confession. My name is Randolph Kennedy, not Werts. I did not want to have my shipment associated with my name which has accumulated a rather significant…prominence in my country. For the purposes of security, I used several pseudonyms in transit."

"Ah, where are my manners?" Rodriguez exclaimed. "I was aware of your name and something of your recent history, I have to admit."

He handed Randolph a copy of the previous day's *New York Times*. On the front page was an article by Gwen Chambers telling of the major and failed raid at the Dastrup Spa Resort and of the wholesale arrest and detention of the Utah Militiamen. Randolph's photograph topped the column. He looked over at Rodriguez.

"We have no interest in your business outside of the transactions at our bank. As you know, we are quite stuffy about the uses and dissemination of client information. I will explain in detail once we are in the bank. We do not do business outside the security of our protected walls. Now, please, tell me about your trip. Was it difficult?"

Randolph found himself taking a liking to the slender Indian man. He told Rodriguez about the problems of making all of the arrangements, the hard sleeping quarters, and the lack of food. The banker seemed to be genuinely sympathetic. The driver pulled up in front of the bank.

Rodriguez leaned forward, "Please take us to the rear entrance, Maéwo," he said.

The driver wheeled the large gray limo around the building and pulled up to a heavy appearing metal door where two armed guards stood. They unslung their M-16s as the limo doors opened.

Rodriguez nodded towards the burly driver, and said aside to Randolph, "He is ni-Vanuatu and is named for his home island. Shall we go out?"

Maéwo was holding open the limo door. He had already signaled to the guards to relax.

"After you," Randolph said.

Together Randolph and Rodriguez entered the building through the heavy steel security door and then passed through an ornate wood door and walked into a marble-floored hallway.

"This way, if you please," Rodriguez requested.

The two men stepped into a spacious elevator decorated with tasteful wood reliefs. The elevator moved silently to the fourth floor. The two men were alone in its cabin.

"My office is just here," said Rodriguez. "Please make yourself comfortable. I shall return momentarily."

Randolph sat in a plush velvet armchair and sank into its luxury. On the floor beneath his feet was a handsome hand knotted silk Kashmir carpet, and on the walls hung exquisite Aubussons of Château David D'Angers, the Cathedral of Saint-Gatien, and the Abbey Fontevrault. Rodriguez's desk chair was protected by a fussy antimacassar that showed the grease marks from the Indian's pomaded hair. On the teak table beside the chair stood an ornate brass umbrella holder with several sizes of umbrellas, a gold-headed ebony cane, and a gnarled Malacca wood walking stick. On the hand-carved coffee table in the center of the room sat an antique Sèvres vase full of jewel orchid foliage with extravagantly patterned leaves and Brassia orchids with their huge, delicate flowers. Also on the table, there was a copy of the latest National Geographic in a gold-embossed Moroccan leather cover. The rich calmness of the room was soothing. Randolph had not realized how tired he was. *Piper's Galliard* by Dowland was playing softly in the background. Randolph had vivid thoughts of happy times with Irene and of small circles of paper stuck to his mirror that said "*LUV*".

The next thing of which he was aware was Rodriguez's hand gently nudging him awake.

"I have taken the liberty of securing a fruit compote for you. I think you will find it quite nice."

There were chunks of vividly colored fresh tropical fruits and a tangy pink sherbet floating in freshly squeezed orange juice. It was delicious and reviving. After he had eaten a sizable portion of the offering, Rodriguez presented a small tray of crackers, brie, and pâté de foie gras. There was also a brownish dip that Randolph did not recognize.

"Tahini, Mr. Kennedy," said Rodriguez, reading his client's mind. "It is a Middle-Eastern paste made from sesame seeds. This is mixed with baba gha-noush and hummus. It is very good for you, and I am sure you will like it."

Randolph did. He had not realized how hungry he was.

"I will explain procedures in a moment. First, allow me to tell you of the banking laws in Vanuatu that govern our transactions. Once we have a con-tract, you have the right to deposit any amount of funds you wish in our bank in person or by wire in any currency you desire at the day's exchange rate plus a point two percent handling fee. You may deposit cash, checks, money orders, bearer bonds, or you may transfer stocks or bonds that will be traded at the day's market rates. The bank charges a flat ten percent fee to handle cash.

"We do not request—nor even allow—any information to be taken as to the source of the funds, save it be the bank and account number or such formal data as is necessary to complete the transaction. You may withdraw any amount from your account at any time; and by any of the conventional methods; but you must follow our national banking procedures of identification to the letter each time you perform a transaction, however large or small and no matter how often. No information as to the use of the funds may be asked of you, and none will be given out to anyone whatever by the bank.

"We do not pay interest on accounts. That is forbidden by our country's laws. On the contrary, we charge a flat one percent per year on all funds remaining in the bank and at the time of placement of a deposit. A one percent fee is levied on the value of the account at the start of each fiscal year, which is January first. We are forbidden by law from charging more or less. We have the most secure banking laws in the world, Mr. Kennedy. Our armed forces exist almost exclusively to protect our banks and our banking customers. Our laws are quite draconian when it comes to protecting the privacy of our customers. Be warned that asking questions of others' banking practices is an offense in this country. That includes most emphatically foreign government officials. We impose more sentences on foreign tax snoopers than on any other type of person. To be safe, we do not discuss the bank or mention accounts on the outside. Otherwise, you will find our citizens and our banking guests to be most hospitable and communicative."

Randolph continued to listen attentively.

"The security of your privacy is determined by laws that govern our citizens in regards to bank procedures. Any transmission of any bank account information—however miniscule—is punishable by an automatic prison sentence of five years without the possibility of parole. Extensive transfers of information in any form can warrant a maximum thirty year sentence. We have a special ten year surcharge of prison time for any transmission of banking information to foreign governments.

"You see, if I were to give your account information to the American Internal Revenue Service or the FBI, for example; and if I were to be convicted of such a serious crime, my *minimum* sentence would be fifteen years plus the ten surcharge years. Vanuatu does not have concurrent sentences. Our prisons are most unpleasant, I might add. The diet consists of two meals a day, largely rice and vegetables and thin soup. Prisoners are obliged to do physical work seven days a week for the entirety of their sentences. Rather a daunting and educational process, wouldn't you say?"

"I would say so," Randolph said, "It makes me jumpy even to think about it."

"Furthermore, upon completion of any sentence for a banking crime, the ex-convict citizen is immediately deprived of his or her citizenship and is deported to one of the other Pacific islands. His or her record accompanies the person to ensure that they never work in the financial industry again."

Randolph shook his head.

"And then there is the matter of how the Vanuatu judicial system deals with foreign nationals in general and with officers of foreign governments who break our banking laws. We have an interesting law: if a foreign officer attempts to intimidate, corrupt, extort, or to bribe a Vanuatu bank or government employee—and is found guilty in a court of law—that officer shall be sentenced to hard labor for not less than thirty years. Vanuatu feels no obligation to inform the felon's country, employing agency, friends, or family of his or her conviction or whereabouts. It is a felony to divulge such information. We have conveyed information about our laws and our corrections institutions' procedures to every country, most agencies, and all of the major financial institutions throughout the world. The onus is on the perpetrator."

Randolph was impressed, as he was meant to be.

"So, permit me to say that the disincentive to reveal banking secrets is most potent, and the offense is rare," Rodriguez said. "I can only recall one or two instances of such criminal behavior. The newspapers carried the stories on their front pages for weeks. Neighbors hounded the innocent families into emigrating. The citizens of the country believe religiously in our system. It stands between us and the poverty of our Third World confreres. I think you will note a conspicuous absence of evidence of poverty here. The banking industry is to Vanuatu what the gambling industry is to your Las Vegas. Have you any questions, Mr. Kennedy?"

"No, sir, I think you have been most thorough and clear."

"Good. Then, let us begin setting up your account. Our people will begin inventory on the boxes of baby food as soon as they arrive in the bank's custody."

He smiled broadly at his little joke.

"We should have a strictly accurate accounting in two days' time. The sum appears to be large. You—of course—have the right to attend the counting at any time and for as long as you desire. You should know that our banking laws regarding actual theft or embezzlement are at least as severe as our banking and currency laws. The Copra Producers Bank security for counting your money rivals that at your Fort Knox or at one of your mints."

"I would like to make a few spot checks, if that could be arranged," Randolph told Rodriguez who quickly nodded his acquiescence.

A peculiar small animal crept silently into the room and hopped up onto the arm of Rodriguez's chair. It was gray with dry, wrinkled, hairless skin. The hump-backed animal had large ears, no whiskers, and had haunting golden eyes. Its face was reminiscent of a pug dog. Randolph stared in undisguised wonder at the strange little creature which might have come from another planet for all Randolph knew. It sat licking Rodriguez's arm affectionately. Rodriguez smiled broadly at Randolph's bemusement.

"My pet, do you like it?"

"What is it? Randolph asked, his curiosity overcoming his desire to be courteous.

"A sphynx, or sometimes known as a Moon Cat. It is the rarest cat in the world. Sphynxes cannot mate and produce offspring, and they cannot go outside into the sunlight or be where it is cold or hot."

Randolph shook his head and raised an eyebrow.

Then he smiled and asked, "Is it a good mouser?"

Rodriguez laughed heartily at the incongruity of such an activity on the part of his rare, expensive, and fragile cat. He showed his bright even white teeth in contrast to his nearly black face.

"It is a decadent showpiece, an indulgence of mine. I'm glad you like her. Now…I suppose we should go back to business."

"If that's all of the sideshow, then I suppose we must."

Rodriguez laughed again, delighted that Randolph had enjoyed seeing the strange rare little beast.

He resumed his business face and said, "The account will be set up in your full name. We do not allow any other information to be included. We require that you give us a code word of no more than seventeen letters or numerals and no less than five. The letters and numerals may be freely intermingled. You may choose any language using Arabic letters and numerals. It is no matter that your code may be meaningless or nonsensical. It is a code, after all. The catch is that the account cannot be entered or manipulated in any way without that code and your full name. The other part of the catch is that anyone who can give your full name and can produce your code and the other requirements we make can have access to the account."

"Please give the code some thought. When we have the exact tabulation of your money, we will assign the code to that figure and will lock in the account."

Rodriguez paused to savor a sip of crystalline water from a plastic bottle that had been in a drawer in his desk.

He went on, "All transactions—however distant in the future—require the inclusion of *my* full name—as the account representative—even if so far in the future that I no longer work for the Copra Producers or am dead. I will give you several calling cards to help you. Today's date is also required. I strongly suggest that you memorize the pertinent information and not leave clues lying around. We will also require your signature, which will become part of the unlocking information. Actually, we require you to write a short paragraph so as to allow computer imprinting of your handwriting. We will have you read a simple selection to serve as a voice print. Each time you request a withdrawal or to make a deposit, you will need to send us a high quality cassette tape or CD of you reading the same paragraph. Alternatively—if you prefer to do business from afar—we can identify you over the telephone by connection to the voice printer. Finally, we will finger print you. In order to add or to remove money in the future, you will have to send us a set of standard fingerprints for comparison. You may fax the fingerprints, if that is more efficient.

"If the account remains open upon your death or incapacity, your rightful heirs can perform transactions by sending us copies of all of your physical characteristics as detailed in the list I just recited. I suggest that you make multiple copies of your prints and save them in a completely secure place and that you give that information to someone you trust completely.

"We can make allowances for changes in your handwriting over time, or for most voice changes. However, if you forget your code and fail to keep a copy, there is no recourse. Any questions?"

"I may need to have this all repeated, but for now, this is all I can absorb."

"Place your signature here, please, Mr. Kennedy."

He indicated a line at the bottom of the page.

The two of them then went to the floor below, where Randolph was fingerprinted and voice printed, and he gave a sample of his handwriting. He submitted his code: 47363-263-26643, Arabic numerals that spelled out IRENEANDANNIE.

"Now, for dinner. I am sure you are starved. I apologize for the inconvenience, but I will no endeavor to make it up to you. Are you Jewish or Muslim, by any chance?"

"No, Christian."

"Ah, good. So are most of we islanders. I ask because I would like to take you to a luau, where the main dish is pig, of course. Would that suit you, Mr. Kennedy?"

"If I don't collapse from hypoglycemia first," he laughed.

The mere mention of the luau excited pangs of hunger in his stomach and a Pavlovian salivation.

They traveled by limo to an open field on the outskirts of Vila. A large European Baker style tent—open all around—sat in the center of the grassy field. A small number of obviously native ni-Vanuatu mingled with a panoply of Bedouin sheiks, Japanese industrialists, British oil magnets, Italian automobile makers, and Mafiosi.

Randolph saw a plentitude of Indian and Chinese merchants and not a few men whom he presumed with Yakusa, Russian mafia, and porn stars. There was a scattering of wealthy men and women, who—by their overt gregariousness—Randolph took to be Americans.

The assemblage of exotic people sat in communal harmony on cushions on the ground and ate with their fingers. The meal consisted of luau pig, chicken and fresh pineapple basted with a honey, mustard, soy, and ginger sauce, and liberally sprinkled with Dutch Red peppers served on fragrant Jasmine rice. The second course was Hawaiian hekka, and fresh fruits. The perfect wines came along with each course. Dessert was Death by Chocolate. Randolph ate the sumptuous meal until he was too full and too sleepy to take more. That night in the Hotel Êfaté, he slept the best sleep he had enjoyed in the past four months.

The following day, he went to the bank three times and watched in fascination as his mountain of money was being weighed, counted, and packaged. He had not reckoned on what a gargantuan task it was. He had Devlin had only guessed at the accounting. The boxes of money stacked on pallets had been estimated by weight when they originally entered the vault to give a first approximation to facilitate the processing of the account. Then the bills were fed into counting machines what were whirring like a room full of insects when Randolph first checked. By his third visit, the tedious process of hand counting and recounting, by workers in tight briefs or bikinis, and spot checking and rechecking by supervisors in skin tight pocketless jump suits was underway. They were one-third finished by the time he left after his third visual inspection of the day.

The day after that, he visited the counting room in the morning, then spent the afternoon snorkeling and spear fishing. His hotel was happy to prepare his day's catch for his supper. He shared his bounty with a quartet of corpulent Japanese who ate their portions raw and expressed gratitude to the point of making Randolph uncomfortable. It was not until mid-afternoon of the fourth day that the final tally of the money was completed and confirmed.

Mr. Rodriguez met Randolph in the counting room.

"I suspected that I would find you here, Mr. Kennedy. I think you have a nose for the status of your money. That is most wise in this complex world. I am told that they are finished. We can retire to my office to bring the total and the charges up on my computer. Would you like to accompany me?"

"Glad to," Randolph said buoyantly.

The blue background of the computer screen showed a neat ledger of black print. The charges came to $512,000. Randolph gulped and Jorge Rodriguez laughed affably.

"Read to the final line—the bottom line—as you Americans put it. Perhaps that will cheer you."

The account contained $511,886,729. Randolph could only stare in disbelief. Even seeing the cash itself had not had the staggering impact of visualizing the numbers written out. Randolph was a numbers person.

"Thank you for all of your help, Mr. Rodriguez. I will leave tomorrow morning. I would like to express my gratitude in a more tangible way."

He suppressed a nervous cough.

"I take it that you mean a gratuity, Mr. Kennedy. Please, we are forbidden by our stringent laws to accept any money whatsoever outside the recorded bank charges. Serves to hold down the temptations. Thank you for the thought anyway. If I can be of service in the future, please do no hesitate to let me know. If you would give me your destinations or itinerary, I would be happy to arrange for your travel if you have not already done so."

"That would be most helpful."

"Now, let us share a congratulatory libation," Rodriguez said. "I have a bottle of very fine old Marquis de Caussade Extra S.P. Armagnac. Not the most expensive, but I think the best."

Despite the knowledge of his windfall, Randolph still considered that that bottle of liquor was probably out of his price league.

"Love to," he said.

The lusty single distilled brandy was served at fifty degrees in a Spanish *copita*, a stemmed, tulip-shaped glass.

With the help of Jorge Joachim Rodriguez, Randolph was in San Diego, California, two days later. He called Devlin O'Herligy in Anchorage from his room in the Island Avenue Horton Grand Hotel. He had paid for the hotel with a new VISA card, the arrangements for which were made by Rodriguez. It was in the name of Gerald Werts.

"Dev., "I'll be brief. The delivery went off without a hitch. I left a package of goods with you. Could you please mail it to me at the post office box number I gave you? It would help."

"Consider it done."

Two large boxes of cash came marked, "Orchids-Fragile and Perishable", arrived at P.O. Box 2540, Abilene, Kansas three days later. They were picked up by the addressee, Dan Spencer. Spencer was a heavily bearded man who wore a large Stetson and garish Texas lizard skin cowboy boots. He blended in perfectly with the locals. Spencer's most distinguishing feature was his unfeeling Visigothan blue eyes.

CHAPTER FIFTY-THREE

Hartley Proctor called Nancy Delgado at her office in the J. Edgar Hoover Building.

"Hello, Special Agent Delgado. My name is Hartley Proctor. You may perhaps have heard of me, at least with regards the Randolph Kennedy case."

"Yes, sir, what can I do for you?"

"I represent Mr. Kennedy. You may already be aware of that as well. It has been in the news recently."

"I'm aware."

She felt her pulse quickening. There was no idle reason for this important man to be calling her.

"My client has recently communicated with me by telephone. He has expressed a desire to negotiate a surrender, but he wishes to attach some conditions."

"Like what?"

"Like, surrendering only to you, for one," Proctor said. "And he wishes to do so as a complete surprise to anyone else to minimize the danger to himself. You may appreciate that he is less than sanguine about the assertions and promises of any of the agencies of the United States government. For some reason, he seems to believe that he can trust you to act in an honest and professional way. In short, he expects that you will protect him."

"I will. Where and when?"

Her heart was pounding. She could all but taste success. Perhaps the sweetest taste of all would be seeing Gerald Silberberg's smug face when he first heard the news that she had been the one to make the collar. She wondered if the attorney could hear her excitement. She put up a fight to sound calm and collected.

"In a moment. There are a few conditions. My client wishes to surrender in a controlled public place and with the presence of a reputable and capable member of the press in attendance who is free to take photographs, videos, and the like and to write anything she pleases without government censorship."

"She? I take it you have someone in mind already."

"My client does. He wants Gwen Chambers from the *New York Times* and no one else, to be present from the media. He makes no preconditions on what Ms. Chambers writes or how she uses the information she obtains. He demands that the government treat her the same way. That will have to be a matter put in writing."

"I don't have the authority to grant all of that. Sometimes, what goes on or what is said is useful in the case against a defendant and is held back from the media until the completion of an investigation. Only the director can make that call."

"I'm afraid that brings up more of my client's conditions. He wants a select group present, again to ensure not only his safety but that an accurate dissemination of the proceedings of his surrender be accomplished. He demands a meeting of himself, you, me, Ms. Chambers, and Phillip Craig, the assistant director of the FBI. He further demands the exclusion of the director of the FBI and any representative of the ATF at the surrender meeting. In fact, he requires that those senior appointees I have mentioned by excluded even from knowledge of that meeting. I'm afraid that he is as mistrustful of the current odium of senior politicians as he is of the leading minions of the law."

"I'll run it past Phil Craig. I know that a deputy U.S. attorney named Hernandez is handling the government's case against the ATF agents who participated in the raid. Maybe it would suit your client's desire to limit the number of government officials in the know and involved directly in the surrender to include Hernandez. It is possible that he might want to have a meeting before the surrender is announced with the ATF agents, FBI, and his advocates, and the government's attorneys to air the different points of view. It would focus the government and would probably let Hernandez decide on the spot how vigorously to pursue Mr. Kennedy and how to handle the other issues this case raises."

"I take it that you have been giving this idea some thought."

"I have. There are some pretty strange things about this affair that a full airing couldn't hurt."

"That has merit. I'll talk to my client again. I'll try to get him to agree to the deputy U.S. attorney's date, time, and place and maybe to having ATF agents present. They would have to be under physical control. Thank you for your help. I think it is in all of our best interests to pursue this. I have to warn you, though, any pre-meeting leaks; and the deal's off."

"I'm not your regular FBI agent. You don't have to worry about leaks coming from me. However, I don't want to come to the meeting alone. I want to bring my two very much trusted fellow agents for my own protection and for control of the ATF agents. I want to trust you; and I want to believe that Kennedy is ready to surrender peacefully; but I think it would be foolhardy for me to relinquish *all* self-protection."

"I'll see if that is okay. That you are not the regular FBI agent is a plus which is why my client wanted you to be involved. Good luck in your efforts, Agent Delgado."

"Thanks for the call, Mr. Proctor."

As soon as they broke contact, Nancy told her two compatriots and swore them to secrecy—although they assured her that the swearing was unnecessary—and she knew that. She next put in a call to the U.S. Attorney's Office and asked for Daniel Hernandez.

"This is Hernandez," he said.

It had taken no more than a minute to raise him. Nancy felt that she must have called the wrong government. She never got through that easily.

"This is Special Agent Nancy Delgado—FBI. I just got a call from Hartley Proctor in regards to his client, Randolph Kennedy. I need to talk to you about the call."

"Not on the phone. Meet me on the steps of the Lincoln Memorial in an hour. Would that be convenient for you?"

"I'll be there."

It was commonplace for meetings of substance to be held *al fresco* away from the halls of official Washington where the walls had ears. It did not strike Delgado as unusual.

Delgado and Hernandez sat on the front steps of the Lincoln Memorial looking out across the reflecting pool towards the Washington Memorial obelisk and on to the distant Capitol. They were surrounded by a swirl of laughing, talking, awe-struck, and emotional tourists; and their own presence drew no attention. Nancy recounted her telephone call from Hartley Proctor. Hernandez listened expressionless and did not interrupt. When she had finished, he told her of the upcoming meeting with Quatraine and Drake and their attorneys scheduled for two weeks hence. He suggested that she try and convince Proctor to have his client surrender then and to be part of the information gathering session he planned to hold before rushing to any final decision as to how to dispose of the many disparate aspects of the Kennedy Affair.

"I can only wait for Proctor's call," she told him.

"Give him the message, at least," Hernandez urged.

"Okay. I'll try."

He seemed to have a high degree of confidence that the call from Proctor would come and that the grand confrontation meeting would take place. For the first time in the case, Nancy felt positively buoyant. As soon as she and Hernandez parted company, she called Phil Craig's private line and told him about the day's events. She could hear the hint of glee in his voice.

"Great work, Nancy. Keep it up. For once the score seems to be Christians 1, lions 0."

Gerald Silberberg had his first breakthrough in many weeks on the same day as Delgado and Hernandez had their meeting. SAC Oscar DeLentigo called him from the Anchorage FBI office.

"This is DeLentigo from the Alaska office. I have a new line on your terrorist, Randolph Kennedy."

The call came at a point of lowest morale among Silberberg's troops and was the most welcome communication the at-large senior agent had had in weeks.

"Well, that has to be better than a poke in the eye with a sharp stick. Let's hear it."

"We have continued to monitor the airports and borders routinely since Kennedy's place was raided. It has turned into a low priority effort in the past month or so, but we have kept at it. My intel is a bit dated as a consequence. The lieutenant in charge of the Kennedy Affair from the Wasilla PD, Carl Thompson, called this in. We have a fairly positive ID on a car that matches the description of the one Kennedy is reported to have used when he left the lower forty-eight. It was found sitting in front of a self-storage place, and when the PD came to look it over on a routine call, they found it full of an assortment of current license plates from around the states and from Canada; none of them were properly registered to that vehicle.

"We pressed the airports, and came up with something good, I think. We got a fairly positive ID on a man who shipped out an air freighter full of goods bound for Hawaii two days ago."

"How about Kennedy, himself?"

"That's the best part. As near as we can determine, he was the guy on that plane. Several freight handlers at the airport were sure it was him when we passed around Kennedy's photo. He paid cash for the freight, all 100s. Although that is not in and of it self too unusual, the bundle of 100s raised a few eyebrows."

"Cargo plane?"

"Yes. Delta."

"Sounds good. Do you have the flight number and all of that?"

"Here it is," DeLentigo said and gave the information slowly; so, Silberberg could write it down. "The cash transaction is fairly common; so, it won't be all that helpful in tracing him; but you should be able to follow his trail from Hawaii, presuming that he went on from there. He was apparently aided and abetted by a local here—a Devlin O'Herligy—although we'll never prove it. This guy is one of the local loonies, in charge of the secession movement, and one of the honchos in the North Star Militia. That bunch is probably connected to the nationwide survivalist ultrapatriot Movement, or however you might want to characterize it. We're interrogating him even as you and I are speaking."

"Nice work, DeLentigo. I'll be sure the director's apprised of your efforts. Keep me informed about what you learn from the accomplice. Remember that Coleman, the AG, and the pres. have given a green light for rough interrogation if you need to. We need everything we can squeeze out of this character. I'll leave that up to you because I have a little trip to Hawaii to attend to."

Silberberg alerted his lieutenants immediately after he and DeLentigo rang off. His men were in military transports flying out of Andrews Air Force Base in less than an hour. The FBI COINTELPRO Rapid Response Team was assembled for action in Hawaii six hours later. It took them fourteen cursing hours to track down the firm that unloaded, stored, and transferred Kennedy's cargo two days earlier. For all the difficulty in pinning down the exact flight, they did learn that the cargo consisted of a large number of boxes of Gerber Baby Food. The agents were hampered by the fact that none of the cargo handlers or clerks had ever heard of Randolph Kennedy; none of them recognized his photograph; and it became obvious in the early hours of the Hawaiian investigation that Kennedy had undoubtedly used an alias.

For several hours the FBI agents could not find anyone who could recall a shipment that would fit the needs for what Silberberg presumed was the cargo. He had no description of the cargo itself, and the handlers played dense or did not want to get involved. He and his men left off their questioning of the airport cargo people and concentrated on inspecting nearby holding warehouses. They found no trace of a shipment from Alaska or anything that looked the least bit likely. Six agents spent their days following the paper trails of 142 shipments of goods that came in by air freight on the day in question. They enlisted the assistance of airport police, Honolulu PD, and the local ATF contingent. The best lead involved a transfer to a private, off-airport Air Pacific warehouse of a consignment of goods that originated in Alaska. It was only one of ten received from the large state, but it was the only one with a large enough number of boxes to fit the needs Silberberg envisioned.

It was nine-twenty in the evening when Silberberg's team finally converged on the Air Pacific warehouse. No one was in the warehouse, and there was no indication of how to get hold of anyone. The building was well secured against thieves and it was essentially impossible for the FBI agents to break in.

Silberberg raged in impotent frustration throughout the night as his men tried everything to get hold of someone responsible for the warehouse. His agents called every Air Pacific number they could obtain from the airline and from Honolulu PD. All they accomplished were polite replies to their shouted demands. No executive contacted had the faintest idea about who worked in the warehouse, but all of them suggested that the workers would be back in the morning and could be contacted then. They sympathized with the police effort; but there was—regrettably—nothing they could do. Silberberg could all but see Kennedy slipping away from his net; it was maddening.

He told his number one, "I am going to take that smug SOB if I have to spend the rest of my life doing it. The only good terrorist is a dead terrorist. You guys have my permission to shoot on sight. This is officially a maximum prejudice operation. He is not to get away again!"

The lieutenant took Silberberg's tirade as just that. His boss was over-wrought and frustrated at being thwarted so many times, and he would think better of his intemperate threats later.

The team was stationed in force outside the suspect warehouse from five o'clock in the morning on. The frustrated FBI agents were tightly wound and pacing when the first worker arrived at eight. They surrounded the elderly Japanese man and frightened him half out of his wits.

"I just open the doors and sweep up. The rest, they come in about half an hour. I don't know nothing. Leave me alone," he begged.

Silberberg was tense enough to punch the old man out. His lieutenants edged him away. It was not going to do any good to rag on the old fellow, who obviously knew nothing. The minutes between eight and eight-thirty dragged by with glacial celerity. Then, two dozen cars and trucks drove into the employee parking lot at almost exactly the same time. The employees all rushed towards the entrance door to punch their cards before they were late.

The army of FBI agents swarmed in after them and began firing questions. It was chaotic and confusing to the agents and the cargomen; but finally, after half an hour, Silberberg had a cargo manifest in his hand listing a shipment of 5.1 tons of baby food en route from Honolulu to Fiji. The signature of the shipper was illegible, but his name was listed as John P. Sousa. Silberberg said that that had to be the one; nobody could have come up with a name more phony than that one. The bill had been paid in cash along with a good set of tips, all in 100s. The agents were satisfied that they had their man, and the workmen rushed to get their cards punched for the day's work.

Silberberg was not having a good day. It proved to be impossible to find a commercial flight to Fiji in less than ten hours. The senior agent finally resorted to exercising his extraordinary law enforcement powers and had the Air Force provide him and his team with a special chartered flight to Fiji. There was considerable reluctance on the part of the Air Force personnel, and it took two hours of communications back and forth from Washington before the arrangements could be finalized. Silberberg was nearly apoplectic by the time the plane took off.

Things did not go any better for him and the team in Fiji. The island nation proved to be a tough nut to crack. Landing permission took up precious time; customs and immigration procedures were conducted at the usual tedious pace—the American sense of urgency did not register as an emergency to the Fijian officials. The air freight computers at the Nandi Airport logging cargo manifests were down—a not infrequent occurrence. Papers were unfiled and unlogged. No one had the remotest memory of baby food coming off a plane in recent days, although the Fijian agents pointed out helpfully that American baby food was very popular in the islands; and they saw many shipments come in and go out.

"Great," Silberberg said.

No one knew of any such cargo going on to anywhere else in recent days, but then, many of the people at work today had not been there in the past week. Silberberg was afraid he was going to have a stroke. The more he raged at the Fijians, the less they seemed to hear, the slower they seemed to move, and the less they seemed to comprehend. Angry outbursts on the part of the Americans produced a profound cessation in the locals' ability to speak English. The team made no progress until the five lieutenants convinced Silberberg that he was now part of the problem, not part of the solution.

A black agent from the team proved to be the answer. His skin color seemed to invoke a less distrustful response from the Fijians. The agent was a soft spoken Southerner with a slow, gentle patois of rural Mississippi. He was able to talk with the heretofore unhelpful locals enough to glean the tidbit that "a nice white man" had brought a big load of baby food for the island. The men he talked to thought the shipment left for local hospitals as best as they could recall. The black agent was unaware of the ingrained helpfulness of the Fiji Islanders. If it proved difficult to be helpful, they filled in gaps with information that seemed to fit and delivered the message as fact. It did not seem illogical or untoward that several separate contributors gave widely differing versions of the same helpful information once they opened up to the African-American agent.

Silberberg and his agents wasted the rest of the day checking out all of the hospitals, clinics, pediatricians' offices, humanitarian aid centers, and grocery stores.

By the following morning, the airport computers were up and running again. Silberberg had resigned himself to the pace of island life and had calmed down by necessity. He knew he could not force his own frenetic pace on these people; he was a guest—after all—and he presumed that they had a genetic deficiency that prevented them from moving rapidly. It was hot, and he found himself not wanting to move all that fast himself on the second day in Fiji.

Finally—after two hours of coaxing—the computer in the short-term cargo holding area yielded up the nugget Silberberg and the team was after. A shipment consisting of a large number of boxes of baby food left the morning after it came in, bound for the Republic of Vanuatu. It was unclear just where in Vanuatu. The team had two choices—Bauerfield near Vila, the capital, on the island of Éfaté, or Pekoa near Luganville on Espirito Santo.

"Espirito Santo is the biggest island, these little black men in skirts tell me," Silberberg said, "let's head there."

The good news for the team was that they had a U.S. Military airplane, because the next commercial flight to Vanuatu was not until the following day. The bad news was that Vanuatu would not give permission for an American military plane to land on their territory. They were wary of an attack from the aggressive country from which they had withheld information for so many years. India and Japan had convinced the minister of Transport of the wisdom of keeping out all foreign militarists as a means of preventing a coup or allowing anyone of the E-8 nations from entering the country in force and compelling the weak army to give in and to make the bankers open their books and vaults to the information starved invaders. Silberberg ordered, demanded, cajoled and threatened. The State Department made polite inquiries and requests. The U.S. Air Force tried gentle persuasion with counterparts in the Vanuatu Defense Force. The result: after six hours of effort, the Minister of Transport remained adamant. His country would not even consider the possibility. The individuals were welcome as guests, but their plane was forbidden.

It had become a personal crusade for Silberberg. He knew that he had given up extremely valuable time in these futile efforts—time that Kennedy undoubtedly would be using to his advantage. The senior agent pursued his crusade with such intense vigor through every military, police, and diplomatic channel that he caused his team to miss even the commercial flight the following afternoon. He raged at his lieutenants—blaming them for that oversight—but he had to capitulate to reality.

The Task Force Response Team flew out on Air Pacific the morning after that. That is, twelve members of the 112 member team did. There were only enough seats for the dozen agents. The remainder would have to wait until the next afternoon when they would be able to charter a private aircraft with enough seats to fly them all to the Republic of Vanuatu.

The first dozen agents ran into much the same response in Pekoa as they had encountered in Fiji. There was no evidence of anyone remotely resembling Randolph Kennedy or any other American having arrived in Pekoa by passenger or cargo flight in the past week. There was no evidence of any large consignment of boxes having come into Espiritu Santo in recent memory. The lead agent telephoned Silberberg and gave him the information.

"Don't believe it," Silberberg said. "It's just the same old lazy run-around. Keep pushing. This is just the same song, second verse from what we heard in Fiji."

He sent his black agent by the next commercial flight to Espiritu Santo to persuade "the pygmies" to give up their secrets. It was to no avail. Silberberg finally decided to give up on the larger island and to go instead to Éfaté.

This posed a new problem. The charter aircraft Silberberg had hired did not have a license to fly into the Vila airport. It was too large. In a rage, Silberberg had to settle for sending a small advance party to the capital city from Pekoa on Air Vanuatu, the interisland airline.

Air Vanuatu operated on a shoestring. It was a private company and flew with some irregularity due to any number of vagaries of economics, weather, availability or lack of availability of spare parts, and the changing needs of its island customers, many of whom could not afford to pay. Silberberg did come into a piece of luck. The fact that he could pay in hard currency was a definite plus. That made it possible for the airfield manager of the private airfield to have the badly needed wheel strut flown in from Vila promptly. That enabled the vintage plane to be repaired the following day, an unheard of luxury.

Air Vanuatu was not equipped and had never had a reason to fly at night. The scheduled flight was luckily in the morning, two days after Silberberg himself had arrived on Espiritu Santo. By then, the entire team had reassembled. The senior agent was once again frantic. Most of the rest of the agents found it expedient to avoid their chief because they were unable to suppress a certain inner merriment at the unfolding of the KeyStone Kops follies in which they were playing starring roles.

Randolph Kennedy had left Éfaté while the KeyStone Kops languished on Espiritu Santo. Gerald Silberberg was a much chastened man by the time he tucked his tail between his legs and began the arduous exercise of getting back to the states. He left behind only three agents—who were Ivy League educated CPAs—to try and learn what they could about Kennedy's activities in Vanuatu; and as importantly, to learn everything there was to know about the boxes of money he undoubtedly had brought in clandestinely. The remaining agents knew it had to be for banking; the island was well-know for its off-shore banking industry. The fugitive was hardly in a position to take a tropical vacation, and Vanuatu fell somewhat short of a tourist destination.

Silberberg and his army returned to Washington; it took them six days. The three remaining agents decided that a direct approach was likely to be met with resistance, given the reputation for bank privacy the country prided itself in. They—instead—made up cover stories and began to probe the banks of Vila for their secrets. When that failed after a two-week effort, they marched en masse and in threat into the Vanuatu Copra Producers Bank. It was the first one on their list for their new strong-arm approach. The bank executive they encountered was a mild-mannered, amicable, Indian islander with the unlikely name of Jorge Joachim Rodriguez.

CHAPTER FIFTY-FOUR

When Randolph arrived back in the states, he contacted Hartley Proctor on a burner cell phone per their pre-arranged signal. He had put an ad in the *Washington Post* personals reading: "Homeless man seeking information on his family. Contact Ephraim at the Holy Bible Shelter." The ad ran two days, and at five p.m. sharp on the second day, Randolph dialed Proctor's private office number. He called from New Bedford, Massachusetts.

Proctor picked up the line, but said nothing.

"It's me," Randolph said. "Were you able to make all of the arrangements?"

"Yes, except for a few loose ends. The deputy U.S. attorney already had a meeting scheduled for a week from now with the ATF agents involved in your case—the ones who may have committed felonies—and their attorneys to establish positions and to determine whether or not to move ahead with a grand jury or indictments. As you may already know, one of the agents has copped a plea and has been granted immunity. I think the U.S. Attorney's Office has its sights set higher; so, it seems to me to be the opportune for you to come in. We can take advantage of the government's and the public's shift of focus away from you. The deputy U.S. attorney suggested that you participate in that meeting, and I concur. I believe the attention is going to be on the bad cops, and you will be more or less an adjunct in that meeting. I also think it is our one chance to find out what else the government has in mind."

"Where is that meeting scheduled to take place?"

"I presume at the U.S. Attorney's Office in the Justice Building in D.C.— on Saturday. Wherever, I can let you know at the last minute. I think you need to come in a day or so early to let us complete our plans and defense."

"I can get there only one day early. I'll get a hotel room in the city and give you a call then. We can meet in my hotel. In the meantime, I have a lot to do."

"All right, be careful. I will expect to see you next Friday, then."

When Randolph rang off, Proctor called Gwen Chambers at the paper and told her that the meeting was a go for the following Saturday. He then called Daniel Hernandez at the U.S. Attorney's Office to confirm that his client would be available for surrender and to attend the meeting, but all parties had to keep the matter sub rosa until then. Hernandez told Proctor that it was likely to be one of the most memorable meetings of either of their lives, if the two of them could pull it off.

Daniel Hernandez weighed his options. He could conduct the meeting and then convey the results up the chain of command like a good appointee. He knew full well that spin doctors at each level would manipulate, frustrate, and procrastinate the ends of justice. It was always the job of presidential loyalists to protect their client no matter what the cost to themselves, to the public, or to the truth. Hernandez knew that he could simply weigh the evidence like the prosecutor he was; and, in all likelihood, enter a bill of indictment against the two low men on the totem pole. No one would be critical of him for doing that. It was the prudent thing to do, the way a good party loyalist would do. Or, he could go with his gut in opposition to everyone who might advise him—his wife, his colleagues, and his bosses—and involve the potential major culprits from the beginning and let the chips fall where they may.

He shrugged. He had been at this long enough anyway. He made up his mind. First, he called the presidential switchboard, then the Attorney General's Office, and arranged for a conference call among himself, the personal lawyer for the president, the attorney for the AG, the White House counsel, and the Attorney General's Office counsel. Had he left anyone out? No one he cared about.

The lawyers were by nature curious and by profession defensive. They were all intrigued at the arrangement for the call, coming as it did from a deputy U.S. attorney with something of a reputation for being a maverick. Hernandez had not informed any of them of the nature of the business to be discussed. He had played this one so close to his vest that he had no even used his administrative assistant in the process.

Secretaries informed their principles that everyone was in attendance on the line.

The White House Senior Counsel, Vera Trimble, said, "We're anxious to hear what you have to say, Mr. Hernandez. Please proceed."

"For the record, this conversation is being recorded, ladies and gentlemen. You will hear intermittent beeping noises. That is to alert you to the recording. If any of you objects to being recorded, you may be excused; but I strongly advise you to hear me out before you make up your mind."

"Is this necessary—the recording—I mean?" the president's personal counsel asked.

"Abundantly so, counselor. From this point on, everything I say or do in regards to the matters for discussion today will be reproducible for a court of law. It might be wise for you to do the same. Eight days from today, on Saturday, the fifth, at ten in the morning, I will convene an informal inquiry into certain aspects of the Randolph Kennedy Affair. I will be acting in my official capacity as a deputy U.S. attorney. I have two ATF agents in my custody who, along with their attorneys, will be present to give testimony. The reason I have called you is that both of them have indicated an involve-ment—a conspiracy, if you will—on the part of the collection of politicians belonging to the President's Final Battle in the War on Drugs and Illegal Weapons Task Force, including the president and the attorney general."

There were several audible sharp inhalations that came in over the tele-phone lines.

"While there is no obligation for you or your principles to be present, you are hereby invited. Because of other considerations I cannot divulge, only you attorneys and your principles, if they should so choose, may be in attendance.

"I will give you fair warning. A member of the press will be in attendance and will have ad libitum privilege to communicate the story to the media. This is expressly to avoid shrouding this procedure in the usual cloak of mystery. There have been far too many secrets in this matter already, ladies and gentlemen."

"Now, look here, Mr. Hernandez," protested the president's personal counsel.

"Mr. Harrelson," Daniel Hernandez said sharply, "there will be no control by any other agency in this matter. There will not even be the appearance of influence. It will be public. You can be there and act, or you can react; but the light of day will shine on these proceedings."

"We'll see about that. Your superiors will have a say. If I had a crystal ball, I would predict that you will be out of a job before this grand stand meeting of yours ever takes place. The proper order of things is to submit an outline of the meeting and the anticipated testimony, and we can assess the need for a meeting. The president cannot tolerate blatant displays of disloyalty in her administration, and no law requires her to do so. Stand down, sir. Let us all have a chance to review the propriety of this meeting of yours."

There were three faint beeps on the line.

"And stop the recording this instant."

"I believe I have made my position clear, and I'm done except for telling you that any leaks about this will come from you, not me. I suggest you keep this under wraps until the actual meeting. A word to the wise—I believe it is in the best interests of your clients to keep this quiet. I am acting in accordance with my sworn duties as a legal officer of the United States. No one is above the law, ladies and gentlemen. The law will not be shunted aside. The meeting will proceed as outlined in eight days. Good day."

He paused long enough to avoid an accusation of disrespect or discourtesy, then hung up, conjuring in his mind's eye the consternation that now undoubtedly reigned at the other ends of his call.

In less than five minutes, the chief U.S. attorney was on Hernandez's line, politely suggesting that he reconsider any rash action. Hernandez asked if the chief had been contacted and if he had considered the propriety of accepting calls from the White House regarding matters that involved an investigation of their activities. The chief said that he wished only to assure Hernandez that he would allow no interference or taint of influence to fall on his department in the pursuit of its sworn duty. He backpedaled with alacrity. Hernandez smiled into his telephone hand piece. He knew that he held one nearly invincible trump card at this point—the implicit threat that if his meeting did not take place, then the matter might rise to the full attention of Congress, and a political "independent counsel" might be appointed. It was always good to be the lesser of evils.

Randolph watched the mid-morning Fox News Channel in his unassuming room in the International Motor Inn located at the junction of the major 5 and 805 Freeways in San Ysidro, a couple of miles from the Mexican border at Tijuana. He kept only half his mind on the news that the Gay Pride parade was to take place that morning and the details of the parade route and the incredibly diverse participants lined up for the event. He chose the motel because it was extremely busy and was located in an extraordinarily high motor traffic area. It was a little down at the heels, not the sort of place where guests struck up conversations with other guests. Mexican nationals used the motel regularly when they came across on San Diego shopping sprees or for business. The motel was very accommodating to the Mexicans, who constituted the life's blood of the place. He had eight days before he had to be in Washington for his all important meeting with the U.S. attorney, and he knew that he had to use that time very efficiently.

Randolph's identity as Jaime Hidalgo Cortez and his choice of paying his bills in cash did not excite the slightest interest. That he looked like a Nordic was of no interest either. He was automatically assumed to be one of the haughty ten percent of Mexicans who had retained the purity of their European Spanish heritage. His middle name, Hidalgo, was a contraction of the older "*Hijo de Algo*"—son of someone, the 'someone' being one of importance. He was careful to be generous with the help at the motel to reinforce that image.

He had to be mindful of several pitfalls of using this old fake identity, one he should have discarded long ago. First of all, this identity was on record with the Utah State Police for a traffic violation, and the feds had found it and had spread his ID picture around the nation. Second, he no longer looked anything like his ID photos. It was obvious that he could not use the phony ID for more than a few days. He went about as little as possible, ever mindful of the possibility of being recognized or followed by police. He made it a point to pay cash for anything he wanted to avoid use of a credit card which might require him to show ID.

Randolph lost himself for the rest of the morning in the crowds of onlookers at the gay and lesbian art exhibits, watched the gay rights parade while sitting between a doctor from Fresno and a flaming transvestite who had come down from the Tenderloin in San Francisco. He blended into the crowd by wearing tough-guy leathers including a black leather cap slouched down over his forehead.

He ate lunch with a commune of women who invited him to join them to prove that they were as tolerant of Deviants—heteros—as they wished the rest of the population would be towards them. The woman next to him had bared breasts with rings in her nipples, and her look dared him to comment. He and she shared a few bottles of Dos Equis beer, foie gras with pineapple and cinnamon, chicken breasts with hijiki seaweed, and for dessert, a shiitake and garlic Napoleon. The meal seemed as foreign and diverse as the company, but they both served to cloak Randolph in anonymity, the purpose of his venturing out.

On the way back to his hotel, he stepped out of the plague of locals swelled with the influx of Gay Pride Week revelers and into a gay bar called Spike to use the bathroom. He used the opportunity to look over his shoulder to see if he was being tailed. That was unnecessary as it turned out. No self-respecting policeman or woman—even the gay ones—would have dreamt of stepping foot in to the notorious hang out. It only took Randolph a trip to the bathroom to be convinced. He opened the door, stepped in, then stepped smartly back out. He did not want to allow into his memory bank any further images of the activities between four or five consenting adults that he saw in his glance into that "Gentlemen's Comfort Room" as the sign said. No bladder pressure was worth another peek inside.

He returned to the International Motor Inn at two in the afternoon and changed into a pair of impeccable white linen trousers, huaraches without socks, and a guayabera shirt. He suspended his valuables inside a wallet attached to a stout string around his neck and tucked in under the guayabera. It had been no trouble to buy a used car in San Ysidro or to find Baja California license plates. He bought Mexican insurance from the car dealer.

Randolph chose to cross the border in mid afternoon, the busiest time of the day. The examination of his Mexican passport was perfunctory since he was going in the direction of Mexico, and who cared? It was the other direction of travel that he could expect scrutiny of Mexican documents.

Randolph knew exactly where he was headed. Half a year on the lam had provided an education in the jargon and about the haunts and practices of people who wished to conduct their lives with a minimum of scrutiny. He made his way slowly through the heart of Tijuana. His progress was impeded by the activities of a fiesta. Ahead of him ran a person in a paper mâché figure costume of a chicken being chased by a dreadful, long-clawed lizard-like monster. When his car ground to a stop at an intersection, he asked an American tourist what was going on.

"It's a Chupacabra festival!"

"What's it about?" Randolph asked, intrigued.

"The Chupacabra is the Goat Sucker!" the American reveler explained with a note of finality.

Randolph raised an eyebrow.

"The Chupacabra is the beast that drains blood from its victims—mostly goats and dogs, but sometimes people."

That made the whole thing clear—a salute to a monster that sucked blood from animals. Randolph pushed ahead without joining in the general merriment of the populace. Maybe it was like opera; the audience wasn't supposed to understand it.

He drove straight through Tijuana on Mexico Highway 1—the Ensenada *Cuota* or toll road. Beyond Tijuana, the highway rambled on south past Rosarito Beach—which was little more than an extension of San Diego for middle-class Americans who wanted to live rich. The beauty of the coast road was interrupted by billboards and banners touting—often in fractured Spanglish—the condominiums, resorts, and restaurants along the way. He passed through Ensenada, stopping on the wharf to eat *tapas*, fish tacos, and *natilla Española*. He ate his delicious lunch seated beside a kiosk advertising "attorney for tourist protection". Big-eyed peninsulare children sat staring at him unabashedly.

Satiated from his meal and still savoring the taste of cinnamon sugar from his dessert he made his way on down the west coast of the Baja Peninsula. The road was excellent, and he made good time. He drove the 200 kilometers from Ensenada to San Quintin in three hours. It was quarter to seven when he passed through an area of strange cirio trees, called *boojum* by locals. In the growing dusk, the long, slender, sinuous, spiny branches of the trees—some of which were 600 years old—looked like tentacles of a giant landlocked squid. South of those trees, he consulted his Fonatur map, then turned onto a newly paved side road to Bahia de los Angeles. He stopped at the lone motel, "Domingo's MotorMotel for Tourists", and entered the unairconditioned lobby.

It was frightfully hot, and Randolph knew he was in for a miserable stay. Out of the car for even the few minutes it took to walk to the motel lobby, he was covered with a profuse sweat. California was named by Hernan Cortez. When the conquistador first saw the broiling landscape, he called it "Cali fornia"—the hot furnace. Lower California was the hottest furnace. Randolph registered, got fuel at the one service station, paying twice the price of gas as he had in San Diego, bought a strawberry Popsicle at the Conasupo store, and walked along the beach looking at the calm waters of the bay. He could see the tiny Isla la Raza with its hordes of birds. The only other building in the area besides the motel, the small national grocery store, and the gas station, was a tiny bait and boat rental shop. The hamlet's isolation was conducive to relaxation, and the heat made him sleepy; so, he returned to his room and tried to nap in the bake oven heat.

At eleven that evening a quiet rap came on his door. He cautiously looked out. A forbidding looking Mexican man stood holding his hands palms open to show that he did not have a weapon. Randolph bit his lip thoughtfully, took in a deep breath, and let the man in. The man's voice was soft and melodious in contrast to his fierce demeanor. He introduced himself.

"I yam Pedro Otero."

His cousin in the International Motor Hotel in San Ysidro had referred Randolph to him.

"I yam a *Californio*, a *beduino, Señor.* I come. I go. Today, I yam here to serve you.

Neither man's grasp of the other's language was adequate for small talk; so, they got down to business immediately.

"What you need, *Señor*?"

"*Tres pasaportes* with mi own photo. *Tres diferentes* addresses."

Pedro gave him a look that signified a failure to communicate. Randolph looked up "address" in his phrase book.

"*Dirrecciones*," he said.

Pedro nodded his understanding.

"*Y* driver licenses, *tambien*?"

"*Si.*"

"*Y* birthaday *certificados*?"

"*Si, todos.*"

"*Estara my costoso!*" Pedro said with emphasis.

It was Randolph's turn to look blank.

"*La costa este espensiva.*"

Randolph had no difficulty understanding that. It was no more than he expected.

Pedro went out to his truck and returned with some simple photographic equipment, He posed Randolph for digital pictures; and when he was finished, he took Randolph's money and left, promising to return on the next evening.

Randolph got up early in the morning and got out of the sweltering motel, took time to rent a *panga*—a small fishing boat—and with the help of the local fisherman/boat renter, he caught three yellowtail. He gave the fish to the man's family. He ambled about the desert floor among the cholla, creosote, and mesquite, and watched out for the red rattlesnakes common in Baja. The motel owner's wife—a Paipai Indian named Tressie, one of the line of original people not exterminated by the diseases brought in by the Jesuits and their missions—made him meals of lobster tacos, fried *agave, leche, queso*-stuffed Anaheim chilies, empanadas stuffed with curried goat, *frijolitos*, and Oaxacan stew spiced with *hoja santa*.

Pedro met Randolph as the fugitive was walking in the relative coolness of early dusk that Saturday evening. Two hours later, Randolph departed Bahia de los Angeles with three new United States identities. He destroyed his old Jaime Hidalgo Cortez passport; it had outlived its usefulness. The workmanship on the new IDs was flawless. From San Quintin, he called Vanuatu and spoke with Jorge Joachim Rodriguez long enough to find the names of several discreet banks in Mexico, D.F. and to inquire how Rodriguez's Sphynx was getting along.

He learned that select Mexican banks were the financial havens for Hispanic drug lords because the banks in question loved cash, and they did not ask a lot of questions. They hated nosy gringos. Randolph left his car in Ensenada and flew on Mexican Airlines to Mexico City that night. The next morning, Sunday, the Mexican banks accommodated Randolph by helping him open accounts in several banks in American cities and by establishing "correspondent" relationships with the banking corporations involved.

The hand of Jorge Rodriguez was evident in getting the banks to do business on the Sabbath. He had paved the way with a glowing account of Randolph's riches. Randolph opened accounts in the correspondent banks in the names of his new identities, using the new name only and obtaining a code number of his choice. Randolph made it simple to remember; his code number was the numerals of his birthday in reverse. Mexico did not have strict disclosure laws. He had only "correspondent" accounts at those American banks—courtesy of the solicitous Mexican clerks—adding another layer of complexity for U.S. financial probers to penetrate. With that done, Randolph destroyed all of his remaining false IDs, hid the new ones that Pedro Otero had created in a false pocket in his valise, and flew back to Ensenada.

CHAPTER FIFTY-FIVE

Sunday at noon, Randolph retraced his journey to leave Mexico. In Tijuana he found a new car and California license plates for a hefty price. The conversation with the car salesman contained references to *autopartes, parkiar* brakes, *carros, trockes,* and some other Spanglish terms not found in the Spanish-English dictionary. The salesman proudly informed Randolph that there was no *leakiendo* from the radiator. With his new car, Randolph entered the six lanes of traffic waiting to cross the border back into the United States.

In front of him an innocent-looking minivan was pulled off to the side lane for a thorough contraband check. The driver appeared to be an elderly Midwesterner, and he was protesting vehemently. The customs and immigration officer bent down to inspect Randolph's documents but had to excuse himself to assist in subduing the elderly protester.

"You can't do this. I will see my congressman. You'll be checking out Eskimos next week," the old man yelled.

The officer returned to Randolph. Traffic had backed up another 200 yards during the time he had been distracted. The officer looked hot and harried.

"Tough day, officer?"

"You'd better believe it."

He cast a scornful look in the old man's direction, but his training forbade him to say anything. "Passport, birth certificate, or driver's license, please."

Randolph handed him the appropriate passport and driver's license from his new collection.

"Where're you from, Mr. Pennington?"

"Ballwin, Missouri."

"May I see your registration, sir?"

This was the moment Randolph had been dreading. The registration he had been given at the Tijuana used car lot looked pretty phony even to him. The license plates on the car bore no resemblance to the vehicle on which they were attached.

The officer took the papers and began to look at them perfunctorily.

In front of them, the old man who had been causing the disturbance earlier had now fallen to the ground along side his minivan.

"Lend us a hand!" shouted one of the officers who had been dealing with the man. "Heart attack, I think."

"Pass on through, sir, have a pleasant day," Randolph's officer requested pragmatically and rushed to assist in CPR.

Randolph exhaled a grateful sigh that he had not had to undergo stringent scrutiny and pulled out into the six lane traffic slowly moving into San Diego.

It was a week before Gerald heard anything from his agents in Vanuatu. The communication was a to-the-point telephone call that came at three o'clock in the morning. The people in charge at the opposite end of the line were not concerned with the inconvenience caused by the time difference, and they insisted that Silberberg accept the calling charges.

"Boss, we only get two minutes. Barnes, Deckington, and I are in a Vanuatu jail. It's a pit, literally. Seems that we somehow violated their securities laws. Didn't matter that we were FBI—seemed to make things worse, in fact. The man who turned us in—a guy named Rodriguez—said we could expect thirty years. You gotta do something to get us out of here. We won't last a year."

"Be good soldiers," Silberberg said. "I'll get right on it. We'll take care of the little brown…"

The line went dead. The two minutes were not quite up, but the censor at the other end of the line took umbrage at the ethnic slur she presumed was coming and cut them off.

Silberberg put his forehead onto the palms of his hands and tried to rub out the headache that was beginning.

Barnes, Deckington, and Haverford sank into a deep depression; the call to Silberberg was the only one they were to be allowed during the entire judicial process; and if the information they were being given by the Vanuatu officials was accurate, it would be their last communication for thirty years. Jeremy Barnes was astounded to learn that his status as a sworn agent of the FBI was going to do nothing to protect him. Peter Deckington was only now coming to grips with the fact that his American citizenship would not avail him anything, and he would not even be able to contact the U.S. Consulate in Vila... ever. Stephen Bartholomew Haverford III remained outwardly confident that this was a nightmare that would be corrected as soon as he could convince these obstinate brown monkeys that it meant something to be the scion of the Haverford shipping family, a Yale graduate with a masters in international finance, a CPA, and a Special Agent of the Federal Bureau of Investigation for the United States of America. It would be quite a tale to tell the folks back home when it was all over. Inwardly, he did not feel quite that confidant.

According to his tickets, Leif Erik Sorensen boarded the first class section of Delta Flight 328 from San Diego bound for Honolulu at four-ten that Sunday afternoon. His driver's license gave Sorensen an address in Minneapolis. His license photograph was that of Randolph Kennedy. Randolph enjoyed the flight which he had paid for with a new VISA card that his Minneapolis bank had been all too happy to provide him on short notice through its branch in San Diego. It was so much simpler to be able to use the card like everyone else instead of having to explain away his wanting to use cash. Randolph enjoyed the flight, sleeping most of the way, tired after his hot drive out of Mexico.

He spent the day in the Kahala Mandarin Oriental Hotel on the dolphin lagoon in Oahu. In Honolulu on Monday morning he established savings and checking accounts at the Bank of Hawaii in the Ala Moana Mall on Kapiolani Boulevard and at the Hale Ewa branch of the First Hawaiian Bank on the north shore of Oahu. Both accounts were in the name of Leif Erik Sorensen and were branch links to the bank corporations he had contacted from Mexico. He arranged with Jorge Joachim Rodriguez in Vila to transfer funds to his Mexican banks, and it was a simple matter to wire-transfer those funds to his new American accounts.

Randolph took a little time to enjoy the sun, sea air, sand and food. After completing his banking business, he turned left from the hotel and walked until he was standing in front of the nearby Waialae Country Club and got directions from the locals going home from their night's work about the best things to do, to see, and to eat.

The directions came from a language peculiar to the island, "You must go to a poke contest."

His informants explained to Randolph about Hawaii's raw fish and Samoan snails marinated in mixtures of sesame, rice vinegar, fish sauce, ginger, garlic, and lemon grass. The avidly helpful islanders slipped comfortably into explanations that included *mouka*—towards the mountains, and *makai*—towards the sea or towards Diamond Head or *Ewa*—towards the direction away from Diamond Head.

He breakfasted on chocolate croissants at the buffet in the Plumeria Beach café, lunched outdoors on appetizers—duck won ton with tangerine sauce and lemon grass chicken brochettes with peanut sauce—at the Indigo Restaurant on Nu'uamma Avenue. He napped in a sleep of the just on a canopy bed swathed in white muslin.

Randolph returned on the night flight to San Francisco, traveling this time as Terrence Pennington from Ballwin, Missouri, the same identity he had used to return to the U.S. from Mexico. He checked into the Stanford Court Hotel. Tuesday morning he spent arranging new bank accounts at Federal Indemnity of San Francisco, and First Federal of Oakland in the name of Terrence Pennington. The transactions were, once again, made effortless by his previous arrangements through the Mexican correspondence banks.

Next, Randolph took the noon flight to Buffalo, New York, on United under his final alias, Orrin Hendersen, whose address was on Baseline Road in the heart of Grand Island. He now had three and a half days before his fateful meeting with the U.S. attorney. Randolph was beginning to feel a little pressure. He again arranged two accounts. One of them was in the Marine Midland Bank in the city center, and the other was in the suburbs in Williamsville Village in the M&T Bank. As with the financial transactions in the other cities, the new accounts were in that city's respective alias. In Buffalo and at the Marine Midland and the M&T, he was in business as Orrin Hendersen.

He told each new account executive that they should expect substantial additions to the account in short order. That afternoon, he drove to New York City in a rented Ford and opened four accounts with Merrill Lynch in as many offices, transferring funds from the bank account corresponding to the name on the new account. At each branch, he arranged to have them provide him with a new Signature Preferred Client VISA card.

Randolph used his own name and ID at the main office on the fourth floor of the World Financial Center on Liberty Street and paid by wire transfer directly from the Vanuatu Copra Producers Bank. Because the amount was going to be very substantial, the broker waited patiently and at a discrete distance while Randolph went through the necessary, but tedious, identification procedures with his Vanuatu bank. The eager account executive recognized neither Randolph's face nor his name. He only registered the large numbers Randolph presented to him. The remainder of the day, Randolph spent establishing accounts at Shearson Lehman and Piper Jaffrey.

That evening, he settled into the Marriott Marquee using his Signature card under his Orrin Hendersen alias. He went to the hotel's business center and began to work. Though it had been less than a full day since his last vetting and set of transactions, he took an hour to go through the rigmarole of identifying himself to Mr. Rodriguez in Vanuatu.

"Mr. Rodriguez, please," he asked as soon as the receptionist at the Copra Producers Bank responded to his call.

"I will get Mr. Rodriguez presently."

In a few seconds, the distinctive Oxford clipped tones of Jorge Joachim Rodriguez came through. The connection was as clear as if he had been calling across town.

"How may I be of service?"

"This is Randolph Kennedy. Perhaps you remember me, Mr. Rodriguez."

"Indeed I do," he laughed. "You have had a busy time of late. How can I help you now?"

"I wish to make wire transfers to two banks in Honolulu."

"Not a problem. First, please identify yourself. It is a formality, but a necessary one, however repetitive."

Randolph placed the copy of his fingerprints in the fax modem and sent it off to Vanuatu. While that operation was underway, he read the prearranged paragraph required for the voiceprint. He had done the same things for each new brokerage account only hours earlier; so, the procedure was becoming almost routine.

"Those identifiers check out, sir," said Rodriguez. "Could I now have your code, please?"

"43363-263-26643."

The images of Irene and Annie formed in Randolph's mind as he recited the numbers. He was mildly disturbed that it was becoming more difficult to picture his lost wife and daughter, and the process of bringing their faces to his consciousness was taking longer.

"That is correct. Please give my name and particulars, if you would."

Randolph recited to the banker his own name and the date of establishment of Randolph's account with the bank.

"That is correct and completes the transaction. I hope it has not proved to be too cumbersome."

"No, not at all. I'm beginning to get the hang of it."

'How much would you like to transfer, to where, and in what currency?"

"Forty million to the Bank of Hawaii and sixty million to First Hawaiian Bank. U.S. currency."

He gave Rodriguez the electronic addresses of the banks and his account numbers.

"Will there be anything else, Mr. Kennedy?"

"No, thank you, that completes my transaction."

"I have one thing to tell you before we close, Mr. Kennedy. It seems that some of your country's FBI people were in Vanuatu trying to secure information regarding your accounts at our bank and at several others. Let me assure you that none was given. The criminals involved are currently incarcerated and are awaiting trial. It can take up to a year to have one's trial in Vanuatu. I thought you might like to know about that."

Randolph laughed.

"I appreciate the intelligence. My best to you and the bank. Keep up the good work."

He waited until he had verification of the transfers from his Vanuatu Copra Producers Bank account to each of his Hawaiian banks. Then he arranged for seven transfers to his stateside banks and investment house accounts. Randolph made the money trail as complex as he could. He moved numbers from Vanuatu to Hawaii, from Hawaii to San Francisco, then from San Francisco to New York, Minneapolis, and Buffalo in a dizzying set of combinations and permutations of sending bank and account information to the receiving institutions. To open his bank accounts originally, he had deposited varying amounts of cash, from $4000 to as much as $8500, always keeping below the $10,000 limit for mandatory reporting of cash transactions. Now, he merely moved numbers electronically around the country—and around the world to his banks. At the end of an hour of hectic telephoning and with considerable help from the obliging Marriott staff, Randolph had set into motion the first steps in making his three aliases very rich men.

He knew it would have to be temporary. His aliases would have to have their lives be fleshed out to include occupations, regular deposits and withdrawals, charitable donations, pay taxes, and the like. He was going to have to effect moves, changes of banks, and the creation of businesses. He had made a good start; it had to be enough before his fateful meeting on Saturday. He knew that he had to become a true expert in laundering money, but he would have to be able to be free to do that. Loss of his freedom loomed large in his thinking right then.

Randolph shopped for clothes in the Marriott's exclusive stores, buying several handsome dark suits, a dozen fitted white pinpoint cotton shirts, underwear, socks, and an assortment of ties and shoes to augment his severely depleted wardrobe,. He splurged and bought an expensive leather brief case into which he placed his remaining cash on Hand—about $200,000 in a mix of denominations.

Early the next morning—Thursday—when he was satisfied that he had completed his business and his wardrobe was adequate, he checked out of the Marriott Marquis and took the Marriott limousine to JFK Airport and flew to Washington on the first hourly flight he could arrange. It was still before business hours when he arrived in D.C.

He hailed a cab from the waiting line at Dulles and went directly to the Library of Congress. He sought out the help of one of the library's information specialists to find what he needed. He spent the next several hours pouring over the available books and periodicals on the subjects of offshore banking laws and practices, regulations regarding the transferal of funds, and the implications of creating false identities to obscure possession and location of large estates.

He worked at a frantic pace. When he was persuaded that he had absorbed all he could at the library, he took a cab to the Washington Bar Association building and inquired into legal firms. He was able to get an appointment with a renowned tax attorney who was a foreign law expert, and a corporation specialist. His ability to pay a retainer of $100,000 and his own experience as a CPA were most helpful in working with the lawyer—at $500 an hour—to establish a plan to create estates for his aliases. He and his new attorney worked until nearly ten o'clock that night with the help of a small army of attorneys, accountants, and secretaries to complete the documentation that would create corporations, holding companies, trusts, and shells for the dispersal of his money—all quite legal—and in his own name. He did not tell the Washington attorney that he intended to clone their work, with minor alterations, so that his now well-to-do aliases, Terrence Pennington, Leif Erik Sorensen, and Orrin Hendersen would become the ultimate owners of similarly labyrinthine and virtually impenetrable corporate structures. When that was concluded, he cancelled all of his banking and business ties in his own name in New York. He changed the names on the investment accounts to the identities of his aliases. No one questioned the changes, and the name of Randolph Armstrong Kennedy disappeared from corporate and banking history.

When they concluded the day's efforts, the attorney and his firm were committed to contract with the Rand Company in Los Angeles and with the Trumps in New York to obtain property, with Merrill Lynch in New York to flesh out a veritable stock empire, and with a recently phenomenally successful small high tech company in Provo, Utah, to head hunt for officers for a controlling company charged with buying up small, vigorous, and potentially successful, but currently struggling companies in need of funding. The principle proviso in contracting with a company was that one of Randolph's aliases would become the titular CEO. He instructed his law firm to allow for generous repayment schedules, not to ask for high stock ownership, and accepted limited control in the companies.

He was spent and had done all that he could do. He called Hartley Proctor from his business attorney's private office and let him know that he was staying at the Shoreham. He took a cab over to his hotel, handed over his luggage to a bellman, and completed the formalities of registration. He used his Hendersen VISA card.

Randolph threw off his clothes and collapsed into bed. The next morning—Friday—he got up early and returned to the attorneys' office building. There, he spent three hours interfacing with Jorge Joachim Rodriguez and his new corporate attorneys to execute a new assortment of wire transfers including a series of six transfers of funds from Vanuatu to an account in Grand Cayman Island owned by "The Devlin, himself" according to official records. He placed $14,000,000 in that account and felt that he had now squared accounts with Devlin and with the North Star Militia to whom he owed his financial freedom.

He also regarded the payment as the means to get them out of his life. Without informing the widow of Wasilla policeman, Alex Tolberg, Randolph created a $2,000,000 trust fund naming her as both the trustee and the beneficiary. He falsified the documents to give the credit to the Disabled Police United Benevolent Fund of Alaska. It was an act of contrition for the one death that came from his booby traps that he deeply regretted. He would never be able to forgive himself fully for that, but it was a little something. He had learned to be philosophical—nothing he had done could be undone.

The most time consuming part of his time with his new lawyers that morning was to start them working on establishing elaborately detailed fictitious lives for his aliases and to prevent connection of any of those aliases with him. The attorneys set about to make the paper men into reclusive taxpayers, philanthropists, notable citizens in their communities, and frequent travelers. The law firm was well compensated for their participation in the questionable enterprise. If he could remain free, Randolph knew he would have a lifetime career to keep up the charade, fleshing out the details of the phony lives, making the paper entities seem to live through e-mails, faxes, telephone calls, snail mail, and without personal contacts. He recognized the difficulties inherent in his project and in what he was asking of the law firm. It would always be a Potemkin village at best.

He was satisfied that he had done all he could to launch his new monied life—lives. He was very tired and decided to return to the Shoreham for a nap before meeting Hartley Proctor.

CHAPTER FIFTY-SIX

His room was on the third floor. He stepped off the elevator lost in thought and ran bodily into a man hurrying into the elevator, equally absorbed in his own agenda. The fit young man was dressed in a light gray suit, white shirt, and subdued tie, and black wing-tip Florsheims. A silent alarm went off in Randolph's head as he instinctively reached out to prevent the two of them from falling. The man's arm was rock hard, and he had a gun in a holster in his left armpit. Randolph's antennae told him that this was a federal agent, an enemy. The man's eyes caught Randolph's with a querying, haven't-we-met-before? look.

Randolph had a hot surge of adrenaline.

"Excuse me," he said.

"Don't mention it, my fault," the young man said.

He entered the elevator, and Randolph reacted with pure animal instinct. He waited until the elevator door closed and then he turned and ran for the stairs mildly hampered by his briefcase. He descended the stairs two at a time, and ran out of the stair well and into the lobby without paying attention to the other people in the crowded public room. Without looking back, he walked very briskly to the revolving front doors of the hotel. He thought he heard the man call out—maybe it was only his imagination—but he made no effort to respond. He made it a point to step into the throngs walking down the busy thoroughfare. He hurriedly swept off his suit jacket and walked bent over to alter his rapidly identifiable features as seen from a distance behind his retreating figure.

The elevator door closed on the FBI agent who took only a moment to connect with the fact that he had just had a physical encounter with public Enemy Number One. He stepped out of the elevator and into the lobby. There, he punched out the numbers for the emergency desk at the FBI Building on his cell phone. As he called he looked about to see if he could catch a glimpse of the fugitive, but he could not. It was evident that the man was now on the third floor of the prestigious hotel.

Randolph quickened his pace and turned left at the next corner and made his way onto 14th Street. He looked over his shoulder frequently. He saw the mass of pedestrians on the sidewalk, but no one obviously on his tail. He ratcheted up his velocity another notch, trying to move quickly but not to draw attention to himself.

The FBI agent's call took him through three formal steps that required him to communicate his identification number, his name, and to state repeatedly that he had a red code emergency.

After several minutes, he heard, "Silberberg."

The voice of the third most powerful and the most feared official in the Federal Bureau of Investigation came across with all of its timbre of cold command.

"Special Agent David Gardner, sir. I have just seen Randolph Armstrong Kennedy."

Randolph turned into an army-navy surplus store on 14th Street near the corner of H Street. It was full of crisp new camouflage fatigues, tents, and Tee shirts with insignias of the various branches of the armed forces. Others were embroidered with images in bright colors that did not necessarily correspond to anything that might have been worn by a serviceman or woman. In fact, there was not a real piece of military surplus in the entire store and nothing used. The country's last war ended a couple of years previously. He looked around very quickly, selected an olive drab Tee shirt imprinted with the marine emblem on its left breast and "Semper Fidelis" curving across the back. He found a gray, black, and white camo jacket that fit. His last selection was a floppy boonie rat hat that slouched down over his forehead and hid much of his face. He paid cash.

"Do you have a change room? I want to wear my stuff out," Randolph asked the clerk.

"Behind the bivouac bags," the clerk said with no effort to show interest in his customer, and pointed in the general direction.

Randolph left the store dressed in camo clothing except for his suit pants and Bruno Magli shoes. He knew the outfit was incongruous, but it was all he could come up with on such short notice. He quickly walked into the middle of the pedestrian crowd and was pleased to see that he was not dressed so very differently than many of the young men and women milling about him.

Silberberg reacted to Agent Gardner's call with a start.

"You absolutely certain, Agent...?"

"Gardner, sir. And, yes, I am about as certain as an eyewitness can be, given the known problems with such evidence."

He wanted to leave himself a little wiggle room.

"I'll go with it, but if I cry havoc and let slip the dogs of war for nothing, you had better have a good hole to hide in for the rest of your natural life, understand?"

"Fully."

"When and where?"

"About seven to ten minutes ago, maybe less. He was getting off the Shoreham Hotel elevator. I bumped into him—literally—as he was leaving the elevator on the third floor, and I was entering it. I am now in the lobby, and I have not seen anything of him. I don't think he realized that I was in law enforcement; so, my best judgment is that he is still on the third floor."

"How was he dressed?"

"Expensive dark charcoal gray suit, red patterned power tie, no hat. He had a briefcase, black leather, I think."

"What are you doing right now?"

"Waiting for instructions."

"Hit the street. Ask anyone and everyone if they saw our man. I will throw a net over a ten-block area. Now move, but keep in sight of the hotel. I will be there shortly to talk to you."

Silberberg put down the receiver and pushed his emergency APB alert button. He spoke a few words into a recorder and thereby launched the largest dragnet in the capital city's history.

Special Agent Gardner ran through the lobby and out onto the street and began collaring people right and left demanding to know if they had seen Kennedy. Most of them gave him a blank look or gestured with their heads at the hundreds of pedestrians passing by. At least a quarter of the men moving along either side of the street fit the description Gardner just gave to the blasé Washingtonians.

Randolph knew he had to get lost, and he had to rest. He had let himself get so tired and so absorbed in his projects of the past few days that he had let down his guard. His nine lives were about used up; he knew that. He was so fatigued—even with the adrenaline rush—that it was evident that he would no longer be able to act or react sufficiently quickly or intelligently to protect himself if he did not lie down and close his eyes very soon. He could try and secrete himself in some abandoned basement or attic or in some junkyard, but he knew that every cop in three states would be searching for him. He had successfully eluded manhunts before—but this was their turf—and they might get lucky. Even a blind hog finds an acorn sometimes, he thought ruefully. The best plan was to hide in the open. His first task was to find enough people crowded into one space.

He put a dollar token into a *Washington Post* newspaper box, pulled out the day's paper, and swiftly perused it until he found the day's activities summary. There were garden expositions, dog shows, African folk dancers, bridge, chess and croquet tournaments, and a list of demonstrations with legal parade permits. He went down that list carefully. Randolph rejected as unlikely to attract the kinds and numbers of people he needed or the wrong ethnic or gender mix: an African Women in Action parade, two competing anti-cruelty to animals rallies, and a Teamster's strike at Walter Reed Army Hospital. What did catch and hold his eye was an announcement that the Gay Pride March for Dignity was underway at the Mall even as he stood reading, and was touted to be the largest gathering of homosexuals in one place and for one purpose in the history of the world.

Law enforcement personnel and vehicles burst onto the streets from all parts of the city, converging on Silberberg's ten-block area. D.C. Metro Police with a full complement of SWAT officers, county deputy sheriffs, Maryland and Virginia state troopers, FBI, and ATF agents were out in full force. Secretaries frantically called all off-duty officers and told them to report to their stations. Others rushed to print up photocopies of Randolph Kennedy for distribution on the streets. Silberberg demanded and received permission for TV and radio simulcast to announce the dragnet and to enlist the help of the citizens of the city.

Silberberg's 112 officer COINTELPRO unit turned the Shoreham Hotel upside down. They went through every room on the third floor inch by inch to the severe and complaining inconvenience of the guests and hotel management. The officers raced through the rest of the hotel until they had given every room at least a cursory look. They wasted four hours at the hotel and caused their leader a dangerous rise in his blood pressure when they finally came up empty handed. Most of the rooms had full suitcases in them, and many had no identifying papers. There was nothing helpful on the third floor or in the hotel.

The law enforcement army scoured the ten square block area of the city; every niche, nook, and cranny, every garage, loft, attic, basement, abandoned building, culvert, grove of trees, and alley was invaded, inspected, and rejected. Nothing, not a hint of Kennedy.

Less than ten minutes after Agent Gardner contacted Silberberg, no one got in or out of the cordoned area. The counter-terrorist chief and his hand picked unit left the Shoreham while the search was still in progress with instructions not to take down the terrorist unless absolutely necessary without contacting Silberberg first. He set up a mobile command center with satellites.

"We have sixteen sightings, Chief," one of the satellite vehicles reported after meeting with the D.C. Metro precinct captain. "Metro has men following up on every one of them."

"Any of them look to be any good?" asked Silberberg.

He planned to expropriate the best one or two for his immediate unit.

"Two by my reckoning."

"Give."

"A flower seller saw a man hurrying down the street, stop, remove his coat and tie, and rush on with the crowd. Seemed out of place and suspicious in retrospect," he reported. "And the next lead was from a dogwalker, one of those guys who take pampered rich people's mutts around the neighborhood and scoops up their poop; so, the dowagers won't have to mix with the riffraff."

"Save me the egalitarian characterizations, Special Agent. Get on with it."

"Yes, sir. This dogwalker thinks he saw a guy fitting our perp's description going into an army-navy surplus store on 14th. He's less sure, but thinks he may have seen the same guy come out in camo."

"You got the address of that store?"

"Yes, sir."

The agent checked his notes and then quickly read it to Silberberg.

"Okay, good work. Keep at it."

Silberberg clicked off.

He turned to his driver and barked, "Get me to 14th and H as fast as this crate can move; red lights and sirens, and God help the lame and the blind in our rush."

As Silberberg's command truck made a dangerous mid-traffic U-turn on N Street and began to roar along 14th, Randolph Kennedy walked into the periphery of the crowd on Madison Drive near the grassy center of the Mall. Most of the people at the fringe of the still gathering gay rights crowd were curious straights and foul-mouthed hecklers. Randolph had to push his way to get through to the cement perimeter of the Mall itself. As he drew closer to the front, the character of the crowd rapidly changed to clusters of women and groups of men with linked arms who were discordantly singing *We Shall Overcome*. The colors on the clothing and hair were more vivid; the amount of skin being exposed was more flagrant; and the hair styles were from another planet. There were— among the eccentrics—men and women dressed in conservative professional suits and dresses—with no clear correlation of gender with dress—men and women dressed in military uniforms, neat and fit and carrying placards that read, "Don't Ask, Don't Tell". Randolph gravitated towards that subgroup.

"Hi, brother, glad to see you out," said a uniformed marine gunny sergeant next to him when Randolph finally chose a place to stop where he felt that he had a decent field of vision but was still more or less enveloped by the milling crowd.

It was disconcerting to see the spit-and-polish noncom sporting nose and ear rings in his tough, craggy face. Most arresting was the fact that the sergeant was wearing lipstick.

"Wouldn't miss it for the world," Randolph responded enthusiastically.

"Like your rig," the sergeant told him, drawing up close to Randolph. "You military?"

"Ex," Randolph lied.

"Got the look," the gunny said, and placed his hand lightly on Randolph's forearm. "You live near the Mall?"

Randolph's first impulse was to jerk his arm away and make a vociferous protest that he was not one of them. His second—more radical thought— was to punch the guy's lipsticked face and establish his bona fides as a hetero beyond question. In his mind it was one thing to accept gays in the military when it was a "no ask, no tell, no problem" arrangement. Under President Gore, the gay activists had succeeded in overturning all obstacles and in obtaining full open rights in the military, including the privilege of wearing makeup and jewelry by both genders. It had always bothered Randolph to see a march in which one out of eight male soldiers wore any of a combination of a fisted Gay Pride emblems, lipstick and rouge, and facial adornments including tattoos and piercings. It was quite another thing beyond passive acceptance to have such a man touching him.

He gritted his teeth and said, "No, I'm from out of town. You?"

"Coupla blocks is all," the marine said, and smiled with prominent newly capped teeth that were glowingly white.

He moved his hand up to grip Randolph's biceps.

"Hard arm,"

He gave Randolph an appreciative look.

"You work out?"

"No, not really, just do a lot of physical stuff."

"Hey, I'm physical stuff," said the gunny, and winked at Randolph conspiratorially.

He actually winked. Randolph fought to keep down the feeling of nausea. He looked over shoulder of his companion of the moment in the direction of the National Museum of Natural History towards the demarcation line between the gays and the straights that was now being forcibly delineated by mounted park rangers and uniformed D.C. Metro officers. Every now and again he thought he could see gray suited men carrying radios moving through the lines in either direction. It was hard to be certain with the large and mobile crowds and with the sun setting.

CHAPTER FIFTY-SEVEN

The COINTELPRO command truck double parked in front of the army-navy surplus store. Silberberg checked the address he had written down. It was correct.

"Let's go stir something up," he ordered and stepped out onto the pavement.

The five federal officers marched briskly to the store. One man walked through the alley to the rear; one stationed herself at the front door; and the remaining three entered the poorly lit and dingy store. Silberberg walked up to the store clerk, who was pouring over the *Police Gazette* and did not have time to be interrupted by a customer right at that moment. He would pay attention when it came time for the guy to pay. Silberberg's two companion officers began to walk carefully through the store's displays of wares that were arranged more like the dishabille of a morning after than that of an intentional retail establishment.

Silberberg showed his badge and ID. The clerk did not deign to look up. Silberberg rapped a steely fist down on the countertop rattling coffee cups and full ashtrays.

Satisfied that he had the little man's attention, he said, "You had a man come in here in a suit a little while ago and bought some of your stuff. You remember him?"

Silberberg held a photo of Randolph Kennedy in the face of the clerk.

"Nope, we get lotsa people."

"Did you get a lot of people this afternoon?"

"Reg'lar."

"Look, you cretin, see this badge? I am not here to dick around with you."

He shoved the badge and ID almost into the clerk's nose. He got the man's attention.

"Now, here's what you are going to do in the next thirty seconds. First you are going to look hard at this picture, and you are going to tell me simply—yes or no—whether this man was here. Second, you are going to tell me what he bought. You got that?"

"Yeah. You don't have to get pushy, ya know. I got rights."

He looked at Silberberg's hard eyes and decided that his rights were not all that important at that moment. It was better for him to look and get rid of this mean-looking dude.

"Gimme see that picture."

Silberberg picked up the wanted poster from the counter and pushed it at the now cooperative clerk. The man studied it assiduously, making the task look like real work—real slow work. Silberberg presumed that the man was evidently exercising cerebral synapses that had been dormant for some time.

"I think that's the dude. Came in the place wearin' a white shirt and nice suit pants, carryin' his coat and tie. Had real fancy shoes, those funny lookin' queer froggy kind."

That thought seemed to cause a block. The clerk's face registered vacancy.

"And what did he buy? Out with it! Keep with me!" Silberberg prodded in exasperation.

"Oh, yeah," the clerk resumed, "Camo," he offered.

"What color? What style? C'mon don't make me drag every little bit out of you."

"Urban commando. You know, the gray, black, and white stuff. He got a jacket and a boonie-rat cap. Didn't get no pants. Seemed like he was in some kind of hurry."

"That all?"

"Yeah, I think so. Maybe…no."

"For the love of…"

"He bought one of them real lookin' marine Tee shirts," the clerk responded quickly.

"Anything else?"

"Nope. He walked outta here lookin' kinda funny in black suit pants, lawyer guy shoes, and camo. He had a brief case, and he stuffed his nice clothes into it when he moved outta here in a big hurry."

Silberberg turned on his heels and headed for the exit. His men shook their heads to indicate that their quarry was no longer in the store.

"Get his description with the camo out on an updated APB," Silberberg said as they were heading back to their vehicle.

The five officers ran for the truck.

"We'll drive around until somebody gives a sighting. Call Metro and get them started on a building to building canvass."

The clerk gave the finger to the departing FBI agents and said aloud to the empty room, "Don't think nuthin' of it. Glad to help the FBI anytime."

He gave them the finger with both hands when he was sure the officers were well out of sight.

Nancy Delgado heard the news of the manhunt from Romaine Terrife when he returned from his late lunch.

"Nancy, Maybe you oughta go out more. There is a manhunt on for our guy, Kennedy. More cops in this town than when every law enforcement officer in the country converged on Chicago after John Dillinger when they heard that he had a movie date with some dame in a sexy red dress."

"Are we invited?" she asked, her attention focused on her associate's report with full intensity.

"Apparently not. Silberberg and his storm troopers are out in force. I think it's a case of don't call us, we'll call you."

"Figures. I will go nuts just sitting here. But if Kennedy can squeeze under the fence, he or his lawyer will have to be in touch with us. The better part of wisdom and valor is to sit tight."

"And hope that Silberberg and his guys or his spies don't have wind of the meeting at the deputy U.S. attorney's office tomorrow morning."

"Amen to that, brother. I should be a loyal follower and root for the home team even if it screws up our well laid plans, but I can't. We won't have a chance to deal with the man if Silberberg gets his evil clutches on him. I would not like to be the insurance company holding a policy on the life of Randolph Armstrong Kennedy right now. I'll let Proctor know what's up."

Two gray-suited men who might as well have been wearing sandwich boards reading "FBI" began to walk in Randolph's direction, stopping every now and again to question one of the gay marchers or revelers.

Randolph made up his mind and said to his new marine noncom friend, "Hey, man, I don't even know your name. I think it would be great to get to know you better."

There must be a more subtle approach to liaisons like this, Randolph thought; but it was a little late for lengthy courting rituals.

"I'm Dick," Randolph said abruptly.

He almost rolled his eyes at his spontaneous choice of a pseudonym. It was all he could do to keep from laughing out loud.

"Ken," said the gunnery sergeant, and put his arm around Randolph's neck. Randolph suppressed a shudder.

"I'm not into the crowd scene. What do you say to us making the split and heading over to my pad?" asked Randolph's ardent new friend.

"I'm game, thanks. Look, I have to do a couple of things first. How about us getting together in about a half an hour at your place?"

Ken found a piece of scrap paper and quickly scribbled down his address and telephone number. The i's were dotted with little hearts and the period at the end of the address was a happy face.

"Can you read that?"

His voice was husky, betraying his arousal.

"No problem, I'll see you in thirty minutes, then."

"Make it twenty," Ken said and flashed an affectionate grin, one reserved for old lovers.

He chucked Randolph hard on the arm to cement the understanding that they were real guys and sympaticos. He was already moving away in the direction of his pad.

"Do my best," Randolph said, and did his utmost to return the toothy and inviting grin.

The two FBI agents were circling ever closer. Randolph hoped his impromptu disguise would serve, but it seemed to him that he had captured the attention of one of the federal officers and that the man and his partner were headed straight for him through the dense crowd. One of the two officers spoke into his shoulder phone pack.

Chapter Fifty-Seven

Silberberg took the car phone from his subordinate.

"Silberberg," he answered tersely.

He listened intently for a moment, then turned to his driver and ordered, "Turn this unit around and get us to the Mall. Full code!"

He spoke into his handset again, "Don't go for him yet unless he makes a break for it. We need to surround the place and move in with full force. This guy is dangerous, and we can't let him get away again."

One of the agents in the backseat asked, "Got a good sighting, boss?"

"We have two agents who have the terrorist in sight right now."

"Fantastic! Want me to call Metro and the state troopers?"

"No, this is an FBI problem. Put it out on the secure COINTELPRO frequency. I want every man we've got to be at the Mall in three minutes. We've got him this time. I feel it. No need to share with the *untermenshen*. Once we have him, we can put the message out on the open frequency."

"My sentiments exactly, boss."

The radioman signaled the rest of the FBI troops, and the jaws of the trap began to shut on Randolph Kennedy.

Randolph watched the two officers, whose behavior was becoming confusing to him. Twenty yards before they would have been able to reach out and grab him, they separated and veered to the right and to the left to question other gays. He caught them making occasional surreptitious glances in his direction. Maybe he was just being paranoid, Randolph considered. Then he saw two more agents, a man and a woman. There was no question now but that they were making a beeline for him. Even paranoids were right about their suspicions sometimes.

Randolph made the instant decision that his camo outfit and marine shirt were now giving him away. The feds must have gotten to the army-navy store; they were good. He suddenly knelt down and took off his camo jacket and hat, then his marine shirt. It was a hot day, and no one paid him the least attention; there was a lot of exposed skin around him. Men and women all around him were in all stages of making statements by their level of undress—some just short of outright nudity—and a couple of dozen couples—boy-boy, girl-girl—were beginning to make out on the lawn and concrete pathways of the Mall. The gathering was starting to look like a homophile Woodstock without the rain and mud. He threw on his dress shirt, missing half the buttons in his haste, and put on his suit coat over the disheveled shirt.

Sirens blared in the distance, apparently converging on the Mall from all directions.

In a flash of inspiration, he stepped over to a rather down at the heels Gay Pride placard carrier and said, "You want to have these threads, man? I don't have any more use for them."

The placard carrier was too far down at the heels to make a polite protest.

"You serious? Nice stuff. And thanks…brother. We gotta stick together 'gainst the homophobe armies. I'm gonna put these on right now."

Silberberg answered his command truck phone then said excitedly, "The two agents in place still have the perp in sight. He's carrying a placard… says 'Gay Pride'. Can't miss him, they are reporting. He's about dead center in the Mall. Can't this thing go any faster?" he growled, the taste of victory driving him.

"Not and stay alive, sir. I haven't obeyed a stop light or a single traffic law since we left the army-navy store."

At the moment they were hurtling along a one-way street going the wrong way and scattering oncomers onto side streets and alleys and even onto sidewalks.

"Any faster, and we'd be airborne."

Randolph began to move diagonally away from his most recent friend who was waving his placard with renewed gusto, undoubtedly energized by his newly obtained urban commando outfit and by the camaraderie it represented. Randolph felt conspicuous—even in mufti—since he was dressed so much more conservatively than the crowds of demonstrators swirling around him. Only he and the federal officers were wearing business suits.

Two groups of five officers each came running towards Randolph from opposite sides of the Mall. They had their guns drawn. He looked for a place to run, but knew it was hopeless. It was an ignominious end to all of his efforts to remain a successful fugitive until he could give himself up to the safety of the arrangements made by his attorney and the reporter. He had been so close. Maybe he had gotten too cocky making all of those plans for the future.

The running officers converged and were almost on top of him. Randolph bowed his head in quiet submission. He could not possibly fight them.

They ran right on past him.

He could not believe it. Ten overheated federal officers pounced on the harmless and luckless Gay Pride placard bearer. The unfortunate crumpled under the sheer weight of the federal government that had piled on him like a professional football team defense squad. Randolph began to hear shouts of "Gay bashers!" "Homophobe thugs!" "Help a brother!" and "Never again!"

An aroused crowd of surrounding gay and lesbian onlookers—some of them very sturdy folks—began to fall on the officers, who had not taken the time to announce themselves.

Randolph sidestepped and sauntered away from the focus of excitement as fast as he could without compromising his own temporary obscurity. He had gone about fifty yards as the crow flies when he felt an iron hand grip his arm. Randolph turned in the direction of the hand and saw his worst nightmare; he was looking directly into the cruel and triumphant eyes of Gerald Silberberg, the FBI agent in charge of making his life miserable.

There was no doubting that face. Randolph had seen it on TV almost everyday for months. Randolph's heart shriveled into a kernel sized knot.

"Don't move a muscle, Kennedy. I would love to have even the most miniscule excuse to shoot you dead!"

Silberberg's voice was quiet despite the growing din around them, and it dripped with menace. Randolph knew he was faced with an inescapable Hobbesian choice and steeled himself to endure complete submission to the officer in order to save his life.

"You are under..."

A band of Queer Nation self-appointed enforcer-protectors were running to join the crowd swarming over the FBI agents who were hard put to fend off the gaggle of demonstrators who were interfering with their efforts to take the quivering placard carrier into custody.

Randolph had a small inspiration borne of sheer desperation.

"Homophobe! Attacking me! Help! Help!" he shouted over and over.

Silberberg looked at his detainee as if Randolph had taken complete leave of his senses and was momentarily caught up in the mounting confusion.

Randolph wrenched his arm free and yelled at the top of his lungs, "Over here! Homophobe thug! Help me!"

The Queer Nation platoon executed a commendable unitary left turn and swept down on Silberberg and his four fellow officers in a phalanx as determined as a Spartan army. Silberberg began to raise his service automatic. Randolph drew back, and punched the senior FBI agent full in the face as hard as he could. The Queer Nation protectors in their motorcycle leathers and wielding truncheons and brass knuckles launched themselves into the completely startled gray-suited federal officers before any of the FBI agents could mount a credible defense. The Queer Nation brothers were joined by the toughest looking group of women Randolph had ever seen. Their jackets had emblems identifying them as "Hell's Lesbians". They were—if anything—more violent and vengeful than their male counter-parts. Randolph almost felt sorry for the FBI agents.

He was sweating profusely, and his heart was pounding until he was out of breath. There was such a kaleidoscope of action and a cacophony of noise that he simply turned and ran away as fast as he could, occasionally dodging and weaving like a broken field runner. The tumult grew steadily fainter as he ran. He was off the Mall and onto 15th Street headed due north. Metro DCPD black and whites roared down the street, and Randolph forced himself to slow to a less conspicuous pace. No one paid him the least bit of attention. All movement was in the direction of the riot now in full force in the Mall. Randolph trotted to Jefferson Place, found the brownstone just as Ken had described it, and knocked on the door of apartment 303.

He was pouring sweat. His shirt looked as if he had been hosed. Ken opened the door. He was wearing a loosely closed embroidered silk kimono. Randolph groaned inwardly but knew this was the lesser of evils. He met Ken's fulsome grin tooth for tooth.

"C'mon in, buddy, looks like you got caught up in the riot. It's all over the tube. Have a look."

"I actually had to run away from some homophobe thugs. They were brutal," Randolph lamented, hoping that his effort to sound a little effeminate was not overdrawn.

"Poor thing. Take a load off. I'll get you a stiff drink, and you can tell Uncle Ken all about it."

He led Randolph into a tastefully decorated and impeccably neat TV room. There were occasional flounces and ruffles and delicate knick knacks that made Randolph wince, but they were no more than might be expected if a husband and wife lived in the apartment.

Ken trotted over to the bar and, looking back at Randolph almost coquettishly, asked, "Hey, Dick, what's your poison?"

"How about a couple of light beers? I'm dry as a desert floor."

Ken brought a tray with four Coors Lites in chilled fluted glasses.

"Here, now, take your medicine," he offered.

His robe was even less secure now.

Randolph had to make an effort not to look inside to avoid getting Ken more anxious. He had to get control of this situation. He had no place to go, and he could not conceive of a wrestling match with the athletic gunny if his life depended on it. He was on the horns of a dilemma; and—for the for the moment—he could not come up with a solution that would not arouse suspicions.

Randolph downed the two beers almost without taking a breath and let out a slow contented sigh. He closed his eyes and let himself drift. He had not meant to, but he was almost out on his feet before he realized what was happening.

"Hey, bro, you look all done in. You better get some shut-eye before we really get to know each other. We have all the time in the world," Ken said gently.

Randolph was pretty sure that Ken was referring to "know" as in the biblical sense; but he could see the proffered reprieve and would have to worry about fending off Ken's ardor when he had rested; maybe he could put off any activity until tomorrow morning.

"I am whipped. Let me have a shower and some sleep, and I'll be fit company. That okay with you?"

"I'm not really a patient guy, Dick; and I have to say that you have me going; but I guess I can stand it a while longer."

He was leering.

For the third time in his career as a fugitive, Randolph began to give thought to murdering a fellow human being face to face. The thought was more than disturbing; he could not think of any other alternative.

"I'll make it worth your while," Randolph said, almost choking on the bile that welled up from his lie.

Metro DCPD quelled the short lived and spontaneous riot and finally got the media reporters to call it a day. Seven ambulances were eventually called in to cart off the casualties, a significant percentage of whom were law enforcement officers. Gay activist spokespersons were featured on the news that evening decrying the brutal anti-gay Nazi tactics of the riot police. The minions of the law—in their turn—pointed to the lawlessness of "certain elements" that led to the disturbance. Gerald Silberberg had been videoed at the scene telling of the progress of the manhunt for the "most dangerous criminal of our time" and became the quasi-official apologist for the police; after all, they were only doing their sworn duty attempting to arrest Randolph Kennedy, and the "certain elements" attacked them and made it possible for Public Enemy Number One to get away.

"We hold the fugitive, Randolph Kennedy—largely responsible—and we certainly do not, for a minute, blame today's outburst on the majority of our law-abiding gay people. There may have been some who overstepped, and their individual cases are being vigorously investigated. Those individuals— let me repeat—are *not* considered to be representatives of our fine American gay people. This is one more felony to lay at the feet of Randolph Kennedy, Public Enemy Number One."

The background on the screen behind Silberberg was filled with a full frontal view photograph of Randolph Kennedy.

In his office at the J. Edgar Hoover Building, Silberberg excoriated his staff and did not leave himself out. He intensified the search, even calling DFBI Coleman to get him to try and arrange to call out the National Guard. Coleman drew the line at that extreme. Even with that bit of restraint, there were police combing every street in the capital city in cars and on foot, going house-to-house and business-to-business. Every vehicle entering or leaving a twenty square block area was subjected to a time consuming search, and traffic was totally disrupted at Reagan National and at Dulles Airports, the bus stations, and at car rental outlets. A mouse could not escape. Silberberg said as much on national television.

CHAPTER FIFTY-EIGHT

"Hey, sleepyhead. Glad to see you back among the living. I was afraid I would have to call the EMTs. Here, have an eye-opener," an exuberantly alert Ken said when Randolph finally popped open one eye.

It was a Bloody Mary.

Ken was dressed in Oscar De La Renta silk briefs that accentuated his contours. Randolph noted that his fingernails had been freshly manicured, and that the man's toenails had been freshly painted a very fetching pink passion.

"Thanks, Ken. What time is it?"

"Quarter of eight."

Randolph sat bolt upright in bed. Ken was standing close beside him.

"Ken, I forgot. I have an appointment at nine. My life depends on being on time!"

Ken saw that there was no coquettishness or guile in his new-found friend's face. He knew that Randolph was sincere, but he had no intention of allowing the man to get away that easily. He had taken a Viagra, and he had seen the morning news.

"I washed out and pressed your shirt and ironed your suit. You have some time...*Dick*."

The ironic way Ken enunciated Randolph's hastily chosen pseudonym ignited Randolph's adrenocortical system. This was trouble.

"I don't, Ken. Sorry. Much as I would like to go to nirvana with you, I can't this morning. Let's take a rain check until this afternoon, okay?"

"No, it's not okay, chum. You imposed on my considerable hospitality, and I got zip. I know who you are; and I'll tell you; I want a little memory to share with the boys. Now let's get on with a quickie, and you can go without anyone ever being the wiser that you were here. What do you say, sweetie?"

"Thanks for the drink, Ken. Thanks for pressing my clothes, and no thanks for the rest. I don't swing that way; you might as well know that. No offense intended, but I needed your place as a hidey hole, not an introduction to the AIDs culture."

He was standing now, muscles tensed for whatever would come next. He was naked and felt completely vulnerable, but nothing about his demeanor revealed that to Ken.

"The quintessential Judas straight. I should have known. Maybe the cops would like to know what your straight little buns have been doing for the past twelve hours."

He took a step toward the phone.

"Don't," Randolph said in a quiet voice edged in menace.

Ken flexed his considerable muscles and put on his marine gunnery sergeant face.

"And if I do?"

"You think I lived this long on the run by letting people with plans like you just suggested survive?"

It was a flagrant bluff, but Ken could not know that. Randolph had no recourse except intimidation—and if that did not work—as much violence as he could muster, knowing that it would be a losing battle against the marine.

Ken searched Randolph's face for any wavering. When his eyes reached Randolph's, he was convinced that there was not a flicker of pity left in them. The pale irises were the blue of a hard glacier and as cold. He averted his gaze.

"Then, just get out. I don't need the grief. Get out!"

"Sorry, Ken. I can't leave you to let the cops know where I am."

For all of his marine training and bravado, Ken was truly afraid now. He had a fleeting thought that his martial arts training would be inadequate against this cold blooded killer. He instinctively glanced down at the drawer of the bedside table. It was nearer to Randolph by two steps than it was to him.

"It's not worth it, Ken. I'm not worth dying for."

Without removing his eyes from Ken's, Randolph crouched down and felt for the ornamental latch on the drawer. He rummaged very briefly in the drawer and drew out a .357 Magnum revolver. He pushed the firing mechanism off safety, and pulled back the hammer. He took a quick look at the front of the gun to reassure himself that it was loaded.

"That was a naughty thought, my friend. Now you are going to have to spend the day highly inconvenienced."

Randolph gestured to the floor with the gun. Ken sat.

"Hands on the top of your head, fingers intertwined."

Randolph asked quietly, "Where do you keep the duct tape, Ken?"

"Now I should help you tie me up; so, you can kill me? I don't think so."

"Ken, think. If I wanted you dead, you would already be dead. I am either going to kill you right now, or I am going to tie you up. I have no time to dilly-dally. Choose."

It was the coldest voice and the worst threat Ken had ever heard.

"In the pantry. You promise you won't kill me. I'll cooperate. I've been good to you, haven't I?"

He was pleading and it shamed him; but indeed, it was better than the alternative. Besides, no one would ever know. If he lived, it would be him telling the story, not the criminal.

"Crawl on your hands and knees to the pantry. I'll get the tape. If you make me nervous, I'll fire off as many rounds as thing can put out and as fast as it can. I have nothing to lose. How about you?"

Ken scurried along on his hands and knees ignoring the discomfort from the hard wood floor. He was thoroughly beaten and completely subservient now, and he did not even give it a thought. Randolph used the butt of the pistol as a club and whipped it across the back of the crawling sergeant's skull. Ken dropped flat on his face and was still. Randolph felt for a carotid pulse and was relieved to find one. He ran to the kitchen pantry and found the duct tape after a few moments of frustrating search. He twisted the unconscious man's wrists behind his back and taped them with multiple layers. He stuffed a dish cloth in Ken's mouth and wound several layers of the stiff tape around his head to hold the gag in place. Randolph taped Ken's bare ankles so tightly that they could not move, and for good measure taped around his knees as well. Ken began to come around.

Randolph moved swiftly into Ken's bedroom, found his uniform boots and tore the bootlaces out. He returned to the terrified marine and tied his big toes and his thumbs together. He thought for a moment. Ken could still make a noise by thumping his heels on the floor, and Randolph could not take the least chance. He dragged Ken to his bed, then sat him up. He heaved with all his might, and was able to hoist his inert victim to the edge of the bed. He got on the bed and with his full strength was able to pull Ken over onto the mattress. He taped a noose around Ken's neck and fixed it to the iron filigree of the head board and tied his ankles to the foot boards. That ought to be enough, he thought. He looked at his watch. Eight-ten. He had to hurry like he never had before.

He collected himself. The problem was how to get from Ken's apartment to Hartley Proctor's building in three-quarters of an hour. The trick would be to do so undetected and in safety. His excitement had ebbed, and his cognitive forces were back to full function.

Randolph dialed Hartley Proctor's law office on Ken's cell phone.

"Law offices."

"I need to speak to Mr. Proctor. It's urgent."

"Whom shall I say is calling, sir?"

"Tell him it's his most famous client."

"Yes, sir."

If she knew who the caller was, she did not let on. In ten seconds, Proctor answered.

"Proctor here."

"This is Randy. I don't have much time. In case you haven't noticed, my life became somewhat more complicated in the last twenty-four hours. Before we go any further, you don't happen to know who put the cops onto me, do you? Like maybe the lady fibbies or the newspaper woman?"

"I have no idea, but I doubt it is either of them. What would they have to gain? Where are you?"

Randolph knew he had to let down his paranoiac guard. He had no reason to mistrust Proctor. He sucked in a brave breath.

"I need you to drive your big old limousine to pick me up."

He gave Proctor the address.

"Better make it in fifteen minutes. There are cops all over the place, and they will cause delays. I will be wearing a dark suit, ready for the meeting with the deputy U.S. attorney if you still think it's safe and worthwhile."

"I'll be there. It'll take some doing, but I think we can still do the meeting and that the parties are all ready to conduct it in good faith."

"Okay, remember, I'm the most skittish guy on the face of the earth right now. I see a cop, and I will take off. If you are more than twenty minutes, I won't be here; and the meeting is off."

"Look, Randolph, you told me you had to trust someone. I am on your team. Relax on that account."

"As much as I can," Randolph said.

He put down the receiver. He looked around the room carefully and gave it some thought. He replaced the .357 Magnum back in its drawer after wiping off his fingerprints. He could not afford to be caught with a gun in his belt. He hurried around the room and wiped off everything that he could remember having touched. He threw on his pants, shirt, tie, socks and shoes, and his suit coat, picked up his briefcase and checked the contents. Everything was still there. He closed the door to the apartment behind him and tested that it was locked. He descended the stairs to wait behind the glass doors of the apartment building until the limousine came.

The police were methodically moving through the neighborhood with their door-to-door inquiries. Randolph could see them three-quarters of a block away on Jefferson Place. Fifteen minutes passed; and they were less than half a block away; and there was no sign of Hartley Proctor's limousine. He checked his watch. He willed himself to wait a full five minutes more. Time crept by making Randolph more tense by the minute.

A pair of uniformed policemen descended the front stairs of the building two doors down and ascended the stairs of the building next to the one in which Randolph was hiding. He walked back down the hallway to plot an escape route and saw that the rear door led into a small backyard enclosed in a high cinderblock fence—too high to climb over. He was beginning to sense panic. He turned back and saw that the limousine was now parked in front of the apartment building. Randolph ran back to the front door and peered out, up and down the street. Across the street a different pair of police—a man and a woman—rang the entrance buzzer and were admitted inside. He could see no other indication of law enforcement personnel anywhere near and presumed that both sets of cops were inside their buildings going methodically through their search.

He gritted his teeth, and walked out of the apartment building as if he owned the place, as if he always rode to work in a stretch car. Proctor's driver hurried around and opened the door for Randolph, and the lightly sweating fugitive stepped in. The police men came out of the building next to Randolph's and moved to the one in which he had been hiding just as the limo pulled away from the curb. Before they opened the door, the two men gave a perfunctory wave to the unseen occupants of the huge black Mercedes limousine. The driver returned the wave—looked both ways—then completed his move into the heavy post-riot traffic.

CHAPTER FIFTY-NINE

At nine-thirty on that Saturday morning, Daniel Hernandez was gratified to see that most of the scheduled participants in the meeting had arrived except the reporter Gwen Chambers, Nancy Delgado—the FBI agent—Hartley Proctor—the defense attorney—and his client—the notorious Randolph Kennedy—who had been the subject of considerable excitement for the last full day. The participants had all taken chairs around the large meeting table in the U.S. Attorney's Office conference room.

The attorneys were wearing their professional and overly friendly faces. Harrelson—the president's counsel—had a round, bluff, John Bull face, too pink from frequently bending his elbow, Hernandez surmised. His sandy hair—streaked with gray—was plastered in place with heavy mousse to control its tendency to unruliness. Vera Trimble—the White House senior counsel—had her hair done up in a tight bun pulled back from a librarian's uninviting face. The president's two lawyers wore nearly matching navy blue three-piece suits, white shirts, and maroon ties. On Ms. Trimble, the outfit looked appropriate with the only nods to femininity being a flounced hanky in the pocket, a silk cravat tie, and a nearly floor length skirt three inches above her no nonsense black shoes. Harrelson's suit looked as if it belonged to a younger, trimmer brother. He had lost the battle of the bulge.

Ali Mahmood Ajami—attorney for Henry Drake—in contrast to Harrelson, was the picture of impeccable grooming, physical bearing, and attire. Henry Drake sat sullenly at the table in his wheelchair along side Ajami. Stephen Benchley, and his new client—Oliver Quatraine—sat well away from Henry

Drake and Ajami. Benchley and Quatraine were in uniform—blue blazers, red ties, and dress khaki—ready for the joust, half an hour away.

Randolph and Hartley Proctor sat quietly in easy chairs in Hartley's spacious private office. The adrenalin rush of his cliff-hanger escape from the police dragnet encompassing the city had ebbed away leaving a kind of lassitude. He was freshly showered and shaved and had on a new set of clothing. He was immeasurably buoyed up for the time being. Hartley called Nancy Delgado and Gwen Chambers in from the outer office. Nancy came in first. Romaine Terrife and David Bendell waited in the outer office.

"Special Agent Delgado, may I present Mr. Randolph Armstrong Kennedy," Hartley said with exaggerated courtliness as soon as the secretary escorted the FBI agent into the inner office.

Randolph was standing to meet her, hand extended.

"I've waited a long time, Mr. Kennedy."

She acted as if she did not see the proffered hand.

Randolph shrugged.

"I share your enthusiasm," he said.

"I have to tell both of you that a great deal of trust goes into this plan of yours. Every instinct—every bit of my training—tells me to arrest you right now and to sort out the various aspects of this case some other day. My superiors would have my job in a second if they knew that I was party to a plan to let Public Enemy Number One go free out of my sight when I had the chance to put the cuffs on him."

"But you did agree, Agent Delgado," Proctor said matter-of-factly.

"I did, and I will abide by the agreement. I don't have to like it or Mr. Kennedy."

"And I accept responsibility as an officer of the court for Mr. Kennedy's compliance," Hartley said. "I don't think we need to second guess each other. Mr. Kennedy is here of his own free will and at considerable personal risk, you realize. We have put a complex set of actions into motion that should actually serve the cause of justice for a change. Maybe you could agree with me that that would be a refreshing innovation."

"Indeed," she said.

Gwen Chambers was formally ushered in and was formally introduced, although they had already met. Randolph, Gwen, Nancy, and Hartley all chatted about everything except the impending meeting until nine-thirty. It was agreed that Nancy and Gwen would go to the meeting along with Terrife and Bendell. They left immediately.

After the two women left, Hartley asked, "Ready, Randy?"

"As I'll ever be," Randolph said.

His face was nervous and drawn. He was glad for the support afforded by the attorney and the two women, however grudging the FBI agent had been. Neither could exactly be described as being on his side.

"Let's go. I don't want to be late," Proctor said. "We'll take my limo and avoid curious onlookers. We can enter from the rear of the building. Hernandez told me the way and arranged for the security people to grease the skids."

Gwen was shown into Hernandez's office and took her seat at the far end of the table. Romaine and David entered the room and stood stationed on either side of the door. Nancy stood immediately inside the door and directly in front of it.

At one minute to ten, Deputy U.S. Attorney Daniel Hernandez glanced at his watch. It was the first small break in the stoical Apache's assurance. There was a firm knock on the heavy oak door. The security guard opened it from the outside. In walked Hartley Proctor in his custom tailored $1400 suit. His drawn, intelligent, Jewish face had curious unsympathetic eyes that took in the opposition with a calculating look. Close behind him, and to the enormous surprise of almost everyone in the room came Randolph Kennedy. The conversational level raised a decibel. Every head cranked around to get a good look at the elusive and famous criminal.

Nancy Delgado stepped forward.

"Special Agent Delgado?" Proctor asked.

"Yes, sir."

"I am attorney Hartley Proctor. I represent Randolph Armstrong Kennedy. Permit me to introduce you. Agent Delgado, meet Randolph Kennedy. Mr. Kennedy, this is Nancy Delgado, Special Agent of the FBI. I believe you have been seeking Mr. Kennedy. Please note for the record that he is here to surrender himself to you of his own free will and choice. He seeks an assurance that you and your colleagues will protect him from harm while he is in custody. Please observe that he is fit, well, and free of any bruises or signs of injury at this moment before surrender."

"So noted, sir."

Again, she did not offer her hand, and neither did Randolph.

"Mr. Kennedy, I am hereby placing you under arrest for the crimes of conspiracy, terrorism, multiple murder, and attempted murder, aggravated assault on a Colorado police officer, illegal use of a firearm in the commission of a felony, grand larceny, gun smuggling, drug trafficking, and interstate flight to avoid prosecution. Would you extend your hands, please?"

Gwen and Hernandez's secretary had both turned on their recording machines at the stroke of ten and were recording every word. Gwen made an evident show of recording the surrender on her compact video camcorder.

Randolph put out his hands to be handcuffed.

"I will now read you your rights under Miranda versus Arizona."

She read each of the rights from a card, asking him each time if he understood. He answered perfunctorily.

"May we take our seats, Mr. Deputy U.S. Attorney?" asked Proctor, mindful of decorum and the video camera.

"Please do. It's time to start. From here on out we are on the record. For that record, I will first have every participant introduce himself or herself and state briefly why he or she is included."

The introductions took two minutes. The people sitting around the table looked glumly at one another.

"This is a formal inquiry into the events surrounding the twenty-sixth of June, last year. For the record, I am Deputy U.S. Attorney Daniel Hipolito Hernandez. I will be conducting this inquiry. Also—for the record—there are several persons who can be considered targets of inquiry and prosecution here. Each of them has his or her attorney in attendance. Randolph Kennedy—heretofore a fugitive from justice—has just been placed under arrest by Special Agent of the Federal Bureau of Investigation, Nancy Delgado. He is presently restrained—per policy—in handcuffs.

"I would be naïve if I did not expect considerable disagreement today. I will—therefore—attempt to delineate the ineluctable facts as best as I have been able to determine them and seek stipulation from all present so as to avoid unnecessary expenditure of time in areas upon which we can agree. Please be informed that a verbatim transcript is being recorded and will be saved for use as evidence if required in a court of law. By prior arrangement, Ms Gwen Chambers—a reporter for the *New York Times* newspaper—is present and will make public the findings and events of this gathering."

The president's two attorneys rolled their eyes at one another at Hernandez's last statement.

"Now, these are the facts as I see them."

Hernandez commanded the attention of every participant in the room for the next hour with a precise and succinct, but detailed rendition of what was known about the events leading up to the assault the previous year, the ATF attack itself, and the aftermath. He did not include references to alleged participation of the president, the attorney general, or other members of the FBG Task Force. He alluded to the allegations of crimes by Drake and Quatraine.

"Anyone need a break?" he asked.

Two attorneys left for the bathroom. Hernandez passed the carafe of ice water down the table.

When the participants reassembled, Hernandez said, "You will now have your turn. Those about whom allegations have been made will be given an opportunity to tell their own stories uninterrupted. I don't want to hear the word 'objection'. This is a fact finding meeting, not a court of law. No allegation will be disposed of today. When the targets of interest in this case are done with their presentations, their own attorneys and I may ask questions. We will stay here until everyone has had his or her say. Mr. Drake, you may be first."

Drake and Kennedy stared daggers at each other—looks of the purest hatred. Drake began his narrative, reading from a prepared statement. His attorney— Ali Mahmood Ajami—followed along, reading and listening intently.

"I am Henry Drake, agent of the Bureau of Alcohol, Tobacco, and Firearms. I was in charge of the field operation against Randolph Kennedy. I am obligated to tell you that I have been granted full immunity from prosecution in return for full disclosure."

With that, the entire *dramatis personae* riveted their eyes on the wheelchair-bound ATF agent. Real fear showed on the faces of Oliver Quatraine and the attorneys for the president and the attorney general.

"I collected and collated evidence, including videotaping, that Randolph Kennedy, the man sitting there in handcuffs, was a member of a syndicate of gun and drug traffickers and did personally move illegal weapons into his own home."

He went on to tell of the disastrous raid, painting Kennedy as a calculating killer, murdering officers from his vantage point inside his home, and with the use of lethal booby traps. He did not spare himself. He admitted taking the evidence from the Ketchikan Federal Evidence Impound Room to use in bolstering and ensuring the ATF's case against Kennedy. He insisted that they had other evidence prior to the raid, but that he had been overzealous in his efforts to ensure a conviction. He pointed out that the drugs and guns had never actually been used to incriminate Kennedy. He made a strong point that his surveillance officers—one whom was dead—had witnessed the terrorist entering but not leaving the house on the day and night of the raid.

He concluded with a matter-of-fact statement that, "I, personally, was shot by the defendant Kennedy and rendered paraplegic and permanently wheel-chair-ridden."

When Drake finished the reading of his statement, Daniel Hernandez looked directly at him.

"Mr. Drake, did you see Mr. Kennedy pull the trigger on the firearm that caused you injury?"

"I did."

"Did you take money from the impound room in Ketchikan?" he asked pointedly.

Drake had steeled himself for that question.

"No, sir, I did not," he replied without so much as a hint of hesitation.

"You are under oath, and your immunity status hinges on this statement.

Do you wish to change it?"

"No, sir."

"Are you willing to take a polygraph test, Mr. Drake, on the question of what became of the money that was present in the Ketchikan impound room?"

"I will answer for my client," Ajami interjected. "Polygraph results are not allowed as evidence because of their notorious inaccuracies. Consequently, my client will not be taking a polygraph test—not now—and not in the future."

"Thank you, Mr. Ajami," said Hernandez

He turned back to Drake and said, "So, I take it that you were firmly convinced by the evidence you possessed that you had a good case against Randolph Kennedy, that he was a dangerous terrorist who would be unwilling to surrender peacefully, and that you had no other recourse but to employ a preemptive strike in force."

"You got all that right."

The other participants all turned to look briefly at Randolph who was sitting quietly and impassively—handcuffed and docile—alongside his famous attorney.

"Did you receive orders to launch the raid and to plant false evidence from any person or persons in a position of authority over you, sir?"

"Yes, sir. From that man over there, that black man, Agent Oliver Quatraine."

All eyes shifted to Oliver, who squirmed in spite of his resolve to be unemotional. The attorneys for the senior government officials allowed themselves brief knowing smiles.

"Anyone else give such orders?"

Chapter Fifty-Nine

"Objection!" said Harrelson.

"Forget it, Mr. Harrelson. You will have your chance. Remember, this is not a court of law. Keep your pants on."

Ajami interrupted for the second time, "If it please the inquiry, Mr. Hernandez, my client would respectfully decline to answer that particular question for the time being. Please let us hear from the other targeted individuals first and return to my client as necessary."

Drake was showing a trace of unease for the first time. He nervously looked at the attorneys for the president and the attorney general who glared malevolently at him.

"I'll allow that bit of leeway, Mr. Ajami, but neither you nor your client should forget the terms of his immunity. He must give full and true disclosure. I will have nothing less in this room today. I am a patient man—however—and I can wait a bit to get that piece of the truth. Let's hear from Mr. Quatraine now. We can break for lunch when he has finished," Hernandez said.

Quatraine gathered his courage and started his prepared remarks, a careful effort that he and his attorney, Stephen Benchley, had worked on for weeks.

"I am Oliver Wendell Quatraine, agent of the ATF. I was Henry Drake's titular superior during the raid on the Kennedy property. Contrary to what Mr. Drake has just said, I had next to nothing to do with the actual gathering of evidence of planning of the raid. I was responsible for the coordination of the several services involved and subsequent to Mr. Drake's wounding, I assumed full charge. Again—contrary to what Mr. Drake alleges—I did not give orders to plant evidence—and the raid itself was his idea, not mine. He did convince me of Kennedy's guilt and that the perpetrator was present in his house on June the twenty-sixth last year along with crates of illegal arms, probably fully operational machine guns. I was assigned to oversee the raid by my superiors at a very late date in the preparations. On the day of the raid, Mr. Drake showed me the evidence he intended to plant. I told him not to do that, because it was illegal. I did nothing illegal throughout my involvement."

"Have you been granted immunity?" Hernandez asked.

"No, sir, I have not."

"Did you take guns, drugs, or money, any or all of them that was alleged to have been removed from the Ketchikan Impound Locker for the purposes of being planted as evidence against Mr. Kennedy?"

"No."

"But you did know about it?"

"Yes, at the last moment. And—as I testified—I tried to prevent Drake from using that material. I thought I had prevailed; so, in a sense my best answer to your question is 'no, I did not know that evidence was going to be planted'."

He made a concerted effort to keep looking the U.S. attorney in the eye.

For his part, Hernandez had always thought that you could not trust a person who insisted on looking you in the eye.

"Did you receive orders to carry out an illegal raid on Randolph Kennedy or to plant evidence to be used against the target?"

Quatraine and his attorney whispered back and forth to one another for a few minutes. The room became silent. It seemed as if the other participants were holding their breaths.

"No, sir."

The response was hesitant and overly deliberate. The presidential attorneys openly smiled.

"I take it that I phrased the question poorly," Hernandez said.

He wore a perplexed expression. He took his time to think.

He sucked a molar thoughtfully and asked, "Mr. Quatraine, do you have knowledge of an order to anyone authorizing a felonious raid?"

"Objection!" blurted Vera Trimble by instinct.

Hernandez raised a critical eyebrow at the White House attorney. She nodded her mea culpa. There was a sweaty pause. Quatraine's face dissolved into lines of concern, fear, and reluctance. He squirmed to look over at the president's and the attorney general's attorneys. They were now looking at him with the same intense curiosity that gripped everyone else in the room. It was premature for them to register serious negativity. This was the pivotal question of the day, evidently. Quatraine had another whispered conversation with Stephen Benchley, then drew in a long tortured breath.

"I do," he answered, almost in a whisper.

"Beg your pardon, Mr. Quatraine?"

"Yes, sir, I do have such knowledge," he said at full volume and with careful enunciation so that no one could mistake his communication.

Even Randolph Kennedy looked shocked. Every eye in the room was fixed on Oliver Quatraine.

Hernandez took his time, steepling his fingers thoughtfully against his forehead before posing his next questions.

"Who else heard these illegal orders?" he asked surprising everyone.

Hernandez was an expert at dissecting information. He did not need to rush.

Quatraine still appeared hesitant.

Hernandez said, "Don't be coy, Mr. Quatraine. You risk the charge of perjury or contempt here. You have already opened Pandora's box. Like the mythological story, there is nothing left but hope. Give me a name."

"Roger Holdaway, director of the ATF, at one point," Quatraine answered quietly.

Several lawyers eased back in their chairs a little.

"Come on, Mr. Quatraine, you're on a roll. Any more?"

Quatraine replied, "The president, the attorney general, the directors of the DEA, ATF, FBI, and the commander of the coast guard. Mr. Henry Drake, and the assistants to the senior government officials named, and several secretaries and guards were also present when the orders were given."

Lawyers for the senior officials were out of their seats, livid with protest.

"Now see here," one of them fairly shouted, "This is preposterous, unconscionable. This jackal is only trying to shift his blame."

"Now, gentlemen and ladies, no name calling. We will keep it civil, and you will get your turn. Take your seats, or I will have you ejected. You wouldn't want to miss this, now, would you?" ordered Hernandez.

His voice was calm and commanding. They took their seats, showing their disbelief and dissatisfaction by shaking their heads, muttering, and glaring death threats at Oliver Quatraine; but no one said anything further.

Finally, and calmly, Tucker Harrelson spoke, "That is a very serious accusation, let's hear evidence."

"Yes, Mr. Quatraine, that is a very serious accusation. Can you back it up? For instance, tell us about those other witnesses."

"There's Henry Drake, for one; and he's right here. He knows what went on, and he knows that plenty of others know that he knows. He will be indicted for perjury and lose his immunity if he lies and there are enough other witnesses to hang him once it all hits the fan."

He said it deadpan, having regained his confidence. He had nothing to lose.

"I definitely think it is time to revisit Mr. Drake. Tell me, sir, is that true? Did you witness an illegal order to plant evidence from the president, the attorney general? Or from the directors of the senior government bureaus on the Task Force?"

Ajami nudged his client and gave him a small nod.

"Drake said, "Yes, sir, I did.""

"Not just Quatraine giving illegal orders?"

Mr. Ajami interjected, "My client wishes to retract his previous statement wherein he denied that others had given him orders. Mr. Drake, you may answer the question.

"No, sir. The president and the attorney general gave those orders. I was confused earlier. I would not go ahead with the raid or the planting of the evidence unless those two said it in so many words. I wasn't born yesterday."

"And who witnessed that very explicit set of orders?"

"All of the members of the Task Force were there. They heard the orders. They were pretty clear—but you know—the orders were kind of expressed in lawyer language; so, they could maybe be misinterpreted. So, Quatraine and I cornered President Vantassa and AG Thaler afterwards and got it straight and clear. No mistake."

The involved lawyers looked as if they would burst a gasket if they did not rise to the defense of their prominent clients again. Hernandez raised a preventative hand and cast them a reproving look.

"Could seem pretty convenient," he said. "Two agents accused of committing crimes fall back on one of the oldest defenses-'*Befehl ist befehl*—orders are orders' as the Nazis said. Why should we believe you against the president and the chief law officer of our country? Any corroboration at all?"

Drake lowered his head and stared at the papers on his desk as his answer.

"Come, come, Gentlemen, either of you. Is there any evidence of the meeting that you had with the president and the attorney general? Anything at all to help your case?"

Stephen Benchley prodded his client.

Quatraine spoke up in a strong clear voice, free of his former hesitation.

"Before either of us answers, Mr. Hernandez, I want to know if you will put us and our families in the Witness Protection Program?"

He looked pointedly at the president's and the AG's lawyers, who were threatening Drake and him with the virulence of their looks. The lawyers appeared like panthers ready to spring. The animus in their eyes was homicidal.

"It will be done, as of this minute," Hernandez promised.

He, too, turned his gaze to the angry lawyers.

"This is crazy! We're talking about the president of the United States here, and she's being accused by these...these...nothings!" shouted Vera Trimble.

"Be quiet, or I will have you ejected, Madam." Hernandez said with quiet finality.

Trimble lapsed into a sullen silence.

Hartley Proctor leaned over the Randolph and whispered facetiously, "I really don't know why they bothered to invite us. They certainly don't lack for defendants. Those they had aplenty."

Randolph, who had been enjoying the fireworks display, smiled broadly, keeping his head down; so, it would not be obvious. He could not have been happier to see the Philistines getting theirs.

CHAPTER SIXTY

Stephen Benchley—Quatraine's attorney—spoke for the first time, "And, Mr. Hernandez, there is the question of immunity from prosecution. My client deserves at least the same treatment as Agent Drake. I assure you that the evidence he has to offer in corroboration of his statements here today will be entirely sufficient to make the case against his superiors ironclad."

"I'll consider it, once I hear the evidence."

"It doesn't work that way; you know that," Benchley said. "We have to have security in this."

"Tell you what I'll do. If you have strong corroborative evidence, I will grant you immunity from prosecution on all counts to which you confess, Mr. Quatraine. Leave anything out; and we will come after you for that; no transactional immunity. You might want to consider that with regards this missing money."

"Alleged missing money," Benchley said, "There is only circumstantial evidence that there ever was money at the site, or that any money was taken; or, for that matter, if it was taken, that either of these agents did it. Mr. Quatraine denies any such assertion emphatically."

"Point well taken. I think we have an understanding, and on the record, too. That's what I like about above board proceedings; there's no mealy mouthing and wiggling later. All right, Mr. Quatraine, let's here your evidence or see it or whatever it takes. I'm warning you; this better be good."

Benchley reached into his cavernous brief case and withdrew a small tape player and two tape cassettes.

"With your permission, Mr. Hernandez?"

"By all means. The suspense is killing me," Hernandez said, and he spoke for everyone in the room.

Benchley inserted the tape and pushed the on button. The whirring sound of the tape started up.

Quatraine said, "This first tape is from a meeting of the President's Task Force on June twenty-first, last year.

Margaret Thaler's easily recognized voice echoed out of the recording device, "Any way to get an undercover agent into the house to have a look, Drake?"

Drake's unmistakable harsh voice was next, "I don't think so, ma'am. Too little time. Besides, these people are as thick as proverbial thieves. They are the most xenophobic lot I ever encountered. We have not been able to infiltrate an agent; they spot us every time. It's not for want of trying."

AG Thaler: "I am very uneasy about this evidence, Agent Drake. I suppose you are here to suggest a raid. Any other helpful evidence? I would be a whole lot more comfortable if there were."

Agent Drake: "I will guarantee that the evidence will be there, and it will stand up in court, ma'am. My job on it."

The voice of the president of the United States, with the decided Eastern accent familiar to every school child in the country, came next: "Indeed. No more fiascoes. It would be off-with-their-heads for both you and me if we foul up on Kennedy a second time. The reporters would have a field day."

The participants in Hernandez's inquiry looked around the room at each other, embarrassed, as if they were listening in on a lovers' intimate tête-a-tête. The tape cassette continued.

Agent Drake: "I appreciate that, Madam President, believe me, I do. There won't be a screw-up, pardon my language."

The president: "You be certain that the evidence is there and that you go in with whatever you need to do the job. I don't want to hear that some more of my good agents have been hurt. Take care of it. Drop an evidence gun if you have to." There was stifled laughter in the background of the tape.

Then came the whispered voice of DFBI Ted Coleman: "I hope this place is leak proof. That kind of little joke is the sort to derail administrations. We don't even kid around about planting evidence over at our patch."

There was considerable discomfort and fidgeting in Hernandez's conference room.

"Perhaps a little indelicate, sort of gallows humor, but hardly the smoking gun, Mr. Hernandez," snorted the president's personal attorney. "And hardly the stuff to warrant immunity."

"We're not done," Stephen Benchley said with cold determination.

The president's lawyer frowned darkly and made a dismissive gesture. Inwardly, he was beginning to think that this was turning out to be the longest day of his career thus far.

"The next tape was obtained later the same day. It takes place in the office of Senator Tomlinson," Quatraine said while his attorney changed tapes.

"Kentucky Senator Tomlinson?" someone asked.

"The same."

The tape began again, a man's voice: "I'll take you to Madam Butterfly now."

The voice was unfamiliar.

"Just our code for Her Majesty."

AG Thaler: "All right, Drake, the president has your orders."

The president: "Agent Drake, you are involved in a matter of national security. Invoking executive powers vested in me by the McGrath-Hoover Internal Security Act of 1948, and more precisely, by the Program for Apprehension and Detention of Persons Considered Potentially Dangerous to the National Defense and Public Safety of the United States, 'Senate Intelligence Committee Hearings', 1952, volume 6, page 495, I hereby order you to carry out a raid on the premises of Randolph Armstrong in Wasilla, Alaska. Because of the extraordinary sensitivity of this case, I order you to place evidence at the scene if necessary and as necessary to obtain a conviction in the case and to expedite it as rapidly and as certainly as can be done."

AG Thaler: "That's it. You have your orders. Time to get back to work."

Agent Drake: "You know the evidence we plan to use. I'd like to hear that in an order."

The tape contained sounds of footsteps and a door closing at that point.

AG Thaler: "Don't press your luck, Drake. You have your orders, and enough is enough."

The tape ended. President Vantassa's two lawyers kept still. Blank aridity was all they showed in their faces.

Hernandez broke the spell.

"You have your immunity and your witness protection guarantee, Mr. Quatraine. You will be made available to testify if and when that becomes necessary."

Gwen Chambers wanted to jump up and run out to call her office. It was all she could do to keep her seat.

Randolph looked at Hartley Proctor. It seemed the time for him to speak out. Proctor put a cautionary hand on Randolph's arm.

Hernandez slowly turned his attention to Kennedy and Proctor.

"Well," he said in a deliberate voice, "interesting day. What do you have to contribute to it, gentlemen?"

Proctor did the talking.

"We have a suit against the government that should result in a summary judgment given what we have just heard. This is the worst malfeasance I have ever seen. I will entertain a meeting in my office tomorrow at ten to discuss settlement. I will have a copy of those tapes, Mr. Hernandez. I believe the figure named in our suit is not far from the one that we will compromise on tomorrow morning. If I receive any hassle on this, I am going to try my case in the press—starting in the afternoon—until the American public can recite the words of those tapes verbatim from memory. I will depose the president, the attorney general, and every head of department who was present in those meetings. I am going to revise the John Does in the complaint to name each of them."

"There is the small matter of the criminal charges against your client, Mr. Proctor."

"Laughable. When these two gentlemen from the ATF get done presenting their evidence and playing the tape for a grand jury—and I, for one, find them both highly believable witnesses—my client will be given the key to the city and his statue in the Capitol rotunda. Criminal charges!? Ha!"

He looked defiantly at Hernandez.

"It won't come off as quite that simple, Mr. Proctor," Hernandez said, unruffled. "There are dead federal agents, maimed men and women, a cop beaten to a pulp, missing money—a lot of it. I'd like to ask your client, if I may, what his role in all of this is. Who is responsible for all that carnage? Who is going to pay the piper for all of that? I don't find the criminal charges to be all that laughable."

Randolph spoke for the first time since entering the room. Gwen picked up her pen to take written notes in addition to what she was getting on her recorder.

"Mr. Hernandez, until the afternoon of March twenty-second, last year, I was a nobody and liked it that way. I had a lovely wife and the cutest little daughter you ever saw. I had a good job, a reputation to be proud of, expectations for the future. Then a weasel—known euphemistically as a reliable confidential informant—put a bug in the ear of the Bureau of Alcohol, Tobacco, and Firearms, and without even the remotest effort at confirmatory investigation, the ATF thugs attacked my home and killed my entire family. That is a matter of record established in the courts. I fought back to save my life against home invaders who did not announce themselves. That, sir, is the crime I supposedly committed that led directly to the second attack on me. Agent Henry Drake declared a vendetta against me and hounded me even to my new home. He and his bureau were willing to trump up charges and to place illegal evidence at my house to trap me because they could not find evidence against me. There was none, and none has been found to this day.

"They manufactured evidence, destroyed the home I built with my own hands—blew it up and burned it to the ground. They did that. That was not enough for them. I was made Public Enemy Number One without the remotest due cause only to protect themselves against exposure of their flagrant wrongdoing. I have been hounded from one end of the country to the other. My friends and acquaintances have been tormented, tortured, unjustly charged and incarcerated until they lost their homes as well—all for no cause. Then, no one dared to be my friend.

"The civil rights of a whole class of people were summarily done away with, entirely without due process. I was innocent—they thought—but they couldn't go near me. I became a leper, someone the police all over the country had carte blanche to shoot on sight. Open season was declared on me. What you monsters have taken from me is irreplaceable. I could have killed two cops who stopped me. I didn't. And you make *me* out to be a criminal and a killer?"

His jaws were clenched and his grasp on the arms of his chair was white-knuckled.

Gwen Chambers dabbed at the corners of her eyes with her handkerchief, hoping no one would notice.

"I still have unanswered questions, Mr. Kennedy."

Proctor remained silent, his client was doing just fine by himself.

Randolph looked quietly into the deputy U.S. attorney's eyes exhibiting neither fear nor guilt.

"Did you kill those agents when they came to arrest you?"

"In Alaska?"

"Yes," Hernandez clarified.

"No, they did it to themselves.'

Hernandez nodded thoughtfully, "And one thing keeps nagging at me, Mr. Kennedy. "It's that elusive money. You wouldn't happen to know anything about a stack of money, would you?"

Proctor laid his hand on Randolph's forearm, a gesture so slight as to escape notice around the room Randolph said nothing. His face had no more expression than a poker chip.

After several seconds of awkward silence, Hernandez bent his head and look down the table at Randolph in a penetrating gaze.

"And, if you did, I don't suppose you would want to tell me," he said.

When Randolph said nothing for a full two minutes and did not seem to be made uncomfortable by his silence, Hernandez shrugged slightly and answered his own question, "No, I don't suppose you would."

Daniel Hernandez looked at Randolph for a long time. No one in the room spoke during his examination. When he did speak, it was to Hartley Proctor.

"I'm inclined to give a little here, Mr. Proctor. The case for the criminal prosecution has some real weaknesses, and I have to admit that you have some basis for your civil suit…"

He ruminated again for a moment before bringing himself to a commitment.

"I am willing to make an offer, but it will have to be regarded as tentative for the time being. No matter what is suggested or agreed upon here with regards to your client or about the currently unindicted co-conspirators, there will be investigation piled upon investigation. There will be special counsel, and the media microscope. But I think this first round is the most important and doubt that anyone will seriously second guess me.

"So, my offer of compromise is that the criminal case be disposed of and your civil case be dropped, once the results of the investigations are in, and presuming that they corroborate what we've heard today. There would be no prosecution against you in the case in chief or in any of the spin-offs, considering them to be the rotten fruit of a diseased tree. I would require an agreement from you to testify should we have to go to trial against the principles in the future. Can you accept that tentative offer in principle, and with the provisos I listed, Mr. Kennedy?"

Proctor turned to Randolph and spoke quietly, but loudly enough for everyone in the quiet room to hear, "Your call, Randolph. I think we could beat the criminal charges quite handily, and I also think we could pull in well over ten million on the civil case when it was finally over. Your position is very strong. The downside is that you can never tell what will happen with a jury; and the process would certainly take years, upwards of a decade on the civil case. The government would almost certainly demand and probably would get a ruling to keep you locked up until the criminal trial was finished—minimum of two to three years. You have demonstrated that you are a flight risk."

Randolph did not hesitate.

"Take the deal," he whispered.

"All right, Mr. Hernandez, my client accepts your offer. When can we have that on paper?"

"By the close of business today, Mr. Proctor. I'm glad for you and your client, and for me. It will save untold hassle, and so I'm glad for the government and the taxpayers as well. I will release Mr. Kennedy into your custody. You will have full responsibility and will answer to me. I will come down on you like a ton of bricks if he bolts. I'll keep his passport. Is that arrangement acceptable?"

"Yes. We can work out the details of reporting at the time of the written agreement."

"Agent Delgado?" Hernandez asked.

She shook her head in disbelief at the turn of events, but said, "Yes, so long as I am kept fully aware of his whereabouts at all times."

"Fair enough," agreed Proctor.

He nudged Randolph, who gave a small acquiescing shrug.

"He will have the freedom to travel around the country, and no one except you, Mr. Hernandez, Agent Delgado, and I will know where he is. I think you might appreciate that my client does not have full confidence in his government, and its agencies quite yet. Frankly, he still fears for his life and has more confidence in his own devices than in anything the Unites States might arrange."

"I don't have a problem with that," said Agent Delgado. "Although I reserve judgment about his crimes, I believe that—otherwise—we are dealing with a reliable person—a gentleman—if you will. I do have complete confidence in Mr. Proctor. He and I will have to work out the details of reporting."

"And I will be happy to take the responsibility for my client's good behavior. I have that much confidence," added Hartley Proctor for the record.

"We will require a bond," said Nancy.

Proctor nodded.

"It may be premature, and perhaps I am not the one to do so, but I apologize on behalf of the United States of America. I think someone ought to, and it might as well be me," Hernandez said, his attention focused on Randolph. "This is not the sort of thing we do here. It's certainly not what we ought to be doing, anyway. I will exert whatever it takes to see to it that Mr. Kennedy gets his wish to be freed of all entanglements and allowed to go about his business in his own way. Be assured, Mr. Proctor and everyone in this room, I will not rest until every man and woman who thought he or she was above the law feels the full measure of justice in the clear sunlight of public inspection."

Hartley Proctor made a small gesture as if tipping his hat to the deputy U.S. attorney. The rest of the attorneys sat like stones.

"Mr. Kennedy, you owe Mr. Proctor and Ms. Delgado. Don't fail them or cause them to be humiliated because they were willing to extend their trust. If you do, I will undo everything we have agreed upon today and will make it a personal crusade to see to it that you also feel the full weight of the bar of justice. You on the same page with me, sir?"

"Yes, Mr. Hernandez. It is in my best interests to take advantage of the opportunity. I won't fail you."

"I declare this inquiry closed."

Hernandez stood and shuffled his papers together. He was tight lipped with suppressed anger and moral indignation. He looked at the president's and the attorney general's attorneys like the avenging angel.

The participants began to file somberly towards the door.

"Wait up a moment, Mr. Harrelson, and the rest of the attorneys for the presently unindicted coconspirators. There are a few procedural matters we need to discuss with regards to your clients—like how and when to deliver subpoenas. I'm sure you would like to keep your clients from learning about this in the press before hearing it from competent authorities, and I just saw the press hurrying off to a telephone."

CHAPTER SIXTY-ONE

Muriel Vantassa had put in a full morning. The Chinese ambassador met with her and Quentin Richards, Secretary of State. The ambassador sought assurances that the United States would not interfere in his country's current efforts to bring its Taiwanese province into line. Even eight years after absorbing the one-time Republic of China into its monolithic whole, the master country of Asia still found Taiwan to be a thorn in its side. The War on Inflation Committee, the War on National Debt, and the National Bankruptcy Committee followed with success reports that they knew the president loved to hear and rewarded with promotions.

President Vantassa had recognized upon her election that the single most critical issue facing the nation was the $19.5 trillion national debt. The heads of governments of the European Union, the Japanese, and the Chinese and the president of the World Bank had all been nipping at the heels of the U.S. Treasury to pay on the principle of its debt load. The second year of her presidency saw both hyperflation—with 25% to as much as 32% increases in a month—and the failure of the nation to be able even to pay the crippling interest on the national deficit. The People's Republic of China now owned over 70% of the U.S. national debt. For ten years, the nation's total income had been exceeded by its debt.

She had formed two committees that were able to hold off the creditors and their demands to take over the fiscal reins of the U.S. and to bring down the interest rates to a stable 14% with the most austere economic program in American history. Now, nearly six years later, the president had weathered the firestorm that had erupted because of her stingy budgets and the thinly strained relationships among the most powerful economic and political forces on the planet. She was weary from the constant struggle, but pleased with the accomplishments of her administration.

Her war on drugs and illegal weapons was not faring as well. She had resisted the easy way out to legalize drugs and the strongly worded advice of her law enforcement and Justice Department appointees to limit gun confiscations to assault rifles and heavier ordnance and to leave handguns and hunting gear alone. The Militia Movement was growing apace with her every effort to remove their armaments, a perverse statistic in her view. The whole picture was gloomy and frustrating to the well-meaning president. Her last appointment of the morning had been to receive a report on the previous month's activities sponsored by her Final Battle in the War on Drugs and Illegal Firearms Task Force. The news was so discouraging that she kept the reporter—the officer in charge, FBI Director Ted Coleman—standing throughout his presentation.

She asked wearily, after the fifteen minute litany of bad news, "And I don't suppose you're any closer to putting a noose around that Randolph Kennedy's neck, are you?"

"No, ma'am. We have been within inches and hours of him, but he has so much help from the Movement's underground conspiracy that he keeps just ahead of us. My people tracked him to Vanuatu within this month. You can presume that he is moving the money he stole from the Ketchikan raid into their crooked offshore banking setup. But we were too late to get him or to find any evidence of money or deposits. I hardly need tell you that the man incited a riot yesterday in this very city to create a diversion. My man, Silberberg, had his hand on the man's shoulder; we were that close."

The president shook her head in frustration and disbelief. She did not know why she let the Randolph Kennedy Affair nettle her so much when she had truly important things to deal with. She considered Ted Coleman to be a sybarite and an aesthete, qualities she despised personally and presumed to be antithetical to the ability to get things done professionally. She would have sought his resignation months ago if his departure from her administration would only have added fuel to the rumors that her house was in disarray.

Now, she sat contemplatively looking out at the east lawn and idly munching a vegetarian sandwich. Her principle standing rule for her staff was that she was to be left entirely alone and undisturbed while she ate. She thought every human being should have at least that much space and privacy every day. The respite could not be stretched any longer. She had to meet with the leaders of all three parties of Congress to try and hammer out a tripartisan national health service bill. This was the first time that the sacred cow of medical care had been considered by the government since Hillary Clinton had tried to force her program—conceived in secret, and without political or medical input—onto a seething Congress; and Barack Obama's PPACA had been repealed. Vantassa was sure the time was right for a one-party-payer program. The first step was going to be the appointment of a blue-ribbon planning committee, something on the order of the crash program that had been instituted to save the country from bankruptcy.

She pressed the button on her console that indicated that she was ready for her next appointment. A green light flashed back indicating that the delegation was present and accounted for. She signaled for them to be ushered into the Oval Office. Suddenly the door to the Oval Office opened, and her longtime secretary—Olivia Prentiss—walked quickly inside. Her face was pale, and she was trembling.

"What is it?" asked the president, mildly alarmed at her secretary's altered appearance.

"Madam President, I apologize for the interruption...but Mr. Harrelson and Ms. Trimble are here with a U.S. marshal. The attorney general's lawyers are here, too. Mrs. Thaler is coming right over from Justice."

"What's going on?"

"I really don't know. They wouldn't tell me, but they hinted that it had to do with you personally. I said it was very irregular; but Mr. Harrelson said it was for your ears only; and it couldn't wait."

Tucker Harrelson was not an alarmist. He was the coldest fish Muriel Vantassa had ever known, positively unflappable. If he was making this matter—whatever it was—an emergency, then it was probably one of a magnitude to tilt the earth off its axis.

Struggling for calm, President Vantassa said, "By all means, show them in. Get the Congresspersons some treats and convey my apologies."

The four attorneys and a burly man dressed in a tweed sport coat and dark pants with white socks, that identified him automatically as a cop, were ushered in. Olivia Prentiss backed out and closed the door behind her. Tucker Harrelson—her personal attorney—and Vera Trimble—the White House counsel—then introduced Malcolm Tannenbaum and Galen Burke, Margaret Thaler's attorneys. Harrelson gestured to the burly cop.

"This is U.S. Marshal Howard Thomas. He has a subpoena for you."

"We get two dozen subpoenas a week. Doesn't he know that they're all handled by the security division?"

She was irritated by the man's presence and talked about him as if he were not present.

"This is an exception, I'm afraid, Madam President," said Harrelson. "He is under orders from the chief U.S. attorney to hand this subpoena to you personally. Vera and I agree, and that's why we're here."

"Get on with it then; I am busy," President Vantassa snapped acerbically.

Marshal Thomas stepped forward and handed her the papers.

"Muriel Vantassa?" he asked, as if he had been lost in the Congo for the past twenty years of Vantassa's meteoric rise to power.

"Who else, you nincompoop?" she barked.

The marshal did not react.

As soon as the president had the subpoena papers in her hand, he stated, for the record, "You have been served," and left the room.

Vantassa grudgingly and hurriedly skimmed through the documents, first red-faced and angry then pale and chagrined. She unconsciously put her hand over her heart. The attorney general joined the marshal before the president was ready to speak.

Finally, Vantassa asked, "I take it you were present at the inquiry where all of this came out?"

Harrelson nodded.

"What damage control measures have been implemented?"

"Not much yet. The meeting with Daniel Hernandez—the deputy U.S attorney in charge of the investigation—has only been over for half an hour. I'm afraid we're still at the stage of taking incoming fire."

The military language seemed appropriate under the circumstances.

"What incoming?"

"There was a *New York Times* reporter in the room. She has already filed an article. We checked with the editors; they are going to print the article—no matter what—but they want a response from you…from us. They told us they were considering putting out an unprecedented afternoon edition of the *Times* to carry this story. They are scrambling all over the town and in Alaska for anyone and everyone who has had anything to do with the case. They will hold off printing for two hours; so, they can have the administration's statement."

"In all candor, what do you think I should do?"

"First, Madam President, we all think the answer has to come from you personally and not from any representative. The plan should be the old tried and true Clinton program. First, lie and deny, then attack and obfuscate, then prolong and complicate. The Clintons' other rule—both in Bill's and in Hillary's administrations—was to cram as much into the first news cycle as possible. Most news stories are hot for a day, present for a week, and after that, they are old hat or forgotten. We suggest calling William Fitzgerald at the *Times* and give him your categorical denial directly. We will claim executive privilege every step of the way when the U.S. attorneys or anyone else makes a demand. For the press, we will tell them how ardent we are about cooperating. I have alerted the staff. They know that leaks will be investigated and dealt with as breaches of national security."

"Shades of Nixon and the first Clinton," sighed the president.

"Nixon could have held out. He buckled under too soon."

Harrelson enjoyed a certain reputation as a presidential historian and felt that he could deliver such statements from the vantage point of looking backward through the telescope of time. His views in the matter of Nixon were looked upon with skepticism by his colleagues in the White House.

"Margaret, you're in this up to your ears. What do you think?" the president asked her old friend and oldest appointee.

"I tend to agree with Tucker and Vera. We deny and stonewall. It will be up to Congress, and we can get to work this very afternoon on our people there to contain this thing. I hate even to mention it, but the Reformists and the Republicans will try and get a Special Counsel appointed as soon as possible. At the same time, we can start our own groundswell in Congress and with the public to forestall and blunt any talk about impeachment."

At the mention of that dreaded word, the president flinched as if she had been punched in the gut.

"Thank you for your candor, Margaret, Tucker, and Vera. Thank all of you for being here. This will be a test of this presidency; we all know that. We will weather this storm just like all of the others. Bernard Nussbaum, Bill Clinton's presidential counsel, advised an all out fight when Bill was first threatened with Whitewater. He pointed out that the judgment of history would vindicate. That is true here, as well. We have accomplished so much of importance and have so many more major issues to resolve, that it will be my plan to work on being and appearing to be president, and it will be yours to last out the siege."

"We're with you, Madam President," said Margaret Thaler with conviction.

"On a pragmatic level, ladies and gentlemen, here is what I think should be done today," the president said. "I will talk to William Fitzgerald at the *Times*, and I want you to refer all other inquiries to Mfuesa Mfume. He can get out a press release to the other papers. The *Times* will be so busy patting itself on the back for its scoop that it won't have time to alert everybody else. I want our papers to run front-page denials."

The others nodded in acceptance that the charismatic black presidential press officer would be the point man.

"I will schedule a three-network—no Fox News—presidential statement during prime time this evening. Vera, contact all cabinet level officers and the officers of the Task Force for an emergency meeting. We will discuss strategy further. We will have to fine tune legal approaches and, just among those of us in this room, decide who is expendable."

"Yes, ma'am"

"Anything else we need to do today?"

"Nothing that I can think of," said the attorney general.

The others indicated their agreement.

"We'll meet here again tomorrow morning, say eleven," President Vantassa said and pressed her console button to summon Olivia Prentiss. "Olivia?"

"Yes, Madam President?"

"Cancel the rest of my day. No, the rest of my week. I will give you a new schedule on a daily basis, but I don't want any side issues to interfere."

The side issues to which the president was referring were the affairs of the American State.

Gwen Chambers supplied the banner headline for her article: "PRESIDENT TO BE SUBPOENAED AS DEFENDANT IN FELONY". The paper went ahead with its almost unprecedented limited afternoon edition with Gwen's exclusive taking up the three right hand columns above the fold. Only news of the inquiry and the president's alleged complicity and related issues were included in the two-page issue so that it could be saved as a collector's edition by history buffs. Gwen deliberately chose objective unemotional language, and just as deliberately included direct excerpts from Oliver Quatraine's damning tapes.

The president's emphatic denial was included and set apart in a highly visible black bordered box along with a photo. Gwen included Vantassa's statement in the first and in the last paragraphs:

"I categorically deny all of the allegations leveled against me, against Attorney General Thaler, and against the heads of the government's law enforcement agencies. This attack is only to be expected since my administration's war on drugs and illegal firearms has stepped on so many wealthy and dangerous toes. It under-scores our successes and indicates how much still needs to be done with the help of the American public. We will mount an unswerving defense; and, in the end, we will be vindicated."

Randolph thanked Hartley Proctor and left him on the steps of the Justice Building. He declined the attorney's invitation to lunch. Randolph was not in a celebratory mood; the affair did not seem finished and had not achieved closure for him. He remained ill at ease, still something of the fugitive.

"Please keep in touch daily, Randolph, at least for the early weeks. I'll record your calls; so, include a day and date in every call. That way I can provide Agent Delgado and Hernandez with a transcript record. We can avoid even the very appearance of evil—as the churchmen say—if we have that written record," Proctor requested.

"I'll do it," Randolph promised.

When Proctor drove away in his limo, Randolph called Gwen Chamber's office number—he now had her private extension. She was not in; so, he left a message.

"Thanks. I appreciate your objectivity and professionalism. I like to think that you were trying to help as well, that your efforts were somewhat more that just your job. Maybe I just need to think that. But maybe one day when all of the pain dies down…"

He could not finish. He did not know what his feelings were, let alone what Gwen's might be in the future. He was objective enough to realize that she had been quite cool when they met—refusing to shake his hand. He was not going to be decent company for some time to come, and she probably still thought of him as a criminal.

Randolph spent three hours on the phone with his corporate attorneys, brokers, and new business associates—whom he had never met—and made progress in fleshing out lives for his aliases. Then he made preparations for travel.

SAC Gerald Silberberg sat morosely in his office chair surrounded by members of the COINTELPRO unit. They had been hashing and rehashing the ongoing manhunt for Kennedy for three hours since ten that morning. He felt like they were no further ahead than when they started.

The case was getting to him in a serious way. His family doctor had found hypertension and his electrocardiogram had revealed some heart strain during his annual physical the previous day. Silberberg did not have time or patience to follow the doctor's orders that he take time off for rest, eat better, and take blood pressure pills.

"You are a time bomb, Gerald," the overly solicitous old worrier had said.

Silberberg had laughed and said, "I'm gonna live forever. All my male progenitors smoked, drank, caroused and were gourmands. They lived into their nineties. Stop being such an old lady. I'm on a big case, but when it's over, I'll be a good boy."

The group sat at their desks finishing up reports, or just doodling. Silberberg felt a sense of ineradicable tension. He had to see Kennedy in cuffs; it was eating away at his soul.

His private phone rang and jangled his nerves. This had to be important enough to bypass his secretary.

"Silberberg."

"This is Ted Coleman. I have news you're not going to believe. Tucker Harrelson just called. He and Vera Trimble were at a meeting at Justice this morning. Guess who else was there?"

"Sir, with all respect, I am just not in a frame of mind for games."

"Well, you can look at this as good news or bad news or maybe both. Randolph Kennedy surrendered to that Delgado puppet of Phil Craig's. Deputy U.S. Attorney Daniel Hernandez—I think you know him—was in charge of the meeting. Drake and Quatraine got immunity to testify against the president and the attorney general, if you can believe that. Hernandez went crazy apparently; he let Kennedy go under his lawyer's responsibility. I hate to say this, but your involvement is over. We can't lay a glove on him until the whole investigation is done and some sort of legal action is taken against the president."

Silberberg could not believe what he was hearing. This had to be a prank. He let it simmer in his gut for a moment, then with full realization of what the DFBI had just said, that it was true, he felt a sudden ripping sensation in his anterior chest. His left arm became numb. He dropped the phone and jammed both hands against the powerful crushing force that was exploding deep inside his chest. He cried out in mortal agony, turned blue, and toppled to the floor.

Coleman was left dangling. Silberberg's lieutenants scrambled to give CPR to their chief. Someone called 911. The number three man in the FBI hierarchy was dead before the ambulance arrived.

CHAPTER SIXTY-TWO

The meeting with the cabinet level officers and the directors of the Task Force took place at three that afternoon owing to the Herculean efforts of President Vantassa's staff to round up the participants from around the city and even from junkets around the country. Besides the formally named defendants and their personal attorneys, there was a small army of legal staffers and secretaries. It was the equivalent of the old time Mafia arrangements to go to the mattresses. Only the vice-president was absent. She was conspicuously absent, and her administrative assistant at the Naval Observatory office had flatly informed President Vantassa's chief of staff that she would not be in attendance.

President Vantassa had Attorney General Thaler outline the events of the day and the particulars of the charges leveled against them. Thaler had spent her day collating every scrap of information she could find. It irked her that the best source was Gwen Chambers' article in the *New York Times*. Thaler reported that Quatraine and Drake were unreachable, and no one seemed to know where they were being held. No one in the FBI Witness Protection Program or from the U.S. Attorney's Office would talk. The AG had obtained a complete transcript of the inquiry by exercising heavy-handed pressure on the U.S. Attorney's Office, and by providing the necessary manpower to get the transcripts ready. She provided a copy to everyone.

Thaler took a defense attorney's approach to the information and presented in painstaking detail every thing known about the case over the next two hours. She was not interrupted by anyone. Before allowing discussion, the president had light suppers brought in. As was her custom, she did not permit discussion of the problem while the participants were eating.

The nearly invisible White House kitchen staff and butler service served then swept up the dishes and cleaned off the conference table and restored it to a work site. When they disappeared back downstairs, President Vantassa reconvened.

"Let's get back to work, ladies and gentlemen, we have just gotten started. I want to outline our plan of attack so as to avoid any question of what the executive order really is. War has been declared against us, against our Task Force, and we must stick together or fall together in an all-out defense. If ever there was a time for loyalty, this is it. There will be blatant and subtle efforts to subvert our cohesiveness, and you must be able to resist the blandishments to separate you from the rest of the administration. It is in your best interests to do so. If Justice finds a chink in our armor, they will not hesitate to capitalize and to take you down to get at me. Our legal authorities—Tucker Harrelson and Vera Trimble and their staffs—agree that we can hold out against this attack.

"No information is to be given to the press, to Congress, or to Justice without first getting the go-ahead from our defense committee, headed by Tucker. I want you to agree to have your office and home telephones monitored to ensure that no one uses your facilities to convey leaks of information."

That blatant bit of mistrust was not lost on anyone in the room.

"I know that you all are wondering about what we can do about the apparent conflict of interest Margaret has, since she has been named in the complaint. We will keep it simple: she will retain her position as attorney general but will relinquish all involvement in and knowledge of the prosecution's case. It may be a hard sell, since she will then be getting the information that we on the defense side have. It will be a thin line; but for now, at least, we will make it fly.

"Our weakest link, it is obvious—and ironically—our best defense, seems to lie with the ATF."

Roger Holdaway's attention had been drifting to his mountain of work left idling at the office. The president's comment shocked him back to the stark realization that he had already received a criminal subpoena and that he had better give this meeting his full attention. He was prepared to take umbrage at what she was intimating.

"With all due to respect to the fine job that Roger has been doing over there in the Treasury Building, this meeting is occasioned because two of his senior people committed felonies. They have admitted to that under oath. They are the loose cannons here. That Hernandez fellow has coerced them into being willing to testify against all of us and gave them immunity. We can consider them our worst enemies. I'm sure you will agree with that, Roger."

She looked over her podium at the DATF. He sat with a pale face and knitted brow. His mind was churning. He believed he was hearing who was going to be the sacrificial goat.

Ted Coleman had a sudden vivid recollection of Ali Mahmood Ajami, the oily little Persian lawyer for Henry Drake, reciting the biblical hand writing on the wall.

"There, but for the Grace of God, go I," he thought.

"Be good soldiers, all of you. That may entail some sacrifice. I venture to predict that it will not be business as usual at the White House for some time to come, but hang in there."

Roger Holdaway thought that the president had just uttered a couple of the most classical understatements of her career. He foresaw quite clearly the sacrifices and the 'business not as usual' centering on him. He did not like what he foresaw at all; and he was, by nature, disinclined to be the 'good soldier' in the implications of the president's context.

The Senate Judiciary Committee met in emergency closed session the following day. In a freewheeling debate that divided along predictable political party lines, three mutually exclusive interpretations of the data and three uncompromising avenues of approach to the governmental crisis were proposed. After hours of acrimony, the committee was only able to agree on one item—the appointment of a Special Counsel to investigate the matter. The Democrats hurriedly left the committee room after the meeting to begin their campaign to undermine that decision.

Each day for the next ten days, the media carried a new revelation about the Kennedy Affair. The White House and the President's Task Force predictably adopted a siege defense *modus vivendi* despite its own hopes to avoid such a debilitating mental outlook. President Vantassa and her staff had wanted to appear to be taking care of the nation's business in a work-a-day manner rather than concerning themselves with such a minor diversion as the Kennedy Affair. It was not to be.

The venom of the press exceeded their worst predictions. The efficiency of the U.S. Attorneys' Office in investigating and gathering depositions from involved lieutenants in the various law enforcement agencies and White House departments was astounding, sobering, and obviously had been planned for some time. The pace at which the case was mounting against them was unprecedented and many of the weaker souls were beginning to be frightened for themselves. The bureau directors all held their ground and refused to be deposed along with the president and attorney general and the vice-president. VP Chou had been subpoenaed belatedly on general principles. Each of them invoked executive privilege as their escutcheon.

The *New York Times* carried a story that Roger Holdaway knew had to have been leaked purposefully from the leader of the Task Force. He was named by "usually reliable sources" as being the principle target at this point in the U.S Attorneys' Office investigation. Roger was fifty-two years old and had carved himself out a respected place among Atlanta prosecutors before accepting his government post to restore confidence in the ATF after the stretch of bad leadership by Ike Petrovsky. He had been president of the Georgia Bar Association at the time of his appointment to head the ATF. There had never been even the breath of impropriety about his personal life or his career prior to this. Now he was at the vortex of an outright scandal. The humiliation of being named prominently in the *Times* article coupled with the almost certain knowledge that the information came with the White House's blessing caused the usually placid and imperturbable bureaucrat to roil inside.

He could see what was developing: he was to be sacrificed for the good of the group, for people he really did not even like. He knew that his good name, his reputation, and his pension were being steadily eroded away. He would go to prison; so, his fellows in the administration and on the Task Force might go to state dinners, give commencement addresses, pontificate on TV news talk shows, and be given credit for everything good that happened on the planet. Roger Holdaway was a social man; he even admitted to himself that he was something of a climber. He truly enjoyed those things, and it pained him deeply to feel them being taken away from him. Why him and not one or two of the others? Didn't loyalty go both ways? Apparently not.

Muriel Vantassa became a reluctant recluse, depressed and angry. The routine work of the presidency was abandoned after little more than a week after futile attempts to put on a good game face. The media and public were consumed with the stupid Kennedy Affair that had assumed an importance exceeding the China question, the nation's economy, health care reform, and national defense issues—the most burning of which was yet another effort by the DOD to get some of the redundant bases closed.

From everywhere came screams for the appointment of a Special Counsel, and the president's friends in the Senate and the House were finding it ever more difficult to stave off the vote to appoint one. On advice of counsel and by her own judgment and preference, she withdrew from view, meeting only with her "War Cabinet", party and administration loyalists. Her refusal to comply with even the most routine requests for disclosure or for documents was met with overt hostility in the Congress and in the press. The Senate Judiciary Committee—over the protests of the Democrats on the panel— voted by a secure margin to file suit against the president on the tenth day after the story broke and precipitated a constitutional crisis.

The Democratic Senate majority leader and the speaker of the House finally were forced by their respective houses to demand a face-to-face meeting with President Vantassa. Her aides prevailed on her to accept the meeting, if for no other reason than to solicit the members' support in their president's struggle.

"Yes, gentlemen, what do you have for me?" she phrased it as soon as the two senior legislators were seated in the Oval Office.

She looked thin and drawn. She had not bothered to put on makeup. The Senator and the leader of Congress both thought that the president looked haggard and ill. They were concerned.

"Are you all right, Madam President?" the majority leader asked solicitously.

"Just fine," she said. "I wouldn't say that it has been my best year."

She managed a wan smile.

"Yes, I'm fine, but I do need your help."

"Name it," said the speaker.

"Tell me how to handle the subpoena for the Task Force's documentation on the raid on that terrorist's place. You know I can't allow the Congress access to privileged information. The Constitution forbids it. The very office of the presidency would be weakened by that, and I have sworn an oath to defend my office for myself and for all the presidents to come."

The two men had a dreary sense of déjà vu, shades of the Nixon and Clinton investigations. Here was another president knowing from history that stonewalling was tantamount to political suicide and choosing that option none-theless. Neither lawmaker subscribed to this president's point of view.

The speaker offered a compromise, "Madam President, we came with a message. The Senate Judiciary Committee, the ranking members of all three parties; and the House leaders have all come to a conclusion; and it has been a hard debate to get to this. As we all see it, the only recourse at this point is to let us appoint a Special Counsel. If we don't, the case will be in the hands of the Supreme Court this week, and matters will be beyond our control. The Special Counsel option is inevitable either way. The Supreme Court route would mean that the case would move with blinding speed according to all the experts. You will lose every advantage you now enjoy, if they take over."

"Enjoy!?" she muttered. "I haven't *enjoyed* anything for months."

She found the very use of the word out of place, even anachronistic.

"I knew this day was coming, but it arrived so much quicker than anyone could have predicted," the president said sadly. "Our enemies have vast resources at their command, it appears. I suppose I will have to make the compromise. But mark my words, Gentlemen, I will go down fighting for ever scrap. I firmly predict that my presidency will last out its full term before anyone gets at me. It is November. I will gracefully complete my second term of office by this time next year. You can take that to the bank."

Neither man spoke. It was a sad thing to see a person of Muriel Vantassa's stature delude herself so completely.

The president continued, "I cannot imagine that the Congress would really want to appoint a Special Counsel at this precarious juncture in our nation's economic history. The primary election season is just around the corner. We can't deal with a constitutional crisis and an election at the same time. The election itself will occupy all of our time, and a substantial portion of our liquid assets in this country. Do you know what it costs to have a Special Counsel appointed?"

They shook their heads; the cost had not entered into their considerations.

"I have given a lot of thought to this issue, as you might well imagine. I *know* how much it costs. Let me illustrate with a few examples."

She recited facts and figures without resorting to notes.

"The Clinton passport files searches scandal cost the taxpayers $2,863,754. It cost $8,199,256 to investigate Agriculture Secretary Mike Espy. The Housing Department contract scandal mounted to $26,422,885. Whitewater and Monica Lewinsky—remember those two?—cost well over $45,000,000. Iran-Contra came to $47,865,000. How much do you think it would take to remove a twenty-first century sitting president of the United States? Remember, that the figures I just quoted were from the late twentieth century dollars; just consider the effect of inflation on what it could cost to unseat me. How much time do you think it would take? How much of the people's work would get done during that time?"

Her face was flushed and angry. She looked healthier—ready for a fight.

"In all candor, Madam President, this so-called Kennedy Affair has progressed beyond the point that Congress, the Judiciary, or the American people would blanch at another waste of a few million. They all want answers. It has become an emotional, divisive, anger driven issue, and nobody is fretting about the cost of getting at the truth. It has become a crusade. The least painful option open to you, and it is a temporary one, is to accept the nomination of a Special Counsel, in my estimation," the majority leader said.

It was the president's turn to shake her head. She did so less emphatically than she might have when the delegation first arrived in the Oval Office. Her face was drawn, and her eyes were squinting in tense concentration. She felt the first inklings that an intense migraine might be coming on.

"Madam President," the speaker of the House asked, "I don't mean to be indelicate, but have you given any consideration to the succession of your presidency? Has the vice-president been kept abreast of the crisis and is she up to speed on the current domestic and foreign affairs problems?"

"I have not seen the need to include her, quite frankly."

"Again, with respect, ma'am, you know that there is a strong movement afoot to draw up articles of impeachment against you; and in all candor, there is a good deal of support in the lower house for taking that first step. The Congress does not like to be stonewalled. You may be able to take some steam out of the movement and gain some time by allowing the Special Counsel. Perhaps, also, it would be wise to include vice-president Chou, at least quietly, into the information loop, and without drawing her into the crisis personally."

"So she can stay her unsullied and pristine self?"

"In a word, yes. She has to be seen as being as pure as Caesar's wife. She must be kept out of the snares here. Our party could not survive having two successive presidential administrations toppled or just crippled because of a conviction of the chief officer."

"Marianne Chou is vice-president for the simple and innocuous reason that we needed to balance the ticket and to appeal to minority voters. She's a Westerner, for heaven's sake! The woman has not contributed a scintilla to this administration and is a political light weight if ever there was one. It is inconceivable that we could have that woman or any other Asian woman, for that matter, become president. Let's get real," President Vantassa said with knotted facial muscles and dilated pupils.

She wrestled with herself to keep from making further characterizations about the Chinese-American vice-president whom she had held in disdain since before they ran together as candidates.

"I think it was Alben Barkley, Harry Truman's veep, who described his office as 'not being worth a bucket of warm spit'. We all agreed before the election and figured that Mrs. Chou could handle such an office reasonably well. After all, she has had six kids, what could be harder about being the vice-president? I am not about to turn over this office to her, to play Greece to her Rome.

"Once again, I think it was Alben Barkley who put it very well, and in an analogy applicable to the current situation. He was asked once while campaigning in 1947 how he would like the job of vice-president. He responded with a little anecdote. He said, 'a man had two sons. One of them went away to sea to be a sailor, and the other went away to Washington to be the vice-president. Neither of them was ever heard of again.' That is exactly what I think should happen to Marianne Chou."

The Congressional leaders were taken aback by the president's intransigent attitude. It came as no surprise that this president was neither a populist nor an egalitarian, but her outburst had all the overtones of oligarchical hubris and maybe even of racism. The speaker was from Arizona, and did not take kindly to Vantassa's disregard of his half of the country. He and the majority leader found that they had nothing more to say in the face of such obstinacy.

"Well, then, Madam President, we will take our leave. Thank you for your time. It seems unlikely that we will have further meetings," the majority leader said and rose from his chair.

"Thank you for coming by. I wish you success in dealing with the nomination for ambassador to China. Rick Hughs is a good man."

When they left, President Vantassa knew that she had just lost a major battle in her war. Her hard line decision was a burning of the bridges over her Rubicon. The institution of the Special Counsel had been notoriously tenacious, hounding presidents into retirement, into docility, and even following them after their terms of office had ended. She pondered how everyone could have turned on her. She was a good, maybe even a great president. She knew that the core problem was the rapacious media. Then there was the fact that she was a woman and persons of her gender would never really be accepted in this old boy's world. She was only the second woman president in the history of the country. The media and the right wingers had been just as vicious to Hillary Rodham Clinton. Vantassa took some solace in the memory that the plucky little blond liberal had brazened out her scandal, had stonewalled the lot of them, and had left her presidency with her head held high. Muriel Vantassa was adamant about accomplishing the same thing.

Vantassa considered herself to be just as tough as she had been when her father deserted the family when she was twelve, and she had had to become the de facto mother for her four younger siblings while her poor mother worked long hours as a receptionist in a motel. She was still as sharp as she had been when she beat out the patriarchy and was named valedictorian of her class at Princeton. She was no less competitive than when she made law review at Harvard Law or when she beat out a legion of prosecutors for the federal judgeship and was eventually elected governor of Oregon, and then that state's Senator. She still had what it took, and she would not only persist, but she would prevail. She looked down and saw that the knuckles of her fingers, gripping the arms of her swivel chair, were white.

CHAPTER SIXTY-THREE

When Randolph contacted FBI Agent Nancy Delgado by telephone for the tenth time in ten days following the inquiry at the U.S. Attorney's Office, she jotted down the details of his location for the day; the location changed almost daily.

When he had finished his communication, she said, "I have a request for you to speak to Agent Quatraine. He says it's personal."

Randolph paused, "Which one is Quatraine?"

"The black ATF agent. The one in the inquiry who revealed the damning tapes of the Task Force and the president's involvement."

"What does he want? What does 'personal' mean?"

"I'm not sure, Mr. Kennedy, and I am reluctant to try and defend the motives of anyone involved in the Affair. However, he sounded every bit as if he wanted to say something to you man-to-man without anyone else being involved."

"How come I think he's just a stalking horse?" Randolph asked bitterly.

"Maybe it's because you have lost the ability to trust," she answered gently.

Randolph was quiet for a few moments.

Finally, he said, "Maybe I can try and find that character trait again. We'll see. I'll talk to the guy. Talk's cheap. I guess you'll have to make the arrangements, since he's in the WPP."

"It will take some time, but I do have his number. The WPP people would have a small stroke if they even knew that he had called me, let alone that he had given me this confidential number. I'll set up a call—and when you make contact—it will be up to the two of you to make any arrangement beyond that. Tomorrow when you check in I can give you a time and a number. Forget that it was me that did it, okay?"

"Did what?" Randolph responded.

Daniel Hernandez could never get the work of his committee done in any working day. He was now the head of what had developed into its own small law firm within the U.S. Attorney's Office. His law firm had only one case—the Kennedy Affair. Getting at the president had become the overriding goal in what everyone in his firm—and out of it—recognized as a blood sport. The firm decided to hold off on full prosecution of the underlings, feeling that it would be the worst miscarriage of justice if the small fry were scooped up and the big fish went free, and it was bad tactics because some of the underlings were bound to crack and give up solid evidence in return for immunity.

It was—as usual—after ten when he finally left his office and walked through the executive parking terrace to his car. He was lost in thoughts and plans for tomorrow's renewed assault on the fortress White House when a voice startled him.

"Mr. Hernandez?"

It came from behind a van he had just passed. It sounded innocuous enough, but still, it unnerved him.

"Yes?" he replied defensively, "Who is it? What do you want?"

He looked for an escape route. With all of the heat of controversy that he had engendered, he could easily imagine someone being provoked enough to attack him. By virtue of his office, he could carry a gun; but he had never bothered to look into it. Right now, a concealed weapon would be a comfort. He was particularly vulnerable, being tired and run down from the weeks of over work.

"I need to talk to you somewhere absolutely private. I need protection. It has to be secret."

"I can arrange that. What is this about? What do you have for me?"

Hernandez was beginning to think he might be dealing with a crank.

The voice from the darkness lowered to a mere whisper, "I'm Roger Holdaway. I'm willing to testify, but I have to have immunity. That's the bottom line for me. I can't be prosecuted or jailed or fined or humiliated by the government."

"I can't promise anything, Mr. Holdaway, until I see what you can contribute to the case at hand that makes you more important as a witness than as a defendant. I presume you are here about the Kennedy Affair."

"Of course, what else?" Holdaway snapped testily. "There is nothing else going on in this country."

His nerves were frayed to the breaking point.

Hernandez could hear that in the man's distraught voice and did not respond in kind to Holdaway's rudeness. He decided to tread very lightly.

"Come to my office tomorrow evening. It is private and safe there."

"Not your office!"

Holdaway's voice was shrill.

"Okay, take it easy. We can meet in Georgetown. I know a little bar—a gay bar called Maxies—where no one pays any attention to anyone else… religiously. I've used it for meetings for years."

Hernandez knew that Holdaway would be leery. It was all the man would need—to be caught in a queer bar and make the evening news.

Holdaway seemed very tense and hesitant. His answer took several minutes to come out.

"All right. Can we do it tonight?"

Hernandez felt his heart sink. No rest again. He was not sure how much longer he was going to be able to keep this up. He was not getting any younger. His work schedule was like a litigator's weeks during a trial. He sighed.

"I suppose so. You think it's that urgent?"

Footsteps echoed in the distance on the same level of the parking terrace. Holdaway slipped away into the shadows. In half an hour the two men met in the shadows of the parking lot of Maxies, then they entered the smoky, dark bar separately. They took a booth near the back.

"So give," said Hernandez in the most affable voice he could muster at this late hour.

"I need a little drink first. I'm about shot," Holdaway said.

He put down a double scotch before he felt like he had had enough liquid courage to prop him up.

"I can corroborate the testimony of my two agents. I'm willing to do it under oath. I'd like to do it as soon as possible. I only ask two things—no less than transactional immunity and that you keep me out of the spotlight as much as possible. I don't really want to testify before Congress with the klieg lights, TV cameras, and all. I want your word as a gentleman on that."

His voice was plaintive.

Hernandez had his reliable witness—the director of one of the premier U.S. government law enforcement bureaus. It was not quite the FBI; but Holdaway would do, and might well do to bring down the FBI director. He could nail everyone else with the corroborative testimony that this witness could provide.

"Deal," he said. "You be in my office tomorrow morning at six o'clock. We can depose you by eight at the latest, and you can be back on your patch in time for regular business hours, nobody the wiser. We'll keep the fact of your deposition secret until we have to use it as a pry bar against the president and her main lieutenants. That's as far as I can go. And I will tell you this only one time. You will tell my office the truth, the whole truth, and nothing but the truth. One deviation—however slight—and the whole deal's off. I will subpoena your testimony as a hostile witness and as a criminal defendant without immunity if you fail me. I go for the jugular. You have been warned."

"All right," the thoroughly cowed DATF said. "I'll see you tomorrow morning. I want to come in through your rear door."

Hernandez gave Holdaway the directions.

"I have to get out of here. This place gives me the creeps."

At the moment two strippers, not so obviously male, were teasing a cheering and whistling audience of men who were none too obviously male themselves.

At nine o'clock, after the DATF's deposition, Daniel Hernandez went home took a short-acting sleeping pill and scarcely moved in his bed until noon the next day giving himself a much needed refreshing sleep. He awakened happy for the first time in a month and ready to tilt at then windmills of his world.

"Ezzzi," he said to his wife of thirty-five years, as she brought him brunch in bed, "I have been a lousy husband for most of this year, but the end is in sight. Thanks for hanging in there for me."

Ezmerelda Hernandez smiled her comforting smile and replied, "it's my job. I am well aware that this new information from the DATF is what you've been looking for and will crack your case in the public eye. I am no longer the naïve girl you married, Daniel. I am very well aware that the road ahead as you tackle the presidency is going to be brutal, and I will stick it out for you. I will be here in our house for you every day. You must promise me that you will let it go when you come to our house and let me take care of you. I don't care that much about the case, or about the crooked president, or about the fame or the controversy. I care about you. You must not give yourself a stroke or a heart attack over this. I will never forgive you if you do."

Ezmerelda almost never made long statements. Daniel knew that she meant every word and had his interests at heart. He also knew that she was right. He vowed to take care of himself; so, he could endure what was coming until the entire war was over.

"Thanks, my dear. I will rely on you, and I promise to be good boy."

Ezmerelda rolled her eyes and offered her man her quiet loving smile.

Back in his office that afternoon—for the first time in the nearly three months that Daniel Hernandez had been pursuing the Kennedy Affair and patiently collecting reams of evidence—he felt trepidations. He had read and reread the deposition from Roger Holdaway. It was the final piece he needed, the virtual smoking gun. Jurists, congressmen, and senators, who might not be ready to believe a pair of disgraced ATF agents and an erstwhile criminal fugitive presenting evidence against the president of the United States, were going to sit up and take notice of Holdaway's testimony. A full and frank confession from a near cabinet level director of one of the most powerful federal bureaus had to have considerable weight.

Hernandez's misgivings centered not on his arguably having too little evidence to ask for an indictment against the president and her chief underlings. His problem was that he had a surfeit of evidence. He had come to the realization that he had boxes full of papers that would surely bring down the administration of the president. In a way inexplicable to himself, he felt guilty about that. He believed in the presidency as he believed in his country. Like most American citizens, he wanted to hold on to the security of believing in the core goodness of the sitting president. He knew that was naïve, that his dreadful knowledge so painstakingly accumulated, was the verifiable truth. There could always be a new president, perhaps one in whom the trust of the people could safely repose, but it was not President Muriel Vantassa.

Hernandez knew that what he was about to do was fundamental to the preservation of the Anglo-American rule of law over the dominance of the individual—a tyrant—but it gave him no sense of satisfaction. He recalled that he was only following the lead of the knights who at Runnymede in June, 1215, forced the Magna Charta on tyrannical King John. The 39th paragraph extracted the far-reaching promise, "The King must live by the law." Hernandez had his duty to do. He slowly pushed himself out of his swivel desk chair to do it.

Roger Holdaway had given names, dates, and portions of conversations that made it crystal clear that the president, the attorney general, and the heads of the federal law enforcement agencies on the Final Battle in the War on Drugs and Illegal Firearms Task Force were guilty of a criminal conspiracy under the cover-all guise of the national security requirement. Holdaway had a near encyclopedic memory; his deposition testimony was reminiscent of White House Counsel John Dean in the Watergate Hearings so long ago. He even looked a little like Dean. To his credit, he did not blink when he detailed his own complicity.

Daniel no longer held any of the high ranking officials on his defendants and witness individually or collectively in the slightest degree of respect. He was spurred by his deep reverence for the offices they held. The people involved were a riffraff of knaves, and he was going to be their undoing. He picked up his transcript summary booklet and walked to the office of the Chief U.S. Attorney, LaVerl Taylor—the nation's prosecutor—and knocked on his inner office door. He was expected.

"Come in, Daniel."

Hernandez entered, took the seat proffered him, and accepted a fruit juice. Taylor was a Mormon from California, who was not only a teetotaler, but he would not allow coffee, tea, or even Coke to be served in his office, let alone alcohol.

"Well, Daniel, how close are you?"

"I'm there, LaVerl."

He felt curiously depressed.

"You sure? There can't be any mistakes or loopholes in this one. We serve an arrest warrant—and there's something amiss in your work—our jobs are gone. Only if the evidence is so good that it is insurmountable and unassailable will we be able to save ourselves. We still won't know if a new administration will want a couple of giant killers or gadflies. I'll tell you frankly, my friend, I wish I had never heard of the Kennedy Affair."

"That's two of us, LaVerl, but here we are."

He slid the Holdaway deposition transcript across the chief's cherry wood desktop. Taylor sighed before picking it up.

"I cleared my appointment calendar for the day. You and I are going to do nothing but go over this evidence to look for flaws."

The chief U.S. attorney was dead serious. Even his desk was free of its usual clutter down to the pictures of his large family.

"I have had an independent summary done by Lyons, Watts, Simpson, and Morehouse," Hernandez said.

He named a large firm of criminal defense attorneys he had hired on a consulting basis to look at the evidence from a defender's point of view. Walter Simpson was one of the recognized constitutional scholars in the country.

"Smooth move, Daniel. I am sure you have been entirely thorough. I'll start with Holdaway's deposition. I presume that he's the star witness in this mess. We can go over the rest after that. How long do you think it will take?"

"Until mid to late afternoon tomorrow, if we use the summaries. A month if we go over every page with a magnifying glass."

"We're lawyers, and I suppose that we should go over it in detail, but I feel familiar enough with the raw evidence to let the summaries suffice for the present need. You know that we are eventually going to have to go over the whole magilla."

He punched his secretary's button. The sharply dressed young man came in a moment later. Taylor had insisted on having a male secretary to avoid even the appearance of impropriety that might be raised by being alone in his office with a woman. Being a Mormon Stake President was an exacting calling which LaVerl Taylor took very seriously.

"Yes, sir?" the secretary asked.

"Jake, I want to have an appointment this afternoon, about four, with Justice Nielson to discuss the issuance of warrants. He's half expecting me. I will have Judge Thatcher sign the warrants and with the Supreme Court Justice involved to monitor every step; we will get this right, at least procedurally. Then make an appointment for Mr. Hernandez, the speaker of the House, the Senate majority leader, the vice-president, and me to meet with President Vantassa day after tomorrow, first thing in the morning. Arrange a call to be accepted from me to Vantassa's chief of staff shortly before that scheduled meeting. I want to give them a little forewarning."

The secretary took no notes. He nodded his understanding and left them alone.

"Call him back, Jake. I want to run something by you before we make that final decision, okay?"

For the next hour, Taylor poured over the transcript of Holdaway's catharsis. That he had left nothing out, spared himself nothing, came through resoundingly. Hernandez had asked every question in every possible way, and Holdaway had never wavered and had never altered his testimony. Hernandez made sure that the plea bargain arrangements were a prominent part of the official record to avoid any appearance that it was a secret and to defuse the defense's expected attack on the witness's credibility. The evidence was fully condemnatory, *la ultima gota*—the final coffin nail. It was inescapable.

Taylor heaved a resigned sigh, a melancholy sound. His face mirrored the sentiment.

"We have a couple of choices. We can be political and wait to give the information to the new Special Counsel. We can give it to the politicians and let them deal with it in their own way."

"Or we can do the right thing, the professional thing, and treat this like any other criminal arrest," Hernandez broke in.

He kept his face impassive—a trait he inherited from his Apache progenitors—but he was determined not to let this case escape from the control of the legitimately empowered prosecutors. He did not like the direction Taylor seemed to be heading.

"Um-hmmh," LaVerl mused shaking his head.

Reluctance was conspicuous in his voice and on his face.

LaVerl went on, taking note of his deputy's dubious look, "we don't even know if we *can* indict a sitting president. It'll be new ground. I don't think it's right to sit on this until a Special Counsel can go through the months and months of rehash. It is my responsibility and yours, Daniel. And so it must be after all the wavering and pain. You heard the appointments scheduled for tomorrow.

Daniel interrupted, "serve the papers the following morning. Take the chief U.S. marshal with you, and have him serve the formal arrest papers. Don't even think about this with anyone else in the room. No forewarnings to anyone. We are well past the point of daintiness or even common courtesy, boss. This is the first salvo in an outright war where no one will take prisoners. We cannot let one syllable of our intentions leak out to the press. The hyenas will have their day soon enough. I do not want our office to have the slightest taint in the handling of any of this. Any objections to any of that, Mr. Chief U.S. Attorney?"

LaVerl Taylor smiled at his ardent deputy.

"Nor from me. I'm willing to backtrack on any suggestion I might ever have made about the courtesies, but I have to be certain that you and I will see this to the end, that I won't get thrown under the bus. I trust you, boss. I will be the Pancho to your Don Quixote all the way. I thought you'd never get to it.

"The only thing, though, LaVerl; I vowed that this whole mess would be given its proper public display. If—somehow—the powers that be are able to suppress or prevent this arrest and indictment and the information that led up to it, I reserve the right to publish abroad any and all of the information. I have made copies and have stored them in a safe place outside the office to ensure that I am not thwarted by politics."

"Fair enough. I'm sure you know the personal cost to you and your career, Daniel. Just keep it close to your vest until there is a chance for a proper service of the warrants. I'll put the steps in motion to have the other arrests take place at exactly the same time. The press will get wind of it the second this goes into motion. They will be able to sniff the blood and will come a baying."

Hernandez and Taylor worked over the summaries and checked and rechecked portions of suspect raw data to be sure that there were no glaring omissions, distortions, or unprovable assertions. Hernandez and his "firm" had done the work thoroughly and with scrupulous accuracy. They broke off at six that evening to allow themselves to remain fresh. At three-thirty the following day, they were finished.

"Keep this in your safe, Daniel. I'm off to Justice Nielson's. I will come back with the vetted arrest warrants. Meet me here at eight sharp tomorrow. We can go over any last-minute preparations for the actual arrests."

CHAPTER SIXTY-FOUR

Randolph called Nancy Delgado at ten the next morning as she had suggested.
"Hi, Mr. Kennedy. Anything new about your location today?"

"No, ma'am. Same as yesterday."

Her caller ID confirmed that.

"Okay, I have a number for Agent Quatraine. He wants you to call him this afternoon at exactly three-ten EST. What do you want me to tell him?"

"I'll call. Nobody should expect much—no feel good get-togethers, sing-alongs, or group hugs. We won't be having a friendly beer, and we won't get to be pals who go to ball games together. I'll talk to him, though."

"I'll let him know. Here's the number."

She gave it to him and a brief set of instructions about the security precautions for the call.

Randolph wrote it all down.

"I'll call you tomorrow, same time, same station. Good-bye Agent Delgado."

"Good-by, Mr. Kennedy."

At five past three, the same day, Randolph entered a telephone booth in Queens as Delgado had instructed, waited just short of five minutes, then dialed the number the FBI agent had given him.

"Hello, is this Mr. Kennedy?" came Quatraine's deep voice.

"It is. What's this about, Agent Quatraine?"

"It'd be easier if you called me Oliver. I am no longer an agent. As a matter of fact, I'm no longer Oliver Quatraine. I'm in a phone booth, away from my keepers for a little while."

Randolph said nothing.

After an awkward pause, Quatraine asked tentatively, "You still there?"

"Yeah."

Quatraine shrugged, "Look, Mr. Kennedy, I just wanted to clear the air a little, get a few things off my chest."

"Go ahead. You asked for the call. I'm listening."

Randolph was intentionally brusque and unfeeling which sounded a bit harsh even to him. However, he thought that it was not his place to have to give the man absolution—even if he were inclined—which he was not.

Quatraine gave a little sigh, "Anyway, man, I wanted to say that I'm sorry. I'm speaking for myself. It was terrible what happened to your wife and little girl and what happened twice to you at the hands of the ATF. Maybe you could understand that I haven't done so well at their hands either. I'm black, and that's about as low as you can be on the ATF preference list. I have been treated like colored trash; so, I do have some small appreciation of what you've been through."

"*No you don't,*" thought Randolph, but he did not interrupt.

"That's beside the point. As one man to another, I just wanted to tell you that I was very reluctant about the raid and had my doubts about the evidence against you from the beginning. I should have spoken up more forcefully before the second raid ever happened."

"*You and two dozen others,*" Randolph thought disdainfully. "*It's a little late, don't you think, you pathetic coward.*"

"The truth of it is that I didn't. I'm ashamed of that, ashamed of my part in the raid. I feel terrible about it. I needed to say that to you. Maybe when you think about me—if you ever do—you could see some balance. I destroyed my career by bringing out those tapes of the president ordering the illegal placement of the evidence against you. I think that helped your case. Maybe you could take that as an extenuating circumstance someday when you have a chance to ponder all of this. Anyway, I'm sorry," Oliver said, and it was obviously heartfelt.

"I've heard you out, Mr. Quatraine. I guess I feel that it was something decent to come out of this wretched mess. I have to tell you. It's too little and too late. You know that."

"I'd like you to accept my apology. I will understand if you won't."

Randolph was beginning to feel like something of a jerk, but he could not let go of his anger. Maybe it was his pride, who knows? But there was nothing left in him to feel any real compassion for this man who had helped bring so much harm to him and his wife and his little girl.

It occurred to Oliver to tell Kennedy that it had been him that had telephoned a warning on the night of the raid, but he dismissed the thought presuming that it would seem to be too self-serving; or worse, it might sound like a lie.

Randolph said, "I'm sorry that I can't find a way to forgive you. Maybe some day. I can't love or trust anymore. I was just an ordinary working stiff with a fine little family. I had feelings for them, but now I'm a straw man. I used to be a gung ho American, and now I can only look on the country as my adversary. I never hated before, and now I'm consumed with it—against the ATF and everybody in it, and if the truth be known, I guess I hate the United States. I would like to get over that feeling, but I can't. Maybe if or when I do, I can reconsider my inability to say that I accept your apology. I have to admit that it was a very decent thing for you to do, and you are alone in having done so."

"This is a personal apology, Mr. Kennedy. I don't speak for the ATF or for the federal government or any other group."

"I'm still in a state of confusion, Oliver. I recognize that I am a long way short of being blameless. I hope you can believe someday that it was never my intention to hurt anyone. The booby traps seemed essential at the time, and I still think I would be dead now if I hadn't had them. I can't shake the guilt and sorrow I have that men are dead because of me—even one of my friends. I don't even know if I'm making an apology. I just needed to say that to someone."

Both men knew that they were like trains passing in the night. It was too soon for them to have enough healing to be able to deal with the Affair rationally. Perhaps in time…

"Maybe we could get together some time, Randolph. I mean, maybe we could talk things out. I don't have anyone except my wife I can unload on, and she wasn't involved; so, she can't really appreciate how I feel. I think maybe you might need to talk to someone who knows as well. Who knows? Maybe in time we could be sort of friends."

"I guess I might come to like that. Let's give it some time, Oliver. We've both got some healing to do."

They said good-bye. Randolph felt as if he had shed some weight. Perhaps the chip on his shoulder was a trifle lighter after talking to Oliver Quatraine.

As soon as LaVerl Taylor's secretary called to make the appointment for the following day and gave the list of attendees, Grace Shabazz Omotonpareti, President Vantassa's dragon lady chief of staff, was all but certain what was in the offing. The U.S. attorney, U.S. marshal, a Supreme Court justice, and the leaders of both houses of Congress, were not making a casual social call. Omotonpareti had dreaded this day ever since the news began to break about the Kennedy Affair. The Special Counsel appointed in a nearly unanimous vote in Congress had just begun his investigation. President Vantassa had scornfully rejected even the institution of the S.C. and certainly had deplored any application of the institution to her. Omotonpareti wondered what could be so ominous so early in the process.

She was a pragmatist, a South Side of Chicago black activist pragmatist. She knew what the end of the manifest blood lust was going to be. Like the rest of the White House aides—however—she had not expected anything definitive until after the president's term of office had ended, and certainly not before the S.C. had submitted his report. The very abruptness of this request for a formal meeting was profoundly unsettling.

She walked from her office in the West Wing to the presidential secretary's desk.

"I have to see her immediately," Omotonpareti said.

She put down the meeting agenda for the secretary to note. All meetings with the president had to be approved by the chief of staff in advance—and that was Grace Shabazz Omotonpareti, who was standing in front of her. Olivia Prentiss made note of the radical change to the day's lineup. It always gave Omotonpareti a little thrill to be able to gain access to the most powerful leader in the Western world with nothing more than her say-so. Grace was a girl who had had a baby out of wedlock at the age of thirteen. She had legally changed her name from Maybelle Struthers—rural unwed mother on welfare—to the aristocratic African sounding name of Omotonpareti, a name she had made up herself. She had come a long way and had long ago done away with her old victim persona.

"Show her in," came the voice of the president over the intercom.

Even discounting the distortions of electronic voice transmission, the weariness in the president's voice came across.

"I know the way," Grace said and forced a smile.

The door to the Oval Office was four feet from where she was standing. She entered.

"Good afternoon, Grace," said the president, her tone flat.

"Madam President," Grace said and gave a deferential little bow of her head, "I need to alert you to the implications of your first appointment tomorrow. At ten you are scheduled to meet with several Justice Department and congressional people and with a Supreme Court justice."

She passed the president a copy of the following day's meeting agenda.

Vantassa's brow knitted into a tight scowl. The implications were evident without having to be explained by her chief of staff.

"Let me guess what this's about," President Vantassa grumbled.

She shook her head in mild disbelief. Dealing with this Kennedy Affair was like killing cockroaches. You could stomp them, burn them, poison them, drown them, or whatever; and they got up again and kept coming on relentlessly.

"Any particulars" she asked.

"None given, Madam President. If I may venture to be so bold, I do have a strong premonition."

"Your premonitions are never wrong, Grace. That's what I dislike about them so much. Why are they coming?"

"The grouping has arrest written all over it. It looks to me like a lynching party, pure and simple."

"I could refuse to meet, could order the doors barred, or take a sudden trip to Europe," President Vantassa said mirthlessly.

"Or get on Air Force One and just fly around, or go to the doomsday shelter, or anything that takes you away from this room," Omotonpareti added gently.

"What I should do is refuse any such unprecedented affront to the office of the president. I remain firmly convinced that no one has the right to arrest or to indict a sitting president."

"It would be a significant fight, Madam President. I'll handle it any way you want me to. Just give the word."

"All right, consider your duty done, Grace. I will have to ponder this. Cancel everything else between now and then. I am going to the quarters to think. National emergency is the only excuse for disturbing me."

When Grace went back to her office, Muriel Vantassa started to tremble. To make a decision this crucial, she had to know.

"Get that Hernandez fellow on the phone," she ordered Olivia.

"The president for you, Mr. Hernandez," Daniel's secretary announced.

"Hello, Madam President," he said.

"I am correct in my understanding that you are in charge of the Justice Department's investigation of the Kennedy Affair, am I not?"

"That's correct. But ma'am you really should not be calling me. It is improper, and under the circumstances, could appear to be an attempt to influence an investigation in which you are a target."

"Don't give me the good government sermon, Hernandez. I need a little truth. I understand that you take pride in dispensing it. I want to know with a simple yes or no, are you planning to serve an arrest warrant on me tomorrow?"

"I will answer that, Madam President, but first I have to have an assurance that you will not warn other potential arrestees or leave the jurisdiction."

She had her answer.

"You have my word."

"Wishing you no disrespect, ma'am, but I still need to record that request and answer. A leak or warning to others would constitute interference with a criminal investigation or even aiding and abetting flight of a fugitive to avoid arrest and prosecution should any of the targeted individuals decide to bolt, and that is a felony."

"*Bolt!*" she snorted.

There were a series of distracting clicks and scrapes over the line, then three quiet, high-pitched beeps.

"I have the recording device in place. Do you still want me to answer your question about the potential that you may be arrested tomorrow?"

"Record away. I'm a lawyer. I know my rights."

"For the record, Madam President, would you please rephrase your question?"
She did.

"The answer is yes," he said. "We are going to formalize the proceedings. We have a criminal arrest warrant to be served on you."

"And who else?"

"I'm afraid I can't divulge that, Ma'am."

"It doesn't take a brain surgeon to figure it out, I suppose. Thank you for your courtesy, Mr. Hernandez. I will see you in the morning, but be aware that I do not believe that an arrest warrant can be legally served on a sitting president."

Her voice was as wintry as the February day outside.

President Vantassa called all of her senior aides, including every cabinet secretary, to an extraordinary White House meeting that evening. She told all of them of the new development and swore them to secrecy, asking them to grant her this much—that she be allowed to make the first move in this end-game scenario. What she wanted from them was advice.

"What should I do? How should I respond?"

Casper Wilson from Communications offered more stonewalling; the strategy had been working well enough thus far. Kevin Trevaine from State wanted her to go before the American people that very night and tell them everything, appeal to their capacity for forgiveness, and throw herself on the mercy of public opinion. Zerminger from Commerce suggested an emergency meeting with the congressional leaders of the Democratic Party to enlist their support in a protracted battle—divide the Congress along party lines and dig in.

Margaret Thaler, speaking for the Justice Department, was the last to offer her opinion.

"Madam President, this is the final test of your embattled presidency. You have a precedent from Nixon. Fire Hernandez and his boss—that wimp, LaVerl Taylor. You must not cave in to them. You must fight. We will all fight with you. I will appoint new U.S. attorneys. Fire the Special Counsel; you can do that, too. Talk to the American people, just as Secretary Trevaine suggested, except my take is that you should go on the offensive. Tell them you are innocent, that your political enemies and the media are trying to destroy you as you are trying to finish of the criminal cartels that have such inordinate power over our society."

"And if you do," Tucker Harrelson said in his deep somber voice that commanded the attention of the gathering, "the Congress will proceed immediately to drawing up articles of impeachment, if they have not already gotten them ready. Under the Constitution, they will have no other choice. I should imagine that the Senate could be ready for an impeachment trial in less than three months, all partisan politics and maneuvers in the House notwithstanding. They, too, will have no choice.

"You, on the other hand, have a choice. You will have that choice until ten o'clock tomorrow morning when the U.S. marshal serves the arrest papers. If you are impeached, you lose your pension and privileges. If you resign before being removed from office, you can keep them. It is as simple and ugly as that. Nixon fought right up until he was informed that articles were about to be served on him by the Congress. Then, he did the only prudent thing; he resigned. His vice-president became president and pardoned him. Maybe Marianne Chou could be persuaded to come through; so, the indictments won't amount to a hill of beans. I guess my strongest advice is that you mend fences with the vice-president tonight and get her to grant you immunity."

Vera Trimble spoke up now, "Speaking as the presidential counsel, and hopefully as a friend, I have to agree in principle with Tucker. I have one caveat to amend his recommendation. Whatever anyone does, stay away from the vice-president. Any approach, and she will feel duty bound to reject a clemency bid. The only thing that saved Nixon was that he had a good relationship with his vice-president, Gerald Ford, and the president was wily enough to leave the matter entirely to the discretion of Ford. Ford was able to take the high road and offer the presidential pardon in the interests of healing the divisions of the country. In this case, the relationship with your vice-president is nowhere near as cordial as witnessed by the fact that she has been snubbed by not receiving an invitation to this meeting. It is too late to change that, but she is the best hope. Give Vice-President Chou a chance to come through."

Every cabinet officer put in his or her suggestion before the meeting came to an acrimonious end shortly after midnight. No one felt that he or she was the winner, and no consensus was achieved. President Vantassa thanked them all for their candor and proffered help. Once again she enjoined them to silence. She took her leave and retired to her bedroom. She opened her bottle of Ambien sleeping pills and for a moment considered taking all of them. Muriel Vantassa believed suicide to be cowardly; and, although she admitted to faults, cowardice was not one of them. She took one white pill. The president spent the night deep in thought; sleep never intruded despite having taken the pill.

Well past midnight the anguished president dialed one of the foremost religious leaders of the country for guidance—Daniel Martin Larousse, pastor of the Crystal Cathedral in Los Angeles.

The pastor's sleepy voice mumbled into his private telephone receiver.

"Hullo, what is it?"

"Pastor Larousse?"

"Yes, Pastor Larousse here. Who is this?"

The voice was very familiar, yet he could not place it with certainty.

"Muriel Vantassa, Daniel, President Vantassa."

He was awake instantaneously, charged with adrenalin.

"Yes, Madam President, what can I do for you?"

"I know it is late, Daniel, and I won't keep you. I am terribly troubled, and I feel I have nowhere else to turn. You are—no doubt—aware of the serious attacks on the presidency of late."

"I certainly am, Madam President. You have my deepest concern. I hold you in my prayers daily."

"Thank you for that, Daniel. I was wondering only if you could guide me on some scriptural reading that might bring me relief or perhaps inspiration. That is the only reason I disturbed you."

Pastor Larousse paused for half a minute. His voice was sober.

"Madam President, I am aware of your soul's complaint. I suggest that you immerse yourself in the *Book of Job*. I think you will find wisdom and solace there."

It was her turn to pause.

"Daniel, I am embarrassed to confess that I am unsure where the *Book of Job* is found."

Pastor Larousse gave a soft indulgent laugh, "*Old Testament*, President Vantassa, between *Esther* and the *Psalms of David*. And the other suggestion is that you read the *23rd Psalm* until you have it memorized."

"Thank you, Pastor. You have been most kind. Get back to sleep. Sorry to have disturbed you."

"Glad to be able to serve. I will pray for you, Madam President."

"I will be happy to accept your intercession, Daniel. I need all the help I can get. Good night."

"Good night, Madam President."

President Vantassa adjusted the pillows on her bed and turned on her reading light. She turned to *Job* in the *King James Version of the Old Testament*, comfortable with the solemnity of its antiquarian language. The president read of Job's afflictions at the hands of God and Satan and the philosophical advice of his well-meaning friends, likening herself to the poor man who was put upon through no fault of his own. She found a verse that summed up the sorry state of her life that night.

"My days are swifter than a weaver's shuttle, and are spent without hope."

For the first time in her adult life, she broke down and wept. She begged for guidance from the God that she had mocked for so long.

CHAPTER SIXTY-FIVE

Randolph Kennedy spent his second nearly sleepless night pondering his own great decision. The problems of running four separate lives in the complex society of the United States were approaching the level of being overwhelming. Taxes were a threatening two-pronged issue for him. The IRS, state, and local levies would slowly erode his fortune to nil because he had so little to shelter wealth without becoming overtly public. The sophisticated investigative and accounting resources of the national taxation apparatus would eventually prove his undoing. The IRS would expose him and—like a proverbial a house of cards—his contrived empire would be blown over whether it took a year or ten years or more. He knew that much intuitively and by observation of unfortunate accounting clients of his who had chosen to play fast and loose with the U.S. tax service that possessed all the power of a totalitarian regime's secret police. The answer had come quite by serendipity. The question Randolph lay pondering was whether the solution was worth the cost.

He was in a king-size bed in the best hotel—the El Rey—in Belmopan, Belize, the 52 year old artificial capital of the country. The city was comparable to Brazilia, the Brazilian creation. Randolph had a headache that came from his night of indiscretion at the Jazzy J, the city's only nightclub. His mouth carried the foul aftertaste from the Garo Habano he had smoked before falling fitfully asleep. The sound system in the room was softly playing *Et Iterum Venturus Est* from Bach's Mass in B Minor. He lay sweating—nervous sweating—in the air-conditioned comfort of his luxury room. He had tried to read the newspaper but had become bored with the article on *"Hispanization of Belize"*, a thinly disguised piece of alien bashing, written by one of the nation's Creole intellectuals who despised the growing Mestizo population.

Randolph had taken the serious risk of violating his agreement with Proctor, Delgado, and Hernandez by leaving the United States on a false passport because of advice he had received from a telemarketing stockbroker from Fort Lauderdale, Florida. The telemarketer had caught Randolph quite by chance when Randolph was having a moment of weakness. His first inclination had been to hang up as he usually did with unsolicited marketers, but the caller—Enrique Calle Cortez—had been so smooth and apparently knowledgeable that Randolph had succumbed and had invested $17,500 in a high tech digital information systems company. Cortez had assured him that the company was in a stock ascendancy while the vast majority of high tech stocks and the NASDAQ were in a several weeks long decline. To his great surprise, the broker proved to be legitimate; and the broker's company to be stable. It was not the scam Randolph's skepticism had presumed given the terrible reputation of most of the other Fort Lauderdale telemarketing enterprises. Randolph made $4000 in two weeks, just as Cortez had promised.

In the course of the conversation with Cortez after getting the profit, Randolph had complained of the seemingly insoluble problems of taxation for a person in his bracket—80% outlay to all taxing sources. Enrique Cortez suggested Belize and a plan that was completely successful and had been so for fifty years—one that was only modestly painful—if one could lay aside his conscience.

Randolph had been in Belize for two days and had learned that what Enrique Cortez had told him about the postage stamp country on the northeast coast of Central America was true. Belize was a nation of 300,000 people, having increased by 100,000 in the previous fifteen years. The official national language was English—more or less—owing to its long-time colonial and now client relationship with England. It was generally clean and free of the grinding poverty of its neighbors, even though its economy was a modest one.

Most of the people still believed in *obeah* or black magic; and few of them—except the Mennonites—believed that hard physical work or a fast pace was good for a person. Belize had no armed forces. Its only regional military only regional military competitor—Guatemala—no longer manifested any hostility since the two countries had long since settled their border disputes peacefully. With that, Belize had disbanded its army because it was too expensive. The country boasted ninety percent literacy, a developing cultural tradition, and an open invitation to outsiders to come in and enrich the cultural life. It welcomed foreign investment with a very generous set of taxation statutes.

The streets of Belmopan were nearly devoid of traffic. The city was observed to be "quiet" by tourists, unpopular and "dead" by Belizans. Automobiles were all but outlawed, and most of the traffic moved in electric carts. There was not a single historical monument in the entire capital city. Another item on the downside for both tourists and locals was the fact that the country had a complex and long set of rules and regulations that would make Singapore seem *laissez faire*.

For two days, Randolph had enjoyed the Yucatan Peninsula dry season, with temperatures averaging no more than 80 degrees during the days as he frequented the world-class shops on the main thoroughfares and browsed in the American style malls. He found high-tech computer equipment, auto-mobiles, and replacement parts for export, yachting facilities, diverse ethnic restaurants, gentleman's clubs, a cornucopia of staple foods, and a busy popu-lace. The uncrowded streets held the diverse ethnicity of the country: Mopan and Kekchi Mayan Indians, Garifuna or Garinagu, descendants of mixed escaped African slaves and Carib Indians who fled to British Honduras in the 1820s, Mennonites, Creoles, Mestizos, East Indians, and indecipherable con-glomerates of all of these. That mix was further complicated by the admixture of Syrian, Lebanese, Chinese, Taiwanese, and American peoples with whom their genetic and racial identities were irretrievably blurred.

During siesta, Randolph made complex phone calls to Nancy Delgado, Daniel Hernandez, and Hartley Proctor. He learned from a family of American expats that it was possible to use a Cayman Island telephone exchange to make his call appear to have come from wherever in the U.S. that he wanted. It worked perfectly.

He went out for a late afternoon stroll when the city was beginning to come alive. Here and there small groups of people, young and old, and of all ethnici-ties, began *brumming*—dancing the *wanaragua*—or watching a good natured bit of man-woman verbal bantering. The sexually transmitted disease scourge evidently concerned the leaders of the country. Prominently displayed on a billboard in Market Square was a sign that read, "IF YOU WA MEK LOVE, WEAR A GLOVE," sponsored by the National AIDs Prevention Control Program. The Ls in the sign were ensheathed in saggy condoms. Street ven-dors sold trinkets, tee shirts, and food: *Meegan's*—rice and beans, not to be confused with beans and rice which came separated—*hamadilly* or armadillo, *gibnut*—cooked forest rodent—cowfoot soup, seaweed shake, and *behave bruda*—behave brother—a red snapper fish soup containing an assortment of ground foods and the whole head of a grouper.

A short walk from his hotel brought Randolph to the Bull Frog Inn, and he found himself in the hotel's pub that outLondoned the best of the old country. He was shown to a table towards the back of the bar where it was darker and cooler. The pub was crowded, and he had to sit at the table with another patron.

"Would you care to share a Negus with me?" the pleasant man already at his table asked.

He wore a monocle, a cream-colored, tropical weight planter's suit, a heavily starched safari shirt, and a brilliantly colored cravat. He also wore a Panama hat with a wide band that matched his cravat. The only incongruity in this vacationing Britisher was his face. He was an Aztec or Mayan with skin the color of old bronze. The monocle and white outfit made him look like the lead actor in a native production of a play about Sir Henry Morton Stanley and David Livingston.

"I'm not familiar with the drink, sorry," replied Randolph, careful to smile and be friendly.

"My favorite, sir. Mix of port, hot water, lemon juice, brown sugar, and nutmeg. Named for the late Colonel Francis Negus."

The idea of having a hot drink did not appeal to Randolph.

"I think I'll pass for something cold," he said.

"The peach melba is toppers here," his new friend suggested in his strained BBC accent. "I'm Neville Delmaine, by the way."

"Pennington, Terrence Pennington," Randolph replied, glad to remember his latest alias, "nice to meet you."

The pub's nightly entertainment started up—Garifuna people playing their unique music called Punta rock. It was cacophonous, almost as loud as the average Hard Rock Café. The music was all *gomboy* drums, hand-clapping, and loud singsong vocal rhythms. A child passed their table selling *boledo*— lottery tickets—adding her clear soprano voice to the din. Delmaine shooed her away, not looking at her. He took care not to look down on the child's eyes from above, knowing that to do so would cause the little girl to be cross-eyed when she grew up.

Unable to make himself heard by his tablemate for the moment, Randolph nodded his head and ordered. He spent a peaceful hour considering his situation over a pint of Guinness Stout, a bowl of Peach Melba, and a Bakewell tart.

Intermittently—when they could hear each other—his expatriate British friend filled Randolph in on his life's history. Neville's family had accepted the offer of British citizenship when British Honduras had been granted its independence and became Belize. His father had returned to the Britain to reap the reward of his expertise in the fledgling shipping industry of Belize which enabled shipping magnets to have a smooth and profitable transition, and Neville had remained in Belize. His education, mannerisms, preferences, religion, and prejudices, were a Gordian knot of British and Belizan. He knew everything worth knowing about the little country and freely imparted of his expertise to Randolph.

At the end of the afternoon, Randolph knew the ins and outs of the shipping, dairy, and mining industries of Belize. He learned that the country was crying out for accountants: an American CPA could all but name his own price, and that nudged Randolph a step closer to adopting the country as his own. Neville shared with him the history of the British and American Women's' Competition—the Wightman Tennis Cup, the inside dirt on King Charles and his latest significant other, the derby at old Epsom Downs, the scandal in the Belize House of Representatives occasioned by evidence of bribery over grapefruit concentrate and cigarettes in Orange Walk, and the paradise that Belize had become because of its liberal tax laws. Randolph was becoming hooked.

There were no taxes for citizens. Belize maintained a very strict set of rules regarding extradition to other countries, especially the United States. For that reason, increasing numbers of U.S. citizens were electing to renounce their citizenship and to swear allegiance to Belize. In accordance with U.S. law, Belize citizens were able to travel to and from the United States without a visa and almost at will. They could stay in the United States for 120 days a year, earn money, own land, run businesses, all without having to pay taxes there. The Bel-Ams—as they were called—tended to return to Belize mainly at festival times or to see to their businesses briefly before returning to cooler regions.

Randolph would be a Belizan billionaire. Sitting back in his comfortable pub chair looking at but not quite paying attention to an intense game of darts, and enjoying the drone of his tablemate's nasal voice, Randolph could think of no pragmatic reasons for not renouncing America and embracing the vibrant little country. His tax problems would vanish, and he would be able to manipulate his money openly. It would only be one of several score of changes he had made in the direction of his life in the last couple of years.

He had to make an effort to think of anything the United States had done for him lately.

Neville Delmaine confirmed what Enrique Cortez had told Randolph. The process of renunciation of American citizenship was the very model of simplicity: appear at the U.S. embassy, fill out a brief form, sign a short document renouncing all privileges and responsibilities of U.S. citizenship, and sign a document that indicated that the signer understood the consequences of renunciation. Becoming a citizen of Belize—if the petitioner had money and particularly if the petitioner declared his intention to establish a business that would employ five people or more—was equally simple and did not even require the services of an attorney.

Randolph fully intended to become part of the growing dairy industry run largely by the Mennonite citizens of the country. He had already approached the Grimmer family—the largest dairying family in Belize—and had received a favorable response. Putting up a shingle to open a CPA office would be simplicity itself. Randolph searched for a downside to the question of renunciation, and came up with nothing. In his mind, the die was cast.

CHAPTER SIXTY-SIX

On the morning of Friday, February 18, Randolph took his first shower of the day, picked through his portmanteau that he had not bothered to unpack, and dressed in tropical linens, a mesh cotton dress shirt, and a tie made by a Belize mestizo self-help cooperative he had found on one of Belmopan's quaint side streets. He took a London style cab to the U.S. embassy, overpaid the driver, and got out. On the sidewalk was a man trying to sell a caged jaguarmundi and a keel-billed toucan and a woman in a bright hand-woven skirt and dark waist-length braids playing a string harp.

Randolph presented his American passport to the marine guard and entered the handsomely refurbished neocolonial building. It was exactly nine in the morning, and the embassy had just opened for business. The floor of the reception hall—the commons room—was polished parquet with a handsome British Axminster carpet in the center of the room. The walls were painted a cream color; the ceilings were twelve feet high and trimmed with ornate cornices. The commons room was all dignity, security, and correctness, and reflected the power of its owners, the people of the United States.

Randolph took his place in a short line of American citizens of all colors and backgrounds queued up to see the busy clerk to obtain the renunciation documents; and while he waited, he vacillated in a welter of indecision. Whether it was nostalgia, a dormant sense of patriotism, or merely fear of breaking with the old and embracing the new, Randolph felt a distinct ill-at-ease shiver.

In Washington D.C., at six o'clock that same morning, Muriel Vantassa gave up the charade of lying in bed as if she might yet fall asleep. She had been awake all through the night; and now, it felt to her as if it were mid-afternoon. She looked in her bathroom mirror and did not at all like what she saw. Her face was pasty, approaching blotched and haggard. Her eyes had dark circles beneath them and lacked their former luster. Where she had once had laugh lines, she now had wrinkles. She radiated the enthusiasm of a Volga boatman about to start another day. The president determined that she would not let them see her looking defeated however the day went. She worked for half an hour with makeup and was embarrassed at her own frivolity, but the results were good. She no longer looked as if she had been dead for two days.

Vantassa was not hungry, but she forced herself to eat a good breakfast and felt better for having done so. Although it was not really cold, she felt chilly and put an afghan made of Astrakhan karakul lamb wool over her shoulders. The beautiful hand made blanket was a gift from the Sultan of Oman.

At seven-thirty, the usual starting time for her work day, she went to the Oval Office. It seemed foreign to her—and for some reason—she felt out of place there. For the first time in days, she became aware that there was a pile of work that had lain neglected for three months while she had been fighting the malaise brought on by the Kennedy Affair. Part of why she had a vague sense of nervous distress was that she ordinarily could not stand to leave things undone. She had been compulsive about leaving a clear desk at the close of each work day. She picked up the beige telephone on her desk and touched the button for the White House operator. Her own regular staff would not be in for another hour.

"Yes, Madam President?"

"Get me the multi-network executive media service, please."

"Yes, ma'am."

There was a pause of about a minute.

"I have the officer in charge on the line, Madam President."

"Thank you. Before I talk to him, please call the vice-president and ask her to come to the Oval Office now."

"I will, ma'am. Is there anything more?"

"No."

"Madam President?" came the eager young man's voice through the telephone line.

"I wish to make an announcement this morning at ten-thirty. It will be of national importance and will necessarily need to be carried by all five networks."

The young man gulped. This was his worst dread, to be the one on call when the president made some program disrupting request.

"I will work on it, ma'am," he said, unable to keep a slight quaver out of his voice.

"Young man, don't work on it, do it. I will expect the crews at eight o'clock, half an hour from now. There is always a slant of journalists and ready action mobile crews stationed all around the White House. You can arrange it. That is the reason your service exists. Now get to work."

"Yes, ma'am."

In half an hour the crew from TBS arrived and set up in the Oval Office. They had drawn the long straw and were to provide the feed to all the other networks. There would be no reporters.

Daniel Hernandez, U.S. Marshal Avery Cassell, the speaker of the House, the Senate majority leader, and Supreme Court Justice Nielson were admitted to the Oval office corridor for their ten o'clock appointment but were stopped by marine guards from approaching the Office itself. They watched with bemusement at the preparations of TBS crews.

"Let's find a TV set," Hernandez said pragmatically, "I think we are going to miss something pertinent if we don't. I rather think we are about to be upstaged."

The five senior government officials were on their own. All staffers were in a state of frenetic activity getting ready for the announcement by the president and could not be bothered with interlopers, however important they were. No one in the place had any better idea what President Vantassa had in mind than did the Justice Department and congressional leaders who were now huddled in front of a TV set in an unnamed side room. They were tense with anticipation and mystified at the unfolding events.

The *Today Show* host turned his head towards the far side of his set, nodded his head, and disappeared from the screen. Peter Dragonivich—the news anchor for TBS—appeared on the screen. He was not quite his usual perfectly groomed self and seemed slightly hurried.

"Ladies and gentlemen, the president has just requested time for a brief message of national importance. TBS, in cooperation with the other four networks, has provided this time. She will be speaking in a few minutes. We are as unaware of the content of the president's message as you are. I have spoken with the White House Chief of Staff, Grace Shabazz Omotonpareti, and she cannot shed any light on the question. After the president's remarks, we will provide commentary. The leaders of the opposition parties are standing by with their comments. Please bear with us."

The cameras provided file footage of the White House, of its grounds, of the city of Washington D.C., and its more prominent monuments and buildings. Strains of classical music flowed in the background. The tension was at an all-time high in the White House. Then the Marine Band recording of "Hail to the Chief" came on full strength. It was ten-thirty in the morning of Friday, February 18, 2022. The video cam showed the Oval Office very briefly then panned in on the president's face.

The television sets around the ornate U.S. Embassy in Belmopan came on all at once and unannounced in a dramatic and somewhat unnerving synchrony. Randolph turned to his right to look at the set nearest him. The familiar face of Peter Dragonivich appeared and mouthed words that were not yet connected to the video portion of the program being received in Belize. The embassy employees and patrons looked at the television sets wonderingly. When the White House Marine Band struck up the presidential introductory music, there was a look of intense interest on the faces of all the people in the room. None of the Americans spoke. When the president began to speak, all other activity in the commons room came to a halt. The audio portion of the broadcast was now coming through with excellent clarity.

"My fellow Americans, you are all aware of the crisis that has beset your government for the past several months. I have been accused of what amounts to high crimes and treason—felonies—in regards to what has become popularly known as the Kennedy Affair. I will make my remarks brief and to the point. I have been a believer in applying Occam's Razor and cutting to the important part of a communication. That is the tack I shall take today. I readily admit to having been overzealous in the pursuit of criminals who plague our country. I categorically deny having committed any crimes."

Margaret Thaler, sitting with the staffers in the chief of staff's office across from the Oval Office, raised her fist in a black power gesture of triumph that had become the standard salute of the nation's liberals and grinned at the vindication of her position in the heavy debate of the previous night.

The president continued, "Nevertheless, I am all too aware that the function of government has been impaired. I could accurately say that the executive branch is all but unable to perform its duty because of the constant bombardment by the press and my detractors in and out of government in what has become a feeding frenzy by them. I swore an oath to uphold the Constitution. Beyond that, I swore that I would faithfully fulfill the duties of this office."

Thaler said loudly enough that everyone in the chief of staff's room could hear, "I knew she would hang tough. That woman is made of good steel. History will vindicate her."

CHAPTER SIXTY-SEVEN

In the embassy in Belize, Randolph—like every other American in the building—found his attention riveted to the television set. For the moment, he had entirely forgotten why he was in that place. Like the rest of his fellows in the room, he heard the message: the United States was going to enter a crisis such that the Constitution would hang in the balance. It was deeply disheartening, even for the men and women who were there for the express purpose of renouncing their citizenship.

In Washington, President Vantassa paused long enough to sip from a cup of water. She was afraid that she would cough or choke in front of the national and international audience and that would be misinterpreted as a show of emotion. Her sense of dignity would be shattered by such a mistake.

"My fellow Americans, and my friends around the world," she resumed. "I have studied this situation very carefully and have compared it to similar constitutional crises of the past. We cannot have a government gridlocked by such a division."

She paused for another sip, and took a deep breath. The people of the nation—and that included the about-to-be ex-Americans in Belmopan, Belize—held their collective breaths. President Vantassa summoned an inner core of strength and seemed to grow more resolute in front of the cameras.

She forcibly brought to her mind the passage in *Job* that had so arrested her attention during the previous sleepless night.

"'If I justify myself, mine own mouth shall condemn me; if I say I am perfect, it shall prove me perverse,'" the *Book of Job* says. "Therefore, faced with an insoluble dilemma, and effective immediately, I shall, in the interests of the greater good of the people of the United States of America, hereby resign my office as president. God bless America."

She stood up and walked purposefully from the room with a dozen cameras in pursuit.

Daniel Hernandez was the first person in the delegation's room to awake from the state of shock.

"Marshal, come with me now. Gentlemen, please follow me. We need to place Citizen Vantassa under arrest now, before we have to chase her down the West Wing hall."

The vice-president was ushered into the Oval Office. Mrs. Chou appeared calm and poised, whatever turmoil might have been roiling in her breast at that moment. The TBS cameras focused on her and let others pursue the departing former president.

Hernandez stepped into the hallway, followed immediately by the U.S. marshal. Walking down the hall towards them was a gaunt faced shell of a woman who had—until twenty seconds before—been the most powerful person in the world. The marshal stepped in front of Hernandez. A roving cameraman followed Vantassa with his lens and caught the confrontation for the world.

"Muriel Vantassa?"

"Yes."

She was surprised and sullen, irritable, and vulnerable.

"I am U.S. Marshal Avery Cassell. You are under arrest for conspiracy, for felonious malfeasance in office by ordering murder and assault on a United States citizen, for ordering—under the cloak of authority—the felonious placement of illegal evidence at a crime scene to obstruct justice and to deprive a United States citizen of his constitutional rights to equal justice under the law."

She winced at the application of the obscure 1874 law making it a crime to deny constitutional rights. She had regarded herself and her Task Force as resourceful when they had applied the old law to corrupt Southern sheriffs who had the hubris to regard themselves as being the personification of the law.

"You have no right. How dare you invade the White House; this is mutiny!" she shouted, breaking her resolve to remain in control.

"No, madam, this is justice, and this is what justice looks like." Daniel Hernandez said. "No one—and I mean no one—is above the law. Even the president must obey the law."

He was fully aware of his paraphrase of the Magna Charta.

"Marshal, do your duty," he ordered.

Cassell placed Citizen Vantassa's wrists in handcuffs and intoned the ritualized formula of the Miranda decision. In the hallway ahead of them, the protests of Margaret Thaler could be heard. Those protests were stilled when a second U.S. marshal placed her under arrest. The delegation ushered the former president out of the White House and into ignominy.

Randolph Kennedy was next in line to meet the embassy secretary to obtain his renunciation of citizenship documents when the televised evaporation of Muriel Vantassa's administration took place. He watched Supreme Court Justice Adolph Nielson swear in Marianne Chou as the new president. It was ten forty-nine in the morning. Randolph made note of that moment then turned and walked out of the embassy.

-END-

"I weep for you, the Walrus said,
"I deeply sympathize."
With sobs and tears, he sorted out
Those of largest size.
Holding his pocket handkerchief,
Before his streaming eyes.
"Oysters," said the Carpenter,
"You've had a pleasant run!
Shall we be trotting home again?"
But answer was there none.
And this was scarcely odd because
They'd eaten every one.
　　　　　　　　-Lewis Carroll

NOTE

ATF's CREDIBILITY ATTACKED BY JUDGES, AGENTS

John Solomon, Associated Press Writer
As quoted in the *Daily Herald*, Provo, Utah, Tuesday, June 3, 1997

Washington — Still on the rebound from Waco and the Good Ol'
Boys Roundup, the Bureau of Alcohol, Tobacco, and Firearms now
is enduring attacks on its integrity from judges and its own agents.

In criminal and civil cases, judges have concluded ATF witnesses
were not credible, had "failed to adhere to the high ethical standards
expected of federal law enforcement" and had shown a "reckless disregard for the truth…"

And during a training seminar at headquarters in Washington, a
training supervisor declared that the agents "always testify" in court
that the agency's firearms registration database is 100 percent accurate "even though we know that isn't always the case."

None of the agents involved in a dozen cases in which questions
of credibility were raised has ever been disciplined, according to a
review by the *Associated Press*.

Agents were cited in 1996 for events that included drunkenness and racist behavior at gatherings dubbed Good Ol' Boys Roundups in Tennessee. And several were reprimanded for the 1993 botched raid on the Branch Davidian compound at Waco, Texas. In the latter, the government concluded ATF supervisors made false statements to cover up errors...

In Ohio, a federal appeals court recently upheld a judge's 1992 ruling throwing out a search warrant that had been used to confiscate more than fifty weapons in the home of a convicted felon.

U.S. District Judge John M. Manos ruled the affidavit submitted by agent Stephen Wells was wrought with "serious omissions and misrepresentations and stale information" and that a key paragraph was "highly unreliable and defies credulity."

"In his zeal to secure a search warrant, Agent Wells displayed a reckless disregard for the truth as evidenced by his affidavit and changed testimony," Manos concluded...

Judge Stephen E. Manrose ruled the agency "failed to adhere to the high ethical standards expected from federal law enforcement agencies" and may have engaged in an "intentional disregard of the law..."

www.ingramcontent.com/pod-product-compliance
Lightning Source LLC
Chambersburg PA
CBHW071329020726
47502CB00001B/30